COLETTE
The Complete Claudine

COLETTE

The Complete Claudine

Claudine at School

Claudine in Paris

Claudine Married

Claudine and Annie

TRANSLATED BY ANTONIA WHITE

AVENEL BOOKS
NEW YORK

This Omnibus edition was previously published in separate volumes
under the titles:

Claudine at School, copyright © 1956 by Farrar, Straus & Cudahy, Inc.
(now Farrar, Straus and Giroux, Inc.);
originally published in French as *Claudine à l'école*
Claudine in Paris, copyright © 1958 by Martin Secker & Warburg, Ltd.;
originally published in French as *Claudine à Paris*
Claudine Married, copyright © 1960 by Martin Secker & Warburg, Ltd.;
originally published in French as *Claudine en ménage*
Claudine and Annie, copyright © 1962 by Martin Secker & Warburg, Ltd.;
originally published in French as *Claudine s'en va*

This 1984 edition is published by Avenel Books,
distributed by Crown Publishers, Inc.,
by arrangement with Farrar, Straus and Giroux, Inc.

Mnaufactured in the United States of America

Library of Congress Cataloging in Publication Data
Colette, 1873–1954.

The Complete Claudine.

Contents: Claudine at School—Claudine in Paris—
Claudine Married—Claudine and Annie.
1. Colette, 1873–1954—Translations, English.
I. Title.
PQ2605.028A287 1984   843'.912   84-7073
ISBN: 0-517-448521

h g f e d c b a

CONTENTS

Claudine at School

My name is Claudine, I live in Montigny; I was born there in
1884; I shall probably not die there. My *Manual of Departmental
Geography* expresses itself thus: "Montigny-en-Fresnois, a pretty
little town of 1,950 inhabitants, built in tiers above the Thaize; its
well-preserved Saracen tower is worthy of note. . . ." To me, those
descriptions are totally meaningless! To begin with, the Thaize
doesn't exist. Of course I know it's supposed to run through the
meadows under the level-crossing but you won't find enough water
there in any season to give a sparrow a foot-bath. Montigny "built in
tiers"? No, that's not how I see it; to my mind, the houses just
tumble haphazard from the top of the hill to the bottom of the
valley. They rise one above the other, like a staircase, leading up to a
big chateau that was rebuilt under Louis XV and is already more
dilapidated than the squat, ivy-sheathed Saracen tower that crum-
bles away from the top a trifle more every day. Montigny is a village,
not a town: its streets, thank heaven, are not paved; the showers roll
down them in little torrents that dry up in a couple of hours; it is a
village, not even a very pretty village, but, all the same, I adore it.

The charm, the delight of this countryside composed of hills and
of valleys so narrow that some are ravines, lies in the woods—the
deep, encroaching woods that ripple and wave away into the
distance as far as you can see. . . . Green meadows make rifts in
them here and there, so do little patches of cultivation. But these do
not amount to much, for the magnificent woods devour everything.
As a result, this lovely region is atrociously poor and its few
scattered farms provide just the requisite number of red roofs to set
off the velvety green of the woods.

Dear woods! I know them all; I've scoured them so often. There are the copses, where bushes spitefully catch your face as you pass. Those are full of sun and strawberries and lilies-of-the-valley; they are also full of snakes. I've shuddered there with choking terror at the sight of those dreadful, smooth, cold little bodies gliding just in front of my feet. Dozens of times near the "rosemallow" I've stopped still, panting, when I've found a well-behaved grass snake under my hand. It would be neatly coiled up, like a snail-shell, with its head raised and its little golden eyes staring at me: it was not dangerous, but how it frightened me! But never mind all that: I shall always end by going back there, alone or with my friends. Better alone, because those girls are so young lady-ish that they annoy me. They're frightened of being scratched by brambles; they're frightened of little creatures such as hairy caterpillars and those pretty heath-spiders that are as pink and round as pearls; they squeal, they get tired—in fact, they're insufferable.

And then there are my favourites, the great woods that are sixteen and twenty years old. It makes my heart bleed to see one of those cut down. No bushy undergrowth in *them* but trees like pillars and narrow paths where it is almost night at noon, where one's voice and one's steps resound in a disturbing way. Heavens, how I love them! I feel so much alone there, my eyes lost far away among the trees, in the green, mysterious daylight that is at once deliciously peaceful and a little unnerving because of the loneliness and the vague darkness. . . . No small creatures in those great woods; no tall grasses; but beaten earth, now dry, and sonorous, now soft on account of the springs. Rabbits with white scuts range through them and timid deer who run so fast that you can only guess their passage. Great heavy pheasants too, red and golden, and wild boars (I've never seen one) and wolves. I heard a wolf once, at the beginning of winter, while I was picking up beech-nuts—those nice, oily little beech-nuts that tickle your throat and make you cough. Sometimes storm-showers surprise you in those woods; you huddle under an oak that is thicker than the others and listen to the rain pattering up there as if on a roof. You're so well-sheltered that when you come out of those depths you are quite lost and dazzled and feel ill at ease in the broad daylight.

And the fir-woods! Not very deep, these, and hardly at all mysterious. I love them for their smell, for the pink and purple heather that grows under them and for the way they sing in the wind. Before you get to them, you have to go through dense forest; then suddenly you have the delicious surprise of coming out on the edge of a lake; a smooth, deep lake, enclosed on all sides by the woods, far, far away from everything! The firs grow on a kind of island in the middle; you have to straddle bravely across on a fallen tree-trunk that bridges the two banks. Under the firs, you light a fire, even in summer, because it's forbidden; you cook any old thing, an apple, a pear, a potato stolen from a field, some wholemeal bread if you've nothing better. And there's a smell of acrid smoke and resin—it's abominable but it's exquisite.

I have lived ten years of wild rovings, of conquests and discoveries, in those woods; the day when I have to leave them my heart will be very heavy.

Two months ago, when I turned fifteen and let down my skirts to my ankles, they demolished the old school and changed the headmistress. The long skirts were necessitated by my calves; they attracted glances and were already making me look too much like a young lady. The old school was falling into ruins. As to the Headmistress, poor good Madame X, forty, ugly, ignorant, gentle and always terrified in the presence of the Elementary School inspectors, Doctor Dutertre, our District Superintendent of Schools, needed her place for a protégée of his own. In this part of the world, what Dutertre wishes, the Minister wishes too.

Poor old school, dilapidated and unhygienic, but so amusing! The handsome buildings they are putting up now will never make me forget you!

The rooms on the first floor, the ones belonging to the masters, were cheerless and uncomfortable. The ground floor was occupied by our two classrooms, the big girls' and the little girls'; two rooms of incredible ugliness and dirtiness, with tables whose like I have never seen since. They were worn down to half their height by constant use and, by rights, we ought to have become hunchbacks after six months of sitting over them. The smell of those classrooms, after the three hours of study in the morning and in the afternoon, was literally enough to knock you down. I have never had schoolmates of my own kind, for the few middle-class families of

Montigny send their children as a matter of course to boarding-school in the main county town. Thus the school's only pupils were the daughters of grocers, farmers, policemen and, for the most part, of labourers; all of them none too well washed.

The reason I find myself in this strange *milieu* is that I do not want to leave Montigny. If I had a Mamma, I know very well that she would not have let me stay here twenty-four hours. But Papa—*he* doesn't notice anything and doesn't bother about me. He is entirely wrapped up in his work and it never occurs to him that I might be more suitably brought up in a convent or in some Lycée or other. There's no danger of my opening his eyes!

As companions therefore, I had—and still have—Claire (I won't give her surname) who made her First Communion with me, a gentle girl with beautiful, soft eyes and a romantic little soul. She spent her time at school becoming enamoured (oh! platonically, of course!) of a new boy every week and, even now, her only ambition is to fall in love with the first idiot of an Assistant-Master or Road-Surveyor who happens to be in the mood for "poetical" declarations.

Then there's the lanky Anaïs who, no doubt, will succeed in entering the portals of the school at Fontenay-aux-Roses, thanks to a prodigious memory which takes the place of real intelligence. She is cold, vicious and so impossible to upset that she never blushes, lucky creature! She is a positive pastmistress of comedy and often makes me quite ill with laughing. Her hair is neither dark nor fair; she has a yellow skin, no colour in her cheeks, and narrow black eyes, and she is as tall as a bean-pole. Someone quite out of the ordinary, in fact. Liar, toady, swindler and traitress, that lanky Anaïs will always know how to get out of any scrape in life. At thirteen, she was writing to some booby of her own age and making assignations with him; this got about and resulted in gossip which upset all the girls in the school except herself. Then there are the Jauberts, two sisters—twins actually—both model pupils. Model pupils! Don't I know it! I could cheerfully flay them alive, they exasperate me so much with their good behaviour and their pretty, neat handwriting and their silly identical flat, flabby faces and sheep's eyes full of maudlin mildness. They swat all the time; they're bursting with good marks; they're prim and underhand and their breath smells of glue. Ugh!

And Marie Belhomme, a goose but such a cheerful one! At fifteen, she has as much reasoning power and common sense as a rather backward child of eight; she overflows with colossally naïve remarks that disarm our maliciousness and we are very fond of her. I'm always saying any amount of disgraceful things in front of her because, at first, she's genuinely shocked and then, the next minute, she laughs wholeheartedly, flinging up her long, narrow hands as high as they'll go. "Her midwife's hands" Anaïs calls them. Dark, with a matt complexion, long, humid black eyes and an innocent nose, Marie looks like a pretty, timid hare. These four and myself make up an envied set this year; from now on we rank above the "big girls" as aspirants to the elementary School Certificate. The rest, in our eyes, are mere scum; lower orders beneath contempt! I shall introduce a few more of my schoolmates in the course of this diary for it is definitely a diary, or very nearly one, that I am about to begin. . . .

When Madame X received the notice of her dismissal, she cried about it for an entire day, poor woman—and so did we. This inspired me with a strong aversion for her successor. Just when the demolishers of the old school made their appearance in the play-ground, the new Headmistress, Mademoiselle Sergent, arrived. She was accompanied by her mother, a fat woman in a starched cap who waits on her daughter and admires her and who gives me the impression of a wily peasant who knows the price of butter but is not bad at heart. As for Mademoiselle Sergent, *she* seemed anything but kindly and I augured ill of that redhead. She has a good figure, with well-rounded bust and hips, but she is flagrantly ugly. Her face is puffy and permanently crimson and her nose is slightly snub between two small black eyes, deep-set and suspicious. She occupies a room in the old school which does not have to be demolished straight away and so does her assistant, the pretty Aimée Lanthenay who attracts me as much as her superior repels me. Against Mademoiselle Sergent, the intruder, I keep up a fierce and rebellious attitude. She has already tried to tame me but I've jibbed in an almost insolent way. After a few lively skirmishes, I have to admit that she is an unusually good headmistress; decisive, often imperi-ous, with a strength of purpose that would be admirably clear-sighted if it were not occasionally blinded by rage. If she had more command over herself, that woman would be admirable. But, if one resists her, her eyes blaze and her red hair becomes soaked with sweat. The day before yesterday I saw her leave the room so as not to throw an ink-pot at my head.

At recreation-time, since the damp cold of this wretched autumn doesn't make me feel in the least inclined to play games, I talk to Mademoiselle Aimée. Our intimacy is progressing very fast. Her nature is like a demonstrative cat's; she is delicate, acutely sensitive to cold, and incredibly caressing in her ways. I like looking at her nice pink face, like a fair-haired little girl's, and at her golden eyes with their curled-up lashes. Lovely eyes that only ask to smile! They make the boys turn and look after her when she goes out. Often, when we're talking in the doorway of the little crowded classroom, Mademoiselle Sergent passes by us on the way back to her room. She doesn't say a word but fixes us with her jealous, searching looks. Her silence makes us feel, my new friend and I, that she's furious at seeing us "hit it off" so well.

This little Aimée—she's nineteen and only comes up to my ears—chatters, like the schoolgirl she still was only three months ago, with a need for affection and with repressed gestures that touch me. Repressed gestures! She controls them from an instinctive fear of Mademoiselle Sergent, clutching her cold little hands tight under the imitation fur collar (poor little thing, she has no money like thousands of her kind). To make her less shy, I behave gently (it isn't difficult) and I ask her questions, quite content just to look at her. When she talks, she's pretty, in spite of—or because of—her irregular little face. If her cheekbones are a trifle too salient, if her rather too full mouth, under the short nose, makes a funny little dint at the left side when she laughs, what marvellous golden-yellow eyes she has to make up for them! And what a complexion—one of those complexions that look so delicate but are so reliable that the cold doesn't even turn them blue! She talks and she talks—about her father who's a gem-cutter and her mother who was liberal with her smacks, about her sister and her three brothers, about the hard training-college in the country-town where the water froze in the jugs and where she was always dropping with sleep because they got up at five o'clock (luckily the English mistress was very nice to her), about the holidays at home where they used to force her to go back to housework, telling her she'd do better to cook than to sham the young lady. All this was unfolded in her endless chatter; all that poverty-stricken youth that she had endured with impatience and remembered with terror.

Little Mademoiselle Lanthenay, your supple body seeks and demands an unknown satisfaction. If you were not an assistant mistress at Montigny you might be . . . I'd rather not say what. But how I like listening to you and looking at you—you who are four years older than I am and yet make me feel every single moment like your elder sister!

My new confidante told me one day that she knew quite a lot of English and this inspired me with a simply marvellous idea. I asked Papa (as he takes Mamma's place) if he wouldn't like me to get Mademoiselle Aimée Lanthenay to give me lessons in English grammar. Papa thought the idea a good one, like most of my ideas, and to "clinch the matter", as he says, he came with me to see Mademoiselle Sergent. She received us with a stony politeness and, while Papa was explaining *his* idea to her, she seemed to be approving it. But I felt vaguely uneasy at not seeing her eyes while she was talking. (I'd noticed very quickly that her eyes always tell what she is thinking without her being able to disguise it and I was worried to observe that she kept them obstinately lowered.) Mademoiselle Aimée was called down and arrived eager and blushing. She kept repeating "Yes, Monsieur", and "Certainly, Monsieur", hardly realising what she was saying, while I watched her, highly delighted with my ruse and rejoicing in the thought that, henceforth, I should have her with me in more privacy than on the threshold of the small classroom. Price of the lessons: fifteen francs a month and two sessions a week. For this poor little assistant mistress, who earns sixty-five francs a month and has to pay for her keep out of it, this was a windfall beyond her dreams. I believe, too, that she was pleased at the idea of being with me more often. During that visit, I barely exchanged a couple of sentences with her.

The day of our first lesson! I waited for her after class while she collected her English books and off we went to my home! I'd arranged a comfortable corner for us in Papa's library—a big table, pens and exercise-books, with a good lamp that only lit the table. Mademoiselle Aimée, extremely embarrassed (why?) blushed and said with a nervous little cough:

"Now then, Claudine, you know your alphabet, I think?"

"Of course, Mademoiselle. I also know a little grammar. I could easily do that little bit of translation. . . . We're cosy here, aren't we?"

"Yes, very cosy."

I asked, lowering my voice a little as I did when we were having our gossips:

"Did Mademoiselle Sergent mention my lessons with you again?"

"Oh, hardly at all. She told me it was a piece of luck for me—that you'd give me no trouble if you were only willing to work a little—that you could learn very quickly when you wanted to."

"Was that all? That's not much! She must have been sure you'd repeat it to me."

"Now, now Claudine, we're not working. In English there is only one article . . . , etc., etc."

After ten minutes of serious English, I questioned her again.

"Did you notice she didn't look at all pleased when I came with Papa to ask to have lessons with you?"

"No . . . Yes . . . Well, perhaps. But we hardly spoke to each other that evening."

"Do take off your jacket, it's always stifling in Papa's room. How slim you are—one could snap you in two! Your eyes are awfully pretty by this light."

I said that because I thought it and also because it gave me pleasure to pay her compliments—more pleasure than if I had received them on my own account. I enquired:

"Do you still sleep in the same room as Mademoiselle Sergent?"

This proximity seemed odious to me but how could she do otherwise? All the other rooms had already been stripped of their furniture and the men were beginning to take off the roof. The poor little thing sighed:

"I have to, but it's too tiresome for words. At nine o'clock I go to bed at once—quick, quick—and she comes up to bed later on. But it's unpleasant all the same, when the two of us are so ill-at-ease together."

"Oh, I do feel so frightfully sorry for you! It must be maddening for you to have to dress in front of her in the morning! I should loathe to have to show myself in my chemise to people I don't like!"

Mademoiselle Lanthenay started as she pulled out her watch.

"Really, Claudine, we're not doing a thing! We simply must work!"

"Yes . . . . Did you know they're expecting some new assistant-masters?"

"I know. Two. They're arriving tomorrow."

"That'll be amusing! Two admirers for you!"

"Oh, be quiet, do. To begin with, all the ones I've seen were so stupid that I wasn't a bit tempted. And, besides, I know the names of these two already. Such ludicrous names—Antonin Rabastens and Armand Duplessis."

"I bet those two idiots will go through our playground twenty times a day. They'll make the excuse that the boys' entrance is cluttered up with builder's rubbish. . . ."

"Listen, Claudine, this is disgraceful. We haven't done a stroke today."

"Oh, it's always like that the first day. We'll work much better next Friday. One has to have time to get going."

In spite of this convincing reasoning, Mademoiselle Lanthenay felt guilty about her own laziness and made me work seriously to the end of the hour. Afterwards, I accompanied her down to the bottom of the street. It was dark and freezing and it upset me to see this small shadow going off into that cold and that blackness to return to the Redhead with the jealous eyes.

This week we've enjoyed some hours of pure bliss because they've been using us big ones to clear the loft and bring down all the books and the old lumber with which it was crammed. We had to hurry: the builders were waiting to pull down the first storey. There were mad gallops through the attics and up and down the stairs. At the risk of being punished we ventured, the lanky Anaïs and I, right on to the staircase leading to the masters' rooms, in the hopes of at least catching a glimpse of the two new assistants who had remained invisible since their arrival. . . .

Yesterday, in front of a door left ajar, Anaïs gave me a shove. I stumbled and pushed the door right open with my head. Then we burst into giggles and stood rooted to the spot on the threshold of this room, obviously a master's and, luckily, empty of its tenant. Hastily, we inspected it. On the wall and on the mantelpiece were large chromolithographs in commonplace frames: an Italian girl with luxuriant hair, dazzling teeth and eyes three times the size of her mouth; as a companion-piece, a swooning blonde clutching a spaniel to her blue-ribboned bodice. Above the bed of Antonin Rabastens (he had stuck his card on the door with four drawing-pins) hung entwined pennants in the French and Russian national colours.

What else? A table with a wash-basin, two chairs, some butterflies stuck on corks, some sentimental songs lying about the mantelpiece, and not a thing besides. We stared at all this without saying a word, then suddenly we escaped towards the loft at full speed, oppressed by an absurd fear that Antonin (one simply *can't* be called Antonin!) might be coming up the stairs. Our trampling on those forbidden steps was so noisy that a door opened on the ground-floor—the door of the boys' classroom—and someone appeared, enquiring in a funny Marseilles accent:

"What on earrth's going on? For the last half-hour, have I been hearing *hosses* on the staircase?"

We had just time to catch a glimpse of a tall, dark youth with healthy ruddy cheeks. . . . Up there, safe at last, my accomplice said, panting:

"Just suppose, if he knew we'd come from his room!"

"Well, suppose he did! He'd be inconsolable at having missed us."

"Missed us!" went on Anaïs with icy gravity, "He looks like a tough chap who wouldn't be likely to miss you."

"Go on, you great slut!"

And we went on with the clearing-out of the loft. It was fascinating to rummage among the pile of books and periodicals to be carried down and that belonged to Mademoiselle Sergent. Of course, we had a good look through the heap before taking them down and I noticed it contained Pierre Loüys' *Aphrodite* and several numbers of the *Journal Amusant*. Anaïs and I regaled ourselves excitedly with a drawing by Gerbault entitled *Whispers behind the Scenes*. It showed gentlemen in black evening clothes occupied in tickling charming Opera dancers, in tights and ballet-skirts, who were twittering and gesticulating. The other pupils had gone downstairs; it was getting dark in the attic and we lingered over some pictures that made us laugh—some Albert Guillaumes that were far from suitable for young ladies.

Suddenly, we started for someone had opened the door and was asking in a garlicky voice: "Hi! who's been making this infernal row on the staircase?"

We stood up, looking very serious, our arms loaded with books and said, very deliberately: "Good morning, Sir," fighting down an agonising desire to laugh. It was the big assistant-master with the jolly face we'd seen just now. So then, because we're both tall and look at least sixteen, he apologised and went away, saying: "A thousand pardons, young ladies." So we danced behind his back in silence, making devilish faces at him. We arrived downstairs late and were scolded. Mademoiselle Sergent asked me: "What on earth were you doing up there?" So I ostentatiously put down the pile of books at her feet with the daring Aphrodite and the numbers of *Journal Amusant* on top, folded back to display the pictures. She saw them at once; her red cheeks turned redder than ever but she recovered herself at once and remarked: "Ah! Those are the Headmaster's books you have brought down. Everything gets so mixed up in that loft we all use. I'll give them back to him." And there the sermon ended; not the least punishment for the two of us. As we went out, I nudged Anaïs whose narrow eyes were crinkled with laughter.

"Hmm, the Headmaster's got a broad back!"

"Claudine, can you *imagine* that innocent collecting bits of dirt! I wouldn't be surprised if he believes babies are found under gooseberry bushes!"

For the Headmaster is a sad, colourless widower. One hardly knows he exists for he only leaves his classroom to shut himself up in his bedroom.

The following Friday, I took my second lesson with Mademoiselle Aimée Lanthenay. I asked her:

"Are the new masters pursuing you already?"

"Oh! As it happens, Claudine, they came yesterday to 'pay their respects'. The nice boy who swaggers a bit is Antonin Rabastens."

"Known as 'the pearl of the Canebière'; and the other one, what's *he* like?"

"Slim, handsome, with an interesting face. He's called Armand Duplessis."

"It would be a sin not to nickname him 'Richelieu'."

She laughed:

"A name that'll stick to him all through the school, you wicked Claudine! But what a savage! He doesn't say a word except Yes and No."

My English mistress seemed adorable to me that night under the library lamp. Her cat's eyes shone pure gold, at once malicious and caressing, and I admired them, not without reminding myself that they were neither kind nor frank nor trustworthy. But they sparkled so brilliantly in her fresh face and she seemed so utterly at ease in this warm, softly-lit room that I already felt ready to love her so much, so very much, with all my irrational heart. Yes, I've known perfectly well, for a long time, that I have an irrational heart. But knowing it doesn't stop me in the least.

"And *she,* the Redhead—doesn't she say anything to you these days?"

"No. She's even being quite amiable. I don't think she's as annoyed as you think to see us getting on so well together."

"Pooh! *You* don't see her eyes. They're not as lovely as yours, but they're more wicked. . . . Pretty little Mademoiselle, what a darling you are!"

She blushed deeply and said, with complete lack of conviction:

"You're a little mad, Claudine. I'm beginning to believe it, I've been told so so often!"

"Yes, I'm quite aware that other people say so, but who cares? I like being with you. Tell me about your lovers."

"I haven't any! You know, I think we shall see plenty of the two assistant-masters. Rabastens strikes me as very 'man of the world' and Duplessis will follow in his footsteps. By the way, did you know that I shall probably get my little sister to come here as a boarder?"

"I don't care a fig about your sister. How old is she?"

"Your age. A few months younger, just on fifteen."

"Is she nice?"

"Not pretty, as you'll see. A bit shy and wild."

"Sucks to your sister! I say, I saw Rabastens in the loft. He came up on purpose. He's got a Marseilles accent you could cut with a knife, that hulking Antonin!"

"Yes, but he's not too ugly. . . . Come along, Claudine, let's get down to work. Aren't you ashamed of yourself? Read that and translate it."

But it was no good her being indignant: work made no progress at all. I kissed her when we said goodbye.

The next day, during recreation, Anaïs was in the act of dancing like a maniac in front of me, hoping to reduce me to pulp and keeping a perfectly straight face all the while, when suddenly Rabastens and Duplessis appeared at the playground gate.

As we were there—Marie Belhomme, the lanky Anaïs and

myself—their lordships bowed and we replied with icy correctness. They went into the big room where the mistresses were correcting exercise-books and we saw them talking and laughing with them. At that, I discovered a sudden and urgent need to fetch my hood, which I had left behind on my desk. I burst into the classroom, pushing open the door as if I had no idea that their Lordships might be inside. Then I stopped, pretending to be confused, in the open doorway. Mademoiselle Sergent arrested my course with a "Control yourself, Claudine" that would have cracked a water-jug and I tiptoed away like a cat. But I'd had time to see that Mademoiselle Aimée Lanthenay was laughing as she chatted to Duplessis and was setting herself out to charm him. Just you wait, my hero wrapped in Byronic gloom! Tomorrow or the day after there'll be a song about you or some cheap puns or some nicknames. That'll teach you to seduce Mademoiselle Aimée. But . . . all right, what is it? Were they calling me back? What luck! I re-entered, looking very meek.

"Claudine," said Mademoiselle by way of explanation "Come and read this at sight. Monsieur Rabastens is musical but not so musical as you are."

How amiable she was! What a complete changeover! *This* was a song from *The Chalet*, boring to tears. Nothing reduces my voice to a shred like singing in front of people I don't know, so I read it correctly but in an absurdly shaky voice that became firmer, thank heavens, at the end of the piece.

"Ah, Mademoiselle, allow me to congratulate you. You sing with such *forrce!*"

I protested politely, mentally sticking out my tongue (my *tonngue*, he'd say) at him. And I went off to find the *otherrs* (it's catching) who gave me a welcome like vinegar.

"Darling!" the lanky Anaïs said between her teeth, "I hope you're in everyone's good books now! You must have produced a smashing impression on those gentlemen, so we shall be seeing them often."

The Jauberts indulged in covert, sneering giggles of jealousy.

"Let me alone, will you? Honestly, there's nothing to foam at the mouth about because I happened to read something at sight. Rabastens is one hundred and fifty per cent a southerner and that's a species I detest. As to Richelieu, if he comes here often, I know quite well who the attraction is."

"Well, who?"

"Mademoiselle Aimée, of course! He positively devours her with his eyes."

"Own up," whispered Anaïs. "It's not him you're jealous of, so it must be her. . . ."

That insufferable Anaïs! That girl sees everything and what she doesn't see, she invents!

The two masters re-entered the playground; Antonin Rabastens expansive and smiling at us all; the other nervous, almost cowed. It was time they went away; the bell was on the point of ringing for the end of recreation and their urchins in the neighbouring playground were making as much noise as if the whole lot had been simultaneously plunged in a cauldron of boiling water. The bell rang for us and I said to Anaïs:

"I say, it's a long time since the District Superintendent came. I shall be awfully surprised if he doesn't turn up this week."

"He arrived yesterday. He's sure to come and poke his nose in here."

Dutertre, the District Superintendent of Schools, is also the doctor to the orphanage. Most of the children there attend the school and this gives him double authorisation to visit us. Heaven knows he makes enough use of it! Some people declare that Mademoiselle Sergent is his mistress. I don't know if it's true or not. What I am prepared to bet is that he owes her money. Electoral campaigns cost a lot and this Dutertre, who hasn't a penny, has set his heart, in spite of persistent failure, on replacing the dumb, but immensely rich old moron who represents the voters of Fresnois in the Chambre des Députés. And I'm absolutely certain that passionate redhead is in love with him! She trembles with jealous fury when she sees him pawing us rather too insistently.

For, I repeat, he frequently honours us with his visits. He sits on the tables, behaves badly, lingers with the older ones, especially with me, reads our essays, thrusts his moustache into our ears, strokes our necks and calls us all "*tu*" (he knew us when we were *so* high!) flashing his wolf's teeth and his black eyes. We find him extremely amiable but I know him to be such a rotter that I don't feel in the least shy with him. And this scandalises my schoolfriends.

It was our day for the sewing-lesson. We were plying our needles lazily and talking in inaudible voices. Suddenly, to our joy, we saw white flakes beginning to fall. What luck! We should be able to make slides; there'd be lots of tumbles; we'd have snowball fights. Mademoiselle Sergent stared at us without seeing us, her mind elsewhere.

Tap, tap on the window-panes! Through the whirling feathers of the snow, we could see Dutertre knocking on the glass. He was all wrapped up in furs and wore a fur cap. He looked handsome in them, with his shining eyes and the teeth he is always displaying. The first bench (myself, Marie Belhomme and the lanky Anaïs) came to life; I fluffed up my hair on my temples. Anaïs bit her lips to make them red and Marie tightened her belt by a hole. The Jaubert sisters clasped their hands like two pictures of First Communicants: "I am the temple of the Holy Ghost."

Mademoiselle Sergent leapt to her feet, so brusquely that she upset her chair and her footstool, and ran to open the door. The sight of all this commotion made me split with laughter. Anaïs took advantage of my helplessness to pinch me and to make diabolical faces at me as she chewed charcoal and indiarubber. (However much they forbid her these strange comestibles, all day long her pockets and her mouth are filled with pencil-stubs, filthy black indiarubber, charcoal and pink blotting-paper. Chalk, pencil-lead and such like satisfy her stomach in the most peculiar way: it must be those things she eats that give her a complexion the colour of wood and grey plaster. At least I only eat cigarette-paper and only one special kind of that. But that gawk Anaïs ruins the store from which they give out the school stationery. She asks for new "equipment" every single week to such an extent that, at the beginning of term, the Municipal Council made a complaint.)

Dutertre shook his snow-powdered furs—they looked like his natural hide. Mademoiselle Sergent sparkled with such joy at the sight of him that it didn't even occur to her to notice if I were watching her. He cracked jokes with her and his quick, resonant voice (he speaks with the accent they have up in the mountains) seemed to warm up the whole classroom. I inspected my nails and let my hair be well in evidence, for the visitor was directing most of his glances at us. After all, we're big girls of fifteen and if my face looks younger than my age, my figure looks eighteen at least. And my hair is worth showing off, too. It makes a curly flying mass whose colour varies according to the season between dull chestnut and deep gold and contrasts, by no means unattractively, with my coffee-brown eyes. Curly, as it is, it comes down almost to my hips. I've never worn plaits or a chignon. Chignons give me a headache and plaits don't frame my face enough. When we play prisoners' base, I gather up my heap of hair, which would make me too easy a victim, and tie it up in a horse's tail. Well, after all, isn't it prettier like that?

Mademoiselle Sergent finally broke off her enraptured conversation with the District Superintendent and rapped out a: "Girls, you are behaving extremely badly!" To confirm her in this conviction, Anaïs thought it helped to let out the "Hpp . . ." of suppressed hysterical giggles without moving a muscle in her face. So it was at me that Mademoiselle shot a furious glance which boded punishment.

At last Monsieur Dutertre raised his voice and we heard him ask: "They're working well, here? They're keeping well?"

"They're keeping extremely well," replied Mademoiselle Sergent. "But they do little enough work. The laziness of those big girls is incredible!"

The moment we saw the handsome doctor turn towards us, we all bent over our work with an air of intense application as if we were too absorbed to remember he was there.

"Ah! Ah!" he said, coming toward our benches. "So we don't do much work? What ideas have we in our heads? Is Mademoiselle Claudine no longer top in French composition?"

Those French compositions, how I loathe them! Such stupid and disgusting subjects: "Imagine the thoughts and actions of a young blind girl." (Why not deaf-and-dumb as well?) Or: "Write, so as to draw to your own physical and moral portrait, to a brother whom you have not seen for ten years." (I have no fraternal bonds, I am an only child.) No one will ever know the efforts I have to make to restrain myself from writing pure spoof or highly subversive opinions! But, for all that, my companions—all except Anaïs—make such a hash of it that, in spite of myself I am "the outstanding pupil in literary composition".

Dutertre had now arrived at the point he wanted to arrive at and I raised my head as Mademoiselle Sergent answered him:

"Claudine? Oh, she's still top. But it's not *her* fault. She's gifted for that and doesn't need to make any effort."

He sat down on the table, and swinging one leg and addressing me as "*tu*" so as not to lose the habit of doing so:

"So you're lazy?"

"Of course. It's my only pleasure in the world."

"You don't mean that seriously! You prefer reading, eh? What do you read? Everything you can lay hands on? Everything in your father's library?"

"No, Sir. Not books that bore me."

"I bet you're teaching yourself some remarkable things. Give me your exercise-book."

To read it more comfortably, he leant a hand on my shoulder and twisted a curl of my hair. This made the lanky Anaïs turn dangerously yellow; he had not asked for her exercise-book! I should pay for this favouritism by surreptitious pin-pricks, sly tale-telling to Mademoiselle Sergent and being spied on whenever I talked to Mademoiselle Lanthenay. She was standing near the door of the small classroom, that charming Aimée, and she smiled at me so tenderly with her golden eyes that I was almost consoled for not having been able to talk to her today or yesterday except in front of my schoolmates. Dutertre laid down my exercise-book and stroked my shoulders in an absent-minded way. He was not thinking in the least about what he was doing, evidently . . . oh, *very* evidently. . . .

"How old are you?"

"Fifteen."

"Funny little girl! If you didn't look so crazy, you'd seem older, you know. You'll sit for your certificate next October?"

"Yes, Sir, to please Papa."

"Your father? What on earth does it matter to him? But you yourself, you're not particularly eager at the prospect?"

"Oh yes, I am. It'll amuse me to see all those people who question us. And besides there are concerts in the town then. It'll be fun."

"You won't go on to the training-college?"

I leapt in my seat.

"Good heavens, no!"

"Why so emphatic, you excitable girl?"

"I don't want to go there any more than I wanted to go to boarding-school—because you're shut up."

"Oho! Your liberty means as much as all that to you, does it? Your husband won't have things all his own way, poor fellow! Show me that face. Are you keeping well? A trifle anaemic, perhaps?"

This kindly doctor turned me towards the window, slipped his arm round me and gazed searchingly into my eyes with his wolfish stare. I made my own gaze frank and devoid of mystery. I always have dark circles under my eyes and he asked me if I suffered from palpitations and breathlessness.

"No, never."

I lowered my lids because I felt I was blushing idiotically. Also he was staring at me too hard! And I was conscious of Mademoiselle Sergent behind us, her nerves tense.

"Do you sleep all night?"

I was furious at blushing more than ever as I answered:

"Oh, yes, Sir. All night long."

He did not press the point but stood upright and let go my waist.

"Tcha! Fundamentally, you're as sound as a bell."

A little caress on my cheek, then he went on to the lanky Anaïs who was withering on her bench.

"Show me your exercise-book."

While he turned over the pages, pretty fast, Mademoiselle Sergent was fulminating in an undertone at the First Division (girls of twelve and fourteen who were already beginning to pinch in their waists and wear chignons), for the First Division had taken advantage of authority's inattention to indulge in a Witches' Sabbath. We could hear hands being smacked with rulers, the squeals of girls who were being pinched. They were letting themselves in for a general detention, not a doubt of it!

Anaïs was suffocated with joy at seeing her exercise-book in such august hands but no doubt Dutertre did not find her worth much attention for he passed on after paying her a few compliments and pinching her ear. He lingered some minutes by Marie Belhomme whose smooth, dark freshness attracted him but she was promptly overwhelmed with shyness. She lowered her head like a ram, said Yes when she meant No and addressed Dutertre as "Mademoiselle". As to the two Jaubert sisters, he complimented them on their beautiful handwriting, as might have been foretold. At last, he left the room. Good riddance!

We still had ten minutes to go before the end of class; how could we use them? I asked permission to leave the room so that I could surreptitiously gather up a handful of the still-falling snow. I made a snowball and bit into it: it was cold and delicious. It always smells a little of dust, this first fall. I hid it in my pocket and returned to the classroom. Everyone round me made signs to me and I passed the snowball round. Each of them, with the exception of the virtuous twins, bit into it with expressions of rapture. Then that ninny of a Marie Belhomme had to go and drop the last bit and Mademoiselle Sergent saw it.

"Claudine! Have you gone and brought in snow again? This is really getting beyond the limit!"

She rolled her eyes so furiously that I bit back the retort "It's the first time since last year", for I was afraid Mademoiselle Lanthenay might suffer for my impertinence. So I opened my *History of France* without answering a word.

This evening I should be having my English lesson and that would console me for my silence.

At four o'clock, Mademoiselle Aimée appeared and we went off happily together.

How nice it was there with her in the warm library! I pulled my chair right up against hers and laid my head on her shoulder. She put her arm round me and I squeezed her supple waist.

"Darling little Mademoiselle, it's such ages since I've seen you!"

"But . . . it's only three days. . . ."

"What does that matter? . . . Don't talk, and kiss me! You're very unkind; time seems short to you when you're away from me. . . . Do they bore you frightfully, these lessons?"

"Oh, Claudine! On the contrary, you know you're the only person I can ever really talk to and I'm only happy when I'm here."

She kissed me and I purred. Then, suddenly, I hugged her so violently that she gave a little shriek.

"Claudine, we *must* work!"

I wished English grammar to the devil! I much preferred to lay my head on her breast while she stroked my hair or my neck and I could hear her heart beating breathlessly under my ear. How I loved being with her! Nevertheless, I had to take up a pen and at least pretend to be working! But really, what was the point? Who could possibly come in? Papa? Nothing less likely! Papa shuts himself up like a hermit in the most uncomfortable room on the first floor, the one where you freeze in winter and roast in summer and there he remains blindly absorbed, deaf to the noises of the world, busy with . . . But, of course . . . you haven't read, because it'll never be finished, his great work on the *Malacology of the Region of Fresnois* and you'll never know that, after complicated experiments and anxious vigils that have kept him bending for hours and hours over innumerable slugs enclosed in little bell-glasses and wire cages, Papa has established the following epoch-making fact: In one day, a *limax flavus* devours as much as 0.24 grammes of food whereas the *helix ventricosa* only consumes 0.19 grammes in the same time! How could you expect that the budding hope of such discoveries would leave a passionate malacologist any paternal sentiment between seven in the morning and nine at night? He's the best and kindest of men— between two orgies of slugs. Moreover, he watches me live—when he has time to—with positive admiration. He's astonished to see me existing "like a real human-being". This fact makes him laugh, with his small deep-set eyes and his noble Bourbon nose (wherever did he get that royal nose?) into his handsome beard that's streaked with three colours—red, grey and white. And how often I've seen that beard shining with traces of slime from the slugs!

I asked Aimée carelessly whether she'd seen the two friends, Rabastens and Richelieu, again. She became excited, which surprised me:

"Ah! I forgot, I hadn't told you. . . . You know we sleep over at the infant-school now because they're pulling down everything. . . . Well, yesterday evening, I was working in my room round about ten o'clock and when I was closing the shutters before going to bed, I saw a tall shadow walking to and fro under my window, in all this cold! Guess who it was!"

"One of those two, of course."

"Yes! But it was Armand. Would you ever have believed it of that shy chap?"

I said no, but, actually I didn't find it at all hard to believe. That tall, dark creature with the sombre, serious eyes seemed to me much less of a nonentity than the hearty Marseillais. Nevertheless I saw that Mademoiselle Aimée's bird-like head was completely turned by this mild adventure. I asked her:

"What? Do you already find him as interesting as all that, that solemn crow?"

"No, of course not! I'm amused, that's all."

That was that, and the lesson ended without further confidences. It was only when we went out into the dark passage that I kissed her with all my might on her charming, slim white neck and in the tendrils of hair that smelt so nice. She's as amusing to kiss as a warm, pretty little animal and she returned my kisses tenderly. Oh, I'd have kept her with me all the time if only I could!

Tomorrow would be Sunday. No school. What a bore! It's the only place I find amusing.

That particular Sunday, I went to spend the afternoon where Claire lives—my sweet, gentle partner at my First Communion. She hasn't been coming to school for a year now. We walked down the Chemin des Matignons which runs into the road leading to the station. It's a lane that's leafy and dark with greenery in summer; in these winter months there aren't any leaves, of course, but you're still sufficiently hidden there to be able to spy on the people sitting on the benches along the road. We walked on the crackling snow. The frozen puddles creaked musically under the sun with the charming sound, that's like no other, of ice breaking up. Claire whispered about her mild flirtations with the boys at the ball on Sunday over at Trouillard's; rough, clumsy boys. I quivered with excitement as I listened to her.

"You know, Claudine, Montassuy was there too and he danced the polka with me, holding me tight against him. At that very minute, my brother, Eugène, who was dancing with Adèle Tricotot, let go of his partner, and jumped up in the air and banged his head against one of the hanging lamps. The lamp-glass turned upside down and that put out the lamp. While everyone was staring and saying "Ooh!" whatever d'you think happened? That fat Féfed turned off the other lamp and everything was black as black . . . nothing but one candle right at the very far end of the little bar. My dear, all the time old mother Trouillard was fetching some matches, you heard nothing but screams and laughs and the sound of kisses. My brother was holding Adèle Tricotot just beside me and she kept on sighing like anything and saying "Let go of me, Eugène" in a muffled voice as if she'd got her skirts over her head. And that fat Féfed and his partner had fallen over on the floor. They were laughing and laughing, so much that they simply couldn't get up again!"

"What about you and Montassuy?"

Claire turned red with belated modesty.

"Ah, that's just what I was going to tell you. . . . The first minute, he was so surprised to see the lamps go out that he only kept on holding my hand. Then he put his arm round my waist again and said very quietly: 'Don't be frightened.' I didn't say a word and I could feel him bending over me and kissing my cheeks. Ever so gently, feeling his way, and it was actually so dark that he made a mistake (Claire, you little hypocrite!) and kissed my mouth. I enjoyed it so much—it made me feel simply marvellous. . . . In fact I was so excited that I nearly fell over and he had to hold me up by hugging me tighter still. Oh! he's nice, I love him!"

"Well, what happened after that, you slut?"

"After that, old mother Trouillard lit the lamps again, grumbling like anything. She swore that if such a thing ever happened again, she'd bring a complaint and they'd have the dances stopped."

"The fact is, it really was going a bit far! . . . Ssh . . . be quiet. . . . Who's that coming?"

We were sitting behind the briar-hedge, quite near the road that ran a couple of yards below us. There was a bench on the edge of the ditch so it was a marvellous hide-out for listening without being seen.

"It's those two masters!"

Yes, it was Rabastens and the gloomy Armand Duplessis who were walking along and talking. What an unhoped-for bit of luck! The coxcomb, Antonin, wanted to sit down on that bench because of the pale sunshine that had warmed him a little. We were about to hear their conversation and we shuddered with joy in our field, right above their heads.

"Ah!" said the southerner with satisfaction, "one's quite *warrm* here. Don't you agree?"

Armand muttered some vague remark. The man from Marseilles started up again. He was going to do all the talking, I was certain!

"You know, *I* like this part of the world. Those two schoolmistress ladies are extremely pleasant. I admit Mademoiselle Sergent is ugly! But that little Mademoiselle Aimée is a smart girl! I feel decidedly pleased with myself when she looks at me."

The sham Richelieu sat up straight; his tongue was loosened:

"Yes, she's attractive, and so charming! She's always smiling and she chatters away like a hedge-sparrow."

But he promptly regretted his expansiveness and added in a different voice: "She's a very charming young lady. You're certainly going to turn her head, Don Juan!"

I nearly burst out laughing. Rabastens as Don Juan! I had a vision of him with his round head and plump cheeks adorned with a plumed hat. . . . Up there, straining towards the road, the two of us laughed at each other with our eyes, without moving a muscle of our faces.

"But, goodness me," went on the heartbreaker of the elementary school, "she's not the only pretty girl round here. Anyone would think you hadn't noticed them! The other day, in the classroom, Mademoiselle Claudine came in and sang quite charmingly (I may say that I know what I'm talking about, eh?) and she's not a girl you'd overlook, with that hair flowing down her back and all round her and those very naughty brown eyes! My dear chap, I believe that girl knows more about things she oughtn't to know than she does about geography!"

I gave a little start of astonishment and we might easily have been discovered for Claire let off a laugh like a gas-escape which might have been overheard. Rabastens fidgetted on his bench beside the absorbed Duplessis and whispered something in his ear, laughing in a ribald way. The other smiled; they got up; they went away. The two of us up there were in ecstasies. We danced a war-dance of joy, as much to warm ourselves as to congratulate ourselves on this delicious piece of spying.

On my way home, I was already ruminating on various alluring tricks to excite that hulking ultra-inflammable Antonin still more. It would be something to pass the time during recreation when it rained. And I who believed he was in process of plotting the seduction of Mademoiselle Lanthenay! I was delighted that he wasn't trying to make up to her, for that little Aimée struck me as being so amorous that even a Rabastens might have succeeded—who knows? It's true that Richelieu was even more smitten with her than I had supposed.

At seven o'clock in the morning, I arrived at school. It was my turn to light the fire, worse luck! That meant breaking up firewood in the shed and ruining one's hands; carrying logs, blowing on the flames and getting stinging smoke in one's eyes. . . . Good gracious, the first new building was already rising high and the boys' school, identical with it, had got most of its roof on! Our poor old half-demolished school looked like a tiny hovel by these two buildings that had so quickly sprouted out of the ground. The lanky Anaïs joined me and we went off to break up firewood together.

"D'you know, Claudine, there's a second assistant mistress arriving today, and we're all going to be forced out of house and home. They're going to give us classes in the Infants' School."

"What a brilliant idea! We shall catch fleas and lice. It's simply filthy over there."

"Yes, but we'll be nearer the boys' classroom, old thing."

(Anaïs really is shameless! However, she's perfectly right.)

"That's true. Now, you twopenny-halfpenny fire, are you going to catch or not? I've been bursting my lungs for the last ten minutes. Ah, I bet Monsieur Rabastens blazes up a lot quicker than you do!"

Little by little, the fire made up its mind to burn. The pupils arrived; Mademoiselle Sergent was late (Why? It was the first time). She came down at last, answered our "Good morning" with a preoccupied air, then sat down at her desk saying: "To your places" without looking at us and obviously without giving us a thought. I copied down my problems while I asked myself what thoughts were troubling her and I noticed, with uneasy surprise, that from time to time she darted quick looks at me—looks that were at once furious and vaguely gratified. Whatever could be up? I was not comfortable in my mind: not at all. I began to search my conscience. . . . I couldn't think of anything except that she'd watched us going off for our English lesson, Mademoiselle Lanthenay and me, with a barely-concealed, almost rueful anger. Aha! so we were not to be left in peace, my little Aimée and I? Yet we were doing nothing wrong! Our last English lesson had been so delightful! We hadn't even opened the dictionary, or the *Selection of Phrases in Common Use,* or the exercise-book. . . .

I meditated, inwardly raging as I copied down my problems in wildly untidy writing. Anaïs was surreptitiously eyeing me, obviously guessing something was up. I looked again at that terrible Redhead with the jealous eyes as I picked up my pen which I'd dropped on the floor by a lucky piece of clumsiness. But . . . but she'd been crying. . . . I couldn't possibly be mistaken! Then why those angry, yet almost pleased glances? This was becoming unbearable; it was absolutely essential to question Aimée as soon as possible. I didn't give another thought to the problem to be transcribed:

"*. . . A workman is planting stakes to make a fence. He plants them at such a distance from each other that the bucket of tar, in which he dips their* *lower ends to a depth of 30 centimetres, is empty at the end of 3 hours. Given that the quantity of tar which remains on the stake equals 10 cubic centimetres, that the bucket is a cylinder whose radius at the base is 0.15 metres and whose height is 0.75 metres and is three-quarters full, that the workman dips 40 stakes an hour and takes about 8 minutes' rest during that time, what is the number of stakes and what is the area of the property which is in the form of a perfect square? State also what would be the number of stakes necessary if they were planted 10 centimetres further apart. State also the cost of this operation in both cases, if the stakes cost 3 francs a hundred and if the workman is paid 50 centimes an hour."*

Must one also say if the workman is happily married? Oh, what unwholesome imagination, what depraved brain incubates those revolting problems with which they torture us? I detest them! And the workmen who band together to complicate the amount of work of which they are capable, who divide themselves into two squads, one of which uses one-third more strength than the other, while the other, by way of compensation, works two hours longer! And the number of needles a seamstress uses in twenty-five years when she uses needles at 50 centimes a packet for eleven years, and needles at 75 centimes for the rest of the time but if the ones at 75 centimes are . . . etc., etc. . . . And the locomotives that diabolically complicate their speeds, their times of departure and the state of health of their drivers! Odious suppositions, improbable hypotheses that have made me refractory to arithmetic for the rest of my life!

"Anaïs, come up to the blackboard."

The lanky bean-pole stood and made a secret grimace, like a cat about to be sick, in my direction. Nobody likes "coming up to the blackboard" under the black, watchful eye of Mademoiselle Sergent.

"Work out the problem."

Anaïs "worked it out" and explained it. I took advantage of this to study the headmistress at my leisure: her eyes glittered, her red hair blazed. . . . If only I could have seen Aimée Lanthenay before class! The problem was finished at last, thank goodness. Anaïs breathed again and returned to her place.

"Claudine, come to the blackboard. Write down the fraction $\frac{3325}{5712}, \frac{806}{925}, \frac{14}{56}, \frac{302}{1052}$ (Lord preserve me from fractions divisible by 7 and by 11, also from those divisible by 5, by 9 and by 4 and 6, and by 1.127) and find their highest common factor."

That was what I had been dreading. I began dismally and I made some idiotic blunders because my mind wasn't on what I was doing. How swiftly they were reprimanded by a sharp movement of the hand or a frown, those small lapses I permitted myself! At last I got through it and returned to my place, followed by a "No witticisms here please!" because I'd replied to her observation "You're forgetting to wipe out the ciphers" with:

"Ciphers must always be wiped out—they deserve to be."

After me, Marie Belhomme went up to the blackboard and produced howler after howler with the utmost good faith. As usual, she was voluble and completely self-confident when wildly out of her depth; flushed and undecided when she remembered the previous lesson.

The door of the small classroom opened and Mademoiselle Lanthenay entered. I stared at her avidly. Oh, those poor golden eyes had been crying and their lids were swollen! Those dear eyes shot one scared look at me and were then hurriedly averted. I was left in utter consternation; heavens, whatever could *She* have been doing to her? I turned red with rage, so much so that Anaïs noticed and gave a low, sneering laugh. The sorrowful Aimée asked Mademoiselle Sergent for a book and the latter gave it to her with marked alacrity, her cheeks turning a deeper crimson as she did so. What could all that mean? When I thought that the English lesson did not take place till tomorrow, I was more tormented by anxiety than ever. But what was the good? There was absolutely nothing I could do. Mademoiselle Lanthenay returned to her own classroom.

"Girls!" announced the wicked Redhead. "Get out your school-books and your exercise-books. We are going to be forced to take refuge for the time being in the Infants' School."

Promptly all the girls began to bustle about with as much frenzied energy as if their stockings were on fire. People shoved each other and pinched each other, benches were pushed askew, books clattered to the floor and we scooped them up in heaps into our big aprons. That gawk Anaïs watched me pile up my load, carrying her own luggage in her arms; then she deftly tweaked the corner of my apron and the whole lot collapsed.

She preserved her expression of complete detachment and earnestly contemplated three builders who were throwing tiles at each other in the playground. I was scolded for my clumsiness and, two minutes later, that pest Anaïs tried the same experiment on Marie Belhomme. Marie screamed so loud that she got some pages of Ancient History to copy out. At last our chattering, trampling horde crossed the playground and went into the Infants' School. I wrinkled my nose: it was dirty. Hastily cleaned up for us, it still smelt of ill-kept children. Let's hope the "time being" isn't going to last too long!

Anaïs put down her books and promptly verified the fact that the windows looked out on the Headmaster's garden. As for me, I'd no time to waste in contemplating the assistant-masters; I was too anxious about the troubles I foreboded.

We returned to the old classroom with as much noise as a herd of escaped bullocks and we transported the tables. They were so old and so heavy that we bumped and banged them about as much as possible in the hope that one of them would completely come to bits and collapse in worm-eaten fragments. Vain hope! They all arrived whole. This was not our fault.

We didn't do much work that morning, which was one good thing. At eleven, when we went home, I prowled about trying to catch a glimpse of Mademoiselle Lanthenay, but without success. Had *She* put her under lock and key then? I went off to lunch so seething with suppressed rage that even Papa noticed it and asked me if I had a temperature. . . . Then I returned to school very early, at quarter-past twelve, and hung about, bored, among the few children who were there; country girls who were lunching at school off hard-boiled eggs, bacon, bread-and-treacle and fruit. And I waited vainly, torturing myself with anxiety!

Antonin Rabastens came in (at least this made a diversion) and bowed to me with all the grace of a dancing bear.

"A thousand pardons, Mademoiselle. By the way, haven't the lady *teacherrs* come down yet?"

"No, Sir, I'm waiting for them. I hope they won't be long for 'absence is the greatest of all ills!'" I had already expatiated half a dozen times on this aphorism of La Fontaine's in French essays which had been highly commended.

I spoke with a sweet seriousness. The handsome Marseillais

listened, with an uneasy look on his kindly face. (He'll begin to think I'm a bit crazy, too.) He changed the subject.

"Mademoiselle, I've been told that you read a great deal. Does your father possess a large library?"

"Yes, Sir, two thousand, three hundred and seven volumes precisely."

"No doubt you know a great many interesting things. And I realised at once, the other day—when you sang so charmingly—that you had ideas far beyond your age."

(Heavens, what an idiot! Why couldn't he take himself off? Ah! I was forgetting he was a little in love with me. I decided to be more amiable.)

"But you yourself, Sir, I've been told you have a beautiful baritone voice. We hear you singing in your room sometimes when the builders aren't making a din."

He turned red as a poppy with pleasure and protested with enraptured modesty. He wriggled as he exclaimed:

"Oh, Mademoiselle! . . . As it happens, you'll soon be able to judge for yourself, for Mademoiselle Sergent has asked me to give singing-lessons to the older girls who are studying for their certificate. On Thursdays and Sundays. We're going to begin next week."

What luck! If I had not been so preoccupied, it would have been thrilling to tell the news to the others who knew nothing about it as yet. How Anaïs would drench herself in eau-de-Cologne and bite her lips next Thursday! How she would pull in her leather belt and coo as she sang!

"What? But I know nothing whatever about it! Mademoiselle Sergent hasn't said a word to us."

"Oh! Perhaps I shouldn't have mentioned it? Would you be good enough to pretend you don't know?"

He implored me with ingratiating movements of his torso and I shook my head to fling back my curls which weren't in the least in my way. This hint of a secret between us threw him into ecstasies. It was obviously going to serve as a pretext for glances full of understanding—exceedingly commonplace understanding on his part. He went off, carrying himself proudly, with a farewell that already had a new touch of familiarity.

"Good-bye, Mademoiselle Claudine."

"Good-bye, Sir."

At half-past twelve, the rest of the class arrived and there was still no sign of Aimée. I refused to play, pretending that I had a headache, and, inwardly, I chafed.

Oh! Oh! Whatever did I see? The two of them had come down, Aimée and her redoubtable chief; they had come down and were crossing the playground. And the Redhead had taken Mademoiselle Lanthenay's arm—an unheard-of proceeding! Mademoiselle Sergent was talking very softly to her assistant who, still a little scared, was raising her eyes towards the other who was much taller than herself. Those eyes already looked reassured and pretty again. The spectacle of this idyll turned my anxiety to chagrin. Before they had quite reached the door, I rushed outside and hurled myself into the midst of a wild game of "Wolf", yelling "I'm playing!" as if I were yelling "Fire!" And, until the bell rang for class, I galloped till I was out of breath, now chasing, now being chased, doing all I could to stop myself from thinking.

During the game, I caught sight of the head of Rabastens. He was watching over the wall and enjoying the sight of these big girls running about and showing—some, like Marie Belhomme, unconsciously and others, like the gawky Anaïs, very consciously indeed—calves that were pretty or ludicrous. The amiable Antonin honoured me with a gracious smile, an excessively gracious one. I did not think it necessary to return it, on account of my companions, but I arched my chest and tossed my curls. It was essential to keep this young man entertained. (In any case, he seems to me a born blunderer destined to put his foot in it on every conceivable occasion.) Anaïs, who had noticed him too, took to kicking up her skirts as she ran so as to exhibit legs which, however, were far from attractive, also to laughing and uttering bird-like cries. She would have acted flirtatiously in the presence of a plough-ox!

We went indoors and opened our exercise-books, still panting from our exertions. But, after a quarter of an hour, Mademoiselle Sergent's mother appeared and announced to her daughter, in a barbaric dialect, that two new girls had arrived. The class bubbled over with excitement: two "new ones" to tease! And Mademoiselle left the room, very politely asking Mademoiselle Lanthenay to look after the class. Aimée arrived and I sought her eyes so as to smile at her with all my anxious tenderness. But she gave me back a far from confident look and my heart swelled absurdly as I bent over my knitting. . . . I've never dropped so many stitches! I dropped so many that I had to go and ask Mademoiselle Aimée for help. While she was trying to remedy my mistakes, I whispered to her: "Good afternoon, my sweet darling little Mademoiselle. . . . Heavens, whatever's the matter? I'm worn to shreds with not being able to speak to you." She looked round her uneasily and answered, very low:

"I can't tell you anything now. Tomorrow, at our lesson."

"I'll never be able to wait till tomorrow! Suppose I pretend Papa wants to use his library tomorrow and ask if you can give me my lesson this evening?"

"No. . . . All right, yes, ask her. But go back to your place at once—the big ones are staring at us."

I said "Thank you" out loud to her and went and sat down again. She was right. That gawk Anaïs was watching us closely, trying to guess what had been going on these last two or three days.

Mademoiselle Sergent returned at last, accompanied by two insignificant young things whose arrival caused a little stir on the benches.

She installed these newcomers in their places. The minutes dragged slowly by.

When, at last, it struck four, I went straight off to find Mademoiselle Sergent and I asked her, in one breathless burst:

"Mademoiselle, it would be awfully kind of you if you'd let Mademoiselle Lanthenay give me my lesson tonight instead of tomorrow night, Papa's got someone coming to talk business in the library so we won't be able to stay there."

Ouf! I had brought out my sentence without pausing for breath. Mademoiselle frowned, studied my face for a moment, then made up her mind:

"Very well. Go and tell Mademoiselle Lanthenay."

I rushed off and did so. She put on her hat and coat and I bore her off, quivering with anxiety to know all.

"Ah, how glad I am to have you to myself for a little. Tell me quick, whatever's gone wrong?"

She hesitated, beating about the bush.

"Not here. Wait. It's difficult to tell you all about it in the street. We'll be at your home in a minute."

In the meantime, I squeezed her arm in mine but her smile was not the charming one of all the other times. As soon as the door of the library shut behind us, I took her in my arms and kissed her. I felt as if she had been kept imprisoned far away from me for a month, that poor little Aimée with those shadows under her eyes and those pale cheeks! Had she suffered very much, then? Yet the looks she gave me struck me as embarrassed rather than anything else, and she seemed feverish rather than sad. Moreover, she returned my kisses very hurriedly—and I don't at all like being kissed in double quick time!

"Come on, tell me . . . tell me everything right from the beginning."

"But it's not a very long story. . . . In fact, nothing much happened at all. It was Mademoiselle Sergent . . . well, she wanted . . . I mean, she preferred . . . she thought these English lessons were preventing me from correcting the exercise-books and making me go to bed too late. . . ."

"Look here, for goodness' sake, don't waste time. And tell me the truth. She doesn't want you to come any more?"

I was trembling with anguish; I gripped my hands between my knees to make them keep still. Aimée fidgeted with the cover of the Grammar and began to tear off a strip where it was gummed. As she did so, she raised her eyes towards me. They had grown scared again.

"Yes, that's it. But she didn't say it the way you said it, Claudine. Listen to me a moment. . . ."

I did not listen to a word; I felt as if I were dissolving with misery. I was sitting on a little stool on the floor, and, clasping my arms round her slim waist, I beseeched her:

"Darling, don't go away. . . . If you only knew, I'd be too utterly wretched! Oh, find some excuse, make up something, come back, don't leave me! It's sheer bliss for me, just being with you! Doesn't it give *you* any pleasure at all? Am I just like Anaïs or Marie Belhomme to you? Darling, do, *do* come back and go on giving me English lessons! I love you so much. . . . I didn't tell you . . . but now you can't help seeing I do! . . . Come back, I implore you. She can't beat you for it, that red-haired beast!"

I was burning with fever and my nerves were becoming more and more frayed at feeling that Aimée's were not vibrating in sympathy. She stroked my head as it lay on her lap and only interrupted now and then with a quavering "my little Claudine!" At last her eyes brimmed over and she began to cry as she said:

"I'm going to tell you everything. It's too wretched—you make me too unhappy! Well, last Saturday, I couldn't help noticing *She* was being much nicer to me than usual. I thought she was getting used to me and would leave the two of us in peace so I was awfully happy and pleased. And then, towards the end of the evening, when we were correcting exercise-books at the same table, I suddenly looked up and saw she was crying. And she was looking at me in such a peculiar way that I was absolutely dumbfounded. Then, all at once, she got up from her chair and went off to bed. The next day, after being awfully nice to me all day, when I was alone with her in the evening and was just going to say good night, she suddenly asked me: 'You're very fond of Claudine, aren't you? And, no doubt, she returns your fondness?' And, before I had time to answer, she fell into a chair beside me and sobbed. And then she took my hands and said all sorts of things that simply took my breath away. . . ."

"What things?"

"Well . . . she said to me: 'My dear little thing, don't you realise you're breaking my heart with your indifference? Oh, my darling girl, how could you possibly not have noticed my great affection for you? My little Aimée, I'm jealous of the tenderness you show to that brainless Claudine who's quite definitely a little unhinged. . . . If you'd only just not hate me, oh! if you'd only love me a little, I'd be a more tender friend than you could ever imagine. . . .' And she looked into the very depths of my soul with eyes like red-hot pokers."

"Didn't you answer her at all?"

"Of course not! I hadn't time to! Another thing she said was: 'Do you think they're very useful to her or very kind to me, those English lessons you give her? It tears my heart every time I see the two of you go off together! Don't go there—don't ever go there again! Claudine won't give it another thought in a week's time and I can give you more affection than she's capable of feeling!' Claudine, I assure you, I no longer had any idea what I was doing. She was mesmerising me with those crazy eyes of hers and, suddenly, the room began to go round, and my head swam; and for two or three seconds, not more, I couldn't see anything at all. I could only hear her saying over and over again, and sounding terrified 'My God!

. . . My poor little girl! I've frightened her . . . she's so pale, my little Aimée, my darling!' And, immediately after that, she helped me to undress, in the most kind, affectionate way, and I slept as if I'd spent the entire day walking. . . . Claudine, my poor pet, you realise there was simply nothing I could do about it!"

I was stunned. So she had passionate friendships, that volcanic Redhead! At heart, I was not tremendously surprised; it was bound to end that way. Meanwhile, I sat there, utterly overwhelmed; faced with Aimée, this frail little creature bewitched by that Fury, I did not know what to say. She dried her eyes. It seemed to me that her distress was over with her tears.

"But you . . . don't you love her at all?"

She answered, without looking at me:

"No, of course not. But, really, she does seem to be awfully fond of me and I never suspected it."

Her answer froze me completely. After all, I'm not completely out of my mind yet and I understand what people are trying to say to me. I let go her hands which I was holding and I stood up. Something had been broken. Since she was unwilling to admit frankly that she was no longer with me against the other, since she was hiding her deepest thoughts, I thought all was over. My hands were ice-cold and my cheeks were burning. After a painful silence, I was the first to speak:

"Dear Aimée of the lovely eyes, I implore you to come just once more to finish up the month. Do you think she will agree?"

"Oh, yes! I'll ask her."

She said it promptly and spontaneously, already sure of getting anything she wanted out of Mademoiselle Sergent now. How fast she was receding from me and how fast the other had triumphed! Cowardly little Lanthenay! She loved comfort like a warmth-starved cat and knew very well that her chief's friendship would be more profitable to her than mine! But I did not mean to tell her so or she would not come back for the last lesson and I still cherished a vague hope. . . . The hour was over and I escorted Aimée to the door. In the passage, I embraced her fiercely, with a touch of despair. Once I was alone, I was surprised not to find myself feeling quite as sad as I believed myself to be. I had expected a tremendous, absurd explosion but, no, what I felt was more like a chill that froze me. . . .

At supper, I broke in upon Papa's musings.

"Papa, you know those English lessons of mine?"

"Yes, I know. You're quite right to take them. . . ."

"Please listen. I'm not going to take any more."

"Ah, they tire you, do they?"

"Yes, they get on my nerves."

"Then you're quite right."

And his thoughts flew back to his slugs—if they had ever left them.

The night was shot through with stupid dreams. Mademoiselle Sergent, as a Fury, with snakes in her red hair, was trying to embrace Aimée Lanthenay who ran away, screaming. I tried to go to her rescue but Antonin Rabastens held me back. He was dressed all in pastel pink and he pulled me back by the arm, saying: "Listen, do listen! Here's a lyrical ballad that I sing and I'm really enraptured with it." Then he warbled in his baritone:

> *"Beloved friends, when I am dead,*
> *Plant a sad pillow on my grrave. . . ."*

He sang it to the tune of: "Ah, how my French blood thrills with pride, to see her soldiers marching by!" An absurd night and one that did not rest me in the least.

I arrived late for school and contemplated Mademoiselle Sergent, secretly surprised to think that this audacious Redhead had had such success. She darted malicious, almost mocking looks at me, but I was so tired and dispirited that I had no heart left to answer her back.

When class was over, I saw Mademoiselle Aimée lining up the little ones in file (it was as if I had dreamt the whole of yesterday evening). I said good morning to her in passing; she looked tired, too. Mademoiselle Sergent was not there. I stopped and said:

"Are you feeling all right this morning?"

"Yes, of course, thank you. You look very dark under the eyes, Claudine."

"Maybe. Any fresh news? The scene didn't start up again? Is she still as amiable to you as ever?"

She blushed and looked embarrassed.

"Oh, yes. Nothing more's happened and she's being very nice.

I . . . I think you don't know her properly . . . she's not in the least like what you imagine. . . ."

Slightly nauseated, I let her go stammering on. When she had got her sentence well and truly entangled, I interrupted her:

"Perhaps you're the one who's right. You'll come on Wednesday for the last time?"

"Oh, indeed I will. I've asked her. It's all fixed. Definitely."

How quickly things change! Since that scene yesterday evening, we had already begun to speak differently to each other. Today I did not dare to show a trace of the vociferous misery I had let her see last night. At all costs, I must make her laugh a little.

"How are your love-affairs? Is the handsome Richelieu going on all right?"

"Who do you mean? Armand Duplessis? Oh, yes, he's going on splendidly. Sometimes he stays two hours in the shadows under my window. But yesterday night, I let him know that I'd noticed him and he went striding away at a great rate, on those long legs of his—they're just like the legs of a compass. And when Monsieur Rabastens wanted to bring him along the day before yesterday, he refused to come."

"You know, Armand is seriously keen on you. I know what I'm talking about. I overheard a conversation between those two masters last Sunday. Quite by chance, by the roadside. And . . . I'll only tell you this much! . . . Armand has got it badly. Only try and tame him—he's a wild bird."

She was all animation now and wanted all the details, but I ran off.

Let me try and think about the singing-lessons we are to have from the seductive Antonin Rabastens. They're to begin on Thursday. I shall put on my blue skirt, with the pleated blouse that shows off my figure, and my apron. Not the big black apron I wear on weekdays with the close-fitting bib (though it's quite becoming), but the pretty little pale blue embroidered one I wear at home on Sundays. And that's all. I'm not going to take too much trouble for his friendship or my dear, kind little schoolmates will notice.

Aimée, Aimée! It really is a pity that she's flown away so soon, that charming little bird who might have consoled me for all those geese! Now, I feel quite certain that last lesson will serve no purpose at all. With a small nature like hers, frail and egotistical, a nature that likes its pleasures but knows how to look after its interests, it is useless to struggle against Mademoiselle Sergent. I only hope that this great disappointment will not sadden me for long.

Today, at recreation, I played madly to shake myself up and to get warm. Anaïs and I, grasping Marie Belhomme firmly by her "midwife's hands", made her run till she was breathless and panting for mercy. Afterwards, under penalty of being locked up in the lavatories, I forced her to recite Théraméne's speech on the death of Hippolyte in a loud, intelligible voice.

She declaimed Racine's alexandrines in a martyred voice and then escaped, flinging up her arms. The sisters Jaubert struck me as impressed. Good! If they don't like the classics, they'll be presented with modern verse on the next occasion.

The next occasion was not long delayed. Hardly had we got back into the classroom than we were clamped down to exercises in round and cursive handwriting in view of the approaching exams. For most of us had appalling writing.

"Claudine, you will dictate the examples while I go and find places for the younger ones' class."

She went off to the "Second Class" who, dislodged in their turn, were about to be installed goodness knows where. This promised us a good half-hour to ourselves.

I began:

"Children, today I am going to dictate to you something highly entertaining."

Chorus of "Ah!"

"Yes, some gay songs taken from *Wandering Palaces*."

"That sounds awfully nice, even from the title," observed Marie Belhomme with conviction.

"You're absolutely right. Are you ready? I'll begin."

> *"On the identical slow curve*
> *Whose slowness is implacable*
> *Ecstatically there vacillates and sinks*
> *The complex present of slow curves"*

I paused. The lanky Anaïs didn't laugh because she didn't understand. (Neither did I.) And Marie Belhomme, with her usual good faith, exclaimed: "But you know quite well we've already done geometry this morning! And besides that all sounded too difficult. I haven't written down half what you said."

The twins rolled four defiant eyes. I went on, imperturbably:

"The selfsame autumn sees those curves homologous.
Parallel to your grief on the long autumn evenings,
Flattening the slow curve of things and your brief birdlike hoppings."

They followed laboriously, without making any further efforts to understand. I felt a delicious satisfaction at hearing Marie Belhomme complain once more and stop me:

"Wait a bit, wait a bit . . . you're going much too fast. . . . The slow curve of what?"

I repeated: "*The slow curve of things and your brief birdlike hoppings.* . . . Now copy that out for me, first in round script, then in cursive. . . ."

These supplementary writing-lessons, designed to satisfy the examiners at the end of July, were my joy. I dictated the most extravagant things and I had immense pleasure in hearing these daughters of grocers, cobblers and policemen meekly reciting and writing down parodies of the Romantic School or of Francis Jammes' murmuring lullabies. I collected all these for the benefit of my dear little companions from the reviews and magazines my father received. And he certainly received plenty! All the periodicals from the *Revue des Deux Mondes* to the *Mercure de France* accumulated in our house. Papa confided to me the duty of cutting their pages: I allocated to myself the duty of reading them. For someone had to read them! Papa merely gave them a superficial, absent-minded glance, since the *Mercure de France* deals very seldom indeed with malacology. As for myself, I found them highly instructive, if not always comprehensible, and I used to warn Papa when the subscriptions were running out. "You must renew yours, Papa, or you'll lose the good opinion of the postman."

That gawk Anaïs, who is lacking in knowledge of literature—it's not her fault—muttered sceptically:

"These things you dictate to us at writing-lessons, I'm sure you deliberately make them up."

"What a thing to say! These are lines dedicated to our ally, the Czar Nicholas, so there!"

She could not call my bluff but her eyes remained incredulous.

Re-enter Mademoiselle Sergent who took one look at what we had written.

"Claudine!" she expostulated, "Aren't you ashamed of dictating such absurdities to them? You'd do better to learn some arithmetic theorems by heart, that would be more useful to everyone!"

But there was no conviction behind her scolding, for in her secret heart, she's rather amused by these hoaxes. All the same, I listened without a smile and my resentment returned at feeling her so near me, this woman who had forced the affections of that unreliable little Aimée. . . . Heavens! It was half-past three and in half an hour she would be coming to my home for the last time.

Mademoiselle Sergent rose from her seat and said:

"Shut your exercise-books. The big ones who are taking their Certificate, stay behind. I have something to say to you."

The others went off, deliberately dawdling over putting on their hoods and shawls. They were annoyed at not being able to stay and listen to the announcement, obviously bristling with interest, that was about to be made to us. The red-haired Headmistress addressed us and, in spite of myself, I had to admire, as always, her clear-cut voice and the decision and precision of her phrases.

"Girls, I imagine you have no illusions about your apparent inability to grasp even the rudiments of music. I make an exception of Claudine who plays the piano and reads fluently at sight. I might well let her give you lessons, but you are too lacking in discipline to obey one of your classmates. As from tomorrow, you will come on Sundays and Thursdays at nine o'clock to practise tonic sol-fa and sight-reading under the direction of Monsieur Rabastens, the assistant-headmaster, as neither Mademoiselle Lanthenay nor myself are in a position to give you lessons. Monsieur Rabastens will be assisted by Mademoiselle Claudine. Try not to behave too disgracefully. And be here at nine o'clock tomorrow."

I added a muttered: "Dis-miss!" that was caught by her redoubtable ear. She frowned, only to smile afterwards, in spite of herself. Her little speech had been delivered in such a peremptory tone that it practically called for a military salute—and she had realised it. But, to tell the truth, it looked as if I could no longer annoy her. This was discouraging. She must be very sure indeed of her triumph to display such magnanimity!

She went away and everyone began excitedly talking at once. Marie Belhomme simply could not get over it.

"Really, I say, making us have lessons with a young man! It's a bit thick! Still, it'll be amusing all the same. Don't you think so, Claudine?"

"Yes. One's got to have *some* slight distraction."

"Won't you be simply terrified, giving us singing-lessons with one of the masters?"

"It doesn't mean a thing to me. I don't care twopence either way."

I didn't listen much. I was waiting, with inward trepidation, wondering why Mademoiselle Aimée Lanthenay did not come at once. Anaïs was in raptures. Her face wore a sneering grin; she was clutching her ribs, as if she were convulsed with laughter, and jostling Marie Belhomme who groaned without knowing how to defend herself. "Ha, ha!" mocked Anaïs "you'll make a conquest of the handsome Antonin Rabastens. He won't be able to resist them long—those long, slim hands of yours, those midwife's hands! And your dainty waist and your eloquent eyes! Aha! my dear—this romantic story's going to end in a marriage!" She grew wildly excited and began to dance about in front of Marie whom she had harassed into a corner and who was hiding her unlucky hands and protesting at the unseemly remarks.

Still Aimée did not come! My nerves were so much on edge that I could not keep still and went and prowled as far as the door of the staircase leading to the "temporary" (still!) rooms of the mistress. Ah! I had been right to come and look! Up there on the landing, Mademoiselle Lanthenay was all ready to set off. Mademoiselle Sergent was holding her by the waist and talking to her very low, with an air of tender insistence. Then she gave Aimée, whose veil was pulled down, a long kiss. Aimée let herself be kissed and yielded graciously; she even stopped and turned back as she went down the stairs. I escaped without their having noticed me but, once again, I felt very unhappy. Wicked, wicked little thing to have broken away from me so quickly to bestow her caresses and her golden eyes on that woman who had been our common enemy! . . . I no longer knew what to think. . . . She joined me in the classroom where I had remained rooted to the spot in a brown study.

"Are you coming, Claudine?"

"Yes, Mademoiselle. I'm ready."

Out in the street, I no longer dared to question her—what would she reply? I preferred to wait till we got home and merely to make conventional conversation on the way. I observed that it was cold, foretold that we should have more snow and that the singing-lessons on Sundays and Thursdays would probably be amusing. . . . But I spoke without conviction and she too realised, that all this chatter meant nothing at all.

When we were settled under the lamp in the library, I opened my exercise-books and I looked at her. She was prettier than she had been the other evening; a little paler and there were shadows round her eyes that made them look larger.

"Are you tired? You look as if you were."

She was embarrassed by all my questions. Whyever should she be? She turned quite pink again and looked everywhere but at me. I was certain she felt vaguely guilty about me. I went on remorselessly:

"Tell me, is she still being so frightfully friendly towards you, the loathsome Redhead? Have the rages and the kisses of the other night started up again?"

"No, of course not. . . . She's being very kind to me. . . . I assure you she takes tremendous care of me. . . ."

"She hasn't 'mesmerised' you again?"

"Oh no, there's no question of that. . . . I think I exaggerated a little the other evening because my nerves were rather on edge."

As she said it, her face became very confused. I didn't care—I wanted to know the truth. I went up close to her and took her hands—her tiny little hands.

"Oh darling, do tell me what else! Don't you want to say anything more to your poor Claudine who was so wretched the day before yesterday?"

But anyone would have said that she had managed to restrain herself and had suddenly decided to say nothing. By degrees she assumed a calm little expression, artificially natural, and looked at me with those clear, untruthful cat's eyes of hers.

"No. Look, Claudine, I assure you that she leaves me completely in peace and that she's even gone out of her way to be very kind. You and I made her out to be much nastier than she is, you know. . . ."

What was that cold voice and those eyes that were shuttered in spite of being open to their widest extent? It was her classroom voice and that I couldn't stand. I thrust back my desire to cry, so as not to make a fool of myself. So it was all over between us then? And if I tormented her with questions, shouldn't we part at loggerheads?

. . . I took up my English Grammar; there was nothing else to do. She opened my exercise-book with marked alacrity.

That was the first—and the only—time I took a serious lesson with her. With a heart swelling and ready to burst, I translated whole pages of:

"*You have some pens but he had not a horse.*"

"*We should have your cousin's apples if he had plenty of penknives.*"

"*Have you any ink in your ink-pot? No, but I have a table in my bedroom, etc., etc.*"

Towards the end of the lesson, that extraordinary Aimée asked me point-blank:

"My little Claudine, you aren't angry with me?"

I was not altogether lying when I answered:

"No. I'm not *angry* with you."

It was almost true. I did not feel angry, only unhappy and exhausted. I escorted her to the door and I kissed her, but she turned her head so much away as she held out her cheek that my lips almost touched her ear. The heartless little thing! I watched her go off under the lamppost with a vague desire to run after her. But what would have been the good?

I slept pretty badly and my eyes proved it. There were shadows under them that reached to the middle of my cheeks. Luckily, that rather becomes me. I noticed this in the looking-glass as I was fiercely brushing my hair (quite golden this morning) before setting off for the singing-lesson.

I arrived half an hour too early and I couldn't help laughing when I found two out of my four classmates already installed in the school! We inspected each other closely and Anaïs gave an approving whistle at my blue dress and my charming apron. She had trotted out for the occasion the apron she wears on Thursdays and Sundays. It's red, embroidered in white and makes her look paler than ever. Her hair was done in a "helmet" with the puff in front pushed well forward, almost overhanging her forehead and she'd squeezed herself till she could hardly breathe into a new belt. Charitably, she observed out loud that I looked ill but I replied that it suited me to look tired. Marie Belhomme came running in, harum-scarum and scatter-brained as usual. She too had adorned herself, in spite of being in mourning. Her big frilly collar of ruched crêpe made her look like a bewildered black Pierrot. With her long, velvety eyes and her lost, innocent expression, she was quite charming. The two Jauberts arrived together, as always, ready to behave irreproachably and never to raise their eyes and to speak ill of all the rest of us after the lesson. We warmed ourselves, clustered round the stove, as we teased the handsome Antonin in advance. Attention! Here he was. . . . A noise of voices and laughter sounded nearer and nearer, then Mademoiselle Sergent opened the door, followed by the irresistible assistant-master.

Rabastens was a splendid sight! He wore a fur cap and a dark blue suit under his overcoat. He removed his cap and coat on entering, after a "Young ladies!" accompanied by a low bow. He had decorated his jacket with a rust-red chrysanthemum in the best of taste and his grey- green tie, patterned with interlacing white circles, was highly impressive. He had obviously knotted it with studious care in front of the mirror. In a flash, we were all demurely lined up, our hands surreptitiously pulling down our blouses to smooth out the faintest trace of unalluring creases. Marie Belhomme was already enjoying herself so whole-heartedly that she gave a loud giggle and then stopped, frightened at her own audacity. Mademoiselle Sergent knitted her terrible eyebrows and was obviously annoyed. She had given me a look as she came in. I thought: "I bet her little friend already tells her every single thing!" I kept obstinately assuring myself that Aimée was not worth so much misery but I was not in the least convinced by my own arguments.

"Young ladies," said Rabastens in his guttural voice. "Would one of you be good enough to lend me her book?"

The lanky Anaïs hurriedly offered her copy of Marmontel's piano pieces so as to get herself noticed and was rewarded with an exaggeratedly affable "Thank you." That hulking fellow must practise his manners in front of the long mirror of his wardrobe. It is true that he doesn't possess a wardrobe with a long mirror.

"Mademoiselle Claudine," he said to me with a fascinating ogle (fascinating for him, I mean), "I am charmed and extremely honoured to become your colleague. For you give singing-lessons to these young ladies, do you not?"

"Yes, but they are not in the least obedient to one of their own classmates" Mademoiselle Sergent cut in sharply. She was becoming impatient with all this chit-chat. "With your assistance, Monsieur, she will obtain better results. Otherwise they will fail in their Certificate, for they do not seem to have grasped even the rudiments of music."

Well done! *That* would teach the gentleman to spin out meaningless phrases! My companions listened with unconcealed astonishment; no one had ever displayed such gallantry towards them before. What reduced them to stupefaction were the compliments lavished on me by the fulsome Antonin.

Mademoiselle Sergent took the "Marmontel" and indicated the gulf his new pupils refused to cross, some from inattentiveness, some from sheer inability to understand. The one exception was Anaïs whose memory allowed to her to learn all the sol-fa exercises by heart without having to beat time and without distorting them. How true it was that they "had not grasped even the rudiments of music", those little duffers! And, as they made it a kind of point of honour not to obey me, they were certainly going to be marked "zero" in the forthcoming exam. This prospect enraged Mademoiselle Sergent who could not sing in tune and so could not act as a singing-teacher, any more than could Mademoiselle Lanthenay, who had never properly recovered from a long-ago attack of laryngitis.

"Make them sing one by one to begin with," I said to the southerner (he was beaming and preening himself like a peacock at being in our midst). "They all make mistakes in time, every single one of them, but not the same mistakes. And, up to now, I haven't been able to stop them."

"Let's see, Mademoiselle . . . ?"

"Marie Belhomme."

"Mademoiselle Marie Belhomme, would you do this exercise for me in tonic sol-fa?"

It was a little polka in G, totally innocent of any nasty traps, but poor Marie, who couldn't be less musical, has never been able to sol-fa it correctly. Under this direct attack, she was seized with tremors; her face turned crimson and her eyes swam.

"I'll beat one silent bar, then you'll begin on the first beat: *Ray, te, te, lah, soh, fah, fah* . . . Not awfully difficult, is it?"

"Yes, Sir" answered Marie who had quite lost her head from shyness.

"Good. I'll begin. . . . One, two, one . . ."

"*Ray, te, te, lah, soh, fah, fah,*" twittered Marie in a voice like a hen with a sore throat.

She had not missed the opportunity of beginning on the second beat! I stopped her.

"No, do listen! One, two, *Ray, te, te* . . . have you got it? Monsieur Rabastens is beating one empty bar. Start again."

"One, two, one . . ."

"*Ray, te, te* . . ." she began again fervently, making the same mistake! To think that, for three whole months, she's been singing that polka out of time! Rabastens intervened, patient and discreet.

"Allow me, Mademoiselle Belhomme. Would you please beat time along with me."

He took her wrist and guided her hand.

"You'll understand better this way: one, two, one . . . But, come on! Sing!"

She did not begin at all, this time! Scarlet as a result of this unexpected gesture, she had completely lost countenance. I was immensely amused. But the handsome baritone, highly flattered at the poor little thing's distress (she was as fluttered as a linnet) made a point of insisting. That gawk Anaïs had her cheeks puffed out with suppressed laughter.

"Mademoiselle Anaïs, may I ask you to sing this exercise, to show Mademoiselle how it should be done?"

That one needed no pressing! She cooed her little piece "with expression", lingering on the high notes and being none too correct in her time. Still, she knew it by heart and her rather absurd way of singing a sol-fa exercise as if it were a sentimental song pleased the southerner who congratulated her. She tried to blush, couldn't manage to, and was obliged to confine herself to lowering her eyes, biting her lips and drooping her head.

I said to Rabastens:

"Sir, would you make us go through some of the two-part exercises? I've done everything I could but they still don't even begin to know them."

I was in a serious mood that morning: firstly, because I didn't feel much like laughing; secondly, because, if I played the fool too much during this first lesson, Mademoiselle Sergent would stop the others. Moreover, I was thinking of Aimée. Wasn't she going to come downstairs this morning? Only a week ago, she'd never have dared lie in bed so late!

With my mind on all this, I gave out the parts; the firsts to Anaïs, reinforced by Marie Belhomme; the seconds to the two new boarders. As for myself, I would come to the rescue of whichever turned out to be the weaker. Rabastens supported the seconds.

Then we executed the little duet, I standing by the handsome Antonin who trolled out "Ah! Ahs!" full of expression in his baritone as he leant over in my direction. We must have made an extraordinarily funny group. That incorrigible southerner was so preoccupied in displaying his charms that he made mistake after mistake, without anyone noticing it, of course. The stylish chrysanthemum he wore in his buttonhole fell out and dropped on the floor. When he had sung his piece, he picked it up and threw it on the table, saying, as if he were appealing for personal compliments: "Well, I think that didn't go too badly, do you?"

Mademoiselle Sergent damped his enthusiasm by replying:

"Yes, but let them sing by themselves without you or Claudine. Then you'll see."

(I could have sworn, from his discomfited looks, that he had forgotten what he was here for. He's going to be a first-class teacher, that Rabastens! So much the better! When the Headmistress doesn't come to the lessons, we'll be able to do exactly what we like with him.)

"Yes, I'm sure, Mademoiselle. But if these young ladies will take a little trouble, I'm sure they'll soon come to know enough to satisfy the examiners. The standard in music is very low indeed, as you must be the first to realise."

Well, well, so he was getting his own back now, was he? He couldn't have found a better way of bringing home to the Redhead that she was incapable of singing a scale. She understood the spite behind the remark and averted her sombre eyes. Antonin went up a little in my esteem, but he had antagonised Mademoiselle Sergent who said sharply:

"I wonder if you would be good enough to make these children practise some more? I should rather like them to sing one by one so as to acquire a little self-possession and confidence."

It was the turn of the twins who possessed non-existent, uncertain voices without much sense of rhythm, but those two plodders always get by, they work with such exemplary diligence! I can't stand those Jauberts, so virtuous and so modest. And I could just see them working at home, going over each exercise fifty times, before coming to the Thursday lessons, the irreproachable sneaks.

To end up with, Rabastens "gave himself the pleasure," as he said, of hearing me sing. He asked me to read the most boring things at sight, ghastly sentimental songs and airs adorned with gargling runs and trills whose out-of-date *coloratura* seemed to him the last word in art. From vanity, because Mademoiselle Sergent was there, and Anaïs too, I sang my best. And the unspeakable Antonin went into ecstasies; he got himself completely tied up in tortuous compliments, in labyrinthine sentences from which I deliberately did not try to extricate him. I was enjoying myself too much listening to him with my eyes riveted on his with earnest attention. I don't know how he would have got to the end of a sentence crammed full of parentheses if Mademoiselle Sergent had not come up to us and asked:

"Have you given these girls some pieces to study for homework during the week?"

"No," he had given them nothing at all. He could not get it into his head that he had not been summoned here to sing duets with me!

But whatever had become of little Aimée? I simply had to know. So I deftly overturned an inkpot, taking care to get plenty of ink on my fingers. Then I let out an "Oh!" of desolation, spreading out all my fingers like spiders. Madame Sergent took the time to remark that this was typical of me and sent me off to wash my hands under the pump.

Once outside, I wiped my fingers with the blackboard sponge to take off the worst of it, then I searched about, peering into every corner. Nothing in the house. I went outside again and walked as far as the little wall that separated us from the Headmaster's garden. Still nothing. But no! There were people talking on the other side. Who? I leant over the little wall to look down into the garden which is a yard or two lower than our playground and there, under the leafless hazels, in the pallid sunshine, so faint you could hardly feel it, I saw the sombre Richelieu talking to Mademoiselle Aimée Lanthenay. Two or three days ago I'd have stood on my head and waved my feet in astonishment at this spectacle, but my recent great betrayal had slightly inured me to shocks.

That shy, unsociable Duplessis! At the moment, he had found his tongue and no longer kept his eyes lowered. Had he burnt his boats then?

"Tell me, Mademoiselle, didn't you suspect? Oh, do say you did!"

Aimée, her face quite pink, was quivering with joy. Her eyes were more golden than ever and they kept alertly watching and listening all about her as he spoke. She gave a charming laugh to indicate that she hadn't suspected anything at all, the liar!

"Come, you must have suspected when I used to spend my evenings under your windows. But I love you with all my might . . . not just to flirt for a term and then go off on my holidays and forget you. Will you listen to me seriously, as I am speaking to you now?"

"Is it as serious as all that?"

"Yes, I assure you it is. Will you authorise me to come and talk to you tonight in the presence of Mademoiselle?"

Oh, bother! I heard the door of the classroom opening: they were coming to see what had become of me. In two bounds I was far from the wall and almost beside the pump. I flung myself on my knees on the ground and when the Headmistress, accompanied by Rabastens, came up to me, she found me energetically rubbing the ink on my hands with sand, "because water won't take it off".

This was a great success.

"Leave off doing that," said Mademoiselle Sergent, "you can take it off at home with pumice-stone."

The handsome Antonin addressed a "Good-bye" to me that was both gay and melancholy. I had stood up and I gave him my most undulating toss of the head which makes my curls ripple softly all down my cheeks. Behind his back, I laughed: the great hobblede-hoy, he thought he had completed my conquest! I returned to the classroom to fetch my hood and I walked home brooding over the conversation I had overheard behind the little wall.

What a pity I hadn't been able to hear the end of their amorous dialogue! Aimée would have consented, without being pressed, to accept the attentions of this inflammable but honest Richelieu and he was quite capable of asking her to marry him. What is it that makes people so infatuated with this little woman who, strictly speaking, isn't even pretty. She's fresh, it's true, and she has magnificent eyes; but, after all, there are plenty of beautiful eyes in really pretty faces, yet all the men stare at her! The builders stop mixing their mortar when she passes by, winking at each other and clicking their tongues. (Yesterday, I heard one of them say to his mate as he pointed her out: "Strewth, I wouldn't half like to be a flea in her bed!") The boys in the streets put on swank for her and the old gentlemen who frequent the Café de la Perle and take their Vermouths there every evening discuss with interest "that little girl who teaches at the school, who makes your mouth water like a fruit tart that isn't sugared enough". Builders, retired businessmen, headmistress, schoolmaster, why do they all fall for her? As for myself, I'm not quite so interested in her since I've discovered what a traitress she is. And I feel quite empty; empty of my tenderness; empty of my fierce misery of that first evening.

They've been pulling it down fast and now they've nearly pulled it down altogether, poor old school! When they were demolishing the ground floor, we watched, with great curiosity, the discovery of some double walls. We had always thought those walls thick and solid; now they turned out to be as hollow as cupboards with a kind of black passage between them where there was nothing but dust and an appalling, ancient, repulsive stench. I took much pleasure in frightening Marie Belhomme by telling her that these hiding-places had been built in the old days for the walling-up of women who were unfaithful to their husbands and that I'd seen white bones lying among the rubble. She looked at me with wide, scared eyes and asked: "Is it really true?" Then she hurried to the walls to "see the bones". The next minute, she was back at my side.

"I didn't see a thing. It's just another of your fibs you're telling me!"

"May I lose the use of my tongue this instant if those hiding-places in the walls weren't hollowed out for a criminal end! And, besides, you're a nice one to tell me I'm fibbing, considering you've got a chrysanthemum hidden in your Marmontel—the one Monsieur Antonin Rabastens was wearing in his buttonhole!"

I shouted this at the top of my voice because I had just caught sight of Mademoiselle Sergent coming into the playground, with Dutertre in her wake. Oh! we see *him* often enough, to do him justice! And what noble devotion to duty that doctor must have to be incessantly leaving his clinic to come and ascertain whether the state of our school is satisfactory! That school is dispersing, bit by bit at the moment; the first class to the Infants' School, the second over there to the Town Hall. No doubt he fears that our education may be suffering from these successive displacements, the worthy District Superintendent!

They had heard, the two of them, what I had just said—naturally, I'd done it on purpose!—and Dutertre seized the opportunity to come over to us. Marie wanted to sink into the ground. She moaned and hid her face in her hands. But he was decent enough to be all smiles as he approached. He slapped the silly noodle on the shoulder and she trembled with alarm:

"Little one, what's that devilish Claudine saying to you? Do you preserve the flowers our handsome assistant wears? Mademoiselle Sergent, your pupils' hearts are thoroughly awakened, you know! Marie, do you want me to tell your mother so as to make her realise that her daughter's no longer a child?"

Poor Marie Belhomme! Quite incapable of answering one word, she stared at Dutertre, she stared at me, she stared at the Headmistress, with eyes like a startled fawn and was on the verge of tears. . . . Mademoiselle Sergent, who was not entirely delighted at the opportunity the District Inspector had found of gossiping with us, watched him with jealous and admiring eyes. She did not dare carry him off. (I knew him well enough to guess he might easily refuse to go.) As for me, I was rejoicing in Marie's confusion, in Mademoiselle Sergent's impatient displeasure (so her little Aimée wasn't enough for her any more, then?) and also at the sight of our good doctor's obvious pleasure at staying beside us. Apparently my eyes must have expressed my mingled feelings of rage and satisfaction for he laughed, showing his pointed teeth.

"Claudine, what's making your eyes sparkle like that? Is it devilment?"

I answered "Yes" with my head, merely tossing my hair without speaking, an irreverence that drew Mademoiselle Sergent's bushy eyebrows together in a frown. . . . I didn't care. She couldn't have everything, that nasty Redhead; her District Superintendent and her little assistant. No, definitely not. . . . More offhandedly than ever, Dutertre came close to me and slipped his arm round my shoulders. The lanky Anaïs watched us with curiosity, screwing up her eyes.

"Are you feeling well?"

"Yes, Doctor, thank you very much."

"Be serious." (As if *he* were being serious!) "Why have you always got those dark shadows under your eyes?"

"Because the good Lord made them like that."

"You oughtn't to read so much. I bet you read in bed?"

"A little, not much. Mustn't one?"

"We-ell. . . . All right, you can read. What *do* you read? Come on, tell me."

He was getting excited and he gripped my shoulders with a brusque gesture. But I'm not so stupid as I was the other day and I didn't blush—at least, not yet. The Headmistress had decided to go and scold the little ones who were playing with the pump and drenching themselves. How she must be boiling inwardly! My heart danced at the thought!

"Yesterday, I finished *Aphrodite.* Tonight I shall begin *La Femme et le Pantin.*"

"Indeed? You *are* going the pace! Pierre Loüys? The deuce! Not surprising that you . . . I should very much like to know how much you understand of all that. Everything?"

(I don't think I'm a coward, but I shouldn't have liked to continue this conversation alone with him in a wood or on a sofa; his eyes glittered so! Besides, he obviously imagined I was about to confide smutty secrets to him. . . .)

"No, I don't understand it all, unfortunately. But quite a lot of things, all the same. Then I've also read, last week, *Susanne* by Léon Daudet. And I'm just finishing *L'Année de Clarisse.* It's one of Paul Adam's and I simply adore it!"

"Yes, yes. And do you get to sleep afterwards? . . . But you'll tire yourself, if you go on like that. Take a little care of yourself, it would be a pity to wear yourself out, you know."

What was he really thinking? He looked at me from so close to, with such a visible desire to caress me—to kiss me—that, suddenly, a shameful burning flush covered my face like rouge and I lost my self-assurance. Perhaps *he* was frightened too—of losing his self-possession—for he let me go, breathing hard. He left me after giving my hair a stroke right down from my head to the tip of my longest curls, as if he were stroking the back of a cat. Mademoiselle Sergent came up to us again, her hands shaking with jealousy, and the two of them went off together. I saw them talking very fast to each other: she seemed to be anxiously imploring him while he lightly shrugged his shoulders and laughed.

They ran into Mademoiselle Aimée and Dutertre stopped, lured by her seductive eyes, and joked with her familiarly. She looked flushed, and a little embarrassed, but pleased. This time Mademoiselle Sergent displayed no jealousy; on the contrary. . . . Whereas my heart always jumps a trifle when that little creature appears. Ah! How badly that's all turned out!

I buried myself so deep in my thoughts that I didn't notice that gawk Anaïs executing a war-dance round me.

"Will you leave me in peace, you filthy monster! I don't feel like playing today."

"Oh yes, *I* know! You've got the District Superintendent on your mind. . . . My goodness me, you don't know which one to listen to these days—Rabastens, Dutertre, who else? Have you made your choice? And what about Mademoiselle Lanthenay?"

She whirled round me, her eyes diabolical in a face that was motionless but secretly furious. For the sake of getting some peace, I flung myself on her and pounded her arms with my fists: she yelled at once, like a coward, and made her escape. I pursued her and hemmed her in in the corner by the pump where I poured some water on her head, not much, just the dregs of the communal drinking-cup. She lost her temper completely.

"You know, that's idiotic. That's not the thing to do. I happen to have a cold. You're making me cough!"

"Cough away! Doctor Dutertre will give you a free consultation . . . and throw in a little something extra!"

The arrival of the lovelorn Duplessis interrupted our quarrel. He was transfigured, since two days ago, that Armand! His radiant eyes proclaimed that Aimée had granted him her hand, along with her heart and her faith, all tied up in one parcel! But when he observed his sweet fiancée joking and laughing over there between Dutertre and the Headmistress, with the Superintendent teasing her and Mademoiselle Sergent encouraging her, his eyes clouded. Aha! So I wasn't the only one who was jealous! I really believe he would have turned round and gone away if the Redhead herself hadn't called out to him. He ran up to them with great strides and bowed low to Dutertre who shook his hand familiarly, as if congratulating him. The pale Armand blushed, became radiant once more and looked at his little fiancée with tender pride. Poor Richelieu, I feel distressed about him! I don't know why, but I've an idea that this Aimée, who half-pretends to be unconscious and who commits herself so hastily, will bring him no happiness. Anaïs was so busy watching the group, determined not to miss a single gesture, that she forgot all about abusing me.

"I say," she whispered to me very low, "what are they doing all together like that? Whatever's up?"

I blurted out:

"What's up is that Monsieur Armand—the compass—Richelieu—has gone and asked for Mademoiselle Lanthenay's hand and she's bestowed it on him and they're engaged! And, at this particular moment, Dutertre is congratulating them. *That's* what's up!"

"Ah! . . . Is that really true? You mean, he's asked for her hand, *to get married*?"

I couldn't help laughing; she had let the word out so naturally, with a guilelessness that was quite unlike her! But I did not let her vegetate in her innocent surprise.

"Run—run and fetch something—it doesn't matter what—from the classroom and listen to what they say. If I go, they'll be suspicious at once!"

She dashed off. As she passed the group, she adroitly lost her wooden sabot (we all wore sabots in the winter) and kept her ears stretched as she put it on again, taking as long as possible. Then she vanished and reappeared, ostentatiously carrying her mittens which she slipped on her hands as she returned to me.

"What did you overhear?"

"Monsieur Dutertre was saying to Armand Duplessis: 'I am not going to wish you good luck, Monsieur. That would be superfluous when you're marrying such a girl as this.' And Mademoiselle Aimée Lanthenay lowered her eyes—like this. But, honestly, I'd never have believed it was all fixed up—as definite as all that!"

I was astonished too, but for a different reason! Aimée was going to get married and this no longer produced any effect on Mademoiselle Sergent? There must certainly be something behind all this that I knew nothing about! Why should she have gone to such lengths to conquer Aimée, why made those tearful scenes, only to hand her over now, with no further regrets, to this Armand Duplessis whom she hardly knew? The devil take them both! Now, once again, I'd got to wear myself to a frazzle to discover what was at the bottom of all this. After all, it may well be that she's only jealous of women.

To clear my mind, I organised a big game of "he" with my classmates and the "country bumpkins" of the second division who were becoming sufficiently grownup to be allowed to play with us. I drew two lines about three yards apart, stationed myself in the middle as "he" and the game began, punctuated by shrill cries and by a certain number of falls for which I was responsible.

The bell rang and we went in for the deadly boring needlework lesson. I took up my tapestry with disgust. After ten minutes, Mademoiselle Sergent left us, on the pretext of having to give out some material to the "little class" which, homeless once again, was temporarily (of course!) installed in an empty room near us in the Infants' School. I was quite ready to bet that, in point of fact, the Redhead was going to spend more time on her little Aimée than on handing out supplies.

After I'd done about twenty stitches in my tapestry, I was seized with a sudden access of stupidity which prevented me from knowing whether I should change the shade to fill in an oak-leaf or whether I should keep the same wool with which I had just finished a willow leaf. So I went out, work in hand, to ask advice from the omniscient Headmistress. I crossed the corridor and went into the little classroom. The fifty small girls shut up in there were squealing, pulling each other's hair, laughing, dancing about and drawing funny men on the blackboard. And not a sign of Mademoiselle Sergent, not a sign of Mademoiselle Lanthenay! This was becoming very queer! I went out again and pushed open the door of the staircase: no one on the stairs! Suppose I went up? Yes, but whatever should I say if I were found there? Pooh! I would say that I was coming to look for Mademoiselle Sergent because I'd heard her old peasant of a mother calling her.

Ssh! I went upstairs in my gym shoes, very quietly, leaving my sabots below. Nothing at the top of the stairs. But the door of one room stood slightly ajar and, promptly, my one thought was to look through the opening. Mademoiselle Sergent, sitting in her big armchair, luckily had her back to me. She was holding her assistant on her lap, like a baby. Aimée was sighing softly and fervently kissing the Redhead who was clasping her tight. Well done! No one could say this Headmistress bullied her subordinates! I could not see their faces because the back of the chair was too high, but I didn't need to see them. My heart pounded in my ears and, suddenly, I dashed down the staircase on my silent rubber soles.

Three seconds later, I was back in my place next to the lanky Anaïs who was busy reading the *Supplément* and looking at the picture with much delectation. So that she shouldn't notice I was upset, I asked to look too, as if I were really interested! There was a seductive story by Catulle Mendés which I should have enjoyed, but my mind was not much on what I was reading; it was still far too full of what I had spied on up there! I had got more than I asked for and I certainly had not believed their caresses were as ardent as that. . . .

Anaïs showed me a drawing by Gil Baër of a slim young man, without a moustache, who looked like a woman in disguise. Carried away by reading the *Carnet de Lyonnette* and some amorous pieces by Armand Sylvestre, she said, with troubled eyes: "I've got a cousin who looks like that. His name's Raoul. He's at college and I go and see him in the holidays every summer." This revelation explained her relatively virtuous behaviour recently; she hardly ever wrote to boys nowadays. The sisters Jaubert were putting up a great show of being scandalised on account of this naughty magazine while Marie Belhomme overturned her ink-pot to come and have a look. When she had looked at the pictures and read a little, she fled, flinging up her long hands and crying: "It's disgusting! I don't want to read the rest before recreation!" She had hardly sat down again and begun to mop up her spilt ink than Mademoiselle Sergent returned, grave but with rapt, sparkling eyes. I stared at that Redhead as if I were not sure she was the same person I had seen kissing upstairs.

"Marie, you will write me a composition on the subject of clumsiness and bring it to me at five o'clock this afternoon. Girls, tomorrow a new assistant-mistress, Mademoiselle Griset, will be arriving. You won't have anything to do with her; she will only be taking the lower class."

I was on the point of asking: "And Mademoiselle Aimée—is she leaving then?" But the answer came of its own accord.

"Mademoiselle Lanthenay is wasting her intelligence in the second class. Henceforward, she will give you history lessons, also drawing and needlework, in here, under my supervision."

I looked at her and smiled, nodding my head as if to congratulate her on this decidedly satisfactory arrangement. This roused her temper at once and she said, frowning: "Claudine, how much have you done to your tapestry? All that? You certainly haven't exhausted yourself!"

I put on my most idiotic expression as I replied:

"But, Mademoiselle, I went to the second class just now to ask if I was to use Number 2 green for the oak-leaf and there wasn't anyone there. I called up the staircase to you but there wasn't anyone there either."

I spoke slowly and loudly, so that all the noses bent over the knitting and the sewing were raised inquisitively. Everyone was listening avidly; the bigger girls were wondering what the Headmistress could be doing so far away, abandoning the pupils to their own devices. Mademoiselle Sergent turned a darker crimson still and answered hastily: "I had gone to see where it would be possible to put the new assistant. The school building is nearly finished—they're drying it out with big fires—and no doubt we shall soon be able to move into it."

I made a gesture of protest and apology which meant:

"Oh! It's not for me to know where you were . . . you could only be where your duty called you." But I felt a savage satisfaction at the thought that I could have replied: "No, zealous teacher, you couldn't care less about the new assistant. It's the other one, Mademoiselle Lanthenay, who takes up all your thoughts, and you were up in your room with her, kissing her full on the mouth."

While I was hatching rebellious thoughts, the Redhead had regained her self-control. Exceedingly calm now, she addressed the class in a precise voice. . . .

"Take your exercise-books. The ones marked: *French Composition*. Explain and comment on the following thought: 'Time does not respect what has been done without him.' You have one hour and a half."

Oh, anguish and despair! What ineptitudes have got to be trotted out again now? I don't care a button whether time respects what is done without inviting him or not! Always subjects like that, or worse! Yes, worse—because it's almost New Year's Eve and we shan't escape the usual little set-piece about New Year gifts: venerable custom of giving and receiving (*mem*: i before e except after c) same; joy of children, tender emotion of parents; sweets, toys, etc;—not forgetting the touching note on the little poor children who don't get any presents and whom we must help on this day so that they may have their share of joy!—Horror, horror!

While I inwardly raged, the others were already scribbling their "roughs". That gawk Anaïs was waiting for me to begin so that she could model her opening on mine and Marie Belhomme had already filled a page with ineptitudes—sentences that contradicted one another and reflections quite beside the point. After yawning for a quarter of an hour, I made up my mind and wrote straight into my "Fair-Copy" book without doing a rough, much to the indignation of the others.

At four o'clock, as we came out of school, I realised, without regret, that it was my turn to sweep up with Anaïs. Normally this chore revolts me but today I didn't care. Actually, I would rather do it than not. As I was going off to fetch the watering-can, I ran at last into Mademoiselle Aimée. Her cheeks were flushed and her eyes shining.

"Good afternoon, Mademoiselle. When's the wedding?"

"What! But . . . these children always know everything! But it's not decided yet . . . at least, the date isn't. It'll be in the long vacation, probably. . . . Tell me, you don't think he's ugly, Monsieur Duplessis?"

"Ugly—Richelieu ugly? No, of course not. He's much better than the other one, ever so much better! Do you love him?"

"But, naturally I do, since I'm taking him for my husband!"

"As if that were a reason! Don't give me silly answers like that—do you think you're talking to Marie Belhomme? You don't love him in the least—you think he's nice and you want to get married to see what it's like. And out of vanity, too, to annoy your friends at the Training College who'll stay old maids. That's all there is to it! Don't play too many tricks on him, that's the best I can wish him, because he certainly deserves to be loved better than you'll ever love him."

It came out slap! And I promptly turned on my heels and ran off to fetch water to sprinkle the floor. She stayed there rooted to the spot, abashed. At last she went off to supervise the sweeping of the junior classroom or to tell her dear Mademoiselle Sergent what I had just said. Let her go! I didn't want to bother any more about those two crazy women, one of whom wasn't crazy at all. I was so excited that I sprinkled recklessly; I even sprinkled Anaïs's feet and the geography maps, then I swept till my arms ached. It was a relief to tire myself out like that.

Singing-lesson. Enter Antonin Rabastens wearing a sky-blue tie. "Hail, fair sun!" as the Provençal girls used to say to Roumestan. Goodness, Mademoiselle Aimée Lanthenay was there too, followed by a little creature even smaller than herself, who moved with unusual suppleness and seemed to be about thirteen. She had a rather flat face, green eyes, a fresh complexion and silky, dark hair. This little girl suddenly stopped in the doorway, overcome with shyness. Mademoiselle Aimée turned towards her, laughing: "Now then, come along, don't be frightened: Luce, do you hear?"

So it was her sister! I had completely forgotten this detail. She had talked to me about this sister, who would probably be coming to school, in the days when we were friends. . . . It struck me as so funny, her bringing along this little sister, that I pinched Anaïs, who clucked, and I tickled Marie Belhomme who miaowed and I executed a silent two-step behind Mademoiselle Sergent's back. Rabastens found these pranks charming and little sister Luce stared at me with her slit-like eyes. Mademoiselle Aimée began to laugh (she laughs at everything these days, she's so happy!) and said to me:

"Now *please*, Claudine, don't frighten her out of her wits as a start. She's shy enough by nature as it is."

"Mademoiselle, I will protect her like my own personal virtue. How old is she?"

"She was fifteen last month."

"Fifteen? Well, after that, I'll never trust anyone again! I thought she was a good thirteen."

The little thing, who had turned quite red, looked down at her feet—they were pretty, too. She nestled against her sister and clutched her arm for reassurance. Aha! I'd give her courage!

"Come along, little girl, come over here to me. Don't be afraid. This gentleman, who displays such intoxicating ties in our honour, is our good singing-master. You'll only see him on Thursdays and Sundays, unfortunately. Those big girls there are some of your classmates—you'll soon get to know them. As for me, I'm the model pupil, the rarest of all birds. I never get scolded ('strue, isn't it, Mademoiselle?) and I'm always good, like I am today. I'll be a second mother to you!"

Mademoiselle Sergent was amused though she tried not to show it; Rabastens was admiring, and the eyes of the new girl expressed doubts of my sanity. But I let her alone; I'd had all the fun I wanted with that Luce. She stayed close to her sister who called her "little silly" and I had lost interest in her. I asked right out, making no bones about it:

"Where are you going to put this child to sleep, as nothing's finished yet?"

"With me," replied Aimée.

I pinched my lips, I looked the Headmistress straight in the face and I said, very distinctly:

"Frightful bore for you, that!"

Rabastens laughed behind his hand (did he know something?) and emitted the opinion that perhaps we might begin to sing. Yes, we might; and we actually did sing. The little new girl dissociated herself completely and remained obstinately mute.

"You don't know this music well, Mademoiselle Lanthenay *Junior?*" inquired the exquisite Antonin, smiling like a commercial traveller.

"I know it a little, Sir," answered little Luce in a faint, lilting voice that must have been pleasant to hear when it was not strangled with terror.

"Very well, then?"

Very well then, nothing. Why couldn't he leave the child in peace, that dandy of the Canebière?

At that very moment, Rabastens whispered to me: "Anyway, if these young ladies are tired, I think the singing-lessons are waste of time!"

I glanced all round me, startled at his audacity in speaking to me under his breath. But he was right; my companions were occupied with the new girl, coaxing her and speaking gently to her and she was answering happily, quite reassured by finding herself kindly received. As to that cat Lanthenay and her beloved tyrant, huddled together in the embrasure of the window that looked on to the garden, they had completely forgotten us. Mademoiselle Sergent had put her arm round Aimée's waist; they were talking very low—or not talking at all, which came to the same thing. Antonin, whose gaze had followed mine, could not stop himself from laughing.

"They get on tremendously well together!"

"They certainly do. It's touching, this friendship, isn't it, Sir?"

The big simpleton did not know how to hide his feelings and blurted out, very low:

"Touching? I'd call it embarrassing for the others! Sunday night, I went to take back the music books and those ladies were here in the classroom, with no light on. I came in—after all it's a public place, this classroom—and, in the dusk, I caught sight of Mademoiselle Sergent and Mademoiselle Aiméee, close together kissing like hot cakes. Do you imagine they moved aparrt? Not a bit of it! Mademoiselle Sergent just turrned round and lannguidly asked: 'Who's there?' Well, I'm harrdly what you'd call shy, but all the same, I just stood there, looking at them like a dumb ox."

(Let him talk as much as he liked, our candid assistant-master; I had nothing to learn from *him*! But I was forgetting the most important thing.)

"What about your colleague, Sir? I imagine he's awfully happy now he's engaged to Mademoiselle Lanthenay?"

"Yes, poorr boy. But, to my mind, it's nothing to be so happy about."

"Oh? Why ever not?"

"Hmm. The Headmistress does anything she likes with Mademoiselle Aimée—not very pleasant for a future husband. I'd be annoyed if my wife were dominated like that by someone otherr than myself."

I privately agreed with him. But the others had finished interviewing the newcomer and it was prudent for us to stop talking. Back to singing then, but no . . . it was no good. Who should dare to enter at that moment but Armand, disturbing the tender whispering of the two women? He stood enraptured beside Aimée who flirted with him, fluttering her eyelids with their curling lashes, while Mademoiselle Sergent watched them with the tender eyes of a mother-in-law who has married off her daughter. My classmates resumed their conversations and carried them on till the clock struck the hour. Rabastens was right. What queerr, sorry, what queer singing-lessons!

This morning, on coming to school, I saw a pale young girl standing in the entrance. She had dull hair, grey eyes and a skin with no bloom on it, and she was hugging a woollen shawl over her shoulders with the heart-rending air of a thin, cold, frightened cat. Anaïs pointed her out to me with a thrust of her chin, making a grimace of displeasure. I shook my head pityingly and said to her, very low: "*There's* someone who's going to be unhappy here, you can see that at a glance. The two others get on too well together not to make her life a misery."

Little by little, the other pupils arrived. Before going inside, I observed that the two school buildings were being finished at a prodigious pace; apparently Dutertre had promised a large bonus to the contractor if everything was ready on the date he had fixed. He must do a good deal of underhand jobbery, that creature!

Drawing lesson, under the direction of Mademoiselle Aimée Lanthenay. "Reproduction in line of any everyday object." This time it was a cut-glass decanter, placed on Mademoiselle's desk, that we had to draw. These drawing lessons were invariably gay, since they furnished a thousand pretexts for getting up: one discovered "impossibilities"; one made blots of Indian ink wherever they were least desirable. Promptly, the usual storm of complaints broke out. I opened the attack:

"Mademoiselle Aimée, I *can't* draw the decanter from where I am—the stove-pipe hides it!"

Mademoiselle Aimée, deeply occupied in tickling the red hair on the nape of the Headmistress's neck (the latter was writing a letter), turned towards me.

"Bend your head forward. You can see it then, I think."

"Mademoiselle," took up Anaïs "I *can't* see the model *at all*, because Claudine's head gets in the way!"

"Oh, how irritating you are! Turn your table round a little, then you can both see."

It was Marie Belhomme's turn now. She moaned:

"Mademoiselle, I haven't any more charcoal. And the sheet of paper you've given me has got a tear in the middle and so I *can't* draw the decanter."

"Oh!" grated Mademoiselle Sergent, exasperated. "Have you finished bothering us, all of you? Here's a sheet of paper, here's some charcoal and now, don't let me hear one more word from any of you or I'll make you draw an entire dinner-service!"

There was a terrified silence. You could have heard a fly breathe . . . for five whole minutes. At the sixth minute, a faint buzzing began again; someone dropped a sabot; Marie Belhomme coughed; I got up to go and measure the height and breadth of the decanter with outstretched arm. The lanky Anaïs did the same, as soon as I had finished, and took advantage of the fact that one had to shut one eye to crumple her face into frightful grimaces that made Marie laugh. I finished sketching the decanter in charcoal and I got up to go and fetch the Indian ink from the cupboard behind the desk where the two mistresses sat. They had forgotten us; they were talking to each other in low voices and laughing. Now and then Mademoiselle Aimée drew back with a shocked little grimace which became her very prettily. In fact, they were now so little inhibited by our presence that it wasn't worth restraining ourselves either. Very well, now was our chance!

I shot out an inviting "Psst!" that brought all the heads up, and, indicating the loving Sergent-Lanthenay couple to the class, I stretched out my hands in benediction over their two heads, from behind. Marie Belhomme burst out laughing with delight, the Jauberts lowered reproving noses, and, without having been seen by the interested parties, I buried myself once more in the cupboard, took out the Indian ink and brought it back to my place.

In passing, I looked at Anaïs's drawing. Her decanter resembled herself; it was too tall and had too long and thin a neck. I wanted to warn her of this but she didn't hear me; she was too absorbed in preparing some "goonygoonya" in her lap to send to the new arrival in a pencil-box, the great pest! (Goonygoonya is charcoal pounded into Indian ink so as to make an almost dry mortar that stains unwary fingers deeply, likewise frocks and exercise-books.) That poor little Luce was going to blacken her hands and dirty her drawing, when she opened the box, and would get scolded. To avenge her, I snatched Anaïs's drawing and drew, in ink, a belt, with a buckle, encircling the waist of the decanter. Underneath, I wrote: *Portrait of the Lanky Anaïs.* She raised her head at the very moment I finished writing and pushed her box of goonygoonya over to Luce with a gracious smile. The little thing turned red and thanked her. Anaïs bent once more over her drawing and let out a resounding "Oh!" of indignation which recalled our cooing teachers to reality.

"What's all this? Anaïs, you've gone mad, I presume?"

"Mademoiselle, look what Claudine's done on my drawing!"

Swelling with rage, she took it up to the desk and laid it down. Mademoiselle Sergent cast a stern eye over it, then, suddenly, burst out laughing. Rage and despair on the part of Anaïs who would have wept with spleen if tears didn't come so hard to her. Resuming her gravity, the Headmistress declared: "This kind of joke isn't going to help you to get satisfactory marks in your exam, Claudine. But you've made quite an accurate criticism of Anaïs's drawing for it was indeed too tall and too narrow." The great weedy thing returned to her place, frustrated and embittered. I told her:

"That'll teach you to send goonygoonya to that child who hasn't done a thing to you!"

"Oho! So you want the little one to make up for your lack of success with her elder sister—that's why you defend her with so much ardour!"

Wham!

That was a tremendous slap which resounded on her cheek. I'd aimed it with all my might, adding a "Mind your own business" for good measure. The class, completely out of hand, buzzed like a bee-hive; Mademoiselle Sergent descended from her desk for so serious an affair. It was so long since I had hit one of my companions that people were beginning to believe I had become rational. (In the old days, I had the annoying habit of settling my quarrels on my own, with kicks and blows, without thinking it necessary to tell tales like the others.) My last battle dated back more than a year.

Anaïs was crying over the table.

"Mademoiselle Claudine," said the Headmistress severely "I insist on your controlling yourself. If you are going to start hitting your companions again, I see myself being forced to refuse to admit you any longer to the school."

But her words fell flat: my blood was up. I smiled at her so insolently that she promptly lost her temper.

"Claudine, lower your eyes!"

I did not lower a thing.

"Claudine, leave the room!"

"With pleasure, Mademoiselle!"

I left the room but, outside, I realised that I was bareheaded. I went back at once to collect my hat. The class was dismayed and silent. I noticed that Aimée had gone up close to Mademoiselle Sergent and was talking to her in a rapid, very low voice. I had not reached the doorway before the Headmistress called me back:

"Claudine, come here. Go and sit down in your place. I do not want to expel you, since you'll be leaving the class after the Certificate. . . . And, after all, you are not a mediocre pupil, though you are often a bad pupil, and I have no wish to deprive myself of you except as a last resort. Put your hat back in its place."

What that must have cost her! She was still so shaken that her heartbeats made the pages of the exercise-book she was holding flutter. I said: "Thank you, Mademoiselle," very modestly. Then, seated once more in my place beside the tall Anaïs, who was silent and a little frightened by the scene she had provoked, I thought with astonishment about the possible reasons which could have decided this vindictive Redhead to recall me. Had she been afraid of the effect it might produce in the principal town of the district? Had she thought I should chatter at the top of my voice, that I should tell everything I knew (at least), all the irregularity in this school, the pawing of the big girls by the District Superintendent and his prolonged visits to our teachers? What about the way those two ladies frequently abandoned their classes in order to exchange endearments behind closed doors? What about Mademoiselle Sergent's decidedly broad taste in reading (*Journal Amusant*, unsavoury Zolas and worse still) and the handsome, gallant assistant-master with the sentimental baritone who flirted with the girls who were taking their Certificate? Wasn't there a whole heap of suspicious things the parents did not know about because the big ones who found the School amusing never told them and the little ones hadn't got their eyes open? Had she dreaded a semi-scandal which would gravely endanger her reputation and the future of the handsome

School which was being built at considerable expense? I believe so. And moreover, now that my temper had cooled, like her own, I preferred to remain in this hole where I had more fun than anywhere else. Feeling quite good again, I looked at Anaïs's mottled cheek and whispered to her gaily:

"Well, old thing? That keeping you warm?"

She had been so terrified of my expulsion, since I could have accused her of being the cause of it, that she bore me no resentment.

"I should just think it is keeping me warm! You've got a jolly heavy hand, you know! You must be crazy to fly into a rage like that."

"Come on, let's forget it. I think I must have had a rather violent nervous twitch in my right arm."

Somehow or other, she managed to rub out the "belt" of her decanter and I finished off mine. Mademoiselle Aimée corrected our drawings with feverish, shaky fingers.

This morning I found the playground empty—or very nearly. On the staircase of the Infants' School, a great deal of talking was going on; voices were calling to each other and shrieking: "Do be careful!"— "Gosh, it's heavy!" I rushed up.

"What's everyone doing?"

"You can see for yourself," said Anaïs. "We're helping their ladyships to move out of here and go into the new building."

"Quick, give me something to carry!"

"There's plenty of stuff up there—go and find some."

I went upstairs into the Headmistress's room, the room where I had spied at the door. I was inside it at last! Her old peasant mother, her starched cap all askew, entrusted me and Marie Belhomme with carrying down a big hamper containing all her daughter's toilet things. She does herself well, the Redhead! Her dressing-table was furnished with every conceivable object: large and small cut-glass bottles, nail-buffers, scent-sprays, tweezers and powder-puffs. There was also a huge washbasin and jug. All those weren't at all the typical toilet accessories of country schoolmistresses. To be sure of this, one had only to look at Mademoiselle Aimée's toilet things, as well as those belonging to that pale, silent Griset, which we transported afterwards—a basin, a water-jug of very modest dimensions, a little round mirror, a toothbrush, some soap, and that was all. Nevertheless, that little Aimée was very smartly dressed, especially these last few weeks, all bedizened and scented. How did she manage it? Five minutes later, I noticed that the bottom of her water-jug was dusty. Good; *that* problem was solved.

The new building, which contained three classrooms and a dormitory on the first floor, together with the assistant-mistresses' little rooms, was still too chilly for my taste, and smelt disagreeably of plaster. Between the two, they were erecting the main municipal building which would comprise the Town Hall on the ground floor and various private apartments on the first and would link up the two wings already completed.

As I was coming downstairs again, I had the marvelous idea of climbing the scaffolding, as the builders were still at lunch. In a moment I had skimmed up a ladder and was wandering about among the "scaffolds" and thoroughly enjoying myself. Bother! There were the workmen coming back! I hid behind a piece of masonry, waiting for a chance to climb down again, but they were already on the ladder. Well, those two wouldn't give me away, even if they did see me. I knew both of them well by sight.

They lit their pipes and began to chat.

"You can bet your boots, I wouldn't lose any sleep over *that* one."

"Which one d'you mean?"

"That there new teacher what come yesterday."

"Coo, she don't half look miserable—not a bit like them other two."

"Don't you talk to me about them other two, they fair make me sick. I'm fed up with them, anyone'd think they was husband and wife. Every blooming day, I see them from here and every blooming day it's the same thing. They starts kissing like anything, then they shuts the window and you can't see nothing more. Don't you so much as mention 'em again! Oh, I grant you the little one's a nice juicy piece, but I'm through, I tell you. And that other master who's going to marry her! That chap must have his eyes stuck together with mud to do such a bloody silly thing!"

I was enjoying myself hugely, but, as the bell was ringing for school, I only had just time to climb down on the inside (there were ladders all over the place), and I arrived, white with plaster and mortar. I was lucky to get off with a sharp: "Where have you sprung from? If you get yourself so dirty, you won't be allowed to help with moving the furniture again." I was jubilant at having heard the builders talk about those two women with so much good sense.

Reading out loud. *Selected passages.* Bother! To distract myself, I unfolded on my lap a copy of the *Écho de Paris*, brought in case of boring lessons: I was enjoying Lucien Muhlfeld's thrilling *Mauvais Désir*, when Mademoiselle Sergent called upon me: "Claudine, read on from there." I hadn't the faintest idea where we had got to, but I hurriedly stood up, determined to "do something desperate" rather than let my paper be pinched. At the very moment I was thinking of upsetting an ink-pot, tearing a page out of my book or shouting "Long live Anarchy!", someone knocked at the door. . . . Mademoiselle Lanthenay rose, opened the door and effaced herself and Dutertre appeared.

Had that doctor buried all his patients then, that he had so much spare time? Mademoiselle Sergent ran to meet him; he shook hands with her, glancing meanwhile at little Aimée, who had turned bright pink and was laughing in an embarrassed way. But why? She wasn't as shy as all that! All those people were beginning to wear me out by forcing me to be incessantly trying to find out what they were thinking or doing. . . .

Dutertre had obviously seen me, since I was standing up, but he contented himself with smiling at me from a distance and remained close to those two females. All three of them were chatting together in an undertone: I sat down demurely and watched. Suddenly, Mademoiselle Sergent—who had not left off lovingly contemplating the handsome District Superintendent—raised her voice and said: "You can go and see for yourself now, Monsieur; I'll go on with the children's lesson and Mademoiselle Lanthenay will show you the way. You'll easily identify the crack I was telling you about. It runs from top to bottom of the new wall, on the left of the bed. It's decidedly worrying in a new house and I can't sleep with an easy mind." Mademoiselle Aimée did not answer and made a slight gesture of objecting. Then she changed her mind and disappeared, ahead of Dutertre who held out his hand to the Headmistress and shook hers vigorously, as if to thank her.

I certainly did not regret not having been expelled, but, however used I was to their astonishing behaviour and their peculiar morals, this dumbfounded me. I asked myself what she hoped to gain by sending this chaser of skirts and this young girl off together to her room to examine a crack which, I was ready to swear, was nonexistent.

"There's a *cracked* story for you!" I whispered this observation into the ear of the gawky Anaïs. She gripped her knees together and chewed india-rubber frantically to show her delight in these dubious happenings. Fired by her example, I pulled a packet of cigarette-papers out of my pocket (I *only* eat the kind called *Nil*) and chewed enthusiastically.

"I say, old thing," said Anaïs, "I've discovered something gorgeous to eat."

"What? Old newspapers?"

"No—the lead in these pencils that are red one end and blue the other—you know the kind. The blue end is slightly better. I've already pinched five from the stationery cupboard. It's delicious!"

"Give me a bit to try. . . . No, not up to much. I'll stick to my *Nil*."

"Idiot, you don't know what's good!"

While we were talking in whispers, Mademoiselle Sergent was making little Luce read aloud. But she was too preoccupied to listen to her. I had an idea! What excuse could I invent to get that child put beside me in class! I would try and make her tell me all she knew about her sister Aimée. She would probably talk all right . . . all the more as she followed me, whenever I went through the classroom, with startled, curious eyes that had a hint of a smile in them. They were green eyes—a strange green that turned brown in shadow—and edged with long, black lashes.

What a long time they were staying over there! Wasn't she going to come and hear us our geography, that shameless little creature?

"I say, Anaïs, it's two o'clock."

"Well, what of it? Nothing to moan about! Wouldn't be half bad if we got off having to be heard the lesson. Done your map of France, old thing?"

"So, so. . . . Haven't finished the canals. I say, it wouldn't do for the Regional Inspector to turn up today. He'd find everything in a fine old mess. You look. . . . Mademoiselle Sergent isn't paying any attention to us . . . she's got her nose glued to the window!"

Anaïs was suddenly convulsed with laughter.

"What can they be doing? I can see Monsieur Dutertre from here, measuring the width of the crack."

"Do you think it's wide, the crack?" asked Marie Belhomme innocently. She was shading in her mountain chains by rolling an unevenly sharpened drawing-pencil over her map.

Such guilelessness made me give a spurt of laughter. Had it been too loud? No, Anaïs reassured me.

"Go on, you needn't worry. Mademoiselle's so absorbed, we could dance in the classroom without getting ourselves punished."

"Dance? Want to have a bet with me that I will?" I said, getting up quietly.

"Oh! I bet you two glass alleys that you won't dance without catching a verb to write out!"

Delicately, I removed my sabots and placed myself in the middle of the classroom between the two rows of tables. Everyone raised their heads: obviously the promised feat had excited lively interest. Now for it! I threw back my hair which was getting in my way, I picked up my skirt between two fingers and I began a "red-hot polka" which roused no less general admiration for being silent. Marie Belhomme was exultant and could not restrain a yelp of delight, deuce take her! Mademoiselle Sergent started and turned round, but I had already hurled myself back on my bench like lightning and I heard the Headmistress inform the little idiot, in a distant, bored voice:

"Marie Belhomme, you will copy me out the verb *to laugh* in medium round hand. It is really very tiresome that big girls of fifteen cannot behave themselves properly unless one has one's eye on them."

Poor Marie had a good mind to cry. Still, one shouldn't be as silly as that! And I promptly claimed the two marbles from Anaïs who handed them over with somewhat ill grace.

What could those two crack-observers be up to? Mademoiselle Sergent was still looking out of the window. It struck half-past two; they could not be much longer now. At least she must be made aware that we had noticed the unwonted absence of her little favourite. I coughed, but without success. I coughed again and asked in a virtuous voice, the voice of the Jauberts:

"Mademoiselle, we have some maps for Mademoiselle to look over. Is there a geography lesson today?"

The Redhead turned round sharply and shot a glance at the clock. Then she frowned with annoyance and impatience.

"Mademoiselle Aimée will be back in a moment. You know quite well that I sent her over to the new school. You can go over your lesson while you are waiting—you can never know it thoroughly enough."

Good! It was quite possible we shouldn't have to recite our homework today. There was much joy and a buzz of activity as soon as we knew we had nothing to do. Then the comedy of "going over the lesson" began. At each table, a girl took up her book while her neighbour closed hers and was supposed to repeat the lesson or to answer the questions her companion asked her. Out of twelve girls, the Jaubert twins were the only ones who really went over their work. The rest asked each other fantastic questions, preserving earnest, diligent expressions and serious lips that seemed to be reciting under their breath. The gawky Anaïs had opened her atlas and was interrogating me:

"What is a lock?"

I answered, as if I were repeating something by heart:

"Tst! Don't go and bore me with your old canals: look at Mademoiselle's expression, it's more amusing."

"What do you think of the conduct of Mademoiselle Aimée Lanthenay?"

"I think she's frequenting shady haunts with the District Superintendent, overseer of cracks."

"What is known as a 'crack'?"

"A fissure, sometimes called in French a *lézarde* or a female lizard. This lizard should normally be found in a wall but it is sometimes met with elsewhere, even in places completely sheltered from the sun."

"What is known as a 'fiancée'?"

"A hypocritical little slut who plays tricks on an assistant-master who's in love with her."

"What would you do in the place of the said assistant-master?"

"I'd give the District Superintendent a good hard kick on the backside and I'd give the little pet who takes him off to observe cracks a couple of smart slaps."

"What would be the result of that?"

"The arrival of another assistant-master and another assistant-mistress."

The lanky Anaïs hoisted up her atlas from time to time to giggle behind it. But I had enough. I wanted to go outside, to try and see *them* coming back. The only thing was to employ vulgar means.

"Mmmselle? . . ."

No reply.

"Mmmselle, beg pard'n, c'n I leave the room?"

"Yes, go, and don't be long."

She said it carelessly and listlessly: obviously her whole mind was over there in the room where the new wall might be cracked. I went out hurriedly, ran over to the lavatories (they were "temporary" too!) and stayed close to a door, pierced with a lozenge-shaped hole, ready to take refuge in the loathsome little kiosk if anyone came. At the very moment I was about to return despairingly to the classroom—for, alas, the customary time had elapsed—I saw Dutertre emerging (all alone) from the new school, putting on his gloves with a satisfied air. He was not coming back here but going straight off to the town. Aimée was not with him, but I didn't care; I had seen enough already. I turned to go back to the classroom but suddenly drew back, frightened. Twenty paces away—behind a new wall six foot high which sheltered the boys' little "convenience" (exactly like ours and equally temporary)—there had appeared the head of Armand. Poor Duplessis, pale and ravaged, was staring in the direction of our new school. I saw him for five seconds, then he disappeared, running at full speed along the path that led to the woods. I was not laughing any more. What was going to be the end of all this? I went indoors, quickly, without further lingering.

The class was still seething. Marie Belhomme had drawn a set of squares on the table and was gravely playing a pleasant game of noughts and crosses with the newly-arrived little Lanthenay—poor little Luce!—who must find this a fantastic school. And Mademoiselle Sergent was still looking out of the window.

Anaïs, who was in process of colouring the portraits of the most hideous men in the *History of France* with crayons, welcomed me with a "Come on, what did you see?"

"No more joking, old thing! Armand Duplessis was spying on them over the wall by the lavatories. Dutertre has gone back to the town and Richelieu's dashed off, running like a madman!"

"Go on! I bet you're telling lies!"

"I assure you I'm not. This is no time for lying. I saw it, on my honour, I did! My heart's in a positive flutter!"

The hope of the drama that might ensue kept us silent for a moment. Anaïs asked:

"Are you going to tell the others?"

"Good heavens, no. Those dunderheads would spread it all over the place. Only Marie Belhomme. I say, Marie!"

I told all to Marie whose eyes grew rounder than ever and who prophesied: "It'll all end badly!"

The door opened and we all turned our heads in a single movement. It was Mademoiselle Aimée, a little out of breath and her colour high. Mademoiselle Sergent ran up to her and checked, only just in time, the hug she was on the point of giving her. The Headmistress had come to life again; she drew the little slut over to the window and questioned her avidly. (And what about our geography lesson?)

The prodigal child showed no excessive emotion as she gave brief answers which did not appear to satisfy the curiosity of her worthy superior. To a more anxious question she replied "No," shaking her head with a mischievous sigh. At that, the Redhead heaved a sigh of relief. We three, at the front table, looked on, rigid with attention. I felt some alarm for that immoral little thing. I would definitely have warned her to beware of Armand but the other, her tyrant, would promptly have alleged that I had gone and denounced her behaviour to Richelieu, by means of anonymous letters, perhaps. So I refrained.

They were beginning to irritate me with their whisperings! So I decided to make an end of them. I emitted a low "hush!" to attract my classmates' attention and we began to buzz. At first the buzz was no more than a continuous bee-like hum; then it rose and swelled until it forced an entrance into the ears of our infatuated teachers, who exchanged an uneasy glance. But Mademoiselle Sergent boldly took the offensive:

"Silence! If I hear any buzzing, I shall keep the class in until six o'clock! Do you suppose we can give you regular lessons as long as the new school remains unfinished? You are old enough to know that you ought to work on your own when one of us is prevented from acting as your teacher. Give me an atlas. Any girl who does not know her lesson without one mistake will do one extra homework for a week!"

Whatever you may say, she's got character, that ugly, passionate, jealous woman; everyone was silent the moment she raised her voice. The lesson was recited at top speed and no one felt any inclination to be frivolous for we could feel a threatening breeze blowing, laden with extra work and detentions. While this was going on, I thought that nothing would console me if I were not present at the meeting of Armand and Aimée; I would rather have got myself expelled (much as that would have cost me) than not see what would happen.

At five minutes past four, when the daily "Shut your books and get into line" sounded in our ears, I went off, sorely against my will. Well, the exciting, unhoped-for tragedy wasn't billed for today! I would arrive early at school tomorrow so as to miss nothing of what might happen.

The next morning, having arrived long before the official time, I had time to kill. So I began a desultory conversation with the shy, melancholy Mademoiselle Griset who was as pale and nervous as ever.

"Do you like it here, Mademoiselle?"

She looked all round her before answering:

"Oh, not very much. I don't know anyone. I feel a little dull."

"But isn't your colleague nice to you . . . and Mademoiselle Sergent too?"

"I . . . I don't know. No, really, I don't know if they're nice; they never pay any attention to me."

"How extraordinary!"

"Yes . . . at meals they talk to me a little, but once the exercise-books are corrected they go off and I'm left all alone with Mademoiselle Sergent's mother who clears the table and then shuts herself up in the kitchen."

"And where do they go off to, the two of *them*?"

"Why, to their room."

Did she mean to their *room* or their *rooms*? Poor little wretch! She certainly earned her seventy-five francs a month!

"Would you like me to lend you some books, Mademoiselle, if you're bored in the evenings?"

(What joy! Her face turned almost pink with it!)

"Oh, I should love that. . . . Oh, how very kind of you . . . you don't think it would annoy the Headmistress?"

"Mademoiselle Sergent? If you think she'd even know, you've still got illusions about the interest that Redhead takes in you!"

She smiled, almost confidently, and asked me if I would lend her *Roman d'un Jeune Homme Pauvre* which she was just longing to read! Certainly, she should have it tomorrow, her romantic novelette. I felt sorry for her, poor abandoned creature! I might easily have raised her to the rank of an ally, but how could one rely on this pathetic, anaemic, far too timid girl?

The favourite's sister, little Luce Lanthenay, came up with noiseless steps, at once pleased and scared to be talking to me.

"Good morning, little monkey: say 'Good morning, Your Highness' to me. Say it at once. Did you sleep well?"

I stroked her hair roughly. This did not seem to displease her and she smiled at me with her green eyes that were exactly like those of Fanchette, my beautiful cat.

"Yes, Your Highness, I slept well."

"Where do you sleep?"

"Up there."

"With your sister Aimée, of course?"

"No, she has a bed in Mademoiselle Sergent's room."

"A bed? Have you seen it?"

"No . . . I mean, yes . . . it's a divan. Apparently it can be opened up into a bed. She told me so."

"She told you so? Fathead! Dim donkey! Nameless object! Scum of the human race!"

She was terror-stricken for I had punctuated my abuse with lashes with a book-strap (oh, not very hard lashes!) and, when she vanished up the stairs, I shouted this crowning insult after her: "Twirp of a female! You deserve to be like your sister!"

A divan that opened up! It would be easier for me to open up this wall! Upon my word, kids like that don't notice anything! Yet she looks vicious enough, that child, with those eyes that slant up at the corners. . . .

The gawky Anaïs arrived while I was still panting and asked what was the matter with me.

"Nothing at all. I've merely beaten little Luce to teach her a thing or two."

"Is there any news?"

"None at all. No one's come down yet. D'you want to play marbles?"

"What game? Haven't got nine alleys to play 'Square'."

"But I've got the two I won off you. Come on, we'll have a chase."

We had a very lively chase: the marbles received knocks hard enough to splinter them. While I was taking a long aim for a difficult shot, Anaïs exclaimed "Ssh! Look there!"

It was Rabastens who was coming into the playground. Moreover the handsomest of Antonins was already got up to kill and radiant—far too radiant. His face lit up at the sight of me and he came straight up to us.

"Young ladies! . . . How the excitement of the game makes you glow with lovely colour, Mademoiselle Claudine!"

The lout could hardly be more absurd! But, all the same, just to annoy Anaïs, I looked at him complacently and thrust out my chest and fluttered my eyelashes.

"What brings you over to us so early, Sir? Those ladies, our mistresses, are still up in their rooms."

"The fact is, I don't quite know what I *have* come to say, except that Mademoiselle Aimée's fiancé didn't dine with us last night. Some people declare that they met him, looking ill; anyhow he still hasn't returned. I think he's in a bad way and I should like to warn Mademoiselle Lanthenay of the disturrbing state of her fiancé's health."

"The disturrbing state of her fiancé's health. . . ." He expresses himself well, that Marseillais! He ought to set himself as "announcer of deaths and serious accidents". So the crisis was approaching! But though yesterday I myself had been thinking of putting Aimée on her guard, now I no longer wanted him to go and warn her. So much the worse for her! I felt malicious and greedy for excitement this morning and I deliberately set out to keep Antonin at my side. Nothing could be simpler: it was enough to open my eyes innocently wide and to droop my head so that my hair fell loose all about my face. He swallowed the bait at once.

"Sir, do please tell me if it's true that you write charming verses? I've heard people in the town say so."

It was a lie, of course. But I'd have invented anything to stop him from going upstairs to the schoolmistresses. He blushed and stammered, overcome with delight and surprise:

"Who could have told you? . . . But no . . . no . . . I certainly don't deserve . . . It's extraordinary, I didn't think I'd ever mentioned it to a soul!"

"You see how fame has betrayed your modesty! (I should begin to talk like him in a minute.) Would it be indiscreet to ask you . . ."

"I entreat you, Mademoiselle . . . you see me utterly confused. . . . All I could offer you to read would be some humble poems, amorous . . . but chaste! (He spluttered.) I should never, naturally, have dared to allow myself . . ."

"Sir, isn't the bell ringing for the boys to come in to class over on your side?"

If only he'd go away, if *only* he'd go away! In a moment Aimée would come down, he would warn her, she would be on her guard and we shouldn't see a thing!

"Yes . . . but it isn't time yet. It's those fiendish urchins hanging on to the chain . . . you can't leave them a second! And my colleague still hasn't come. Ah, it's harrd work being all on one's own to keep an eye on everything!"

No one can say he isn't frank! This method of "keeping an eye on everything" which consists in coming and saying sweet nothings to the big girls can't exhaust him unduly.

"You see, Mademoiselle, I shall have to go and be severe. But Mademoiselle Lanthenay . . ."

"Oh, you can always tell her at eleven o'clock, if her fiancé's still absent . . . which would surprise me! Perhaps he'll be coming back any minute now?"

Oh, for goodness' sake go and be severe, you great blundering oaf! You've bowed enough and smiled enough; be off with you, vanish! At long last, he did.

The lanky Anaïs, rather vexed at the master's lack of attention to her, disclosed to me that he was in love with me. I shrugged my shoulders. "Come on, let's finish our game. It's more fun than talking insane nonsense."

The game ended while the others were arriving and the teachers were coming down at the last moment. Those two never let each other out of sight! That little horror of an Aimée was lavishing girlish wiles on the Redhead.

We went into class and Mademoiselle Sergent left us in the hands of her favourite who asked us the results of the problems set the day before.

"Anaïs, to the blackboard. Read out the terms of the problem."

It was a fairly complicated problem but the lanky Anaïs, who is gifted for arithmetic, moved with remarkable ease among mail-coaches, watch-hands and proportional shares. Then—horror!—it was my turn.

"Claudine, to the blackboard. Extract the square root of two million, seventy-three thousand, six hundred and twenty."

I professed an intolerable loathing for those little things you have to extract. And, as Mademoiselle Sergent wasn't there, I suddenly decided to play a trick on my ex-friend; she had only herself to blame, the fickle wretch! I hoisted the standard of rebellion. Standing in front of the blackboard, I shook my head and said gently: "No."

"What do you mean, no?"

"No, I don't want to extract roots today. It doesn't appeal to me."

"Claudine, have you gone mad?"

"I don't know, Mademoiselle. But I feel that I shall fall ill if I extract this root or any other like it."

"Do you want a punishment, Claudine?"

"I want anything in the world, except roots. It isn't because I'm disobedient, it's because I can't extract roots. I'm awfully sorry, I assure you."

The class jumped for joy; Mademoiselle Aimée lost patience and raged.

"Once and for all, will you obey me? I shall report you to Mademoiselle Sergent and then we shall see."

"I repeat, I'm simply in despair."

Internally, I shrieked at her: "Nasty little bitch, I'm not going to show *you* any consideration. On the contrary, I'll do everything I can to annoy you."

She descended the two stairs from the desk and advanced on me, in the vague hope of intimidating me. With great difficulty, I stopped myself from laughing and preserved my expression of respectful regret. . . . That tiny little thing! Upon my word, she only came up to my chin! The class was enjoying itself hugely; Anaïs was eating a pencil, both the wood and the lead, in great mouthfuls.

"Mademoiselle Claudine, are you going to obey, yes or no?"

With exaggerated mildness, I began again; she was quite close to me, so I lowered my voice a trifle:

"Once again, Mademoiselle, make me do anything you like . . .

give me fractions to reduce to the same denomination, similar triangles to construct . . . *cracks to verify* . . . anything, anything at all. But not that, oh *not* square roots."

The rest of the class, with the exception of Anaïs, had not taken it in, for I had slipped in my impertinence quickly, without stressing it. The other girls were merely amused by my resistance but Mademoiselle Lanthenay had received a shock. Turning scarlet, she lost her head and said shrilly:

"That's . . . that's too much! I shall go and call Mademoiselle Sergent. . . . Oh, it's really too much!"

She made a bee-line for the door. I ran after her and caught her up in the corridor while the class laughed uproariously, shrieked with joy and climbed up on the benches and stood on them. I held Aimée back by her arm while she tried with all her feeble strength to throw my hands off. She did not say a word; she did not look at me and she kept her teeth clenched.

"Now will you listen to me when I speak to you! We've got beyond the stage of making small-talk, you and I. I swear to you that if you report me to Mademoiselle Sergent, I shall go straight and tell your fiancé the story of the crack. *Now* do you still mean to go up to the Headmistress's room?"

She had stopped dead, still without saying a word; her eyes were obstinately lowered and her mouth compressed.

"Come on, say something! Are you coming back to the classroom with me? If you don't come back at once, *I* shan't go back either; I shall go and warn your Richelieu. Hurry up and choose."

At last, she opened her lips and whispered, without looking at me: "I won't say anything. Let me go, I won't say anything."

"You really mean it? You realise that if you tell the Redhead about it, she won't be able to keep it to herself for five minutes and I shall soon know. You really mean it? It's a . . . promise?"

"I won't say anything, let me go. I'll come straight back to the classroom."

I let go her arm and we went back without a word. The noise of the hive stopped abruptly. My victim, at the desk, laconically ordered us to make a fair copy of the problems. Anaïs asked me under her breath: "Did she go up and tell?"

"No, I made my humble excuses. You see, I didn't want to push a joke like that too far."

Mademoiselle Sergent did not return. Her little assistant retained her shut face and her hard eyes till the end of the class. At half-past ten, we were already thinking about going home. I took some cinders from the stove to stuff them in my sabots, an excellent means of warming them—officially forbidden, that goes without saying. But Mademoiselle Lanthenay's mind was far from cinders and sabots! She was sullenly ruminating her anger and her golden eyes were two cold topazes. I didn't care. In fact, I was even delighted.

Whatever was that? We pricked up our ears. Shouts; a man's voice cursing, mingled with another voice trying to drown it . . . were some of the builders having a fight? I did not think so; I sensed something else. Little Aimée was standing up, very pale; she too felt that something else was coming. Suddenly Mademoiselle Sergent flung herself into the classroom; the crimson had fled from her cheeks.

"Girls, go home at once. It isn't time, but that doesn't matter. . . . Off with you, off with you—don't get into line. Do you understand, get out!"

"Whatever's the matter?" shrieked Mademoiselle Lanthenay.

"Nothing, nothing . . . but get them to go and don't *you* stir from here. Better lock the door. . . . Haven't you gone yet, you little idiots!"

Obviously, circumspection had gone to the winds! Rather than leave the school at such a moment, I would have let myself be flayed alive! I went out in the general scurry of my bewildered classmates. Outside, the vociferating voice could be clearly heard. . . . Good heavens! It was Armand, more livid than a drowned man, his eyes hollow and wild. He was stained green all over with moss, and there were twigs in his hair—he had obviously slept in the woods. . . . Mad with rage after that night spent in brooding over his misery, he wanted to rush into the classroom, yelling and brandishing his fists: Rabastens was holding him back with both arms and rolling his eyes in terror. What a fuss! What a scene!

Marie Belhomme fled, frightened out of her wits, the Second Division behind her; Luce vanished—I had just time to catch her malicious little smile; the Jauberts had run to the playground-door without turning their heads. I could not see Anaïs but I could have sworn she was huddled in some corner and not losing any of the spectacle.

The first word I heard distinctly, was "Trollops!" Armand had dragged his panting colleague right into the classroom where our mute mistresses stood clasping each other tight. He shouted: "Whores! I'm not going to go without telling you what you are, even if I do lose my job for it! Filthy little bitch! Ah, so you let yourself be fumbled for money by that swine of a District Inspector! You're worse than a street walker but *that* one there is even worse than you, that damned redhead who's making you like herself. Two bitches, two bitches, you're two bitches, this house is . . ." I did not hear what. Rabastens, who must have double muscles like Tartarin de Tarascon, succeeded in dragging away the unfortunate man who was choking with insults. Mademoiselle Griset, losing her head, pushed the little girls, who were coming out of the small classroom, back into it again and I escaped, my heart rather shaken. But I was glad that Duplessis had exploded without further delay for Aimée could not now accuse me of having warned him.

When we returned in the afternoon, the one and only person we found there was Mademoiselle Griset who repeated the same phrase to each new arrival. "Mademoiselle Sergent is ill and Mademoiselle Lanthenay is going home to her family; you're not to come back to school for a week."

Fine, so off we went. But, honestly, this is no ordinary school!

DURING the week of unexpected holidays which this commotion procured for us, I went down with measles. This compelled me to spend three weeks in bed, then another fortnight convalescing. And they kept me in quarantine still another fortnight on the pretext of "school safety". If I hadn't had books and Fanchette, however should I have got through it! That doesn't sound very kind to Papa, yet he looked after me as if I were a rare slug. Convinced that one must give a little invalid everything she asks for, he brought me *marrons glacés* to make my temperature go down! Fanchette spent a whole week on my bed, washing herself from ears to tail, playing with my feet through the blanket and nestling in the hollow of my shoulder as soon as I stopped smelling of fever. I returned to school, a little thinner and paler, and immensely curious to see that extraordinary "teaching staff" again. I'd had so little news during my illness! No one came to see me, not even Anaïs or Marie Belhomme, for fear of possible infection.

Half-past seven was striking when I entered the playground on a morning in late February that was as mild as spring. At once I was surrounded and everyone made a fuss of me. The two Jauberts conscientiously asked me whether I was completely cured before coming near me. I was a little stunned by all this noise. At last they let me breathe and I hastily asked the lanky Anaïs the latest news.

"I'll tell you all. Armand Duplessis has left, to begin with."

"Sacked or sent somewhere else, poor old Richelieu?"

"Only sent somewhere else. Dutertre got busy finding him another post."

"Dutertre?"

"Naturally! If Richelieu had talked, that would have stopped the District Superintendent from ever becoming a Deputy. Dutertre has been solemnly saying all over the town that the unfortunate young man had had a very dangerous attack of brain-fever and that they'd called him in, as school doctor, just in time."

"Ah! So they called him in just in time? Providence had planted the remedy next door to the ill. . . . And Mademoiselle Aimée? Sent away too?"

"Certainly not! Oh, *she's* in no danger! By the end of a week, he didn't appear any more. And she was giggling with Mademoiselle Sergent just as usual."

It was too much! That odd little creature who had neither heart nor brain, who lived without memory and without remorse, would begin all over again. She would humbug an assistant-master and romp with the District Superintendent until there was another crisis and she would live quite contentedly with that jealous, violent woman who was going to pieces as a result of these adventures. I hardly heard Anaïs telling me that Rabastens was still there and was constantly inquiring after me. I'd forgotten him, that pathetic lout Antonin!

The bell rang but it was the new school that we trooped into now. And the central building that linked the two wings was almost finished.

Mademoiselle Sergent installed herself at the desk that was all new and shining. Farewell the old ricketty, scarred, uncomfortable tables; now we sat down at handsome sloping ones, provided with benches with backs to them and desks with hinged lids. We were only two to a bench now; instead of the lanky Anaïs, I now had as my neighbour . . . little Luce Lanthenay. Luckily the tables were extremely close together and Anaïs was near me, at a table parallel to mine, so that we could gossip together as comfortably as before. They had put Marie Belhomme beside her for Mademoiselle Sergent had intentionally placed two "lively" ones (Anaïs and me), next to two "torpid" ones (Luce and Marie) so that we should shake them up a little. We certainly would shake them up! At least I would, for I could feel all the rebelliousness that had been suppressed during my illness boiling up in me. I took in my new surroundings and arranged my books and exercise-books, while Luce sat down and watched me with a sidelong, timid glance. But I didn't deign to speak to her yet: I merely exchanged remarks about the new school with Anaïs who was avidly nibbling some unknown substance that looked to me like green buds.

"Whatever are you eating—old crab-apples?"

"Lime buds, old thing. Nothing so good. Now's just the moment, when it's getting on for March."

"Give us a bit? . . . Really, it's awfully good. It's sticky, like the gum on fruit-trees. I'll get some off the limes in the playground. And what other hitherto unknown delicacies are you stuffing yourself with nowadays?"

"Oh, nothing startling. I can't even eat coloured pencils any more. This year's lot are gritty. Beastly—absolute rubbish. However, to make up for that, the blotting-paper's excellent. There's also something good to chew, but not to swallow . . . the samples of handkerchief linen that the Bon Marché and the Louvre send out."

"Ugh! That doesn't appeal to me in the least. . . . I say, young Luce, are you going to try and be good and obedient sitting here beside me? Otherwise, I promise you slaps and pinches. So beware!"

"Yes, Mademoiselle," answered the little thing, looking none too reassured, with her lashes downcast on her cheeks.

"You can say '*tu*' to me. Look at me, so as I can see your eyes? That's right. Now, you know that I'm mad, I'm sure you've been told that. Well, if anyone annoys me, I become furious and I bite and scratch, especially since my illness. Give me your hand: there, that's what I do."

I dug my nails into her hand; she did not squeal, only tightened her lips.

"You didn't yell, good. I'll put you through questioning at recreation."

In the Second classroom, whose door had been left open, I had just witnessed the entrance of Mademoiselle Aimée. Fresh, curled, and rosy, she wore her coaxing, mischievous expression and her eyes were more velvety and golden than ever. Little trollop! She flashed a radiant smile at Mademoiselle Sergent who forgot herself for a moment in contemplating her, then came out of her ecstasy and addressed us sharply:

"Your exercise-books. History essay: *The war of 1870.* Claudine," she added more gently "Can you do this essay in spite of not having followed the classes these last two months?"

"I'm going to try, Mademoiselle: I'll do the essay with less detailed development, that's all."

I did, in fact, dash off a little essay. It was excessively short and, when I got towards the end, I lingered over it and applied myself to it, spinning out the last fifteen lines so as to be able to spy and ferret out what was going on about me. The Headmistress, the same as ever, preserved her expression of concentrated passion and jealous daring. Her Aimée, who was carelessly dictating problems in the other classroom, wandered closer and closer while she read aloud. All the same, last winter, she did not have that confident, coquettish walk—the walk of a spoilt pussy-cat! Now she was the adored, cherished little animal that is developing into a tyrant, for I caught glances from Mademoiselle Sergent that implored her to find some pretext to bring her over to her, glances to which the scatterbrained creature replied with capricious shakes of her head and amused eyes that said No. The Redhead, who had definitely become her slave, could bear it no longer and went across to her, asking very loud: "Mademoiselle Lanthenay, you haven't got the Attendance Register in your room, have you?" Good, she had gone; they were chattering in whispers. I took advantage of this solitude in which we were left to put little Luce through a severe inquisition.

"Ah, ah, let that exercise-book alone, will you and answer my questions. Is there a dormitory upstairs?"

"Oh yes. We sleep there now, the boarders and me."

"All right. You're a dolt."

"Why?"

"That's none of your business. Do you still have singing-lessons on Thursdays and Sundays?"

"Oh, we tried to have one without you, Mademoiselle . . . Claudine, I mean, but it didn't go a bit well. Monsieur Rabastens doesn't know how to teach us."

"Good. Has the cuddler been here while I was ill?"

"Who's that?"

"Dutertre."

"I can't remember. . . . Oh yes, he did come once, but not into the classrooms. And he only stayed a few minutes talking to my sister and Mademoiselle Sergent in the playground."

"Is she nice to you, the Redhead?"

Her slanting eyes darkened.

"No . . . she tells me I've no intelligence . . . that I'm lazy . . . that my sister must have taken all the intelligence in the family as she's taken all the beauty. . . . Anyway, it's always the same story wherever I've been with Aimée: people only pay attention to her and *I'm* pushed into the background. . . ."

Luce was on the verge of tears in her fury against this sister who was more "fetching" as they say here and who thrust her aside and eclipsed her. For all that, I didn't think her any better than Aimée: only shyer and more timid because she was used to remaining lonely and silent.

"Poor kid! You've left friends over there, where you used to be?"

"No, I didn't have any friends. The girls were too rough and used to laugh at me."

"Too rough? Then it upsets you when I beat you or push you about?"

She laughed, without raising her eyes:

"No, because I realise that you . . . that you don't do it cruelly, out of beastliness . . . well, that it's a kind of joke and you don't really mean it. It's like when you call me 'dolt', I know it's only for fun. In fact, I quite like feeling a bit frightened, when there isn't the least danger."

Tralala! They're both alike, these two little Lanthenays; cowardly, naturally perverse, egotistical and so devoid of all moral sense that it's amusing to watch them. All the same, this one detested her sister and I thought I could drag any number of revelations about Aimée out of her by cramming her with sweets and also by beating her.

"Have you finished your essay?"

"Yes, I've finished . . . but I didn't know the stuff a bit . . . I'm sure I'll get rotten marks. . . ."

"Give me your exercise-book."

I read her essay, which was very so-so; then I dictated some things she'd forgotten and remodelled her sentences a little. She was in a welter of joy and astonishment and observed me slyly, with surprised, enchanted eyes.

"There, you see, it's better like that. . . . Tell me, do the boarders in the boys' school have their dormitory opposite yours?"

Her eyes lit up with mischief.

"Yes, and at night they go to bed the same time as we do, on purpose. And, you know, the windows have no shutters so the boys try and see us in our chemises. We lift up the corners of the curtains to look at *them* and it's no good Mademoiselle Griset keeping watch on us till the light's put out. We always find a way of pulling a curtain right up, all of a sudden, and that makes the boys come back every night to spy."

"Well, well! You have a gay time undressing up there!"

"We certainly do!"

She was becoming lively and more familiar. Mademoiselle Sergent and Mademoiselle Lanthenay were still together in the Second classroom. Aimée showed the Redhead a letter and the two of them burst out laughing, but they kept their laughter very low.

"Do you know where your sister's ex-Armand has gone to bury his sorrows, young Luce?"

"No, I don't. Aimée never talks to me about her private affairs."

"I thought as much. Has she got her room upstairs too?"

"Yes, the nicest and most comfortable of the assistant-mistresses' rooms—much prettier and warmer than Mademoiselle Griset's. Mademoiselle's had curtains with pink flowers put in it and linoleum on the floor, my dear, and a goatskin rug. And they've enamelled the bed white. Aimée even wanted to make me believe that she'd bought all these lovely things out of her savings. I told her straight: 'I'll ask Mamma if it's true.' Then she said: 'If you mention it to Mamma, I'll have you sent back home on the excuse that you're not working.' So, as you can imagine, there was nothing for me to do but keep my mouth shut."

"Ssh. Mademoiselle's coming back."

And, indeed, Mademoiselle was approaching, abandoning her tender, laughing expression for her school-mistress's face.

"Have you finished, girls? I am going to dictate you a problem in geometry."

Dolorous protests arose, demanding another five minutes' grace. But Mademoiselle Sergent was not moved by these supplications, which were repeated three times a day, and began calmly to dictate the problem. Heaven confound similar triangles!

I was careful to bring sweets to school often with the object of seducing young Luce completely. She took them, hardly saying thank you, filled her little hands with them and hid them in an old mother-of-pearl rosary-case. For ten sous' worth of too-hot English peppermints, she would have sold her big sister and one of her brothers into the bargain. She opened her mouth, breathed in the air so as to feel the cold of the peppermint and exclaimed: "My tongue's freezing, my tongue's freezing," her eyes rapturous. Anaïs shamelessly begged sweets of me, stuffed her cheeks with them, then hastily asked again, with an irresistible grimace of affected disgust:

"Quick, quick . . . give me some more to take the taste away— those had gone bad."

As if by chance, while we were playing "He", Rabastens came into the playground, bearing some exercise-books or other as an excuse. He feigned an amiable surprise at seeing me again and profited by the occasion to thrust a love-song under my nose. He proceeded to read its amorous words in a cooing voice. Poor noodle of an Antonin, you're no longer any use to me now—and you never were *much* use! The very most you're good for is to keep me amused for a little while and to excite the jealousy of my schoolfriends. If only you'd go away. . . .

"Monsieur, you'll find those ladies in the end classroom. I think I saw them coming downstairs . . . weren't they, Anaïs?"

Thinking I was sending him away on account of the malignant glances of my companions, he threw me an eloquent look and departed. I shrugged my shoulders at the "Hmm-Hms" I heard from the lanky Anaïs and from Marie Belhomme and we went on with an exciting game of "turn-the-knife" in which the beginner, Luce, made mistake after mistake. She's young, poor thing, she doesn't know! The bell rang for class.

It was a sewing-lesson, a test for the examination. That is to say they made us do the samples of sewing, demanded in the exam, in one hour. We were handed out small squares of linen and Mademoiselle Sergent wrote up on the blackboard, in her clear writing, full of strokes like hammers:

Buttonhole.—Ten centimetres of whipping. Initial G in marking-stitch. Ten centimetres of hem in running-stitch.

I groaned at this announcement because I could just manage the buttonhole and the whipping but the running-stitch hem and the initial in marking-stitch were things I didn't "execute to perfection", as Mademoiselle Aimée noted with regret. Luckily I had recourse to a simple and ingenious device. I gave little Luce, who sews divinely, some sweets and she worked a marvellous G for me. "We must help one another." (Very appropriately, we had commented on this charitable aphorism only the day before.)

Marie Belhomme had confected a letter G that looked like a squatting monkey and, in her usual cheerful, crazy way, was roaring with laughter at her own work. The boarders, with their heads bent and their elbows held in were talking imperceptibly as they sewed. From time to time they exchanged meaning looks with Luce in the direction of the boys' school. I suspected that, at night, they spied some amusing spectacles from the vantage-point of their peaceful white dormitory.

Mademoiselle Lanthenay and Mademoiselle Sergent had exchanged desks; it was Aimée who invigilated our sewing-lesson while the Headmistress was making the girls in the Second class read aloud. The favourite was occupied in inscribing the title of an Attendance Register in a beautiful round hand when her Redhead called out to her from the distance:

"Mademoiselle Lanthenay!"

"What do you want?" cried Aimée. Thoughtlessly, she used the familiar "*tu*".

There was a stupefied silence. We all looked at each other: Anaïs began to clutch her ribs so as to be able to laugh longer; the two Jauberts bent their heads over their sewing; the boarders slyly dug each other with their elbows; Marie Belhomme burst out in a stifled laugh that sounded like a sneeze, and, at the sight of Aimée's face of consternation, I exclaimed out loud:

"Ah! She's so awfully kind!"

Little Luce was hardly laughing at all. It was obvious that she must have heard them address each other in that intimate way before. But she was staring at her sister with mocking eyes.

Mademoiselle Aimée turned on me furiously:

"Anyone may happen to make a mistake at times, Mademoiselle Claudine! And I apologise to Mademoiselle Sergent for my slip of the tongue!"

But the latter, having recovered from the shock, was quite aware that we would not swallow the explanation. She shrugged her shoulders as a sign of giving up in face of the irremediable blunder. This made a gay finale to the boring sewing-lesson. I'd badly needed this sprightly distraction.

When school was over at four o'clock, I did not go straight home. Instead, I astutely forgot an exercise-book and came back. I knew that, during the time for sweeping, the boarders took turns to carry water up to their dormitory. I did not know that dormitory yet; I wanted to visit it and Luce had told me: "Today, *I'm doing the water*." Treading like a cat, I climbed upstairs, carrying a full pail in case of awkward encounters. The dormitory had white walls and a white ceiling and was furnished with eight white beds. Luce showed me hers but I hadn't the faintest interest in her bed! I went straight to the windows which did, indeed, let one see into the boys' dormitory. Two or three big boys of fourteen or fifteen were prowling about it and looking in our direction: as soon as they saw us, they laughed and gesticulated and pointed to their beds. A lot of scamps! All the same, how tempting they are! Luce, shocked or pretending to be, hurriedly shut the window. But I'm pretty sure that, at bedtime, she displays less prudishness. The ninth bed, at the end of the dormitory, was placed under a kind of canopy that shrouded it in white curtains.

"That," explained Luce "that's the mistress on duty's bed. The assistant-mistresses are supposed to take it in turn, week by week, to sleep in our dormitory."

"Ah! So it's sometimes your sister Aimée, sometimes Mademoiselle Griset?"

"Well, of course . . . that's how it ought to be . . . but up to now, it's always Mademoiselle Griset. . . . I don't know why."

"Ah, so you don't know why? Hypocrite!"

I gave her a bang on the shoulder; she complained, but without conviction. Poor Mademoiselle Griset!

Luce went on enlightening me:

"At night, Claudine, you simply can't imagine what fun we have when we go to bed. We laugh, we run about in our chemises, we have pillow-fights. Some of the girls hide behind the curtains to get undressed because they say it embarrasses them. The oldest one, Rose Raquenot, washes so little that her underclothes are grey by the end of the three days she wears them. Yesterday, they hid my nightdress so I had to stay in the wash-room, absolutely naked. Luckily Mademoiselle Griset came along! Then we make fun of one of them who's so plump she had to powder herself all over with starch so as not to chafe herself. Oh, and I'd forgotten Poisson who wears a nightcap that makes her look like an old woman and who won't undress till we've all left the wash-room. Oh, believe me, we have heaps of fun!"

The wash-room was scantily furnished with a big zinc-covered table on which stood a row of eight basins, eight tablets of soap, pairs of towels and eight sponges. All these objects were exactly alike: the linen was marked in indelible ink. It was all very neatly kept.

I inquired:

"Do you have baths?"

"Yes . . . and that's something else that's frightfully funny! In the new wash-house they heat up a huge wine-vat full of water . . . as big as a room. We all get undressed and we cram ourselves into it to soap ourselves."

"Quite naked?"

"Of course—how'd we manage to soap ourselves otherwise? Rose Raquenot didn't want to strip, of course, because she's too thin. If you could only see her," added Luce, lowering her voice, "She's got practically nothing on her bones, and it's absolutely flat on her chest, like a boy! But Jousse is just the reverse. She's like a wet-nurse, *they* are as big as that! And the one who wears an old woman's nightcap—you know, Poisson—she's got hair all over like a bear, and she's got blue thighs."

"What do you mean, blue?"

"Yes, really blue. Like when it's freezing and your skin's blue with cold."

"It must be most engaging!"

"Oh, no, it certainly isn't. If I were a boy, I wouldn't be a bit keen on having a bath with her!"

"But mightn't it have more effect on *her*, having a bath with a boy?"

We giggled, but I started at the sound of the voice and the footsteps of Mademoiselle Sergent in the corridor. So as not to be caught, I hid myself under the canopy reserved for the unique occupation of Mademoiselle Griset. Then, when the danger had passed, I escaped and dashed downstairs, calling out "Good-bye" under my breath.

Next morning, how good my dear countryside looked! How gaily my pretty Montigny was sunning itself in this warm, precocious spring! Last Sunday and Thursday, I'd already ranged through the delicious woods, full of violets, with my co-First Communicant, my gentle Claire. She told me all about her flirtations . . . ever since the weather had turned mild her "follower" arranged for them to meet in the evening at the corner of the Fir Plantation. Who knows if she won't end up by going too far! But it's not *that* which attracts her. Provided someone pours out choice words she doesn't quite understand, provided someone kisses her and goes down on his knees and everything happens *like it does in books* . . . well, she's perfectly satisfied.

In the classroom, I found little Luce collapsed over a table, sobbing fit to choke herself. I raised her head by main force and saw that her eyes were swollen as big as eggs, she'd dabbed them so much.

"Oh! Really! You look far from beautiful like that! What's the matter, little thing! What are you *blubbing* about?"

"She . . . she . . . beat me!"

"Do you mean, your sister?"

"Ye-e-es!"

"What had you done to her?"

She dried her eyes a little and began to tell her story.

"You see, I hadn't understood my problems, so I hadn't done them. That put her in a temper, so she said I was a dolt, that it wasn't worth while our parents' paying my fees, that she was disgusted with me, and so on and so on. . . . So I answered back: 'Oh, you bore me stiff.' Then she beat me, she slapped my face. She's a beastly, horrible scold. I loathe her."

There was a fresh deluge.

"My poor Luce, you're a goose. You shouldn't have let yourself be beaten, you should have thrown her ex-Armand in her teeth. . . ."

The sudden scare in the little thing's eyes made me turn round: I caught sight of Mademoiselle Sergent listening to us from the doorway. Help! What was she going to say?

"My compliments, Mademoiselle Claudine. You are giving this child some pretty advice."

"And you a pretty example!"

Luce was terrified by my reply. As for me, I didn't care in the least. The Headmistress's fiery eyes were glittering with rage and emotion! But this time, too subtle to lose her temper openly, she shook her head and merely observed:

"It's lucky the month of July is not far off, Mademoiselle Claudine. You realise, don't you, that it's becoming more and more impossible for me to keep you here?"

"Apparently. But, you know, it's due to our misunderstanding each other. Our relationship got off on the wrong foot."

"Go off to recreation, Luce," she said, without answering me.

The little thing did not wait to be told twice. She left the room at a run, blowing her nose. Mademoiselle Sergent went on:

"It's entirely your own fault, I assure you. You showed yourself full of ill-will towards me when I first arrived and you have repelled all my advances. For I made you plenty of them, though it was not my place to do so. All the same, you seemed to me intelligent—and pretty enough to interest me . . . who have neither sister nor child."

Hanged if I'd ever thought of it. . . . I couldn't have been more clearly told that I would have been "her little Aimée" if I'd been willing. Well, well! No, that meant nothing to me, even in retrospect. Nevertheless, it would have been me of whom Mademoiselle Lanthenay would have been jealous at this very moment. . . . What a comedy!

"That's true, Mademoiselle. But, as fate would have it, it would have turned out badly all the same, on account of Mademoiselle Aimée Lanthenay. You put so much fervour into acquiring her . . . friendship—and into destroying any she might have for me!"

She averted her eyes.

"I did not seek, as you pretend I did, to destroy. . . . Mademoiselle Aimée could have gone on giving you her English lessons without my preventing her. . . ."

"For goodness' sake don't say that! I'm not quite an idiot and there are only the two of us here! For a long time I was furious about it, devastated even, for I'm very nearly as jealous as you are. . . . Why did you take her? I've been so unhappy, yes, there, you can be pleased, I've been so unhappy! But I realise now that she didn't care for me—who *does* she care for? I've realised too that she's not really worth much: that was enough for me. I've thought that I'd do quite enough foolish things without committing the folly of wanting to take her away from you. There! Now the only thing I want is that she shouldn't become too much the little queen of this school and that she shouldn't over-torment that little sister of hers who's fundamentally no better—and no worse—than she is, I assure you. . . . I never tell tales at home—never—about anything I may see here. I shan't come back again after the holidays and I shall sit for the Certificate because Papa's got it into his head that he's keen on it and because Anaïs would be only too delighted if I didn't pass the exam. . . . You might leave me in peace till then—I don't torment you at all nowadays. . . ."

I could have gone on talking for a long time, I think, but she was no longer listening to me. I was not going to contend with her for her little darling, that was all she had been interested to hear. Her gaze had become introspective: she was pursuing an idea of her own. She roused herself, suddenly becoming the Headmistress again, after this conversation on an equal footing, and said to me:

"Hurry out to the playground, Claudine. It's after eight, you must get into line."

"What were you chattering so long about in there with Mademoiselle?" demanded the lanky Anaïs. "Does that mean you're matey with her, now?"

"Two girls together, my dear!"

In the classroom, little Luce squeezed up close to me, threw me affectionate looks and clasped my hands. But her caresses irritated me; I only like hitting her and teasing her and protecting her when the others upset her.

Mademoiselle Aimée came into the classroom like a whirlwind, exclaiming in a loud whisper: "The Inspector! The Inspector!" There was an uproar. Anything is an excuse for disorder here; under cover of arranging our books with impeccable neatness, we opened all our desks and chattered hurriedly behind the lids. The lanky Anaïs sent all the completely distracted Marie Belhomme's exercise-books flying and prudently thrust a *Gil Blas Illustré*, that she had concealed between two pages of her *History of France,* into her pocket. I myself hid Rudyard Kipling's marvellously-told stories of animals (there's a man who really knows about them!)—though they were hardly very reprehensible reading. We buzzed, we stood up, we gathered up papers, we took out the sweets hidden in our desks, for this venerable Blanchot, the Inspector, has eyes that squint but that poke into everything.

Mademoiselle Lanthenay, in her own classroom, was hustling the little girls, tidying her desk, shouting and flapping about. And, now, from the third room, there appeared the wretched Griset, in great dismay, demanding help and protection.

"Mademoiselle Sergent, will the Inspector ask to see the little ones' exercise-books? They're dreadfully dirty . . . the smallest ones can only do pothooks. . . ." The malicious Aimée laughed in her face; the Headmistress replied with a shrug: "You'll show him whatever he asks to see, but if you think he'll bother with your urchins' copy books!" And the pathetic, dazed creature returned to her classroom where her little beasts were making an appalling din, for she hadn't a ha'porth of authority.

We were ready, or as near as maybe. Mademoiselle Sergent exclaimed: "Quick, get out your selected pieces! Anaïs, spit it out at once, that slate-pencil you have in your mouth! On my word of honour, I'll turn you out in front of Monsieur Blanchot if you go on eating those revolting things! Claudine, couldn't you stop pinching Luce Lanthenay for one single instant? Marie Belhomme, take those off at once, those three scarves you have on your head and round your neck. And also take that stupid expression off your face. You're worse than the little ones in the Third Class and not one of you is worth the rope to hang you with!"

She simply had to discharge her nervous irritation. The Inspector's visits always upset her because Blanchot was on good terms with the Deputy who detested his possible successor Dutertre, who was Mademoiselle Sergent's protégé, like poison. (Heavens, how complicated life is!) At last everything was more or less in order; the lanky Anaïs stood up, looking quite alarmingly tall, her mouth still dirty from the grey pencil she had been nibbling, and began *The Dress* by that maudlin poet Manuel:

> *In the wretched garret where daylight scarce could pierce*
> *Wife and husband argued in a quarrel fierce. . . .*

Only just in time! A tall shadow passed across the panes giving on to the corridor; the entire class shuddered and rose to its feet—out of respect—at the moment when the door opened to admit old Blanchot. He had a solemn face framed in large pepper-and-salt whiskers and a formidable Franche-Comté accent. He pontificated, he chewed his words enthusiastically like Anaïs chewing indiarubber, he was always dressed with a stiff, old-fashioned correctness; what an old bore! Now we were in for a whole hour of him! He would be sure to ask us idiotic questions and prove to us that we ought all to "embrace the career of teaching." I'd rather do even that than embrace *him*!

"Young ladies! . . . Sit down, my children."

"His children" sat down, modest and mild. I wished to goodness I could get away. Mademoiselle Sergent danced attendance on him with an expression at once respectful and malevolent, while her assistant, the virtuous Lanthenay, shut herself up in her own classroom.

Monsieur Blanchot placed his silver-headed cane in a corner and promptly began to exasperate the Headmistress (well done!) by drawing her over to the window to talk about Certificate syllabuses, zeal, assiduity and all that sort of thing! She listened, she replied: "Yes, Inspector." Her eyes had retreated under her brows; she was obviously longing to hit him. He had finished boring her; now it was our turn.

"What was that girl reading when I came in?"

Anaïs, the "girl" in question, hid the pink blotting-paper she was chewing and broke off the narrative, obviously a scandalous one, she was pouring into the ears of Marie Belhomme. The latter, shocked and crimson but attentive, rolled her birdlike eyes with a modest dismay. Smutty Anaïs! What could those stories possibly be?

"Come, my child, tell me what you are reading."

"*The Dress*, Sir."

"Kindly continue."

She began again, with an air of mock intimidation, while Blanchot examined us with his dirty-green eyes. He was severe on any hint of coquetry and he frowned when he saw a black velvet ribbon on a white neck or curly tendrils escaping over forehead and temples. He always scolded *me* every time he visited us about my hair, which was always loose and curly, and also about the big white pleated collars I wore on my dark dresses. Although these had the simplicity I like, they were attractive enough for him to find my clothes appallingly reprehensible. The lanky Anaïs had finished *The Dress* and he was making her logically analyse (oh, my goodness!) five or six lines of it. Then he asked her:

"My child, why have you tied that black velvet about your neck?"

Now we were in for it! What did I tell you? Anaïs, flummoxed, answered idiotically that it was "to keep her warm". Cowardly fat-head!

"To keep you warm, you say? Don't you think a scarf would have served that purpose better?"

A scarf! Why not a woollen muffler, you doddering old bore? I couldn't help laughing and this drew his attention to myself.

"And you, my child, why is your hair not properly done and hanging all loose instead of being twisted up on your head and secured with hairpins?"

"Sir, that gives me migraines."

"But you could at least plait it, I presume?"

"Yes I could, but Papa doesn't like me to."

I can't tell you how he irritated me! After a disapproving little smack of his lips, he went and sat down and tormented Marie Belhomme about the War of Secession, one of the Jauberts about the coastline of Spain and the other about right-angled triangles. Then he sent me to the blackboard and ordered me to draw a circle. I obeyed. It was a circle . . . if you chose to call it one.

"Inside it, inscribe a rose-window with five lights. Assume that it is lit from the left and indicate with heavy strokes the shadows the petals receive."

That didn't bother me at all. If he'd wanted to make me calculate figures, I'd have been in a hopeless mess but I knew all about rose-windows and shadows. I got through it quite well, much to the annoyance of the Jauberts who were sneakingly hoping to see me scolded.

"That's . . . good. Yes, that's not bad at all. You're sitting for the Certificate Examination this year?"

"Yes, Sir, in July."

"Then, no doubt, you wish to enter the Training College afterwards?"

"No, Sir. I shall go back home."

"Indeed? As a matter of fact, in my opinion, you have not the slightest vocation for teaching. Very regrettable."

He said that exactly as if he were saying: "In my opinion, you are an infanticide." Poor man, let him keep his illusions! But I could only wish he had been able to see the Armand Duplessis drama or the way we were left on our own for hours while our two mistresses were upstairs, billing and cooing. . . .

"Be so good as to show me your Second Class, Mademoiselle."

Mademoiselle Sergent took him off to the Second classroom where she remained with him to protect her little darling against inspectorial severity. I profited by his absence to sketch a caricature of old Blanchot and his huge whiskers on the blackboard. This sent the girls into ecstasies. I added donkey's ears, then I quickly rubbed it out and went back to my place. Little Luce slipped her arm coaxingly under mine and tried to kiss me. I pushed her away with a light slap and she pretended that I was "simply horrid"!

"Simply horrid! I'll teach you to take liberties like that with me! Try and muzzle your feelings and tell me if it's still always Mademoiselle Griset who sleeps in the dormitory."

"No, Aimée's slept there twice two days running."

"That makes four times. You're a duffer; not even a duffer a total nitwit! Do the boarders keep quieter when it's your chaste sister who's sleeping under the canopy?"

"Not a bit. And one night even, when one of the girls was ill, we got up and opened a window . . . I even called out to my sister to give us some matches because we couldn't find any, and she didn't budge. She didn't breathe any more than if there were no one in the bed at all! Does that mean that she's a very heavy sleeper?"

"Heavy sleeper! Heavy sleeper! What a goose you are! Good Lord, why have You allowed beings so utterly deprived of intelligence to exist on this earth? They make me weep tears of blood!"

"What have I done now?"

"Nothing! Oh, nothing at all! Only here come some thumps on your back to improve your heart and your wits and teach you not to believe in the virtuous Aimée's alibis."

Luce squirmed over the table in mock despair, ravished at being bullied and pummelled. But I had suddenly remembered something:

"Anaïs, whatever were you telling Marie Belhomme that raised such blushes that the nation's over the Bastille pale beside them?"

"What Bastille?"

"Never mind. Tell me quick."

"Come a bit closer."

Her vicious face was sparkling; it must have been something very sordid.

"All right, then. Didn't you know? Last New Year's Eve, the Mayor had his mistress at his house—the fair Julotte—and, besides, his secretary had brought a woman from Paris. Well, at dessert, they made them both undress . . . take off even their chemises, and they did the same. And they set to and danced a quadrille like that, old dear!"

"Not bad! Who told you that?"

"It was Papa who told Mamma. I was in bed, only they always leave my bedroom door open because I pretend I'm frightened and so I hear everything."

"Your home life must be far from dull. Does your father often tell stories like that?"

"No, not always such good ones. But sometimes I roll about in my bed with laughing."

She told me some more pretty dirty bits of gossip about our neighbourhood: her father works at the Town Hall and knows every scrap of scandal in the district. I listened to her and the time passed.

Mademoiselle Sergent returned: we had only just time to open our books at random, but she came straight up to me without looking at what we were doing.

"Claudine, could you make your classmates sing in front of Monsieur Blanchot? They know that pretty two-part song now— *Dans ce doux asile*."

"*I'm* perfectly willing. Only it makes the Inspector so sick to see me with my hair loose that he won't listen!"

"Don't say silly things, this isn't the day for them. Hurry up and make them sing. Monsieur Blanchot seems decidedly dissatisfied with the Second Class; I'm counting on the music to smooth him down."

I had no difficulty in believing that he must be decidedly dissatisfied with the Second Class: Mademoiselle Aimée Lanthenay occupies herself with it whenever she has nothing else to do. She gorges her girls with written work so as to be able to chat peacefully with her dear Headmistress while they're scribbling. I was perfectly willing to make the girls sing, whatever it cost me!

Mademoiselle Sergent brought back the odious Blanchot: I ranged our class and the first division of the Second in a semi-circle and entrusted the firsts to Anaïs and the seconds to Marie Belhomme (unfortunate seconds!). I would sing both parts at once; that's to say I'd quickly change over when I felt one side weakening. Off we went! One empty bar: one, two, three.

> *Dans ce doux asile*
> *Les sages sont couronnés,*
> *Venez!*
> *Aux plaisirs tranquilles*
> *Ces lieux charmants sont destinés. . . .*

What luck! That tough old pedagogue nodded his head to the rhythm of Rameau's music (out of time, as it happened), and appeared enchanted. It was the story of the composer Orpheus taming the wild beasts all over again.

"That was well sung. By whom is it? By Gounod, I believe?" (Why does he pronounce it *Gounode?*)

"Yes, Sir." (Don't let's annoy him.)

"I was sure it was. It is an extremely pretty piece".

(Pretty piece yourself!)

On hearing this unexpected attribution of a melody of Rameau's to the author of *Faust*, Mademoiselle Sergent compressed her lips so as not to laugh. As to Blanchot, now serene once more, he uttered a few amiable remarks and went away, after having dictated to us—as a Parthian shot—this theme for a French composition:

"Explain and comment on this thought of Franklin's: Idleness is like rust, it wears a man out more than work."

Off we go! Let us contrast the shining key, with its rounded contours which the hand polishes and turns in the lock twenty times a day, with the key eaten away with reddish rust. The good workman who labours joyously, having risen at dawn, whose brawny muscles, etcetera; etcetera. . . . Let us set him against the idler, who lying languidly on oriental divans, watches rare dishes etc; etc. . . . succeed each other on his sumptuous table etc; etc. . . . dishes which vainly attempt to reawaken his appetite etc; etc. . . . Oh, that won't take long to hash out!

Nonsense, of course, that it isn't good to laze in an armchair! Nonsense, of course, that workers who labour all their life don't die young and exhausted! But naturally one mustn't say so. In the "Examination Syllabus" things don't happen as they do in life.

Little Luce was lacking in ideas and whining in a low voice for me to provide her with some. I generously let her read what I had written; she wouldn't get much from me.

At last it was four o'clock. We went off home. The boarders went upstairs to eat the refreshments Mademoiselle Sergent's mother had prepared for them. I left with Anaïs and Marie Belhomme after having looked at my reflection in the window-panes to make sure my hat wasn't crooked.

On the way, we shared a sugar-loaf and castigated Blanchot as if we were breaking it over his back. He bores me stiff, that old man, who wants us always to be dressed in sackcloth and wear our hair scraped back.

"All the same, I don't think he's awfully pleased with the Second class," remarked Marie Belhomme. "If you hadn't wheedled him round with the music!"

"What d'you expect?" said Anaïs, "Mademoiselle Lanthenay doesn't exactly over-exert herself with anxiety over the welfare of her class."

"The things you say! Come, come, she can't do everything! Mademoiselle Sergent has attached her to her person—she's the one who dresses her in the morning."

"Oh, that's bunkum!" Anaïs and Marie exclaimed both at once.

"It isn't bunkum in the least! If ever you go into the dormitory and into the mistresses' rooms (it's awfully easy, you've only to take some water up with the boarders), run your hand over the bottom of Mademoiselle Aimée's basin. You needn't be afraid of getting wet, there's nothing but dust in it."

"No, that's going a bit far, all the same!" declared Marie Belhomme.

The lanky Anaïs made no further comment and went away meditating; no doubt she would pass on all these charming details to the big boy with whom she was flirting that week. I knew very little about her escapades; she remained secretive and sly when I sounded her about them.

I was bored at school; a tiresome symptom and quite a new one. Yet I wasn't in love with anyone. (Indeed, perhaps that was the reason.) I was so apathetic that I did my schoolwork almost accurately, and I was quite unmoved as I watched our two mistresses caressing each other, billing and cooing and quarrelling for the pleasure of being more affectionate than ever when they made it up. Their words and gestures to each other were so uninhibited nowadays that Rabastens, in spite of his self-possession, was taken aback by them and spluttered excitably. Then Aimée's eyes would gleam with delight like those of a mischievous cat and Mademoiselle Sergent would laugh at seeing her laughing. Upon my word, they really were amazing! It's fantastic, how exacting the little thing has become! The other changes countenance at the faintest sigh from her, at a pucker of her velvety eyebrows.

Little Luce is acutely conscious of this tender intimacy: she watches every move, hot on the trail, and learns things for herself. Indeed she is learning a great deal for she seizes every opportunity of being alone with me, and brushes up against me coaxingly, her green eyes almost closed and her fresh little mouth half-open. But no, she doesn't tempt me. Why doesn't she transfer her attentions to the lanky Anaïs who is also highly interested in the goings-on of the two love-birds who serve us as teachers in their spare moments and who is extremely surprised at them, for she is oddly ingenuous in some ways?

This morning I beat little Luce to a jelly because she wanted to kiss me in the shed where they keep the watering-cans. She didn't yell but began to cry until I comforted her by stroking her hair. I told her:

"Silly, you'll have plenty of time to work off your superfluous feelings later on, as you're going on to the Training College!"

"Yes, but *you're* not going on there!"

"No, thank goodness! But you won't have been there two days before two "Third Years" will have quarrelled over you, you disgusting little beast!"

She let herself be insulted with voluptuous pleasure and threw me grateful glances.

Is it because they've changed my old school that I'm so bored in this one? I no longer have the dusty "nooks" where one could hide in the passages of that rambling old building where one never knew whether one was in the staff's quarters or in our own and where it was so natural to find oneself in a master's room that one hardly needed to apologise on returning to the classroom.

Is it because I'm getting older? Can I be feeling the weight of the sixteen years I've nearly attained? That really would be too idiotic for words.

Perhaps it's the spring? It's also too fine—almost indecently fine! On Thursdays and Sundays I go off all alone to meet my First Communion partner, my little Claire, who's heavily embarked on an absurd adventure with the Secretary at the Town Hall who doesn't want to marry her. From all accounts, there's an excellent reason that prevents him! It seems that, while he was still at college, he underwent an operation for some peculiar disease, one of those diseases whose "seat" is never mentioned, and people say that, if he still wants girls, he can never again "satisfy his desires". I don't understand awfully well, in fact I don't really understand at all, but I'm sick and tired of passing on to Claire what I've vaguely learnt. She turns up the whites of her eyes, shakes her head, and replies, with an ecstatic expression: "Oh, what does that matter, what does that matter? He's so handsome, he has such a lovely soft moustache and, besides, the things he says to me make me quite happy enough! And then, he kisses me on the neck, he talks to me about poetry—and sunsets—whatever more d'you expect me to want?" After all, if that satisfies her . . .

When I've had enough of her ravings, I tell her I'm going home to Papa so that she'll leave me on my own. But I don't go home. I stay in the woods and I hunt out a particularly delicious corner and lie down there. Hosts of little creatures scamper over the ground under my nose (they even behave extremely badly sometimes, but they're so tiny!) and there are so many good smells there—the smell of fresh plants warming in the sun. . . . Oh, my dear woods!

I arrived late at school (I find it hard to go to sleep: my thoughts start dancing in my head the moment I turn out the lamp), to find Mademoiselle Sergent at the mistress's desk, looking dignified and scowling, and all the girls wearing suitable prim, ceremonious expressions. Whatever did all that mean? Ah, the gawky Anaïs was huddled over her desk, making such tremendous efforts to sob that her ears were blue with the exertion. I was going to have some fun! I slid in beside little Luce, who whispered in my ear: "My dear, they've found all Anaïs's letters in a boy's desk and the master's just brought them over for the Headmistress to read!"

She was, indeed, reading them but very low, only to herself. What bad luck. Heavens, what bad luck! I'd cheerfully have given three years of Antonin Rabastens's life to go through that correspondence. Oh! would no one inspire the Redhead to read us two or three well-chosen passages out loud? Alas, alas, Mademoiselle Sergent had come to the end. . . . Without a word to Anaïs, who was still hunched over her table, she solemnly rose and walked over, with deliberate steps, to the stove beside me. She opened it, deposited the scandalous papers, folded in four, inside; then she struck a match, applied it to the letters, and closed the little door. As she stood up again, she said to the culprit:

"My compliments, Anaïs, you know more about these things than many grown-up people do. I shall keep you here until the exam, since your name is entered for it, but I shall tell your parents that I absolve myself from all responsibility for you. Copy out your problems, girls, and pay no more attention to this person who is not worth bothering about."

Incapable of enduring the torture of having Anaïs's effusions burn, I had taken out the flat ruler I use for drawing while the Headmistress was majestically declaiming. I slipped the ruler under my table and, at the risk of getting caught, I used it to push the little handle that moved the damper. No one saw a thing: perhaps the flame, thus stifled of draught, would not burn everything up. I should know when class was over. I listened; the stove stopped roaring after a few seconds. Wouldn't it soon strike eleven? I could hardly keep my mind on what I was copying, on the "two pieces of linen which, after being washed, shrank $1/19$ in length and $1/22$ in breadth; they could have shrunk considerably more without my being interested.

Mademoiselle Sergent left us and went off to Aimée's classroom, no doubt to tell her the good story and laugh over it with her. As soon as she had disappeared, Anaïs raised her head. We stared at her avidly: her cheeks were blotched and her eyes were swollen from having been violently rubbed, but she kept her eyes obstinately fixed on her exercise-book. Marie Belhomme leant over to her and said with vehement sympathy: "I say, old thing, I bet you'll get a fearful wigging at home. Did you say lots of awful things in your letters?" Anaïs did not raise her eyes but said out loud so that we should all hear: "I don't care a fig, the letters weren't mine." The girls exchanged indignant looks: "My dear, would you believe it! My dear, what a liar that girl is!"

At last, the hour struck. Never had break been so long in coming! I dawdled over tidying my desk so as to be the last one left behind. Outside, after having walked fifty yards or so, I pretended I'd forgotten my atlas and I left Anaïs in order to fly back to school: "Wait for me, will you?"

I dashed silently into the empty classroom and opened the stove: I found a handful of half-burnt papers in it which I drew out with the most tender precautions. What luck! the top and bottom ones had gone but the thick wad in the middle was almost intact; it was definitely Anaïs's writing. I took the packet away in my satchel so as to read them at home at leisure, and I rejoined Anaïs, who was quite calm, and strolling about while she waited for me. We set off again together: she stared at me surreptitiously. Suddenly, she stopped dead and gave an agonised sigh. . . . I saw her gaze was anxiously fixed on my hands and then I noticed they were black from the burnt papers I had touched. I wasn't going to lie to her—certainly not. I took the offensive:

"Well, what's the matter?"

"So you went and searched in the stove, eh?"

"Certainly I did! No danger of my losing a chance like that of reading your letters!"

"Are they burnt?"

"No, luckily: here, look inside."

I showed her the papers, keeping a firm hold on them. She darted positively murderous looks at me but did not dare pounce on my satchel, she was too sure I'd thrash her! I decided to comfort her a little; she made me feel almost sorry for her.

"Listen, I'm going to read what isn't burnt—because I just can't bear not to—and then I'll bring you the whole lot back this afternoon. So I'm not such a beast after all, am I?"

She was highly mistrustful.

"Word of honour! I'll give you them back at recreation before we go into class."

She went off, helpless and uneasy, looking even longer and yellower than usual.

At home, I went through those letters at last. Immense disappointment! They weren't a bit what I'd imagined. A mixture of silly sentimentalities and practical directions: "I always think of you when there's moonlight. . . . Do make sure, on Thursday, to bring the corn-sack you took last time, to Vrimes' field; Mamma would kick up a shindy if she saw grass-stains on my frock!" Then there were obscure allusions which must have reminded young Gangneau of various smutty episodes. . . . In short, yes, a disappointment. I would give her back her letters which were far less amusing than her cold, whimsical, humorous self.

I gave them back to her; she could not believe her own eyes. She was so overjoyed at seeing them that she couldn't resist making fun of me for having read them. Once she'd run and thrown them down the lavatory, she resumed her shut, impenetrable face, without the faintest trace of humiliation. Happy disposition!

Bother, I've caught a cold! I stay in Papa's library, reading Michelet's absurd *History of France,* written in alexandrines. (Am I exaggerating a bit?) I'm not in the least bored, curled up in this big armchair, surrounded by books, with my beautiful Fanchette for company. She's the most intelligent cat in the world and she loves me disinterestedly in spite of the miseries I inflict on her, biting her in her pink ears and making her go through the most complicated training.

She loves me so much that she understands what I say and comes and rubs against my mouth when she hears the sound of my voice. She also loves books like an old scholar, this Fanchette, and worries me every night after dinner to remove two or three volumes of Papa's big Larousse from their shelf. The space they leave makes a kind of little square room in which Fanchette settles down and washes herself; I shut the glass door on her and her imprisoned purr vibrates with a noise like an incessant, muffled drum. From time to time, I look at her; then she makes me a sign with her eyebrows which she raises like a human being. Lovely Fanchette, how intelligent and understanding you are! (Much more so than Luce Lanthenay, that inferior breed of cat!) You amused me from the moment you came into the world; you'd only got one eye open when you were already attempting warlike steps in your basket, though you were still incapable of standing up on your four matchsticks. Ever since, you've lived joyously, making me laugh with your belly-dances in honour of cockchafers and butterflies, your clumsy calls to the birds you're stalking, your way of quarrelling with me and giving me sharp taps that re-echo on my hands. Your behaviour is quite disgraceful: two or three times a year I catch you on the garden walls, wearing a crazy, ridiculous expression, with a swarm of tom-cats round you. I even know your favourite, you perverse Fanchette—he's a dirty-grey Tom, long and lean, with half his fur gone. He's got ears like a rabbit's and coarse, plebeian limbs. How can you make a *mésalliance* with this low-born animal, and make it so often? But, even at those demented seasons, as soon as you catch sight of me, your natural face returns for a moment, and you give me a friendly mew which says something like: "You see what I'm up to. Don't despise me too much, nature has her urgent demands. But I'll soon come home again and I'll lick myself for ages to purify myself of this dissolute life." O, beautiful Fanchette, your bad behaviour is so remarkably becoming to you!

When my cold was over, I observed that people at school were beginning to get very agitated about the approaching exams; we were now at the end of May and we "went up" on the 5th of July! I was sorry not to be more moved, but the others made up for me, especially little Luce Lanthenay, who burst into floods of tears whenever she got a bad mark. As for Mademoiselle Sergent, she was busy with everything, but most of all, with the little thing with the beautiful eyes who kept her "on a string". She'd blossomed out, that Aimée, in an astonishing way! Her marvellous complexion, her velvety skin and her eyes, "that you could strike medals out of", as Anaïs says, make her into a spiteful and triumphant little creature. She is so much prettier than she was last year! No one would pay any more attention now to the slight crumpling of her face, to the little crease on the left of her lip when she smiles; and, anyhow, she has such white, pointed teeth! The amorous Redhead swoons at the mere sight of her and our presence no longer restrains her from yielding to her furious desire to kiss her darling every two minutes.

On this warm afternoon, the class was murmuring a *Selected Passage* that we had to recite at three o'clock. I was almost dozing, oppressed by a nervous lassitude. I was incapable of any more effort, when all of a sudden I felt I wanted to scratch somebody, to give a violent stretch and to crush somebody's hands; the somebody turned out to be Luce, my next-door neighbour. She found the nape of her neck being clutched and my nails digging into it. Luckily, she didn't say a word. I fell back into my irritated listlessness. . . .

The door opened without anyone having even knocked: it was Dutertre, in a light tie, his hair flying, looking rejuvenated and pugnacious. Mademoiselle Sergent sprang to her feet, barely said good afternoon to him and gazed at him with passionate admiration, her tapestry fallen unheeded on the floor. (Does she love him more than Aimée? or Aimée more than him? Curious woman!) The class had stood up. Out of wickedness, I remained seated, with the result that, when Dutertre turned towards us, he noticed me at once.

"Good afternoon, Mademoiselle. Good afternoon, little ones. *You* seem in a state of collapse!"

"I'm floppy. I haven't a bone left in me."

"Are you ill?"

"No, I don't think so. It's the weather—general slackness."

"Come over here and let's have a look at you."

Was all that going to start over again . . . those medical pretexts for prolonged examinations? The Headmistress launched looks of blazing indignation at me for the way I was sitting and for the way I was talking to her beloved District Superintendent. I decided to put myself out and obey. Besides, he adores these impertinent manners. I dragged myself lazily over to the window.

"One can't see here because of that green shadow from the trees. Come out into the corridor, there's some sunlight there. You look wretched, my child."

Triple-distilled lie! I looked extremely well. I know myself: if it was because I had rings round my eyes that he thought I was ill, he was mistaken. It's a good sign when I have dark circles under my eyes, it means I'm in excellent health. Luckily it was three in the afternoon, otherwise I should have been none too confident about going out, even into the glass-paned corridor, with this individual whom I mistrust like fire.

When he had shut the door behind us, I rounded on him and said:

"Now, look here, I *don't* look ill. Why did you say I did?"

"No? What about those eyes with dark circles right down to your lips?"

"Well, it's the colour of my skin, that's all."

He had seated himself on the bench and was holding me in front of him, standing against his knees.

"Shut up, you're talking nonsense. Why do you always look as if you were cross with me?"

". . . ?"

"Oh yes, you know quite well what I mean. You know, you've got a nice, funny little phiz that sticks in one's head once one's seen it!"

I gave an idiotic laugh. If only heaven would send me some wit, some smart repartee, for I felt terribly destitute of them!

"Is it true you always go for walks all by yourself in the woods?"

"Yes, it's true. Why?"

"Because, you little hussy, perhaps you go to meet a lover? You're so well chaperoned!"

I shrugged my shoulders.

"You know all the people round here as well as I do. Do you see any of *them* as a possible lover for me?"

"True. But you might be vicious enough. . . ."

He gripped my arms and flashed his eyes and his teeth. How hot it was here! I would have been only too pleased if he would have let me go back to the classroom.

"If you're ill, why don't you come and consult me at my house?"

I answered too hurriedly "No! I won't go . . ." and I tried to free my arms, but he held me firmly and raised burning, mischievous eyes to mine. They were handsome eyes too, it's true.

"Oh, you little thing, you charming little thing, why are you frightened? You're so wrong to be frightened of me! Do you think I'm a cad? You've absolutely nothing to fear . . . nothing. Oh, little Claudine, you're so frightfully attractive with your warm brown eyes and your wild curls! You're made like an adorable little statue, I'll swear you are. . . ."

He stood up suddenly, clasped me in his arms and kissed me; I hadn't time to escape, he was too strong and virile, and my head was in a whirl. . . . What a situation! I no longer knew what I was saying, my brain was going round and round. . . . Yet I couldn't go back to the classroom, all red and shaken as I was, and I could hear him behind me. . . . I was certain he was going to want to kiss me again. . . . I opened the front-door, rushed out into the playground and dashed up to the pump where I drank a mug of water. Ouf! . . . I must go back. . . . But he must be ambushed in the passage. Ah! After all, who cares! I'd scream if he tried to do it again. . . . It was because he's kissed me on the corner of the mouth, which was the best he could do, that beast!

No, he wasn't in the corridor. What luck! I went back into the classroom and there I saw him, standing by the desk and calmly chatting to Mademoiselle Sergent. I sat down in my place; he looked at me searchingly and inquired.

"You didn't drink too much water, I hope? These kids, they swallow mugfuls of cold water, it's shockingly bad for the health."

I was bolder with everyone there.

"No, I only drank a mouthful. That was quite enough, I shan't take any more."

He laughed and looked pleased:

"You're a funny girl. But you're not a complete idiot."

Mademoiselle Sergent did not understand, but the uneasiness that puckered her eyebrows gradually smoothed itself out. All that remained was her contempt for the deplorable manners I displayed towards her idol.

Personally, I was furious with him: he was stupid! The lanky Anaïs guessed that something was up and could not restrain herself from asking me: "I say, did he examine you awfully close to, to make you so upset?" But I certainly wasn't going to tell *her*. "Don't be an idiot! I tell you, I went out to the pump." Little Luce, in her turn, rubbed herself against me like a fidgety cat and ventured to question me: "Do tell me, Claudine darling, whatever made him take you off like that?"

"To begin with I'm not 'Claudine darling' to *you*. And, besides, it's none of your business, you little rat. He had to consult me about the standardisation of pensions. And that's that."

"You never want to tell me anything. And *I* tell *you* all!"

"All what? A fat lot of use it is to me to know that your sister doesn't pay her board or yours either—and that Mademoiselle Olympe heaps her with presents—and that she wears silk petticoats—and that . . ."

"Ssh! Oh, *please*, stop! I'd be absolutely done for if they knew I'd told you all that!"

"Then, don't ask *me* anything. If you're good, I'll give you my lovely ebony ruler, the one with the brass edges."

"Oh, you *are* sweet! I'd like to kiss you but that annoys you. . . ."

"That'll do. I'll give it you tomorrow—if I feel like it!"

For my passion for "desk-furniture" was becoming appeased, which was yet another very bad symptom. All my classmates (and I used to be just like them) were crazy about "school equipment". We ruined ourselves on exercise-books of cream-laid paper bound in shimmering tinfoil with a moiré pattern, on rosewood pencils, on lacquered penholders shiny enough to see one's face in, on olive-wood pencil-boxes, on rulers made of mahogany or of ebony, like mine, which had its four edges bound with brass and which made the boarders, who were too poor to afford one like it, green with envy. We had big satchels like lawyers' brief cases in more-or-less crushed more-or-less Morocco. And if the girls didn't have their school text-books sheathed in gaudy bindings for their New Year presents, and if I didn't either, it was simply and solely because they were not our own property. They belonged to the Town Council which generously provided us with them on condition we left them at the School when we left it never to return. Moreover, we loathed those bureaucratic books; we didn't feel they belonged to us and we played horrible tricks on them. Unforeseen and fantastic mishaps befell them: some of them had been known to catch fire at the stove, in winter; there were others over which inkpots took a particular delight in upsetting; in fact, they attracted disaster! And all the affronts put upon the dreary "Council Books" were the subject of long lamentations from Mademoiselle Lanthenay and terrible lectures from Mademoiselle Sergent.

Lord, how idiotic women are! (Little girls, women, it's all one.) Would anyone believe that, ever since that inveterate wolf Dutertre's "guilty attempts" on my person, I've felt what might be called a vague pride? It's very humiliating to me, that admission. But I know why; in my heart of hearts, I tell myself: "If that man, who's known heaps of women, in Paris and all over the place, finds me attractive, it must be because I'm not remarkably ugly!" There! It was a pleasure to my vanity. I didn't really think I was repulsive, but I like to be sure I'm not. And besides, I was pleased at having a secret that the lanky Anaïs, Marie Belhomme, Luce Lanthenay and the others didn't suspect.

The class was well trained now. All the girls, even down to those in the Third Division knew that, during recreation, they must never enter a classroom in which the mistresses had shut themselves up. Naturally, our education hadn't been perfected in a day! One or other of us had gone in at least fifty times into the classroom where the tender couple was hiding. But we found them so tenderly entwined, or so absorbed in their whisperings or else Mademoiselle Sergent holding her little Aimée on her lap with such total lack of reserve that even the stupidest were nonplussed and fled as soon as the Redhead demanded: "What do you want *now*?", terrified by the ferocious scowl of her bushy eyebrows. Like the others, I frequently burst in and sometimes even without meaning to: the first few times, when they saw it was me and they were too close together, they hastily got up or else one of them would pretend to pin up the other's loosened hair. But they ended up by not disturbing themselves on my account. So I no longer found it entertaining.

Rabastens doesn't come over any more: he has declared over and over again that he is "too intimidated by this intimacy" and this expression seemed to him a kind of pun which delighted him. As for *them*, they no longer think of anything but themselves. They dog each other's footsteps and live in each other's shadow: their mutual adoration is so absolute that I no longer think of tormenting them. I almost envy their delicious oblivion of everything else in the world.

There! I was sure it would happen sooner or later! A letter from little Luce that I found when I got home, in a pocket of my satchel.

"MY DARLING CLAUDINE,—I love you very much. You always look as if you didn't know anything about it and that makes me die of misery. You are both nice and nasty to me, you don't want to take me seriously, you treat me as if I were a little dog: you can't imagine how that hurts me. But just think how happy we could be, the two of us; look at my sister Aimée with Mademoiselle, they're so happy that they don't think of anything else now. I implore you, if you're not annoyed by this letter, not to say anything to me tomorrow morning at school, I'd be too embarrassed at that moment. I'll know very well, just from the sort of way you talk to me during the day, whether you want to be my great friend or not.

I kiss you with all my heart, my darling Claudine and I count on you, too, to burn this letter because I know you wouldn't want to show it so as to get me into trouble, that's not your way. I kiss you again very lovingly and I'm longing so impatiently for it to be tomorrow!

Your little LUCE."

Good heavens no, I *don't* want to! If that appealed to me, it would be with someone stronger and more intelligent than myself, someone who'd bully me a little, whom I'd obey and not with a depraved little beast who has a certain charm, perhaps, scratching and mewing just to be stroked, but who's too inferior. I don't love people I can dominate. I tore up her letter straight away, charming and unmalicious as it was, and put the pieces in an envelope to return them to her.

The next morning I saw a worried little face pressed against the windows, waiting for me. Poor Luce, her green eyes were pale with anxiety! What a pity, but all the same I couldn't, just for the sake of giving her pleasure. . . .

I went inside; as luck would have it, she was all alone.

"Look, little Luce, here are the bits of your letter. I didn't keep it long, you see."

She said nothing and took the envelope mechanically.

"Crazy girl! Besides whatever were you doing up there . . . I mean up there on the first floor . . . behind the locked doors of Mademoiselle Sergent's room? That's where that leads you! *I* can't do anything for you."

"Oh!" she said, prostrated.

"But yes, my poor child. It isn't from virtue, you can be sure. My virtue's still far too small, I don't trot it out and about yet. But you see, in my green youth I was consumed by a great love. I *adored* a man who died making me swear on his deathbed never to . . ."

She interrupted me, moaning:

"There, there, you're laughing at me again. I didn't want to write to you, you've no heart. Oh, how unhappy I am! Oh, how cruel you are!"

"And besides, you're deafening me! What a row! What d'you bet I give you a few kicks to bring you back to the straight and narrow path?"

"Oh, what do I care! Oh, I could almost laugh!"

"Take that, you little bad lot! And give me a receipt."

She had just been dealt a heavy slap which had the effect of promptly silencing her. She looked at me stealthily with gentle eyes and began to cry, already comforted, as she rubbed her head. How she loves to be beaten; it's astounding.

"Here come Anaïs and lots of the others, try and look more or less respectable. They'll be coming in to class in a moment, the two turtle-doves are on their way down."

Only a fortnight till the Certificate! June oppresses us. We bake, half asleep, in the classrooms; we're silent from listlessness: I'm too languid to keep my diary. And in this furnace heat, we still have to criticise the conduct of Louis XV, explain the role of the gastric juices in the process of digestion, sketch acanthus leaves and divide the auditory apparatus into the inner ear, the middle ear and the outer ear. There's no justice on the earth! Louis XV did what he wanted to do, it's nothing to do with *me*! Oh Lord, no! With *me* less than anyone!

It was so hot that it made one lose one's desire to make oneself look attractive—or rather, the fashion palpably changed. Now we displayed our skin. I inaugurated dresses with open square necks, something on medieval lines, with sleeves that stopped at the elbow. My arms were still rather thin, but nice all the same, and, as to my neck, I back it against anyone's. The others imitated me: Anaïs did not wear short sleeves but she profited by mine to roll her own up to the shoulders; Marie Belhomme displayed unexpectedly plump arms above her bony hands and a fresh neck that would be fat later on. Oh Lord, what *wouldn't* one display in a temperature like this! With immense secrecy, I replaced my stockings with socks. By the end of three days, they all knew it and told each other about it and implored me under their breath to pull my skirt up.

"Let's see your socks . . . are you really wearing them?"

"Look!"

"Lucky devil! All the same, *I* wouldn't dare."

"Why? Respect for the decencies?"

"No . . . but . . ."

"Shut up, I know why. . . . You've got hair on your legs!"

"Oh, you liar of all liars! You can look. . . . I haven't any more than you have. Only I'd be ashamed to feel my legs quite bare under my dress!"

Little Luce exhibited some skin shyly—skin that was marvellous-

ly white and soft. The gawky Anaïs envied this whiteness to such an
extent that she pricked her arms with needles on sewing-days.

Farewell to repose! The approach of the examinations, the honour
that our possible successes would reflect on this fine new school had
at last dragged our teachers from their sweet solitude. They kept us,
the six candidates, in close confinement; they pestered us with
endless repetitions; they forced us to listen, to remember, even to
understand, making us come in an hour before the others and leave
an hour after them! Nearly all of us became pale, tired and stupid;
some of us lost appetite and sleep as a result of work and anxiety. I
myself remained looking almost fresh, because I didn't worry
overmuch and I have a matt skin. Little Luce did too; like her sister
Aimée, she possesses one of those enviable, indestructible pink and
white complexions. . . .
We knew that Mademoiselle Sergent was going to take us all
together to the principal town of the Department and we should stay
with her at the same hotel. She would take charge of all the expenses
and we would settle our accounts on our return. But for that cursed
exam, we should have found this little trip enchanting.

These last days have been deplorable. Mistresses and pupils alike
have been so atrociously nervy that they explode every other
minute. Aimée flung her exercise-book in the face of a boarder who
had made the same idiotic mistake for the third time in an arithmetic
problem, then promptly fled to her own room. Little Luce was
slapped by her sister and came and threw herself in my arms for me
to comfort her. I hit Anaïs when she was teasing me at the wrong
moment. One of the Jauberts was seized, first with a frantic burst of
sobbing, then with a no less frantic attack of nerves, because, she
screamed, "she would never manage to pass! . . ." (wet towels,
orange-flower water, encouragements). Mademoiselle Sergent, also
exasperated, made poor Marie Belhomme, who regularly forgets
next day what she learnt the day before, spin round like a top in
front of the blackboard.
I can only rest properly at night in the top of the big walnut-tree,
on a long branch that the wind rocks . . . the wind, the darkness,
the leaves. . . . Fanchette comes and joins me up there; each time I
hear strong claws climbing up, with such sureness! She mews in

astonishment: "What on earth are you doing up in this tree? *I'm*
made to be up here, but you . . . it always shocks me a little!" Then
she wanders about the little branches, all white in the blackness, and
talks to the sleeping birds, ingenuously, in the hope they'll come and
obligingly let themselves be eaten—why, of course!

It's the eve of our departure. No work today. We took our
suitcases to school (a dress and a few underclothes; we're only
staying two days).

Tomorrow morning, we all meet at half-past nine and go off in old
Racalin's evil-smelling omnibus which will cart us off to the station.

It's over. We returned from the main town yesterday, triumphant
all except (naturally) poor Marie Belhomme, who was ploughed.
Mademoiselle Sergent is thoroughly puffed-up over such a success. I
must tell the whole story.

On the morning of our departure, we were piled into old Racalin's
omnibus. He happened to be dead-drunk and drove us crazily,
zigzagging from one ditch to the other, asking us if he was taking us
all to be married, and congratulating himself on the masterly way he
was bumping us about: "Be going ever sho eashy, bear't I? . . ."
while Marie uttered shrill cries and turned green with terror. At the
station, they parked us in the waiting-room. Mademoiselle Sergent
took our tickets and lavished tender farewells on the beloved who
had come along to accompany her thus far. The beloved, in a frock
of unbleached linen, and wearing a big, artless hat under which she
looked fresher than a convolvulus (that bitch of an Aimée!) excited
the admiration of three cigar-smoking commercial travellers who,
amused at this departure of a batch of schoolgirls, had come into the
waiting-room to dazzle us with their rings and their witticisms, for
they found it irresistible to let out the most shocking remarks. I
nudged Marie Belhomme to warn her to listen; she strained her ears
but could not understand: however I couldn't draw diagrams to help
her out! The gawky Anaïs understood perfectly well and wore
herself out in adopting graceful attitudes and making vain efforts to
blush.

The train puffed and whistled: we grabbed our suitcases and
surged into a second-class carriage. It was overheated to the point of

suffocation; luckily the journey only lasted three hours! I installed myself in a corner so as to be able to breathe a little and we didn't talk at all on the way, it was so entertaining to watch the landscape flying past. Little Luce, nestling beside me, slipped her arm under mine but I extricated myself, saying: "Let go, it's too hot." Yet I had on a dress of cream tussore, very straight and smocked like a baby's, clasped at the waist with a leather belt that was wider than my hand and had a square opening in front. Anaïs, brightened up by a red linen frock, looked her best; so did Marie Belhomme, who was in half-mourning, wearing mauve linen with a black flower-pattern. Luce Lanthenay had kept to her black uniform and wore a black hat with a red bow. The two Jauberts continued to be non-existent and drew out of their pockets some lists of questions that Mademoiselle Sergent, disdainful of this excessive zeal, made them put back again. They couldn't get over it!

Factory chimneys appeared, then scattered white houses that suddenly huddled closer together and became a crowd; the next moment, we were at the station and were getting out. Mademoiselle Sergent hustled us towards an omnibus and soon we were bumping along over grievous cobblestones, like cat's skulls, towards the Hôtel de la Poste. Idlers were strolling about the streets, which were gay with bunting, for tomorrow it was St. Someone-or-other's day—a great local feast—and the Philharmonic would be in full blast in the evening.

The manageress of the hotel, Mme. Cherbay, a fat, gushing woman who came from the same part of the country as Mademoiselle Sergent, fussed over us. There were endless staircases, then a corridor and . . . three rooms for six. That had never occurred to me! Who would they put to share with me? It's stupid; I hate sleeping with other people!

The manageress left us to ourselves, at last. We burst out chattering and asking questions; we opened our suitcases. Marie had lost the key of hers and was bewailing the fact: I sat down, tired already. Mademoiselle said ruminatively: "Let's see, I must get you fixed up. . . ." She stopped, trying to find the best way of installing us in pairs. Little Luce slid silently up to me and squeezed my hand: she hoped they would thrust us both into the same bed. The Headmistress made up her mind: "The two Jauberts, you'll sleep together. You, Claudine, with . . ." (she looked at me in a pointed way but I neither flinched nor fluttered an eyelash) ". . . with Marie Belhomme, and Anaïs with Luce Lanthenay. I think that will work out quite well." Little Luce was not at all of this opinion! She picked up her luggage with a crestfallen look and went off sadly with the gawky Anaïs to the room opposite mine. Marie and I settled ourselves in; I tore off most of my clothes so as to wash off the dust of the train and we wandered about ecstatically in our chemises behind the shutters that were closed because of the sun. A chemise, *that* was the only rational, practical dress!

There was singing in the courtyard. I looked out and saw the fat proprietress sitting in the shade with the hotel servants and some young men and girls; they were all bawling sentimental songs: "Manon, behold the sun!" as they made paper roses and garlands of ivy to decorate the front of the building, tomorrow. The courtyard was strewn with pine-branches; the painted iron table was loaded with bottles of beer and glasses; the earthly paradise, in fact!

Someone knocked: it was Mademoiselle Sergent. I let her come in, she didn't embarrass me. I received her in my chemise while Marie hurriedly pulled on a petticoat, out of respect. However, she didn't look as if she had noticed it, and merely told us to hurry up: luncheon was ready. We all went downstairs. Luce complained about their room; it was lit from above, they hadn't even the resource of looking out of the window!

The hotel's set luncheon was bad.

As the written exam took place next day, Mademoiselle Sergent enjoined us to go up to our rooms and make one last final revision of what we felt weakest on. What point in being here just for *that*? I'd much rather have gone to see Papa's charming friends, the Xs, who were excellent musicians. . . . She added: "If you're good, tonight you shall come down with me after dinner and we'll make roses with Madame Cherbay and her daughters." There were murmurs of joy: all my companions exulted. But not me! I felt no intoxication at the prospect of making paper roses in a hotel courtyard with that fat manageress who looked as if she were made of lard. Probably I let this be seen, for the Redhead went on, suddenly irritated:

"I'm not forcing anyone, naturally; if Mademoiselle Claudine thinks she ought not to join us . . ."

"Honestly, I *would* rather stay in my room, Mademoiselle. I'm afraid I'd be so totally useless!"

"Stay there, then, we'll do without you. But, in that case, I fear I shall be forced to take the key of your room with me. I am responsible for you."

This detail had not occurred to me and I did not know what to reply. We went upstairs again and we yawned all the afternoon over our books, our nerves frayed with the suspense of waiting for tomorrow. It would have been much better for us to go out for a walk, for we didn't do any good, none at all. . . .

And to think that tonight I was going to be locked in! Locked in! Anything that's in the least like imprisonment makes me rabid: I lose my head as soon as I'm shut up. (When I was a child, they could never send me to boarding-school because I used to fall into swoons of rage at realising that I was forbidden to go out of the door. They tried twice when I was nine. Both times, on the very first night, I dashed to the windows like a stunned bird; I screamed, bit and scratched, then fell down unconscious. They had to set me at liberty again and I could only "stick it" at this fantastic school in Montigny because there, at least, I didn't feel "trapped" and I slept in my own bed at home.)

Certainly, I wasn't going to let the others see it, but I was sick with nervous tension and humiliation. I wasn't going to beg to be let off; she'd be far too pleased, that beastly Redhead! If she'd only leave me the key on the inside! But I wasn't going to ask her for anything at all, I didn't want to! I only prayed the night would be short. . . .

Before dinner, Mademoiselle Sergent took us for a walk along the river: little Luce, quite overcome with pity, tried to console me for my punishment:

"Listen, if you asked her to let you come downstairs, I'm sure she would, if you asked her nicely. . . ."

"Don't worry! I'd rather be triple-locked in for eight months, eight days, eight hours and eight minutes."

"You're awfully silly not to want to! We'll make roses—and we'll sing—and we'll . . ."

"Such pure pleasures! I shall pour some water on your head."

"Ssh! Be quiet! But truly, you've spoilt our day. I shan't feel a bit gay tonight, because you won't be there."

"Don't get sentimental. I shall sleep, I shall gather strength for the 'great day' tomorrow."

We dined again at the common table with commercial travellers and horse-dealers. The gawky Anaïs, obsessed with the idea of getting herself noticed, gesticulated wildly and upset her glass of wine and water over the white cloth. At nine, we went upstairs again. My companions armed themselves with little shawls against the coolness that might come later and, as for me—I went back into my room. Oh, I put a good face on it, but I listened with far from kindly feelings to the key that Mademoiselle Sergent turned in the door and carried off in her pocket. . . . There, I was all alone. . . . Almost at once, I heard them in the courtyard. I could have had an excellent view of them from my window but not for anything in the world would I have admitted my regrets by showing any curiosity. Very well, what then? There was nothing to do but go to bed.

I had already taken off my belt when, suddenly, I stood stock-still before the dressing-table in front of the communicating-door that it blocked. That door opened into the neighbouring room (the bolt was on my side) and the neighbouring room gave on to the corridor. . . . I recognised the finger of Providence in this, it was undeniable . . . Never mind, come what might, I didn't want the Redhead to be able to triumph and say to herself: "I shut her in!" I buckled on my belt again and put on my hat. I wasn't going to be so silly as to go into the courtyard, I was going to see Papa's friends, those charming hospitable Xs, who would give me a warm welcome. Ouf! How heavy that dressing-table was! It made me hot. The bolt was hard to push back, it needed exercise, and the door grated as it opened, but it *did* open. The room I entered, holding my candle high, was empty; there were no sheets on the bed. I ran to the door, the blessed door which was not locked and which opened angelically on to the adorable corridor. . . . How easily one breathes when one is not under lock and key! I mustn't let myself get caught! But there wasn't a soul on the stairs, not a soul at the reception-desk . . . everyone was making roses. Go on making roses, good people, go on making roses without me!

Outside, in the warm darkness, I laughed very softly; but I had to get to the X's house. . . . The trouble was that I didn't know the way, especially at night. Pooh! I would ask. First of all, I resolutely followed the course of the river, then, under a lamp-post, I decided to ask a passing gentleman "the way to the Place du Théâtre, please?" He stopped and leant down to have a good look at me: "But, my lovely child, allow me to take you there, you'll never find it all by yourself. . . ." Botheration! I turned on my heels and fled precipitately into the shadows. At last I asked a grocer's boy, who was pulling down the iron curtain of his shop with a tremendous din, and then, after walking street after street, often pursued by a laugh or a cheeky call, I arrived in the Place du Théâtre. I rang the bell of the house I knew.

My entrance interrupted the trio for violin, 'cello and piano which two fair-haired sisters and their father were playing: they all got up excitedly: "You here? How? Why? All alone!"—"Wait, let me explain and do forgive me." I told them about my imprisonment, my escape and the Certificate tomorrow; the little fair girls laughed like mad. "Oh, that's funny! No one but you would think of such marvellous stunts!" Their Papa laughed too, indulgently: "Come along, don't be frightened. We'll take you back, we'll obtain your forgiveness." Thoroughly nice people!

So we went on making music, with no remorse. At ten o'clock, I thought I ought to go and I managed to persuade them to let only an old servant take me back. . . . Nevertheless I wondered what on earth the peppery Redhead would say to me!

The servant came into the hotel with me and I discovered that my companions were still in the courtyard, occupied in crumpling up roses and drinking beer and lemonade. I could have returned to my room unnoticed but I preferred to stage a little effect so I presented myself modestly to Mademoiselle who leapt to her feet at the sight of me. "Where have you come from?" With my chin, I indicated the servant accompanying me and she meekly produced her set speech: "Mademoiselle spent the evening at the Master's with the young ladies." Then she murmured a vague good night and vanished. I was left alone (one, two, three!) with . . . a fury! Her eyes blazed, her eyebrows knitted together till they touched, while my stupefied classmates remained standing, their half-finished roses in their hands. From Luce's brilliant glances and Marie's scarlet cheeks and Anaïs's feverish appearance, it looked to me as if they were a little tight; of course, there was no harm in *that*. Mademoiselle Sergent did not utter a word; either she was trying to find adequate ones or else she was forcibly controlling herself so as not to explode. At last she spoke, but not to me. "Let us go upstairs, it's late." So it was in my room that she was going to burst out? Very well, then. . . . On the stairs, all the girls stared at me as if I had the plague: little Luce questioned me with her imploring eyes.

In the room, there was, at first, a portentous silence; then the Redhead interrogated me with weighty solemnity:

"Where were you?"

"You know very well . . . at the X's . . . some friends of my father's."

"How did you dare leave your room?"

"How? You can see for yourself. I pulled out the dressing-table that barred that door."

"This is the most odious insolence! I shall inform your father of your monstrous behaviour. No doubt it will give him intense pleasure."

"Papa? He'll say: 'Good gracious, yes, that child has a passion for liberty', and he'll wait impatiently for you to finish your story so that he can eagerly bury himself again in the *Malacology of Fresnois*."

She noticed that the others were listening and turned on her heels. "Off to bed, all of you! If your candles aren't out in a quarter of an hour, you'll have me to deal with! As to Mademoiselle Claudine, she is no longer my responsibility and she can elope this very night, if she pleases!"

Oh! shocking! Really, Mademoiselle! The girls had disappeared like frightened mice and I was left alone with Marie Belhomme who declared:

"It's absolutely true that they can't shut you up! *I'd* never have had the brainwave of pulling out the dressing-table!"

"I had an anything but boring time. But do stir your stumps a little so that she doesn't come back to blow out the candle."

One sleeps badly in a strange bed and, besides, I glued myself all night against the wall so as not to brush against Marie's legs.

In the morning, they woke us up at half-past five: we got up in a state of torpor and I drenched myself in cold water to rouse myself a little. While I was splashing, Luce and the lanky Anaïs came in to borrow my scented soap, ask for a corkscrew, etc. Marie begged me to start plaiting her chignon for her. They were an amusing sight, all those little creatures, still half-asleep and wearing next to nothing.

We exchanged views on ingenious precautions to take against the examinations. Anaïs had copied out all the history dates she wasn't sure of on the corner of her handkerchief (*I* should need a table-cloth!). Marie Belhomme had contrived to make a minute atlas which could be slipped into the palm of her hand. On her white cuffs, Luce had written dates, fragments of royal reigns, arithmetic theorems—a whole manual. The Jaubert sisters had also put down quantities of useful information on strips of thin paper which they rolled up in the tubes of their penholders. They were all very anxious concerning the examiners themselves; I heard Luce say: "In arithmetic, it's Lerouge who takes the oral questions; in physics and chemistry, it's Roubaud . . . apparently he's an absolute beast; in literature, it's old Sallé . . ."

I broke in:

"Which Sallé? The one who used to be Principal of the college?"

"Yes, that's the one."

"What luck!"

I was delighted that I was to be questioned by this extremely kind old gentleman whom Papa and I knew very well; he would be good to me.

Mademoiselle Sergent appeared, concentrated and taciturn at this zero hour before battle.

"You haven't forgotten anything? Let's be off."

Our little squad crossed the bridge, mounted through various steep streets and lanes and eventually arrived in front of a battered old porch, on whose door an almost-effaced inscription proclaimed it to be the *Rivoire Institute.* It had once been the Girls' Boarding-School, but had been deserted for the past two or three years on account of its decrepitude. (Why did they park us *there?*) In the courtyard that had lost half its paving-stones, some sixty girls were chattering vivaciously, in well split-off groups; the schools didn't mix with each other. There were some from Villeneuve, from Beaulieu and from a dozen country-towns in the district; all of them clustered in little groups round their respective Headmistresses and making copious and far from charitable remarks about the other schools.

The moment we arrived, we were stared out of countenance and criticised from top to toe. I was singled out for particularly sharp scrutiny on account of my white dress with blue stripes and my big floppy lace hat which stood out against the black of the uniforms. As I smiled insolently at the candidates who were glaring at me, they turned away in the most contemptuous way imaginable. Luce and Marie flushed under the stares and shrank back into their shell: the gawky Anaïs exulted in the consciousness of being so hypercritically examined. The examiners had not arrived yet; we were merely marking time. I was getting bored. A little door without a latch yawned open on a dark corridor, lit at the far end by a luminous pane. While Mademoiselle Sergent was exchanging icily polite remarks with her colleagues, I slipped quietly into the passage: at the end was a glass door—or the remains of one—;I lifted the rusty latch and found myself in a little square courtyard, by a shed. It was overgrown with jasmine and clematis, and there was a little wild plum-tree and all sorts of charming weeds, growing unchecked. On the ground,—admirable find!—some strawberries had ripened and smelt delicious.

I promptly decided to call the others to show them these marvels! I went back to the playground without attracting attention and I informed my companions of the existence of this unknown orchard. After nervous glances at Mademoiselle Sergent who was talking to an elderly headmistress, at the door which had still not opened on the examiners (they sleep late, those chaps), Marie Belhomme, Luce Lanthenay and the lanky Anaïs made up their minds, but the Jauberts refrained. We ate the strawberries, we plundered the clematis, we shook the plum-tree; then, hearing an even louder hullabaloo in the front courtyard, we guessed that our torturers had arrived.

As fast as our legs could carry us, we dashed back along the corridor; we arrived just in time to see a file of black-clad gentlemen, by no means handsome ones, entering the ancient building in solemn silence. In their wake, we climbed the staircase, the sixty-odd of us making a noise like a squadron of cavalry. But, on the first floor, they halted us on the threshold of a deserted study-room; we had to allow their Lordships to instal themselves. They sat down at a big table, mopped their brows and deliberated. What about? the advisability of allowing us to enter? But no, I was certain they were exchanging observations about the weather and chatting about their trifling affairs while we were held back with difficulty on the landing and the stairs on to which we overflowed.

Being in the front rank, I was able to observe these great men: a tall, greying one with a gentle, grandfatherly expression—kind old Sallé, twisted and gouty, with his hands like gnarled vines—a fat short one, his neck swathed in a shot-silk cravat worthy of Rabastens himself—that was Roubaud, the terrible, who would question us tomorrow in "science".

At last, they decided to tell us to come in. We filled this ugly old room, with its indescribably dirty plaster walls, scored all over with inscriptions and pupils' names. The tables were appalling too, scarred with penknives and black and purple from inkpots upset over them in former days. It was shameful to intern us in such a hovel.

One of the gentlemen proceeded to allot us our places; he held a big list in his hand and carefully mixed all the schools, separating the girls from the same district as widely as possible, so as to avoid any communication between them. (Didn't he realise one could always convey information?) I found myself at the end of a table, by a small girl, in mourning, with large, serious eyes. Where were my classmates? Far away, I caught sight of Luce who was sending me despairing signs and looks; Marie Belhomme was fidgeting about at a table just in front of her. They would be able to pass information to each other, those two weak vessels. . . . Roubaud was going round distributing large sheets of writing-paper, stamped in blue on the top left-hand corner, and sealing-wafers. We all understood the routine; we had to write our names in the corner, along with that of the school where we had done our studies, then to fold over this corner and seal it. (The idea was to reassure everyone about the impartiality of the criticisms.)

This little formality over, we waited for them to be kind enough to dictate something to us. I looked about me at the little unknown faces, several of which made me feel sorry for them, they were already so strained and anxious.

Everyone gave a start; Roubaud had broken the silence and spoken: "Spelling test, young ladies, be ready to take it down. I shall repeat the sentence I dictate only once."

There was a great hush of concentration. No wonder! Five-sixths of these little girls had their whole future at stake. And to think that all of those would become schoolmistresses, that they would toil from seven in the morning till five in the afternoon and tremble before a Headmistress who would be unkind most of the time, to earn seventy-five francs a month! Out of those sixty girls, forty-five were the daughters of peasants or manual labourers; in order not to work in the fields or at the loom, they had preferred to make their skins yellow and their chests hollow and deform their right shoulders. They were bravely preparing to spend three years at a Training College, getting up at five a.m. and going to bed at eight-thirty p.m. and having two hours recreation out of the twenty-four and ruining their digestions, since few stomachs survived three years of the college refectory. But at least they would wear hats and would not make clothes for other people or look after animals or draw buckets from the well, and they would despise their parents. And what was I, Claudine, doing here? I was here because I had nothing else to do and so that, while I was undergoing the ordeal of being questioned by these professors, Papa could mess about in peace with his slugs. I was also there "for the honour of the School", to obtain one more Certificate for it, one more glory for this unique, incredible, delightful School. . . .

They had crammed this dictation with so many participles and laid so many traps of ambiguous plurals that all the sentences were so twisted and inverted that the piece ended by making no sense at all. It was puerile!

I was pretty sure I had made no mistakes; all I had to do was to be careful about the accents, for they counted stray accents hovering in the wrong place over words as half-mistakes and quarter-mistakes. While I was reading it through again, a little ball of paper, very deftly aimed, landed on my exam sheet; the lanky Anaïs had written to me asking: "Should there be an s to *trouvés*, in the second sentence?" She hadn't the faintest idea, that Anaïs! Should I lie to her? No, I disdained her own usual methods. Raising my head, I signalled an imperceptible "Yes" and, calmly, she made the correction.

"You have five minutes for revision," announced the voice of Rombaud; "the handwriting test will follow."

A second and larger ball of paper arrived. I looked about me: it came from Luce whose anxious eyes were seeking mine. But . . . but she was asking for four words! If I sent back the ball, I was sure it would get pinched. I had an inspiration, a really brilliant one: I took the black leather satchel containing pencils and charcoal (the candidates had to provide everything themselves) and, using a little bit of plaster torn off the wall as chalk, I wrote down the four words that were worrying Luce. Then I suddenly lifted the satchel above my head, with its virgin side turned towards the examiners who, in any case, weren't paying much attention to us. Luce's face lit up; she made some hurried corrections: my neighbour, the girl in mourning, who had observed the scene, spoke to me:

"I say, you, aren't you frightened?"

"Not much, as you see. Got to help one another a bit."

"Yes . . . of course. Still, I wouldn't dare. You're called Claudine, aren't you?"

"Yes. How did you know?"

"Oh, you've been 'talked of' for quite a time. I'm from the school at Villeneuve; our mistresses used to say about you: 'She's an intelligent girl but as impudent as a cock-sparrow and her tomboyishness and the way she does her hair set a very bad example. All the same, if she chooses to take the trouble to exert herself, she'll be a redoubtable competitor in the exam.' You're known at Bellevue too; they say you're a bit crazy and more than a bit eccentric."

"Charming women, your teachers! But they're more interested in me than I am in them. So tell them they're only a pack of old maids who are furious because they're running to seed. Tell them that from me, will you?"

Scandalised, she said no more. Besides, Roubaud was promenading his plump little pot-belly between the tables and gathering up our papers which he carried up to the others of his species.

Then he distributed other sheets of paper to us for the handwriting test and went off to inscribe four lines on the blackboard in a "beautiful hand".

Tu t'en souviens, Cinna, tant d'heur et tant de gloire, etc., etc. . . .

"Young ladies, you are asked to execute a line of thick cursive, one of medium cursive, one of fine cursive, one of thick round-hand, one of medium round-hand, one of fine round-hand, one of thick slanting-hand midway between round and cursive, one of medium and one of fine. You have one hour."

It was an hour of rest, that hour. The exercise was not tiring and they were not very exacting about handwriting, the round hand and the slanting suited me all right because they almost amounted to drawing; my cursive is vile; my looped letters and my capitals have considerable difficulty in keeping the prescribed number of "bodies" and "half-bodies". Never mind! I was feeling hungry when we got to the end of the period.

We fairly flew out of that depressing, musty room into the playground to rejoin our anxious teachers who were clustered in the shade that was not even cool. Promptly there was a torrential outburst of words and questions and laments: "Did it go well? What was the subject for dictation? Did you remember the difficult phrases?"

"It was this—that—I put '*indication*' in the singular—*I* put it in the plural—the participle was invariable, wasn't it, Mademoiselle?—I wanted to correct it, and then, after all, I left it—such a difficult dictation! . . ."

It was past twelve and the hotel was so far away. . . .

I was yawning from starvation. Mademoiselle Sergent took us to a nearby restaurant, as our hotel was too far away to walk back there in this oppressive heat. Marie Belhomme wept and wouldn't eat, disheartened by three mistakes she had made (and every mistake took off two marks!). I told the Headmistress—who seemed to have forgotten all about my escapade of last night—our methods of communicating; she laughed over them, delighted, and merely cautioned us not to do too many rash things. During examinations, she egged us on to the worst kinds of cheating; all for the honour of the school.

While we were waiting for the period of French Composition, we were nearly all of us dozing on our chairs, overcome with heat. Mademoiselle was reading the illustrated papers and got up, after a glance at the clock: "Come along, children, we must go. . . . Try not to make yourselves out too stupid in the paper you're just going to do. And you, Claudine, if you're not marked eighteen out of twenty for French Composition, I'll throw you in the river."

"I'd be cooler there, at least!"

What dolts these examiners were! The most obtuse mind would have grasped that, in this crushing heat, we should have written more lucid French essays in the morning. But not they. Whatever were we capable of, at *this* hour?

Though full, the playground was more silent than this morning and their lordships were keeping us waiting again! I went off by myself into the walled garden: I sat down under the clematis, in the shade, and I closed my eyes, drunk with drowsiness. . . .

There were shouts and calls: "Claudine! Claudine!" I started up, only half-awake for I had been well and truly asleep, to find myself faced with Luce, looking terrified as she shook me to my feet and dragged me along with her. "But you're crazy! But you don't know what's happening! My dear, we went in a quarter of an hour ago! They've dictated the synopsis of the essay and then at last Marie Belhomme and I plucked up courage to say you weren't there . . . they looked for you . . . Mademoiselle Sergent! out in the fields— and I thought maybe you were strolling about here. . . . My dear, you aren't half going to catch it, up there!"

I dashed up the staircase, Luce after me: a mild hullabaloo arose at my entrance and their Lordships, red from a prolonged luncheon, turned towards me:

"You had forgotten all about it, Mademoiselle? Where were you?" It was Roubaud who had spoken to me, half amiable, half thoroughly nasty.

"I was in the garden over there. I was having a siesta." A pane of the open window showed me my dim reflection; I had mauve clematis petals in my hair, leaves on my frock, a little green insect and a lady-bird on my shoulder; my hair was in wild disarray. . . . The general effect was not unattractive. . . . At least, I could only presume so, for their Lordships considered me at length and Roubaud asked me point-blank:

"You don't know a picture called *Primavera*, by Botticelli?" Aha! I was expecting that.

"Yes, I do, Sir. . . . I've been told that already."

I had cut the compliment off short and he pinched his lips with annoyance. The black-coated men laughed among themselves; I went to my place, escorted by these reassuring words mumbled by Sallé, a worthy man, although he was too short-sighted to recognise me, poor fellow: "In any case, you're not late. Copy the synopsis written on the blackboard, your companions have not begun yet." There, there, he needn't have been frightened—I wasn't going to scold him!

Forward, French Composition! This little adventure had given me new heart.

"*Synopsis*—Develop the thoughts and comments aroused in you by these words of Chrysale: 'What matter if she fails to observe the laws of Vaugelas,' etc."

By unheard-of luck, it was not too stupid or too repellent a subject. All round me I could hear anxious and agonised questions, for most of these little girls had never heard of Chrysale nor of *Les Femmes Savantes*. They were going to make a splendid hash of it! I couldn't help laughing over it in advance. I prepared a little elucubration that wasn't too silly, adorned with various quotations to prove that one knew one's Molière tolerably well; it went quite well and I ended up by being quite oblivious to what was going on about me.

As I looked up in search of a recalcitrant word, I noticed that Roubaud was deeply absorbed in sketching my portrait in a little notebook. *I* was quite agreeable, and I resumed the pose without appearing to do so.

Paf! Yet another little ball had dropped. It was from Luce: "Can you write me one or two general ideas? I'm in a hopeless mess, I'm simply wretched. I send you a kiss from the distance." I looked at her and saw her poor little face was all blotched and her eyes red. She answered my look by a despairing shake of the head. I scribbled down everything I could for her on a bit of tracing-paper and launched the ball, not in the air—too dangerous—but along the ground in the aisle that separated the two rows of tables, and Luce deftly put her foot on it.

I titivated up my final version, developing the things that pleased *them* and displeased *me*. Ouf! Finished! I could have a look at what the others were doing. . . .

Anaïs was working without raising her head, sly and secretive, her left arm curved over her paper to prevent her neighbour from copying. Roubaud had finished his sketch and it was getting late, though the sun was almost as high as ever. I was exhausted: tonight I would go to bed virtuously with the others, with no music. I went on observing the classroom; a whole regiment of tables in four ranks, extending right down to the end; the bent black figures of little girls of whom all one could see were smooth chignons or hanging plaits, tight as ropes; very few light dresses, only those of elementary schools like ours; the green ribbons at the necks of the boarders from Villeneuve made a splash of colour. There was a great hush, disturbed only by the faint rustle of paper being turned over or by a sigh of weariness. . . . At last, Roubaud folded up the *Fresnois Monitor*, over which he had dozed a little, and took out his watch: "Time is up, young ladies. I will collect your papers!" A few faint groans were heard; the little things who hadn't finished took fright and asked for five minutes' grace which was granted them; then the examiners collected up the fair copies and left us. We all stood up, yawning and stretching, and, before we had reached the bottom of the staircase, the groups had re-formed. Anaïs rushed up to me:

"What did you put? How did you begin?"

"You bore me stiff. . . . You don't imagine I learnt all that stuff by heart?"

"But your rough?"

"I didn't do one—only a few sentences that I licked into shape before I wrote them down."

"My dear, you'll get a terrific scolding! *I've* brought my rough out to show to Mademoiselle."

Marie Belhomme had also brought her rough out, so had all the others, including all the girls from other schools: it was always done.

In the playground, still warm from the sun that had now withdrawn from it, Mademoiselle Sergent was sitting on a little low wall, reading a novel: "Ah! Here you are at last! Your roughs, quick . . . let me see that you haven't made too many howlers."

She read them and pronounced on them: Anaïs's, it seemed, was not "devoid of merit"; Luce's "had good ideas" (mine, to be exact) "not sufficiently developed"; Marie's was "full of padding, as usual"; the Jauberts' essays were "very presentable."

"Your rough, Claudine?"

"I didn't do one."

"My dear child, you must be mad! No rough on an examination day! I give up all hope of ever getting any rational behaviour out of you. . . . Well, was your essay bad?"

"Oh no, Mademoiselle, I don't think it was bad."

"It's worth what? Seventeen?"

"Seventeen? Oh, Mademoiselle, modesty forbids me . . . seventeen, that's a lot. . . . After all, they ought to give me at least eighteen!"

My companions stared at me with envious spite. "That Claudine, she isn't half lucky to be able to foretell what marks she'll get! Let's hasten to add that it's no merit to her, she's naturally good at it and that's that; she does French essays as easily as anyone else fries eggs" . . . and so on and so on!

All about us, candidates were chattering in a shrill key, showing their roughs to their teachers, exclaiming, giving "*Ahs*" of regret at having missed out an idea . . . twittering like little birds in an aviary.

That night, instead of escaping into the town, I lay in bed, side by side with Marie Belhomme, discussing this great day with her.

"The girl on my right," Marie told me, "comes from a convent school. Just imagine, Claudine, this morning, when they were giving out the papers before Dictation, she brought a rosary out of her pocket and was saying it under the table. Yes, my dear, a rosary with huge round beads, something like a pocket abacus. It was to bring her luck."

"Pooh! If that doesn't do any good, it doesn't do any harm either. . . . What's that I hear?"

What I heard, or thought I heard, was a tremendous row in the room opposite ours, the one where Luce and Anaïs slept. The door opened violently and Luce, in a brief chemise, flung herself into the room, distracted:

"Please, *please* . . . protect me . . . Anaïs is being so *horrid*. . . ."

"What's she been doing to you?"

"First she poured water in my boots, and then, in bed, she kicked me and she pinched my thighs, and, when I complained, she told me I could sleep on the bedside mat if I wasn't satisfied!"

"Why don't you call Mademoiselle?"

"All very well, call Mademoiselle! I went to the door of her room, she wasn't there, and the girl who was going along the passage told me that she'd gone out with the manageress. . . . So now what am I going to do?"

She was crying, poor kid! She was so small in her daytime chemise that showed her slim arms and her pretty legs. Decidedly, she would be much more seductive quite naked and with her face veiled. (Two holes for the eyes, perhaps?) But this was not the moment to speculate about such matters; I jumped out of bed and ran across to the room opposite. Anaïs occupied the middle of the bed, with the blanket pulled right up to her chin: she was wearing her wickedest face.

"Look here, what's come over you? Won't you let Luce sleep with you?"

"I don't say that. Only she wants to take up all the room, so I pushed her."

"Rot! You pinched her—and you poured water in her boots."

"Sleep with her yourself, if you want to. *I'm* not keen to."

"Anyway her skin's much fresher than yours! True that's not saying much."

"Oh go on, go on. Everyone knows you're as keen on the little sister as you are on the big one!"

"You just wait, my girl. I'm about to change your ideas."

Only in my chemise as I was, I hurled myself on the bed, tore off the sheets and grabbed the lanky Anaïs by her two feet. In spite of the nails she silently dug into my shoulders, I dragged her down from the bed on her back, with her feet still in my hands and I called out: "Marie, Luce, come and look!"

A little procession of white chemises ran in on bare feet and everyone was scared. "Hi! Separate them! Call Mademoiselle!" Anaïs did not scream; she waved her legs and threw me devouring glances, desperate to hide what I was revealing as I dragged her along the floor—yellow thighs and a pear-shaped behind. I had such a frantic desire to laugh that I was frightened I would let go of her. I explained the situation:

"The fact is that this great gawk Anaïs I'm holding doesn't want to let little Luce sleep with her, that she pinches her, that she puts water in her boots and that I want to make her keep quiet."

There was silence and a marked chill. The Jauberts were too prudent to lay the blame on either of us two. At last I let go of Anaïs's ankles and she got up, hastily pulling down her chemise.

"Into bed with you now, and try and leave this kid in peace or you'll get a thrashing that'll tan your hide."

Still silent and furious, she ran to her bed, and huddled down into it, her face to the wall. She's an incredible coward and blows are the only thing in the world she fears. While the little white ghosts were scurrying back to their rooms, Luce got timidly into bed beside her persecutor, who was now as motionless as a sack. (My protégée told me next day that Anaïs had not stirred all night, except to fling her pillow on the floor out of rage.)

No one mentioned the story to Mademoiselle Sergent. We were far too busy thinking about the day that lay before us! Arithmetic and drawing tests and, in the evening, they would put up the lists of the candidates admitted to the oral exam.

After gulping down some chocolate, we made a hurried departure. It was already warm at seven o'clock. Feeling more used to things, we took our places ourselves and we chattered, with decent moderation, while we waited for their Lordships. Already we felt more at home; we slipped ourselves in without banging ourselves between the bench and the table; we arranged our pencils, penholders, indiarubbers and scrapers in front of us with an air of being quite accustomed to doing so; it was remarkably convincing, that air. We very nearly displayed personal fads.

The masters of our destinies made their entrance. They had already lost some of their prestige; the least shy ones looked at them tranquilly, as if they knew them quite well. Roubaud, who was sporting a pseudo-Panama hat in which he obviously fancied himself very smart, became quite fidgety and said impatiently: "Come along, young ladies, come along! We're late this morning, we must make up for lost time." I liked that! So, just now, it had been our fault that they hadn't been able to get up in good time. At top speed, the tables were strewed with sheets of paper; hurriedly we sealed the corners to hide our names; hurriedly the revved-up Roubaud broke the seal of the big yellow envelope bearing the official stamp of the Examining Faculty and drew out of it the redoubtable statement of the problems:

"*First Question.*—A certain man bought $3^{1}/_{2}$ per cent. stock at the rate of 94 francs, 60 centimes, etc."

I longed for hail to batter through his pseudo-panama! Operations on the Bourse drive me frantic: there are brokerages of $1/_{8}$ per cent. that I have all the torment in the world not to forget.

"*Second Question.*—The Theory of Divisibility by 9. You have one hour."

My goodness, that was none too much. Luckily I'd learnt divisibility by 9 for so long that it had finally stuck in my mind. Once again I'd have to put in order all the necessary and sufficing conditions—what a bore!

The other candidates were already absorbed and alert; a faint whispering of numbers, of muttered calculations, arose above the bent heads.

The first problem was finished. After having begun each calculation all over again twice (I so often make mistakes!) I obtained a result of 22,850 francs as the gentleman's profit: a pretty profit! I had confidence in this round and reassuring number but all the same, I wanted the support of Luce who conjures with figures in a masterly way. Several competitors had finished and I could see none but satisfied faces. In any case most of these little daughters of grasping peasants or shrewd seamstresses are gifted for arithmetic to an extent that has often amazed me. I might have asked my dark-haired next-door-neighbour, who had also finished, but I mistrusted her discreet and serious eyes, so I therefore concocted a ball, which flew off and fell under Luce's nose, bearing the figure 22,850. The child joyfully signalled me a "Yes" with her head. Satisfied, I then asked my neighbour: "How much have you got?" She hesitated and murmured, with reserve: "I've over 20,000 francs."

"So've I, but how much more?"

"I told you . . . more than 20,000 francs. . . ."

"All right, I'm not asking you to lend me them! Keep your 22,850 francs, you're not the only one who's got the right result. You're like a black ant—for various reasons!"

A few girls near us laughed; my interlocutor, not even offended, folded her hands and lowered her eyes.

"Have you finished, young ladies?" bellowed Roubaud. "I restore you your liberty. Be in good time for the drawing test."

We returned at five minutes to two to the ex-Rivoire Institute. What disgust, what a desire to run away the sight of that dilapidated prison induced in me!

In the best-lit part of the classroom, Roubaud had disposed two circles of chairs; in the centre of each, a stand. What were they going to put on it? We were all eyes. The examiner-cum-factotum disappeared and returned bearing two glass jugs with handles. Before he had placed them on the stand, all the girls were whispering: "My dear, it's going to be frightfully difficult, because of being transparent!"

Roubaud announced:

"Young ladies, for the drawing test, you are at liberty to sit where you choose. Reproduce these two utensils (utensil yourself!) in line, the sketch in charcoal, the finished outline in drawing-pencil. You are strictly forbidden to use a ruler or anything whatever that resembles one. The sheets of cardboard that you should all have brought with you will serve you as drawing-boards."

He had not finished speaking before I had already flung myself into the chair I had my eye on, an excellent place from which one saw the jug in profile, with the handle at the side. Several followed my example and I found myself between Luce and Marie Belhomme. "Strictly forbidden to use a ruler for the lines of construction?" Nonsense, everyone knew what *that* meant! My companions and I had in reserve strips of stiff paper a decimetre long and marked off in centimetres, very easy to conceal.

We had permission to talk, but we made little use of it; we preferred to make grimaces, arm outstretched and one eye shut, in order to take measurements with the charcoal-holder. With a little dexterity, nothing was simpler than to draw the construction-lines with a ruler (two strokes which divided the sheet cross-wise and a rectangle to enclose the belly of the jug).

From the other circle of chairs came a sudden small commotion, stifled exclamations and Roubaud's severe voice: "It wouldn't need more than that, Mademoiselle, to have yourself excluded from the examination!" It was a wretched girl, a skimpy, puny little thing, who had got caught, ruler in hand, and was now sobbing into her handkerchief. Roubaud became extremely nosy and examined us at close quarters, but the marked strips of paper had disappeared as if by magic. In any case, we didn't need them any more.

My jug was coming on beautifully, with a well-curved belly. While I was complacently considering it, our invigilator, distracted by the timid entry of the school-mistresses who had come to find out "if the French composition had been good on the whole", left us alone. Luce gave me a gentle tug: "*Do* tell me if my drawing's all right; it looks to me as if something's wrong with it."

After examining it, I explained to her:

"Why, of course—it's got the handle too low. It makes it look like a whipped dog that's tucking its tail in."

"What about mine?" asked Marie from the other side.

"*Yours* is hunchbacked on the right side: put an orthopedic corset on it."

"A what?"

"I'm telling you you ought to put some cotton wool on the left, it's only got 'advantages' on one side. Ask Anaïs to lend you one of her false bosoms." (For the lanky Anaïs inserts two handkerchiefs in the gussets of her stays and all our gibes haven't succeeded in making her decide to give up this childish padding.)

This back-chat threw my neighbours into a state of uncontrollable gaiety. Luce flung herself back in her chair, exposing all the fresh teeth in her little cat-like jaw as she laughed. Marie blew out her cheeks like the bellows of a bagpipe. Then suddenly they both stopped, petrified in the midst of their joy—for the terrible pair of blazing eyes belonging to Mademoiselle Sergent had cast a Medusa look at them from the far end of the room. And the session was concluded in irreproachable silence.

They put us out, feverish and noisy at the thought that, this very evening, we should read, on a big list nailed to the door, the names of the candidates who had qualified for the Orals next day. Mademoiselle Sergent had difficulty in restraining us: we were making an intolerable noise chattering.

"Are you coming to look at the names, Marie?"

"Gracious, no! If I wasn't on it, the others would jeer at me."

"*I'm* coming," said Anaïs. "I want to see the faces of those who haven't qualified."

"And suppose you were one of them yourself?"

"All right then, I don't have my name written on my forehead. I'd know how to put on a beaming expression so that the others wouldn't look pitying."

"That's enough! You're bursting my eardrums," said Mademoiselle Sergent sharply. "You'll see what you'll see—and take care I don't come alone, this evening, to read the names on the door. To begin with, we're not going back to the hotel; I've no desire to make that trek twice more; we'll dine at the restaurant."

She asked for a private room. In the species of bathroom they allotted to us, where the light fell drearily from above, our effervescence petered out. We ate like so many little wolves, without saying a word. Our hunger appeased, we took it in turn to ask, every ten minutes, what time it was. Mademoiselle tried vainly to calm our jangled nerves by assuring us there were too many entrants for their Lordships to have been able to read all the essays before nine o'clock; we went on seething all the same.

We did not know what to do with ourselves in this cellar! Mademoiselle Sergent would not take us out of doors; I knew why: the garrison was off duty at that hour and the red-trousered soldiers, out to cut a dash, did not stand on ceremony. Already, on the way to dinner, our little band had run the gauntlet of smiles, tongue-clickings and the sound of blown kisses; these manifestations had exasperated the Headmistress who had machine-gunned these audacious infantrymen with her scowls, but it would have needed more than that to reduce them to order!

The declining day, and our impatience, made us peevish and ill-natured; Anais and Marie had already exchanged spiteful remarks, their feathers ruffled like two fighting hens; the two Jauberts appeared to be meditating on the ruins of Carthage and I had thrust little Luce away with a sharp elbow when she wanted to be cuddled. Luckily, Mademoiselle, whose nerves were almost as much on edge as ours, rang, and asked for some light and two packs of cards. Good idea!

The brightness of the two gas-jets restored our morale a little and the packs of cards made us smile.

"I say, let's play *trente-et-un*!"

"Come on, then!"

The two Jauberts did not know how to play! All right, they could go on reflecting on the frailty of human destiny; we others were going to play cards while Mademoiselle read the papers.

We had a good time. We played badly and Anais cheated. And, every now and then, we stopped in the middle of a game, our elbows on the table and our faces strained, to ask: "Whatever time is it?"

Marie gave vent to the opinion that, as it was dark, we shouldn't be able to read the names; we should have to take matches with us.

"Silly, there'll be street-lamps."

"So there will! . . . But suppose that, just in that very place, there wasn't one?"

"All right," I said very low, "I'll steal a candle from the candlesticks on the mantelpiece and you bring the matches. . . . Let's go on playing. . . . Knave of Clubs and two aces!"

Mademoiselle Sergent draw out her watch; we did not take our eyes off her. She stood up; we followed her example so abruptly that chairs fell over. All our excitement surged up again, we danced over to get our hats, and, while I was looking in the glass to put mine on, I pinched a candle.

Mademoiselle Sergent put herself to unheard-of-trouble to prevent us from running; passers-by laughed at this swarm of girls which was forcing itself not to gallop and we laughed back at the passers-by. At last, the door glittered before our eyes. When I say glittered, I am using the word in a literary way . . . for, after all, there actually wasn't a lamp-post! In front of that closed door, a crowd of agitated shadows was screaming, jumping for joy or lamenting; they were our competitors from the other schools. Sudden, brief match-flares, soon extinguished, and flickering candle-flames lit up a great white sheet pinned to the door.

Nothing would stop us: we dashed forward, brutally shoving away the small, milling silhouettes; no one paid the least attention to us.

Holding the stolen candle as straight as I could, I read and divined, guided by the initials in alphabetical order: "Anaïs, Belhomme, Claudine, Jaubert, Lanthenay." All of us! All! What joy! And now came the verifying of the number of marks. The minimum of marks required was 45; the total was written beside the names, the detailed marks between two brackets. Mademoiselle Sergent, in ecstasy, transcribed into her notebook: "Anaïs 65, Claudine 68—what did the Jauberts get? 63 and 64, Luce 49, Marie Belhomme 44½. What? 44½? But you've not qualified then? Whatever's this you're telling me?"

"No, Mademoiselle," said Luce, who had just gone up to verify. "It's 44¾ . . . she's qualified with a quarter of a mark short . . . by a special favour of those gentlemen."

Poor Marie, quite out of breath from the terrible fright she had just had, gave a long sigh of relief. It was decent of those chaps to have overlooked her quarter of a mark but I was afraid she would make a mess of the Oral. Anaïs, once her first joy was over, charitably held up a light for the new arrivals, while spattering them with melted wax, horrid girl!

Mademoiselle could not calm us, not even by dousing us with the cold water of this sinister prediction: "You're not at the end of your troubles yet. I should like to see your faces tomorrow night after the Oral."

With difficulty she got us back to the hotel, skipping about and singing in the moonlight.

And later on, when the Headmistress was in bed and asleep, we got out of our beds and danced, Anaïs, Luce, Marie and I (not the Jauberts, of course). We danced wildly, our hair flying, holding out our brief chemises as if for a minuet.

Then, at a fancied noise from the direction of the room where Mademoiselle reposed, the dancers of this unseemly quadrille fled with suppressed giggles and a rustling of bare feet.

The next morning, waking up too early, I ran in to "scare the life out of" the Anaïs-Luce couple which was sleeping in an absorbed, conscientious way. I tickled Luce's nose with my hair; she sneezed before she opened her eyes and her dismay woke Anaïs who grumbled and sat up, cursing me. I exclaimed, with immense seriousness: "But don't you know what time it is? Seven o'clock, my dear, and the Oral's at half-past." I let them hurl themselves out of bed and put on their stockings and I waited till they'd buttoned up their boots before telling them it was only six, that I'd seen it wrong. This didn't annoy them as much as I'd hoped.

At a quarter to seven, Mademoiselle hustled us, hurried us over our chocolate, insisted on our casting a glance through our history summaries while we ate our slices of bread-and-butter and finally pushed us out into the sunlit street, completely dazed. Luce was armed with her pencilled cuffs, Marie with her tube of rolled-up paper, Anaïs with her miniature atlas. They clung to these little life-saving planks even more than yesterday for today they had to talk; talk to their Lordships whom they did not know; talk in front of thirty pairs of malicious little ears. Anaïs was the only one who looked cheerful; she did not know the meaning of intimidation.

In the dilapidated courtyard, there were far fewer candidates today; so many had fallen by the wayside between the written exam and the oral! (That was good; when they admit a lot to the written, they turn down a lot for the oral.) Nearly all of them looked pale, yawned nervously and complained, like Marie Belhomme, of a tight feeling in their stomachs . . . that disturbing stage-fright!

The door opened to admit the black-garbed men: we followed them silently to the room upstairs, stripped today of all its chairs. In each of the four corners, behind black tables (or rather, tables that had once been black) an examiner seated himself, solemn, almost lugubrious. While we were taking in this stage-setting, feeling both curious and fearful, as we stood massed in the doorway, embarrassed by the vast space we had to cross, Mademoiselle gave us a push: "Go on! Go on, for goodness' sake! Are you going to take root here?" Our group advanced more boldly, in a bunch: old Sallé, gnarled and shrivelled, stared at us without seeing us, he was so incredibly short-sighted; Roubaud was playing with his watch-chain, his eyes abstracted; the elderly Lerouge was waiting patiently and consulting the list of names; and, in the embrasure of a window, a fat lady, Mademoiselle Michelet, was enthroned, with sol-fa charts in front of her. I nearly forgot another one, the bad-tempered Lacroix, who was grumbling and furiously shrugging his shoulders as he turned over the pages of his books and seemed to be having a fierce argument with himself; the girls, terrified, were telling each other he must be "an absolute beast"! *He* was the one who made up his mind to growl out a name: "Mademoiselle Aubert!"

The said Aubert, an overgrown girl, limp and stooping, started like a horse, squinted and promptly became stupid. In her desire to do the right thing, she bounded forward, shouting in trumpet-like tones, and with a strong peasant accent: "But here I be, Surr!" We all burst out laughing and that laugh we hadn't thought of repressing raised our spirits and cheered us up.

That bulldog of a Lacroix had frowned when the unfortunate girl had bellowed her "But here I be!" of distress and had replied: "Who's denying it?" As a result, she was in a pitiable state.

"Mademoiselle Vigoureux!" called Roubaud. *He* was taking the alphabet by the tail. A plump little thing hurried forward; she wore the white hat, wreathed in daisies, of the Villeneuve school.

"Mademoiselle Mariblom!" barked old Sallé, who thought he was taking the middle of the alphabet and was reading it all wrong. Marie Belhomme advanced, crimson, and seated herself on the chair opposite old Sallé; he stared at her and asked her if she knew what the Iliad was. Luce, just behind me, sighed: "At least, she's begun—the great thing is to begin!"

The unoccupied competitors, of whom I was one, dispersed shyly, scattered themselves about the room and went to listen to their colleagues sitting on the stool of repentance. I myself went off to the examination of the Aubert girl to give myself a little entertainment. At the moment I approached, old Lacroix was asking her: "So you don't know who married Philip the Handsome?"

Her eyes were starting out of her head and her face was red and glistening with sweat; her mittens revealed fingers like sausages: "He married . . . no, he didn't marry . . . Surr, Surr," she cried all of a sudden, "I've forgotten. Everything!" She was trembling; big tears rolled down her cheeks. Lacroix looked at her, vicious as the plague: "You've forgotten everything? With what remains, you get a nice zero."

"Yes, yes," she stammered. "But it doesn't matter, I'd rather go off back home, I don't care. . . ."

They took her away, hiccuping with great sobs. Through the window, I heard her outside, telling her mortified teacher: "Honest I'd rather look after Dad's cows, so I would. An' I'll never come back here, I won't. An' I'll take the two o'clock train, so I will."

In the classroom, her schoolmates were discussing the "regrettable incident", grave and disapproving. "My dear, can you imagine her being so idiotic! My dear, if they'd asked me a question as easy as that, I'd have been only too pleased, my dear!"

"Mademoiselle Claudine!"

It was old Lerouge who was asking for me! Ugh! Arithmetic. . . . Luckily he looked like a kindly Papa. . . . I saw at once that he wouldn't do me any harm.

"Let's see, my child, now could you tell me something about right-angled triangles?"

"Yes, sir, though, actually, I don't much care for them."

"Now, now! You make them out worse than they are. Let's see, construct me a right-angled triangle on this blackboard, and then you'll give its dimensions and then you'll talk to me nicely about the square on the hypotenuse. . . ."

One would have to be pretty determined, to get oneself ploughed by a man like that! So I was as meek as a lamb with a pink ribbon round its neck and I said everything I knew. Actually, it didn't take long.

"But you're getting along splendidly. Tell me, as well, how one recognises that a number is divisible by 9, and I'll let you off any more."

I rattled off: "sum of the digits . . . necessary condition . . . adequate condition."

"You can go, my child, that's enough."

I stood up with a sigh of relief and found Luce behind me. She said: "You're lucky, I'm so glad you were." She said it charmingly:

for the first time, I stroked her neck without laughing at her. Goodness! It was me again! One hadn't time to breathe!

It was the porcupine, Lacroix; things were getting hot! I installed myself; he looked at me over the top of his eye-glasses and said: "Ha! What was the War of the Two Roses?" After the names of the leaders of the two factions, I stopped dead.

"And then? And then? And then?"

He irritated me. I burst out:

"And then, they fought like ragamuffins for a long time, but that hasn't stuck in my memory."

He stared at me, amazed. I'd get something thrown at my head in a moment!

"Is that how you learn history, my good girl?"

"Pure chauvinism, Sir. I'm only interested in the history of France."

Incredible luck: he laughed!

"I'd rather deal with impertinent girls than stupefied ones. Tell me about Louis XV (1742)."

"All right. That was the period when Madame de la Tournelle was exercising a deplorable influence over him. . . ."

"Good heavens! You're not being asked about that!"

"Excuse me, Sir, it's not my own invention, it's the simple truth . . . the best historians . . ."

"What d'you mean? the best historians . . ."

"Yes, Sir, I read it in Michelet—with full details!"

"Michelet! but this is madness! Michelet, get this into your head, wrote a historical novel in twenty volumes and he dared to call that the *History of France*! And you come here and talk to me of Michelet!"

He was excited, he banged on the table, but I stood up to him. The young candidates round us stood transfixed, not believing their ears; Mademoiselle Sergent had approached, gasping, ready to intervene. . . . When she heard me declare:

"Anyway, Michelet's less boring than Duruy! . . ."

She flung herself against the table and protested in anguish:

"Sir, I implore you forgive . . . this child has lost her head: she will withdraw at once. . . ."

He interrupted her, mopped his brow and panted:

"Let her alone, Mademoiselle, there's no harm done. I hold to my own opinions, but I'm all in favour of others holding to theirs. This young person has false ideas and bad reading-habits, but she is not lacking in personality—one sees so many dull ones!—Only you, my peruser of Michelet, try and tell me how you would go, by boat, from Amiens to Marseilles or I'll chuck you a 2 that will give you a painful surprise!"

"Leaving Amiens by embarking on the Somme, I go up . . . etc., etc., . . . canals . . . etc., and I arrive at Marseilles only after a period varying between six months and two years."

"That isn't *your* business. Mountain-system of Russia, and step lively."

Alas, I cannot say that I shine outstandingly in the knowledge of the mountain-system of Russia, but I got through it more or less except for some gaps which seemed regrettable to the examiner.

"And the Balkans . . . you're cutting them out, then?"

That man spat out his words like a fire-cracker.

"Certainly not, Sir, I was keeping them as a final titbit."

"That's all right. Be off with you."

People drew back rather indignantly to let me through. Those dear little pets!

I relaxed; no one had summoned me, so I listened with horror to Marie Belhomme who was answering Roubaud that "to prepare sulphuric acid, you pour water on lime and then that begins to boil; then you collect the gas in a balloon-flask." She wore the expression that always meant enormous howlers and boundless stupidities; her huge, long, narrow hands gripped the table; her eyes, like those of a brainless bird, rolled and glittered; she poured out monstrous ineptitudes with extreme volubility. There was nothing to be done; even if one had whispered in her ear, she wouldn't have heard! Anaïs was listening to her too and enjoying herself with all her kindly soul. I asked her:

"What have you got through, already?"

"Singing, history, joggraphy."

"Nasty old Lacroix?"

"Yes. What a swine! But he asked me easy ones, Thirty Years' War, the Treaties . . . I say, Marie's off the rails!"

"Off the rails seems to me putting it mildly."

Little Luce, excited and astounded, came up to us:

"I've passed joggraphy, and history, I answered well. . . . Oh, I *am* bucked!"

"Hullo, twirp! I'm going to have a drink at the pump, I can't hold out any longer. Anyone comin' too?"

Not one of them was; either they weren't thirsty or they were afraid of missing a summons. Downstairs, in a kind of parlour, I found the Aubert girl, her cheeks still blotched with red from her recent despair and her eyes swollen. She was writing to her family, at a little table, calm now and pleased to be going back to the farm. I said to her:

"Look here, didn't you *want* to know anything just now?"

She raised her calf's eyes.

"Makes me frightened, all that do, and gets me in ever such a state, it do. Mother sent me to boarding-school, father he didn't want it, he said I'd do best looking after the house like my sisters, and doing the washing and digging the garden. Mother, she didn't want it—it was her as they listened to. They made me ill, trying to make me learn—and you see how I come over today. I said as it would happen! Now they'll have to believe me!"

And she went on tranquilly writing her letter.

Upstairs, in the classroom it was hot enough to kill one. The girls, nearly all red and shiny (lucky I haven't any tendency to redness!), were scared and tense, straining their ears to hear their names called and obsessed with the idea of not making stupid answers. Wouldn't it soon be twelve o'clock so that we could go?

Anaïs returned from physics and chemistry; *she* wasn't red, how could she be red? I believe that, even in a boiling cauldron she would remain yellow and cold.

"Well, everything all right?"

"Thank goodness, I've finished. You know Roubaud's taking English into the bargain: he made me read sentences and translate; I don't know why he squirmed when I read in English . . . isn't he idiotic?"

It was the pronunciation! Bother! It was pretty obvious now that Mademoiselle Aimée Lanthenay, who gave the lessons, did not speak English with excessive purity. And, as a result, any moment now that imbecile of a Professor was going to make fun of me because *I* didn't pronounce better! Still another delightful episode! I was enraged to think that idiot was going to laugh at me.

Midday at last. Their Lordships rose and we proceeded to the usual shindy of our departure. Lacroix, his hair bristling and his eyes starting out of his head, announced that the merry little party would begin again at 2.30. Mademoiselle sorted us out with difficulty from the swirling tide of chattering young things and took us off to the restaurant. She was still stiff with me on account of my "odious" conduct with old Lacroix; but I didn't care! The heat weighed down on me; I was tired and mute. . . .

Oh, the woods, the dear woods of Montigny! At that very hour, how well I knew how they hummed! The wasps and flies that tippled in the flowers of the limes and the elders made the whole forest vibrate like an organ; and the birds did not sing, for, at midday, they perched upright on the branches, seeking the shade, preening their feathers and peering into the undergrowth with bright, shifting eyes. I would be lying at the edge of the Fir Plantation from which I could see the whole town down there below me with the warm wind in my face, half dead with well-being and laziness.

. . . Luce saw me far away, completely in another world, and tugged my sleeve, giving me her most fetching smile. Mademoiselle was reading the papers; my classmates were exchanging sleepy scraps of conversation. I complained and Luce protested gently:

"And you never talk to me any more, either! All day we're passing exams, in the evening we go to bed and at meals you're in such a bad temper that I don't know when to find you any more!"

"Perfectly simple! Don't look for me!"

"Oh, that's not a bit nice of you! You don't even notice all my patience in waiting for you, the way I put up with your always pushing me away. . . ."

The gawky Anaïs laughed like a door that needed oiling and the little thing stopped, highly intimidated. All the same it is true that she has unshakable patience. And to think that so much constancy won't avail her in the least; sad! sad!

Anaïs was pursuing an idea of her own: she had not forgotten Marie Belhomme's incoherent answers and, amiable bitch, she kindly asked the poor wretch who was sitting dazed and motionless:

"What question did they ask you in physics and chemistry?"

"It's of no importance," growled Mademoiselle crossly. "Whatever they asked her, she'll have given nonsensical answers."

"I can't remember now," said poor, flummoxed Marie. "Sulphuric acid, I think. . . ."

"And what did you say?"

"Oh, luckily I knew a bit, Mademoiselle; I said that you poured water on lime and that the bubbles of gas that form were sulphuric acid. . . ."

"You said that?" articulated Mademoiselle, gritting her teeth as if she were longing to bite. . . .

Anaïs gnawed her nails with delight. Marie, thunderstruck, did not utter another word and the Headmistress, rigid and red in the face, marched us off, walking very fast. We trotted behind her like little dogs, practically hanging our tongues out under the sun that beat down on us.

We no longer paid the least attention to our alien competitors and they did not look at us either. The heat and our jangled nerves had taken away all desire to show off and all animosity. The girls from the Villeneuve High School, the "apple-greens" as we called them—because of the green ribbons round their necks, that appalling harsh green which is the special prerogative of boarding-schools—still put on prudish, disgusted airs when they came anywhere near us (why? we shall never know); but everyone was settling down and relaxing. Already we were thinking about our departure tomorrow morning and brooding deliciously on how we'd rile our rejected schoolmates, the ones who hadn't been able to enter on account of "general weakness". How the gawky Anaïs was going to preen and strut and talk about the Training College as if she owned it! Pooh! I hadn't enough shoulders to shrug.

The examiners reappeared at last; they were mopping their faces and looked ugly and shiny. Heavens, I should hate to be married in weather like this! The mere idea of sleeping with a man who was as hot as they were. . . . (In any case, in summer, I should have two beds. . . .) Moreover, the smell in that overheated room was appalling; it was obvious that a great many of those little girls were anything but fastidious about their underclothes. I would have done anything to get away.

I collapsed on a chair and vaguely listened to the others as I awaited my turn; I saw the girl, the luckiest one of all, who had "finished" first. She had endured all the questioning; now she could breathe again as she crossed the room to the accompaniment of compliments, envious glances and cries of "You're jolly lucky!" Soon another one followed her and joined her in the playground where the "released" were resting and exchanging their impressions.

Old Sallé, slightly unbent by this sun which warmed his gout and his rheumatics, was taking a forced rest as the girl he was waiting for was occupied elsewhere. Suppose I risked a tentative assault on his virtue? Very quietly, I went up and sat down on the chair opposite him.

"Good morning, Monsieur Sallé."

He stared at me, settled his glasses, blinked—and still did not recognise me.

"Claudine, you know?"

"Ah . . . fancy that! Good morning, my dear child! Is your father well?"

"Very well, thank you."

"Well now, how's the exam going? Are you satisfied? Will you soon be finished?"

"Alas, I'd like to be! But I've still got to get through physics and chemistry, literature—which is your department—English and music. Is Madame Sallé well?"

"My wife's gadding about in Poitou; she'd do much better to be looking after me but . . ."

"Listen, Monsieur Sallé, now you've got me here, do get me over the literature."

"But I haven't got to your name, not nearly! Come back a little later on. . . ."

"Monsieur Sallé, whatever would it matter?"

"Matter? It would matter that I was enjoying a moment's respite and that I had thoroughly deserved it. And besides, it's not in the programme; we mustn't break the alphabetical order."

"Monsieur Sallé, be a dear. You need hardly ask me anything. You know that I know much more than the syllabus demands about books that count as literature. I'm a book-worm in Papa's library.

"Er . . . yes, that's true. I can certainly do that for you. I had intended to ask you what were the bards and the troubadours and the *Roman de la Rose,* and so on."

"You can set your mind at rest, Monsieur Sallé. The troubadours, I know all about *them.* I always see them in the person of the little Florentine Singer, like this . . ."

I stood up and struck the pose: my body leaning forward on the right leg and old Sallé's green umbrella doing duty as a mandoline. Luckily we were quite alone in that corner! Luce stared at me from the distance and gaped with surprise. Poor gouty old man, it amused him a little and he laughed.

"And they wore a velvet cap and curly hair, very often even a piebald costume (in blue and yellow, it looks particularly well); their mandoline hung on a silken cord and they sang that little thing out of the *Passer-By:* 'My sweet one, April's here.' That, Monsieur Sallé, is how *I* see the troubadours. We have also the First Empire troubadour."

"My child, you're a little crazy but I find you refreshing. Just Heaven! What on earth can you possibly call troubadours of the First Empire? Speak very low, my little Claudine—if their Lordships saw us . . ."

"Ssh. The First Empire troubadours, I knew all about them from the songs Papa used to sing. Listen carefully."

I hummed very softly:

> *Burning with love, setting forth to the wars,*
> *His helm on his head and his lyre in his hand,*
> *A troubadour sings to the maid he adores,*
> *Looking his last on his dear native land:*
> *   'My country, she calls me,*
> *   My sweetheart enthrals me,*
> *For love and for glory, I'd gladly be slain,*
> *Such is the troubadour's merry refrain?'*

Old Sallé roared with laughter:

"Good Lord, how absurd those people were! Of course I know we shall be just as absurd in twenty years' time, but that idea of a troubadour with a helmet and a lyre! . . . Run away quick, child, you'll get a good mark; kind regards to your father, tell him I'm devoted to him and that he teaches his daughter fine songs!"

"Thank you, Monsieur Sallé, good-bye. Thank you again for not asking me any questions. I won't say a word—don't worry!"

What a thoroughly nice man! This had slightly restored my courage and I looked so cheerful that Luce asked me:

"Did you answer well, then? What did he ask you? Why did you take his umbrella?"

"Ah! I'll tell you! He asked me very difficult things about the troubadours, about the shape of the instruments they used; lucky I happened to know all those details!"

"The shape of the instruments . . . no, honest, I shudder at the thought he might have asked me that! The shape of the . . . but it's not in the syllabus! I shall tell Mademoiselle!"

"Right, we'll make a formal complaint. Have *you* finished?"

"Yes, thanks! I've finished. I've got a hundred pounds weight off my chest, I assure you! I think there's only Marie left to go through it now."

"Mademoiselle Claudine!" said a voice behind us. Aha! It was Roubaud. I sat down in front of him, decorous and reserved. He assumed a pleasant manner—he is the most polished of the local professors—and I talked back, but he still had a grudge against me, vindictive creature, for having too hastily brushed aside his Botticellian compliment. It was in a slightly peevish voice that he asked me:

"You haven't fallen asleep under the leaves today, Mademoiselle?"

"Is that a question that forms part of the programme, Monsieur?"

He gave a slight cough. I had made a shocking blunder to vex him. Well, it couldn't be helped:

"Kindly tell me how you would set about procuring yourself ink."

"Good heavens, Sir, there are lots of ways: the simplest would be just to go and ask for some at the stationer's on the corner. . . ."

"A pleasant joke, but not enough to obtain you lavish marks. . . . Will you try and tell me what ingredients you would use to fabricate ink?"

"Nut gall . . . tannin . . . iron monoxide . . . gum . . ."

"You don't know the proportions?"

"No."

"Pity! Can you tell me something about mica?"

"I've never seen it anywhere except in the little panes in the doors of stoves."

"Really? Once more, a pity! The lead in pencils, what is it made of?"

"Graphite, a soft stone that is cut into thin rods and enclosed between two halves of a wooden cylinder."

"Is that the only use of graphite?"

"I don't know any others."

"As usual, what a pity! Only pencils are made with it?"

"Yes, but a great many are made; there are some mines in Russia, I think. People consume a fabulous quantity throughout the entire world, especially examiners who sketch portraits of candidates in their notebooks. . . ."

(He blushed and fidgeted.)

"We will pass on to English."

Opening a little collection of Miss Edgeworth's *Tales,* he said:

"Please translate a few sentences for me."

"Translate, yes, but read . . . that's another matter!"

"Why?"

"Because our English mistress pronounces it in a ridiculous way. And I don't know how to pronounce it otherwise."

"Pooh! What does that matter?"

"It matters that I don't like making a fool of myself."

"Read a little, I'll pull you up at once."

I read but in a very low voice, hardly articulating the syllables and I translated the sentences before I had uttered the last words. Roubaud burst out laughing, in spite of himself, at such eagerness not to display my deficiency in English and I felt like scratching his face. As if it were my fault!

"Good. Will you give me some instances of irregular verbs, with their form in the present tense and in the past participle?"

"To see, I saw, seen. To be, I was, been. To drink, I drank, drunk. To . . ."

"That's enough, thank you. Good luck, Mademoiselle."

"Too kind of you, Sir."

I discovered the next day that that hypocrite had given me extremely bad marks, three below the average, so that I would have been ploughed if my marks for written work, especially for French Composition hadn't pleaded in my favour. Beware of these underhand men in pretentious neckties who stroke their moustaches and pencil your portrait while giving you surreptitious looks! It was true that I had annoyed him, but the fact remains that straightforward bulldogs like old Lacroix are worth a hundred of him!

Delivered from physics and chemistry as well as English, I sat down and busied myself with making my disordered hair look slightly more artistic. Luce made a bee-line for me and obligingly rolled my curls round her finger, kittenish and cuddling as usual! She certainly had courage, in a temperature like that!

"Where are the others, baby?"

"The others? Oh, they've all finished, they're down in the playground with Mademoiselle. And all the girls from the other schools who've finished are down there too."

The room was, in fact, rapidly emptying.

That fat kind Mademoiselle Michelot summoned me at last. She was red and exhausted enough to make Anaïs herself feel sorry for her. I sat down; she studied me with big, puzzled, good-natured eyes, without saying a word.

"You are . . . musical, Mademoiselle Sergent told me."

"Yes, Mademoiselle, I play the piano."

She threw up her arms and exclaimed:

"Then you know much more about it than I do."

It was a cry from the heart; I couldn't help laughing.

"Dear me, now! Listen . . . I'm going to make you read at sight and that'll be all. I'll find you something difficult, you'll get through it without any trouble."

The "something difficult" she found was a fairly simple exercise which, being all in semiquavers, with seven flats in the key-signature, had seemed to her "black" and redoubtable. I sang it *allegro vivace*, surrounded by a circle of admiring little girls who sighed with envy. Mademoiselle Michelot nodded her head, and, without further insistence, awarded me a 20 which made the audience turn green.

Ouf! So it was actually over! Soon I would be back in Montigny; I would return to school, run about the woods, watch the frolics of our instructresses (poor little Aimée, she must be languishing, all by herself!). I tore down to the playground; Mademoiselle Sergent was only waiting for me and stood up as soon as she saw me.

"Well! Is it all over?"

"Yes, thank the Lord! I've got twenty for music."

"Twenty for music!"

My companions shouted the words in chorus, unable to believe their ears.

"It only needed that—that you should *not* have got twenty for music," said Mademoiselle, with an air of detachment, but secretly flattered.

"All the same," said Anaïs, annoyed and jealous, "twenty for music, nineteen for French Composition . . . if you've got a lot of marks like those!"

"Don't worry, sweet child, the elegant Roubaud will have marked me extremely stingily!"

"Because?" inquired Mademoiselle, promptly uneasy.

"Because I didn't have much to say to him. He asked me what wood they made flutes out of, no, pencils, something of that sort, and then something or other about ink . . . and about Botticelli. . . . Quite frankly, the two of us didn't 'click'."

The Headmistress's brow darkened again.

"I should have been extremely surprised if you *hadn't* done something idiotic! You'll have no one but yourself to blame if you fail."

"Alas, who knows? I shall blame it on Monsieur Antonin Rabastens—he has inspired me with a violent passion and my studies have suffered deplorably as a result."

At this, Marie Belhomme clasped her midwife's hands and declared that, if she had a lover, she would not say it so brazenly. Anaïs looked at me out of the corner of her eye to find out if I were joking or not, and Mademoiselle, shrugging her shoulders, took us back to the hotel, lagging and dropping behind and dawdling so much that she invariably had to wait for someone at every turning. We had dinner; we yawned. At nine o'clock we were smitten again with the fever of going to read the names of the elect on the gates of that ugly Paradise. "I shan't take any of you," declared Mademoiselle, "I shall go alone and you will wait here." But there arose such a concert of groans that she relented and let us come.

Once again we took candles as a precaution, but this time they were not needed; a benevolent hand had hung a big lantern over the white notice on which our names were inscribed . . . there, I'm going a little too fast in saying "our" . . . suppose mine wasn't to be found in the list? Anaïs would have fainted from joy! Luckily in the midst of exclamations, shoves from behind and much clapping of hands, I read out: Anaïs, Claudine, etc., . . . All of us, in fact! Alas, no, not Marie: "Marie's failed," murmured Luce. "Marie's not on it," whispered Anaïs, hiding her malicious delight with considerable difficulty.

Poor Marie Belhomme remained rooted to the spot, her face quite white, in front of the cruel sheet which she studied with her glittering, birdlike eyes huge and round: then the corners of her mouth pulled down and she burst into noisy tears. . . . Mademoiselle took her away, annoyed; we followed, without giving a thought to the passers-by who looked back. Marie was moaning and sobbing out loud.

"Come, come, little girl" said Mademoiselle. "You're being unreasonable. You can try again in October, you'll have better luck. . . . Why think, that gives you two more months to work in. . . ."

"Oh, oh!" wailed the other, inconsolable.

"You'll pass, I tell you! Look, I promise you that you'll pass! Now are you satisfied?"

This affirmation did, indeed, have a happy result. Marie no longer did more than give little grunts, like a month-old puppy when you stop it from sucking the teat and walked along dabbing her eyes.

Her handkerchief was wringing wet and she ingenuously wrung it out as we walked over the bridge. That bitch of an Anaïs said in an undertone: "The papers announce a high rise in the river Lisse." Marie, who had heard, burst into uncontrollable laughter mixed with the remains of sobs, and we all laughed wildly too. And, in a flash, the unstable head of the ploughed candidate had veered round to joy, like a weathercock; she thought how she was going to pass in October and became positively gay. And nothing seemed more appropriate to us, that heavy, sultry night, than to take a skipping-rope and skip in the square (all of us, yes, even the Jauberts!) up till ten o'clock under the moon.

The next morning, Mademoiselle had already come round and shaken us in our beds at six o'clock, though the train didn't leave till ten! "Get up, get up, you little ticks; you've got to pack your things and have your breakfast, you'll have none too much time!" She was throbbing with violent trepidation, her sharp eyes gleamed and sparkled; she hustled Luce who was staggering with sleep and pommelled Marie Belhomme who, in her nightdress and slippers, was rubbing her eyes without regaining any clear consciousness of the everyday world. *We* were all utterly exhausted but who would have recognised in Mademoiselle the duenna who had chaperoned us these last three days? Happiness transfigured her; she was going to see her little Aimée again. From sheer joy, she kept smiling beatifically at nothing in the omnibus that took us back to the station. Marie seemed a little melancholy about her failure, but I think it was out of duty that she put on a contrite expression. And we chattered wildly, all at once, each one telling the story of her exam to five others who were not listening.

"Old thing!" screeched Anaïs. "When I heard that he was asking me the dates of the . . ."

"I've forbidden you a hundred times to call each other 'old thing'," broke in Mademoiselle.

"Old thing," went on Anaïs under her breath, "I only just had time to open my little notebook in my hand; the most terrific thing is that he saw it—cross my heart he did—and he didn't say a word!"

"Oh, you liar of liars!" cried the honest Marie Belhomme, her eyes starting out of her head, "I was there, I was watching, he didn't see anything at all—he'd have taken it away from you . . . they certainly took the ruler away from one of the Villeneuve girls. . . ."

"You'd better keep your mouth shut! Or run along and tell Roubaud that the Dog's Grotto is full of sulphuric acid!"

Marie hung her head, turned red and began to cry again at the remembrance of her misfortunes. I made the gesture of opening an umbrella and Mademoiselle once more emerged from her "delicious anticipation":

"Anaïs, you're a pest! If you torment one single one of your companions, I'll make you travel alone in a separate compartment."

"The smoking compartment, naturally," I observed.

"*You* were not being asked your opinion. Pick up your bags and wraps, don't stand there like stuffed dummies!"

Once in the train, she paid no more attention to us than if we did not exist; Luce went to sleep, with her head on my shoulder; the Jauberts became absorbed in the contemplation of the fields that slipped past and of the white and dappled sky; Anaïs bit her nails; Marie declined into a doze, along with her affliction.

At Bresles, the last station before Montigny, we began to fidget a little; ten minutes more and we should be there. Mademoiselle pulled out her little pocket-mirror and verified the set of her hat, the disorder of her rough frizzy red hair, the cruel crimson of her lips. Absorbed and palpitating with excitement, her expression was almost demented. Anaïs pinched her cheeks in the wild hope of bringing a faint touch of red to them; I put on my immense, riotous hat. For whom were we taking so much pains? Not for Mademoiselle Aimée, certainly, in the case of us small fry. . . . Oh, well! for no one, for the station officials, for the omnibus-driver, old Racalin, a sixty-year-old drunkard, for the half-wit who sold the papers, for the dogs who would be trotting along the road.

There was the Fir Plantation, and the Bel Air wood, and then the common, and the goods station; then, at long last, the brakes squeaked! We jumped out behind Mademoiselle who had already rushed to her little Aimée, who was hopping gaily about on the platform. She had crushed her in such a fierce embrace that the frail assistant-mistress had suddenly turned red, stifled by it. We ran up to her and welcomed her in the manner of good little schoolgirls: ". . . 'morning, Mmmselle! . . . H'are you, Mmmselle?"

As it was fine and we were in no hurry, we stuffed our suitcases into the omnibus and returned on foot, strolling the whole way between the high hedges where milkwort blossomed, blue and winey pink, and *Ave Marias* with their flowers like little white crosses. Happy to be off the leash, to have no French History to revise or maps to colour, we ran in front of and behind those ladies who walked arm-in-arm, close together and keeping in perfect step. Aimée had kissed her sister and given her a tap on the cheek, saying: "There, you see now, little canary-bird, one gets through somehow, in spite of everything!" And, after that, she had only eyes and ears for her tall friend.

Disappointed once again, poor Luce attached herself to my person and followed me like a shadow, muttering jeers and threats: "It's truly worth while splitting one's head to get compliments like that! . . . What a couple of guys those two look; my sister hanging on the other like a basket! . . . In front of all the people going by, it's enough to make you weep!" They couldn't have cared less about the people going by.

Triumphal return! Everyone knew not only where we came from but the results of the examination which Mademoiselle had telegraphed: people were standing in their doorways and made friendly signs to us. . . . Marie felt her distress increasing and effaced herself as much as possible.

The fact of having left the School for a few days made us see it more clearly on returning to it. It was finished, perfect to the last detail, white and spotless. The Town Hall stood in the middle, flanked by the two schools, boys' and girls'; there lay the big playground, whose cedars they had mercifully spared, with its small, formal, typically French clumps of shrubs, and the heavy iron gates—far too heavy and too redoubtable—that shut us in. There stood the water-closets with six compartments, three for the big girls, three for the little ones (in a touching concession to modesty, the big girls' lavatories had full doors and the little ones' half-doors); upstairs were the handsome dormitories whose shining window-panes and white curtains were visible from outside. The unfortunate ratepayers would be paying for it for years to come. Anyone might think it was a barracks, it was so handsome!

The girls gave us a noisy welcome. Since Mademoiselle Aimée had kindly confided the supervision of her own pupils and that of the First Class to the chlorotic Mademoiselle Griset during her little trip to the station, the classrooms were strewn with papers, and littered with sabots that had been used as missiles and the cores of wind-fallen apples. . . . At a frown from Mademoiselle Sergent, everything was restored to order; creeping hands picked up the apple-cores and feet stretched out and silently resumed possession of the scattered sabots.

My stomach was crying out and I went off to lunch, delighted to see Fanchette again, and the garden, and Papa; my white Fanchette, who had been baking herself and growing thinner in the sunshine, welcomed me with sharp, surprised mews; the green garden, neglected and overgrown with plants which had strained upward and grown immensely tall to find the sunlight the great trees hid from them; and Papa who welcomed me with a hearty, affectionate slap in the hollow under my shoulder:

"What on earth's become of you? I never see you these days!"

"But, Papa, I've just come back from passing my exam."

"What exam?"

I assure you there is no one like him! Obligingly, I recounted to him the adventures of the last few days, while he tugged his great red and white beard. He seemed pleased. No doubt, his experiments in cross-breeding slugs had furnished him with unhoped-for results.

I allowed myself four or five days of rest and of wandering over to the Matignons where I found Claire, my co-First Communicant, dripping with tears because her lover had just left Montigny without even deigning to inform her. In a week she will possess another fiancé who will leave her at the end of three months; she is not cunning enough to hold the boys and not practical enough to get herself married. And, as she obstinately insists on remaining virtuous, this may go on for a long time.

Meanwhile, she was looking after her twenty-five sheep, a slightly comic-opera, slightly absurd little shepherdess, with the big mushroom hat that protected her complexion and her chignon (the sun fades one's hair, my dear!), her tiny blue apron embroidered in white, and the white novel, with its title *En Fête!* lettered in red, that she concealed in her basket. (It was I who had lent her the works of Auguste Germain to initiate her into Life! Alas, maybe I shall be responsible for all the appalling errors she'll commit.) I was convinced that she found herself poetically unhappy—a pathetic, deserted fiancée—and that, when she was by herself, she delighted in assuming nostalgic poses, "her arms dropped, like useless weapons", or her head bowed, half-buried under her dishevelled hair. While she was telling me the meagre news of the past four days, along with her misfortunes, it was I who kept an eye on the sheep and urged the bitch after them: "Fetch them, Lisette! Fetch them over there!" and I who uttered the warning "Prrr . . . my beauty!" to stop them from touching the oats: I'm used to it.

"When I found out what train he was leaving by," sighed Claire, "I arranged to leave my sheep with Lisette and I went down to the level crossing. At the barrier, I waited for the train—it doesn't go too fast there because it's uphill. I saw him, I waved my handkerchief, I blew him kisses, I *think* he saw me. . . . Listen, I'm not certain, but it looked to me as if his eyes were red. Perhaps his parents forced him to come back home. . . . Perhaps he'll write to me. . . ."

Keep it up, romantic little thing, hope costs nothing. If I tried to dissuade you, you wouldn't believe me.

After five days of loafing about the woods, scratching my arms and legs on brambles, bringing home armfuls of wild pinks, cornflowers and campions, and eating bitter wild cherries and gooseberries, curiosity seized me again and I felt a homesick longing for the School. So I went back to it again.

I found them all—that is the big ones—sitting on benches in the shade, working lazily at "exhibition pieces"; the little ones, under the covered-in part, were in process of splashing each other at the pump; Mademoiselle was in a wicker armchair, her Aimée at her feet on an inverted flower-box, lounging and whispering. At my arrival, Mademoiselle Sergent started and swung round in her seat.

"Ah, there you are! That's lucky! You've certainly taken your time! Mademoiselle Claudine runs wild in the fields without giving a thought to the fact that the prize-giving is approaching and that the pupils don't know a note of the part-song they're supposed to be singing at it!"

"But . . . isn't Mademoiselle Aimée a singing teacher then? Isn't Monsieur Rabastens (Antonin) one either?"

"Don't talk nonsense! You know perfectly well that Mademoiselle Lanthenay can't sing, her voice is too delicate to permit her to. As to Monsieur Rabastens, apparently they've been gossiping in the town about his visits and his singing lessons. Good heavens, what a filthy hole this is for tittle-tattle! The long and short of it is, he won't be coming back. We can't do without you for the part-songs and you take advantage of the fact. This afternoon, at four o'clock, we will divide up the parts and you will copy out the verses on the blackboard."

"*I'm* perfectly willing. What's the song this year?"

"*The Hymn to Nature.* Marie, go and get it—it's on my desk. Claudine is going to begin to din it in to you."

It was a chorus in three parts, the typical kind of thing that schoolgirls sing. The sopranos twittered earnestly:

> *O'er the distant fields they ring.*
> *As the morning hymn they sing,*
> *Echoing sweetly to the sky. . . .*

Meanwhile, the mezzos, echoing the rhymes in "ing", repeat "ding, ding, ding" to imitate the Angelus bell. The audience would love it.

So that delightful life was about to begin; a life consisting in shouting myself hoarse, in singing the same tune three hundred times over, in returning home voiceless, in losing my temper with those little girls who were congenitally lacking in the faintest sense of rhythm. If at least they gave me a present for doing all this!

Anaïs, Luce and a few others luckily had a good aural memory and, after the third repetition, could follow me with their voices. We stopped because Mademoiselle said: "Enough for today"—it would have been too cruel to make us sing for long in that African temperature.

"And, one other thing," added Mademoiselle. "It's forbidden to hum the *Hymn to Nature* between lessons. Otherwise you'll murder it, you'll distort it out of all knowledge and you'll be incapable of singing it properly at the prizegiving. Get on with your needlework now and don't let me hear you talking too loud."

They kept us big ones out-of-doors so that we could execute in greater comfort the marvellous pieces of needlecraft destined for the exhibition of *hand work*! (Could these works be done in any way except "by hand"? I don't know of any "foot work".) For, after the distribution of prizes, the entire town would come and admire the display of our work. Two classrooms would be filled with samples of lace, tapestry and beribboned lingerie laid out on the study-tables. The walls would be hung with open-work curtains, crochet bedspreads mounted on coloured linings, bedside rugs of green wool moss (in brushed-up knitting) dotted with imitation red and pink flowers, also in wool, and with chimney-piece borders in embroidered plush. . . . These grown-up little girls liked the underclothes they displayed to be glamorous, so their main exhibits consisted of sumptuous pieces of lingerie—batiste chemises embroidered with tiny flowers, with marvellous yokes; frilly drawers gartered with ribbons; camisoles scalloped top and bottom—all displayed over linings of red, blue and mauve paper with labels on which the maker's name was inscribed in beautiful round handwriting. All along the walls were ranged stools worked in cross-stitch on which reposed either the horrible cat whose eyes were made of four green stitches with a black one in the middle or the dog with the crimson back and the purplish paws, from whose mouth lolled a turkey-red tongue.

Obviously it was the underclothes that principally interested the boys who came, like everyone else, to see the exhibition. They lingered over the flowered chemises and the beribboned knickers, nudged each other, laughed and whispered monstrous comments.

It is only fair to say that the Boys' School boasted its own exhibition, rivalling our own. If they did not offer exciting lingerie for public admiration, they displayed other marvels; cleverly-turned table-legs, twisted columns (my dear! they're the most difficult of all), samples of woodwork in "dovetailing", cardboard boxes dripping with glue, and, above all, clay models—the joy of the Headmaster who modestly christens this room "*Sculpture Section*"—models which claim to reproduce the friezes of the Parthenon and other bas-reliefs but are all blurred, bloated and pitiable. The *Drawing Section* is no more consoling: the heads of the Brigands of the Abruzzi squint, the King of Rome has a boil, Nero grimaces horribly, and President Loubet in a tricolour frame (woodwork and paste-board combined) obviously wants to be sick (because he's thinking about his minister, explains Dutertre, still furious at not being a Deputy). On the walls, grubby wash-drawings, architectural plans and the "anticipated (*sic*) general view of the Exhibition of 1900"—a water-colour which deserves the prize of honour.

So, during the time that still separates us from the holidays, we shall leave all our books on the shelf, we shall work lazily in the shade of the walls, incessantly washing our hands—a pretext to go for a stroll—so as not to stain light wools and white fabrics—with damp fingers. All I am exhibiting is three pink lawn chemises, cut like a baby's, with matching knickers—closed ones. This last detail scandalises my companions who unanimously find it "indecent"—on my word of honour!

I installed myself between Luce and Anaïs who herself was sitting next to Marie Belhomme for, from force of habit, we keep together in a little group. Poor Marie! She had to work again for the exam in October. . . . Since she was fretting to death in the classroom, Mademoiselle took pity on her and let her come with us; she sat there reading Atlases and Histories of France; when I say "reading"—her book was open on her knees, she bent her head and glanced sideways in our direction, straining her ears to catch everything we said. I could foresee the result of the October exam!

"I'm parched with thirst! Have you got your bottle?" Anaïs asked me.

"No, didn't think of bringing it, but Marie's sure to have hers."

Still another of our immutable, absurd customs, those bottles. As soon as the weather turned really hot, it was agreed that the water in the pump became undrinkable (it is at any season), and each one brought along a bottle of some cool drink at the bottom of her little basket—sometimes in her leather satchel or her canvas bag. There was great rivalry as to who could produce the most fantastic mixture and the most unnatural liquid. No cocoa, that was for the baby class! For us water mixed with vinegar which blanches the lips and gnaws at the stomach; acid lemonades; mint drinks, confected oneself with the fresh leaves of the plant; brandy, pinched from home and thickened with sugar; the astringent juice of green gooseberries that made one's mouth water. The lanky Anaïs bitterly deplored the departure of the chemist's daughter who at one time used to provide us with bottles of spirits of peppermint diluted with far too little water, or sometimes with a patent concoction called eau de Botot. I myself, being a simple nature, confined myself to drinking white wine with a dash of Seltzer water, sugar and a little lemon. Anaïs indulged too freely in vinegar and Marie in extract of liquorice, so concentrated that it was almost black.

As the use of bottles was forbidden, each one, I repeat, brought her own, stoppered with a cork through which was thrust a quill. This arrangement allowed us to drink, by bending forward on the pretext of picking up a cotton-reel, without displacing the bottle lying in its basket, its beak sticking out. At the little quarter-of-an-hour recreation (at half-past nine and half-past three), everyone rushed to the pump to pour water over the bottles and cool them a little. Three years ago, a little girl fell down with her bottle and blinded herself in one eye; her eye is all white now. After this accident, they confiscated all the receptacles, every single one, for the space of a week . . . then, someone brought hers back, an example followed by someone else the next day . . . and, a month later, the bottles were functioning regularly again. Perhaps Mademoiselle did not know of this accident which happened long before her arrival—or else she preferred to shut her eyes so that we should leave her in peace.

Nothing has been happening, to tell the truth. The heat has taken away all our high spirits. Luce besieges me less with her importunate caresses; inclinations to quarrel hardly arise before they die down at once; it is general slackness, of course, and the sudden storms of July that catch us unawares in the playground and sweep us away under tremendous downpours of hail.—An hour later, the sky is cloudless.

We played a wicked joke on Marie Belhomme, who had boasted of coming to school without any drawers on, on account of the heat.

There were four of us, one afternoon, sitting on a bench in the following order:

Marie—Anaïs—Luce—Claudine.

After having had my plan duly explained to them in undertones, my two neighbours got up to wash their hands and the middle of the bench remained empty, leaving Marie at one end and me at the other. She was half asleep over her arithmetic. I got up suddenly; the bench tipped over: Marie, startled awake, fell, her legs in the air, with one of those squawks like a slaughtered hen which are her personal speciality, and showed us . . . that she was, indeed, wearing no drawers. There was an outburst of howls and tremendous laughs; the Headmistress wanted to lecture us but could not, being in fits of laughter herself. Aimée Lanthenay preferred to take herself off so as not to present her pupils with the sight of herself writhing like a poisoned cat.

Dutertre had not been here for ages. He was said to be at some bathing-resort where he was basking in the sun and flirting (but where did he get the money?). I could just see him in white flannels, wearing belts that were too broad and shoes that were too yellow; he adores those rather flashy get-ups. He would look very much of a flashy adventurer himself in those light colours—his face too sun-tanned and his eyes too bright—with his pointed teeth and his black moustache that has a rusty look as if it has been singed. I have never given another thought to his sudden attack in the glass-paned corridor; the impression had been sharp, but short—and besides, with him, one knows perfectly well that it means nothing! I am probably the three hundredth little girl he has tried to lure to his house; the incident is of no interest either to him or to me. It would have been if the attempt had succeeded, that's all.

Already, we were giving a great deal of thought to what we should wear for the prizegiving. Mademoiselle was getting herself a black silk dress embroidered by her mother, an exquisite needlewoman, who was working a design all over it, in satin-stitch; a pattern of big bunches of flowers and slender garlands that ran round the hem of the skirt and branches that climbed over the bodice—all in subtle, muted shades of violet silk. It was an extremely distinguished affair, a little "old-ladyish" perhaps, but impeccably cut. Always dressed in dark, simple things, the chic of our Headmistress's clothes eclipses all the lawyers' and tax-collectors' and shopkeepers' and retired businessmen's wives' in the place! It is her little revenge—the revenge of an ugly woman with an excellent figure.

Mademoiselle Sergent was also concerned about dressing her little Aimée charmingly for this great day. They had ordered samples of stuff from the Louvre and the Bon Marché and the two friends, deeply absorbed, made their selection together in our presence, in the playground where we sat working in the shade. I thought that this was going to be a dress that would not cost Mademoiselle Aimée much; really, she would be very wrong to act otherwise. It was not with her seventy-five francs a month—from which she had to deduct thirty francs for her board (which she did not pay), another thirty for her sister's (which she saved) and twenty francs she sent to her parents, as I knew from Luce—it was not, I declare, with these emoluments that she would pay for the charming dress of white mohair of which I had seen the pattern.

Among the schoolgirls, it was very much the thing not to seem in the least concerned about what one was going to wear for the prizegiving. All of them were brooding over it a month in advance and tormenting their Mammas to be allowed ribbons or lace or at least alterations which would bring last year's dress up to date—but it was considered good taste to say nothing about it. We asked each other with detached curiosity, as if out of politeness: "What's your dress going to be like?" And we appeared hardly to listen to the answer, made in the same off-hand, contemptuous tone.

The gawky Anaïs had asked me the routine question, her eyes elsewhere and her face vacant. With an absentminded look, and sounding quite indifferent, I explained: "Oh, nothing startling . . . white muslin . . . a crossed fichu on the bodice, with the neck cut down to a point . . . and Louis XV sleeves with muslin frill, stopping at the elbows. . . . That's all."

We were always all in white for the prizegiving, but the dresses were trimmed with light ribbons; these rosettes, bows and sashes whose colour, which we insisted on changing every year, greatly preoccupied us.

"The ribbons?" inquired Anaïs in an artificial manner.

(I had been expecting that.)

"White too."

"My dear, a real bride then! You know, lots of them are going to look as black in all that white as fleas on a sheet."

"True. Luckily, white suits me quite well."

(Fume, dear child! Everyone knows that with your yellow skin, you're forced to put red ribbons or orange ones on your white frock so as not to look like a lemon.)

"What about you? Orange ribbons?"

"Goodness, no! I had *them* last year! Louis XV ribbons, striped, in two materials, faille and satin, ivory and scarlet. My dress is cream wool."

"Me," announced Marie Belhomme, who had not been asked anything. "It's white muslin with periwinkle-blue ribbons, a mauvey blue, awfully pretty!"

"Me," said Luce, as usual, nestling in my skirts or crouched in my shadow, "I've got the dress, only I don't know what ribbons to put on it; Aimée would like them blue. . . ."

"Blue? Your sister's a dolt, saving the respect I owe her. With green eyes like yours, one doesn't choose blue ribbons—that sets one's teeth on edge. The hatshop in the square sells very pretty ribbons, in green and white glacé . . . your dress is white?"

"Yes . . . white muslin."

"Good! Now, bully your sister into buying you green ribbons."

"No need to, I'm the one who's buying them."

"Better still. You'll see, you'll look charming; there won't be three who'll dare risk green ribbons, they're too difficult to wear."

That poor kid! At the least kind thing I say to her without meaning to, her face lights up. . . .

Mademoiselle Sergent, in whom the forthcoming exhibition inspired certain anxieties, hustled us and hurried us up; it snowed punishments, punishments that consisted in doing twenty centimetres of lace, a metre of hem or twenty rows of knitting after class. She herself was working, too, at a pair of magnificent muslin curtains which she embroidered very prettily indeed when her Aimée left her time to. That charming sluggard of an Assistant, lazy as a cat as she is, sighed and yawned over fifty tapestry stitches, in front of all the pupils and Mademoiselle told her, without daring to scold her, that "it was a deplorable example to us". Whereupon the *in*subordinate tossed her work in the air, looked at her friend with sparkling eyes and flung herself on her, nibbling her hands. The big ones smiled and nudged each other; the little ones did not raise an eyebrow.

A large paper, bearing the seal of the Prefecture and the stamp of the Town Hall, which Mademoiselle found in the letter-box, has greatly disturbed this morning which happens, for once, to be cool. All heads are busy about it—and all tongues. The Headmistress unfolded it; read it; re-read it, and said nothing. Her giddy little companion, impatient at not being in the know, snatched it with lively, insistent paws and uttered such loud cries of "Ah!"s and "That's going to cause a lot of fuss" that we were violently intrigued and positively palpitating.

"Yes," Mademoiselle said to her, "I was told about it, but I was waiting for the official confirmation; he's a friend of Doctor Dutertre's. . . ."

"But that's not all. You must tell the school, because they're going to hang out the flags, they're going to have illuminations, they're going to have a banquet. . . . Just look at them, they're sizzling with impatience!"

Sizzling? Weren't we just!

"Yes, we must announce it to them. . . . Young ladies, try and listen to me and to take in what I say! The Minister of Agriculture, Monsieur Jean Dupuy, is coming to the main town on the occasion of the forthcoming Agricultural Show, and he will take advantage of this to come and officially open the new schools: the town will be decorated with flags and bunting and illuminated; there will be a reception at the station . . . and now I'm bored with you all—you'll soon know all about it because the town-crier will announce it. Only try and 'get a move on' more than you're doing at the moment so that your samples of work will be ready."

Profound silence. And then babel broke loose! Ejaculations burst out, everyone talked at once and the tumult grew, pierced by a shrill little voice: "Is the Minister going to ask us questions?"

We howled down Marie Belhomme, the duffer who had asked that.

Mademoiselle made us get into line, although it wasn't time yet, and left us screeching and chattering while she went off to sort out her ideas and make arrangements in view of the unheard-of-event which was brewing.

"Old thing, what have *you* got to say about that?" Anaïs asked me in the street.

"I say that our holidays will begin a week earlier. That's no joy to me. I'm bored stiff when I can't come to school."

"But there's going to be celebrations and balls and fun and games in the square."

"Yes, and heaps of people to parade in front of, I know just what's in your mind! You know, we shall be very much in the public eye. Dutertre, who's an intimate friend of the new Minister (it's because of him that this newly-fledged Excellency's risking himself in a hole like Montigny), will put us forward. . . ."

"No! D'you really think so?"

"Definitely! It's a plot he's hatched to get the Deputy pushed out!"

She went off radiant, dreaming of official celebrations during which ten thousand pairs of eyes would contemplate her admiringly!

The town-crier had announced the news: we were promised endless joys; arrival of the ministerial train at nine o'clock; the municipal authorities, the pupils of the two Schools, in fact every most outstanding member of the population of Montigny would await the Minister near the station, at the entrance to the town and would conduct him through the decorated streets to the bosom of the Schools. There, on a platform, he would speak! And in the great reception-room of the Town Hall he would banquet, along with a numerous company. After that, distribution of prizes to grown-up people (for Monsieur Jean Dupuy was bringing along a few little green and purple ribbons for those to whom Dutertre was under an obligation—a master-stroke the latter had brought off). In the evening, a great ball in the banqueting room. The brass band of the principal town of the district (something very special!) would graciously lend its assistance. Finally the Mayor invited the inhabitants to hang out flags and bunting on their dwellings and to decorate them with greenery. Ouf! What an honour for us!

This morning, in class, Mademoiselle solemnly announced to us—we saw at once that great things were brewing—the visit of her dear Dutertre who would give us, with his customary obligingness, ample details about the way in which the ceremony was to be ordered.

Whereupon, he did not come.

It was only in the afternoon, just before four o'clock, at the moment when we were folding away our lace and knitting and tapestry-work into our little baskets that Dutertre arrived, as usual, like a whirlwind, without knocking. I had not seen him since his "attempt"; he had not changed. He was dressed with his usual carefully thought-out negligence—coloured shirt, almost white jacket and trousers, a big, light-coloured, sailor-knotted tie tucked into the cummerbund that served him as a waistcoat. Mademoiselle Sergent, like Anaïs, like Luce, like Aimée Lanthenay, like all of them, found his taste in clothes supremely distinguished.

While he was talking to those ladies, he let his eyes wander in my direction, long eyes, tilting up at the outer corners—the eyes of a vicious animal, which he knew how to make gentle. He won't catch me again letting him take me out into the corridor; those days are over!

"Well, little ones," he exclaimed. "You're pleased to be seeing a Minister?"

We answered in vague, respectful murmurs.

"Attention! You're going to give him an elegant reception at the station, all in white! That's not all, you must offer him bouquets, three of the big ones, one of whom will recite a little compliment; yes, definitely!"

We exchanged looks of feigned shyness and untruthful fright.

"Don't behave like little geese! There must be one in pure white, one in white with blue ribbons, one in white with red ribbons, to symbolise a flag of honour. Eh! Eh! not a bad little flag at all! You're in it, of course, in the flag, you (that was *me*) . . . you're decorative and besides I want you to be seen. What are your ribbons for the prizegiving like?"

"As it happens, this year, I'm white all over."

"That's fine, you little virginal type, you'll be the middle of the flag. And you'll recite a speech to my friend the Minister. He won't be bored looking at you, you know!"

(He was completely crazy to let out things like that here! Mademoiselle Sergent would kill me!)

"Who's got red ribbons?"

"Me!" shrieked Anaïs who was palpitating with hope.

"Right, you then. I'm quite agreeable."

It was a half-lie on the part of Anaïs, who was determined at all costs to be in the picture, since her ribbons were striped.

"Who's got blue ones?"

"Me, S-sir," stammered Marie Belhomme, choking with terror.

"That's fine, you won't make a repulsive trio. By the way, about the ribbons, don't spoil the ship for a ha'porth of tar, let yourselves go, I'm doing the paying! (Hum!) Magnificent sashes, fine dashing bows—and I'm buying you bouquets to match your colours!"

"So far ahead!" I observed. "They'll have plenty of time to get faded."

"Be quiet, you little hoyden, you'll never develop the bump of reverence. I like to think you've already developed two others more pleasantly situated?"

The entire class burst into enthusiastic giggles; Mademoiselle gave a sickly smile. As to Dutertre, I could have sworn he was drunk.

They threw us out before he left. I was bombarded with cries of: "My dear, there's no denying it, you're always the lucky one!" "All the honours for you, as usual!" "It wouldn't have been anyone else, no fear!" I did not answer a word but went off to comfort poor little Luce who was heartbroken at not having been chosen as one of the flag. "There, there, green will suit you better than anything. . . . And, besides, it's your own fault. Why didn't you put yourself forward like Anaïs?"

"Oh," sighed the little thing, "it doesn't matter. I lose my head in front of lots of people and I should have done something silly. But I'm glad that you're reciting the compliment and not that great gawk Anaïs."

Papa, when informed of the glorious part I was to play in the opening of the schools, wrinkled his Bourbon nose and inquired:

"Ye gods! Am I going to have to show myself over there?"

"Certainly not, Papa. You remain in the shadow!"

"Then you really mean I haven't got to bother about you?"

"Really and truly not, Papa. Don't change your usual ways!"

The town and the School are upside down. If it goes on like this, I shall no longer have time to describe anything in my diary. This morning we were in class by seven o'clock, though class was hardly the word! The Headmistress had had enormous parcels of tissue-paper sent over from the main town; pink, pastel blue, red, yellow and white. In the central classroom, we gutted the parcels—the biggest girls were constituted chief assistants—and off we went, counting the huge flimsy sheets, folding them in six lengthwise, cutting them into six strips and tying these strips in little bundles which were carried to Mademoiselle's desk. She scalloped them along the edges with pinking-shears, then Mademoiselle Aimée distributed them to the entire First Class and the entire Second Class. Nothing to the Third; those kids were too little—they would ruin the paper, the pretty paper of which every strip would become a crumpled, bloated rose at the end of a wire stalk.

We lived in a state of ecstasy! Text-books and exercise-books slept in closed desks and it was a question of who could get up first and rush off at once to the School, now transformed into a florist's workroom.

I no longer lingered lazily in bed and I was in such a hurry to get there in good time that I fastened my belt in the street. Sometimes we were all assembled in the classrooms already when their Lady-ships came down at last. They were taking things easy too, in the matter of costume! Mademoiselle Sergent displayed herself in a red cotton dressing-gown (without any corsets, proudly); her winsome assistant followed her, in bedroom slippers, her eyes sleepy and tender. The atmosphere has become completely homely; the day before yesterday, Mademoiselle Aimée, having washed her hair, appeared in the morning with her hair down and still damp. Her golden hair was as fine as silk, rather short and curling softly at the ends; she looked like a scamp of a little page and her Headmistress, her kind Headmistress, devoured her with her eyes.

The playground was deserted; the drawn serge curtains enveloped us in a blue, fantastic twilight. We made ourselves comfortable; Anaïs left off her apron and turned up her sleeves like a pastry-cook; little Luce, who hopped and ran behind me all day long, had pulled up her dress and her petticoat like a washerwoman, a pretext for displaying her rounded calves and slender ankles. Mademoiselle, moved to pity, had allowed Marie Belhomme to shut away her books. Wearing a linen blouse with black and white stripes and looking, as usual, rather like a Pierrot, she flapped around with us, cutting the strips crooked, making mistakes, catching her feet in the wire, in utter despair or swooning with joy all in the same minute, but so gentle and inoffensive that we didn't even tease her.

Mademoiselle Sergent stood up and with a brusque gesture, drew the curtain on the side that overlooked the boys' playground. We could hear, from the school opposite, the braying of harsh, badly-pitched young voices; it was Monsieur Rabastens teaching his pupils a Republican song. Mademoiselle waited a moment or two, then waved her arm. The obliging Antonin promptly came running up, bareheaded, with a La France rose adorning his buttonhole.

"Would you be kind enough to send two of your boys over to the workshop and make them cut this brass-wire into lengths of twenty-five centimetres?"

"Rright away, Mademoiselle! Are you still working at your flowers?"

"We shan't be finished for a long time; it needs five thousand roses for the school alone and we're also commissioned to decorate the banqueting room!"

Rabastens went off, running bareheaded under the ferocious sun. A quarter of an hour later, there was a knock on our door which opened to admit two big boobies of fourteen or fifteen, bringing back the lengths of wire. Not knowing what to do with their lanky bodies, they stood there, red-faced and stupid, excited to find themselves in the midst of fifty little girls who, bare-necked and bare-armed, with their bodices undone, laughed mischievously at the two boys. Anaïs brushed against them in passing, I gently stuffed serpentine trails of paper into their pockets; they escaped at last, both pleased and sorry, while Mademoiselle was prodigal of "Shs's" to which we paid scant attention.

Along with Anaïs, I was a folder and cutter; Luce tied up the bundles and carried them to the Headmistress; Marie put them in a heap. At eleven in the morning, we left everything and formed into a group to rehearse the *Hymn to Nature*. Towards five o'clock, we smartened ourselves up a little; tiny mirrors emerged from pockets; some smaller fry of the Second Class obligingly stretched their black aprons behind the panes of an open window and, in front of this sombre looking-glass, we put on our hats again, I fluffed up my curls, Anaïs pinned up her collapsing chignon, and we went off home.

The town was beginning to be as stirred-up as we were; just think, Monsieur Jean Dupuy was arriving in six days' time! The boys went off in the morning in carts, singing at the top of their lungs and whipping the sorry steed in the shafts with all their might. They went out into the municipal wood—and into private woods too, I'm quite sure—to choose their trees and mark them; firs in particular, elms and velvety-leaved aspens would perish in hundreds; at all costs, honour must be done to this newly-made Minister! In the evening, in the square and on the pavements, the girls crumpled paper roses and sang to attract the boys to come and help them. Good heavens, how they must speed the task! I could see them from here, going at it with both hands!

Carpenters removed the mobile screens from the great room in the Town Hall where the banquet was to be held; a huge platform sprouted in the courtyard. The district Doctor-Superintendent Dutertre made brief and frequent appearances, approved everything that was being built, slapped the men on the back, chucked the women under the chin, stood drinks all round and disappeared, soon to return. Happy countryside! During this time, the woods were ravaged, poaching went on day and night, there were brawls in the taverns and a cow-girl at Chêne-Fendu gave her newborn child to the pigs to eat. (After a few days, they stopped the prosecution; Dutertre having succeeded in proving that the girl was not responsible for her actions. . . . Already, no one bothered any more about the affair.) Thanks to these methods, he was poisoning the countryside but, out of a couple of hundred scoundrels, he had constituted himself a bodyguard who would murder and die for him. He would be made a Deputy. What else mattered!

As for us, good heavens! *We* made roses. Five or six thousand roses is no light matter. The little ones' class was busy to the last child making garlands of pleated paper in pastel colours which would float all over the place at the whim of the breeze. Mademoiselle was afraid that these preparations would not be finished in time and gave us provisions of tissue paper and wire to take away every afternoon when school was over. We worked at home, after dinner, before dinner, without respite: the tables in all our houses were loaded with roses—white, blue, red, pink and yellow ones—full-blown, crisp and fresh on the end of their stalks. They took up so much room that one didn't know where to put them; they over-flowed everywhere, blooming in multi-coloured heaps, and we carried them back in the morning in sheaves, looking as if we were going to wish relatives a happy birthday.

The Headmistress, bubbling over with ideas, also wants to construct a triumphal arch at the entrance to the Schools: the side-pillars are to be built up with pine-branches and dishevelled greenery, stuck with quantities of roses. The pediment is to bear this inscription, in letters of pink roses on a ground of moss:

WELCOME TO OUR VISITORS!

Charming, isn't it?

I've had my inspiration too: I have suggested the idea of crowning the flag—meaning us three—with flowers.

"Oh, yes," Anaïs and Marie Belhomme screeched delightedly.

"That's fixed then. (Hang the expense!) Anaïs, you'll be crowned with poppies; Marie, you'll be diademmed with cornflowers and, as for me, whiteness, candour, purity, I shall wear . . ."

"What? Orange blossom?"

"I've still a right to it, Miss! More than *you* have, no doubt!"

"Do lilies seem immaculate enough to you?"

"You make me *sick*! I shall choose marguerites; you know perfectly well the tricolour bouquet is made up of marguerites, poppies and cornflowers. Let's go down to the milliner's."

Looking disdainful and superior, we made our choice. The milliner took our head measurements and promised "the very best that could be made".

The next day we received three wreaths which grieved me to the heart; diadems that bulged in the middle like the ones country brides wear; how on earth could one look pretty in that? Marie and Anaïs, enraptured, tried theirs on in the midst of an admiring circle of juniors; *I* said nothing, but I took my accessory home where I quietly took it to pieces. Then, on the same wire frame, I recon-structed a fragile, slender wreath with the big, starry marguerites placed as if by chance, ready to drop away; two or three flowers hung in bunches about my ears, a few trailed behind in my hair; then I tried my creation on my head. I'm only telling you that much! No danger of my letting the two others in on it!

An additional job has descended on us: the curl-papers! You don't know, you couldn't be expected to know. Learn then that, at Montigny, a schoolgirl could not assist at a prizegiving, or at any solemnity, without being duly curled or waved. Nothing strange in that, certainly, although those stiff corkscrews and excessive twistings make the hair resemble teasled brooms more than anything else. But the Mammas of all these little girls, seamstresses, women market-gardeners, wives of labourers and shopkeepers have neither the time, nor the wish, nor the skill to put all those heads in curl-papers. Guess to whom this work, sometimes far from appetising, reverts? To the teachers and to the pupils of the First Class! Yes, it's crazy, but you see it's the custom and that word is the answer to everything. A week before the prizegiving, juniors badger us and inscribe themselves on our lists. Five or six for each of us, at least! And for one clean head with pretty, supple hair, how many greasy manes—not to mention inhabited ones!

Today we began to put these creatures, ranging from eight to eleven years old, in curl-papers. Squatting on the ground, they abandoned their heads to us and, for curlers, we used pages from our old exercise-books. This year, I was only willing to accept four victims and chosen, moreover, among the clean ones; each of the other big girls was being hairdresser to six little ones! A far from easy job, since nearly all girls in the country round here possess great bushy manes. At midday, we summoned our docile flock: I began with a fair-haired little thing with fluffy hair that curled softly by nature.

"Why, whatever are you doing here? With hair like that, you want me to frizz it in curl-papers? It would be a massacre!"

"Fancy! But of *course* I want it curled for me! Not curled, on a Prizeday, on a day a Minister's coming! Whoever heard of such a thing!"

"You'll be as ugly as the fourteen deadly sins! You'll have stiff hair, sticking out all round your head like a scarecrow. . . ."

"I don't care. At least, I'll be curled."

Since she insisted! And to think they all felt as she did! I was prepared to bet that Marie Belhomme herself . . .

"I say, Marie, you who've got natural corkscrews, I'm sure *you'll* stay as you are, won't you?"

She screeched with indignation at the idea:

"Me? Stay as I am? Don't you think it! I'd arrive at the prizegiving with a flat head!"

"But *I'm* not going to frizz myself."

"My dear, you curl tight enough. And besides your hair goes into a "cloud" quite easily . . . and besides everyone knows your ideas are never the same as everyone else's."

As she spoke she was vivaciously—too vivaciously—rolling the long locks, the colour of ripe wheat, of the little girl who was sitting in front of her, buried in her hair—a bush from which there occasionally issued shrill squeaks.

Anaïs, not without deliberate malice, was maltreating her patient, who was howling.

"Well, she's got too much hair, this one," she said, by way of excuse. "When you think you've finished, you're only half-way. You wanted it—you're here—try not to scream!"

We curled, we curled . . . the glass-paned corridor was filled with the rustle of the folded paper we twisted into the hair. . . . Our work achieved, the juniors stood up with a sigh of relief and displayed heads bristling with wisps of paper on which one could still read "Problems . . . morals . . . Duc de Richelieu . . ." During the next four days they will go about the streets and the School, looking utter little frumps, without the least shame. But it's the custom and that's that.

. . . Our life had become completely disorganised. We were always out-of-doors, trotting hither and thither, carrying home or bringing back roses, begging—we four, Anaïs, Marie, Luce and I—requisitioning flowers, real ones this time, to decorate the banqueting-hall. Sent by Mademoiselle, who counted on our innocent young faces to disarm the conventional, we went into the houses of people we had never seen. It was thus we paid a visit to Paradis, the Registrar, because rumour accused him of being the possessor of dwarf rose-trees, little marvels. All shyness gone, we burst into his peaceful office with: "Good morning, Monsieur!

We've been told you have some lovely rose-trees, it's for the flower-stands in the banqueting-hall, you know, we've been sent by etc., etc." The poor man muttered something into his great beard and led us out, armed with a pair of secateurs. We departed with our arms loaded with pots of flowers, laughing, chattering, cheekily answering back the people who, at the entrance to each street, were all busy erecting the framework of triumphal arches. They called out to us: "Hi! You nice little pieces, there! Want someone to lend a hand? We'll find you one, all right. . . . Hoy! look out! There's one just going to fall! You're losing something, pick it up!" Everyone knew each other; everyone addressed each other familiarly as "*tu*". . . .

Today and yesterday, the boys went off in the carts at dawn and did not come back till sunset, buried under branches of box, larch and *arbor vitae*, under cartloads of green moss that smelt of the bogs; afterwards they went off drinking, as usual. I have never seen these gangs of ruffians in such a state of excitement; normally they don't care a fig about anything, even politics. Now they emerged from their woods, their hovels, from the bushes where they spied on the girls who looked after the cows, to embower Jean Dupuy! It was beyond all comprehension! Louchard's gang, six or seven ne'er-do-wells who had pillaged the forests, went by, singing, invisible under heaps of ivy that trailed behind them, rustling softly.

The streets fought among themselves in rivalry; the Rue du Cloître erected three triumphal arches because the Grande-Rue had planned two, one at each end. But the Grande-Rue, put on its mettle, constructed a marvellous affair, a medieval castle, all in pine-branches trimmed even with shears, with pepper-pot turrets. The Rue des Fours-Barraux, just by the School, came under the rural-arty influence of Mademoiselle Sergent. It confined itself to covering the houses on either side with a complete tapestry of long-tressed, dishevelled branches and then putting battens across from each house to the one opposite and covering this roof with hanging masses of intertwining ivy. The result was a delicious arbour, dusky and green, in which voices were muted as if in a thickly-curtained room; people walked to and fro under it for sheer pleasure. Furious at this, the Rue du Cloître lost all restraint and linked its three triumphal arches together with clusters of mossy garlands stuck with flowers so as to have *its* arbour too. Whereupon, the Grande-Rue calmly set to and took up its pavements and erected, in their stead, a wood! Yes, honestly, a real little wood on either side with young trees that had been uprooted and replanted. It would only have needed a fortnight of this furious emulation for everyone to be cutting each other's throats.

The masterpiece, the jewel, was our School—rather our Schools. When it was all finished, not a square inch of wall would be visible under the greenery, the flowers and the flags. Mademoiselle had requisitioned an army of young men; the bigger boys and the assistant-masters, all of whom she directed with a rod of iron; they obeyed her without a murmur. The triumphal arch at the entrance had now seen the light of day; standing on ladders, the two mistresses and the four of us had spent three hours "writing" in pink roses on the pediment:

WELCOME TO OUR VISITORS

while the boys amused themselves by ogling our calves. From up above, from the roofs and windows and all the rough surfaces of the walls, there flowed and rippled such a cascade of branches, of red, white and blue material, of ropes masked with ivy, of hanging greenery and trailing roses that the huge building seemed to undulate from base to summit in the light wind and to be gently swaying. You entered the School by lifting a rustling curtain of flower-decked ivy and the fairy-like atmosphere continued inside. Ropes of roses outlined the corners, were festooned from wall to wall and hung at the windows: it was adorable.

In spite of our activity, in spite of our bold incursions on garden-owners, this morning we saw ourselves on the point of being short of flowers. General consternation! Curl-papered heads bent forward agitatedly around Mademoiselle who was brooding, with knitted brows.

"All the same, I've got to have some!" she exclaimed. "The whole stand on the left hasn't any at all; we must have flowers in pots. You Rovers, come here at once!"

"Here, Mademoiselle!"

We sprang up, all four of us (Anaïs, Marie, Luce, Claudine); we sprang forth from the buzzing throng, ready to dash away.

"Listen. You're to go and see old Caillavaut. . . ."

"Oh! ! ! . . ."

We hadn't let her finish. You must realise that old Caillavaut is a miser, a regular Harpagon, slightly mad, spiteful as the plague and immensely rich. He owns a magnificent house and grounds which no one is allowed to enter but himself and his gardener. He is feared for being extremely malicious, hated for being a miser and respected as a living mystery. And Mademoiselle wanted us to go and ask him for flowers! She couldn't have realised what she was doing!

". . . Now, now, now! anyone would think I was sending off lambs to the slaughterhouse! You'll soften his gardener's heart and you won't even *see* old Caillavaut himself. Anyway, what if you do? You've got legs to run away with, haven't you? Off you go!"

I took the three others off, though they were far from enthusiastic, for I was conscious of a burning desire, tinged with vague apprehension, to penetrate into this old maniac's domain. I urged them on: "Come on, Luce, come on, Anaïs! We're going to see terrific things, we'll be able to tell the others all about it . . . Why, they can be counted on the fingers of one hand, the people who've been inside old Caillavaut's place!"

Confronted with the great green door, where flowering, over-scented acacias overhung the wall, no one dared to pull the bell-chain. Finally, I gave it a violent tug, thereby setting off a terrifying tocsin; Marie took three steps towards flight, and Luce, trembling, hid bravely behind me. Nothing happened; the door remained shut. A second attempt was equally unsuccessful. I then lifted the latch, which yielded, and, like mice, we crept in one by one, uneasily, leaving the door ajar. A great gravel courtyard, beautifully kept, lay in front of the fine white house whose shutters were closed against the sun; the courtyard expanded into a green garden, rendered deep and mysterious by its thick clumps of trees. . . . Rooted to the spot, we stared without daring to move; still no one to be seen and not a sound. To the right of the house were greenhouses, closed and full of marvellous plants. . . . The stone staircase widened out gently as it descended to the level of the gravel courtyard; on each step there were flaming geraniums, calceolarias with little tiger-striped bellies, dwarf rose-trees that had been forced into too much bloom.

The obvious absence of any owner restored my courage.

"I say, are you coming or not? We're not going to take root in the gardens of the Sleeping-Miser-in-the-Wood!"

"Ssh!" whispered Marie in terror.

"What d'you mean, ssh? On the contrary, we must call out! Hi, over there! Monsieur Caillavaut! Gardener!"

No answer; all remained silence. I went over to the greenhouses, and, pressing my face against the panes, I tried to make out what was inside; a kind of dark emerald forest, dotted with splashes of brilliant colour that must certainly be exotic flowers. . . .

The door was locked.

"Let's go," whispered Luce, ill at ease.

"Let's go," repeated Marie, even more anxious.

"Suppose the old man jumped out from behind a tree!"

This idea made them flee towards the door; I called them back at the top of my voice.

"Don't be such dolts! You can see there isn't anyone here. Listen . . . you're each going to choose two or three pots, the best ones on the stone steps. We'll carry them off back there, without saying anything and I think we'll have a huge success!"

They did not budge; definitely tempted, but nervous. I seized two clumps of "Venus' slippers", speckled like tit's eggs, and I made a sign that I was waiting. Anaïs decided to imitate me and loaded herself with two double geraniums; Marie imitated Anaïs, Luce too, and we all four walked discreetly away. Near the door, absurd terror seized us again; we crowded each other like sheep in the narrow opening of the door and we ran all the way to the School where Mademoiselle welcomed us with cries of joy. All at once, we recounted our Odyssey. The Headmistress, startled, remained in perplexity for a moment, then concluded light-heartedly:

"Well, well, we shall see! After all, it's only a loan . . . a slightly forced one." We've never, never heard one mention of it since, but old Caillavaut has put up a bristling defence of spikes and broken tiles on his walls (this theft earned us a certain prestige; they're connoisseurs in brigandage here). Our flowers were placed in the front row and then, goodness me!, in the whirlwind of the ministerial arrival, we completely forgot to return them; they now embellish Mademoiselle's garden.

For a good long time now, this garden has been the one single subject of discord between Mademoiselle and that great fat woman, her mother. The latter, who has remained an out-and-out peasant, digs, weeds, tracks snails to their last retreats and has no other ideal than to grow beds of cabbages, beds of leaks, beds of potatoes—enough to feed all the boarders without buying anything, in fact. Her daughter's refined nature dreams of deep arbours, flowering shrubs, pergolas wreathed in honeysuckle—in short, of useless plants! As a result, one could alternately see Mother Sergent giving contemptuous hacks with her hoe at the little lacquer-trees and weeping birches and Mademoiselle stamping an irritated heel on the borders of sorrel and the odorous chives. This battle convulses us with joy. I must be just and also admit that, everywhere else except in the garden and in the kitchen, Madame Sergent effaces herself completely, never pays us a visit, never gives her opinion in discussions and bravely wears her goffered peasant's bonnet.

The most amusing thing, in the few hours that now remained to us, was arriving at the School and going home again through the unrecognisable streets, transformed into forest paths and parklike landscapes, all fragrant with the penetrating smell of cut firs. It was as if the woods that encircled Montigny had invaded it, had come in and almost buried it. . . . One could not have dreamed of a prettier, more becoming decoration for this little town lost among the trees . . . I cannot bring myself to say more "adequate", it's a word I simply loathe.

The flags, which will make all these green alleys ugly and commonplace, will all be in place tomorrow, not to mention the Venetian lanterns and the fairy-lights. What a pity!

No one felt embarrassed with us; the women and boys called out to us as we passed: "Hi! you there, you've got the trick of it! Come on, come and 'elp us a bit sticking in these roses!"

We "'elped" willingly. We climbed up ladders: my companions let themselves—all for the Minister's sake, of course!—be tickled around the waist and sometimes on the calves: I must say that no one ever allowed themselves those little pranks on the daughter of the "Gentleman of the slugs". In any case, with these boys who don't give it another thought once their hand is removed, it's inoffensive and not even annoying; I can understand the girls from the School falling in with the general behaviour. Anaïs allowed all liberties and yearned after still more; Féfed carried her down from the top of the ladder in his arms. Touchard, known as Zero, stuffed prickly branches of pine under her skirts; she gave little squeaks, like a mouse caught in a door, and half closed swooning eyes, without strength even to pretend to put up a defence.

Mademoiselle let us rest a little, for fear we should be too limp and tired on the great day. Besides, I really could not see what remained to be done; everything was decked with flowers, everything was in place; the cut flowers were soaking their stalks in buckets of cool water in the cellar; they would be scattered all over the place at the last moment. Our three bouquets arrived this morning in a big, fragile packing-case; Mademoiselle did not want us even to unnail it completely: she removed one slat, and slightly lifted up the tissue-paper which shrouded the patriotic flowers and the cotton-wool from which came a damp smell: then old Madame Sergent promptly took the light case, in which rattled crystals of some salt that I don't know and that prevents flowers from fading, down to the cellar.

Nursing her principal subjects, the Headmistress sent us off, Anaïs, Marie, Luce and me, to rest in the garden under the hazels. Slumped in the shade on the green bench, our minds were almost blank; the garden hummed. As if stung by a fly, Marie Belhomme gave a start and suddenly began to unwind one of the big curl-papers that, for three days, had been quivering round her head.

". . . 't 'you doing?"

"Seeing if it's curled, of course!"

"And supposing it isn't curled enough?"

"Why, I'll wet it tonight when I go to bed. But you can see—it's very curly—it's fine!"

Luce followed her example and gave a little cry of disappointment.

"Oh! It's as if I hadn't done anything to it at all! It corkscrews at the end, and nothing at all higher up—or next to nothing!"

She had, in fact, the kind of hair that is supple and soft as silk and that escapes and slips out of one's fingers and out of ribbons and will only do what it wants to do.

"So much the better," I told her. "That'll teach you. Look at you . . . thoroughly miserable at not having a head like a bottle-brush!"

But she refused to be comforted, and, as I was weary of their voices, I went further off and lay down on the gravel, in the shade of the chestnut trees. I hadn't any distinct notions in my head; I was aware only of heat, of lassitude. . . .

My dress was ready, it was a success . . . I should look pretty tomorrow, prettier than the gawky Anaïs, prettier than Marie: that wasn't difficult, but it pleased me all the same. . . . I was going to leave school; Papa was sending me to Paris to a rich, childless aunt; I should make my début in the world, and a thousand blunders at the same time. . . . How should I do without the country, with this hunger for green, growing things that never left me? It seemed insane to me to think that I should never come here again, that I should never see Mademoiselle any more, or her little Aimée with the golden eyes, or the scatterbrained Marie, or the bitch Anaïs, or Luce, always greedy for blows and caresses. . . . I should be unhappy at not living here any more. Moreover, now that I had the time, I might as well admit something to myself; that, in my heart of hearts, Luce attracted me more than I liked to own. It's no good reminding myself that she has hardly any real beauty, that her caressing ways are those of a treacherous little animal, that her eyes are deceitful; none of this prevents her from possessing a charm of her own, the charm of oddity and weakness and still innocent perversity—as well as a white skin, slender hands, rounded arms and tiny feet. But she will never know anything about it! She suffers on account of her sister whom Mademoiselle Sergent took away from me by main force. Rather than admit anything, I would cut out my tongue!

Under the hazels, Anaïs was describing her dress for tomorrow to Luce. I walked towards them, in an ill-natured mood, and I heard:

"The collar? There isn't any collar! It's open in a V in front and at the back, edged with a runner of silk muslin and finished with a cabbage-bow of red ribbon. . . ."

" 'Red cabbages, known as curly cabbages, demand a meagre, stony soil'; the ineffable Bérillon teaches us. That fills the bill perfectly, eh, Anaïs? Scarlet runners, cabbages . . . that's not a dress, it's a kitchen-garden."

"My lady Claudine, if you've come here to say such witty things, you can stay on your gravel. We weren't pining for your company!"

"Don't get in a temper. Tell us how the skirt's made, what vegetables are being used to give it a relish? I can see it from here—there's a fringe of parsley all round!"

Luce was highly amused; Anaïs wrapped herself in her dignity and stalked off; as the sun was getting low, we got up too.

Just as we were shutting the garden gate, we heard bursts of silvery laughter. They came nearer and Mademoiselle Aimée passed us, giggling, as she ran, pursued by the amazing Rabastens who was pelting her with flowers fallen from the bignonia bush. This ceremonial opening by the Minister authorises pleasant liberties in the streets—and in the School too, apparently! But Mademoiselle followed behind, frowning and turning pale with jealousy: further on, we heard her call out: "Mademoiselle Lanthenay, I've asked you twice whether you've told your class to assemble at half-past seven." But the other, in wild spirits, enchanted to be playing with a man and annoying her friend, ran on without stopping and the purple flowers caught in her hair and glanced off her dress. . . . There would be a scene tonight.

At five o'clock, the two ladies assembled us with considerable difficulty, scattered all over the building as we were. The Headmistress decided to ring the dinner-bell, thereby interrupting a furious galop that Anaïs, Marie, Luce and I were dancing in the banqueting-room under the flower-decked ceiling.

"Girls," she cried, in the voice she used for great occasions, "you're to go home at once and get to bed in good time! Tomorrow morning, at half-past seven, you're all to be assembled here, dressed and your hair done, so that we don't have to bother about you any more! You will be given your streamers and banners; Claudine, Anaïs and Marie will take their bouquets. . . . All the rest . . . you'll see when you get here. Be off with you now, don't ruin the flowers as you go through the doors and don't let me hear so much as a mention of you till tomorrow morning!"

She added:

"Mademoiselle Claudine, you know your complimentary speech?"

"Do I know it! Anaïs has made me rehearse it three times today."

"But . . . what about the prizegiving?" risked a timid voice.

"Oh! the prizegiving, we'll fit that in when we can! In any case, it's probable that I shall just give you the books here and that this year there will be no public prizegiving, on account of the opening."

"But . . . the songs, the *Hymn to Nature*?"

"You'll sing them tomorrow, before the Minister. Now, vanish!"

This speech had caused consternation to quite a number of little girls who looked forward to the prizegiving, as a unique festive occasion in the year; they went off perplexed and discontented, under arches of flower-decked greenery.

The people of Montigny, exhausted but proud, were taking a rest, sitting on their doorsteps and contemplating their labours; the girls used the rest of the dying day to sew on a ribbon or to put some lace round an improvised low neck—for the great ball at the Town Hall, my dear!

Tomorrow morning, as soon as it was light, the boys would strew the route of the procession with cut grass and green leaves, mingled with flowers and rose-petals. And if the Minister Jean Dupuy wasn't satisfied, he must be extremely hard to please, so he could go to blazes!

The first thing I did when I got up this morning was to run to the looking-glass; goodness, one never knew, suppose I'd grown a boil overnight? Reassured, I made my toilet very carefully: I was admirably early, it was only six o'clock: I had time to be meticulous over every detail. Thanks to the dryness of the air, my hair went easily into a "cloud". My small face is always rather pale and peaky, but, I assure you, my eyes and mouth are not at all bad. The dress rustled lightly; the underskirt of plain unspotted muslin, swayed to the rhythm of my walk and brushed softly against my pointed shoes. Now for the wreath. Ah, how well it suited me! A little Ophelia, hardly more than a child, with those amusing dark shadows round the eyes! . . . Yes, they used to tell me, when I was little, that I had a grown-up person's eyes; later, it was eyes that were "not quite respectable": you can't please everyone and yourself as well. I prefer to please myself first of all. . . .

The tiresome thing was that tight round bouquet which was going to ruin the whole effect. Pooh! it didn't matter since I was to hand it over to His Excellency. . . .

All white from head to foot, I set off to the School through the cool streets; the boys, in process of "strewing" called out coarse, monstrous compliments to the "little bride" who fled in shyness.

I arrived ahead of time, but I found about fifteen of the juniors already there, little things from the surrounding countryside and the distant farms; they were used to getting up at four in summer. They were comical and touching; their heads looked enormous with their hair frizzed out in harsh twists and they remained standing up so as not to crumple their muslin dresses, rinsed out in too much blue, that swelled out stiffly from waists encircled by currant-red or indigo sashes. Against all this white their sunburnt faces appeared quite black. My arrival had provoked a little "ah!" from them, hastily suppressed. Now they stood silent, greatly awed by their fine clothes and their frizzed hair, rolling an elegant handkerchief, on which their mother had poured some "smell-nice", in their white-cotton-gloved hands.

Our two lady mistresses had not appeared but, from the upper floor, I could hear little footsteps running. . . . Into the playground came pouring a host of white clouds, beribboned in pink, in red, in green and in blue; in ever-increasing numbers the girls arrived—silent for the most part, because they were extremely busy eyeing each other, comparing themselves and pinching their lips disdainfully. They looked like a camp of female Gauls, those flying, curly, frizzy, overflowing manes, nearly all of them golden. . . . A clattering troop poured down the staircase; it was the boarders—always a hostile and isolated band—for whom their First Communion dresses still did duty on festive occasions. Behind them came Luce, dainty as a white Persian, charming with her soft, fluttering curls and her complexion like a newly-opened rose. Didn't she only need a happy love-affair, like her sister, to make her altogether beautiful?

"How lovely you look, Claudine! And your wreath isn't a bit like the two others. Oh, you *are* lucky to be so pretty!"

"But, kitten, do you know I find *you* amusing and desirable in your green ribbons? You certainly are an extremely odd little animal! Where's your sister and her Mademoiselle?"

"Not ready yet. Aimée's dress does up under the arm, just fancy! It's Mademoiselle who's hooking it up for her."

"I see. That may take quite a time."

From above, the voice of the elder sister called: "Luce, come and fetch the pennants!"

The playground was filled with big and little girls and all this white, in the sunlight, hurt one's eyes. (Besides, there were too many different whites that clashed with each other.)

There was Liline, with her disturbing Gioconda smile under her golden waves, and her sea-green eyes; and that young beanpole of a "Maltide", covered to the hips in a cascade of hair the colour of ripe corn; there was the Vignale family, five girls ranging from eight to fourteen, all tossing exuberant manes that looked as if they had been dyed with henna. There was Nannette, a little slyboots with knowing eyes, walking on two deep blonde plaits as long as herself and as heavy as dull gold—and so many, many others. Under the dazzling light, all these fleeces of hair blazed like burning bushes.

Marie Belhomme arrived, appetising in her cream frock and blue ribbons, quaint under the crown of cornflowers. But, good heavens, how big her hands were under the white kid!

At last, here came Anaïs and I sighed with relief to see how awful her hair looked in stiff, corrugated waves; her wreath of crimson poppies, too close to her forehead, made her complexion look like a corpse's. With touching accord, Luce and I ran to meet her and burst out into a concert of compliments: "My dear, how nice you look! Honest, my dear—*definitely*—there's nothing so becoming to you as red! It's a complete success!"

A little mistrustful at first, Anaïs dilated with pleasure and we staged a triumphal entry into the classroom where the children, their numbers now complete, greeted the living *tricolore* flag with an ovation.

A religious silence descended: we were watching our two mistresses walk slowly and deliberately, step by step, down the stairs, followed by two or three boarders loaded with pennants on the end of long, gilded lances. As to Aimée, frankly I have to admit it; one could have eaten her alive, she was so attractive in her white dress of glistening mohair (merely a slim sheath with no seam at the back!) and her rice-straw hat trimmed with white gauze. Away with you, little monster!

And Mademoiselle looked at her with fond, brooding eyes, moulded, herself, in the black dress embroidered with mauve sprays that I have already described to you. *She* can never be pretty, that bad-tempered Redhead, but her dress fitted her like a glove and one was only aware of the eyes that sparkled from under the fiery waves crowned by an extremely smart black hat.

"Where is the flag?" she demanded at once.

The flag came forward, modest and pleased with itself.

"That's good! That's . . . very good! Come here, Claudine . . . I knew you'd be at your best. And now, seduce that Minister for me!"

She rapidly reviewed her white battalion, arranged a curl here, pulled a ribbon there, did up Luce's skirt which was gaping, slid a reinforcing hairpin into Anaïs's chignon and, having scrutinised everything with her redoubtable eye, seized the bundle of various inscriptions: *Long live France! Long live the Republic! Long live Liberty!*

Long live the Minister! . . . etc., twenty pennants in all which she distributed to Luce, to the Jauberts, to various chosen souls who crimsoned with pride and held the shaft upright like a candle, envied by the mere mortals who were fuming.

Our three bouquets, tied with a shower of red, white and blue ribbons, were taken with infinite precautions out of their cotton-wool-like jewels. Dutertre had used the money of the secret funds to advantage; I received a bunch of white camellias, Anaïs one of red camellias; the big bouquet of great velvety cornflowers fell to Marie's share, since nature, not having foreseen ministerial receptions, had neglected to produce blue camellias. The little ones pushed forward to see and already slaps were being exchanged, along with shrill complaints.

"That's enough!" cried Mademoiselle. "Do you think I've got time to be a policeman? Come here, flag! Marie on the left, Anaïs on the right, Claudine in the middle, and forward march. Hurry up and get down into the playground! It would be a fine thing if we missed the arrival of the train! Banner-bearers, follow in fours, the tallest in front. . . ."

We descended the steps into the courtyard without waiting to hear more; Luce and the tallest ones walked behind us, the pennants of their lances flapped lightly above our heads; followed by a trampling like sheep, we passed under the arch of greenery—WELCOME TO OUR VISITORS!

The whole crowd which awaited us outside, a crowd in its Sunday best, excited and ready to shout "Long live—it doesn't matter what!" let out a huge "Ah!" at the sight of us, as if we were fireworks. Proud as little peacocks, our eyes lowered, but inwardly bursting with vanity, we walked delicately, our bouquets in our clasped hands, treading on the strewn leaves and flowers that kept down the dust. It was only after some minutes that we exchanged sidelong looks and rapturous smiles, in a daze of bliss.

"We're having a gorgeous time!" sighed Marie, gazing at the green paths along which we proceeded slowly between two hedges of gaping onlookers, under the leafy arches which filtered the sunshine, letting a charming, artificial daylight sift through, as if in the depths of a wood.

"We certainly are! You'd think all the festivities were for us!"

Anaïs did not breathe a word, too absorbed in her dignity, too busy searching out among the crowd, that made way before us, for boys whom she knew and whom she thought she was dazzling. Not beautiful today, nevertheless, in all that white—no, certainly *not* beautiful! . . . but her narrow eyes sparkled with pride all the same. At the cross-roads of the Market, they shouted to us: "Halt!" We had to let ourselves be joined by the boys' school, a whole dark procession which was only kept in regular ranks with infinite difficulty. The boys seemed thoroughly contemptible to us today, sunburnt and awkward in their best suits; their great, clumsy hands held up flags.

During the halt, we all three turned round, in spite of our importance: behind us Luce and her like leant like warriors on the spears of their pennants; the little thing was radiant with vanity and held herself straight, like Fanchette when she is showing off; she kept laughing low from sheer pleasure! And, as far as eye could see, under the green arches, with their starched, full-skirted dresses and their bushy manes, stretched the deep ranks of the army of female Gauls.

"Forward march!" We set off again, light as wrens; we went down the Rue du Cloître and eventually we passed that green wall made of trimmed yew that represented a fortified castle. As the sun struck hot on the road, they halted us in the shade of a little acacia wood just outside the town, there to await the arrival of the Ministerial carriages. We relaxed a little.

"Is my wreath keeping on all right?" inquired Anaïs.

"Yes . . . see for yourself."

I passed her a little pocket-mirror that I had prudently brought and we made sure that our head-dresses were in position. . . . The crowd had followed us, but too tightly packed in the road, it had broken down the hedges that bordered it and was trampling down the fields, regardless of the second crop. The boys, delirious with excitement, carried bunches of flowers and flags, not to mention bottles! (I was sure of this because I had just seen one stop, throw back his head and drink from the neck of one that held a litre.)

The "Society" ladies had remained at the gates of the town and were seated, some on the grass, some on camp-stools, but all under parasols. They would wait there, it was more refined; it was unbecoming to show too much enthusiasm.

Over there, flags floated over the red roofs of the station, towards which the crowd was hurrying; the noise of it retreated into the distance. Mademoiselle Sergent, all in black, and her Aimée, all in white, already out of breath from supervising us and trotting beside us, sat down on the grass, lifting up their skirts so as not to get green stains on them. We waited, standing. We had no desire to talk—I went over in my head the rather absurd little complimentary speech, composed by Antonin Rabastens, that I should have to recite in a moment:

Mr. Minister,—The children of the schools of Montigny, bearing the flowers of their native countryside . . .
(If anyone has ever seen fields of camellias here, let them say so!)
. . . come to you, full of gratitude. . . .

Boom!!! A fusillade bursting out at the station brought our mistresses to their feet.

The shouts of the populace came to us in a muffled roar, that suddenly grew louder and came nearer, with a confused din of joyous cries, the tramp of innumerable feet and the gallop of horses' hooves. . . . Tense, we all watched the spot where the road turned. . . . At last, at last the vanguard came in sight: dusty urchins trailing branches and bawling; then floods of people; then two broughams that glittered in the sun and two or three landaus from which emerged arms waving hats. . . . We watched them, all eyes. . . . The carriages approached at a slowed-down trot; they were there, in front of us. Before we had time to come to ourselves, the door of the first brougham was opening, ten steps away from us.

A young man in black evening clothes jumped out and offered his arm to support the Minister of Agriculture. The great man had not a ha'porth of distinction, in spite of the pains he took to appear imposing to us. I even found him slightly ridiculous, this haughty little gentleman, stout as a bullfinch, who was mopping his undistinguished brow and his hard eyes and his short, reddish beard for he was dripping with sweat. After all, *he* wasn't dressed in white muslin—and black cloth in this heat! . . .

A minute of interested silence greeted him, then, immediately, came extravagant cries of "Long live the Minister! Long live Agriculture! Long live the Republic! . . ." Monsieur Jean Dupuy thanked them with a cramped, but adequate gesture. A fat gentleman, embroidered in silver, wearing a cocked hat, his hand on the mother-of-pearl hilt of a little sword, came and placed himself on the left of the illustrious man; an old general with a little white goatee, a tall, bent man, flanked him on the right. And the imposing trio came forward, escorted by a troop of men in black evening clothes adorned with red ribbons, rows of decorations or military medals. Between the heads and shoulders I made out the triumphant face of that blackguard of a Dutertre. He was acclaimed by the crowd who made much of him as being both the Minister's friend and the future Deputy.

I sought Mademoiselle's eyes and asked, with my chin and my eyebrows: "Should I get on with the little speech?" She signalled "Yes" and I advanced with my two acolytes. A startling silence suddenly descended;—Heavens! How was I going to dare to speak in front of all those people? If only I wasn't choked with that beastly stage-fright!—First of all, keeping well together, we dived into our skirts in a magnificent curtsy that made our dresses to "fuiiii" and I began, my ears buzzing so much that I couldn't hear my own voice:

Mr. Minister,—The children of the schools of Montigny, bearing the flowers of their native countryside, come to you, full of gratitude . . .

And then my voice suddenly became firmer and I went on, clearly articulating the prose in which Rabastens guaranteed our "unshakable loyalty to Republican institutions", as calm now as if I were reciting Eugène Manuel's *The Dress* in class. In any case, the official trio wasn't listening to me; the Minister was reflecting that he was dying of thirst and the two other great personages were exchanging appreciative remarks in whispers:

"Mr. Prefect, wherever does that little peach spring from?"

"Not the faintest idea, General. She's as pretty as a picture."

"A little Primitive (he too!). If she looks in the least like a Fresnois girl, I'll eat my . . ."

"Pray accept these flowers of our maternal soil!"—I concluded, offering my bouquet to His Excellency. Anaïs, looking supercilious as she always does when she is aiming at being distinguished, handed hers to the Prefect, and Marie Belhomme, crimson with emotion, presented hers to the General.

The Minister mumbled a reply in which I caught the words "Republic . . . solicitude of the Government . . . confidence in the loyalty"; he got on my nerves. Then he remained motionless and so did I; everyone was waiting expectantly, then Dutertre bent down to his ear and prompted him: "Come on, you must kiss her!"

Thereupon he kissed me, but clumsily (his harsh beard scratched me). The brass band of the main town blared the *Marseillaise*, and, doing an about-turn, we marched towards the town, followed by the banner-bearers; the rest of the Schools made way for us and, leading the majestic procession, we passed under the "fortified castle", and returned once more under the leafy arches. All about us, people were shouting in a shrill, frenzied way, but we honestly gave no sign that we heard anything! Erect and crowned with flowers, it was the three of us they were acclaiming, quite as much as the Minister. . . . Ah! if I had any imagination, I should have seen us at once as three king's daughters, entering some "loyal town" with their father; the girls in white would be our ladies-in-waiting, we would be being escorted to the tournament where the noble knights would dispute for the honour of . . . Heaven send that those wretched boys hadn't overfilled the little coloured lamps with oil earlier this morning! With the jolts those urchins were giving to the posts on which they were perched, yelling, we should be a nice sight! We did not talk, we had nothing to say to each other; we had quite enough to do throwing out our chests the way people do in Paris and leaning our heads in the direction of the wind to make our hair stream out. . . .

We arrived in the front-courtyard of the Schools, we halted and massed in close formation. The crowd surged in on all sides, beat up against the walls and climbed up on to them. With the tips of our fingers, we rather icily pushed away our companions who were over-anxious to surround us and overwhelm us. There were sharp exchanges of "Do be careful!" "Well, *you* needn't look as much as if butter wouldn't melt in your mouth! You've had enough people staring at you all the morning!" The lanky Anaïs greeted these jeers in disdainful silence; Marie Belhomme became fidgety; I restrained myself with great difficulty from pulling off one of my strapless shoes and applying it to the face of the bitchier of the two Jauberts who had slyly jostled me.

The Minister, escorted by the General, the Prefect and a host of councillors, secretaries and I don't know what else (I'm not up in that world) who had forced a way for him through the crowd, had mounted the platform and installed himself in the handsome, over-gilded armchair that the Mayor had specially provided from his own drawing-room. A meagre consolation for the poor man who was tied to his bed with gout on that unforgettable day! Monsieur Jean Dupuy sweated and mopped himself; what would he not have given for it to be tomorrow! Still, that's what he's paid for. . . . Behind him, in concentric semi-circles, sat the district councillors and the municipal council of Montigny . . . all those perspiring people couldn't smell very agreeable. . . . Well, and what about us? Was it over, our glory? Were we to be left down there, without anyone so much as offering us a chair? That was really too much! "Come on, all of you, we're going to sit down." Not without difficulty, we made ourselves a gangway as far as the platform, we, the flag, and all the pennant-bearers. There, lifting my head, I hailed Dutertre in an undertone—he was chatting, leaning over the back of the Prefect's chair right at the edge of the platform. "Sir, hi, Sir! Monsieur Dutertre, I say! . . . Doctor!" He heard that appeal better than the others and bent down, smiling and showing his fangs: "It's you! What do you want? My heart? I give it to you!" I was quite sure he was drunk already.

"No, Sir, I'd much rather have a chair for myself and some others for the girls with me. They've abandoned us there all by ourselves, with the mere mortals—it's heartrending."

"That cries out for justice, pure and simple. You shall all sit in tiers on the steps so that the populace can at least refresh its eyes while we're boring them with our speeches. Up with the lot of you!"

We did not wait to be asked twice. Anaïs, Marie and I climbed up first, with Luce, the Jauberts and the other pennant-bearers behind us. Their lances got caught and entangled in each other and they tugged them furiously, their teeth gritted and their eyes lowered because they thought the crowd was laughing at them. A man—the sacristan—took pity on them and obligingly collected the little flags and carried them away; no doubt the white dresses, the flowers and the banners gave the good fellow the illusion that he was assisting at a slightly more secular Corpus Christi procession, and, from long force of habit, he removed our candles—I mean our flags—at the end of the ceremony.

Installed and enthroned, we gazed at the crowd at our feet and the Schools in front of us, those Schools so charming today under the curtains of greenery and flowers, under all that quivering decoration that hid their bleak, barrack-like look. As to the vulgar herd of our schoolmates, left standing down below, who stared at us enviously, and nudged each other and gave sickly smiles, we disdained them.

On the platform, there was a scraping of chairs and some coughing: we half-turned round to see the orator. It was Dutertre; he was standing up, in the middle, lithe and bowing, and preparing to speak without notes, empty-handed. A deep hush descended. One could hear, as at High Mass, the shrill weeping of a small child who was pining to get away, and, just as at High Mass, it raised a laugh. Then:

Mr. Minister,
. . . .

He did not speak for more than two minutes; his speech was deft and ruthless, packed with fulsome compliments and subtle scurrilous allusions, of which I probably only understood a quarter. It was savage against the Deputy and charming towards all the rest of humanity; towards his glorious Minister and dear friend—they must have done some dirty deals together—towards his dear fellow-citizens, towards the Headmistress, "so unquestionably of the very highest order, Gentlemen, that the number of awards and certificates gained by her pupils dispenses me from any other encomium," . . . (Mademoiselle Sergent, seated down below, modestly lowered her head beneath her veil); even, believe it or not, towards *us:* "flowers carrying flowers, a feminine flag, patriotic and enchanting." At this unexpected thrust, Marie Belhomme lost her head and covered her eyes with her hand, Anaïs renewed her vain efforts to blush, and I could not prevent myself from rippling my spine. The crowd looked at us and smiled at us, and Luce winked at me. . . .

. . . *of France and of the Republic!*

The clapping and the shouts of applause lasted five minutes, so violent that they went *bzii* in one's ears; while they were dying down, the lanky Anaïs said to me:

"My dear, d'you see Monmond?"

"Where? . . . Yes, I see him. Well, what about him?"

"He keeps staring all the time at that Joublin girl."

"Does that give you corns?"

"No, but honest! He must have queer tastes! Just look at him!

He's making her stand on a bench and he's holding her up! I bet he's feeling if she's got firm calves."

"Probably. Poor Jeannette, I wonder whether it's only the arrival of the Minister that's put her in such a state of excitement! She's as red as your ribbons and she's trembling all over. . . ."

"Old thing, do you know who Rabastens is getting off with?"

"No."

"Look at him, you'll soon see."

It was true; the handsome assistant-master was fixedly gazing at someone. . . . And that someone was my incorrigible Claire, dressed in pale blue, whose lovely, rather melancholy eyes were dwelling with satisfaction on the irresistible Antonin. . . . Good! My First Communion partner was caught again! It wouldn't be long before I should be hearing romantic descriptions of meetings, of delights, of desertions. . . . Lord, how hungry I was!

"Aren't you hungry, Marie?"

"Yes, I am a bit."

"*I'm* dying of starvation. I say, do you like the milliner's new dress?"

"No, I think it's loud. She thinks the more a dress shrieks at you, the smarter it is. The Mayoress ordered hers from Paris, did you know?"

"Fat lot of good *that's* done her! She wears it like a dog dressed-up. The watchmaker's wife has got on the same bodice she wore two years ago!"

"Yes, I know! Bet she wants to give her daughter a dowry so she's got good reason, poor thing!"

The revered little Jean Dupuy had stood up and was beginning his reply in a dry voice, wearing an air of importance that was highly diverting. Luckily, he did not speak for long. Everyone clapped, including ourselves, as loud as we could. It was amusing, all those heads waving, all those hands beating in the air down there at our feet, all those black mouths yelling. . . . And what glorious sunshine over it all! a trifle too hot. . . .

There was a scuffling of chairs on the platform; all their Lordships were getting up. They signed to us to go down; they led the Minister away to feed; now we could go off to lunch!

With great difficulty, tossed about in the crowd which kept pushing in opposite directions, we managed at last to get out of the courtyard into the square where the cohorts were thinning out a little. All the little girls in white were going off, alone or with the immensely proud Mammas who were waiting for them; the three of us were going to separate, too.

"Did you enjoy yourself?" asked Anaïs.

"Certainly I did. It went off very well—it was great fun!"

"Well, to my mind . . . Somehow, I thought it would have been more amusing. . . . It needed a bit of livening-up, in fact!"

"Shut up, you give me a pain! I know what *you* thought it needed. You'd have liked to stand up and sing something, all by yourself on the platform. Then the whole thing would have immediately seemed much gayer to you."

"Go on, you can't hurt *my* feelings. Everyone knows what those polite remarks mean from *you*!"

"As for me," confessed Marie, "I've never enjoyed myself so much in my life. Oh! What he said about us . . . I didn't know where to hide myself! . . . What time do we have to be back?"

"Two o'clock precisely. That means half-past two, you can be quite sure the banquet won't be finished before that. Good-bye, see you very soon!"

At home, Papa enquired with interest:

"Did he speak well, Méline?"

"Méline! Why not Sully? It's Jean Dupuy, you know, Papa!"

"Yes, yes."

But he found his daughter pretty and looked at her with satisfaction.

After lunch, I tidied myself up; I rearranged my wreath of marguerites, I shook the dust off my muslin skirts and I waited patiently for two hours, fighting off with all my might a violent desire to take a siesta. Heavens, how hot it would be down there!— "Fanchette, don't touch my skirt, it's muslin. No, I'm not going to catch flies for you, can't you see I'm receiving the Minister?"

I went out once again; the streets were already humming and rang with the sound of footsteps, all of which were going downhill towards the Schools. Nearly all my schoolmates were already there when I arrived; red faces, muslin skirts already limp and crumpled; the crisp freshness of this morning had gone. Luce was stretching and yawning; she had eaten her lunch too fast; she was sleepy; she was too hot; she could "feel herself growing claws". Anaïs alone remained the same; just as pale, just as cold, neither languid nor excited.

Our two mistresses came down at last. Mademoiselle Sergent, her cheeks burning, was scolding Aimée who had stained the hem of her skirt with raspberry juice; the spoilt little thing sulked and shrugged her shoulders and turned away, refusing to see the tender beseeching in her friend's eyes. Luce eagerly watched all this, fuming and sneering.

"Now, now, are you all of you here?" scolded Mademoiselle, who, as usual, was visiting her personal resentments on our innocent heads. "Whether you are or not, we're leaving now. I've no desire to hang . . . to wait about here for an hour. Get into line—and quicker than lightning!"

We needn't have hurried! Up there, on that enormous platform, we marked time for ages, for the Minister lingered endlessly over his coffee and all that went with it. The crowd, herded like sheep down below, looked up at us and laughed, with the sweating faces of people who have lunched heavily. . . . The "Society" ladies had brought camp-stools; the innkeeper from the Rue du Cloître had set out benches, which he was hiring out at two sous a place; and the boys and girls had piled on to them, shoving each other; all those people, tipsy, coarse and cheerful, waited patiently, exchanging loud ribaldries which they shouted to each other from a distance with tremendous laughs. From time to time, a little girl in white forced her way through to the steps of the platform, climbed up and got herself hustled and pushed into the back rows by Mademoiselle whose nerves were on edge from all these delays and who was champing her bit under her eye-veil. She was even more furious on account of little Aimée who was making great play with her long lashes and her lovely eyes at a group of draper's assistants who had bicycled over from Villeneuve.

A great "Ah!" heaved the crowd towards the doors of the banqueting-room which had just opened to let out the Minister, even redder and more perspiring than this morning, followed by his escort of black dress-suits. Already people made way for him with more familiarity, with smiles of recognition: if he stayed here three days, the rural policeman would be tapping him on the stomach, asking him for a tobacconist's shop for his daughter-in-law who's got three children, poor girl, and no husband.

Mademoiselle massed us on the right-hand side of the platform, for the Minister and his confederates were going to sit on this row of seats, the better to hear us sing. Their Lordships installed themselves; Dutertre, the colour of Russia leather, was laughing and talking too loud, drunk, as if by accident. Mademoiselle threatened us under her breath with appalling punishments if we sang out of tune, and off we went with the *Hymn to Nature:*

> *Lo, the sky is tinged with morning,*
> *Glowing beams grow brighter yet:*
> *Haste, arise! the day is dawning,*
> *Honest toil demands our sweat!*

(If it's not content with the sweat of the official cortège, honest toil must demand a great deal!)

The small voices were a little lost in the open air; I did my very utmost to superintend the "seconds" and the "thirds" simultaneously. Monsieur Jean Dupuy vaguely followed the beat by nodding his head; he was sleepy, dreaming of the report in the *Petit Parisien.* The wholehearted applause woke him up; he stood up, went forward and clumsily complimented Mademoiselle Sergent who promptly turned shy, stared at the ground and retired into her shell. . . . Queer woman!

We were dislodged and the pupils of the boys' School took our place. They had come to bray in chorus a completely imbecile song:

> *Sursum corda! Sursum corda!*
> *Up all hearts! this noble order*
> *Be the cry that spurs our soul!*
> *Rally, brothers, thrust aside*
> *All that might our wills divide,*
> *March on firmly to the goal!*
> *Fling cold selfishness away,*
> *Traitors, who for wealth betray,*
> *Are not such a bitter foe*
> *To the burning love we owe*
> *As patriots to . . . etc., etc. . . .*

After them, the brass-band of the main town, "The Friendly Club of Fresnois", came to shatter our ears. It was excessively boring, all this! If I could only find a peaceful corner. . . . And then, since no one was paying the least attention to us, upon my word, I left without telling anyone. I went back home, I undressed and I lay down till dinner-time. Why not? I should be fresher at the ball!

At nine o'clock, I was standing on the steps in front of the house, breathing in the coolness that was falling at last. At the top of the street, under the triumphal arch, ripened paper balloons in the shape of huge coloured fruits. All ready, my gloves on, a white hood under my arm, a white fan clasped in my fingers, I waited for Marie and Anaïs who were coming to fetch me. . . . Light footsteps and well-known voices were heard approaching down the street, it was my two friends. . . . I protested:

"Are you mad? To leave for the ball at half-past nine! But the room won't even be lit up—it's ridiculous!"

"My dear, Mademoiselle said: 'It'll begin at half-past eight. In this part of the world, they're like that, you can't make them wait. They'll rush off to the ball as soon as they've wiped their mouths!' That's what she *said*."

"All the more reason not to imitate the boys and girls round here! If the 'dress-suits' dance tonight, they'll arrive about eleven, as people do in Paris, and we shall already have lost our bloom from dancing! Come into the garden for a little with me."

They followed me, much against their wills, into the dusky tree-lined paths where my cat Fanchette, dressed in white, like us, was dancing after moths, capering like a crazy creature. . . . She mistrusted the sound of strange voices and climbed up into a fir-tree, from which her eyes followed us, like two tiny green lanterns. In any case, Fanchette despised me these days: what with the examination, and the opening of the Schools, I was never there any more. I no longer caught her flies, quantities of flies, that I impaled in a row on a hatpin and which she picked off delicately in order to eat them, coughing occasionally because of a wing stuck uncomfortably in her throat; I hardly ever gave her coarse cooking-chocolate now or the bodies of butterflies, which she adored, and sometimes, in the evening, I went so far as to forget to "make her room" between two volumes of Larousse.—Patience, Fanchette darling! Soon I shall have all the time in the world to tease you and make you jump through a hoop because, alas! I shall never be going back to the School. . . .

Anaïs and Marie could not keep still and only answered me with absent-minded *Yeses* and *Noes*—their legs were itching to dance. All right, we would go since they were so desperately keen to be off! "But you'll see that our lady mistresses won't even have come downstairs!"

"Oh! You know, they've only got to come down the little inside staircase to find themselves right in the ballroom; they'll take a peep now and then through the little door to see whether it's the right moment to make their entrance."

"Exactly. Whereas if we arrive too early, we'll look utter fools, all by ourselves—except for three cats and a calf—in that enormous room!"

"Oh! You're simply maddening, Claudine! Look! If there's nobody there, we'll go up the little staircase and rout out the boarders and we'll go downstairs again when the dancers have arrived!"

"All right. In that case, I'm quite willing."

To think I had feared that this great room would be a desert! It was already more than half-full of couples who were gyrating to the strains of a mixed orchestra (mounted on the garlanded platform at the far end of the room); an orchestra composed of Trouillard and other local violinists, trombonists and cornet-players mingled with sections of "The Friendly Club of Fresnois" in gold-braided caps. All of them were blowing, scraping and banging, far from in unison but with tremendous spirit.

We had to push our way through the hedge of people who were looking on and cluttering up the main doorway. Both the double doors were flung open for it was here, you realise, that a self-constituted vigilance committee took up its station! It was here that disapproving remarks and cackles were exchanged about the young girls' dresses and the frequency with which certain couples danced together.

"My dear! Fancy showing as much of one's skin as that! What a little hussy!"

"Yes, and showing what? Just bones!"

"Four times, *four times* running she's danced with Monmond! If only I were her mother, I'd give her what-for to teach her a lesson, I'd send her straight home to bed!"

"Those gentlemen from Paris, they don't dance like we do here."

"They certainly don't! You'd think they were afraid of getting themselves broken, they exert themselves so little. Now, our boys here, that's something like! They enjoy themselves without minding how hard they go at it!"

It was the truth, even though Monmond, a brilliant dancer, was restraining himself from doing flying leaps with outspread legs, "with reference to" the presence of the people from Paris. A dashing young spark, Monmond, over whom there was fierce rivalry! A lawyer's clerk, with a girl's face and black curly hair, how could you expect anyone to resist him!

We made a timid entrance, between two figures of a quadrille, and we walked slowly and deliberately across the room to go and seat ourselves on a sofa against the wall—three model little girls.

I had been fairly sure, in fact, I had seen for myself that my dress suited me and that my hair and my wreath made my little face look very far from contemptible—but the sly glances and the suddenly rigid countenances of the girls who were resting and fanning themselves made me quite convinced of it and I felt more at my ease. I could examine the room without apprehension.

The "dress-suits", ah! there weren't many of them! All the official group had taken the six o'clock train; farewell to the Minister, the General, the Prefect and their suite. There remained some five or six young men, mere secretaries, but pleasant and civilised, who were standing in a corner and seemed to be prodigiously amused at this ball, the like of which they had obviously never seen before. The rest of the male dancers? All the boys and young men of Montigny and its neighbourhood, two or three in badly cut evening clothes, the rest in morning-coats; paltry accoutrements for this evening party that was supposed to be an official occasion.

The female dancers consisted entirely of young girls, for, in this primitive countryside, a woman ceases to dance as soon as she is married. They had spared no expense tonight, the young ones! Dresses of pink muslin and blue muslin that made the swarthy complexions of these little country girls look almost black, hair that was too sleek and not puffed out enough, white cotton gloves, and, in spite of the assertions of the gossips in the doorway, necks that were not cut nearly low enough; the bodices stopped their décolletage too soon, just where the flesh became white, firm and rounded.

The orchestra warned the couples to set to partners and, amidst the fan-strokes of the skirts that brushed our knees, I saw my First Communion partner, Claire, languid and altogether charming, pass by in the arms of the handsome assistant-master, Antonin Rabastens, who was waltzing furiously, wearing a white carnation in his buttonhole.

Our lady mistresses had still not come down (I was keeping assiduous watch on the little door of the secret staircase, through which they would appear) when a gentleman, one of the "dress-suits", came and made his bow to me. I let myself be swept off; he was not unattractive; too tall for me, but solidly built, and he waltzed well, without squeezing me too tight, and looking down at me with an amused expression. . . .

How idiotic I am! I ought to have been aware of nothing else but the pleasure of dancing, of the pure joy of being invited before Anaïs who was staring at my partner with an envious eye . . . and, yet, during that waltz, I was conscious only of unhappiness, of a sadness, foolish perhaps, but so acute that I could only just keep back my tears. . . . Why? Ah, because . . . —no, I can't be utterly sincere, I can only give a hint or two . . . —I felt my soul overwhelmed with sorrow because, though I'm not in the least fond of dancing, I should have liked to dance with someone whom I adored with all my heart. I should have liked to have that someone there so that I could relieve my tension by telling him everything that I confided only to Fanchette or to my pillow (and not even to my diary) because I so wildly needed that someone, and this humiliated me, and I would never surrender myself except to the someone whom I should completely love and completely know—dreams, in short, that would never be realised!

My tall waltzer did not fail to ask me:

"You like dancing, Mademoiselle?"

"No, Monsieur."

"But then . . . why are you dancing?"

"Because I'd rather be doing even that than nothing at all."

We went twice round the room in silence and then he began again:

"May one observe that your two companions serve you as admirable foils?"

"Oh, heavens, yes, one may! All the same Marie is quite attractive."

"You said?"

"I said that the one in blue isn't ugly."

"I . . . don't much appreciate that type of beauty. . . . Will you allow me to ask you here and now for the next waltz?"

"Yes, certainly."

"You haven't a dance-programme?"

"That doesn't matter: I know everyone here, I shan't forget."

He took me back to my seat and had hardly turned his back before Anaïs complimented me with one of her most supercilious "My dears!"

"Yes, he really is charming, isn't he? And you'd never believe how amusing it is to hear him talk!"

"Oh! Everyone knows *your* luck's right in today! *I've* been asked for the next dance, by Féfed."

"And me," said Marie, who was radiant, "by Monmond! Ah! Here comes Mademoiselle!"

Here, in fact came both ladies. They stood framed in turn in the little doorway at the far end of the room; first, little Aimée who had only changed into an evening top, an all-white, filmy bodice from which emerged delicate, dimpled shoulders and slim, rounded arms; in her hair, just above the ear, white and yellow roses made the golden eyes look more golden still—they had no need of them to make them sparkle!

Mademoiselle Sergent, still in black, but trimmed with sequins this time, wore a dress that was cut only very slightly low at the neck, revealing firm, amber-tinted flesh. Her foaming hair cast a warm shadow over her ill-favoured face and made her eyes shine out; she really looked quite well. Behind her came the serpentine train of the boarders, in white, high-necked dresses, all very commonplace. Luce rushed up to me to tell me that she made herself "décolletée" by tucking in the top of her dress, in spite of her sister's opposition. She had been right to do so. Almost at the same moment, Dutertre entered by the big main door; red, excited and talking too loud.

On account of the rumours that circulated in the town, the whole room was keenly watching these simultaneous entries of the future Deputy and his protégée. But neither of them fluttered an eyelash: Dutertre went straight up to Mademoiselle Sergent, greeted her and, as the orchestra was just beginning a polka, he boldly swept her off with him. She, flushed and with her eyes half-closed, did not talk at all and danced . . . very gracefully, upon my word! The couples re-formed and attention was turned elsewhere.

Having conducted the Headmistress back to her place, the District Superintendent came up to me—a flattering attention, very much remarked. He mazurkaed violently, without waltzing, but whirling round too much, squeezing me too tight and talking too much into my hair:

"You're as pretty as a cherub!"

"In the first place, Doctor, why do you call me '*tu*', like a child? I'm practically grown-up."

"No, have I got to restrain myself? Just look at this grown-up person! . . . Oh, your hair and that white wreath! How I'd love to take it off you!"

"I swear that *you* won't be the one who'll take it off!"

"Be quiet, or I'll kiss you in front of everyone!"

"No one would be surprised—they've seen you do it to so many others. . . ."

"True. But why won't you come and see me? It's not fear that stops you, you've got thoroughly naughty eyes. . . . You just see, I'll catch you again one of these days; don't laugh, you'll end by making me lose my temper!"

"Pooh! Don't make yourself out so wicked—I don't believe you."

He laughed, showing his teeth, and I thought to myself:

"Talk as much as you like: next winter, I'll be in Paris and you'll never run into me there!"

After me, he went off to whirl round with little Aimée, while Monmond, in an alpaca morning-coat, invited me to dance. I didn't refuse, certainly not! Provided they're wearing gloves, I'm very willing to dance with the local boys (the ones I know well) who are charming to me, in their way. Then I danced again with my tall "dress-suit" of the first waltz up till the moment when I took a little breather during a quadrille so as not to get flushed and also because quadrilles seem to me ridiculous. Claire joined me, gentle and languishing, softened tonight with a melancholy that became her. I questioned her:

"Tell me, is everyone talking about you because the handsome schoolmaster's being so assiduous?"

"Oh, do you think so? . . . They can't say anything, because there's nothing to say."

"Come on! You're not going to pretend to make mysteries with me, are you?"

"Good heavens, no! But it's the truth—there really is nothing! . . . Look, we've met twice, tonight's the third time. He talks in a way that's absolutely . . . captivating! And just now he asked me if I ever went for walks in the evening in the Fir Plantation."

"Everyone knows what that means. What's your answer going to be?"

She smiled, without speaking, with a hesitant, yet longing expression. She would go. They're odd, these little girls! Here was one who was pretty and gentle, docile and sentimental and who, from the age of fourteen, had got herself deserted by half a dozen lovers in succession. She didn't know how to manage them. It was true that I shouldn't have the least idea how to manage them either, in spite of all the magnificent arguments I put up.

A vague giddiness was coming over me, from spinning round and, above all, from watching others spin round. Nearly all the "dress-suits" had left, but Dutertre was whirling round with tremendous enthusiasm, dancing with all the girls he found attractive or who were merely very young. He swept them off their feet, turned their heads, crushed them nearly to death and left them dazed, but highly flattered. After midnight, the hall became, from minute to minute, a homelier affair; now that the "foreigners" had gone, everyone was among their own friends again, the public of Trouillard's little dancing and drinking place on holidays—only one had more room to move in this big, gaily-decorated room and the chandelier gave a better light than the three oil-lamps of the *cabaret*. The presence of Doctor Dutertre did not make the boys feel shy, very much the reverse; already Monmond had stopped restraining his feet from sliding over the parquet floor. They flew, those feet, they sprang up above people's heads or shot wildly apart in prodigious "splits". The girls admired him and giggled into their handkerchiefs scented with cheap eau-de-Cologne. "My dear, isn't he a scream? There's nobody like him!"

All of a sudden, this enthusiastic dancer shot past, as brutally as a cyclone, carrying his partner like a parcel, for he had betted a "boocket of white wine", payable at the buffet installed in the courtyard, that he would "do" the whole length of the room in six steps of a galop; everyone had gathered round to admire him.

Monmond won his bet, but his partner—Fifine Baille, a little slut who brought milk to the town to sell, and something else too, for anyone who wanted it—left him in a furious temper and cursed him!

"You great clumsy b——! You might easy have gone and split me dress! You ask me to dance again, and I'll clout you over the ear!"

The audience was convulsed with laughter and the boys took advantage of their being jammed together to pinch, tickle and stroke whatever was within reach of their hands. It was becoming altogether too gay; I would soon go home to bed. The lanky Anaïs, who had at last vanquished a lingering "dress-suit", was promenading about the room with him, fanning herself, and giving high, warbling laughs, rapturous at seeing the ball warming up and the boys getting excited; there would be at least one of them who would kiss her on the neck, or elsewhere!

Where on earth had Dutertre got to? Mademoiselle had ended by driving her little Aimée into a corner and was making a jealous scene; after leaving her handsome District Superintendent, she had once more become tyrannous and tender; the other was listening, shaking her shoulders, her eyes far away and her brow obstinate. As to Luce, she was dancing desperately,—"I'm not missing one"— passing from arm to arm without getting breathless; the boys did not think her pretty but, once they had asked her to dance, they came back again; she felt so supple and small, melting into their arms, light as a snowflake.

Mademoiselle Sergent had disappeared now, vexed perhaps by seeing her favourite waltzing, in spite of her objurgations, with a tall fair counter-jumper who was squeezing her tight and brushing her with his moustache and his lips without her objecting in the least. It was one o'clock, I wasn't enjoying myself a bit any more and I was going home to bed. During the break in a polka (here, they dance the polka in two parts, between which the couples promenade arm-in-arm round the room in Indian file), I stopped Luce as she was passing and forced her to sit down for a minute.

"Aren't you getting tired of all this business?"

"Be quiet! I could dance for a whole week on end! I can't feel my legs. . . ."

"So you're thoroughly enjoying yourself?"

"I've no idea! I'm not thinking about anything at all, my head's in a whirl, it's simply marvellous! Still I like it awfully when they hold me tight. . . . When they hold me tight and we're doing a fast waltz, it makes me want to scream!"

What was that we suddenly heard? The trampling of feet, the shrill cries of a woman who was being hit, screamed insults. . . . Were the boys fighting amongst themselves? But no, the noise definitely came from upstairs! The screams suddenly became so shrill that the couples stopped their promenade; everyone became anxious and one good soul, the gallant and absurd Antonin Raba-stens, rushed to the door of the inside staircase and opened it . . . the tumult grew louder and I was thunderstruck to recognise the voice of Mademoiselle Sergent's mother, that harsh old peasant-woman's voice, yelling quite appalling things. Everyone listened, nailed to the spot, in absolute silence; their eyes fixed on that little doorway from which so much noise was coming.

"Ah! you bitch of a girl! It serves you right! Yes, I've broken my broom-handle on his back, that swine of a doctor of yours! Yes, I've given him a good whack on the bum all right! Ah, I've smelt a rat a good long time now! No, no, my beauty, I'm not going to hold my tongue, I don't care a f——, I don't for the fine folk at the ball! Let 'em hear, they'll hear a nice thing to be sure! Tomorrow morning, no, not tomorrow—this very minute—I'm packing my bag. I won't sleep in such a house, I won't! You dirty little beast, you took advantage of him being drunk and incapable (*sic*) to get him into bed with you, that fellow that'll grub in any muck-heap! So *that's* why you got a rise in pay, you bitch on heat, you! If I'd made you milk the cows like I did, you'd never have come to this! But you'll suffer for it, I'll shout it everywhere, I'd like to see them point their fingers at you in the streets, I'd like to see you a laughing-stock! He can't do nothing to me, your dirty dog of a District Superintendent, however much him and the Min'ster's in each other's pockets; I gave him such a whack that he ran away from me. He's frightened of me, he is! Comes and does his filthy business here, in a room where I make the bed with my own hands every morning—and doesn't even lock the door! Runs off he does, half in his shirt and nothing on his feet, so that his dirty boots are still there! Look, there's his boots—take a good look at 'em!"

We could hear them being thrown down the stairs, bumping against the steps; one fell right down to the bottom and lay in the doorway, in the full glare of light, a patent-leather boot, all shining and elegant. . . . No one dared touch it. The infuriated voice grew less loud, retreated along the passages to the accompaniment of banging doors, and suddenly ceased. Then everyone looked at each other; no one could believe their own ears. The couples, still arm-in-arm, stood there perplexed, keyed-up for what might happen next; then, little by little, sly smiles appeared on mocking lips and ran all through the room, gradually turning into bantering laughter till the band on the platform caught the infection and laughed as heartily as everyone else.

I looked round for Aimée and saw that she was as white as the bodice of her dress, her eyes were stretched wide, staring at the boot, the focal point of the entire room's gaze. A young man charitably went up to her, and offered to take her outside for a little to recover herself. . . . She cast panic-stricken glances all around her, then burst into sobs and rushed hurriedly from the room. (Weep, weep, my girl, these painful moments will bring you hours of even sweeter pleasures.) After this flight, no one hesitated to restrain their wholehearted amusement; everyone was nudging each other and saying: "I say, did you see *that*!"

It was then that I heard just beside me a hysterical laugh, a piercing, suffocating laugh, vainly stifled in a handkerchief. It was Luce, who was writhing, doubled-up, on a sofa, crying with pleasure, and wearing such an expression of unmitigated bliss on her face that *I* was overcome with laughter too.

"You've not gone out of your mind, have you, Luce, laughing like that?"

"Ah! Ah! . . . oh! let me alone . . . it's too good. . . . Oh! I'd never have dared to hope for that! Ah! Ah! I can go now, that'll keep me bucked for ages. . . . Lord, how that's done me good! . . ."

I took her off into a corner to calm her down a little. In the ballroom, everyone was chattering hard and no one was dancing any more. . . . What a scandal there would be in the morning! . . . But a violin launched a stray note, the cornets and trombones took it up; a couple timidly began a polka step, two others imitated them, then all the rest followed suit; someone shut the little door to hide the scandalous boot and the dance started up again, all the gayer and wilder for having witnessed such a comic, such a totally unexpected interlude! As for myself, I was going home to bed, completely happy at having crowned my schooldays with such a memorable night.

Farewell to the classroom; farewell, Mademoiselle and her girl friend; farewell, feline little Luce and spiteful Anais! I am going to leave you to make my entry into the world;—I shall be very much astonished if I enjoy myself there as much as I have at school.

Claudine in Paris

1

Today, once again, I am beginning to keep my diary. It was forcibly interrupted during my illness—my serious illness. For I really believe I've been very ill indeed!

I still don't feel any too strong even now, but the time when I had high fever and was in such utter despair seems a long while ago. Of course I can't conceive that people live in Paris for pleasure, of their own free will, but I do begin to understand that one can get interested in what goes on inside these huge six-storeyed boxes.

For the honour of my notebooks, I shall have to explain why I come to be in Paris; why I've left Montigny, that beloved, quite fantastic school where Mademoiselle Sergent, oblivious of Mrs. Grundy's comments, continues to cherish her little Aimée while the pupils kick up a hullabaloo; why Papa has deserted his slugs and so on. Oh dear, there's so much to tell. . . . I shall be awfully tired by the time I've finished! Because, you know, I'm thinner than I was last year and a little taller too. In spite of having turned seventeen the day before yesterday, I barely look sixteen—let me look at myself in the glass. Yes . . . no doubt about it!

Pointed chin, you're attractive but don't, I implore you, overdo that point. Hazel eyes, you persist in being hazel and I can't blame you for it; but don't retreat under my eyebrows with that excessive modesty. Mouth, you're still my mouth, but so pale that I can't resist rubbing those short, colourless lips with petals pulled from the red geranium in the window. (Incidentally it only gives them a horrid, purplish tinge that I promptly lick off.) As to you my poor little white, anaemic ears, I hide you under my curly hair and secretly look at you from time to time and pinch you to make you redden. But it's my hair that's the worst of all. I can't touch it without wanting to cry. . . . They've cut them all off, just below the ear—my auburn ringlets, my lovely, smoothly-rolled ringlets! To be sure, the ten centimetres that remain to me are doing their utmost; they curl and fluff out and are growing as fast as ever they can. But I'm so miserable every morning when I involuntarily make the gesture of lifting up my mane before soaping my neck.

Papa, with that magnificent beard of yours, I'm nearly as furious with you as I am with myself. You simply can't imagine a father like mine! Just you listen.

When his great treatise on the *Malacology of Fresnois* was nearly finished, Papa sent a large portion of his manuscript to Masson, a publisher in Paris. From that day on, he was devoured by an appalling fever of impatience. What! His 'galleys' corrected and sent off to the Boulevard Saint-Germain in the morning (eight hours journey by rail) had not arrived back at Montigny that self-same night? Ah! Doussine the postman heard some home truths. "Filthy Bonapartist of a postman, not bringing me my proofs! He's a cuckold, it serves him right!" And the compositors . . . my goodness me! Threats of scalping these perpetrators of scandalous printer's errors and anathemas against these "vermin of Sodom" were boomed out all day long. Fanchette, my beautiful cat, who is a very correct person, raised indignant eyebrows. November was rainy and the neglected slugs died one after the other. So much so, that, one evening, Papa, with one hand in his tri-coloured beard, declared to me: "My book isn't getting on at all, the printers don't give a damn for me. The most reasonable (*sic*) thing to do would be for us to go and live in Paris." This proposal completely bowled me over. Such simplicity, combined with such utter craziness, excited me and all I asked was a week to think it over. "Be quick about it," added Papa, "I've got someone for our house. What's-his-name wants to rent it." Oh the duplicity of the most guileless fathers! This one had already arranged everything behind my back and I had no inkling of this threatened departure!

Two days later, at school, where, on Mademoiselle's advice, I was vaguely thinking of working for my Higher Certificate, that gawk Anaïs was even more shrewish than usual. I couldn't stand any more of it so I said, with a shrug, "Come off it, old thing. Anyway, you won't be able to bore me stiff much longer. In a month's time, I'm going off to live in Paris." The stupefaction she hadn't time to hide absolutely delighted me. She rushed up to Luce: "Luce! You're going to lose your great friend! My dear, you'll weep tears of blood when Claudine goes off to Paris! Hurry up, cut off a lock of your hair, exchange your last vows of eternal friendship: you've only just time!" Luce was petrified. She spread out her fingers like palm-leaves, opened her green, lazy eyes to their fullest extent and shamelessly burst into loud tears. She got on my nerves. "Yes, I really am going. And I shan't be the least bit sorry to see the last of the whole lot of you!"

At home, having made up my mind, I gave Papa my solemn "Yes". He combed his beard complacently and announced:

"Pradeyron is already hunting for a flat for us. Where? I haven't the least idea. Provided I've room for my books, I don't care a damn about the neighbourhood. What about you?"

"I don't care a . . . I mean, I don't mind either."

In reality, I knew nothing whatever about it. How could you expect a Claudine who had never left the big house and the beloved garden of Montigny to know what she wanted in Paris and which neighbourhood to choose? Fanchette knew nothing about it either. But I became agitated and, as in all the great crises of my life, I took to wandering about while Papa, suddenly practical—no, that's going too far—suddenly *active*, flung himself tempestuously into the business of packing.

For a hundred reasons, I preferred to escape to the woods and not to have to listen to Mélie's furious lamentations.

Mélie is fair, lazy and faded. She was once extremely pretty. She does the cooking, brings me water and pilfers fruit from our garden to give it to vague "acquaintances". But Papa assured me that, when I was a baby, she nourished me with "superb" milk and that she is still devoted to me. She sings a great deal and knows by heart a varied repertory of broad, not to say obscene, songs of which I remember quite a number. (And they say I don't cultivate the social graces!) There's a very pretty one:

> *He drank five or six straight off*
> *And never stopped for breath*

Tra la la. . . .
Just to show he liked the stuff
He near drank himself to death
Tra la la . . . , etc., etc.

Mélie tenderly cherishes my defects as well as my virtues. She declares enthusiastically that I'm 'ever so fetching', that I have 'a lovely body' and concludes: "It's a pity you haven't got a young man." Mélie includes the whole of nature in her innocent and disinterested urge to excite and appease the desires of the flesh. In the spring, when Fanchette miaows and purrs and rolls on her back in the garden paths, Mélie obligingly summons the tomcats and attracts them with platefuls of raw meat. Then she sentimentally contemplates the resulting idylls. Standing in the garden, in a dirty apron, she lets the rump of veal or the jugged hare "catch", as she dreamily cups her uncorseted breasts in the palms of her hands as if she were weighing them—a frequent gesture of hers that always manages to irritate me. In spite of myself, I feel vaguely disgusted to think that I was suckled at them.

All the same, if I were just a silly little fool and not a very sensible girl, Mélie would obligingly do everything necessary to help me lapse from virtue. But I only laugh at her when she mentions the subject of a lover . . . *no*, thank you very much! . . . and I give her a push and say: "Go and tell that stuff to Anaïs, you'll get a better reception from *her*."

Mélie swore on her mother's blood that she wouldn't come to Paris. I told her: "I don't give a damn whether you come or not." So then she began to make her preparations, prophesying a thousand appalling catastrophes as she did so.

As for me, I wandered along the slushy paths in the rusty woods that smelt of mushrooms and wet moss, gathering the yellow chanterelles that go so well with creamy sauces and casserole of veal. And, little by little, I realised that this move to Paris was sheer madness. Perhaps, if I implored Papa or better still, bullied him? But what would Anaïs say? And Luce, who might think I was staying because of her? No. Hang it all! I needn't do anything about it unless Paris turned out to be too intolerable.

One day, in the clearing of the Valley Wood as I was looking down at the woods, the woods that I love better than anything in the whole world, and up at the Saracen tower that gets lower every year, I saw so clearly and sharply the folly, the misery of going away that I nearly raced down the hill and back to the house to implore them, to *order* them to undo the packing-cases and unwrap the legs of the chairs.

Why didn't I do it? Why did I stay up there, with my mind a blank and my hands icy under my red hooded cloak? The chestnuts, in their husks, fell on me and pricked my head a little, like balls of wool with darning-needles left stuck in them.

I'm skipping a good deal. Farewells at school; a chilly goodbye to the Headmistress (amazing Mademoiselle! With her little Aimée glued to her, she said "au revoir" as if I were coming back that same evening); a mocking farewell from Anaïs: "I don't wish you good luck, old dear. Luck follows you everywhere. No doubt you won't deign to write to me except to announce your wedding"; anguished and tearful farewells from Luce who has confected a little purse for me in yellow and black embroidery silk and exquisitely bad taste. She has also presented me with a lock of her hair in a fancy-wood needle-case. She has "empicated" these souvenirs so that I shall never lose them.

(For those who do not know about the witching spell of "empication", the process is as follows: you place the object O, to be empicated, on the ground; you enclose it between two brackets whose joined ends (XO) cross over each other and inside which you inscribe an X on the left of the object. After that, you can set your mind at rest; the empication is infallible. One can also spit on the object but this is not absolutely indispensable.)

Poor Luce said to me: "Go on, you don't believe I'll be miserable. But you just wait and see what lengths I'm ready to go to. You know, I'm absolutely fed up with my sister and Mademoiselle. There was no one but *you* here, the only thing that kept me going was you. You just wait and see!" I gave the heartbroken creature a great many kisses, on her resilient cheeks and her wet eyelashes and the brown and white nape of her neck; I kissed her dimples and her irregular, too short little nose. She had never had so many caresses from me and the poor child's despair redoubled. Perhaps, for one year, I might have made her very happy. (It wouldn't have cost you as much as all that, Claudine, I know you!) But I don't regret in the least not having done so.

The physical horror of seeing the furniture moved and my little possessions packed up made me shivery and cross, like a cat in the rain. Having to watch the departure of my little ink-stained mahogany desk and my narrow walnut four-poster bed and the old Norman sideboard that serves me as a linen cupboard nearly threw me into hysterics. Papa, more insufferably pleased with himself than ever, paraded about the scene of disaster, singing: *"The English, full of arrogance, Came to set siege to Lorient. And the men of Lower Brittany . . ."* (unfortunately, one cannot quote the rest). I've never detested him so much as I did that day.

At the last moment, I thought I had lost Fanchette. Just as horrified as I was she had fled wildly into the garden and taken refuge in the coal-shed. I had endless trouble recapturing her and shutting her up in a travelling-basket. She was spitting, black all over and swearing like a fiend. When it comes to baskets, the only one she approves of is the meat-basket.

2

THE journey, the arrival and the first days of settling-in are all confused in a general fog of misery. The dark flat, between two courtyards in this dismal, shabby Rue Jacob, reduced me to a broken-hearted stupor. I stood without moving, watching the crates of books arrive one by one, then the uprooted furniture; I watched Papa, bustling and excited, nailing up shelves, pushing his desk from corner to corner, rejoicing out loud at the flat's situation: "Two steps from the Sorbonne, just by the Geographical Society, and the Sainte-Geneviève Library only a stone's throw away!" I heard Mélie moaning over the smallness of her kitchen . . . which is on the other side of the landing and actually one of the best rooms in the flat . . . and I suffered because she served us, on the excuse of the moving-in being unfinished and difficult, with stuff to eat that was . . . unfinished and difficult to digest. I was obsessed with one single idea: "Is it really *me* here, was it really *me* who let this crazy thing happen?" I refused to go out; I obstinately refused to do anything useful; I wandered from one room to another, with a lump in my throat and no appetite whatsoever. By the end of ten days, I looked so queer that Papa himself noticed it and was promptly seized with panic, for he goes to extremes in everything and is nothing if not thorough. He sat me on his knees, against his great tri-coloured beard, and rocked me between his gnarled hands that smelt of fir from putting up so many shelves. . . . I said nothing; I gritted my teeth because I still felt a savage resentment against him. . . . And then, my taut nerves gave way in a tremendous burst of hysteria and Mélie put me to bed, burning hot all over.

After that, a very long time went by. Something like brain-fever, with symptoms of typhoid. I do not think I was very delirious, but I fell into a woeful darkness and I was aware of nothing but my head which ached so dreadfully! I can remember lying for hours on my left side, tracing the outlines of the fantastic fruits printed on my bed-curtains with the tip of my finger. The fruit is a kind of apple with eyes in it. Even now, I have only to look at it to drift off at once into a world of nightmares and dizzy dreams where everything is all mixed up: Mademoiselle, and Aimée, and Luce, a wall that's just going to collapse on me, the spiteful Anaïs, and Fanchette who becomes as big as a donkey and sits on my chest. I can remember, too, Papa bending over me; his beard and his face looked enormous and I pushed him away with my two feeble arms, then pulled my hands back at once because the cloth of his overcoat seemed so harsh and so painful to touch! Last of all, I remember a gentle doctor, a little fair man with a woman's voice and cold hands that made me shudder all over.

For two months, they couldn't comb my hair, and, as my matted curls hurt me when I rolled my head on my pillow, Mélie cut them off with her scissors, quite close to my head. She had to manage as best she could and the result was uneven layers like doorsteps! Heavens, what luck that gawk Anaïs can't see me like this, transformed into a boy! She was so jealous of my chestnut curls and used to pull them slyly during recreation.

Little by little, my taste for life returned. I noticed one morning, when they had been able to sit me up in bed, that the rising sun came into my room and that the striped red and white paper livened up the walls, and my thoughts began to run on fried potatoes.

"Mélie, I'm hungry. Mélie, what's that smell coming from your kitchen? Mélie, my little looking-glass! Mélie, some eau-de-Cologne to wash my ears with! Mélie, what can one see out of the window? I want to get up."

"Oh, my little pet, aren't you getting *aggravating* again? It's because you're better. But you wouldn't be able so much as to stand up on your two feet and the doctor's said you're not to."

"He has, has he? Wait . . . get back . . . don't move! You just see!"

Hop! In spite of the agonised remonstrances and the cries of: "Sakes alive! You'll fall flat on your face, my precious girlie, I'll tell the doctor!" I made a tremendous effort and managed to drag my legs out of bed. . . . Alack! What had they done with my calves? And my knees, how enormous they looked! Gloomily, I got back into bed, already too exhausted to make any more effort.

I've consented to stay fairly good, though I find that "fresh eggs" in Paris have a peculiar taste of printed paper. It's nice in my room: there's a wood fire in it and I like looking at the red and white striped wallpaper (I've said that already), at my double-doored Norman sideboard that contains my small wardrobe of clothes and lingerie; its top is worn and chipped, I've scratched it a bit and spilt some ink on it. It stands against the longest wall of my rectangular room, next to my bed, my walnut four-poster with its chintz curtains (we're out of date) patterned with red and yellow flowers and fruits on a white ground. Opposite my bed, my little old-fashioned mahogany desk. No carpet; by way of a bedside rug, a big white poodle-skin. A tub armchair in tapestry, a little threadbare on the arms. A low chair made of old wood, with a red and yellow straw seat. Another, just as low, enamelled white. And a little square cane table, varnished its natural colour. What a jumble! But the general effect has always seemed exquisite to me. My dressing-table is a Louis XV console with a pink marble top. (It's sheer waste, it's imbecility: it would be infinitely better in its right place in the drawing-room. I know that perfectly well but I'm not Papa's daughter for nothing.) Let us complete the inventory: a big commonplace wash-basin, an impetuous water-jug and, no, *not* a hip-bath. Instead of a hip-bath that freezes your feet and makes ridiculous noises like stage-thunder, a wooden tub, *actually* a 'small wine-vat!' A good Montigny wine-vat, of copper-hooped beech, that I squat in, tailor-fashion, and that rasps the behind pleasantly as one sits in the hot water.

So I meekly eat eggs and, as I'm absolutely forbidden to read, I only read a little (my head begins to swim at once). I can't manage to explain how the joy of waking up gradually clouds over as the day wanes till I'm reduced to melancholy and to curling myself up into an unsociable ball, in spite of Fanchette's attempts to rouse me.

Fanchette, lucky girl, has taken her internment gaily. She has accepted, without protest, a tray of sawdust, hidden in the space beside my bed, in which to deposit her little messes. Leaning over her, I amuse myself by following the phases of an important operation in the expression of her cat's features. Fanchette washes her hind paws carefully, between the toes. Her face is discreet and says nothing. An abrupt pause in the washing: her face is serious, slightly anxious. A sudden change of pose; she sits down on her behind. Her eyes are cold, rather severe. She gets up, takes three steps, and sits down again. Then, irrevocable decision, she jumps off the bed, runs to her tray, scratches . . . and there is nothing at all. The indifferent expression returns. But not for long. Her anxious eyebrows draw together: feverishly, she scratches the sawdust again, tramples it down, looks for a good place and, for three minutes, seems lost in bitter thoughts, her eyes fixed and starting out of their sockets. For she is, deliberately, slightly constipated. At last, she slowly gets up and, with minute precautions, covers up the corpse, wearing the earnest expression suitable to this funereal operation. A little supererogatory scratching *round* the tray, then she goes straight into a loose-limbed, diabolic caper, prelude to a goat-like skipping and leaping, the dance of liberation. At that, I laugh and call out: "Mélie, quick! Come and change the cat's tray!"

I've begun to get interested in the noises in the courtyard. A big, depressing courtyard; at the far end of it, the backside of a black house. In the courtyard itself, anonymous little buildings with tiled roofs . . . tiles like the ones you see in the country. A low dark door opens, I'm told, on the Rue Visconti. I've never seen anyone walking across this courtyard but workmen in blouses and sad, bare-headed women whose busts sag down towards their hips at every step in the way peculiar to worn-out drudges. A child plays there silently, invariably all by himself. I think he belongs to the concierge of this sinister block of flats. On the ground floor of our home—if I dare call it "home", this square house full of people whom I don't know and instinctively dislike—a dirty servant-girl in a Breton coif punishes a poor little dog every morning. No doubt it misbehaves during the night in the kitchen, but oh how it yelps and it cries! Let that girl just wait till I'm well, she shall perish by my hand and no other! Lastly, every Thursday, a barrel-organ grinds out shocking love-songs from ten to eleven, and every Friday a pauper (they say a pauper here and not "an unfortunate" as they do in Montigny), a real classic pauper with a white beard comes and declaims pathetically: "Ladies and gentlemen . . . remember . . . a pore unfortunate! . . . Can't hardly see at all! . . . He looks to your kind 'eartedness! . . . Ladies and gentlemen, please! (one, two, three . . .) . . . *if* you p-p-please!" All this in a little minor sing-song that ends up in the major. I make Mélie throw this venerable old man four sous out of the window; she grumbles and says that I spoil beggars.

Papa, freed from anxiety and radiant in the knowledge that I'm really and truly getting better, takes advantage of this by no longer appearing at home except at meal times. Oh the Libraries and the Public Record Offices—the Nationale, the Cardinale and all the rest—that he tramps through, dusty and bearded and looking like one of the Bourbons!

Poor Papa, didn't he nearly start it all up again one February morning by bringing me a bunch of violets? The smell of the living flowers, their cool touch, suddenly ripped back the curtain of forgetfulness that my fever had stretched over the Montigny I had left . . . Once again I saw the transparent, leafless woods, the roads edged with shrivelled blue sloes and frost-bitten hips, and the village built in tiers, and the tower with the dark ivy—the only thing that remained green—and the white School in the mild, unglittering sunshine. I smelt the musky, rotten smell of the dead leaves; I smelt, too, the vitiated atmosphere of ink and paper and wet sabots in the classroom. And Papa, frantically clutching his Louis XIV nose and Mélie, anxiously fiddling with her breasts, thought I was going to be seriously ill again. The gentle doctor with the feminine voice came rushing up the three flights of stairs and assured them that it was nothing at all.

(I detest that fair man with the light spectacles. I admit that he looks after me well, but, at the sight of him, I put my hands under the sheets, I curl up like a gun-dog and I clench my toes, as Fanchette does when I want to see her claws close to. This feeling is completely unjust but I haven't the least intention of overcoming it. I don't like a man whom I don't know touching me and fingering me and laying his head on my chest to hear if I'm breathing properly. Besides, hang it all, he might at least warm his hands!)

It *was* nothing at all and, actually, I was soon able to get up. And, from that day, my preoccupations took another turn.

"Mélie, whoever's going to make my dresses now?"

"Haven't the faintest idea, my lamby. Why don't you ask Ma'ame Coeur to give you an address?"

Why, Mélie was absolutely right!

Really, it was dense not to have thought of that before, because, good gracious, "Ma'ame Coeur" isn't a distant relative, she's Papa's sister. But this admirable father of mine has always managed, with perfect ease, to keep free of any kind of family ties and duties. I really believe I've only seen her once in my life, Aunt Coeur. I was nine and Papa brought me to Paris with him. She looked like the Empress Eugénie; I think that was to annoy her brother who looks, himself, like Louis XIV. Quite a royal family! She's a widow, this amiable woman, and, as far as I know, has no children.

Each day, I wander a little further through the flat. I'm so thin that I'm quite lost in my flowing dressing-gown of faded purple velveteen, gathered on the shoulders. In the gloomy drawing-room, Papa has installed the furniture from his smoking-room and from the drawing-room at Montigny.

It hurts me to see little low, wide, slightly ripped Louis XVI armchairs side by side with the two Arab tables, the Moorish armchair of inlaid wood and the divan covered with an oriental carpet. Claudine, you'll have to do something about that. . . .

I finger the knick-knacks, I pull out a Moroccan stool, I put the little sacred cow back on the chimneypiece (it's a very old Japanese curio, twice stuck together again, thanks to Mélie), then, all at once, I plump down on the divan, against the glass where my eyes, so much too big, and my hollow cheeks and most, most of all my poor hair in those uneven layers, throw me into black depression. Well, old thing, suppose this moment you had to climb the big walnut-tree in the garden at Montigny? Where's your wonderful nimbleness, where are your agile legs and your monkey's hands that made such a brisk *slap* on the branches when you used to be up at the top in ten seconds? You look like a little girl of fourteen who's been martyred.

One night at the dinner-table, as I nibbled—without seeming

to—some bread crusts that are still strictly forbidden, I questioned the author of the *Malacology of Fresnois.*

"Why haven't we seen my aunt yet? Haven't you written to her? Haven't you been to see her?"

Papa, with the condescension one displays to mad people, asked me gently, with a clear eye and a soothing voice:

"Which aunt, darling?"

Accustomed to his frank absent-mindedness, I made him grasp that I was talking about his sister.

Thereupon he exclaimed, full of admiration:

"You think of everything! Ten thousand herds of swine! Dear old girl, how pleased she'll be to know we're in Paris." He added, his face clouding: "She'll hook on to me like a damn' leech."

Little by little, I extended my walks as far as the book-lair. Papa has put up shelves all round the three walls of the room that gets the daylight from a big window (the only even moderately light room in the flat is the kitchen—though Mélie picturesquely insists that "you can't see in it neither with your head or your tail"), and, in the middle, he has planted his thuya-wood and brass desk, furnished with castors, that rambles into all the corners, laboriously followed by an old low-seated, high-backed armchair of red leather that's gone white at the corners and is split on both arms. The little wheeled ladder to reach the high-perched dictionaries, a trestle-table—and that's all.

Now that I'm getting stronger every day, I come and cheer myself up with the well-known titles of the books and now and then I re-open the Balzac (in Bertall's shocking edition) or Voltaire's *Dictionnaire Philosophique.* What am I doing with this dictionary? Boring myself . . . and learning various undesirable things, nearly always shocking ones (undesirable things are not always shocking; on the contrary). But, ever since I've learnt to read, I've been "Papa's bookworm" and, though I'm not in the least shocked, I don't get over-excited either.

I have explored Papa's "sanctum". That Papa of mine! In his bedroom, hung with a wallpaper strewn with bunches of rustic flowers—a young girl's wallpaper—he has a four-poster too, with its mattress sloped at a vertiginous angle—Papa will only sleep in a sitting position. I will spare you the Empire furniture, the big wicker armchairs cushioned with brochures and scientific reviews, the coloured planks hung all over the place, strewn with slugs, millipedes and various horrid little creatures! On the chimneypiece, rows of fossils that were molluscs a good long time ago. And, on the floor beside the bed, two ammonites as big as cartwheels! Long live Malacology! Our home is the sanctuary of a noble—and I dare to say unsullied—Science.

The dining-room isn't interesting. If the sideboard weren't Burgundian and the big chairs Burgundian too, I'd find it very commonplace. The too-rustic dresser no longer has the dark panelling at Montigny as a background. Having nowhere else to put it, Mélie has placed the big linen-cupboard there. It's beautiful, with its Louis XV panels adorned with musical emblems, but like everything else, it is sad and exiled. It thinks of Montigny, as I do.

When the doctor I dislike told me, with an air of modest triumph, that I could go out, I exclaimed: "Nothing would induce me to!" I said it with such splendid indignation that it left him—it's the only word—stupid.

"Why?"

"Because my hair's been cut off! I won't go out till I've got long hair."

"Very well, my child, then you'll get ill again. You need, you absolutely must have fresh air."

"You make me sick. What I absolutely must have is *hair*."

He went away, mild as ever. Why didn't he get angry? I'd have said some hard things to him to relieve my feelings. . . .

Feeling thoroughly embittered, I studied myself in looking-glasses. I decided that it wasn't so much the shortness of my hair as its unevenness that made me look more than ever like a melancholy cat. The desk scissors to the rescue! They were too big and blunt. My work-box ones? They were too short. Of course there were Mélie's scissors . . . but she uses them for cutting up chickens' guts and splitting gizzards—they disgust me.

"Mélie, tomorrow you're to buy me a pair of cutting-out scissors."

It was a long and difficult job. A hairdresser would have done it quicker and better but my misanthropy concerning everything to do with Paris was still too acute not to shudder at the thought. Oh my poor locks, all cut off at ear-level! The ones in front, amusingly curled, didn't look too bad but I felt thoroughly miserable and furious when I saw, in two glasses, that thin white nape under the stiff little ends that were only slowly making up their minds to grow into spirals, like balsam pods that, when they've shot out their seeds, curl up little by little into corkscrews and dry that shape.

Before I had consented to put one foot out-of-doors, the human species irrupted into my home, represented by the concierge. Exasperated by hearing the Breton servant unjustly beating her unfortunate little dog every morning, I'd spied on her and poured half my big water-jug over her coif.

Five minutes later, enter the portress, a dirty, long-winded woman who had once been handsome. Papa being absent, she stared with some surprise at this pale, arrogant little girl. "Mademoiselle, the Breton girl has said someone emptied a pail. . . ."—"I did. What of it?"—"She says as how it's a reason for her to put up a complaint. . . ."—"My nerves can't put up with *her*. Besides, if she starts beating the dog again, she'll get something worse than water. Do I tell her employers that she spits in the breakfast-cups and blows her nose on the table napkins? If she'd prefer that, she'd better say so!" And the Breton girl has, at last, left that poor dog in peace. Moreover, you know, I've never seen her spit in the cups or blow her nose on the napkins. But she looks perfectly capable of doing so. Besides, as we say at home, she *repulses* me. Isn't that what's called a "generous lie"?

My first outing took place in March. A sharp sun and an acid wind; Papa and myself in a cab with pneumatic tyres. In the red cloak I wore at Montigny and my astrakhan cap I looked like a poor little boy in skirts. (And all my shoes have grown so big!) We took a slow walk in the Luxembourg, where my noble father entertained me with the comparative merits of the Nationale and the Sainte-Geneviève Libraries. The wind dazed me, so did the sun. I thought the big, smooth, tree-lined walks really beautiful but the quantities of children and the absence of weeds shocked me, the one quite as much as the other.

"In re-reading the proofs of my great *Treatise*," Papa told me, "I realised there was still a great deal more delving to be done. I'm astonished, myself, at the superficiality of certain parts. Don't you think it extraordinary, that, with my mental precision, I've only been able to touch on certain important points—of fascinating interest, I venture to say—relating to minute species? But this is no subject for a little girl."

Little girl! Won't he ever condescend to notice that I'm forging ahead fast, leaving my seventeen years behind me? As to minute species, goodness me, I couldn't care less for them! Major species, ditto!

What lots of children, what lots of children! Shall I have as many children as that one day? And who is the gentleman who will inspire me to perpetrate them with him? Ugh, ugh! It's odd how chaste my imagination and my feelings are since my illness. What would people think of a *Great Treatise*—(my work!)—*on the elevating influence of cerebral fevers on young girls?* My poor little Luce. . . . How far advanced the trees are here! The lilacs are shooting out tender leaves. Back there, back there . . . you can still only see brown and varnished buds, at the most some wood-anemones, if that!

On returning from my walk I noticed that the Rue Jacob obstinately maintained its sordid aspect with its pavements freely used as spittoons. Indifferent to the flattery of my faithful Mélie, who pretended that the walk had put back some roses into her "girlie's" cheeks (she's a brazen liar, my faithful Mélie), and depressed by this Paris spring that made me dream too much of the other, the real one, I lay down on my bed, tired out. Then I got up and wrote a letter to Luce. When I'd sealed my letter, I realised, too late, that the poor little goose wouldn't understand a word of it. For it means nothing whatever to her that What's-his-name, the new tenant of our house at Montigny, has lopped the branches of the big walnut-tree because they were trailing on the ground and that the Fredonnes wood is already hazy (you can see it from the School) with the green mist of young shoots! Luce won't be able to tell me, either, whether the corn is springing well or whether the violets at the west fork of the lane that leads to Vrimes are forward or late with their leaves. All she will notice is the unsentimental tone of my letter. She won't understand why I give her so few details about my life in Paris and why the news of my health is confined to this: "I've been ill for two months, but am getting better." It's to Claire, my little Co-First Communicant, that I ought to have written! Today, she would be looking after her sheep in the field at Vrimes or near the Matignons wood, a big cloak over her shoulders and her little round head, with its soft eyes, protected by a scarf coquettishly pinned up like a mantilla. Her sheep would be straying, restrained with difficulty by the good dog Lisette and Claire would be absorbed in a yellow-back novel, one of the ones I had left her when I went away.

So I wrote Claire a nice, affectionate, commonplace letter. French composition: *Letter from a young girl to her friend to tell her of her arrival in Paris.* Oh Mademoiselle! Red-haired and vindictive Mademoiselle, I'm still a little feverish and I can hear your cutting voice, so effective in suppressing all disorder. What are you doing with your little Aimeé at this very moment? I can imagine, I can imagine quite well: and imagining it sends up my "temperature". . . .

3

Papa, whose thoughts I had turned in the direction of Aunt
Coeur, began, during the next few days, to express faint suggestions
of taking me to see her. I emitted loud screams to frighten him.

"Go and see my Aunt? Well, of all the ideas! With my hair like
this and my face like this and not one single new frock! Papa, it's
enough to jeopardise my future and wreck my prospects of marriage!"

(I needn't have protested so much. The eighteenth-century features resumed their serenity.)

"Three dozen herds of swine! I like it devilish well, your cropped
hair! No, what I really mean. . . . Well, the fact is I'm revising a
difficult chapter at the moment. I need at least another week on it."

(Things were going well.)

"Hi, Mélie, you great lazy slut, stir your stumps and look sharp
about it! I've got to get hold of a dressmaker."

One was discovered, who came to "take my orders". She is an old
woman who lives in the house and her name is Poullanx. She has
scruples, she's easily alarmed, she doesn't like tight skirts and she
ostentatiously parades an old-fashioned honesty. When she had
finished a perfectly simple blue cloth dress with fine little tucks on
the bodice and a collar, edged with stitching, that came right up to
my ears (I can show my neck later on when I've grown plumper), she
brought me back all the bits and pieces of stuff, even little snippets
three centimetres wide. She's a dreadful woman with her Jansenist
way of disapproving of the "immodest dresses" that are all the rage at
the moment!

There's nothing like a new dress for making me want to go out. But, however much I brush my hair, it doesn't grow fast. Little by little, the activity of the old Claudine is beginning to reappear. Besides, the fact that there are plenty of bananas about helps to make life bearable. By buying them ripe and letting them rot just a little, bananas are sheer heaven, like eating Liberty velvet! Fanchette thinks they smell disgusting.

During this last fortnight, I received an answer from Luce; a letter in pencil which, I admit, staggered me.

"MY DARLING CLAUDINE,—*You've taken ages to think of me! You really might have thought of me sooner, to give me a little strength to bear all the tortures I've been through. I failed in my Entrance Exam to the Teachers' Training College and, from that day to this, my sister has made me pay for it. For the least thing, she hits me on the head hard enough to dislocate my neck and she refuses to let me have any shoes. I can't ask my mother to let me go back home, she'd beat me too much. And it's no good looking to Mademoiselle to protect me (she's still as crazy as ever about my sister who's led her a pretty dance). I'm writing to you a few lines at a time. I don't want her to pinch my letter. When you were here, those two were a little afraid of you. Now everything's gone—everything went with you, and I'd say goodbye to this world if I weren't so frightened of killing myself. I don't know what I'm going to do but things can't go on like this. I shall run away, I'll go goodness knows where. Don't laugh at me, Claudine. Oh, if I'd only got you here, even if only to beat me, life would still be worth living. The two Jauberts and Anaïs are at the Training College. Marie Belhomme is serving in a shop. There are four new girls who are squits and, as to the violets, I don't know whether they're ahead of time—it's so long since I went for a walk. Goodbye, Claudine darling, if you can find some way of making me less miserable or of coming to see me, please do, it would be an act of charity. I kiss your lovely hair and your two eyes that didn't love me a bit, and your whole face, and your white neck. Don't laugh at me, it isn't any silly little misery to be joked about that's making me cry.*

Your
LUCE."

What are they doing to her, those two horrid women? My poor, inconsistent little Luce, too bad to be good and too cowardly to be bad, I couldn't, all the same, have brought you with me! (besides, I didn't want to). But you've no more peppermints, no more chocolate, and no more Claudine. The new School, the opening of it by the Minister, Doctor Dutertre. . . . How far away I am from all that! Doctor Dutertre, you are the only man up to now who's dared to kiss me—and on the corner of the mouth, too. You excited me and you frightened me: is that all I'm to hope for, to a greater degree, from the man who will definitely carry me away? As regards practical notions of love, it's a trifle meagre. Luckily my theory is far more complete, though there are some obscure patches in it. For even Papa's library can't teach me everything.

Well, that is more or less the summary of my first months in Paris. My "fair-copy book", as we used to say at school, is up to date; it shouldn't be difficult for me to keep it so. I haven't got much to do here. I'm making some charming little chemises for my always needy wardrobe and some little knickers (closed ones). I brush my hair—it's so soon done nowadays—I comb my white Fanchette, who has hardly any fleas left since she became a Parisienne, and install her with her flat cushion on the window-sill so that she can take the air. Yesterday she caught sight of the fat—how can I put it?—*impaired* tom belonging to the concierge and muttered nameless insults at him, from the height of her third storey, in the slightly hoarse, peasant voice of an ex-outdoor cat. Mélie looks after her health and, to prevent constipation, brings her pots of catmint which the poor darling devours. Does she dream of the garden, and of the great chestnut-tree we so often climbed together? I think she does. But she loves me so much she would live with me in the filthiest of hovels.

Escorted by Mélie, I've sampled the charms of the big shops. People stare at me in the street because I'm pale and thin, with short, bushy hair and because Mélie wears a Fresnois peasant coif. Am I at last going to experience the covetous glances of those famous "old gentlemen" who follow young girls? We'll see about that later on: at the moment, I'm busy.

I've principally been engaged in studying the different smells in the Louvre and the Bon Marché. In the linen department, it's intoxicating. Oh Anaïs! You, who used to eat samples of sheets and handkerchiefs, this is your spiritual home! That sugary smell of new blue cottons, does it thrill me or make me want to vomit? Both, I think. Shame on flannel and woollen blankets! They smell exactly like rotten eggs. The smell of new shoes is by no means to be despised, neither is that of leather purses. But they can't compete with the heavenly odour of the thick blue tracing-paper used for embroidery which consoles one for the sickening, cloying smell of the soaps and the scents. . . .

Claire has answered my letter, too. Once again, she's extremely happy. This time, she really *has* found true love. And she informs me she's going to get married. At seventeen, she's really and truly "settling down"! A mean little feeling of annoyance made me shrug my shoulders. (Now, now, Claudine, my dear, how vulgar of you!) "*He's so handsome,*" Claire wrote, "*that I'm never tired of looking at him. His eyes are stars and his beard is so soft! And he's so strong—honestly, I don't weigh more than a feather in his arms! I still don't know when we're going to get married. Mamma thinks I'm ever so much too young. But I'm imploring her to let me as soon as possible. How blissfully happy I shall be to be his wife!*" She enclosed a little photograph of the Loved One with these ravings; he's a broad fellow who looks thirty-five, with an honest, placid face, kind little eyes and a bushy beard.

In her ecstasy, she completely forgot to tell me whether the violets at the west fork of the lane that leads to Vrimes . . .

4

No getting out of it, we've got to go and call on Aunt Coeur, otherwise she'll be annoyed with us when she knows we've been in Paris so long, and I hate family rows. Papa suggested the ingenious idea of warning her in advance of our visit but I fiercely dissuaded him.

"You know, we oughtn't to spoil the pleasure of the surprise. Considering we've been here three months without letting her know, let's go the whole hog and spring it on her in a dramatic way!"

(In that case, if she were out, at least we'd have gained a little time. And we should have done our duty.)

We set off, Papa and I, about four o'clock. Papa was, quite frankly, sublime with his overcoat with the ample red ribbon in the buttonhole and that top-hat whose brim is far too wide and that dominant nose and that tri-coloured beard. His whole appearance—suggesting a retired army officer awaiting the return of the rightful King of France—and his childish, ecstatic expression excited the enthusiasm of the urchins of the neighbourhood and they greeted him with cheers.

I was indifferent to this popularity. I had put on my new dress of perfectly plain blue cloth and on my hair—what was left of it—I'd carefully poised my round black felt hat with the feathers, artfully arranging some curls on my temples and pulling some forward over my eyebrows. My apprehension over the visit made me look ill; it still doesn't take much to make me do that!

Aunt Coeur lives in a magnificent, unattractive new block of flats in the Avenue de Wagram. The rapid lift made Papa uneasy. And, personally, I rather disliked all those white walls and stairs and woodwork. And Madame Coeur was "in". What bad luck!

The drawing-room where we waited a minute or two desperately carried on the whiteness of the staircase. White painted woodwork, frail white furniture, white cushions with light-coloured flowers, white chimney-piece. Great heavens, there wasn't one single dark corner! And *I* can't feel safe and comfortable except in dim rooms and dark woods and deep, heavy armchairs! That "eighteenth-century" white of the windows sets one's teeth on edge like the noise of zinc being scraped. . . .

Enter Aunt Coeur. She was astonished, but extremely agreeable. And how she prided herself on her august resemblance! She had the Empress Eugénie's distinguished nose, her smooth, heavy swathes of greying hair, her slightly drooping smile. Not for anything in the world would she have given up her low (and artificial) chignon or her very full gathered skirt, or the little lace scarf that *flirted* (ha! ha!) round her shoulders that were drooping, like her smile. My good Aunt, how Your Majesty, who reigned before 1870, clashes with this drawing-room all done up in whipped cream that couldn't be more pure 1900!

But she was charming, Aunt Coeur! She spoke a polished French that intimidated me, exclaimed over our unexpected move—it certainly *was* unexpected!—and never stopped staring at me. I couldn't get over hearing someone call Papa by his Christian name. And she used the formal "vous" to her brother.

"But, Claude, this child . . . incidentally she's charming and a completely individual type . . . hasn't really recovered yet. You must have nursed her in your own rough and ready way, poor little thing! What I simply can't understand is why it never entered your head to send for me! You're just the same as ever!"

Papa took his sister's remonstrances very ill, and he so seldom jibs at anything. They obviously seldom see eye to eye with each other and start bickering at once. I began to get interested.

"Wilhelmine, I looked after my daughter perfectly adequately. Incidentally, I had a great deal on my mind, and I can't think of everything."

"And this idea of living in the Rue Jacob! My dear, the new neighbourhoods are far healthier, far airier and far better built and they're no more expensive. I simply don't understand you. . . . Look here, at 145B . . . just a few yards from here, there's a delightful flat, and we'd be practically on each other's doorsteps. . . . We could be always running in and out . . . it would be nice for Claudine and for you too."

(Papa leapt in his chair.)

"Live here? My dear girl, you're the most exquisite woman on earth, but I'd rather be shot than live in your company!"

(Oh, well done, Papa! This time I laughed wholeheartedly and Aunt Coeur seemed stupefied by my being so little upset by their disagreements.)

"Little girl, wouldn't you rather have a pretty, light flat like this than be on that dirty Left Bank where no nice people live?"

"Aunt, I think I prefer the Rue Jacob and the flat there, because light rooms depress me."

She raised her arched, deliberately Spanish-looking eyebrows under her concentric wrinkles and seemed to attribute my demented words to my state of health. Then she began to talk to Papa about their family.

"I have my grandson, Marcel, living here with me—you know, Poor Ida's son (??). He's doing his philosophy course and he's about Claudine's age. I shan't say a word about *him*," she added, radiant. "He's a treasure for a grandmother. You'll see him in a moment: he comes home at five and I'm longing to show him to you."

Papa said "Yes" and looked impressed. But I could see that he hadn't the faintest notion who Ida was or who Marcel was, and that he was already bored at having rediscovered his family! I was thoroughly enjoying myself! But my amusement was entirely inward and I didn't shine in conversation. Papa was dying to go and could only resist the temptation by talking about his great treatise on Malacology. At last, a door banged, there was a light step and the heralded Marcel entered. . . . Heavens, how pretty he was!

I gave him my hand without saying a word, I was staring at him so much. I'd never seen anything so charming! But he was a *girl*! A slip of a girl in breeches! Fair hair, rather long, parted on the right, a complexion like Luce's, blue eyes like a little English girl's and no more moustache than I had. He was blushing, he spoke softly, keeping his head a little on one side and looking down at the ground.

You could have eaten him! Papa, however, seemed insensible to so much far from manly charm, whereas Aunt Coeur devoured her grandson with her eyes.

"You're back very late, darling. I hope nothing happened to you?"

"No, Grandmother," replied the little wonder sweetly, raising his pure eyes.

Papa, who continued to be a hundred miles away, vaguely questioned Marcel about his studies. And I went on staring at this pretty sugar-stick of a cousin! *He*, on the contrary, didn't so much as look at me, and, if my admiration hadn't been so disinterested, I should have felt slightly humiliated. Aunt Coeur, who had exultantly observed the effect produced by her cherub, tried to bring us together a little:

"Marcel, Claudine is the same age as you are, you know. You'll be nice companions for each other. The Easter holidays will soon be here."

I made a brisk movement forward to show that I was all in favour; the boy, surprised at my eagerness, looked up at me with his blue eyes and replied with tempered enthusiasm:

"I'd like that very much, Grandmother, if Madem—if Claudine is willing."

After that, there was no stopping Aunt Coeur. She told us at length about the virtues of her precious darling. "I never even had to raise my voice." She made us stand shoulder to shoulder, Marcel was all that much taller! (*All that much* was three centimetres, hardly worth making such a terrific fuss about!) The treasure condescended to laugh and to become a little livelier. He straightened his tie in front of the glass. He was dressed like a pretty fashion-plate. And that walk, that swaying, gliding walk! That way of turning round, pivoting on one hip! No, he was really too good-looking! I was startled out of my contemplation by the following question from Aunt Coeur. "Claude, you'll both dine here, won't you?"

"Good Lord, no!" exploded Papa, who was dying of boredom. "I've got an appointment at home with . . . with what's-his-name who's bringing me some documents, some doc-u-ments for my treatise. Come along, child, we must be off!"

"I'm *so* sorry, and tomorrow I'm not dining at home. I'm rather booked-up this season, I've stupidly gone and accepted invitations

from all and sundry. How about Thursday? Just ourselves, of
course. Claude, are you listening to me?"

"I'm hanging on your lips, my dear, but I'm damnably late. Till
Thursday, Wilhelmine. Goodbye, young Paul . . . no, Jacques."

I said goodbye too, unwillingly. Marcel saw us to the door, very
polite and correct, and kissed my glove.

We returned in silence through the lighted streets. I haven't got
used yet to being out-of-doors at that hour, and the lights and the
dark passers-by made me nervous and brought a lump into my
throat. I was in a hurry to get home. Papa, released from the
miseries of his visit, gaily hummed songs of the First Empire. "*Nine
months later, a sweet pledge of love.*"

The soft lamplight and the table laid for dinner revived my spirits
and loosened my tongue.

Mélie, I've seen my aunt. Mélie, I've seen my cousin. He's
so-so . . . his hair's combed smooth as smooth . . . he's got a short
parting . . . his name's Marcel."

"Now then, my pet, now then! You're deafening me. Come along,
eat up your nice soupy. So you'll have a young man, and high time
too!'"

"You big fathead! Silly idiot, do you have to be so dense! He's *not*
a young man! Why, I don't even know him! Oh, you make me sick.
I'm going to my room."

And, believe it or not, I *did* go to my room! The very idea
that a little mother's darling like Marcel could be a lover for *me*! If I
found him so attractive and made so little secret of it, it was
precisely because he seemed to me no more of a man than Luce
herself.

The effect of once more seeing people who live like everyone else
and talking to someone other than Fanchette and Mélie was to make
me slightly, but rather pleasantly, feverish and keep me awake part
of the night. The sort of fancies one has at midnight danced through
my head. I was frightened of not knowing what to say to that
amiable Aunt Coeur who had stepped straight out of a Winterhalter
painting; she'd take me for a dolt. Goodness, sixteen years at
Montigny, of which ten were spent at school, hardly develop the gift
of repartee! You emerged from that with just about enough vocabulary to call Anaïs names and to pet Luce. That pretty little girl of a
Marcel probably couldn't even say 'Shut up'. He'd make fun of me

on Thursday if I skinned my bananas with my teeth. And what should I wear for that dinner? I hadn't got an evening frock, I'd have to wear the one I wore for the opening of the Schools: white muslin with a cross-over fichu. He'd think it very dull and ordinary.

The result was that having gone to sleep last night in open-mouthed admiration of that boy whose trousers haven't a single wrinkle in them, I woke up this morning with a strong desire to slap his face. All the same, if Anaïs set eyes on him, she'd be quite capable of raping him! The gawky Anaïs, with her yellow face and her brusque gestures, raping little Marcel made a funny picture. It made me laugh in spite of myself as I went into Papa's book-lair.

To my surprise, Papa wasn't alone. He was talking to a gentleman, a young gentleman who looked quite intelligent and had a square beard. It appeared he was a "first class man", Monieur Maria, you know, who discovered the underground caves at X. . . . Papa had met him in some boring place, the Geographical Society or somewhere else in the Sorbonne and had got excited about these caves—they might contain some hypothetical fossilised slugs! He indicated me to him by saying: "This is Claudine", as he might have said: "This is Leo XIII, of course you know he's the Pope." At which, Monsieur Maria bowed as if he perfectly understood the situation. A man like that who fiddles about all the time in caves—I'm perfectly sure he must smell of snails.

After lunch, I asserted my independence.

"Papa, I'm going out."

(This did not go down as well as I should have expected.)

"Going out? With Mélie, I presume?"

"No, she's got some mending to do."

"What! You want to go out all by yourself?"

I opened my eyes as wide as saucers.

"Gracious, of course I'm going out by myself—what's wrong?"

"What's wrong is that, in Paris, young girls . . ."

"Look here, Papa, you must try and be consistent. At Montigny, I used to wander about the woods all the time. I should have thought that was lots more dangerous than walking along a Paris pavement."

"There's something in that. But I might foresee dangers of another kind in Paris. Read the papers."

"Fie, fie, father, it is an offence to your daughter even to entertain such a supposition!" (Papa did not look as if he understood this elegant allusion. No doubt he neglects Molière as not being sufficiently concerned with slugs.) "Besides, I never read the sensational news items. I'm going to the Louvre—the shop, not the picture gallery. I must be tidy for Aunt Coeur's dinner-party. I haven't got any fine stockings and my white shoes are shabby. Gimme some lovely money. . . . I've only a hundred and six sous."

(In Fresnois they reckon in sous up to six francs, with the exception of sixty sous which they call three francs like anywhere else.)

5

WELL, after all, it's not so terrible going out alone in Paris. I brought back some very interesting observations from my little walk: (1) it's much warmer than in Montigny; (2) your nose is all black inside when you get home; (3) people stare at you if you stand still in front of a newspaper kiosk; (4) people also stare at you when you don't let yourself be disrespectfully treated on the pavement.

Let me narrate the incident that gave rise to observation (4). A very good-looking gentleman followed me in the Rue des Saints-Pères. During the first quarter of an hour, inner jubilation of Claudine. Followed by a very good-looking gentleman, just like in Albert Guillaume's pictures! Second quarter of an hour . . . the gentleman's step came closer; I hastened mine, but he kept his distance. Third quarter of an hour; the gentleman passed me, pinching my behind with a detached expression. A leap in the air from Claudine who raised her umbrella and brought it down on the gentleman's head with typical Fresnois vigour. Gentleman's hat in the gutter, immense delight of passers-by, disappearance of Claudine, overwhelmed by her too sensational success.

Aunt Coeur is very nice. She's sent me, with a friendly note, a necklace, a thin gold chain with little round pearls strung on it at intervals of ten centimetres. Fanchette thinks this piece of jewellery is charming; she has already flattened two of the links and she bites the pearls with her big teeth, like an expert in precious stones.

While I was getting ready for the Thursday dinner-party, I thought about my décolletage. It was very, very modest but suppose

I was going to look too thin? Sitting in my tub, quite naked, I noticed that I had put on a little flesh, but I still needed to put on more. What luck that my neck had stayed round and firm! That saved me. It was a pity about the two little salt-cellars at the base, but they couldn't be helped! I wasted time in the hot water, counting the little bones in my back, measuring whether I was the same length from my groin to my feet as from my groin to my forehead, pinching my right calf because I could feel it in my left shoulder blade. (At every pinch, a funny little sting behind one's shoulder.) And what sheer bliss to be able to hook my feet behind my neck! As that dirty great gangling Anaïs used to say: "It must be frightfully amusing to be able to bite one's toe-nails!"

Good heavens, how tiny my breasts were! (At school, we called them bubs and Mélie says titties.) I thought of our "Competitions" of three years ago, during our rare Thursday walks.

In a clearing of the wood, in a sunken path, we used to sit in a circle—we four big ones—and we used to open our bodices. Anaïs (what cheek!) used to display a morsel of lemon-coloured skin, swell out her stomach and say impudently: "*They've* come on like anything since last month!" Nothing of the sort! The Sahara desert! Luce, pink and white in her coarse schoolgirl chemise—longsleeved chemises without so much as a scallop, that's the rule—uncovered a hardly discernible "centre valley" and two small pink points like Fanchette's nipples. And Claudine? A little arched chest but about as much breasts as a slightly plump boy. Well, after all, at fourteen! The exhibition over, we fastened up our bodices again, each of us with the inner conviction that we had much more of *them* than the three others.

My white muslin dress, well-ironed by Mélie, still seemed attractive enough to me not to feel peevish when I put it on. My poor beautiful hair no longer cascaded over it right down to my hips, but it stood out so amusingly round my head that I didn't languish too much over my vanished mane, that night. Ten thousand herds of swine!—to use Papa's pet expression—at all costs, I mustn't forget my gold chain!

"Mélie, is Papa getting dressed?"

"He's getting dressed all right. Overdoing it, if you ask me. He's bust three stiff collars already. Run along and tie his tie."

I hurried to do so. My noble father had got himself up in a slightly, in fact a *very*, old-fashioned evening suit, but it was impossible for him not to look imposing.

"Hurry up, hurry up, Papa, it's half-past seven. Mélie, you give Fanchette her dinner. My red cloak, and let's be off!"

The white drawing-room, with electric bulbs in all the corners, made me feel that, any moment, I might have an epileptic fit. Papa thinks as I do; he loathes this iced-cake décor so dear to his sister Wilhelmine and said so in no uncertain manner.

"Believe it or not, I'd have myself flogged in public rather than sleep inside this cream bun."

But the pretty Marcel appeared and beautified everything with his presence. How charming he looked! Light and slim in a dinner-jacket, his hair moonlight fair, his translucent skin velvety under the lights like the inside of a convolvulus. While he was saying good evening to us, I noticed that his pale blue eyes were giving me a swift inspection.

Aunt Coeur followed him, dazzling. That dress of pearl-grey silk with flounces of black Chantilly lace, was its date 1867 or 1900? 1867, more likely, only a household-cavalryman must have sat on the crinoline and flattened it somewhat. The two grey bandeaux were very thick and very smooth; in the old days, she must have studied that pale blue gaze under the drooping, worn eyelids so thoroughly from the Comtesse de Téba that it had become second nature. She had a gliding walk, she wore sleeves set into deep armholes and she showed herself full of . . . urbanity. "Urbanity" is a noun that suits her as well as her bandeaux.

No other guests beside ourselves. But, goodness me, how they dress up at Aunt Coeur's! At Montigny, I used to dine in my school pinafore and Papa used to keep on the indescribable garment—cloak, overcoat, coachman's cape, a mongrel product of all three—that he'd put on first thing in the morning to feed his slugs in. If one wears low necks for an intimate family meal, what on earth shall I put on for big dinner-parties? Perhaps my chemise with the pink ribbon shoulder straps. . . .

(Claudine, old thing, enough of these digressions! You must try and eat correctly and not say, when you're handed a dish you don't like: "Take it away, I think it's disgusting!")

Naturally, I was seated beside Marcel. Oh horror, oh misery! The dining-room was white too! White and yellow, but the effect was just as bad. And the crystal and the flowers and the electric light . . . it all made such a shindy on the table, you could positively *hear* it. Honestly, all those sparkles of light gave me an impression of noise.

Marcel, under Aunt Coeur's adoring eye, behaved like a society debutante and asked if I was enjoying myself in Paris. At first, a savage "no" was all he got in reply. But soon I became a little more human, because I was eating a little patty with truffles that would have consoled a widow the day after her bereavement, so I condescended to explain myself.

"You see, I'm quite sure I shall enjoy myself later on. But, up to now, I find it terribly hard to get used to not seeing any leaves. Third floors in Paris don't exactly abound in green 'tillers'."

"In green . . . *what?*"

"In 'tillers'. It's what we call them in Fresnois," I added with a certain pride.

"Oh, it's a Fresnois word, is it? Rather unusual! Gr-r-reen tillers," he repeated teasingly, rolling the *r*.

"I forbid you to mimic me! If you imagine it's more elegant, your Parisian *r* that you rumble in the depths of your throat as if you were gargling!"

"Ugh, you dirty little thing! Are your girl friends like you?"

"I didn't have any girl friends. I don't much care for having girl friends. Luce had a soft skin, but that isn't enough."

"Luce had a soft skin. . . . What a funny way of judging people!"

"Why funny? From the moral point of view, Luce simply doesn't exist. I'm considering her from the physical point of view and I tell you she has green eyes and a soft skin."

"Did you love each other very much?"

(That pretty, vicious face! What wouldn't one say to him to see those eyes light up! Shame on you, you naughty little boy!)

"No, I didn't love her in the least. *She* did, yes. She cried like anything when I went away."

"But. then, which one did you like better?"

My calmness emboldened Marcel. Perhaps he took me for a goose and would gladly have asked me more definite questions but the grown-ups stopped talking for a moment while a manservant with a clerical face changed the plates and we stopped, too. There was already a touch of complicity between us.

Aunt Coeur's tired blue gaze wandered from Marcel to myself.

"Claude," she said to Papa, "look how those two children set each other off. Your daughter's ivory skin and her hair with those bronze lights in it and her deep eyes—all that brunette look some little girls have who aren't really brunettes—make my cherub look fairer than ever. Don't you agree?"

"Yes," replied Papa with conviction. "He's much more of a girl than she is."

Her cherub and I lowered our eyes as becomes children bursting at once with pride and with a desperate desire to giggle. And the dinner pursued its course without further confidences. Moreover, a delicious tangerine ice detached me from all other preoccupations.

I returned to the drawing-room on Marcel's arm. And all at once, no one seemed to know what to do. Aunt Coeur appeared to have some serious things to say to Papa and got rid of us.

"Marcel, my darling, go and show Claudine over the flat. Be nice—try and make her feel a little at home."

"Come along," said the 'darling', "I'll take you to see my room."

It was white, too, just as I had expected. White and green, with slender reeds on a white ground. But so much whiteness eventually aroused in me a secret desire to upset inkpots—heaps of inkpots—over it, to scribble in charcoal all over the walls, to dirty that distemper with blood from a cut finger. . . . Heavens, how perverse I'd become in an all-white flat!

I went straight to the chimneypiece on which I saw a photograph-frame. Excitedly, Marcel switched on an electric light just over our heads.

"That's my best friend . . . Charlie. . . . Almost like a brother. Isn't he good-looking?"

Much too good-looking, in fact. Dark eyes, with curving lashes, the merest hint of a black moustache above a tender mouth, hair parted at the side, like Marcel's.

"I certainly agree he's handsome! Nearly as good-looking as you are," I said sincerely.

"Oh, *much* better!" he exclaimed fervently. "The photograph can't do justice to his white skin and his black hair. And he's such a charming *person*. . . ."

And so on and so on. That pretty Dresden china figure was coming to life at last. I listened, without flinching, to the panegyric of the magnificent Charlie and when Marcel, slightly embarrassed, regained his self-possession, I looked completely convinced and answered quite naturally: "I understand perfectly. You're his Luce."

He took a step backwards and, under the light, I saw his pretty features harden and his sensitive skin turn imperceptibly paler.

"His Luce? Claudine, what do you mean by that?"

With the boldness derived from two glasses of champagne, I shrugged my shoulders and said:

"But, of course. His Luce, his pet, his darling, whatever you call it! One's only got to look at you—do you *look* like a man? That's just why I found you so pretty!"

And as he stood there, perfectly still, staring at me almost icily, I went up closer to him and added, smiling right into his face:

"Marcel, I find you just as pretty at this very moment, believe me. Now, do I look like someone who wants to upset you? I tease you, but I'm not spiteful and there are lots of things I know perfectly well how to keep quiet about—and to listen to without telling anyone else. I shall never be the little female cousin whose unfortunate male cousin feels he's forced to make love to her as they do in books. May I remind you," I went on, laughing, "that you're the grandson of my aunt, what's called my 'Breton nephew'? Marcel, it would be practically incest!"

My "nephew" decided to laugh, but he didn't really want to.

"My dear Claudine, I quite agree that you're not like the little female cousins in 'nice' novels. But I'm afraid that, at Montigny, you've got into the habit of making rather, well—risky—jokes. Suppose there'd been someone listening to us. Grandmother, for example—or your father. . . ."

"I was only giving you tit for tat," I said very sweetly. "And I didn't think it necessary to attract the family's attention when you kept plying me with questions about Luce."

"You had more to lose than I had, if you *had* attracted their attention!"

"Do you think so? I very much doubt it. In the case of girls, those little diversions are just called 'school-girls' nonsense'. But when it comes to boys of seventeen, it's almost a disease. . . ."

He made a violent gesture with his hand.

"You read too much! Young girls have too much imagination to really understand what they read, even if they do come from Montigny."

"I'd managed things badly. That wasn't in the least what I was driving at.

"Have I made you angry, Marcel? I'm a clumsy idiot! All I wanted to do was to prove to you that I wasn't a goose, that I could understand—how can I put it?—*appreciate* certain things. Look, Marcel, you can't really expect me to see you as a great raw-boned schoolboy with enormous feet who'll turn into the perfect type of N.C.O. one day. Just look at yourself! Aren't you, thank heaven, almost exactly like the very prettiest of my schoolfriends? Give me your hand. . . ."

He really ought to have been a girl! All he did was to smile furtively at my over-enthusiastic compliments. He held out his little manicured paw with quite a good grace.

"Claudine, you wicked Claudine, let's get back to them quickly. We'll go through Grandmother's bedroom. I'm not angry any more, only a little flabbergasted still. Let me think things over. . . . It seems to me you aren't too bad a *boy*. . . ."

His sarcasm didn't upset me a bit! To see him sulking and then smiling again, was pure pleasure. I didn't pity his friend with the sweeping eyelashes in the least and I wished them plenty of quarrels with my blessing.

Looking extremely natural—almost unnaturally natural—we continued the tour of the estate. What joy, Aunt Coeur's room was adequate (ghastly word!) to its owner! In it, she had assembled—or exiled—all the furniture that must have been in her room when she was a girl, all the souvenirs of her heyday. The carved rosewood bed, the red damask armchairs that all looked like Their Imperial Majesties' thrones, the tapestry prie-Dieu bristling with oak carvings, the flashy imitation of a Boule desk, console tables galore—they were all there. Damask curtains dripped from the canopy of the bed and the ornate chimneypiece, a shapeless, complicated mass of cupids and acanthus leaves and gilded bronze wreaths, filled me with admiration. Marcel had a supreme contempt for this room and we disputed hotly about the modern style and the merits of beaten egg-white in interior decoration. This aesthetic wrangle allowed us to return, in a calmer frame of mind, to the drawing-room where Papa was yawning like a lion in a cage under the gentle, relentless rain of Aunt Coeur's good advice.

"Grandmother!" cried Marcel, "Claudine's priceless! She likes your bedroom better than all the rest of the flat."

"Funny little girl," said my aunt, caressing me with her languid smile. "My room's very ugly, really. . . ."

". . . But it suits you, Aunt. Don't you think your bandeaux 'clash' with this drawing-room? Thank goodness, you know that perfectly well, because you've kept one little corner of your proper setting!"

It wasn't exactly a compliment perhaps, but she got up and came over and kissed me very sweetly. Suddenly Papa leapt to his feet and consulted his watch.

"Ten thousand herds of . . . ! Sorry, Wilhelmine, but it's five minutes to ten and it's the first time this child has been out since her illness. . . . Young man, go and order us a cab!"

Marcel went out, and quickly returned, with that quick, supple way of swinging round as he went through a doorway, bringing me my red cloak that he dropped deftly on my shoulders.

"Goodbye, Aunt."

"Goodbye, my child. I'm at home on Sundays. It would be too charming of you to come and hand round my tea at five o'clock with your friend Marcel."

Inwardly, I curled up like a prickly hedgehog.

"I don't know how to, Aunt, I've never . . ."

"Now, now, I won't take no for an answer. I must make you into a little person who's as charming as she's pretty! Goodbye, Claude, don't shut yourself up too much in your lair—give a thought now and then to your old sister!"

At the front door, my 'nephew' kissed my wrist a little more lingeringly and accompanied his "Till Sunday" with a knowing smile and a delicious pout and . . . that was that.

All the same, I'd been on the very verge of quarrelling with that boy! Claudine, old thing, will you never cure yourself of that itch to meddle in things that don't concern you, that rather despicable little wish to show that you're artful and knowledgeable and understand heaps of things beyond your age? This urge to astonish people, this craving to disturb people's peace of mind and upset too-placid lives will play you a nasty trick one of these days.

I felt much more at home, back in my own room, squatting on my four-poster bed and stroking Fanchette who had begun her night without waiting for me and lay there trustingly, with her stomach upturned. But—begging your pardon, Fanchette—I recognised those smiling slumbers, those blissful hours of perpetual purring. And I also recognised that filling-out of the flanks and that exceptionally well-licked belly along which the little pink nipples stood out. Fanchette, you had fallen from virtue! But with whom? Good heavens, it was like running one's head against a brick wall! A female cat who didn't go out-of-doors, the concierge's neutered tom . . . who, who could it have been? All the same, I was simply delighted. Kittens in prospect! Compared with this joyous future, even the prestige of Marcel paled.

I asked Mélie for explanations of this mysterious pregnancy. She owned up to everything.

"My lamby, this last time the poor darling did want it so cruel. Three whole days, she was in such a state, she was quite beside herself. So I asked round among the neighbours. The maid downstairs lent me a lovely husband for her, a fine striped grey. I gave him lots of milk to encourage him and our poor darling didn't have to be asked twice . . . they got together straight away."

How she must have been pining, poor Mélie, to act as Cupid's messenger for someone, if only for the cat! She did absolutely right.

Our home has become a meeting-place for various odd people, each more astonishing and more scientific than the last. Monsieur Maria, the Cantal caves one, frequently comes along with that shy man's beard of his. When we meet in the book-lair, he bows awkwardly and makes stammering enquiries about my health, which I lugubriously assure him is "very bad, very bad, Monsieur Maria". I've made the acquaintance of various fat, untidy men with ribbons in their buttonholes whose lives are devoted, I understand, to the cultivation of fossils. . . . Anything but exciting, Papa's friends!

6

A T four o'clock today, Marcel came to see me, "spick and span as if he'd come straight out of a bandbox", as Mélie said. I welcomed him like the sunshine and took him into the drawing-room where he was immensely amused by the arrangement of the furniture and the artificial partition created by the big curtain. "Come along, Nephew, I'm going to show you my room." He contemplated the narrow four-poster and the odd assortment of little bits of furniture with the slightly contemptuous gaiety that Aunt Coeur's bedroom inspired in him, but he was keenly interested in Fanchette.

"How white she is!"

"That's because I brush her every day."

"And fat!"

"That's because she's pregnant."

"Ah! She's . . ."

"Yes. That crazy Mélie brought her a tom-cat because Fanchette nearly went out of her mind while I was ill. The interview had fruitful results, as you see!"

My freedom in speaking about such things obviously made him uncomfortable. I began to laugh and he stared at me with a slightly shocked expression.

"Are you staring at me because I don't talk respectably? Well, that's because, down there in the country, you see cows and dogs and goats getting married very hastily and unceremoniously every day. Down there, it isn't in the least indecent."

"What, not indecent! You know, in Zola's *La Terre*, I realised very well it wasn't as innocent as all that. Peasants don't always watch those things in a purely detached, practical way just as part of the job of farming."

"Your Zola just doesn't understand the first thing about the country. I don't much care for his work in general. . . ."

Marcel wandered about, spying into every corner. What tiny feet he has. He discovered *The Double Mistress* on my desk and wagged his tapering finger at me.

"Claudine, Claudine, I'll tell my uncle!"

"My dear boy, he couldn't care less."

"What an accommodating Papa. I wish Grandmother were as easy-going! Oh, that doesn't stop me reading," he replied to the questioning thrust of my chin. "But, for the sake of peace, I've had to pretend that I'm frightened of the dark and must have a light in my room."

I burst out laughing.

"Frightened! You actually told her you were frightened! Weren't you ashamed?"

"Oh, what on earth does that matter! Grandmother's brought me up—and she does to this day—just like a little girl."

Those last words reminded us so vividly of the scene two evenings ago that we both blushed (he more than I, his skin's so white!). And we were so obviously thinking of the same thing that he asked me:

"Haven't you got a photograph of Luce?"

"No; not a single one."

"I bet that's a lie."

"Word of honour! And, anyway, you'd quite likely think she was ugly. But I'm not coy about Luce—look, here's the only letter she's written me."

He avidly read the pathetic pencil scrawl and this little Parisian who adored sensational news-items became impassioned.

"But it's a drama, a case of illegal restraint! Oughtn't we to get hold of someone and take legal action?"

"What a crazy idea! What on earth has it got to do with you?"

"To do with me? But, Claudine, it's a case of positive cruelty! You read it again!"

To read it, I leant on his fragile shoulder. He smiled, because my hair got into his ear. But I did not lean any harder. I merely said to him:

"You're not cross any more, Marcel?"

"No, no," he said hurriedly. "But, I implore you, do tell me all about Luce. I'll be awfully nice, if you tell me all about Luce! Look . . . I'll bring Fanchette a collar."

"No good, she'd only eat it! My poor boy, there's nothing to tell. Besides, I'm only going to *exchange* confidences with you. Give and take, or nothing doing."

He sulked like a girl, head down and lips pouting.

"Tell me, Marcel, do you often put that face on with your . . . your friend? Tell me his Christian name again?"

"He's called Charlie," my 'nephew' replied, after a moment's hesitation.

"How old? Come on, come on, have I got to drag everything out of you?"

"He's eighteen, but very serious, very mature for his age. Really, the things you've been imagining!"

"Stop it. You make me fed up, d'you hear? We're not going to start all that rot again, are we? Be his girl friend as much as you like, but be a good pal to me just for once and I'll tell you all about Luce. There!"

With his disarming grace, he gently grasped my wrists.

"Oh, you *are* an angel! I've been longing for such ages to hear *real* girls' secrets. Here in Paris, girls are either women or mugs. I say, Claudine, *dear* Claudine, *do* let me be your confidant!"

Was this the icy little piece of perfection of our first meeting? As he talked to me, he held out his hands and made tremendous play with his eyes and his mouth and his whole face to coax a confidence out of me; exactly as I'm sure he did when he was trying to cajole a kiss or a reconciliation. And I was suddenly tempted to invent all sorts of disgraceful things I'd done. He'd tell me others—that he almost certainly *had* done. It was rather beastly of me. But what could you expect? I couldn't get it into my head that I was playing with a boy. If he had put his arm round my waist or kissed me, I'd have scratched his eyes out by now, and that would have been the end of it. The evil arose from the fact that there wasn't any danger. . . .

My 'nephew' was in no mood to give me any time for reflection. He pulled me by my wrists, seated me in my tub-armchair and settled himself on the floor on my chaff-stuffed cushion, hitching up his trousers so that they shouldn't bag at the knees.

"There, now we're nicely settled! Oh, how horrid that gloomy courtyard is! Do you mind if I draw the curtain? And now, tell me how all *that* began?"

In the long glass, I could see the two of us. I must admit we weren't ugly—I've seen worse. But what was I going to invent for him, that avid, fair-haired boy who was sitting so close to me to listen that I could see all the rays of slate-blue over periwinkle-blue that glittered in the irises of his eyes? I told myself sternly I'd only got to remember my schooldays. I needn't go as far as telling actual lies: a little exaggeration perhaps, no more.

"Oh, *I* don't know. That sort of thing doesn't have a definite beginning. It's, it's a gradual transformation of one's everyday life, a . . ."

". . . An *infiltration*. . . ."

"Thank you, Sir. It's obvious *you* know all about it."

"Claudine, Claudine, don't wander off into generalisations. Generalisations are so colourless. Keep your promise, tell me the whole story. First of all, you must describe Luce to me. An Introductory Chapter, only brief!"

"Luce? That's soon done. Small, brown-haired, pink and white, green slits of eyes, curling eyelashes—like yours—too small a nose and a slightly Mongol face. There, I *told* you you wouldn't like that type! Wait. Feet, hands, ankles, all very delicate. My accent, a real Fresnois accent, only more drawling. Untruthful, greedy, wheedling. She was never happy when she hadn't had her daily thrashing."

"Her 'thrashing'? Do you mean you used to beat her?"

"Certainly, that's what I mean, but you mustn't interrupt. 'Silence in the Junior Class or I'll set you twice as many sums for tomorrow!' That was what Mademoiselle used to say when her dear Aimée couldn't keep her pupils in order."

"Who was she, this Aimée?"

"Mademoiselle's—the Headmistress's—Luce."

"Right. Go on."

"I proceed. One morning that it was our turn to break up firewood for the stove in the shed . . ."

"*What* did you say?"

"I said: one morning that it was our turn to break up firewood for the . . ."

"You actually used to break up firewood at that boarding-school?"

"It isn't a boarding-school, it's a day-school. Everyone took it in turns to break up firewood at half-past seven on winter mornings, even in the coldest weather. You've no idea how splinters hurt, when it's freezing! I always had my pockets full of hot chestnuts to eat in class and to warm my hands. And the ones who had to break up the twigs used to hurry to get there early, so as to suck the icicles on the pump by the shed. And I used to bring raw chestnuts too, unsplit ones, to annoy Mademoiselle by putting them in the stove."

"Gosh! Whoever heard of a school like that! But Luce, Luce?"

"Luce moaned more than anyone the mornings she was 'on wood' and used to cling to me for consolation. 'Claudine, I be froze, my hands are peeling, look see, my thumb be all scratted! Cuddle me, Claudine, my darling Claudine.' And she'd snuggle up under my cloak and kiss me."

"How? How?" Marcel impatiently enquired. He was listening with his mouth half-open and his cheeks flushed. "How did she cud . . . kiss you?"

"On the cheeks, of course, and on the neck," I said, as if I'd suddenly become mentally deficient.

"Get away with you, you're just a woman like all the rest!"

"That's most definitely not what Luce thought." (I put my hands on his shoulders to make him keep still.) "Don't get cross, the horrors will come all in good time!"

"Claudine, one minute. Didn't it upset you, her talking dialect?"

"Dialect? You'd have found dialect positively attractive, my young Parisian, spoken in that tearful, sing-song voice and coming from that mouth under the red hood that hid her forehead and ears. All you could see was a little pink nose and two cheeks like velvety peaches—even the cold didn't take the colour out of them! To blazes with dialect!"

"What passion, Claudine! Anyone can see you haven't forgotten her yet."

"Then, one morning, Luce put a letter in my hand."

"Ah! At last! Where is it, that letter?"

"I tore it up and gave it back to Luce."

"That's not true!"

"So you call me a liar, do you? All right, I shall pack you off to Avenue Wagram to see if your cake's nicely browned."

"Sorry! I only meant I could hardly believe it."

"All right, you little beast! Yes, I did give it back to her. Because it suggested things that weren't . . . well, proper. There!"

"Claudine, in heaven's name, don't keep me on tenterhooks."

"She wrote: 'My darling, if you'd only be my best friend, I don't think I'd have anything in the world left to wish for. We should be as happy as my sister Aimée is with Mademoiselle, and I'd be grateful to you my whole life. I love you so much, I think you're so pretty. Your skin is softer than that yellow powder on lily petals. I even love it when you scratch me because you've got little cold nails. . . .' All that sort of thing, you know."

"Ah? . . . That artless humility. . . . But, you know, it's adorable!"

My 'nephew' was in a state of tremendous excitement. If that's what's meant by an impressionable nature, he certainly has one, all right! He wasn't looking at me any more; his eyelashes were fluttering, his cheeks stained with crimson, and his pretty nose had turned pale. I'd never seen anyone in the grip of that particular emotion except Luce, but how much more beautiful *he* was! I suddenly thought: 'If he looked up, if he put his arms round me at this precise minute, what should I do? A little caterpillar crept up my spine. He raised his lashes, thrust his head nearer and passionately implored:

"What next, Claudine, what next?"

He wasn't excited by *me*, of course, but by my story and the details he hoped to hear! Claudine, my girl, if your virtue was ever in danger, it most certainly wasn't then!

The door opened. It was Mélie, making a discreet entrance. I think she has high hopes of Marcel; she sees in him the 'young man' I've hitherto lacked. She brought in my little lamp, closed the shutters, drew the curtains and left us in a warm twilight glow. But Marcel had leapt to his feet.

"The lamp! Claudine, whatever time is it?"

"Half-past five."

"Goodness, Grandmother will flay me! I must go—I promised to be back at five."

"But I thought Aunt Coeur let you have your own sweet way in everything?"

"Yes and no. She's awfully nice but she fusses too much. If I'm back half an hour late, I find her in tears. No joke, I can tell you! And, every time I go out, I have to put up with endless admonitions. '*Do* take care! I nearly die of anxiety when you're out! Whatever you do, don't go through the Rue Cardinet, it's so deserted. Nor by the Etoile, all those carriages when it's getting dark!' And so on and so on. *You've* no idea what it's like, being brought up in cotton-wool! Claudine, come close, whisper. . . . You *will* keep the rest of the story for me, won't you? I *can* trust you, can't I?"

"As much as I can trust you," I said gravely.

"Wicked girl! Give me your paw to kiss. Don't be unkind to your 'nephew' any more—he's awfully fond of you. Goodbye, Claudine—see you soon, Claudine!"

From the doorway, he blew me a kiss from the tips of his fingers, just to tease, and fled with his noiseless steps. It had been a wonderful afternoon! My brain was still on fire from it.

"Come on, Fanchette! A little gym! Come and give your future children a bit of exercise!"

7

My gaiety didn't last. I had a sudden relapse into homesickness for Fresnois and the old school. And why? All because of Bérillon; because of that idiot of a Bérillon, that moron of a Bérillon. I'd been dusting the books in my little desk, the ones I'd piously brought back from school, and I mechanically opened *The Good Country Housewife, Simple notions of rural and domestic economy for use in girls' schools*, by Louis-Eugène Bérillon. This ineffable little book was a source of pure joy to all the big girls in the school (by that time, we hadn't any too many pure joys left) and that great gawk Anaïs and I used to repeat passages aloud over and over again without getting tired of them. On wet days, when we couldn't play marbles or 'He', we used to walk round the new covered-in part of the square playground and put each other posers out of *The Good Housewife.*

"Anaïs, tell me about the *Good Country Housewife* and her ingenuity in the matter of cesspools."

With her little finger in the air and her flat mouth compressed into an inimitable grimace, Anaïs would recite with a solemnity that made me die of laughter:

"In a sequestered spot on the north side of the garden, the good housewife has persuaded her husband to construct, or has constructed herself, with the aid of a few poles, a few planks and some handfuls of broom or rye-straw, a kind of cabin which serves as a convenience." (It runs exactly as I'm telling you. . . .) "This cabin, literally hidden under verdure and the flowers of creepers and climbing plants bears far more semblance to a charming bower of greenery than to a latrine."

"Charming! What truly poetic conception and style! Ah, could I only wander in dreamy meditation to that flowery, perfumed arbour and seat myself there for a moment! . . . But let us pass to the practical side. Kindly proceed, Anaïs."

"As the excrement of five or six persons in the course of one year is amply sufficient to manure one hectare of ground and that nothing in the nature of . . ."

"Ssh, ssh, don't dwell on it!"

". . . In the nature of dung ought to be wasted, the cesspool is either a hole dug in the earth and lined with puddled clay or a kind of deep terra cotta vessel or, quite simply, an old disused wine-vat."

"Farewell, ye vats, the vintages are o'er! My dear child, that is perfect. I shall teach you nothing you do not already know by telling you that it is an excellent idea to mix human dung *very thoroughly* with twice its volume of earth and that five kilos are sufficient to manure one *are* (a hundred square metres) and to make two hundred stink. As a reward for your diligence, I authorise you to kiss Dr. Dutertre, the District Superintendent, five times."

"You're joking," Anaïs murmured dreamily, "but, if it only needed your permission . . ."

Oh Bérillon, how you've amused those smutty little girls, of whom I was one! We used to mime your preface as we declaimed it. Marie Belhomme, that guileless soul, used to raise her 'midwife's hands' to heaven, as, throbbing with heartfelt conviction, she apostrophised the young peasant girl:

"Unhappy child! How great is your error! Ah, in your own interests and for your own happiness, thrust back as detestable the thought of thus leaving your parents and the cottage where you were born! If you knew at what price those, whose luxury you envy, had bought the silk and the jewels with which they deck themselves out!"

"Ten francs a night," broke in Anaïs. "I believe that's the price in Paris!"

It was that sour old Bérillon and his worn binding, with the end-papers adorned with transfers, that brought the school and my little classmates all too vividly back to my mind. Suddenly, I decided to write to Luce. It was a very long time since I'd had news of her; had she perhaps left Montigny?

Nothing amusing, these last few days, I've been out on foot; I've bestirred myself over the question of dresses and hats. A gentleman followed me. I had the unfortunate idea of putting out a pointed tongue at him. At which he exclaimed eagerly: "Oh! Give it me!" That will teach me. The prospect of dispensing tea at Aunt Coeur's? "Bouac!" as that gawk Anaïs used to say—she was marvellous at imitating people being sick. Luckily, Marcel will be there. . . . All the same, I'd infinitely rather drudge away here, even at something boring.

8

O N my next visit to Aunt Coeur, I wore my simple little blue cloth dress; I hadn't any other suitable ones yet. And besides, if I 'put on weight', as I probably shall, the ones I ordered too soon might burst. (Can you see that avalanche of flesh which would overflow its bounds?) Meanwhile I only weigh fifty kilos[1] on the automatic scales in the Place Saint-Germain-des-Prés.

I arrived at half-past four. There was no one in the drawing-room yet, except Marcel who was fluttering about noiselessly. He looked a little pale and there were mauve shadows under his eyes. I think this slightly tired look made him even more attractive. He was arranging flowers in vases and humming under his breath.

"Dear 'nephew', why don't you put on a little white embroidered apron?"

"And would *you* like my trousers?"

"Thanks, I've got some on already. Clumsy! Just look what you're doing! You're putting the little stand upsidaisy."

"Upsi-what?" he said, and burst out laughing.

"Upside down. Isn't there anything you understand? Wherever were you brought up?"

"Here, alas! Claudine, why don't you wear tailored coats and skirts? They'd suit you marvellously."

"Because there isn't a tailor in Montigny."

"But there are plenty in Paris. Would you like me to take you to one? Not to one of the big ones, don't be frightened. Do let's go. I adore anything to do with clothes and fiddling with materials."

[1]110 lb.

"Yes, I'd love to. Who's going to come here today? They'll all be popping their eyes out at me—Suppose I go away?"

"Not worth it. There won't be masses of people to pop—to stare at you! Madame Barmann, for certain, the old tortoise. Possibly . . . Charlie," he said, averting his eyes, "but perhaps he mayn't come. Madame Van Langendonck . . ."

"A Belgian?"

"No, she's a Cypriot."

"What's the point of being Greek if you go and rig yourself up with a name like that? If I were Flemish, it wouldn't occur to me to call myself Nausicaa!"

"Don't blame *me*! I can't do anything about it! Then there'll be some young people who belong to the Barmann set—an old lady Mamma's very fond of and who's always called Madame Amélie—no one knows her surname any more. In fact, hardly anyone . . ."

"Fine. I'm delighted to hear it."

"Claudine. . . . What about Luce?"

"Hush, for goodness' sake! Here's Aunt."

His grandmother was indeed making her entrance, all in rustling silk.

"Ah! My pretty niece! Have you told them to come and fetch you or would you like Marcel to take you home?"

"But, Aunt, I don't need anyone. I came all by myself."

She turned purple under her powder.

"Alone! On foot? In a cab?"

"No, Aunt. In the Panthéon-Courcelles bus."

"Heavens! Heavens! How disgraceful of Claude!"

She did not dare say more. Marcel was watching me sideways and biting his tongue, the wretch. If I laughed, all was lost. He switched on the electric lights and Aunt Coeur emerged from her consternation with a deep sigh.

"Children, I shall have very few friends this week."

Trrrrr. . . . Well, here was one at least. A female one. Hurriedly, I took cover behind the tea-table, and Marcel laughed outright. A humpbacked ball, haloed in iodised cottonwool screwed into ringlets, had rolled up to Aunt Coeur. Madame Barmann's ample form had been coaxed into a sable coat, much too hot for the time of year and she was perspiring under it. On her head was an owl with outstretched wings. Owl above, owl below. The hooked nose, streaked with broken veins, was not lacking in authority and the grey eyes looked like marbles and rolled alarmingly.

"I'm dead beat. I've done eleven miles on foot," announced her harsh voice. "But I've found some wonderful bits of furniture at two old maids' who live in Montrouge. A real expedition! Huysmans would have adored that oddly picturesque jumble of tumble-down houses! I'm hunting all over the place to furnish and decorate our illustrious friend Gréveuille's new house—he has a childlike confidence in me. And, in three weeks' time, one of the shows from La Foire repertory is being done at my house. . . . I don't ask you, dear Madame Coeur, to bring that child with you. . . ."

She looked at Marcel, and then looked at me, without saying another word.

"My niece Claudine," Aunt Coeur hastened to introduce me. "Only just arrived in Paris," she added, beckoning me to come forward, for, to tell the truth, I was in no hurry to move.

From close to, the "illustrious friend's" furnisher stared at me with such insolence that I was in two minds whether I wouldn't suddenly lash out at her broken veins with my fist. But at last she transferred her gaze back to Aunt Coeur.

"Charming," she said roughly. "Will you bring her to me one Wednesday? Wednesdays are, as you know, innocuous."

Aunt Coeur thanked her on my behalf. I didn't unclench my teeth and I trembled so violently as I poured out some tea for the impudent old owl that Marcel was exultant. His eyes sparkled with mockery. He whispered to me:

"Claudine, what are we going to do with you if you throw yourself at people's heads like this? Now, now, restrain this uncontrolled expansiveness a little!"

"Go to blazes!" I muttered furiously. "I can't stand being glared at like that!"

And I went off to my cup of tea, followed by Marcel, much more gracious and girlish than myself, bearing the sandwiches.

Trrrrr. . . . Yet another lady. But charming, this one, with eyes right up to her temples and hair right down to her eyes.

"Madame Van Langendonck," Marcel informed me in a whisper. "The one who's a Cypriot. . . ."

"As her name indicates, exactly."

"Does *she* appeal to you at all, Claudine?"

"She certainly does. She looks like an antelope out on a spree."

The pretty creature! Flying hair, a vast feathered hat tipped forward, rapturous, short-sighted eyes, a frequent soft, all-embracing gesture with her little right hand that glittered with rings. She was approbation incarnate. To Aunt Coeur and Madame Barmann, she said: "Yes," she said: "You're right," she said: "How true that is." She obviously had a conciliatory nature. Her desire to agree with everyone occasionally landed her in certain inconsistencies. She informed us, practically in the same breath: "Yesterday at five, I was shopping in the Bon Marché" and "Yesterday at five, I was at such an interesting lecture". This did not seem to embarrass anyone, herself least of all.

Aunt Coeur called me over:

"Claudine!"

I went, with a good grace, and smiled at the enchanting face presented to me. Promptly, a wild deluge of compliments poured down on my innocent head.

"Isn't she charming! And such an original type! And what a pretty figure! Seventeen? I should have thought she was at least eighteen. . . ."

"Oh, no, that's absurd!" protested the owl Barmann. "She looks much younger than her age."

"Yes, doesn't she? Hardly fifteen."

And so the nonsense went on! Marcel's mock solemnity was beginning to get too much for me, when *trrrrr* . . . a gentleman this time. A tall slim gentleman, an attractive gentleman. He had a dark complexion, a great deal of golden-brown hair that was turning white, young eyes with tired eyelids, and a well-groomed moustache, fair, but streaked with silver. He came in, almost as if this were his own home, kissed Aunt Coeur's hand and, standing under the cruel glare of the chandelier, observed mockingly:

"How it rests one's eyes, the gentle twilight of these modern flats!"

Amused at the joke, I looked at Marcel: he wasn't laughing at all and was contemplating the gentleman in an anything but benevolent way.

"Who's that?"

"It's my father," he answered icily, going up to the gentleman who shook his hand pleasantly and absent-mindedly as one pulls one's gun-dog's ear.

His father! I didn't think it at all funny! I must have looked a perfect idiot. A father with whom he'd been at loggerheads, that was obvious. His son only resembled him very vaguely. The obstinate arch of the eyebrows, perhaps? But all Marcel's features were so refined that one still couldn't be quite sure. What a funny expression, at once cold and submissive, my nephew had put on for the author of his being! In any case, he certainly hadn't proclaimed from the roof-tops that he had a Papa; yet this one seemed to me a father anyone would positively flaunt. But, evidently, with both of them, the call of the blood didn't sound loud enough in their ears to deafen them.

"Things going all right with you, my boy? Working well?"

"Yes, Father."

"You look a little tired to me."

"Oh no, Father."

"You ought to have come to the races with me today. That would have shaken you up."

"Father, I absolutely had to hand round the tea."

"That's true. You absolutely had to hand round the tea. Heaven forbid I should seduce you from such serious duties!"

As the Barmann owl and the Cypriot antelope were deep in conversation, the one authoritative and the other so compliant that her soft agreement blunted every barb, Aunt Coeur risked, less unctuously than usual:

"Renaud, do you really think a racecourse quite the right place for that child?"

"Why not, Madame? He'd see some very eligible people . . . and even more Israelites," he added softly with a sidelong glance at Madame Barmann.

This was absolutely splendid! I was simmering with suppressed joy. If this went on, the English porcelain I was reverently handling would soon be strewing the carpet. Aunt Coeur lowered her eyes and blushed imperceptibly. No doubt about it, he wasn't at all polite but I was thoroughly enjoying myself. (Oh! "Not half having fun, I wasn't!" as Luce would have said.) Marcel was counting the flowers on the velvet upholstery with the expression of a girl who hadn't been asked to dance.

"You betted at the races no doubt," my aunt enquired sadly, with a face of despair.

The gentleman gave a melancholy shake of his head.

"I even went so far as to lose. So I gave twenty francs to the cabby who drove me back."

"Why?" asked his own, raising his eyebrows.

"Because, with what I'd lost, that made it up to a round sum."

"Hpppp. . . ." This was that idiot of a Claudine exploding into a giggle. My cousin . . . (let me see, if he was the father of my nephew, was he my cousin? I was all at sea) . . . my cousin turned his head towards that indecorous laugh.

"Do you know my little niece Claudine, Renaud? My brother Claude's daughter, only just arrived in Paris. She and Marcel are the best friends in the world already."

"I'm anything but sorry for Marcel," declared the gentleman to whom I had offered my hand.

He had only looked at me for a second, but he was someone who knew how to look. A zigzagging look, with an imperceptible pause at the hair, the eyes, the lower part of the face and the hands. Marcel moved away to the tea-table and I prepared to follow him. . . .

"Claude's daughter . . ." my cousin racked his brains. "Oh! wait a minute, I've so little sense of genealogies. . . . But, in that case, Mademoiselle is Marcel's aunt? But this situation is pure vaudeville, isn't it. . . . *Cousin?*"

"Yes, Uncle," I said without hesitation.

"What luck! That'll make me two babies to take to the Circus if your father permits me to . . . you're how old . . . fifteen, sixteen?"

I corrected him, offended.

"Over seventeen!"

"Seventeen . . . yes, those eyes. Marcel, that makes a change for you, eh?—having a girl friend?"

"Oh," I said laughing. "I'm much too much of a boy for him!"

My cousin Uncle, who had followed us to the tea-table, scrutinised me sharply, but I looked such a good little girl!

"Too much of a boy for him? No, definitely not," he said, with a touch of mockery in his voice.

Marcel fidgeted so clumsily with a little enamel spoon that he managed to twist its handle. He shrugged his graceful shoulders and walked out of the room, with his charming, quiet step, shutting the dining-room door behind him. Old Mother Barmann went off, throwing me a highly absurd "Goodbye, little one!" On her way out, she passed a new arrival. This was an old lady with white hair done in bandeaux, looking exactly like dozens of other old ladies, who sat down in two movements and refused tea. What luck!

My cousin Uncle, who had accompanied the owl to the door, returned to the tea-table and asked me for some tea. He demanded cream and, furthermore, two lumps of sugar, also a sandwich, not the top one because it must have got dry, and various other things. But he had the same type of greediness as I had and I didn't get impatient. I found him sympathetic, this cousin Uncle. I was longing to know what was wrong between him and Marcel. He looked as if he were thinking about it himself, and, while still munching a delicious little shortbread biscuit, he asked me in a muffled voice:

"Has my son talked to you about me?"

Misery me! What could I do? What could I say? I dropped my spoon to give myself time, just as I used to drop my pen-holder at school, and, at last, I replied:

"No—at least I don't remember it."

It wasn't a very brilliant effort but it was all I could manage. He didn't look surprised. He went on eating. He wasn't old. He was a father who was still young. His nose amused me; it was slightly aquiline, with mobile nostrils. Under very black lashes, his eyes gleamed dark blue-grey. For a man, his ears weren't ugly. His hair was going white at the temples and fluffed out. At Montigny there was a beautiful silvery dog who had fur just that colour. Without warning, he raised his eyes so suddenly that he caught me looking at him.

"Do you think I'm ugly?"

"No, Uncle, not in the least."

"Not as handsome as Marcel, eh?"

"Ah, no, certainly not! There doesn't exist another boy as pretty as he is. And there can only be very few women who can hold a candle to him."

"Perfectly true! My paternal pride is flattered. My son isn't exactly forthcoming, though, is he?"

"Oh yes, he *is*! He came to see me at home yesterday, all on his own, and we talked away like anything. He's much better brought up than I am."

"Much better than I am, too. But you astonish me by saying he's already paid you a visit. You positively astound me. It's a conquest. I'd like to meet . . . I mean, it would give me great pleasure if you would introduce me to your revered father, Cousin. The Family! First and foremost, I am the most devout upholder of the Family. I am a pillar of tradition."

"And of the turf!"

"Oh! but it really *is* true—that you're shockingly brought up! When can I find your father at home?"

"In the morning, he never goes out. In the afternoon, he goes and sees people who have decorations and stirs up dust in libraries. But not every single day. Anyway, if you really want to come, I'll tell him to stay in. He's still fairly obedient to me about little things."

"Ah, little things! They're the only ones that matter: they take up all the room and there's none left for the big ones. Let's see now . . . what have you seen in Paris up to now?"

"The Luxembourg and the big shops."

"Quite sufficient, in short. Suppose I took you to a concert on Sunday, with Marcel? I think the concerts are 'exclusive' enough this year for my son to consent to risk being seen at them occasionally."

"The big concerts? Oh, yes . . . thank you. I've been longing to go to them, though I don't know much about them. I've so seldom heard good orchestras."

"Good, that's settled. What else? You strike me as a young person who's not difficult to entertain. Dear me, I should like to have had a daughter—I'd have brought her up so well in my own way! What sort of things do you like?"

I lit up.

"Heaps of things! Rotten bananas, chocolates, lime buds, the inside of the tails of artichokes, the 'cuckoo' on fruit-trees . . ." (I didn't stop to explain that 'cuckoo' is our name at home for the gum) "new books and penknives with lots of blades, and . . ."

Out of breath, I burst out laughing because my cousin Uncle had solemnly taken a notebook out of his pocket and was writing in it:

"A moment's respite, I implore you, dear child! Chocolates,

rotten bananas—horror!—inside of artichokes, that's child's play. But, as for lime buds and the cuckoo that perches exclusively on fruit-trees, I don't know any retail-houses in Paris. Can one write direct to the manufacturers?"

What luck! Here was a man who really knew how to amuse children! Why did his son look as if he didn't get on with him? At that very moment, Marcel returned, wearing a much too indifferent expression on his charming mug. My cousin Uncle stood up, the white-haired old lady stood up, the pretty Cypriot Van Langen-donck stood up: general retreat. When these ladies had gone, my aunt enquired:

"Darling, now who's going to take you home to your father? Would you like my maid to?"

"Or why not me, Grandmother?" Marcel suggested charmingly.

"You? . . . Very well, but take a cab by the hour, my pet."

"What, you let him go out in a cab at this hour?" exclaimed my cousin Uncle, so sarcastically that Aunt Coeur noticed it.

"My friend, I'm responsible for his welfare. Who else takes any trouble over this child?"

I did not hear what followed: I went to put my hat and coat on. When I returned, my cousin Uncle had disappeared and Aunt Coeur was very gradually resuming her smile of an old lady who has lodged in the Tuilleries.

Goodbyes, "see you soons", then the cold street after the shut-in warmth of the drawing-room.

We got into a pneumatic-tyred cab on the rank in the Rue Joffroy! The joy of pneumatic tyres hasn't begun to pall on me yet and I admitted it. Marcel smiled, but said nothing. Suddenly, I attacked.

"He's charming, your father."

"Charming."

"Restrain your delirious tenderness, most passionate of sons!"

"What do you expect me to say? I haven't just discovered Papa for the first time today, have I? I've known him for seventeen years."

I shut myself up in wounded discretion.

"Don't sulk, Claudine . . . it's all too complicated to explain."

"You're quite right, my friend. It's nothing whatever to do with me. If you don't make a great fuss of your father, you must have your reasons."

"Most certainly I have. He made Mamma very unhappy."

"For long?"

"Yes . . . for eighteen months."

"Did he beat her?"

"No, of course not! But he was never at home."

"And you? Has he made you very unhappy?"

"Oh, it's not that. But," my 'nephew' explained with controlled fury, "he can be so biting! Our two natures don't harmonise in any way."

He threw out these last words in a disillusioned, theatrical voice that inwardly convulsed me.

"Claudine! The other day, we stopped just at Luce's letter. Do go on from there, please! It's far more interesting than a lot of domestic quarrels and dirty family linen!"

Ah, I'd found *my* Marcel, my pretty Marcel, again. Under the passing gas-lamps, his slender face shone out and disappeared, shone out again and vanished and, every three seconds, I could make out the dimple in his delicate obstinate chin. Quivering, my nerves on edge from my afternoon, from the darkness, from the new faces and the over-strong tea, I snuggled my cold hands comfortably into my 'nephew's' feverishly hot ones. Up to now I'd told him the truth; today it was a question of inventions, something really impressive. I'd got to lie! "Lie like a trooper", as Mélie says.

"Well, then I gave Luce back her 'minced' letter."

"Torn up?"

"Yes. Minced into little bits."

"What did she say?"

"She cried without any shame . . . out loud."

"And . . . was that your last word?"

Ambiguous, and, as it were, slightly shamed silence on the part of Claudine. . . . Marcel thrust his pretty head forward avidly.

"No. . . . She did everything she could to make me yield. When I was '*on water*' . . . you see, we used to carry up water in turn . . . she waited for me in the dormitory till the others had gone down so that she could speak to me. She threatened to weep out loud to annoy me and I got so fed up that I ended up by sitting down on the bed and taking her on my lap. She clasped her little hands behind my neck, hid her face on my shoulder and pointed out the boys' dormitory opposite, over at the end of the playground, where you could see them undressing at night. . . ."

"You could see them un . . . ?"

"Yes, and they used to make signs. Luce laughed very softly into my neck and beat my leg with her heels. I told her: 'Get up . . . *Cave* . . . Mademoiselle's coming!' But she suddenly flung herself on me and began to kiss me wildly. . . ."

"Wildly. . . ." Marcel repeated like an echo and his hands slowly turned cold in mine.

"So then I promptly jumped to my feet and nearly knocked her down. She cried out, very low: 'You're wicked . . . you're wicked! Heartless!' "

"And then?"

"And then I gave her such a real good thrashing that her arms were all blue and her scalp tingling. I can hit jolly hard when I try. She adored that. She hid her face and let herself be beaten, letting out great sighs . . . (The bridges, Marcel, we're nearly there.) Great sighs . . . just like you're doing now."

"Claudine," said his soft, slightly choked voice, "won't you go on and tell me some more? I . . . I simply love these stories."

"So I observe. . . . Only, you know the conditions?"

"Ssh. . . . I know the conditions. Give and take. But," he said, putting his face, with its pink dry mouth and eyes that had grown enormous, quite close to mine, "friendships that are passionate, but chaste and entirely of the heart are more difficult to tell about. I'm afraid of being meagre, as well as clumsy."

"Take care, you're being tempted to tell lies. I shall seal my lips."

"No, no! I shall compel you to talk now! We're there. I'll get out and ring the bell."

When the door was opened, he took my hands again in his moist fingers, squeezed them much too hard and kissed them one after the other.

"My compliments to my uncle, Claudine. And my respects to Fanchette. Claudine, you wonderful, surprising girl! How could I ever have expected all this pleasure would come to me from Montigny?"

That was really quite well said.

At the dinner-table, my nerves became a little calmer as I told Papa (who didn't listen) all about my afternoon and my cousin Uncle. Fanchette, the darling, ran her nose along the hem of my skirt to find out where I'd been. She now had a pretty round belly which she carried gaily and which did not prevent her from leaping after the moths round the lamp. It was no use my telling her: "Fanchette, one shouldn't stretch one's arms up when one's pregnant"; she didn't pay any attention.

As we were eating the Cheshire cheese, Papa, no doubt suddenly inspired by the Holy Spirit, emitted a loud cry.

"What is it, Papa? A new slug?"

"I've got it, I know who he is! All that business had gone clean out of my mind. When one's entire life is occupied with serious things, trifles like that get forgotten. Poor Ida, Marcel, Renaud. . . . I've got it now. Six and thirty swine! Wilhelmine's daughter married this Renaud when she was very young and he wasn't very old either. She bored him, I think. Just fancy . . . a daughter of Wilhelmine's! . . . Well, then she had a son—Marcel. They didn't get along any too well, after the child. A touchy, Puritanical little woman. She said: 'I'm going home to mother.' He said: 'I'll get them to call a cab for you.' Soon after, she died of something or other rapid. There!"

That night, before I went to bed, I said to Mélie, as she was closing the shutters:

"Mélie, I now possess an uncle. No, I mean I've a cousin and a nephew, you understand!"

"You've also got maggots in your brain, at this moment. And look at that cat, now. Ever since she's been in the family way she's always in the drawers and cupboards, a-moithering of everything."

"You must put out a basket for her. Will it be soon?"

"Not for another fortnight."

"But I haven't brought her basket of hay."

"That's a pity. Never mind. I'll buy her a dog-basket with a cushion."

"She won't have anything to do with it. It's too Parisian for her."

"Go on with you! What about the tom from downstairs? *He* wasn't too Parisian for her, was he?"

9

Aunt WILHELMINE came to see me but I wasn't in. She talked to Papa, Mélie told me, and was 'in ever such a state' to find I'd gone out alone. (No doubt she's aware that our neighbourhood is infested with students from the Beaux-Arts Art School.)

I had gone out-of-doors to see some leaves.

Alas! green leaves! they come out early here!

There, at the very most, the hawthorn hedges would be veiled, at long intervals, with that green haze their tiny tender leaves weave for them and that seems to hang from their twigs. In the Luxembourg, I wanted to eat young tree-shoots as I used to at Montigny, but here they're covered with coal-dust and scrunch under your teeth. And never, never once did I breathe the dank smell of rotting leaves and reedy ponds, nor the faintly acrid tang of wind that has blown over woods where charcoal is burning. *There* the first violets would be out, I could see them! The border near the garden wall that faces west would be flowering with little violets—ugly, puny and stunted but with a heavenly smell.

How miserable I am! The excessive warmth of this Paris spring and its mugginess make me feel like nothing so much as a wretched wild animal condemned to live in the zoo. They sell primroses and yellow daisies and daffodils by barrowloads here. But the daisy-balls I make from force of habit don't amuse anyone but Fanchette who has stayed nimble, in spite of her taut little corporation, and handles them deftly, using her paw like a spoon. I am in a thoroughly bad state of mind. . . . Luckily my body is all right: I frequently verify this as I squat in the hot water of my tub and it gives me considerable satisfaction. It's long-limbed and supple and elastic, not very plump, but muscular enough not to seem too thin.

I've kept myself supple, even though I've no longer a tree to climb. One of my efforts was to balance myself in my tub on my right foot and bend back as far as possible with my left leg raised very high, my right arm used as a balancing-pole and my left hand under the nape of my neck. It sounds nothing—but you just try! Flop! Over I went backwards. And, as I hadn't dried myself, my behind made a round wet patch on the floor. (Fanchette, sitting on the bed, stared at me with cold contempt both for my clumsiness and for this unaccountable mania of mine for sitting in water.) But I do other exercises with brilliant success; putting my feet alternately on the nape of my neck or bending back till my head is on a level with my calves. Mélie is full of admiration, but warns me against too much of these gymnastics.

"You'll go and split yourself one of these days!"

After all these intimate diversions, I collapse again into apathy or irritability: my hands too hot or too cold; my eyes languid and over-bright; prickly and edgy all over. I don't say my cross cat's face is ugly, actually it's the reverse, with its cap of curly hair. The one thing I lack, the one thing I need . . . I shall discover it only too soon. And, besides, it would be humiliating. . . .

Up to now, the net result of all this for Claudine has been an unexpected passion for Francis Jammes because that odd poet understands the country and animals and old-fashioned gardens and the importance of the stupid little things in life.

10

Mᴍʏ cousin Uncle came to see Papa this morning. At first Papa was furious at being disturbed, but he promptly became quite human because this man Renaud knows how to be charming and disarming. In broad daylight, he had more white hairs but his face looked younger than when I saw it first and his eyes were an unusual, highly individual slate-colour. He got Papa launched on malacology and my noble father was inexhaustible on the subject. Appalled by this spate of words, I stemmed it by saying: "Papa, I want to let my uncle see Fanchette."

And I carried my uncle off to my room, enchanted to see that he appreciated the little four-poster and the old-fashioned chintz and my beloved, shabby little desk. He deftly massaged and scratched Fanchette's sensitive stomach and cleverly talked cat-language to her. Whatever Marcel says about him, he's *definitely* "all right!"

"My dear child, a white cat and a tub-armchair are indispensable objects in a young girl's room. All that's missing is the nice, suitable novel . . . no, here it is. Good Lord, it's *André Tourette*. What an extraordinary notion!"

"Oh, you'll see plenty of others! You'll have to get used to them. I read everything."

"Everything? Saying a good deal, isn't it? Don't try and shock me . . . that's just ridiculous."

"Ridiculous!" I said, choking with rage. "I'm quite old enough to read what I choose."

"Dear, dear, dear! Certainly your father—incidentally, he's charming—is no ordinary father but . . . well, well, there are some things you'd be none the worse for not knowing. My dear . . ." he added, seeing I was nearly in tears. "I don't want to hurt your feelings. Whatever's come over me to moralise like this? I'm being preternaturally avuncular. Which doesn't prevent *you* from being the prettiest and most delicious of nieces, bibliomania apart. And you're going to give me your little paw in token of peace."

I gave it him. But I suddenly felt miserable. I had been so determined to find that man charming in every possible way.

He kissed my hand. He was the second man who had kissed my hand. And I noticed the difference. Marcel's kiss is the faintest brush, so light and hasty that I don't know whether a pair of lips or a hurried finger has touched my skin. But when it came to his father, I had time to feel the shape of his mouth.

He has gone. He will come back on Sunday to fetch me for the concert. He has gone. . . .

I ask you! An uncle who didn't look in the least the old-fashioned kind! Do *I* nag *him* about his habit of losing his money at the races? He might, quite naturally, reply that he was no longer seventeen and that his name was not Claudine.

And, as if all that weren't enough, I still have no news of Luce.

Claudine is playing at being a fashionable lady. Claudine is ordering herself dress after dress and tormenting the ancient and superannuated Poullanx, dressmaker, as well as Madame Abraham Lévi, milliner. My uncle has assured me that, in Paris, all the milliners are Jewesses. This one, though she's on the Left Bank, displays a liveliness of taste that is rare and refreshing; besides, it amuses her to find hats for my pointed face and short, bushy hair. Before trying them on, she brushes my hair forward roughly, fluffs up the sides, takes two steps backwards and says rapturously: "There! Now you look exactly like Polaire!" Personally, I'd rather look like Claudine. As, from February onwards, the women here plant greenery on their heads, I've chosen two summer hats; a big black crinoline straw with feathers—"makes you look like a millionaire's baby", Madame Lévi declared, pouting amiably into her dark moustache—and another one, russet, trimmed with black velvet. They've got to go with everything. *I* don't share that gawk Anaïs's tastes. She was never happy unless her head was capsizing under three kilogrammes of roses.

And I'm working out still another blue dress. I cultivate blue, not for its own sake, but for the way it sets off the Spanish tobacco colour of my eyes.

No sign of Marcel. I feel vaguely that he's sulking with me. 'Sulking' is too strong a word, but I can sense a muffled resentment. Today, as it's raining, I'm consoling myself with old and new books, with Balzacs I've read over and over again, that have crumbs of long-ago meals hidden between their pages . . . there's a cake-crumb that comes from Montigny—smell, Fanchette! Heartless beast, it didn't mean a thing to her; she was listening to the noises of saucepans in the kitchen! . . . Papa, his tie looking like a shoe-string, pats my head whenever he passes through. How happy that man is in having found the rich fulfilment of life and a fruitful new channel for his energies in slugs . . . who is going to take the place of the slug for *me*?

A letter. Why, yes, it was from Claire!

"*Darling, I've got blissful news to tell you. I'm being married in a month's time to my dear beloved whose photograph I sent you. He is richer than I am; he has no troubles, but that doesn't matter. I'm so happy! He's going to be manager of a factory in Mexico (!!!) and I shall go out there with him. Now you can see life really is like it is in novels. You used to laugh at me in the old days when I told you so. I so much want you to come to my wedding, etc., etc., etc.*"

After that came endless repetitions and all the chatter of a little girl delirious with happiness. She deserves all her joy, that gentle, trusting child—and such a nice decent child, too! That trust and that gentleness, by a miraculous chance, have protected her better than the most knowing artfulness. This wasn't entirely due to her, but it has certainly been the case. I answered her straight away in a letter full of nice, affectionate nothings. And then I stayed sitting there by a little wood fire—shivery, as always, the moment it rains—waiting for night and dinner-time, in a shaming state of misery and dejection.

She was getting married; *she* was seventeen. And I? . . . Oh, if I could only be given back Montigny, and last year, and the year before that, and my turbulent, indiscreet prying into other people's affairs! If I only could have back my disappointed love for Mademoiselle's little Aimée and my sensual bullying of Luce—for I've no one here and don't even want to behave badly!

Whoever would have believed that she was revolving such tearful thoughts, this Claudine, squatting cross-legged in a dressing-gown before the marble chimneypiece and apparently completely absorbed in roasting one side of a bar of chocolate kept upright between a pair of tongs? When the surface exposed to the fire softened, blackened, crackled and blistered, I lifted it off in thin layers with my little knife. . . . Exquisite taste, a mixture of grilled almonds and grated vanilla! The melancholy sweetness of savouring the toasted chocolate and, at the same time, staining one's toenails pink with a little rag soaked in Papa's red ink!

The returning sun showed me the absurdity of my desolation of last night. All the more so because Marcel arrived at half-past five, lively and beautiful as . . . as only Marcel can be. His pongee tie was a dull turquoise that brightened his lips to China rose, an artificial rose like a made-up mouth. Heavens, that little furrow between the nose and the upper lip and the imperceptible down that silvered it! Pure silk velvet at 15 francs 90 a yard wasn't as smooth!

"Nephew, how pleased I am to see you? You're not shocked that I've kept my little apron on?"

"It's charming, your little apron. Keep it on, you make me think (what, already!) of Montigny."

"I don't need to keep it on to make *me* think of Montigny. If you knew how that hurts sometimes!"

"Oh come now, none of that nostalgic nonsense, Claudine! It doesn't suit you a bit!"

His levity was cruel to me at that moment and, no doubt, I gave him a nasty look, for he became tractable and charming.

"Wait a moment. Homesickness! I'm going to breathe on your eyes and it will fly away!"

With his woman's grace, a compound of ease and of extraordinary precision of movement, he caught me round the waist and gently breathed on my half-closed eyes. He kept the game up and finally declared, "You smell of . . . cinnamon, Claudine."

"Why cinnamon?" I asked languidly, leaning against his arm and half tranced by his light breath.

"I don't know. A warm smell, a smell like some exotic sweet-meat."

"So that's it! An oriental bazaar, in fact?"

"No. A bit like Viennese pastry—a smell good to eat. And what do *I* smell of?" he demanded, putting his velvety cheek very close to my mouth.

"New-mown hay", I said, sniffing it. And, as his cheek did not withdraw, I kissed it gently, without pressing. But I would have kissed a bunch of flowers or a ripe peach in just the same way. There are some scents one can only take in properly with one's mouth.

Marcel understood that, it seemed. He did not return my kiss, but drawing back, he said, with an absurd little pout:

"Hay? That's a very artless smell. . . . By the way, are you coming to the concert tomorrow?"

"Certainly. Your father came to see Papa the other morning, didn't you know?"

"No," he said with indifference. "I don't see Papa every day. He hasn't time. And now I must be off, I've only got a minute. Do you know, you ungrateful little girl, whom I'm keeping waiting by staying here? Charlie!"

He burst into a mischievous laugh and fled.

But I fully appreciated the costliness of this favour.

11

"Papa, I'm going to the concert in a moment. Do hurry a little. I'm quite aware that cold fried eggs are a dish for the gods, but all the same, do be quick."

"Inferior creature!" declaimed Papa, shrugging his shoulders. "All women are on a level with the least intelligent of she-asses. I am soaring in the realm of ideas!"

"Take care, you'll upset the water-jug with the tip of your wing. Don't you think my dress suits me?"

"Hmm . . . yes. . . . Is it made from one of last year's garments?"

"Certainly not. You paid for it two days ago."

"No doubt. This household is a bottomless gulf. Is your aunt well?"

"But she came here. Didn't you see her?"

"No—yes—I can't remember; she bores me. Her son's a great improvement on her. Very intelligent! Has views on all sorts of things! Even about malacology, he's not too scandalously ignorant."

"Who do you mean? Marcel?"

"No, no, not the little squit. What's-his-name . . . Wilhelmine's son-in-law, that's the one I mean."

The little squit, the little squit! So Papa didn't care a rap about little squits like that! Not that I think badly of Marcel's father, who attracts me and warms the cockles of my heart, but *really* . . .

The bell. Mélie made haste slowly to answer it. My cousin Uncle and my 'nephew' entered, both resplendent. Marcel, in particular, in a tight-fitting suit too new for my taste; beside his father, he seemed a little diminished.

"My dear sir. . . . How pretty that girl of yours looks in that big black hat!"

"Not bad, not bad," Papa said carelessly, disguising his very genuine admiration.

Marcel examined me critically as usual.

"Do put on suède ones instead of pearl-grey kid; they're prettier with blue."

He was right. I changed my gloves.

All three of us in a closed cab, Marcel on the torturingly narrow pull-down seat, we bowled along towards the Châtelet. As I was quaking inwardly, I said nothing and behaved well. There was no danger of the conversation between Uncle Renaud and his son becoming over-exciting.

"Do you want to see the programme? Here you are. *The Damnation of Faust*. It's not a first performance. . . ."

"It's a first performance for me."

In the square, the spitting sphinxes of the Palm-tree Fountain reminded me of the disgusting game we used to adore at Montigny: standing in a row, five or six of us horrid little girls would fill our cheeks with water and imitate the sphinxes. The one who spat furthest won a marble or some nuts.

At the box-office and on the staircase, my cousin Uncle kept bowing to people or shaking hands with them. Evidently he came here often.

It was badly lit. It smelt of horse-dung. Why did it smell of horse-dung? I asked Marcel under my breath why and he answered: "It's because they're playing *Michael Strogoff* every night." Uncle Renaud installed us in the front row of the dress-circle. Scowling a little at being in such conspicuous seats, I looked round me shyly, but it was difficult to see after coming in from broad daylight, so I felt at my ease. It was all right, there were plenty of ladies! And what a row they were making! All that banging of doors in the boxes, all that pushing about of chairs . . . it was like being in church at Montigny where no one paid any attention to what Father Millet was saying in the pulpit, nor even to the altar.

The Châtelet auditorium was large but ugly and commonplace; the lights showed red in a halo of dust. I can assure you it *did* smell of horse-dung! And all those heads down below—the men's black and the women's beflowered. I wondered, if I threw bread down to those people, whether they'd open their mouths to catch it? When was it going to begin? My cousin Uncle, seeing me pale and nervous, took my hand and kept it between his fingers as a gesture of protection.

A bearded gentleman, with shoulders slightly 'askew', advanced on to the stage and applause (already!) drowned the extremely disagreeable tumult of chatter and of instruments tuning-up. It was Colonne himself. He rapped his desk twice with a little baton, inspected those under his command with an encircling glance, and raised his arm. At the first chords of the *Damnation* a nervous lump rose up from my stomach to my throat and stayed there, nearly choking me. I had hardly ever heard an orchestra and those bows were playing on my nerves. I had a crazy terror of bursting into tears from sheer nervous exasperation and making an utter fool of myself! With tremendous efforts, I mastered this ridiculous feeling and I gently withdrew my hand from my Uncle's so as to get myself under better control.

Marcel was looking round everywhere and making signs with his head towards the gallery where I could make out soft felt hats, long hair, clean-shaven faces and aggressive moustaches.

"Up there," explained the Uncle in a whisper, "are all the people who really matter. Anarchist musicians, writers who will change the face of the world and even extremely nice boys who haven't a penny and love music. It's up there too they put 'the man who protests'. He whistles and utters his obscure maledictions; a military policeman gathers him like a flower, expels him and lets him return discreetly by another door. Colonne has tried engaging one specially at modest fees, but he's given it up. 'The man who protests' must first and foremost have passionate convictions."

At a certain point, I wanted to laugh. It was when Mephistopheles was singing the song of the flea, to such a burlesque accompaniment that Berlioz must have done it on purpose. Yes, I wanted to laugh because the baritone was obviously finding it tremendously difficult not to *act* what he was singing. He restrained himself as much as he could from being diabolical, but he could feel that forked feather waving above his forehead and his eyebrows shaped themselves of their own accord into the traditional circumflex accent.

Right up to the interval, I listened with all my inexpert ears that had had little practice in distinguishing the tones of the various instruments.

"What is it that's singing in the orchestra, among the wood-wind, Uncle?"

"A base flute, I'm pretty sure. We'll ask Maugis in the interval, if you like."

The interval came all too soon, in my opinion. I detest being rationed and having a pleasure cut short without my asking. Where were all those people leaving the auditorium rushing to so fast? Actually, they were only going out into the passages. I glued myself to Marcel's side, but Uncle Renaud authoritatively slipped his own arm under mine.

"Collect yourself, little girl. Even though we're limited to damning Faust today and there won't be any of the latest works from the young men of the new School, I can show you some tolerably well-known faces. And your illusions will strew the ground like flowers from withered garlands!"

"Oh! Is it the music that's inspired you to such eloquence?"

"Yes. The real truth about me is that behind a thinker's brow I have a young girl's soul."

His slate-coloured eyes, indulgent and lazy, smiled at me with a smile that calmed me and gave me confidence. His son, who was rather overdoing being all things to all men, had just gone off to make his bow to Madame Barmann who was dominating and laying down the law in the midst of a group of men.

"Quick, let's escape," my Uncle implored in alarm. "She'll go and quote the latest aphorism of her 'illustrious friend' at us, once we get dragged into her wake!"

"Which illustrious friend? The one she was talking about at Aunt Coeur's the other Sunday?"

"Gréveuille, a very much sought-after member of the Academy whom she . . . subsidises, boards and lodges. Last winter I still used to dine in that set-up and I went off with a slightly embarrassing picture in my mind: the great man installed in front of the Louis XIII chimneypiece and artlessly presenting his two unbuttoned boots to the fire."

"Why hadn't he buttoned them up?" (I put the question to him with a convincing imitation of innocence.)

"Because, of course, he'd just been . . . Claudine, you're intolerable! Anyway, it's entirely my fault. I'm not used to little girls. I've been an Uncle for such a very short time. But I'll watch my step from now on."

"What a pity! It won't be nearly so amusing."

"Ssh, you little horror! As you read *everything*, do you know who Maugis is? I can see him over there."

"Maugis? Yes, he does music criticism—articles all peppered with puns and vulgarities—a hotchpotch of affectation and lyrical enthusiasm that I don't always understand. . . ."

"'Affectation and lyrical enthusiasm!' Goodness, what an amusing niece I've got! Do you know that's not at all a bad criticism? But I'm positively going to enjoy taking you out, chicken!"

"Thanks very much! If I know what those words really mean, you 'took me out' today just out of politeness, didn't you?"

We had come within earshot of the Maugis in question. He was extremely animated and holding forth in a throaty voice that kept choking; he appeared to be in one of his lyrical moods. . . . I went up closer still. No doubt he was giving full vent to his admiration? Bumpetty-bump! (as they say at home when a child tumbles down. . . .) *This* was what I heard:

"No, but did you hear that swine of a trombone baying among the new-blown roses of that night? If Faust could sleep in spite of the rumpus that ass was making, he must have been reading *Fertility* before he dossed down. Besides, what a dung-heap of an orchestra! In the sylphilitic Ballet, there was a putrid little flautist who didn't stick at blowing his confounded nose at the same time the harps were doing their harmonic what-d'you-call-'ems. If I could lay hands on him, I'd stuff his flute up his . . ."

"My friend, my friend," my Uncle soothingly admonished the back of the frenzied speaker. "If you go on, you'll lose all moderation of speech!"

Maugis swung his heavy shoulders round and displayed a short nose, protruding blue eyes under drooping lids and a huge, ferocious moustache above a babyish mouth. Still swelling with righteous fury, his bulging eyes and his congested neck made him look like a slightly froglike little bull. (I have profited by the natural history lessons of Montigny.) But he was smiling now, with a disarming mouth, and, as he bowed, revealing a vast pink pate, I noticed that the whole lower part of the face—the nebulous chin vanishing in rolls of fat and the childish lips—incessantly contradicted the energy of the huge forehead and the short, obstinate nose. I was introduced to him. His response was:

"My dear old chap, why do you bring this young person to this dubious resort? It's so delightful in the Tuilleries with a nice hoop . . ."

I was offended and said nothing. And my dignity immensely amused the two men.

"Is your Marcel here?" Maugis asked my Uncle.

"Yes. He came with his aunt."

"*What!*" exclaimed the critic with a start, "you mean to say that now he's going about openly with his . . ."

"With Claudine," explained my Uncle, shrugging his shoulders. "Claudine here is his aunt. We are a complicated family."

"Ah, Mademoiselle, so you are Marcel's aunt? Interesting irony on the part of fate. Or possibly a happy prognostication."

"If you think you're being funny . . ." growled my Uncle, torn between wanting to laugh and wanting to scold.

"One does one's poor best," replied the other.

What was all that about? There was something there that I didn't understand. It wasn't till long after that I discovered that, in slang, 'aunt' meant young men like Charlie.

The pretty Cypriot, Madame Van Langendonck, swept past us, escorted by six men who all seemed to be equally infatuated with her and whom she caressed impartially with her enraptured gazelle's eyes.

"What a delicious creature! Don't you think so, Uncle?"

"I certainly do. She's one of those women one simply must invite to at-home-days. She's both decorative and inflammatory."

"And," added Maugis, "while the men are gazing at her, they forget to gobble up all the stuffed rolls."

"Who's that you're bowing to, Uncle?"

"An extremely estimable trio."

"Like the César Franck one," broke in Maugis.

"Three inseparable friends," my Uncle went on, "who are always invited together and everyone would be sorry to leave one out. They're good-looking, they're well-behaved, and, incredible as it may seem, absolutely irreproachable and decent. One composes music, charming, very individual music; the second—the one who's talking to Princess De C . . . , sings it like a great artist and the third does extremely clever pastels while he listens to them."

"If I were a woman," concluded Maugis, "I should want to marry all three of them!"

"What are their names?"

"You'll nearly always hear people mention all three together: Baville, Bréda and della Sugès."

My Uncle exchanged a few passing words with the trio, who were a pleasure to look at. One looked like a Valois who had strayed into our midst from another century, slim and high-bred as a heraldic greyhound; this was Baville. The handsome, healthy boy with shadows under his blue eyes and a delicious feminine mouth was the tenor, Bréda. The tall, casual della Sugès, who retained something of the East in his matt complexion and the marked curve of his nose, watched the people go by, as serious as a well-behaved child.

"You're an expert, Maugis. Point out a few notorious specimens to Claudine."

"Specimens of the world and his wife? Cert'nly. It's a charming spectacle to present to a female infant. . . . Here, young *backfisch*, behold, to begin with . . . honour to whom honour is due . . . the fashionable sterilizer dear to all ladies who never, never more, *ovariemore*, wish to combat the depopulation of our beloved country. . . ."

My Uncle could not repress a little gesture of annoyance. He had no need to: my fat showman talked with such obviously deliberate volubility that I didn't manage to catch half his jokes. They got no further than his moustache and I was sorry because my Uncle's irritation proved they were pretty stiff.

Gradually, Maugis modified his tone somewhat as he enumerated further celebrities.

"No, enviable aunt of the enviable Marcel, cast your eyes on one of the critics whom Sainte-Anne envies us; that beard—about which we can sing a roundelay, if you like, that it is gilded with peroxide and golden as ripe corn—that beard is named Bellaigue. Ah, the Scudo of the *Revue des Deux Mondes* ought to have twisted it seven times round his tongue before uttering such blasphemies against Wagner. . . . But much will be forgiven him because he did like

Parsifal. . . . Another critic, that far from handsome little man. . . ."

"The one coming towards us, scraping along the walls?"

"If that wall had a reputation, he wouldn't scrape it, he'd flay it—he's a wriggling, poisonous little snake. . . . Oh, how cantankerous our dear brother is to his brother-critics! When he isn't writing music, he starts up a perfect hullaballoo of disgusting rumours."

"And when he is writing music?"

"He starts up an even more disgusting hullaballoo."

"*Do* show me some more critics!"

"Ugh! They seem to have astonishingly depraved tastes in your native bog, my Princess from a far country. No! I won't show you any more critics because the sole representatives of French musicography here are limited to the two bipeds I have just had the honour of . . ."

"What about the others?"

"The others—who number nine hundred and forty-three and a half (one of them's a legless cripple)—the others never venture inside a concert-hall . . . it wouldn't be any earthly use to them if they did. They piously flog their seats to the ticket-hawkers. They sell their passes and even their 'services'! But let us leave these clodhoppers and contemplate Madame Roger-Miclos of the cameo profile, Blowitz of the gorilla face, Diémer who conceals a piano keyboard, without the black notes, in his mouth, Dutasby the barrister who hasn't missed a single Colonne concert since that day he was weaned."

"Who's that . . . that lovely creature who positively undulates in her dress?"

"Delila, Messalina, the future Omphale, Austria's share of the spoils."

"Please?"

"Haven't you read that in old man Hugo? '*L' Angleterre prit Leygues*' . . . I wonder what the hell she got out of it . . . '*et l'Autriche l'Héglon*'."

I knew about *l'aigle* and *l'aiglon* of course, but this pun was beyond me. So I asked: "And all those other elegant ladies?"

"Nothing, less than nothing. High society and high finance. Gotha and Goldgotha. The pick of the basket and the pick of the pickpockets. They take boxes for the season because it's the thing to do . . . the tiresome thing. . . . They're about as musical as skunks and they all jabber loud enough to drown the orchestra—every one of them from the Marquise de Saint-Fiel, who comes here to buck up the artists she gets to perform in her drawing-room with the sight of her, down to the charming Suzanne de Lizery, that well-kept Greuze, 'The Broken Pitcher', or the dumb girl who wasn't such a mug as to get broken without being put together with gold rivets. Also known as 'the whole duty of man'."

"Why?"

"Because she can't spell."

Judging I'd been sufficiently bewildered, Maugis went off, at the summons of a friend, to have a well-earned beer in the bar. His throat must have been dry after all that eloquence.

I caught sight of Marcel by a pillar in the foyer; he was talking low and fast to a very young man of whom I could see nothing but the nape of a dark neck and very silky hair. I gently pulled my Uncle round the pillar and I recognised the liquid eyes and the white and black face of a certain photograph on the chimneypiece of my 'nephew's' bedroom.

"Uncle, do you know the name of the young man who's talking to Marcel behind the pillar?"

He turned round and swore violently into his moustache.

"Why, it's Charlie Gonzalès of course. He's a bounder, as well as everything else."

"Everything else?"

"Oh, I mean it's not a friendship I feel exactly overjoyed about for Marcel! That boy could hardly look more flashy!"

The ringing of a bell summoned us back. Marcel rejoined us in our seats. I forgot a great many things to listen to Mademoiselle Pregi poignantly lamenting her desertion, and the orchestra held me enthralled; the orchestra in which Marguerite's heart beat in dull throbs. The Invocation to Nature was encored. This time, Engel imperiously tossed his tempestuous hair and at last roused some response in this audience which had hardly been pretending to listen. My Uncle explained: "It's because this audience has only heard the *Damnation* seventy-six times!" Marcel, on my left, puckered his mouth discontentedly. When his father is there, he always looks as if he were annoyed with me.

To the accompaniment of an uproar of sound that I found exhausting, Faust rushed towards the Abyss, and we ourselves, shortly after, towards the exit.

It was still daylight outside and the declining sun was dazzling.

"Do you want some tea, children?"

"No, thank you, Father. Do you mind if I leave you now? I've arranged to meet some friends."

"*Some* friends? That Charlie Gonzalès, I presume."

"Charlie and others," Marcel answered curtly.

"Run along. Only, you know," added my Uncle, in a lower voice, bending down to his son, "the day I've had enough of all this, I shan't hesitate to tell you. . . . I'm not going to stand for a repetition of the Lycée Boileau business."

What business? I was on fire with curiosity to know. But Marcel did not answer. His eyes were black with concentrated fury as he said goodbye and rushed off.

"Are you hungry, my dear?" my Uncle asked again. His disillusioned face had aged in the last few moments.

"No, thank you. I'll go home—if you don't mind putting me in a cab."

"I'll even put myself in it too. I'll take you back."

As a great favour, I begged to go in one with pneumatic tyres that was just passing; I adore that padded, bouncy feeling as you bowl along on them.

We said nothing. The Uncle stared in front of him with a weary, troubled expression.

"I've got things on my mind," he said after ten minutes, answering a question I had not asked. "Talk to me, little girl, distract the old gentleman."

"Uncle, I'd like to ask you how you come to know those people, Maugis and the others?"

"Because I've trailed about all over the place for the last fifteen or twenty years and because it's easy to get to know people in journalism; in Paris, one makes contacts very quickly."

"I'd also like to ask you—but if it's indiscreet, you can put me off—what you do in the ordinary way, if . . . if, well, you have a profession? I'd so much like to know."

"Have I a profession? Alas, I certainly have. I'm the man who 'does' the foreign politics in the *Diplomatic Review.*"

"In the *Diplomatic Review*! But that's most frightfully boring! I mean" (what a ghastly brick! I felt myself turning scarlet) "I mean those are awfully serious articles."

"Don't try and get out of it! Don't gloss it over! You couldn't say anything more flattering: those saving words shall go down to your credit. All my life, I've been regarded by your Aunt Wilhelmine, and by many others, as a contemptible individual who does nothing but amuse himself and amuse his friends. For the last ten years, I've revenged myself by boring my contemporaries. And I bore them in the way they like best—I am well-documented, I am stereotyped, I am pessimistic and peevish! I am atoning, Claudine, I am rising once more in my own esteem. I have produced twenty-four articles—two dozen—on the scoop of the dispatch from Ems. At present, three times a week for the past six months, I deal with the Russian policy in Manchuria, thus procuring myself necessary cash."

"It's incredible! I'm nonplussed!"

"And now, why I'm telling you all this, is another affair. I believe that, under the absurd ambition to appear a grown-up person who doesn't need advice from anyone, you're as violent and enthusiastic as any lonely little girl. I never expand, as you've seen, with that unfortunate little Marcel, and I'm overflowing with pent-up paternity. That's what's loosened your uncle's tongue."

The dear man! I wanted to cry. The music, the nervous strain . . . and something else as well. It was a father like that that I missed and needed. Oh, I don't want to speak ill of mine; it isn't his fault if he's a little peculiar. But this one, I should have adored! With the shyness I always feel when I show what little good I may have in me, I took the risk of saying:

"You know, perhaps *I* might be quite a good safety-valve. . . ."

"I thought as much, I thought as much." (His two great arms closed round my shoulders and he laughed, so as not to seem too emotional.) "I should like people to do things to upset you so that you could come and tell me about them."

I stayed leaning against his shoulders; the rubber tyres purred over the uneven cobbles along the quays and the jingling awakened romantic ideas of driving at night in a post-chaise.

"Claudine, what would you have been doing at Montigny at this very moment?"

I started. Montigny couldn't have been further from my thoughts.

"At this very moment? Mademoiselle would have been clapping her hands for us to come in for the evening class. For an hour and a half, up to six o'clock, we used to ruin our eyes in the dusk or, worse still, in the light of two oil-lamps hung much too high up. Anaïs would have been eating pencil-lead or chalk or fir-wood and Luce would have been begging me, with her cat's eyes, for some of my extra-hot peppermints. The room smelt of the four o'clock sweeping, dust sprinkled with water, ink and unwashed little girl."

"Really unwashed? You don't mean to tell me you were the one and only exception to this hydrophobia?"

"Well, practically. Anaïs and Luce always seemed to me fairly clean. But the others—of course I didn't know them so well—but, honestly, well-brushed hair and smooth stockings and white tuckers sometimes don't mean a thing, you know."

"Lord, as if I didn't know! Unfortunately I can't tell to what extent I *do* know."

"The other girls . . . anyway, most of them . . . didn't have the same ideas as I did about what's dirty and what's clean. Take Célénie Nauphely, for example. . . ."

"Aha! Let's hear what Célénie Nauphely did!"

"Well, Célénie Nauphely used to stand up—she was a big girl of fourteen—at half-past three—half an hour before it was time to go . . . and say out loud, looking very serious and self-important, 'Mademoiselle, can I go, please? I've got to go and suck my sister.'"

"Merciful heavens! Suck her sister?"

"Yes. Just imagine, her married sister, who was weaning a child, had too much milk and her breasts hurt her. So twice a day Célénie used to suck them to relieve her. She pretended she used to spit the milk out again but, all the same, she must have swallowed some of it in spite of herself. Well, the girls used to fuss over her with admiring envy, this suckling infant. The first time I heard her telling all about it, I couldn't eat my next meal. Doesn't it have any effect on you?"

"Don't press the point or I think it most certainly *will* have an effect on me. You certainly open strange vistas on the Fresnois institutions, Claudine!"

"And Héloïse Basseline who found Claire (the girl who made her First Communion with me), with her feet in water one night and said 'I say, have you gone crazy? T'aint Saturday and look at you, washing your feet!' So Claire answered: 'But I wash them every night.' Whereupon Héloïse Basseline went off, shrugging her shoulders, and saying: 'My dear, you're only sixteen and you're as bad as an old maid. They gets sort of funny manias like that!'"

"God in heaven!"

"Oh, I could tell you lots of other things like that. But decency wouldn't permit."

"Come, come, an old uncle."

"No, even so, I'd rather not. By the way, talking of Claire, she's getting married."

"The girl who washes her feet? At seventeen? She's mad."

I jibbed at this.

"What's mad about it? At seventeen one isn't a child any more! I might very well get married myself."

"And to whom?"

Caught unawares, I began to laugh.

"Ah, that's another question! Mr Right is in no hurry to appear. At the moment, my suitors aren't exactly falling over each other. My beauty hasn't made enough general sensation yet."

Uncle Renaud sighed as he leant right back in his seat.

"Alas, you're not ugly enough, you won't go begging long. Some man will fall in love with that lithe figure and the mystery of those elongated eyes. And I shan't have a niece any more and you'll have made a big mistake."

"So I mustn't get married?"

"Claudine, don't imagine I'm demanding quite such devotion to an uncle as that. But I do at least beg you . . . don't marry just anyone."

"All right. Choose me a thoroughly safe, reliable husband yourself."

"You'd better not count on that!"

"Why not? You're so awfully good to me!"

"Because I don't like seeing particularly nice cakes eaten under my very nose. Get out, my dear, we're there."

What he had just said was better than all the other compliments. I knew I shouldn't forget it.

Mélie opened the door to us, one breast cupped in her hand. In the book-lair, I found Papa in deep conference with Monsieur Maria. This hairy scholar, whose existence I frequently forget, spends an hour here nearly every morning but I seldom see him.

When Uncle Renaud had gone, Papa solemnly announced to me: "My child, I have some excellent news for you."

Heavens, what sinister plot was he hatching now?

"Monsieur Maria is willing to act as my secretary and to assist me in my labours."

Thank goodness it was only that! Much relieved, I held out my hand to Monsieur Maria.

"I'm delighted, Monsieur. I'm sure your collaboration will be an immense help to Papa."

I'd never said so much to this shy man before and he took refuge behind his forest of hair, beard and eyelashes without managing to hide his confusion. I suspect this honest youth of secretly having what Maugis would call a "crush" on me. This doesn't annoy me. *That* one would never dream of treating me disrespectfully!

I've had yet another letter from Claire, positively drivelling with happiness. "What fun you must be having!" she wrote, so as to give me the idea she was thinking of me. Having fun? I wouldn't exactly describe it as that. . . . It isn't that I'm bored, but I'm not happy. Don't get the idea that I'm in love with Marcel. No. He arouses my defiance, my interest, a touch of contemptuous tenderness and, physically, the desire to touch him. Just that. All the time I keep wanting to comb his hair, stroke his cheeks, pull his ears, even stick my nails into him now and then, as I used to do to Luce. Also, as I used to do with her too, I want to put one of my eyes close to one of his, lashes to lashes, so as to see the blue stripes in his irises look as if they were dancing. All the same, when one really thinks it over, he is a little like his father on a smaller scale. Yes, *definitely* on a smaller scale.

And still nothing from Luce. It's really very odd, this prolonged silence!

I now possess a tailored coat and skirt, after two fittings at *New Britannia* with Marcel. Those two fittings were enough to make one die of laughter though I kept a perfectly straight face like a real lady.

My 'nephew' was admirable. Sitting on a chair a yard away, in one of the little looking-glass lined fitting-rooms, he made Léone the skirt-fitter and Monsieur Rey the cutter spin round like tops, with an off-handedness I admired. "The dart on the hips a shade further back, don't you agree, Mademoiselle? Not too long, the skirt—just clearing the ground is plenty long enough for the street. Besides, Mademoiselle doesn't know how to walk in very long skirts yet. . . ." (A venomous glance from Claudine who said not a word.) "Yes, the sleeve hangs well. Two little curved pockets on the jacket, to slip her thumbs into when her hands are empty. Claudine, for heaven's sake, keep still for two seconds! Fanchette would fidget less than you do!" The fitter, hypnotised, didn't know what to think. Crouching on all fours on the carpet, she kept glancing up, obviously asking herself: 'He's not her brother because he doesn't say "*tu*" to her but could he be her gigolo?' And when we went off together after the last trying-on, 'the final fitting', Claudine stiff in her white-collared shirt and wearing a 'boater' that failed to subdue her short hair, Marcel said to me, with a sidelong glance:

"I know what you look like, Claudine, but I'll keep my opinion to myself."

"Why? You may as well go on now you've started."

"Certainly not! Respect, family feeling! But that starched collar and that short, curly hair and that straight skirt . . . Oh dear, oh dear! Papa's quite capable of frowning at all that."

Uneasy at once, I asked:

"You think he wouldn't like it?"

"Oh, he'd get used to it. Papa's no saint under all that air of being a champion of outraged morality."

"Thank heaven he's *not* a saint. But he's got taste."

"So have *I* got taste," said Marcel huffily.

"You . . . you've mainly got *tastes,* rather unusual ones, too."

Marcel gave a forced laugh as we climbed the dreary steps up to the Rue Jacob. My 'nephew' gladly agreed to come and have something to eat in my room. We settled down with our laps full of Turkish Delight, over-ripe bananas, cold drinks and salty biscuits. It was hot out-of-doors and cool in my dark bedroom. I risked asking something I'd been keeping back for several days.

"Marcel, what was the business of the Lycée Boileau?"

With his elbow on the arm of the tub-chair and the salt biscuit he was nibbling held between the tips of his slim fingers, Marcel twisted round like a lizard and stared at me. His cheeks were flaming. With his eyebrows drawn together and his mouth open in surprise, what a beautiful little angry god he was! "Tiny as a clove of garlic," but so handsome!

"Ah, so you've heard about that! My compliments. You've got sharp ears. I might reply that . . . it's none of your business."

"You might. But I'm too nice for you to give me such a nasty answer."

"The business of the Lycée Boileau? A piece of sheer infamy that I shan't forget as long as I live. My father . . . perhaps this'll teach you to know him better, as you're so keen on him. What he did to me over that was something absolutely unforgivable."

It was incredible how angry and miserable that boy looked! I was absolutely boiling with curiosity.

"*Do* tell me the whole story."

"Well, you know who I mean by Charlie?"

"I most certainly do!"

"Right. When I first went to the Lycée Boileau as a day-boy, Charlie was due to leave the next year. All those untidy boys with their red wrists and dirty collars simply disgusted me! He was the only one. . . . I had the impression that he was like me, and hardly much older! For a long time he used to look at me without speaking to me, and then, for no earthly reason, we suddenly became friends. It's impossible to resist the attraction of those eyes. I was obsessed by him without daring to tell him and—I have to believe this"— whispered Marcel, drooping his eyelashes, "he was obsessed by me, because . . ."

"He told you so?"

"No, he wrote it to me, alas! But wait. I answered, you can imagine how gratefully! And, after that, we used to see each other outside school, at Grandmother's, and other places. And he taught me to know and love hundreds of things I didn't know existed."

"Hundreds!"

"Oh, don't jump to conclusions and imagine any *Luceries*," protested Marcel, putting out his hand. "Exchanges of ideas, of annotated books, or little souvenirs."

"Go on, schoolgirl!"

"All right, schoolgirl if you like. But most of all, that exquisite correspondence . . . we wrote almost daily . . . until the day . . ."

"Ah, *that* was what I was dreading!"

"Yes. Papa stole one of my letters."

"*Stole* is going a bit far."

"Oh, all right, he said he picked it up off the floor. Anyone less evil-minded than he is might perhaps have guessed that all that affectionate way of writing was . . . was purely poetic. But not he! He flew into a really brutish rage—oh! when I think of it, I don't think there's any injury in the world I wouldn't do him—he hit me! And not only that—he went off to make, as he said, 'the hell of a row' at the school."

"Which you were . . . politely asked to leave?"

"Much worse than that. No, it was Charlie who was expelled. They had the insolence! Otherwise Papa would probably have made 'the hell of a row' in his filthy newspapers. He's quite capable of it."

Avidly, I listened, and admired. His red cheeks, his blue eyes, almost black with fury, and that quivering mouth, its corners tense, perhaps, with a desire to cry. I should never see any girls as lovely as Marcel!

"The letter! Your father kept that, of course?"

He gave a forced laugh.

"Oh, he wanted to, all right! But I'm cunning too. I got it back from him, with a key that opened his drawer."

"Oh! Show it me! Do, *do!*"

With an instinctive gesture towards his breast-pocket, he replied:

"Unfortunately I can't, my dear. I haven't got it on me."

"On the contrary, I'm absolutely certain you have. Marcel, my pretty Marcel, it would be shocking ingratitude for the trust, the beautiful trust your friend Claudine reposes in you!"

I slid insidious hands over him and made my eyes as coaxing as I knew how.

"Little pickpocket! You're not going to take it from me by force? Did one ever see such a girl! I say, let go, Claudine, you'll break one of my nails. Yes, you're going to be shown it. But promise you'll forget it?"

"I swear. By Luce's head!"

He drew out a woman's card-case, Empire green, and extracted a sheet of very thin paper, carefully folded, and scrawled over in minute handwriting.

I gave myself up to savouring the 'poetry' of Charles Gonzalès.

MY DARLING,—*I am going to look up that story of Auerbach's and I shall translate for you the passages that describe the passionate friendship of the two children. I know German as well as I know French, so this translation won't give me the least difficulty. I almost regret this because it would have been a delight to me to endure some hardships for you, my only loved one.*

Oh, yes, my only one! My only loved, my only adored one! And to think your jealousy, always on the alert, is flaring up again! Don't say it isn't, I know how to read between your lines as I know how to read the depths of your eyes and I cannot misunderstand the irritable little sentence in your letter about "the new friend with the too-black curls whose conversation absorbed me so much at the four o'clock break".

This so-called new friend—actually I hardly know him—this little boy "with the too-black curls" (why too?) is a Florentine, Giuseppe Bocci, whom his parents have sent as a boarder to B. . . . , the celebrated philosophy beak, to remove him from the depravity of school friendships; he's certainly got far-seeing parents! This child was telling me about an amusing psychological study one of his compatriots has devoted to the Amicizie del Collegio which this transalpine Kraft-Ebbing apparently defines as a "mimicry of the passionate instinct"—for these materialists, Italian, German or French, all manifest the most disgusting, sham-medical imbecility.

As the pamphlet contains some amusing observations, Giuseppe is going to lend it to me. I asked for it for whom? For you, of course, for you who reward me with this monstrous suspicion. Do you realise how unjust you've been? Then kiss me. Or don't you realise it? In that case, it's I who kiss you.

What a lot of books have been concocted already, all dealing more or less clumsily with this most fascinating and complex question in the world!

To steep myself once more in my faith and my sexual religion, I have re-read Shakespeare's burning sonnets to the Earl of Pembroke and Michelangelo's no less idolatrous ones to Cavalieri. I've also fortified myself by re-reading passages in Montaigne, Tennyson, Wagner, Walt Whitman and Carpenter.

My slender, my adorable child, my supple, living Tanagra, I kiss your throbbing eyes. You know very well that all that unwholesome past I sacrificed without hesitation for you, all that past with its degrading curiosities that now I loathe, seems to me today like some distant, horrible nightmare. Only your tenderness remains, inspiring me, firing me.

Hell! I've got exactly a quarter of an hour left in which to study "The Conceptualism of Abelard". His conceptions must have been of a somewhat peculiar kind, after what he'd had cut off.

Yours, body and soul,

Your Charlie.

When I had finished, I did not know what to say. I was slightly alarmed by these goings-on between boys. It didn't astonish me in the least that Marcel's father should have 'flared up' too. . . . Oh, I was aware—only too aware—that my 'nephew' was extremely tempting—rather more than tempting, even. But the other one? So Marcel kissed him, kissed this phrasemongering, plagiarising Charlie, in spite of the little black moustache? Marcel must be anything but ugly when one kissed him. I gave him a covert glance before handing him back the letter: he wasn't thinking about me at all; he wasn't even considering asking my opinion. With his chin resting on his hand, he was pursuing some private train of thought. His resemblance to my cousin Uncle, obvious at that moment, suddenly upset me and I gave him back the sheets of paper.

"Marcel, your friend writes that sort of letter more prettily than Luce does."

"Yes. . . . But aren't you shocked at such stupid prudery? Punishing an exquisite person like Charlie!"

"Shocked isn't perhaps quite the word, but I am surprised. After all, though there can only be one Marcel in this world, I imagine schools must include other Charlies."

"Other Charlies! Look, Claudine, you can't possibly compare him with those dirty schoolboys who . . . I say, give me something to drink and a piece of Delight! Thinking about all this has made me hot."

He mopped himself with a little blue linen handkerchief. As I hastily offered him a cool drink, he put his card-case down on the wicker table beside him and leant back, feverishly sipping his drink in tiny mouthfuls. He sucked a rose-flavoured piece of Turkish Delight, nibbled a salted biscuit, and lost himself in memories of his Charlie. As for myself, I was so bitten with curiosity that I could have screamed; I asked myself what other letters there might well be in the Empire-green card-case. Now and then (not often, thank heaven) I am seized with these ugly and violent desires to possess something, as fierce as temptations to steal. Certainly, I was perfectly well aware that if Marcel caught me in the act of rummaging among his letters, he would have the right to despise me, and would certainly exploit it, but the thought of this did not make the crimson flush of shame overspread my brow as is customary in all school stories. Sad, but true! With careful negli-

gence, I laid a plate of cakes down on the tempting card-case. If it
worked, it worked.

"Claudine," said Marcel, waking up, "my grandmother finds you
very unsociable."

"It's true. But I don't know how to talk to her. I can't help
it . . . she's practically a stranger to *me*. . . ."

"Anyway, all that isn't of the slightest importance. . . . Heavens!
What an ugly shape Fanchette's getting!"

"Be quiet! My Fanchette is always beautiful. She's very fond of
your father."

"I'm not surprised . . . he's so sympathetic!"

He stood up as he made this amiable remark. He slipped the scrap
of linen into his left pocket . . . would he? No! He'd forgotten about
it. If only he'd hurry up and go! For a second, I remembered Anaïs's
half-burned love-letters that a similar fit of curiosity had made me
take out of the school stove, but I felt not the slightest remorse.
Anyway, he'd been sarcastic about his father—he was a horrid little
boy!

"Are you going? Already?"

"Yes, I must. And, I assure you, I'm always sorry to go. Because
you're the confidante I've always dreamed of—and hardly a bit like a
woman!"

Could anything be more charming! I accompanied him as far as
the stairs to make sure that the door was duly shut and that he would
have to ring the bell if he came up again.

I rushed to the little card-case. It smelt good; Charlie's scent, I
presumed.

In one pocket, there was a photograph of Charlie. A half-length
postcard-size portrait with bare shoulders and a classical fillet
binding his brow and the date "28th December". I looked up the
calendar: "28th December, the Holy Innocents." Certainly, there
were some odd coincidences in the almanack!

There was a bundle of little blue express letters in spiky,
pretentious writing and hit-or-miss spelling; meetings arranged or
postponed. Two telegrams signed . . . Jules! Well, I never! Here
was something that would have made Anaïs gasp till she nearly
dislocated her jaw! Along with these letters, there was a woman's
photograph! Who was she? An extremely pretty creature, excessively slim, with stream-lined hips, wearing a discreetly low-cut dress of
sequin-studded black lace. With her fingers on her lips, she was

blowing a kiss. Under the photograph, the same signature . . . Jules! I simply had to look closer into this! I sharpened my eyes; I went off and fetched Papa's venerable triple magnifying-glass; I examined the picture minutely. "Jules's" wrists seemed a trifle thick perhaps, but not as shockingly so as Marie Belhomme's, to quote only one feminine example; those hips could not be masculine, nor could those rounded shoulders, and yet—and yet—the muscles of the neck under the ear made me hesitate again. Yes, it was definitely the neck of a very young man, I could see it now. . . . Well, that was that! . . . I continued my rummaging.

On the sort of paper a cook uses and written in a cook's style and with a cook's spelling, was some obscure information.

"Take my tip and give the rue Traversière a miss, but you wont run no risk cumming with me to Léons. His place is nice and handy for the Brasserie I was tellig you of and youll see persons there as is worth your while, stable lads from Medrano, eccetera. As to Ernestine and that Weevil, watch out! I dont think Victorine has drawn lotts yet for army service. Rue Lafite, granny will have told you the hotel is saife."

What an extraordinary world! It was this pack of shady characters that Charlie had "sacrificed" to Marcel! And he dared to make capital out of it! What staggered me most of all was that my 'nephew' did not find it revolting to accept the dregs of an affection that swilled round Weevils, soldiers, grooms "eccetera". On the other hand, I understood to perfection that Charlie, sick at last of the too-compliant Juleses—all the same, that incredible photograph!—should have found the novelty adorable. A child who offered him an emotion he had never known before, a child whose scruples it would be delicious to overcome.

He definitely repelled me, this Charlie. My cousin Uncle was perfectly right to get him kicked out of the Lycée Boileau. A dark boy like that probably had hair on his chest!

"Mélie! Quick, run over to Aunt Coeur's! Take a cab—it's to take this little parcel to Marcel with a letter I'm writing to him. You're not to leave it with the porter."

"A letter, gracious me! Of course I'll take it up my own self! You're a lovely girl. Don't you fuss yourself, my pet, it'll get there safe! And no one won't be any the wiser!"

I could safely trust her. Her devotion blazed up at the thought that I was about to kick over the traces. I had no intention of disillusioning her. It gave her so much pleasure.

All the same, it is true that Fanchette is becoming ridiculous to look at! She accepts her 'Parisian' basket on condition that I leave a piece of my old velveteen dressing-gown in it. She kneads this rag energetically, sharpens her claws on it, keeps it warm in a ball under her, or licks it as she dreams of her future family. Her little breasts are swelling and becoming painful; she is possessed by a constant, insatiable craving to be petted and 'fussied' as they say in Montigny.

Mélie, jubilant, brought me back a note from Marcel, thanking me for the return of the card-case. "Thank you, dear, I wasn't worried" (*I don't think!*) "knowing the card-case was in your little hands which I kiss affectionately, discreet Claudine."

"Discreet Claudine." That might be sarcastic as well as an appeal to me to keep silence.

Papa is working with Monsieur Maria; that is to say he is wearing the unfortunate young man out by turning out his books from top to bottom. First of all, he had nailed up twelve shelves on the library wall, to the accompaniment of much swearing, twelve shelves designed to take decimo-octavo volumes. A splendid job! Only, when Monsieur Maria, mild, devoted and dusty, wanted to put the volumes on them, he discovered that Papa had made a mistake of a centimetre in the distance between the shelves so that the books could not stand upright. The result was that all the shelves except one had to be taken down again. You can imagine the stormy cries of "God's thunderbolts!" and "Come down, Eternal Father!" Personally, I was convulsed with laughter over this catastrophe. And all that the divinely patient Monsieur Maria said was: "Oh, it's nothing. We'll just space out the eleven shelves a little more."

Today I received a lovely great box of chocolate creams, bless him, with a letter from my cousin Uncle.

"My charming little friend, your old uncle is sending you this box to make his farewells in his stead. I am sure you won't complain of the substitute. I have to go away on business for eight or ten days. On my return, if you are willing, we will explore some other ill-ventilated haunts of pleasure. Take good care of Marcel who, I'm not joking, gains much from your company. An avuncular kiss on both your paws."

Yes? Well, *I'm* not joking, I'd rather have an uncle and no chocolates. Or, better still, an uncle *and* chocolates. Anyway, these are superb. Luce would sell herself for half the box. Now then, Fanchette, if you want me to murder you, you've only to go on doing that! That wicked creature keeps dipping an only too-efficient paw, curved like a spoon, into the open box. Yet all she'll get are half-shells of chocolates, after I've scooped the cream out with the big end of a new pen-nib.

I haven't seen Marcel for two days. A little ashamed of my laziness about going to see Aunt Wilhelmine, I set off, none too eagerly, to visit her. However, I was dressed to my entire satisfaction. I am delighted with my smoothly-fitting tailored skirt and my light blue zephyr blouse that gives my skin a golden tone. Before saying goodbye to me, Papa enunciated solemnly:

"Be sure and tell my sister that I'm up to my eyes in work and that I haven't got a minute to myself so that she doesn't take it into her head to come and bore me under my own roof! And if anyone is impertinent to you in the street *in spite* of your tender years, give them a good clout on the jaw!"

Armed with this sage advice, I went to sleep for forty minutes in the respectable and evil-smelling Panthéon-Courcelles bus and only woke up at the terminus, Place Péreire. Bother! I almost invariably do that idiotic thing! I had to walk back all the way to the Avenue Wagram where the unfriendly maid stared disapprovingly at my short hair and informed me that "Madame had just gone out". What incredible luck! I didn't waste a second making my escape; I fairly hurtled down the staircase without waiting for the lift.

The green Parc Monceau, with its soft lawns veiled in misty curtains of spray from the sprinklers, attracted me, like something good to eat. There were fewer children there than in the Luxembourg. It was better altogether. But those lawns that are swept like floors! Never mind, the trees enchanted me and the warm dampness I breathed in relaxed me. All the same, the climate of Paris is disgracefully hot. But that sound of leaves, how sweet it was!

I sat down on a bench, but an old gentleman whose hair and moustache had been tinted with a paint-brush, dislodged me by his insistence on sitting on a fold of my skirt and nudging my elbow. Having treated him as an 'old reptile', I walked away with great dignity to another bench. A tiny little telegraph-boy—what on earth was he doing there?—engaged in hopping from one foot to the other and kicking a flat pebble along, stopped and stared at me and screeched: "Ooh, aren't you a naughty girl? You jolly well run off and hide in my bed!" Evidently, the Parc Monceau wasn't the desert. Oh, why wasn't I sitting in the shade of the forest of Fredonnes! Collapsing on a chair against a tree, I fell into a drowse, lulled by the jets of the sprinkler drumming on the broad leaves of the castor-oil plants.

The heat weighed me down and made me feel imbecile, utterly imbecile. Charming, that lady pattering along, but her legs were too short; anyway, three-quarters of the women in Paris have their behinds on their heels. My Uncle was absurd to go off the moment I was beginning to like him so much. My Uncle. . . . He has young eyes, in spite of his incipient crow's feet, and a charming way of leaning towards me when he talks to me. He's travelling on business! Business affairs—or another kind. Mélie, who has a practised eye, answered, when I asked her her impression of him: "Your Uncle's a fine, handsome man, my lamby. A real good all-round worker, for sure."

He must 'trail around' with women, this man with such a sense of duty. Disgusting!

That little woman just passing. . . . Her skirt hung well. She had a walk . . . a walk that I recognised. And that round cheek, fringed in the light with a silvery glisten of fine down . . . I recognised that too. That sketchy little nose, those rather high cheekbones. . . . My heart turned over. With one bound, I was beside her, shouting at the top of my voice: "Luce!"

It was incredible, but it really was she! Her cowardice was proof enough for me. At my shout, she boldly jumped backwards and put her elbow over her eyes. My emotion dissolved into a fit of nervous giggles; I grabbed her by both arms. Her little face with the narrow eyes slanting up to the temples flushed to the ears, then suddenly went pale. At last, she gasped: "What luck it's you!"

I was still holding her by the arms and there was no end to my amazement. How had I ever recognised her? This little slip of a girl whom I'd always seen in a black serge apron and wearing pointed sabots or heavy lace-up shoes, with no hat except the red woollen hood and her hair in a plait on weekdays and a chignon on Sundays—this Luce was wearing a tailored suit better cut than mine, a pale pink blouse of the finest silk under a short bolero and a toque of draped crinoline-straw, turned up with a bunch of roses, that she certainly hadn't bought at the 'inexpensive hats' counter. There were one or two false notes one didn't see at first glance: a clumsy corset, too stiff and not curved enough; hair too flattened down and with no style about it; gloves that were too tight. She takes five-and-a-halfs and had, no doubt, squeezed herself into fives.

But what was the explanation of all this splendour? No two ways about it, my little friend had definitely launched herself on the lucrative path of misdemeanour. Yet how fresh and young she looked, with no powder on her face and no red on her lips!

Standing face to face, staring at each other without saying a word, we must have looked ridiculous. It was Luce who spoke at last.

"Oh, you've had your hair cut off!"

"Yes. You think I look ugly, don't you?"

"No," she said tenderly. "You couldn't look ugly if you tried. You're taller. You look ever so nice. But you don't love me any more, do you? You stopped loving me ages ago."

She had kept her Montigny accent. I listened to it, enchanted, my ears strained to catch her soft, slightly drawling voice. Her green eyes had subtly changed colour ten times since I had been looking at her.

"That's neither here nor there, you little 'wurzit'! Hang it all, what are you doing here and why are you looking so marvellous? Your hat's delicious—tip it a bit further forward. You're not alone, are you? Is your sister here?"

"No, she certainly *isn't* here," replied Luce, with a malicious smile. "I've ditched the whole lot of them. It's a long story. I'm dying to tell you all about it. Honestly, it's like something out of a novel."

Her voice betrayed a fathomless pride; it no longer charmed me.

"But tell away, my little piglet! I've got the whole afternoon to myself."

"What luck! Claudine, please, would you come back to my place?"

"Yes, but on one condition. I shan't find *anyone* there?"

"No, no one. But come along, come along quick. I live in the Rue de Courcelles, only two steps from here."

With my head in a whirl, I went along with her, watching her sideways as we walked. She wasn't very good at holding up her long skirt and she walked with her head a little forward like someone who doesn't feel their hat is very secure. Oh, how much more touching and individual she used to be in a woollen skirt above her ankles, with her plait half-undone, and her slim feet always out of her sabots. Not that she was uglier! I noticed that her freshness and the mutable colour of her eyes produced considerable effect on the male passers-by. She was aware of it; she made eyes, unconsciously and lavishly, at all the amorous dogs we met. Heavens, how queer it all was! I was treading in a world of unreality.

"You're looking at my parasol," said Luce. "Look see, it's got a crystal handle. It cost fifty francs, old thing!"

"Cost whom?"

"Wait till I tell you everything. I must begin at the beginning or I'll get fair moithered."

I adored these local expressions. Contrasting with the elegant clothes, the country accent produced a startling effect! I understood certain chortles that occasionally burst without warning from my 'nephew' Marcel.

We passed through the main entrance of a new block of flats, loaded with white sculptures and balconies. An enormous lift, all lined with mirrors, which Luce manipulated with nervous respect, swept us up.

To whose home was she taking me?

On the top storey, she rang the bell—hadn't she got a key then?—and walked quickly past a starchy maid, dressed like an English one, in black with a ridiculous little white muslin apron. It was no bigger than a Negro's costume . . . you know, the costume that consists of a small square of woven grass, suspended over the stomach by a string.

Luce hurriedly opened one of the doors in the hall; I followed her into a white passage with a dark green carpet: she opened another door, disappeared through it, shut it behind us and flung herself into my arms.

"Luce! Do you want a slap?" I said, recovering my former authority with considerable difficulty, for she was holding my tight and burrowing her cool nose in my neck, under the ear. She raised her head and, without loosening her arms, said, with an ineffable expression of happy slavery:

"Oh yes! *Do* beat me a little!"

But I no longer felt inclined—or did not yet feel inclined—to beat her. You don't pound a four-hundred-franc tailored coat and skirt with your fists and it would have been a pity to flatten that pretty bunch of roses with a box on the ears. I'd gladly have clawed her little hands . . . but she'd kept her gloves on.

"Claudine! Oh, you don't love me the least little bit any more!"

"I can't love you like that to order. I've got to know who I'm dealing with! That blouse didn't grow on your back of its own accord, did it? And this flat? 'Where am I? Is it magic, is it an enchanted dream?' as that beanpole Anaïs used to sing in that acid voice that put one's teeth on edge."

"This is my bedroom," answered Luce, in an unctuous voice. She stood back a little so as to let me admire it.

Too sumptuous, but not too absurd, her bedroom. It was well upholstered for instance! There was white enamel—alas!—but there were chairs and wall-panels covered in almond-green velvet with a shell design—a copy of Utrecht, I think—that flattered one's eyes and enhanced one's complexion. The bed—oh! what a bed! I couldn't resist measuring its width with my two outstretched arms: more than a metre and a half. Madame, more than a metre and a half, they say, is a bed for at least three people! Beautiful curtains of almond-green damask at the two windows, a triple-doored wardrobe with a long glass, a little chandelier), and a big white and yellow striped armchair by the fireplace. And goodness knows what else!

"Luce, are these the fruits of dishonour? *You* know . . . 'the deceptive fruits that leave a taste of ashes in the mouth', if one can believe our old *Moral Tales*."

"You haven't seen the most splendid of all," Luce went on without answering. "Look!"

She opened one of the doors adorned with little carved garlands. "This is the bathroom and dressing-room."

"Thanks. I might so easily have thought it was Mademoiselle Sergent's private oratory."

Paved with tiles, walled with tiles, the bathroom glittered, like

Venice, with a thousand lights (and more). Sakes alive, was it possible? A bath for a young elephant and two tip-up basins as deep as the pond of Barres. On the dressing-table, blonde tortoiseshell that must have cost fantastic sums. Luce rushed to a curious little stool, lifted up the padded top studded with gilt buttons that covered it, like a box-lid, and said ingenuously, displaying the oblong pan, "It's solid silver."

"Ugh! The edges must be awfully cold to sit on. Is your coat-of-arms engraved on the bottom? But tell me everything or I'll buzz off."

"And it's all lit by electricity. *I'm* always frightened of accidents, sparks, something or other that kills you (my sister used to bore us so much with all that stuff at Montigny in physics lessons!). So *when as* I'm all alone at night, I light a little oil lamp. Have you seen my chemises? I've got six silk ones, and the rest Empire with pink ribbons and knickers to match. . . ."

"Empire knickers? I didn't think there was a frenzied demand for them in these days. . . ."

"Oh yes, because the sewing-maid told me that they were Empire, so there! And then . . ." Her face sparkled. She fluttered from one cupboard to another, getting tangled up in her long skirt. Suddenly she pulled up her rustling petticoats with both hands and whispered to me ecstatically: "Claudine, I've got *silk stockings!*"

She had, indeed, silk stockings. They were silk, as I could verify, right up to the thighs. I remembered her legs very well, the little marvels.

"Feel how soft it is!"

"I take your word for it, I take your word for it. But I swear I'll go away if you keep rambling on like this without saying anything!"

"Then let's make ourselves comfortable. Here, in the armchair, plumpy you down. Just a twit, while I pull down the blind, 'cos of the sun."

They were priceless, her lapses into her native speech. In her pink blouse and her impeccable skirt, the effect was pure comic-opera.

"Shall we have a drink? I always keep two bottles of tonic wine in my bathroom. *He* says that'll stop me from getting anaemic."

"*He!* There's a *He!* What luck, now I shall know all! The portrait of the seducer . . . go and fetch it this minute."

Luce went out and returned with a frame in her hand.

"There, that's him," she said without enthusiasm.

It was hideous, this cabinet photo of a fat, almost bald, man of about sixty, perhaps more. He had a bestial look, with jowls like a Great Dane and big calf's eyes! Horrified, I stared at my little friend who was silently contemplating the carpet and fidgeting with one foot.

"Old thing, you've got to tell me all. It's even more interesting than I thought."

Sitting at my feet on a cushion, in the gilded dusk of the lowered blinds, she clasped her hands on my knees. The change in the way she did her hair upset me very much; besides she should never have had it waved. I, in turn, took off my boater and ruffled up my curls to give them some air. Luce smiled at me.

"You look exactly like a boy, Claudine, with your short hair, a jolly nice-looking boy, too! Yet no, when one really looks at you, you've definitely got a girl's face. Yes, a pretty girl's!"

"That'll do. Get on with the story, from the very first scrap right up to today. And do buck up a bit, otherwise Papa will think I've got lost or run over."

"Yes. Well, when you decided to write to me after your illness, *they* were already being as beastly as possible to me. And this and that, and I was a goose and I was a caricature of my sister, and all the time they kept calling me names."

"Are they still getting on well together, your sister and the Headmistress?"

"Goodness me, worse than ever. My sister doesn't even sweep her room any more. Mademoiselle has taken on a little servant girl. And on the least excuse, Aimée pretends she's ill and doesn't come downstairs and it's Mademoiselle who takes her place for nearly all the oral lessons. Better than that: one evening, in the garden, I heard Mademoiselle making a terrible scene with Aimée about a new assistant master. She lost all control of herself: 'One of these days I'll kill you,' she said to Aimée. And my sister burst out laughing and said, looking at her sideways: 'You wouldn't dare, you'd be too sorry afterwards.' And then Mademoiselle began to 'blub' and implored her not to torture her any more and Aimée flung her arms round her neck and they went indoors together. But it wasn't all *that* stuff, I was used to that. Only, I tell you, my sister treated me like a dog and so did Mademoiselle. When I started to ask for some shoes and stockings, my sister sent me packing. 'If the feet of your stockings are in holes, mend them'—that's what she said to me. 'Besides, the legs are good still and as long as the holes can't be seen, it's as if they didn't exist.' It was the same thing with dresses; she had the cheek, the filthy beast, to foist off an old blouse on me that had all gone under the arms. I cried all day because my clothes were in such an awful state; I'd rather have been beaten! Once I wrote home. They never have a penny, as well you know. Mum wrote back: 'Fix things up with your sister, you cost us enough money as it is. Our pig has died of disease and I had fifteen francs to pay the chemist last month for your little sister Julie. You know that at home it's poverty and trouble of every kind, so, if you're hungry, eat your fist.'"

"Go on."

"One day, when I'd tried to frighten my sister, she ended up by laughing in my face and bawling at me: 'If you don't like it here, why don't you go back home then? You could look after the geese. It would be good riddance for us.' That day, I couldn't eat my dinner or get to sleep. The next morning, after class, as I was going up to the refectory, I found Aimée's bedroom door ajar. Her purse was lying on the mantelpiece, by the clock (for she's got a clock, my dear, the dirty pig!). Seeing it there suddenly made my blood run cold. I pounced on the purse, but she'd have been sure to search me and I didn't know where to hide it. I'd still got my hat on, I put on my jacket and I went down to the lavatories and threw my apron down one. I went out again without meeting anyone (everyone was in the refectory by then), and I ran off on foot to catch the 11.39 train to Paris. It was just on the point of starting. I was half-dead from running."

Luce paused for breath and to enjoy the effect of her story. I admit I was stunned. Never would I have believed that chit capable of such impulsive action.

"What next? Hurry up, child, what next? How much was there in the purse?"

"Twenty-three francs. So, when I got to Paris, I had nine francs left. I'd taken third-class tickets, of course. But wait. Everyone knew me at the station and old Racalin asked me: 'Where are you running off to like that, my little dear?' I told him: 'My mother's ill . . . they sent us a telegram. . . . I'm hurrying off to Sementran, my sister can't get away.' And he said, 'That's very worrying for you.'"

"But, once you'd reached Paris, what did you do?"

"I went out of the station and I walked. I asked where the Madeleine was."

"Why?"

"You'll see. Because my uncle—that's him in the photo, lives in the Rue Tronchet, near the Madeleine."

"Your mother's brother?"

"No, her brother-in-law. He married a rich woman who's dead now. He's made simply piles of money himself too, and, of course, he didn't so much as want to hear us starving relations mentioned any more. You'd expect that. I knew his address because Mum, who'd an eye on the money, forced us to write to him, all five of us, on New Year's Day, on flowered paper. So I only went to his place to know where to sleep."

" 'Where to sleep!' Luce, my homage! You're a hundred times wickeder than your sister, and than me too."

"Oh! Wicked? That's not the right word. I just fell into it. I was dying of hunger. I had on Aimée's little old blouse and my school hat. And I found a flat *even* more grand than this one and a manservant who asked me, all sharp like: 'What do you want?' I felt so ashamed, I wanted to cry. I said: 'I want to see my uncle.' Do you know what he said to me, that beast? 'Monsieur has given me orders not to admit any of his relations!' Wasn't it enough to strike you dead? I turned round to go away, but I found myself face to face with a fat gentleman who was just coming in. So from then on, there was no going back! 'What's your name?'—'Luce.' 'Did your mother send you?'—'Oh, no. I came all on my own. My sister was making me so unhappy that I've run away from school.'—'From school? How old are you then?' he asked, and he took me by the arm and made me come into the dining-room. 'I'll be seventeen in four months' time.'—'Seventeen? You don't look it, far from it. What a strange story! Sit down, my child, and tell me all about it.' So then, you see, naturally I brought it all out, how miserable I'd been, and Mademoiselle, and Aimée, and the holey stockings, well, the whole lot. He listened and he kept looking at me with his big blue eyes and he kept pulling his chair up closer. Towards the end, I was so tired that I started to cry! And here was a man who took me on his knees and kissed me and said nice things to me. 'Poor little thing! It's a shame to torment such a nice little girl. Your sister takes after her mother; mark my words, she's a pest. Hasn't she got lovely hair! With her pigtail, you'd say she was fourteen.' And little by little there he was stroking my shoulders and hugging my waist and my hips and kissing me all the time and puffing like a grampus. It disgusted me a bit, but I didn't want to annoy him, you understand."

"I understand perfectly. What happened next?"

"What happened next . . . oh, I couldn't tell you *everything.*"

"Don't be a little hypocrite! You weren't such a prude at school!"

"It's not the same thing. *Before,* he made me dine with him—I was dying of hunger. Such good things, Claudine! 'Goodies' of all kinds—and champagne. After dinner, I'd no idea what I was saying. *He* was as red as a cock, but he didn't get flustered. He came out fair and square with his proposition: 'My little Luce, I'll promise to put you up for a week, to inform your mother—in a way that won't start her yapping—and, later on, to arrange a nice little future for you. But on one condition; you'll do whatever I want you to do. You look to me as if you didn't despise the good things of life and liked your comforts—that goes for me too. If you're absolutely untouched, so much the better for you, because then I'll be nice to you. If you've already trailed around with boys, nothing doing! I've got my ideas and I stick to them.'"

"And then?"

"And then he took me into his bedroom, a lovely red bedroom."

"And then?" I said avidly.

"And then . . . oh, I can't remember. Honest I can't!"

"Do you want a slap to make you talk?"

"Well," said Luce, shaking her head, "actually it's not so funny, you know."

"Ah? Does it really hurt very much?"

"It certainly does! I 'gave tongue' with all my might—and besides his face right up against mine made me hot and his hairy legs scratched me. And he puffed and he panted! As I was 'giving tongue' too much, he said, in a choky voice. 'If you don't scream, I'll give you a gold watch tomorrow.' I tried not to make another sound. Afterwards, I was so all to bits that I cried out loud. *He* kept kissing my hands and saying: 'Swear to me that no one else shall ever have you. I'm too lucky for words, too lucky for words!' But *I* wasn't awfully happy."

"Difficult, aren't you?"

"And then, in spite of myself, all the time I kept thinking about the rape at Ossaire—you remember *that*—the bookseller in Ossaire who raped one of his shopgirls. When the case was on we used to read the *Fresnois Monitor* in secret and we used to learn some sentences by heart. All the same, they did come up at quite the wrong moment, those memories."

"Stop being literary and get on with the rest of the story."

"The rest of the story? Oh dear! . . . Well, the next morning, I just couldn't get over seeing this fat man in my bed. He's so ugly when he's asleep! But he's never been really nasty and sometimes we even have good moments. . . ."

Luce's lowered eyelids hid eyes that were knowing and hypocritical. I wanted to question her, yet, at the same time, I was embarrassed. Surprised at my silence, she looked at me.

"Come on, Luce, get on with it!"

"All right. Well, at first my family tried to find me. But my uncle wrote to them straight away. 'My little darling, I simply warned your mother to leave us in peace and not poke her nose in if she wanted to see the colour of my money after I'm dead. As for you, you can do whatever you like. You've twenty-five louis a month, your food and your clothes. Send them some brass or don't send it them, I don't give a damn either way! But *I* won't send them a farthing!'"

"So you did send some money home?"

Luce's face became diabolical.

"What, *me?* You don't know me! Oh no thanks, I'm too fed up with all they've done to me! Let them starve, d'you hear? . . . starve! I'd see them all starve to death without drinking one single drop less myself! Oh, they haven't denied themselves the pleasure of asking me for money . . . oh ever so nicely, with ever such good manners. D'you know what I answered? I took a sheet of white paper—a big one and I wrote on it: S . . t! Just that!"

She had said the word, a word of four letters.

She stood up and danced about, her pretty pink face positively lit up with ferocity. I couldn't get over it.

Could this really be that timid little girl I had known at school, that poor younger sister who was beaten by Aimée, the favourite, that little Luce of the soft, coaxing ways who was always wanting to

kiss me in the wood-shed? I wondered whether to leave then and
there. This little girl and her uncle, it was all too modern for me.
According to her, she'd actually have let them die of starvation!

"Honestly, Luce, you'd let them . . ."

"Oh! yes, Claudine darling. What's more," she added, with a
forced laugh, "if you only knew, I'm working on my uncle to cut
them right out of his will! Isn't that screamingly funny?"

Obviously, it was screamingly funny.

"So, you're utterly and completely happy?"

She broke off her waltz and pulled a face.

"Utterly and completely? There are snags. I still have to go
carefully with my uncle! He's got a way of saying: 'If you don't want
to, it's all up between us!' that forces me to do as I'm told."

"If you don't want to what?"

"Nothing—lots of things," she answered, with a sweeping gesture. "But he gives me money, too, that I hide under a pile of
chemises and, most of all, oh! most of all, sweets and pastries and
little birds to eat. And even better than that, champagne at dinner."

"Every night? Your skin will get blotchy, my dear!"

"Do you think so? Just take a good look at me. . . ."

It was true that no flower could be fresher. Luce's skin is genuine
fast-dyed material, guaranteed not to spot in rain—or even in mud.

"Tell me, dear Madame. Do you receive company? Do you give
dinner-parties?"

Her face darkened.

"Not possible, with that jealous old thing! He doesn't want to let
me see anyone at all. But" (she lowered her voice and spoke with a
smile that told much), "one can manage things all the same. I've seen
my little friend, Caïn Brunat—you know, the one you used to call
my 'flirt'. He's at the Beaux-Arts, he ought to become a great
painter, and he's going to do my portrait. If you only knew . . ." she
said, with her birdlike volubility. "He's old, my uncle, but he has
impossible ideas. Sometimes he makes me get down on all-fours and
run about the room like that. And he runs after me on all-fours too,
looking like a comic caricature with his great fat stomach. Then he
jumps on me, bellowing: 'I'm a wild beast! . . . look out for
yourself! I'm a bull!'"

"How old is he?"

"Fifty-nine, so *he* says. A bit more, I think."

My head was aching, I was stiff all over. This Luce was too disgusting. You should have seen her describing these horrors! Perched on one foot, with her fragile hands spread wide, a pink ribbon belt buckled round her tiny waist and her soft hair combed back smoothly from her transparent temples, the pretty little boarding-school Miss.

"Luce, while you're off the chain, *do* give me some news of Montigny. Please! No one ever talks to me about it any more. How's that gawk Anaïs?"

"Much as usual; nothing special. She's 'going with' one of the Third Years."

"Not too squeamish a Third Year, I bet! And Marie Belhomme and her midwife's hands? Remember, Luce, when she owned up to us, that in summer she didn't wear any drawers so as to feel her thighs 'stroke each other' when she walked?"

"Yes, I remember *that*. She's serving in a shop. No luck, poor girl!"

"Everyone can't have your luck, you little prostitute!"

"I don't like people to call me that," Luce protested, shocked.

"All right then, shy virgin, tell me about Dutertre."

"Oh, that poor doctor, he flirted with me ever such a lot towards the end. . . ."

"Well? Why not?"

"Because my sister and Mademoiselle had sent him packing good and proper and my sister said to me: 'If *that* happens to you, I'll scratch your two eyes out!' He's having a lot of worries over his politics."

"So much the better! What worries?"

"Hark you now to this story. At a meeting of the Town Council, Dutertre got caught out over the station at Moustier. If he didn't want to go and have it put two kilometres away from the village because that would have been more convenient for Monsieur Corne—you know, the owner of that lovely château on the edge of a road—who'd given him goodness knows how much money!"

"Just like his impudence!"

"So, in the Council, Dutertre tried to carry that through as something quite reasonable and the others didn't kick up any fuss, when suddenly Dr. Fruitier, a thin, dried-up old man, a bit loony, got up and treated Dutertre like the lowest of the low. Dutertre gave him a pretty rough answer, a bit too rough, and Fruitier slapped him right in the face in front of the whole Council!"

"Ah, ah! I can see him from here, old Fruitier! His little white hand—it's all bones—must have made a splendid *clack!*"

"Yes, and Dutertre, absolutely beside himself, kept rubbing his cheek and gesticulating and yelling: 'I shall send my seconds to challenge you!' But old Fruitier calmly replied: 'One doesn't fight a duel with Dutertre, don't force me to print the reason why in all the local papers!' There was a terrific hullabaloo about it in our part of the world, I can tell you."

"I bet there was. Did Mademoiselle make herself ill over it?"

"She'd have died of rage if my sister hadn't consoled her, but the things she said about it! As she wasn't a native of Montigny, there was no stopping her. 'Filthy hole full of brigands and thieves!' And so on and so forth. . . ."

"And Dutertre? Is he a figure of public scorn?"

"Him! Two days afterwards, no one gave it another thought: he hasn't lost *that* of his influence. And the proof is, that at one of the last Council meetings, they got round to talking about the School and saying it was run in a very peculiar way. You realise, all Mademoiselle's goings-on with Aimée are known all over the countryside now: no doubt some of the big girls must have gossiped about it . . . so much so that one of the Councillors demanded that Mademoiselle should be dismissed. Whereupon my Dutertre stood up and announced: 'If the Headmistress is called to account, I shall make it my personal business.' He didn't say anything more but they understood and they started talking about other things because, you know, they're nearly all under some obligation to him."

"Yes, and, besides, he's got them by all sorts of dirty things he knows about them."

"Still it didn't stop his enemies fairly rushing at it or the parish priest talking about it in his sermon the very next Sunday."

"Old Father Millet? Right out in the pulpit? But Montigny must have been put to fire and sword!"

"Yes, indeed. The priest, he shouted: 'Shame on the scandalous object-lessons lavished on youth in your Godless schools!' Everyone realised he was talking about my sister and the Headmistress and, of course, they thoroughly enjoyed it!"

"More, Luce, tell me more. You rejoice my heart."

"Goodness, I can't think of any more. Liline had twins last month. They gave a big official reception for Hémier's son who came home on leave from Tonkin where he's landed an awfully good job. Adèle Tricotot's now got a fourth husband. Gabrielle Sandré, who still looks like a little girl with those babyish teeth of hers, is getting married in Paris. Léonie Mercant is an assistant-mistress in Paris (you know who I mean, that tall shy girl—we used to amuse ourselves by making her blush because she had such a thin skin). I tell you, *all* of them are coming to Paris; it's the rage, it's a positive mania."

"It's not a mania that afflicts me," I said, with a sigh. "Personally, I long to be back *there.* Not so much as when I first arrived, though, because I'm beginning to get attached to . . ."

I bit my lips, worried at having said too much. But Luce is not observant and the flow of her conversation went on, in full spate.

"Well, if you long to be back, you're not a bit like *me.* Sometimes, in that huge bed over there, I dream I'm still at Montigny and that my sister's torturing me with her decimal fractions and the mountain-system of Spain and quadrigeminal peduncles. I wake up in a sweat and I'm always tremendously happy to find I'm here!"

"Beside your kind uncle, who snores."

"Yes, he does snore. However did you know?"

"Oh, Luce, how disarming you can be! But the School, tell me more about the School. Do you remember the jokes we used to play on poor Marie Belhomme? And that wicked devil, Anaïs?"

"Anaïs, she's at the Training College—I've told you that already. She and her 'Third Year', who's called Charretier, are almost like my sister and Mademoiselle. You know, at Training College, the dormitories have two rows of open cubicles, separated by an aisle for the mistress in charge to walk up and down and keep her eye on everyone. At night, they draw a red cotton curtain in front of those cubicles. Well, Anaïs had found a way of going into Charretier's almost every night and she hasn't got caught yet. But it'll end up in disaster. At least, I hope so."

"How do you know all this?"

"From a boarder who lives near us in Sementran and who went there the same term as Anaïs. Apparently that Anaïs looks frightfully ill—an absolute skeleton! She can't find uniform collars small enough to fit her neck. Imagine, Claudine darling, they get up at five there! And I laze in my bye-bye till ten or eleven and I have my morning chocolate there. You know," she added, looking exactly like a sensible, practical housewife, "all that helps one to overlook a lot of things."

But, in my inward mind, I was still far away in Montigny. Luce had squatted down at my feet like a little hen.

"Luce, what have we got for composition for next time?"

"For next time," said Luce, bursting into laughter . . . "we've got: *Write a letter to a girl of your own age to encourage her in her vocation to be a teacher.*"

"No, Luce, that's not it, we've got: *Look below yourself and not above yourself; such is the way to be happy.*"

"Sucks, no, it isn't! It's: *What do you think of ingratitude? Support your opinion by an anecdote invented by yourself.*"

"Is your map finished?"

"No, old thing. Didn't have time to 'ink it in'. I shall get an awful wigging. Just imagine . . . my mountains aren't hatched and my Adriatic coast isn't finished."

I hummed: "Come down to the blue Adriatic . . ."

"And bring all your fish-nets on board," sang Luce, in her small, liquid voice.

Then both of us sang in parts: "Come down, bring your fish-nets on board!"

And we launched into it.

> *Haste down to the sea! Ye fishers, the tide,*
> *Foams round the rocks as it races:*
> *The trusty boat moored too long to the side,*
> *Rocks in the wavelet's embraces.*
> *To the beach, all ye maids of the village.*
> *The harvest is ripe for the tillage.*
> *Come forth from each cellar and attic,*
> *To linger ye cannot afford.*
> *Come down to the blue Adriatic*
> *And bring all your fish-nets on board.*
> *Come down, bring your fish-nets on board.*

"Do you remember, Luce, that was where Marie Belhomme *always* went down two notes, goodness knows why? She started shaking with apprehension ten bars before, but she invariably got it wrong. Chorus, now!

> *'Tis a cool and calm night*
> *For the fishers' delight;*
> *Row fast o'er the wave,*
> *Ye fishermen brave!*

"And now, Luce, the grand arrival of the catch!"

> *Here are sardines,*
> *Of our waters the queens,*
> *Here cuttlefish writhe,*
> *Their tentacles lithe*
> *And fish great and small*
> *Heap the glittering haul*
> *Let us sing jubilee*
> *To the generous sea*
> *Who has granted our wish* ⎱ twice
> *With such harvest of fish.* ⎰

Carried away with enthusiasm and beating time, we sang this preposterous ballad through to the very end and we burst into roars of laughter like the two children we still were. Nevertheless, I felt a little saddened by these old memories, whereas Luce hopped about ecstatically, giving little squeaks of joy, and admiring herself in "her" triple-mirrored wardrobe.

"Luce, don't you ever regret the School?"

"The School? Every time I remember it at meals, I ask for more champagne and I eat enough petits-fours to make me sick, to make up for lost time and for all I've had to put up with. Lord, I wish I'd left school for good and all. But I *haven't*, even now!"

She pointed gloomily towards a folding-screen. I followed the direction of her finger and saw, half-hidden by the silk and lacquer screen, a little wooden desk with a seat attached to it, just like our school-desks at Montigny. It was ink-stained and littered with grammar and arithmetic books. I rushed to it and opened some exercise books filled with Luce's tidy, childish writing.

"Your old exercise books, Luce! Whatever for?"

"No, not my old exercise books, unfortunately—my new ones!

And you'll find my big black apron in the hanging-cupboard in the bathroom."

"What's the idea?"

"Oh, goodness, it's one of my uncle's fancies, the worst one of all! You'll never believe it. Claudine darling," groaned Luce, raising two plaintive arms, "he often makes me do my hair in a plait again and put on a big pinafore and sit down at that desk . . . and then he dictates a problem to me, or the outline of an essay. . . ."

"I don't believe you!"

"Oh, but he *does*. And it's not just a joke: I have to do sums and write essays. The first time, when I said I wouldn't, he flew into a real temper. 'You deserve to be whipped, you're going to be whipped', he kept saying. And his eyes were all shining and his voice was so queer. I was frightened, so I got down to work."

"So this man's interested in your progress as a scholar, is he?"

"It amuses him, it . . . it gets him going. It makes me think of Dutertre who used to read our French essays and keep putting his fingers down our necks at the same time. But Dutertre was much handsomer than my uncle. *Ever* so much," sighed poor Luce, doomed to be an eternal schoolgirl.

I couldn't get over it! That sham-little girl in a black apron, that old schoolmaster questioning her about decimal fractions.

"Believe it or not, Claudine," Luce went on, looking gloomier than ever, "he went for me yesterday, the *beast*, just like my sister at Montigny because I went wrong over some dates in English History. I rebelled, I screamed at him: 'English History, that's Higher Certificate, I've had enough!' My uncle didn't raise his eyebrows, he just closed his book and said: 'If the pupil Luce wants her piece of jewellery, she must recite the Gunpowder Plot to me without one mistake.'"

"And *did* you recite it without one mistake?"

"Lord love us, yes—here's the buckle. It was well worth it—look see the topazes—and the snake's eyes be little diamonds."

"But come, come Luce, this is really all most edifying. You'll be able to sit for your 'Higher' at the next exam session."

"Just you wait," Luce said furiously, shaking her little fist menacingly. "My family's going to pay for all this. Besides, I got my revenge. After that, I cut down my uncle's rations. Last month, I was 'indisposed' for a fortnight. So there!"

"He must have looked decidedly glum!"

"Glum? The things you say!" Luce twittered in delight, leaning back in her armchair and showing all her short little white teeth.

At school she used to laugh just like that when Anaïs had said something extra smutty or spiteful. But personally, I felt shocked. That coarse, fat man she was joking about was too close to us amidst all this tart's luxury. Suddenly, I noticed a charming little crease at the base of her neck that had not been there before.

"Luce, you're putting on flesh!"

"D'you think so? I think I am, too. My skin wasn't exactly black even at Montigny," she said coquettishly, coming close to me, "but now it's even whiter. If only I'd got real breasts! But my uncle likes me better flat. All the same, they're a little rounder than they were at our competitions in the hollow lanes, remember, Claudine? . . . Would you like to see?"

She came closer still, her face sparkling and provocative and, with one hand, deftly undid her pink blouse. The skin above the incipient breasts was so fine and pearly that it looked bluish against the China rose silk. There were pink ribbons threaded through the lace of the chemise (Empire, don't forget!). And her eyes, those green eyes with black lashes, had become strangely languid.

"Oh, Claudine!"

"What is it?"

"Nothing. I'm so pleased to have found you again! You're even prettier than you were at school, even though you're crueller than ever to your Luce."

Her soft, coaxing arms turned round my neck. Heavens, how my head ached and throbbed!

"Whatever scent do you use?"

"Chypre. I smell nice, don't I? Oh, do kiss me. You've only kissed me once. You asked me, didn't I regret anything about the School? I do, Claudine, I regret the little shed where we used to break up the firewood at half-past seven in the morning and where I used to kiss you, and you used to beat me. You used to thrash me good and hard, you cruel girl! But, all the same, tell me, truly, don't you think I'm prettier *now*? I have a bath every morning, I wash myself as much as your Fanchette. Do stay a little longer! Do stay! I'll do absolutely anything you like. Now, put your ear close, let me whisper. I know such lots of things now."

"*No!*"

She was still rubbing up against me and talking to me when I took her by the shoulders and gave her such a brutal push that she tottered back against the handsome three-doored wardrobe and banged her head on it. She rubbed her skull and looked at me, to know whether to cry or not. So I went up to her and gave her a hearty slap. She turned crimson and burst into tears.

"Oh, how *could* you? Whatever have I done?"

"Look here, do you imagine I pick up old men's leavings?"

I put on my boater with a shaking hand (I pricked my head hard with the hatpin); I threw my jacket over my arm and I made for the door. Before Luce realised what was happening, I was in the hall and groping to find the front door. Luce flung herself on me, distraught.

"Claudine, you're mad!"

"Not in the least, my dear. I'm too old-fashioned for you, that's all. It wouldn't work at all, the two of us. My kindest regards to your uncle."

And I hurried downstairs as fast as I possibly could, so as not to see Luce, in tears, with her blouse open over her white breast, sobbing out loud and leaning over the banisters, imploring me to come back.

"Comey back, Claudine darling, comey back!"

I found myself in the street with a splitting headache and the dazed feeling you wake up with after some particularly idiotic dream. It was nearly six o'clock. The eternally dusty air of this filthy Paris seemed to me, this evening, soft and clear. What on earth *was* all this story? I wished someone would pull me by the sleeve and wake me up. I wished a Luce in pointed sabots, with her rebellious hair straying in wisps out of the red woollen hood, would say to me, laughing like a child: "Aren't you a silly, Claudine, to dream such *re*diculous things?"

But it was no use, I didn't wake up. And it was the other Luce I kept seeing, weeping and dishevelled and calling to me in her tear-drenched country accent, so much more pretty and so much less touching than the schoolgirl Luce.

But, in spite of everything, what on earth had come over me when that little thing had implored me, with her slim arms twined about

my neck? Had I become extraordinarily prudish in the course of a
few months? Without mincing words, extraordinarily virtuous? It
was not the first time that incorrigible Luce had tempted me nor the
first time I had hit her. But a whole flood of feeling had surged up in
me. Jealousy, perhaps. A smothered indignation at the thought that
this Luce who used to adore me, who still did adore me in her own
way, had flung herself into the lap of an old gentleman (no, really,
those eyes like a badly-boiled calf's head!). And disgust. Disgust,
yes, definitely! There I was, making myself out completely sophisticated and disillusioned and shouting from the roof-tops "Ha, ha!
you can't teach *me* anything. Ha, ha! *I* read *everything*! And *I*
understand everything even though I *am* only seventeen!" Precisely.
And when it comes to a gentleman pinching my behind in the street
or a little friend *living* what I'm in the habit of reading about, I'm
knocked sideways. I lay about me with my umbrella or else I flee
from vice with a noble gesture. In your heart of hearts, Claudine,
you're nothing but a common everyday decent girl. How Marcel
would despise me if he knew that!

The Panthéon-Courcelles bus came placidly zigzagging alongside
me. Hop! I leapt on it without deigning to wait for it to stop. A
successful jump on to the step of a bus going at full trot consoles me
for many things. Provided Papa hadn't decided, this one day of all
days, to make one of his rare incursions into real life! He might have
thought I'd been out rather a long time and it would have upset me
to have had to lie to him and tell him I'd spent the afternoon with
Aunt Coeur.

My fears were groundless: Papa was up in the clouds as usual.
When I went in, he was surrounded by manuscripts, and he merely
darted a wild look at me over his forest of beard. Monsieur Maria,
almost as quiet as a mouse, was writing at a little table. At the sight
of me he furtively pulled out his watch. *He* was the one who had
worried over my absence!

"Aha!" cried Papa, in his richest tones. "You've more than done
your duty by the family! You went off at least an hour ago."

Monsieur Maria gave a distressed glance at Papa. *He* knew that I
had gone out at two o'clock and that it was now thirty-five minutes
past six.

"Monsieur Maria, you've got eyes like a hare! No, don't take that
badly! Hares have very beautiful eyes, black and liquid. Papa, I

didn't see Aunt Coeur because she'd gone out. But I've seen something much better, I've re-discovered a little friend from Montigny here. Luce, you remember Luce, don't you? She's living in the Rue de Courcelles."

"Luce, ah, I've got it! She's the one who's getting married, who made her First Communion with you."

"More or less right. We talked for ages, as you can imagine."

"And you'll be going to see her often?"

"No, because I can't stand the furniture in her flat."

"What's the husband like? Poisonous, eh?"

"I don't know. I only saw his photograph."

For the last two days, I haven't set foot out-of-doors. I stay in my room or in the book-lair, behind the half-closed shutters that still let in too much heat and too much light. This summer, that has turned threatening, frightens me, I don't know where to hide myself. Suppose I were to fall ill again! I listen to the thunderstorms and, after the showers, I breathe in the damp air, charged with electricity. However boldly I lie to myself, that afternoon with Luce has shaken me more than I like to admit. Mélie, who has given up trying to understand me, aggravates my trouble by talking to me about Montigny; she has had recent and detailed news from there.

"The little girl at Koenet has just had a baby."

"So? How old is she?"

"Thirteen and a half. A fine boy, it seems. The walnut tree at the top of the garden is going to have lots of nuts."

"Shut up, Mélie, I shan't be there to eat them."

"What fine nuts, eh, my lamb? Riddle-me-ree, riddle-me-reeks. Two pairs of buttocks in one pair of breeks."

"Tell me some more news."

"The big *cuisse-de-nymphe* rose is already eaten up with caterpillars (it's the tenant's manservant as wrote to me) and they're amusing themselves killing them all. He must have a tile loose!"

"Well, what do you expect them to do with them? Make them into jam?"

"Don't you go purtending as you don't know! You takes a caterpillar in your hand, you takes him over to another village—Moustier, say—and then all the others follow him!"

"Mélie, whatever are you waiting for? You ought to take out a patent at once. Why, it's pure genius. Is it your own invention, this method?"

"Lordy, no," said Mélie, tucking some faded, fair wisps back under her coif. "*Everyone* knows it."

"Is that all the news?"

"No. Old Cagnat, my cousin, is so bad with his kidneys, that he's completely omnipotent."

"He is, is he?"

"Deary me, yes. His legs have swelled right up to the knees, and what with having an intruding stomach too, he's quite capable, so to speak. What else? The new owners of the château at Pont de l'Orme are turning their park upside down to go in for apisiculture in a big way."

"Pisciculture? But there isn't any water at Pont de l'Orme, is there?"

"It's funny how hard of hearing you are today, my poor girl! I tell you they're building lots and lots of hives so as to go in for apisiculture, there!"

As she was trimming a lamp, Mélie threw me a glance of affectionate contempt. Her vocabulary is full of surprises. One just needs to be on the alert.

It's hot in this hateful Paris! I don't want it to be hot! It isn't the fiery heat, fanned with cool breezes one breathes *there* without too much difficulty, but a mugginess that oppresses me. Lying on my bed, in the afternoon, I think about far too many things, about Marcel who's forgotten me, about my cousin Uncle who's gallivanting about. He's disappointed me. Why was he so kind, so communicative, so almost affectionate with me, if he meant to forget me straight away? It would only have needed a few days, a few words, for us to have been completely at ease with each other and we could have gone out together often. I should like to have got to know the Paris world better with him. But he was a charming bad lot who wouldn't find Claudine adequate as a friend.

The lilies-of-the-valley on the chimneypiece intoxicated me and gave me a migraine. What was the matter with me? My unhappiness over Luce, yes, but something else too—my heart was aching with homesickness. I felt as ridiculous as that sentimental engraving hanging on the wall of Mademoiselle's drawing-room, *Mignon regretting her fatherland.* And I thought I was cured of so many things and had lost so many of my illusions! Alas, my mind kept going back to Montigny. Oh, to clasp armfuls of tall, cool grass, to fall asleep, exhausted, on a low wall hot from the sun, to drink out of nasturtium leaves, where the rain rolls like quicksilver, to ransack the water's edge for forget-me-nots for the pleasure of letting them fade on a table, and lick the sticky sap from a peeled willow-wand; to make flutes of hollow grass-stalks, to steal tit's eggs and rub the scented leaves of wild currants; to kiss, to kiss all those things I love! I wanted to kiss a beautiful tree and the beautiful tree to kiss me back.—"Go for a walk, Claudine, take some exercise."

I can't go for a walk and I won't; it bores me! I prefer to stay at home and get feverish. Do you imagine they smell good, your Paris streets under the sun? And to whom can I tell everything that's weighing on my heart? Marcel would take me off to look at the shops to comfort me. His father would understand me better, but it would frighten me to show him so much of myself. The dark blue eyes of my cousin Uncle seem to guess so many things already, his beautiful, disturbing eyes with the bistred, wrinkled eyelids that inspire confidence—yet, at the very moment when that look says: "You can tell me everything", a smile, below the silvering moustache, suddenly makes me uneasy. And Papa. . . . Papa is working with Monsieur Maria. (Monsieur Maria's beard must make him hot, in this weather. Does he do it up in a little plait at night?)

How I've degenerated since last year! I've lost the innocent pleasure of running about and climbing and jumping like Fanchette. Fanchette doesn't dance any more because of her heavy stomach. I've got a heavy head, but luckily, I haven't any stomach.

I read, I read, I read. Everything. It doesn't matter what. I've nothing but that to occupy me, to take me away from here and from myself. I've no more homework to do. And if I no longer explain, at least twice a year, in a school essay why "Idleness is the mother of all the vices", I understand far better now how it engenders some of them.

12

On Sunday, I went back to see Aunt Wilhelmine, as it was her 'at-home-day'.

The omnibus passed in front of the block of flats where Luce lived. I was afraid of running into her. She would not have hesitated to make a tearful scene in public and my nerves felt none too strong.

My aunt, deflated by the heat, had abandoned her 'at-home', and was slightly surprised by my visit. I did not make much elegant conversation.

"Aunt, things aren't going a bit well. I want to go back to Montigny, I'm fretting in Paris."

"My child, you certainly don't look very well and your eyes are far too bright. Why don't you come and see me more often? Your father, I won't so much as mention him. He's incurable."

"I don't come because I'm bad-tempered and irritated with everything. I'd only hurt you, I'm only too capable of doing that."

"Isn't that surely what they call homesickness? If only Marcel were here! But that secretive little thing probably never told you he was spending the day in the country?"

"He's jolly sensible, he'll see some leaves. Is he all alone? Doesn't that worry you, Aunt?"

"Oh, no," she said, with that sweet smile of hers that hardly ever varied, "he's gone off with his friend Charlie."

"Oh, in that case," I said, getting up suddenly from my chair, "he's in good hands."

Decidedly, this old lady was rather stupid. It wasn't to her either that I would make my confidences and moan that I felt like an uprooted tree. I shifted from one foot to the other, pining to go; she held me back, looking a trifle anxious.

"Would you like to see my doctor? An old doctor, very clever and experienced, in whom I have complete faith?"

"No, I don't want to. He'll tell me to distract myself, and to see people, and to make friends with girls of my own age. Girls of my own age, they're contemptible!"

All the same, that filthy Luce. . . .

"Goodbye, Aunt. If Marcel can come and see me, I'd like that." And I added, to soften my rudeness. "He's the only friend of my own age I have."

Aunt Coeur let me go, this time without attempting to stop me. I had disturbed the placidity of a blind, doting grandmother. Marcel was so much easier to bring up.

Aha, so they were seeking coolness under the trees, on the outskirts of the city, those two pretty boys! The greenness would be making them feel amorous, brightening their cheeks, turning Marcel's blue eyes to aquamarine and lightening the black eyes of his dear friend. It would be gloriously funny if they got caught together! Lord, how I should enjoy myself! But they knew their way about, they wouldn't get caught. They would come back by one of the evening trains, arm in arm, and separate with eloquent eyes. And I—I should be as I was now, all alone.

Shame on you, Claudine! Isn't it ever going to stop, this obsession, this anguish of loneliness?

All alone, all alone! Claire's getting married, I'm left all alone.

Well, my dear, it's your own fault. So stay alone—with your virtue intact.

Yes. But I'm a poor, unhappy little girl who takes refuge at night in Fanchette's soft fur and buries her hot mouth and her black-ringed eyes in it. I swear, I absolutely swear, all this can't be just the boring nervous edginess of a female who needs a husband. *I* need far, far more than a husband.

13

MARCEL has reappeared. Today as the finishing touch to his grey suit—of a grey a turtle-dove might envy—he wore an astonishing buttercup-yellow crêpe-de-Chine cravat. It was folded round the white collar of which only a narrow rim could be seen and draped in front and fastened with pearl-headed pins, like a woman's. I congratulated him on this find.

"Have a nice walk on Sunday?"

"Ah! Grandmother told you? That Grandmother of mine will end up by compromising me! Yes, an exquisite walk. Such weather!"

"And such a friend!"

"Yes," he said, his eyes far away. "A friend who matched the weather."

"It's a second honeymoon, then?"

"Why *second*, Claudine?"

He was in a dreamy, melting mood, looking tired, yet enchanting, his eyelids mauve under his blue eyes. He seemed ready to drop all reserve and make unlimited confidences.

"Tell me about the walk."

"The walk? Nothing to tell about it. We lunched at an inn on the river bank like two . . ."

". . . lovers."

"—drank some *vin rosé*," he went on, without making any protest, "and ate some fried potatoes, and after that there's really nothing to tell. We wandered about on the grass, in the shade. Honestly, I don't know what there was about Charlie that day, he *had* something."

"He had you, that's all."

Surprised at the tone of my voice, Marcel raised his languid eyes and looked at me.

"What an odd face you have, Claudine! A little anxious, pointed face—charming, all the same. Your eyes have got bigger since the other day. Are you ill?"

"Yes and no . . . troubles you wouldn't understand. And also something you would understand. I've seen Luce again."

"Ah!" he cried, clasping his hands in a childish gesture. "Where is she?"

"In Paris. She's here indefinitely."

"And . . . so that's why you're looking so tired, Claudine! Oh, Claudine, what can I do to make you tell me all?"

"Nothing. It won't take long. I met her by chance. Yes, honestly, by chance. She took me home with her. Luxury fittings and furniture, a dress that cost thirty louis. Don't look so startled, old boy!" I said, laughing at his half-open mouth that looked like a surprised baby's. "And then, just as in the old days, she was the loving—too loving—Luce, her arms round my neck, her scent all round me, the over-trusting Luce who told me everything. Marcel, my friend, she's living in Paris with an old gentleman, she's his mistress."

"Oh!" he exclaimed, with genuine indignation. "How terribly that must have hurt you!"

"Not as much as I'd have expected. A little, all the same."

"My poor little Claudine!" he said, throwing his gloves on my bed. "I do understand so well."

In an affectionate, brotherly way, he put his arm round my waist, and, with his free hand, drew my head against him. Were we touching or ridiculous? At that moment, I didn't stop to ask myself. He had his arm round my neck, like Luce. He smelt nice, like her, but of a subtler scent, and, looking up, I could see his fair eyelashes drooping like a shade over his eyes. Was all my nervous tension of that week going to burst into a storm of sobs then and there? No, he would dry my tears, that would wet his well-cut jacket, with a furtive uneasiness. I forced myself to bite my tongue vigorously, a sovereign remedy against impending tears.

"My little Marcel, you're sweet. It's been a comfort seeing you."

"Be quiet. I understand so well. God! If Charlie did such a thing to me!"

Quite pink with selfish emotion, he mopped his temples. What he said struck me as so funny that I burst out laughing.

"Yes, your nerves are all to pieces. Let's go out, shall we? It's been raining and the temperature is quite bearable now."

"Oh yes, do let's go out. That'll calm me down."

"But tell me more. Was she very pressing, did she implore you?"

It never occurred to him for a moment that his insistence would be cruel if one were really suffering; he was trying to get something out of this for himself—what? A rather interesting new sensation.

"Yes, extremely pressing. I ran away, so as not to see her up there, in tears, with her blouse undone over her white skin, calling to me over the banisters to come back. . . ."

My 'nephew' was breathing faster. No doubt this unduly early heat in Paris must be very exhausting.

I left him for a moment and returned wearing the boater I'm so fond of. Marcel, with his forehead against the windowpane, was looking out into the courtyard.

"Where shall we go?"

"Anywhere you like, Claudine, any old where. We'll go and have some iced tea with lemon to revive us. So . . . you won't ever see her again?"

"Never," I said very firmly.

My companion heaved a great sigh. Perhaps he wished my jealousy had been less adamant, so that there would have been further anecdotes.

"We must tell Papa we're going out, Marcel. Come with me."

Papa was in bliss, striding up and down his room and dictating things to Monsieur Maria. The latter raised his head, looked hard at me, looked hard at Marcel, and became gloomy. My noble father's broad shoulders, clad in a waisted frock-coat whose pockets were torn, were raised to their fullest extent to express his contempt for Marcel. Marcel returned the contempt in full but behaved with extreme deference.

"Run along, children. Don't be out long. Keep out of draughts. Bring me back some foolscap, the biggest size you can find, and some socks."

"I brought three quires of foolscap in with me this morning," put in Monsieur Maria, in a mild voice. He had not taken his eyes off me for a moment.

"Splendid. All the same . . . one can never buy too much foolscap."

We went off and I heard Papa, behind the closed door, burst into a hunting-song at the top of his voice.

> *You should just see my thing,*
> *It would give you a start,*
> *It's a fine rosy pink*
> *Like an artichoke's heart.*

"He knows some very odd songs, my great-uncle," observed Marcel, more astonished than ever.

"Yes. He and Mélie between them have a pretty complete repertoire. What always puzzles me is that 'fine rosy pink like an artichoke's heart'. Artichokes with crimson hearts are an unknown species, in Montigny, anyway."

We walked fast so as to get away from the reeking Rue Jacob and the evil-smelling Rue Bonaparte. On the quays one could at least breathe, but here the breath of May smells of asphalt and creosote, alas!

"Where are we going?"

"I don't know yet. You're pretty, you're very pretty today, Claudine. Your tobacco-coloured eyes have something anxious and appealing about them that I've never seen in them before."

"Thank you."

I, too, felt I was looking my best. The shop-windows told me so, even the very narrow ones in which I could only see one eye and a slice of cheek as I passed by. What a weathercock I am! How I had wept for my long hair, and yet this very morning I had cut off three centimetres of my short locks, so as to keep the "curly shepherd-boy" effect. *That's* an expression of my uncle's. The fact is that no other way of wearing my hair could make a better frame for my long eyes and my narrow chin.

People looked at us a good deal, at Marcel quite as much as at me, perhaps he was slightly embarrassing in the full glare of the streets. He kept laughing shrilly, and pivoting round on his hips to see his reflection in shop-windows and lowering his eyelids when men stared at him: these airs and graces of his left me decidedly cold.

"Claudinette, come and have some iced tea in the Boulevard Haussmann. Do you mind if we take the first boulevard to the right after the Avenue de l'Opéra? It's more amusing."

"No streets in Paris amuse *me*. It's so dull walking on the flat all the time. I say, do you know whether your father is back in Paris yet?"

"He hasn't informed me to that effect, dear. Papa goes about a lot. Journalism, 'affairs of honour, affairs of the heart'. You must know that my father is tremendously fond of women, and vice versa," he said, over-emphatically, with the acid voice he uses when he speaks of my cousin Uncle. "Does that surprise you?"

"No, it doesn't surprise me. One out of two—that's not excessive for one family."

"You're charming when you're annoyed, Claudine."

"My little Marcel, do you honestly think I care a fig one way or the other?"

For it was essential to prove that I could lie very convincingly and not to let him see how distressed and uneasy those last words of his had made me feel. I seriously considered withdrawing my confidence from my cousin Uncle. I didn't like the idea of telling my secrets to someone who would go and forget them with 'women'. Besides, it was disgusting! I could hear that Uncle talking to 'women' in that same veiled, seductive voice, the voice that had said such charming, affectionate things to me. When his 'women' were unhappy, did he put his arm round their shoulders to comfort them, as he comforted me, three weeks ago? Oh, *damn*!

Claudine's utterly unreasonable irritation expressed itself by shoving her elbow against the hip of a fat lady who was blocking her path.

"Whatever's the matter with you, Claudine?"

"Oh, shut up, *do*!"

"Temper, temper! Sorry Claudine, I'd forgotten about your trouble. I know just what you're thinking of."

His mind was still running on Luce. His misunderstanding restored my good temper a little. I felt like an unfaithful wife who had been deceived by her lover and who was being comforted by her husband.

Both of us deep in thoughts that we could not tell each other, we reached the Vaudeville. Suddenly, a voice—which I heard even before it uttered a word—whispered to my back: "Good afternoon, model children."

I swung round violently, my eyes blazing, bristling so much that my cousin Uncle burst out laughing. There he was, with another gentleman whom I recognised as Maugis of the concert. Maugis of the concert, plump and pink, was very hot. He mopped his forehead and bowed with an exaggerated deference that I suspected was mocking and that did not help to pacify me.

I stared at Uncle Renaud as if I were seeing him for the first time. His short arched nose and his moustache, the colour of a silvery beaver, were just as I remembered, but had his deep, tired blue-grey eyes changed their expression? I had not realised that his mouth was so small. The sharply-etched little lines on his temples ran right down to the corners of his eyes, but I did not find that altogether unattractive. Ugh! The horrible rake who had just come back from seeing his 'women'! And I studied him for those two seconds with such a vindictive expression that that loathsome Maugis was impelled to remark, shaking his head:

"Now *there's* a face I wouldn't allow to have any pudding . . . without further pretext."

I shot him a glance with intent to kill, but his bulbous blue eyes and his arched eyebrows shammed such an expression of oily sweetness and total innocence that I laughed outright in his face . . . without further pretext.

"These old ladies," observed the abominable Uncle, shrugging his shoulders, "they laugh at the merest trifle."

I did not answer; I did not even look at him.

"Marcel, what's the matter with your girl friend? Have you two been quarrelling?"

"No, Father, we couldn't be better friends. But," he added, with an air of knowledgeable discretion, "I think Claudine has had some worries this week."

"Don't fret yourself too much," insisted Maugis. "Dolls' heads can easily be replaced. I know an excellent place. . . . I can get them for you by the baker's dozen and five per cent. discount for cash."

It was my uncle's turn now to look at me as if he were seeing me for the first time. He signed rather imperiously to Marcel to come and speak to him. As the two of them moved a step or two away, I was left to the mercy of the plump Maugis. He quite amuses me; he's never subtle but he's occasionally funny.

"He's looking his best today, the young man whose aunt you claim to be."

"He certainly is! People stare at him in the street more than they do at me! But I'm not jealous."

"How right you are!"

"He's wearing a lovely cravat, isn't he? But it's really a cravat for a woman."

"Come, come, don't reproach him for having *something* for a woman," said Maugis placatingly.

"And his clothes . . . not one wrinkle to be seen!"

Surely, Marcel could not be telling his father about Luce? No, he wouldn't dare. He'd better *not* dare. No, if he had, my uncle's face would be looking quite different.

"Claudine," he said, returning to us, with his son: "I'd like to take you both to see *Blanchette* next Sunday at the Antoine theatre. But, if you're sulking, what am I to do? Go all alone?"

"No, not all alone. I'll come!"

"And bring your bad temper with you?"

He looked right into my eyes, and I gave in.

"No, I'll be nice. But I've got things on my mind today."

He went on looking at me searchingly; he was trying to guess what was wrong. I turned my head away as Fanchette does from the saucer of milk she both wants and refuses.

"There, I'll leave you now, model children. Where are you off to like that?"

"We're going to have some iced tea, Father."

"That's better than going to a pub," muttered Maugis absently.

"Listen, Claudine," my uncle said in my ear. "I find Marcel very much easier to get on with since you and he have been friends. I think you're a good influence on him, little girl. His old Papa is extraordinarily grateful to you, do you know that?"

I let the two men shake hands with me and we turned our backs to them. A good influence on Marcel? That was something that left me completely cold! Moralising isn't in my line. A good influence on Marcel? Oh Lord, what an utter fool an intelligent man can be!

We drank our iced tea with lemon. But my 'nephew' found me depressing company. I amuse him less than Charlie does and I realise, moreover, that my own diversions are of an entirely different kind. It's not my fault, I can't help it.

14

Tнат night, after dinner, I read vaguely and absent-mindedly while Papa smoked, occasionally bursting into song with one of his barbarous ditties and Mélie wandered about, weighing her breasts. The cat, swollen and enormous, had refused her dinner; she kept purring for no reason and her nose was too pink and her ears hot.

I went to bed late with the window open and the shutters closed, after going through my complicated nightly routine. As usual, I washed all over in hot water, studied myself naked in the long-glass, did my limbering-up exercises. I felt limp and flat. My Fanchette, panting for breath, lay on her side in her basket, trembling and listening to her swollen stomach. I thought it would be soon now.

It certainly was soon! I had hardly blown out my lamp before a loud, despairing *miaooooo* made me leap out of bed. I lit the lamp again and ran, barefoot, to my poor little darling, who was breathing very fast. She put her hot paws imperiously on my hand and looked at me with beautiful, dilated eyes. She was purring wildly, without rhyme or reason. Suddenly, the delicate paws clenched on my hands and there was a second *miaoooo* of distress. Ought I to call Mélie? But, at the first movement I made to get up, Fanchette frantically got up too and tried to run; she was crazy with terror. The only thing to do was to stay. It disgusted me rather, but I wouldn't look.

After a ten minutes calm, the situation became acute. There were swift alternations of furious purring (*frrrr-frrrr*) and terrible cries (*miaooo, miaooooo*). Fanchette's eyes nearly bolted from her head, a spasm convulsed her and . . . I turned away my head. Then the purring resumed and a stirring in the basket informed me that there was something new in it. But I knew only too well that the poor sweet never stopped at one. The cries broke out again, the frantic paw scratched my hand; I kept my head obstinately averted. After three such episodes, at last there was definite calm. Fanchette was empty. I rushed to the kitchen in my nightdress to get her some milk; that would give her time to tidy up all sorts of little things. I delayed, on purpose. When I returned with the saucer, my pretty, exhausted cat was already wearing her 'happy mother' face. I thought I might look now.

On the white and pink stomach, three minute kittens, three grey slugs with black stripes, three little marvels were sucking and wriggling like leeches. The basket was clean, without any trace left: Fanchette has the gift of having kittens as if by magic! I didn't dare touch the little things yet—they were shining from being licked from ear to tail—though the little mother invited me in her poor, cracked voice to admire them, to stroke them. Tomorrow, we shall have to choose and have two of them drowned. Mélie, as usual, will be the Lord High Executioner. And for weeks I shall watch Fanchette being a capricious mother, carrying her striped little one about in her mouth, tossing him up in the air with her paws and being astonished, the incorrigible innocent, that this fortnight-old son doesn't jump up after her on to the chimneypiece and on to the top shelf of the book-case.

My shortened night was full of dreams, in which the extravagant vied with the idiotic. For some time, I've been dreaming more than usual. Mélie wept all the ready tears of her tender soul when she received the order to drown two of the little Fanchettes. It was necessary to choose and to distinguish the sexes. Personally, I've no idea when they're so little and it seems that people more expert than I am make mistakes, but Mélie is infallible. A kitten in each hand, she gave one sure glance at the right place and declared: "This one's the little male. The two others are shes." I restored the little chosen one to Fanchette, who stood on the floor, mewing anxiously. "Take the two others away quick, so that she won't know." All the same, Fanchette did know some were missing; she can count up to three. But this enchanting animal showed up as a rather indifferent mother. After having roughly rolled her tom-kitten over with her paws and her nose to see if the others weren't hidden underneath him, she made up her mind. She would lick that one twice more, that was all.

How many days are there still to go? Four more till Sunday. On Sunday I'm going to the theatre with Marcel and my uncle. I'm indifferent about the theatre; about my uncle, no. My uncle, my uncle. . . . What an idiotic notion to have christened him that! Silly mutt of a Claudine! 'My uncle'—it makes me think of that horrible little Luce. It doesn't worry her in the least to call *him* 'my uncle', that old gentleman who . . . This one, *mine*, in actual fact, is the widower of a first cousin whom I never even set eyes on. In plain French, that's called a cousin. 'Renaud' is better than 'Uncle', it makes him seem younger, it sounds right. Renaud!

How quickly he conquered my bad temper, the other day. It was pure cowardice on my part, not courtesy. Obeying, obeying, that's a humiliation I've never endured—I was going to write savoured. Yes, savoured. It was out of perversity that I gave in, I believe. At Montigny, I'd have let myself be chopped up into small bits sooner than take my turn at sweeping the classroom if I didn't feel like it. But, perhaps, if Mademoiselle had given me a long look with grey-blue Renaud-coloured eyes, I might have obeyed more often, just as I obeyed *him*, all my limbs numb with a new, unknown weakness.

For the first time, I have just been able to smile at the thought of Luce. A good sign: she is becoming remote to me, this little thing who hopped about on one foot as she talked about letting her mother starve to death! . . . She doesn't know; it isn't her fault. She's just a little, velvety animal.

Still two more days before going to the theatre. Marcel is coming too. It isn't the thought of his presence that delights me most; when his father is there, he's a pink and golden little duffer, a slightly hostile little duffer. I like them better separately, Renaud and Marcel.

My mood—and why shouldn't I have 'moods' like anyone else— isn't easy to define clearly. It's the mood of someone who expects that, at any moment, a chimney may fall on their head. I live with my nerves strung up, waiting for this inevitable fall. And when I open the door of a cupboard, or when I turn the corner of a street, or when the post comes in the morning—the post that never brings me anything—my heart gives a slight jump. "Is it going to happen *this* time?"

It's no good staring at the features of my little slug—he's called Limaçon, the kitten, to please Papa and also because he's much more like a snail than a slug, with his beautiful, clearly-marked stripes— it's no good looking enquiringly at his little closed face, rayed with fine lines that converge towards the nose like the face of a yellow and black pansy, the eyes won't open till nine full days have gone by. And whenever I give white Fanchette back her beautiful child, paying her a thousand compliments, she washes him meticulously. Though she loves me to distraction, she privately thinks that I smell horridly of scented soap.

Something has occurred; something really serious! Was it the chimney I was expecting to fall? Probably it was, but, in that case, I ought to feel relieved of my anxious apprehension. Whereas I've still got 'shrunk stomach' as they say in Montigny. This is what happened.

This morning, at ten o'clock, when I was assiduously trying to get Limaçon used to another of Fanchette's teats (he always takes the same one and, in spite of what Mélie says, I am afraid that may deform my lovely cat), Papa came into my room, looking very solemn. It wasn't seeing him look solemn that alarmed me, but seeing him come into my bedroom. He never enters it unless I announce that I'm ill.

"Come along with me for a moment."

I followed him into his book-lair with the meekness of an inquisitive daughter. There I found Monsieur Maria. The mere fact of his being there seemed perfectly normal. But Monsieur Maria, dressed in a brand-new frock-coat at ten o'clock in the morning and wearing gloves—that went beyond the bounds of reasonable possibility!

"My child," began my noble father, with dignified unction, "here is an excellent young man who wishes to marry you. I must tell you at the outset that he has my warmest approval."

I listened with all my ears, attentive but stupefied. When Papa had finished his sentence, I articulated just one idiotic, but sincere word: "What?"

I swear I really hadn't understood. Papa lost a little of his solemnity, but retained all his nobleness.

"Of all the bally idiots! Surely I articulate clearly enough for you to understand without having to repeat myself! This excellent little Monsieur Maria wants to marry you—if necessary, in a year's time, if you're too young. You know, I've rather tended to forget your exact age lately (!). I told him you must be quite fourteen and a half but he declares that you are going on for eighteen; he probably knows better than I. There! And if you don't want him, ten thousand herds of swine, you're hard to please!"

This was superb! I looked at Monsieur Maria, who turned pale beneath his beard and gazed at me with his long-lashed animal eyes. Suddenly feeling extraordinarily light-hearted, without quite knowing why, I darted up to Monsieur Maria.

"You mean it's true, Monsieur Maria? You really and truly want to marry me? You're not joking?"

"Oh! I'm not joking," he said in a low, pathetic voice.

"How terribly, terribly nice of you!"

And I seized both his hands and shook them joyously. He turned crimson, like a setting sun behind a bushy wood.

"So . . . you consent, Mademoiselle?"

"Me? Not on your life!"

Ah! I had been about as tactful as a ton of dynamite! Monsieur Maria stood facing me with his mouth open, obviously feeling he must be going mad.

Papa thought it was his duty to intervene.

"Look here, are you going to keep us in suspense much longer? What does all this mean? First you fling yourself round his neck, then you refuse him. Extraordinary behaviour, I must say!"

"But, Papa, I don't in the least want to marry Monsieur Maria, that's quite definite. I think he's very nice—oh, terribly nice!—to think I'm worthy of such . . . such serious intentions, and that's what I'm thanking him for. But of course, I don't want to *marry* him!"

Monsieur Maria made a faint, pitiful, imploring gesture, but said nothing. He made me feel a brute.

"Eternal Father in heaven!" roared Papa. "Why the devil don't you want to marry him?"

Why? Spreading out both hands, I shrugged my shoulders. Had I any idea why? It was as if they were proposing I should marry Rabastens, the handsome assistant master at Montigny. Why? For the only valid reason in the world—because I didn't love him.

Papa, exasperated, launched into such a resounding volley of oaths that I couldn't attempt to write them down. I waited for the litany to come to an end.

"Oh, Papa! Do you want me to be unhappy then?"

That man of stone did not insist further.

"Idiot child! Unhappy? Of course not. Besides, anyway, you can think things over, you may change your mind. You there, Maria, she may change her mind, mayn't she? Actually, it would be extraordinarily convenient for me if she *did*! I'd have you here all the time and we'd really get on with the job! But, for this morning, positively for the last time, you *don't* want him? Then b—— off, we've got work to do."

Monsieur Maria knew very well that I shouldn't change my mind. He fidgeted with his leather brief-case and searched for his pen without seeing it. I went up to him.

"Monsieur Maria, are you angry with me?"

"Oh no, Mademoiselle, it's not that . . ."

A sudden hoarseness prevented him from going on. I went away on tiptoe, and, alone in the drawing-room, I began to dance a fandango. What marvellous luck! Someone had asked for my hand in marriage! In *marriage*! Someone had thought me pretty enough, in spite of my short hair, to marry. And a sensible young man, too, who knew his own mind, not a pathological case. So, there might be others. . . . Having danced enough, I decided to think of the future.

It would have been childish to deny it, my life was approaching a crisis. The chimney was imminent. It was going to fall on my whirling head; the result might be terrifying or delicious, but fall it inexorably would. I did not feel the slightest need to confide my situation to anyone else in the world. I should not write to Claire, happy Claire: "Oh, dear little friend of my childhood, it is approaching fast, the fateful moment when I foresee that my heart and my life will burst into flower together." I shall not ask Papa: "Oh father mine, what can this be that both oppresses and delights me? Enlighten my young ignorance." . . . He'd only pull a long face, poor Papa! He would twist his tri-coloured beard and mutter perplexedly: "I've never studied that particular species."

Come off it, Claudine, come down to earth. . . . In your heart of hearts, you're not conceited. You wander about the enormous flat, you desert your beloved old Balzac, you stop with a lost, vague look in front of your bedroom glass that shows you a tall slim girl with her hands clasped behind her back, in a red silk pleated blouse and a dark blue serge skirt. She has short hair in big curls, a narrow face with warm ivory cheeks, and long eyes. You think she's pretty, that girl, who looks as if she didn't care a rap for anyone or anything. It's not a beauty that excites the mob but . . . I've definitely got *something*: those who can't see it are either idiots or short-sighted.

I simply *must* look my best tomorrow! My blue coat and skirt will do, and my big black hat, with the little dark blue silk blouse— dark colours suit me best—and two tea-roses tucked into the corner of its square neck, because, at night, they're exactly the same colour as my skin.

Shall I tell Mélie that I've had a proposal of marriage? No, it's not worth it. She'd only answer, "My lamby, you should do as we do at home. Them as proposes to you, try them out first. That way, all's fair and square and no one gets a bad bargain." For her, virginity is something quite worthless. I know her theories. "All a pack of lies, my poor girl! Nothing but a lot of doctors' faddy notions. Before, after, don't you go imagining the men aren't every bit as keen! Go on with you, it's all one to *them*!" Well, I've no lack of good instruction! But decent girls are doomed by fate; they remain decent in spite of all the Mélies in the world!

I got to sleep late, that stifling night. Memories of Montigny drifted through my troubled sleep; thoughts of rustling leaves, of the chilly dawn, of mounting larks with that song we used to imitate at the School by rubbing a handful of glass marbles together. Tomorrow, tomorrow . . . would someone else think me pretty? Fanchette purred softly, her striped Limaçon between her paws. How often my beautiful darling's even purr has soothed me and sent me to sleep.

I dreamed that night. And when the plump, flabby Mélie came in at eight to open my shutters she found me sitting huddled up in a ball with my knees in my arms and my hair over my nose, taciturn and preoccupied.

"Good morning, my precious pet!"

". . . 'morning."

"You're not ill?"

"No."

"Got worries and troubles?"

"No. I had a dream."

"Ah, that's ever so much more serious. Still if you didn't dream a child nor the royal family (sic), there's no harm done. If only you'd dreamt a man's dung, now!"

These predictions, which she had solemnly repeated to me ever since I could understand what she said, didn't seem funny any more. What I *did* dream, I will never tell anyone, not even this exercise-book. It would embarrass me too much to see it in writing.

I had asked that we should have dinner at six o'clock and Monsieur Maria, self-effacing as usual, went off an hour early, eclipsed in his bushy beard, and looking dejected. I have not avoided him at all since the Event; he doesn't embarrass me in the least. I have even been more forthcoming than usual; full of bright, chatty commonplaces.

"What lovely weather, Monsieur Maria!"

"Do you think so, Mademoiselle? It's very oppressive, the west looks black. . . ."

"Ah, I hadn't noticed. It's funny, ever since this morning, I've been imagining it was fine."

At dinner, as I was lingering over the jam soufflé after having toyed with my meat with no appetite, I asked Papa a question.

"Papa, have I got a dowry?"

"Why the hell d'you want to know that?"

"Honestly, you're marvellous! Someone proposed to me yesterday, it might happen again tomorrow. It's only the first refusal that's difficult. You know, proposals are like the old story of the ants and the pot of jam; when one comes along, so do three thousand more."

"Good Lord, three thousand! Mercifully we haven't a vast number of acquaintances. Certainly, pot of jam, you possess a dowry! When you made your First Communion, I put them in charge of Meunier, the solicitor at Montigny, your hundred and fifty thousand francs. They were left you by your mother, a remarkably unpleasant woman. They're safer with him than here, you know, with me, one never knows what might happen."

Now and then he says touching things like that that make you want to kiss him—and I did kiss him. Then I went back to my room, my nerves already on edge because it was getting late, listening for the sound of the bell with my ears strained and my heart limp.

Half-past seven. He certainly wasn't hurrying himself! We should miss the first act! Supposing he wasn't going to come! A quarter to eight. It was revolting! He could at least have sent me a telegram, or even Marcel, this fugitive uncle.

But an imperious *trrr* made me leap to my feet and I saw, in the glass, a strange white face that embarrassed me so much that I averted my head. For some time now, my eyes have taken to looking as if they knew something I did not know myself.

The voice I heard in the hall made me smile nervously; a single voice, that of my cousin Uncle—of my cousin Renaud, I should say. Mélie brought him straight in, without knocking at my door. Her eyes followed him with the flattering gaze of an obedient bitch. He was pale too and obviously on edge; his eyes were glittering. In the artificial light, his silvery moustache looked more golden. If I had dared, I would like to have touched that beautiful, upturned moustache to feel how soft it was.

"So you're all alone, Claudine! Why don't you say something? Has Mademoiselle gone out?"

Mademoiselle was thinking that perhaps he had come straight from one of his 'women' and smiled mirthlessly.

"No, Mademoiselle is just going out . . . with you I hope. Come and say goodbye to Papa."

Papa was charming to my cousin Uncle who is only unattractive to women.

"Take good care of the child; she's delicate. Have you the key to get in with?"

"Yes, I've got my own to get into my flat."

"Ask Mélie to give you ours. I've already lost four, I give up. What's happened to the little boy?"

"Marcel? He's not . . . he's meeting us at the theatre, I believe."

We went downstairs without saying a word. I was as pleased as a child to find a hansom waiting for us below. A coupé from Binder's, drawn by magnificent horses, could not have enchanted me more.

"Are you all right? Would you like me to pull up one of the windows, because of the draught? No, I'll pull them both half up, we'll be so hot otherwise."

I'd no idea whether I was hot, but, heavens, how 'shrunk' my stomach was! A nervous shiver made my teeth chatter; at last I managed to say, with an effort:

"So Marcel's meeting us there?"

No reply. Renaud—how nice that was, just plain Renaud—stared straight ahead, frowning. Suddenly, he turned to me and seized my wrists; this man who was turning grey had such young movements!

"Listen, I lied just now, that was rather mean of me. Marcel isn't coming. I told your father he was and I'm vexed with myself about that."

"What? He's not coming? Why?"

"That's a disappointment for you, isn't it? It's my fault. His too. I don't know how to explain to you. . . . It'll all seem to you so petty. He came to fetch me at my flat in the Rue Bassano, looking charming, with his little face less stiff and secretive than usual. But his tie! A crêpe-de-Chine cravat wound round his neck, draped like the top of a woman's bodice, with pearl pins all over the place, frankly . . . impossible. I said: 'My dear boy, would you do me a great favour and change your tie? I'll lend you one of mine.' He took offence, became insolent and sarcastic and we . . . well, in the end we had a quarrel about something rather too involved to tell you, Claudine. He insisted: 'I'll go in my cravat or I won't go at all.' I slammed the door behind him, and that was that. Are you very angry with me?"

"But," I said, ignoring his question, "you've seen it already, that cravat. He was wearing it the other day when you met us, with Maugis, on the boulevard near the Vaudeville."

He raised his eyebrows and looked extremely surprised.

"You don't say so! Are you sure?"

"Absolutely sure. It's a cravat you couldn't possibly forget. However was it you didn't notice it?"

Leaning back once more against the cushions, he shook his head and said in a rather subdued voice:

"I don't know. I noticed that you had circles round your eyes, and a wild, shy look like an offended deer. And a blue blouse, and a little wisp of curl that kept tickling your right eyebrow."

I said nothing. I felt a little chokey. As he suddenly broke off what he was saying, he tilted his hat over his eyes with the curt gesture of a man who has just said something idiotic and realises it too late.

"Obviously, it's dull for you, just me on my own. I can still take you home again if you'd rather, my dear."

To whom was that aggressive tone really addressed? I only laughed softly, laid my gloved hand on his arm and left it there.

"No, don't take me home. I'm very pleased. You don't get on together, you and Marcel. I prefer seeing you separately rather than together. But why didn't you say all this in front of Papa?"

He took my hand and tucked it under his arm.

"Perfectly simple. I was hurt and annoyed, and I was frightened your father would deprive me of you, dear little compensation. I hadn't, perhaps, deserved you but I had certainly earned you."

"You'd nothing to be frightened about. Papa would have let me go off with you, he does everything I want."

"Oh, I quite realise that," he said, a little irritably, pulling his moustache that was like silver-gilt with the gold wearing off. "Promise me, at least, that you'll always want such eminently reasonable things."

"One never knows, one never knows! What I really *would* like . . . listen, grant me the thing I'm just going to ask you for."

"What banana tree must I plunder? What fabulous artichoke must I strip to its heart? One word, one gesture, one single one . . . and your lap shall be filled with chocolate creams. . . . These meagre hansom-cabs restrict the nobility of my gestures, Claudine, but not, I assure you, of my sentiments!"

All these literary men talk in the same, rather exaggerated, bantering way, but how much less elephantine he was than Maugis who had that horrible Paris working-class accent into the bargain.

"I've never been known to refuse chocolate creams. But . . . I don't want to call you 'Uncle' any more. There, it's out!"

In the passing lights from a shop window, he bowed his head in mock resignation.

"It's come at last. She's going to call me 'Grandfather'. The dreaded hour has struck."

"No, don't laugh. I've been thinking it over for a long time—that you're my cousin and that, if you didn't mind, I might call you . . . Renaud. I don't think it's such a monstrous request."

We were driving up a dimly-lit avenue; he bent down to look at me; I made heroic efforts not to blink. At last he replied:

"Is that all? But begin at once, I implore you. You take years off my age, not as many as I could wish, but at least five already. Look at my temples—haven't they suddenly turned golden again?"

I leant forward to see, but, almost at once, I drew back again. Looking at him so close to made my stomach shrink almost to nothing.

We said no more. From time to time, as the lights came and went, I glanced furtively at his short profile and his eyes, wide open and alert.

"Where do you live . . . Renaud?"

"I told you, Rue de Bassano."

"Is it pretty, your flat?"

"Well, it suits *me*."

"Could I see it?"

"Good Lord, no!"

"Why not?"

"Why, because . . . well . . . it's too . . . too eighteenth-century engraving for you."

"Pooh! What does *that* matter?"

"Let me have the illusion that these things do still matter a little. We're there, Claudine."

"What a pity!"

Before *Blanchette*, I conscientiously enjoyed *Poil de Carotte*. I was enchanted by Suzanne Després's boyish grace and restrained gestures: under the short red wig, her eyes were green, like Luce's. And Jules Renard's clear-cut, incisive dialogue delighted me too.

As I was listening, absolutely still, with my chin thrust forward, all at once I *felt* Renaud was looking at me. I turned my head swiftly; he had his eyes on the stage and an extremely innocent expression. That proved nothing.

During the interval, Renaud walked me about and enquired:

"Are you a trifle calmer now, you nervous little thing?"

"I wasn't nervous," I said, bristling.

"And that delicate, tense little paw that felt so cold on my arm in the cab? Not nervous? Oh dear no, *I'm* the nervous one!"

"You are . . . too."

I had spoken very low, but the faint pressure of his arm showed me that he understood.

During the performance of *Blanchette*, I found myself thinking of the laments—how far away they had receded already—of Mademoiselle's little Aimée. In the days when we were beginning to be fond of each other, she used to confide to me—more crudely than that Blanchette in the play—the horrified aversion she had developed for her own home. The little teacher, already accustomed to the comparative comfort of the School, was revolted by the very thought of her parents' cottage and the whole poverty-stricken, ill-kept, squalling household. She used to tell me endlessly about her fears and miseries, standing in the doorway of the stinking classroom, and shivering like a little half-starved cat in the draught. And Mademoiselle would pass behind our backs, jealous and silent. . . .

My neighbour, who seemed to be listening to my thoughts, asked me almost in a whisper:

"Is it like that in Montigny?"

"Like that, only much worse!"

He did not press me further. Elbow to elbow, we stayed silent; little by little, I relaxed against that kind, reassuring shoulder. At one moment, I lifted my head to him. His intelligent eyes looked down into mine and I smiled at him with all my heart. I have seen that man exactly five times; I have known him all my life.

When it came to the last act, I put my elbow down first and I left a little place on the velvet arm of the stall. His elbow understood perfectly and came to meet mine. I had entirely lost that shrinking sensation in my stomach.

At a quarter to midnight, we left the theatre. The sky was dark, the wind almost fresh.

"Please, Renaud, I don't want to get into a cab straight away. I'd much rather walk along the boulevards—have you got time?"

"My entire lifetime, if necessary," he answered, smiling.

He held me by the arm, firmly, and we walked in step, because I have long legs. Under the electric lights, I could see us walking: Claudine had a strange, exalted little face turned upwards to the stars and her eyes were almost black; the wind streamed through Renaud's long moustache.

"Tell me about Montigny, Claudine, and about yourself."

But I shook my head. It was perfect, as we were. There was no need to talk. We walked fast; I had Fanchette's paws tonight; the ground was like a springboard under my feet.

Lights, bright lights, coloured window-panes, people sitting at tables on a terrace, drinking.

"What's that?"

"It's the Brasserie Logre."

"Oh, I'm so thirsty!"

"I'd like nothing better. But not in this Brasserie."

"*Yes*, here, please! It's all lit up and exciting, it looks amusing."

"But it's arty and tarty, not to mention noisy."

"So much the better! I want to have a drink here."

He pulled at his moustache for a second, then with a gesture that said: "After all, why not?", he shepherded me into the main room. It was not so crowded as he had implied; in spite of the time of year, it was almost possible to breathe. The green tiled pillars awoke thoughts of baths and jugs of cool water.

"Thirsty! Thirsty!"

"There, there, keep calm, you shall have your drink! What a redoubtable child! It would be unwise to refuse *you* a husband."

"I agree," I said, unsmiling.

We were sitting at a little table against a pillar. To my right, under a panel daubed tempestuously with naked Bacchantes, a mirror assured me that I had no ink on my cheek, that my hat was on straight and that my eyes were dancing above a mouth red with thirst, perhaps with a little fever. Renaud, sitting opposite me, had shaky hands and moist temples.

A little moan of covetousness escaped me, aroused by the trail of scent left by a passing dish of shrimps.

"Some shrimps too? Well, well! How many?"

"How many? I've never discovered how many I could eat. A dozen to begin with, after that we'll see."

"And to drink, what? Beer?"

I made a face.

"Wine? No. Champagne? Asti Spumante?"

I flushed with greed.

"Oh! *Yes*!"

I waited impatiently and I watched several beautiful women come

in, wearing light evening cloaks with sparkling embroideries. All
very pretty—crazy hats, over-golden hair, flashing rings. My great
friend, to whom I pointed out each new arrival, displayed an
indifference that shocked me. Were 'his women' more beautiful,
perhaps? I turned suddenly fierce and gloomy. He was surprised
and started quoting edifying authors:

"What? The wind has turned? 'Hilda, whence comes thy sorrow?'"

But I did not answer a word.

They brought the Asti. To drive away my care and to quench my
thirst, I drank a big glass in one gulp. The womaniser opposite me
excused himself for devouring red roast-beef on the grounds he was
dying of hunger. The musky, treacherous fire of the Asti Spumante
made the lobes of my ears begin to burn and my throat feel thirsty
again. I held out my glass and, this time, I drank more slowly, my
eyes half-closed with pleasure. My friend laughed:

"You drink like a baby at the breast. You've all the spontaneous
grace of an animal, Claudine."

"Fanchette has a son, you know."

"No, I didn't know. You ought to have showed him to me! I bet
he's as beautiful as a star."

"Even more beautiful than that. Oh, these shrimps! If you only
knew, Renaud"—each time I called him Renaud, he raised his eyes
and looked at me—"down there in Montigny, they're simply
tiny. . . . I used to go and pick them up with my hands, at
Gué-Ricard, paddling barefoot. These are simply marvellously
seasoned."

"You swear you won't be ill?"

"Good heavens, no! I was going to tell you something else, but
something serious this time. Don't you think there's something
extraordinary about me tonight?"

I thrust my face, rosy from the Asti, towards him. He leant
forward too, and looked at me at such close quarters that I could see
the fine wrinkles on his brownish eyelids; then he turned away,
saying:

"No, not more tonight than the other times."

"Then you're blind! My friend, the day before yesterday, as
recently as that, at eleven o'clock in the morning, I had a pro-po-sal
of marriage!"

"Hell's . . . who was the idiot who . . ."

Rapturous at the effect I had produced, I laughed out loud in ascending scales then stopped suddenly, because people at the other tables had heard and were looking round at us. Renaud was anything but rapturous.

"It's monstrous of you to lead me up the garden path! Of course, I didn't believe a word of it really."

"I can't very well spit, can I? But I give you my word of honour, he *did* propose!"

"Who?"

That "Who?" was anything but benevolent.

"An extremely nice young man—Monsieur Maria—Papa's secretary."

"You refused him . . . naturally?"

"I refused him . . . naturally."

He poured himself out a large glass of the Asti he disliked so much and ran his hand through his hair.

As for me, who never drank anything but water at home, I was observing some extraordinary phenomena. A kind of faint, misty trellis was rising from the table, making a halo round the lights and making objects seem very far away at one moment, and very close at the next.

At the moment when I was trying to analyse my sensations, a well-known voice bellowed from just inside the doorway:

"Kellner! Will you have the goodness to produce some Sauerkraut, mother of heart-burn and some of that insipid, salicylated cocoa that you have the impudence to denominate Munich beer. Liquid velvet, flowing perfumed locks of the Rheintochter, forgive them, they know not what they drink! 'Weia, waga, waga la weia.' . . ."

It was Maugis, lyrical and perspiring, Wagnerising away at the top of his voice, with his flat-brimmed top hat on the back of his head and his waistcoat undone. He had three friends in tow. Renaud could not restrain a gesture of extreme annoyance and tugged his moustache, growling something under his breath.

As he came close to us, Maugis suddenly stopped his garglings from the *Rheingold*, opened his round protruding eyes wide, hesitated a moment, then raised his hand and passed on without greeting us.

"There!" muttered Renaud furiously.

"Whatever is it?"

"It's your fault, child. Most of all it's mine. You oughtn't to be here, alone with me. That imbecile Maugis . . . anyone else would have done the same. Do you think there's any particular point in giving people wrong ideas about you, and about me?"

For one second, I was chilled by his vexed and worried eyes, but the next instant, I revived.

"Was *that* why? You don't mean you're making all that fuss and putting on all that performance of frowns and moral indignation just for *that*? But, I ask you, whatever harm can it do me? Give me something to drink . . . pleashe."

"You don't understand! I'm not in the habit of taking respectable little girls out. A girl as pretty as you, alone with me, what do you expect people to suppose?"

"And what else?"

My drunken smile and my wandering eyes suddenly made it dawn on him.

"Claudine! You aren't, by any chance, a little . . . gay? You're drinking pretty hard tonight, do you at home?"

"At home I swig Evian water," I replied in a kind, reassuring voice.

"Oh Lord! Now we're in a nice mess! What on earth am I going to say to your father?"

"He's gone to bye-byes."

"Claudine, don't drink any more! Give me that full glass this minute!"

"Do you want me to hit you?"

Putting my glass out of reach of his prudent hands, I drank, and I listened to myself being happy. This was not altogether easy to do. The chandelier's misty haloes kept getting bigger and bigger like the halo round the moon when it's going to rain. 'The moon's drinking', as they say in Montigny. Perhaps, in Paris, it's a sign of rain when the chandeliers drink! It's you, Claudine, who've been drinking. Three large glasses of Asti, you little 'wurzit'! How nice it is! It makes one's ears go *sshh, sshh*. The two fat gentlemen eating two tables away, did they really exist? Without moving, they came so close up that I could have sworn I only had to put out my hand to touch them. No, now they were ever so far away. Besides, there wasn't any space between objects; the chandeliers were stuck to the ceiling, the tables stuck to the walls, the fat gentlemen stuck to the light background of the glittering cloaks sitting further away. I exclaimed loudly:

"I understand! It's all in Japanese perspective!"

Renaud raised a despairing arm, then mopped his brow. In the glass to my right, I saw a most extraordinary Claudine with her hair in ruffled feathers, her long eyes full of delicious confusion, her lips bright and wet! That was the other Claudine, the one who had 'run past herself' as they say at home. And opposite her was that silver-streaked gentleman who kept looking at her and looking at her, who wasn't looking at anything *but* her and wasn't eating any more. Oh, I knew perfectly well! It wasn't the Asti, it wasn't the pepper in the shrimps that had intoxicated the little girl; it was that presence, it was that almost black gaze with the lights shining in it.

Completely two people now, I watched myself behaving, I heard myself talking, in a voice that seemed to come from rather far off, and the sensible Claudine, fettered and imprisoned in a glass cell, listened to the crazy Claudine chattering away and could do nothing for her. She couldn't do anything and, moreover, she didn't want to do anything. The chimney, whose collapse I had been dreading, had fallen with a great crash and the dust of its fall made a golden halo round the electric light bulbs. Help, sensible Claudine, above all, don't stir! The crazy Claudine is pursuing her course with the infallibility of the mad and the blind.

Claudine looked at Renaud: she fluttered her lashes, dazzled. Resigned, carried away, swept along in her wake, he sat silent, looking at her, one might say, with even more sorrow than pleasure. She burst out:

"Oh, how happy I am! Oh *you*, who didn't want to come! Aha, when I want something. . . . We won't ever go away from here, will we? If you only knew! I obeyed you the other day, me, Claudine! I've never obeyed anyone except on purpose, before you . . . but obeying, in spite of yourself, when your knees feel nice and nasty at the same time—oh, that must be why Luce liked being beaten so much, you know, Luce? I used to beat her so much, without knowing she was perfectly right, she used to roll her head on the window-sill just where the wood's worn because, during recreations, we split cornies on it. Do you know too what 'cornies' are? One day I wanted to fish some for myself in the pond at Barres and I caught a fever, I was twelve and I had all my lovely hair. You'd like me better, wouldn't you, with my hair long? I've got 'quivers' at the tips of my fingers, a whole 'quiverful'—Do you smell that? A smell of absinthe? The fat gentleman's poured some into his champagne. At school we used to eat green barley sugar flavoured with absinthe; it was considered awfully smart to suck them for ages till they got a long point on them. That gawk Anaïs was so greedy and so patient that the little ones used to bring her their barley-sugars, 'Make mine pointed!' they used to say. Disgusting, wasn't it? I dreamt about you. A wicked dream, too good to be true! But now I'm *somewhere else,* I don't in the least mind telling you. . . ."

"Claudine!" he implored, very low.

The crazy Claudine, leaning towards him, with her two hands laid flat on the tablecloth, kept her eyes on his face. They were wild and held no secrets; a light, straying curl tickled her right eyebrow. She was talking as a vase overflows, this silent, reserved creature. She saw him turn red, then pale; she saw that he was breathing fast, and all this struck her as perfectly natural. But why did he not seem as ecstatic, released from all constraint as she was herself? She dimly asked herself this vague question and answered herself aloud, with a sigh:

"Now, nothing sad can ever happen to me again."

Renaud beckoned the head-waiter with the emphatic insistence of a man saying inwardly: 'Things can't go on like this.'

Claudine said irrelevantly, her cheeks burning, as she nibbled one of her tea-roses:

"How stupid you are."

"Am I?"

"Yes. You've told a lie. You stopped Marcel from coming tonight on purpose."

"No, Claudine."

That very gentle 'no' struck home and sobered her a little. She let herself be put on her feet and drawn towards the door, like a little sleepwalker. Only the floor turned soft under her like asphalt that was still warm. Renaud only just had time to grasp her by one elbow; he guided her, almost carried her into the closed cab and sat down beside her. The cab drove off. With her head buzzing and almost completely blank, Claudine leant against the helpful shoulder. He became anxious.

"Are you feeling ill?"

No reply. Then:

"No. But hold me, because I'm swimming. Everything else is swimming, too. You're swimming too, aren't you?"

He wrapped his arm round her waist, sighing with apprehension. She leant her head against him, but her hat got in the way. She took it off with a fumbling hand and laid it on her lap, then once again she leant her head against the kind shoulder, with the blissful security of someone who has at last reached the end of a long journey. And the sensible Claudine looked on, observed, and gradually began to come closer. A lot of use, *she* was! She was very nearly as demented, that sensible Claudine, as the other one.

Her companion, her beloved friend, had not been able to stop himself from hugging the small body that lay so trustfully abandoned in his arms. He mastered himself and gave her a gentle shake:

"Claudine, Claudine, we're nearly there! Come to! Can you manage to get up the stairs."

"What stairs?"

"Your stairs. The ones in the Rue Jacob."

"You're going to leave me?"

She was sitting up straight now, stiffened like a snake. Bareheaded and dishevelled, her panic-stricken face was one agonised question.

"But look, child, look! Come to your senses. We've both been idiots tonight. It's all my fault this has happened."

"You're going to leave me!" she cried, heedless of the driver's attentive back, "Where do you expect me to go? It's you I want to go with, it's you . . ."

Her eyes reddened and her mouth tightened. She almost screamed:

"Oh, I know! Go away, I know why you want to. You're going to your *women*, the ones you love. Marcel told me you had at least six of them! They don't love you—they'll leave you—they're ugly! You're going to sleep with them, every single one of them! And you'll kiss them, you'll even kiss them on the mouth! And who's going to kiss *me*? Oh! why don't you want me, at least for your daughter? I ought to have been your daughter, your friend, your wife—everything, everything!"

She flung herself on his neck and clung to it, weeping and sobbing.

"There's no one but you in the world, no one but you, and you're leaving me!"

Renaud wrapped her close in his arms; his mouth searched the curly nape, the warm neck, the cheeks salt with tears.

"Leaving you, my sweet, my adorable!"

She fell suddenly silent. She raised her wet face and looked at him with extraordinary intensity. He was panting and pale; his face was young, under the silvery hair; Claudine could feel the muscles trembling in the great arms that held her. He bent down to the little girl's hot mouth; she struggled and leant back, hardly knowing whether she was yielding herself or resisting. The sharp jolt of the cab against the pavement threw them apart, intoxicated, serious and trembling.

"Goodbye, Claudine."

"Goodbye."

"I'm not coming up with you. I'll light your candle. You've got the key?"

"The key, yes."

"I can't come and see you tomorrow; it's tomorrow already. I'll come the day after tomorrow, for certain, at four o'clock."

"At four o'clock."

Meekly, she let him give her hand a long kiss, breathing in, as he bent over it, the faint smell of mild tobacco he carried about him. Then, like a dreamer awakened, she climbed the three flights and went to bed. In her four-poster the crazy Claudine was rejoined— high time too—by the sensible Claudine. But the sensible Claudine, respectful and admiring, timidly effaced herself before the other who had gone straight where Destiny had impelled her. She had marched forward, without once looking back, like a conqueror or someone on their way to the scaffold.

15

LANGUOR. Languor all over. The delicious languor of someone who has been beaten or caressed almost to death. My calves were trembling, my hands were cold, there was a numb feeling in the nape of my neck. And my heart kept beating faster and faster, as if it wanted to catch up with the tick-tock of my little watch, then stopping and starting up again with a *Poum*! So this was true love, the real thing? Yes, because no place was bearable to me but his shoulder, where my lips almost touched his neck when I nestled against it. Then I smiled with pity at the mental image of Marcel's delicate cheeks against Renaud's wrinkled temples. Thank God, no, he wasn't young! Because of that noble, almost lunatic father of mine, I needed a Papa, I needed a friend, I needed a lover. Oh, heavens, a lover! It was hardly worth while having read so much and bragged about my erotic knowledge—entirely theoretical—if that mere word passing through my mind made me clench my teeth and curl up my toes. What should I do in his presence if I couldn't prevent myself from thinking? He would see, he would think about it too. Help, help! Suddenly, I felt dying of thirst.

The open window and the water in my jug helped a little. My candle was still burning on the chimneypiece. Looking in the glass, I was stupefied to see *that* was not more obvious. At four o'clock, in broad daylight, I fell asleep exhausted.

"Are you hungry, my lamb? Your chocolate's been waiting for you since half-past seven and it's going on nine, to be sure. Oh, oh, what a face!"

"What's the matter with it?"

"Something's gone and changed my baby!"

Her sure old servant's instinct took in my tiredness, noticed the crumpled feathers of the hat flung on the chair, exulted in my headache. She got on my nerves.

"Have you finished weighing your breasts like melons? Which one's the ripest?"

But she laughed very softly and went off to her kitchen, singing one of her most outrageous songs.

> *The Montigny girls*
> *Are as hot as live coals*
> *You're surely in luck*
> *When you . . .*

I must confine myself to this brief quotation.

What had really woken me up was the terror of having only dreamt that whole impossible night.

Was *that* how tremendous things happened? Blessed be Asti and highly-seasoned shrimps! Without them, I should certainly never have had the courage.

I might not have had the courage that particular evening, but, some other evening, my heart would have gone *bumpetty-bump* just the same. But he loved me, didn't he? Hadn't he been pale? Wouldn't he have lost his head, like a simple Claudine, but for that unlucky—that lucky—no, I *mean*, but for that *unlucky* pavement in the Rue Jacob that caught the edge of the cab-wheel? No man had ever kissed me on the mouth. His was narrow and alive, with a round, firm lower lip. Oh, Claudine, Claudine, how you are turning into a child again as you feel yourself becoming a woman! As I conjured up his mouth and the passion in his darkened eyes, a delicious distress made me clasp my hands.

Other ideas assailed me too, but I did not in the least want to dwell on them at that moment.

"It certainly does hurt!" echoed Luce's sing-song voice. No, no: she had slept with a swine, that didn't prove anything! Besides, what did it matter? What mattered was that he should be there all the time, that the dear place on his shoulder should always be there ready for me at every hour of the day and the night, and that his great arms should shelter me every time they closed round me. My liberty oppressed me, my independence exhausted me; what I had been searching for for months—for far longer—I knew, with absolute clarity, was a master. Free women are not women at all. He would know all that I didn't know; he would rather despise all that I did know; he would call me "My little silly!" and stroke my hair.

My dream was so vividly real to me that, to reach up to *his* hand, I lowered my forehead and stood on tiptoe, like Fanchette when she wants me to scratch the top of her little flat skull. "You have all the spontaneous grace of an animal, Claudine. . . ." Lunchtime found me thoughtfully examining myself in a handglass, with my hair brushed back from my temples, wondering whether he would like my pointed ears.

Having quickly had enough of orange salad and fried potatoes, I left Papa alone with his coffee into which he daily methodically drops seven pieces of sugar and a morsel of pipe-ash. And I abandoned myself to bitter despair at the thought that I had twenty-seven hours to wait! Read? I couldn't, I could *not*! Strands of silvery-gold hair kept sweeping over the pages of the book. And I could not go out either; the streets swarmed with men whose name was not Renaud, and who would stare at me and try to make an impression on me, the imbeciles!

A small piece of stuff rolled up into a ball in my tubchair managed to extract a smile from me. It was one of my little chemises, begun long ago! Sewing was the thing! Claudine would be needing chemises. Would Renaud like this one? White and filmy, with a charming little lace edge and white ribbon shoulder-straps. . . . Some nights, when I feel particularly pleased with myself, I study myself in front of the glass in my chemise, a tall slim little Madame Sans-Géne with curls over her nose. Renaud *can't* find me ugly. Oh, heavens, I'd be so near, so much *too* near him in nothing but a thin chemise. My trembling hands sewed all crooked and, quite absurdly, I could hear the far-away voice of the favourite, the thin voice of Mademoiselle's little Aimée, at sewing lessons: "Claudine, I implore you, *do* be more careful with your hem-stitching. You're not getting it nice and even. Look at Anaïs's!"

Someone had rung the bell. Breathless, with my heart stopped, I listened, thimble in air. It was he, it was he, he hadn't been able to wait! Just as I was about to get up and run, Mélie knocked, and brought in Marcel.

Stupefaction made me remain seated. Marcel? That was someone I had completely forgotten! For several hours, he had been dead. What, Marcel! Why Marcel, not the other?

Supple and silent, he kissed my hand and sat down on the little chair. I stared at him with a dazed expression. He was rather pale, extremely pretty, slightly doll-like as usual. A little sugar boy.

Vexed by my silence, he urged me:

"Well, come along, out with it!"

"Out with what?"

"Was it fun, last night? What did *somebody* say to explain my not being there?"

I loosed my tongue with an effort:

"He told me you were wearing an impossible tie."

How stupid he was, this boy! Couldn't he see the miracle, then? I should have thought it was blindingly obvious. However, I was not in the least hurry to enlighten him. He burst into a shrill laugh: I winced.

"Ha, ha! . . . an impossible tie! Yes, the whole truth is contained in those three words. What do you think of the story? You know my crêpe-de-Chine cravat, don't you? It was Charlie who gave it me?"

"I think," I said in all sincerity, "that you were quite right not to change it. I think that cravat's exquisite."

"Isn't it? A charming idea, that drapery pinned with pearls! I knew I could trust your taste, Claudinette. However," he added with a polite smile, "it didn't prevent my amiable father from depriving me of that evening with you. I would have brought you home, I was already looking forward to that delicious little moment in the cab. . . ."

Where, oh where had his eyes been all this time? It was positively pitiful, such blindness! He must have heard some wounding things yesterday night, for, at the thought of them, his face had hardened and his mouth become thin.

"Tell me all about it, Claudine. My dear father was exquisite and witty as usual? He didn't treat you, as he did me, as a 'filthy little beast' and a 'child with revolting habits'? God," he fumed, firing up with resentment, "what a swine, what a . . ."

"No!"

I had interrupted with a violence that had brought me to my feet, face to face with him.

Without moving a muscle, he started at me, turned pale, grasped what I meant, and stood up too. There was a silence in which I could hear Fanchette's purring, the tick-tock of my little watch, Marcel's breathing, and the pounding of my heart. A silence that lasted, perhaps, two whole minutes. . . ."

"You too?" he said, at last, in a cynical voice. "I thought Papa didn't go in for young girls. Usually he's all for married women or tarts."

I said nothing: I was past speaking.

"And . . . this is quite recent? Only since last night, perhaps? Thank me, Claudine. After all, you owe this marvellous piece of luck to my cravat."

His delicate, pinched nose was as white as his teeth. I still said nothing; something prevented me.

Standing behind the chair that separated us, he sneered at me. With my hands hanging and my head lowered, I looked up at him; the lace of my little apron fluttered with the beating of my heart. The silence fell once more; interminable. Suddenly, he began to speak again, in a peculiar voice:

"I've always thought you very intelligent, Claudine. And what you're doing at this moment increases my respect for your . . . shrewdness."

Stupefied, I lifted my head.

"I repeat, you're a remarkable girl, Claudine. And I congratulate you, unreservedly, a nice piece of work."

I did not understand. But I quietly moved away the chair that separated us. I had a vague notion that, in a moment or two, it would be in my way.

"Come, come now, you know perfectly well what I mean. After all, though he's got through quite a bit of money, Papa's still well worth your powder and shot."

Quicker than a wasp, I flung all my nails at his face; for the last minute I had been taking aim at his eyes. With a shrill scream, he staggered over backwards, his hands up to his face, then, recovering his balance, he rushed to the glass over the chimneypiece. The lower eyelid was torn and bleeding, a little blood was already staining the lapel of his jacket. In a state of crazy exaltation I could hear myself giving little muffled, involuntary shrieks. He turned round, quite beside himself: I thought he wanted to seize a weapon and I rummaged feverishly in my work-bag. My scissors, my scissors! But he wasn't even thinking of hitting me; pushing me aside, he rushed to the jug and dipped his handkerchief in the water. He was already bending over my basin—what impudence! I was on him in a flash, I grabbed his bent head by its two ears and I pushed him back into the room, screaming at him in a hoarse voice I did not recognise:

"No, no, not here! Run away and get your wounds dressed at Charlie's!"

With his handkerchief over his eye, he picked up his hat and went out, forgetting his gloves. I opened all the doors for him and I listened to his footsteps tottering down the stairs. Then I went back into my bedroom and I stood there, I don't know how long, thinking of nothing at all. At last the limpness of my legs forced me to sit down. This movement started up my thinking mechanism again, and I collapsed. Money! money! He had dared to say that I wanted money! All the same, that was a fine claw-stroke I'd given him—that little piece of skin that hung down—I swear I only missed the eye by less than a centimetre. The coward, he ought to have bashed me on the head! Ugh, the little milksop, mopping himself up. Money! Money! Whatever should I do with it? I'd more than enough for Fanchette and me. Oh, dear Renaud, I'd tell him everything, and I'd nestle close against him, and he would be so kind and sweet that it would make me cry.

That boy I'd scratched—he'd been eaten up with jealousy; disgusting little *girl* of a boy!

Suddenly I understood, and my temples throbbed painfully. It was *his* money, Marcel's money, I should take if I became Renaud's wife; it was *his* money he was trembling for! And how could I prevent that unfeeling boy from believing in Claudine's cupidity? He would not be the only one to believe in it and he'd tell, they'd all tell Renaud that the girl was selling herself, that she'd inveigled the poor man who was going through the dangerous forties. What could I do? What could I do? I wanted to see Renaud, I didn't want Marcel's money, but I wanted Renaud all the same. Suppose I asked Papa for help? Oh, dear—my head ached so dreadfully—oh, my dear, sweet place on his shoulder, must I give it up? No! Rather than that, I'd blow up everything! I'd tie that Marcel up here in my

bedroom and I'd kill him. And afterwards I'd tell the police he'd
tried to seduce me and I'd killed him in self-defence. *There*!

Right up to the time when Fanchette woke me up by mewing that
she was hungry, I remained huddled up in the tub chair, with one
finger on each eye and one finger in each ear, overwhelmed with
wild dreams, black despair . . . and love.

"Dinner? No, I don't want any dinner. I've got a migraine. Make
me some fresh lemonade, Mélie, I'm dying of thirst. I'm going to
bed."

Papa and Mélie, anxious and disturbed, hovered round my bed till
nine o'clock. At last, I could stand it no more and implored them:
"Oh, do go away—I'm so tired."

As I lay in the dark, I could hear the servants down in the
courtyard banging doors and washing dishes. I desperately needed
Renaud! Why hadn't I sent him a telegram straight away? Now it
was too late. Tomorrow would never come. My friend, my dear life,
the man to whom I would trust myself as to a beloved father, the
man with whom I felt alternately ashamed and apprehensive, as if I
were his mistress—then happy and uninhibited as if he had rocked
me in his arms when I was little.

After hours of fever, of painful throbbings in my head, of silent
appeals to someone who was too far away and did not hear, my
demented thoughts began to clear a little. Towards three in the
morning, they gradually shifted back, leaving an empty space in
which, at last, there appeared the Idea. It came with the dawn, the
Idea, with the awakening of the sparrows and the fleeting coolness
that precedes a summer day. Thunderstruck by it, I lay perfectly
still on my back in bed, with my eyes wide open. How simple it was
and how I had tortured myself for nothing! Now I should have
circles round my eyes and drawn cheeks when Renaud came. And
the solution had been staring me in the face all the time!

I didn't want Marcel to think: "Claudine's got her eye on my
money." I didn't want to say to Renaud: "Go away and don't love
me any more." Oh God, that was the last thing I wanted to say to
him! But I didn't want to be his wife either, and, to soothe my
irritable conscience—very well, then, I'd be his mistress!

Revived and refreshed, I went to sleep. I slept like a sack, flat on my stomach, with my face hidden in my folded arms. The declamatory voice of my classic old beggar awoke me. I felt completely relaxed, but startled. Ten o'clock already! "Mélie, throw the old man four sous!"

Mélie did not hear. I slipped on my dressing-gown, and ran into the drawing-room, barefooted, with my hair standing wildly on end. "Old man, here's ten sous. Keep the change!" What a beautiful white beard! No doubt he possesses a country house and an estate, like most of the beggars in Paris. So much the better for him. And, as I was going back to my room, I ran into Monsieur Maria who had just arrived, and who stood still, dazzled by my morning déshabille.

"Monsieur Maria, don't you think that today's going to be the end of the world?"

"Alas, no, Mademoiselle."

"*I* think it is. You just see."

Sitting in my tub of warm water, I studied myself lingeringly and minutely. That down, surely that didn't count as hair on my legs? Bother, my nipples weren't as pink as Luce's, but my legs were longer and more elegant, and I had dimples in my back. I wasn't a Rubens, far from it, but I'm not keen on the 'beautiful butcher's wife' type—neither is Renaud.

Renaud—that name spoken almost aloud when I was dressed in nothing but a beechwood tub—intimidated me a good deal. Eleven o'clock. Still five hours to wait. All was going well. I brushed and brushed my curls, I brushed my teeth, I brushed my nails! Everything must shine, shine, shine! Filmy stockings, a new chemise, knickers to match, my pink corsets, my finely-striped silk petticoat that goes *frou frou* when I move.

Gay as I used to be at the School, active and bustling, I busied myself with anything and everything to stop myself from thinking what might be going to happen. After all, if it was today I was going to offer myself, he might very well take me today if he wanted to—it was entirely up to him. But oh, I hoped he wouldn't want me quite so quickly, quite so suddenly—it wouldn't be in the least like him. I counted on him, yes, far more on him than on myself. For, as they say in Montigny, I'd completely lost my 'rudder'.

16

THE afternoon was hard to get through, all the same. He might not come to see me. At three o'clock I began to play at being a panther in a cage and my ears were stretched to their utmost.

At twenty to four, there was a very faint ring at the bell. But I was not deceived; it was definitely he. Standing with my back against the foot of the bed, I ceased to exist. The door opened and closed behind Renaud. He was bareheaded; he seemed to have grown a little thinner. His moustache trembled imperceptibly and his eyes gleamed blue in the dimness. I did not move; I did not speak. He was taller. He was paler. His face was shadowed, tired, arrogant. Still standing by the door, without advancing into the room, he spoke very low.

"Good afternoon, Claudine."

Drawn to him by the sound of his voice, I went to him and held out my two hands. He kissed them both, but he let them drop again.

"Are you angry with me, little friend?"

I gave an ineffable shrug. I sat down in the armchair. He sat down on the low chair and I quickly went up close to him, ready to throw myself into his arms. Hateful man! He did not seem to understand. He spoke almost under his breath, as if he were frightened:

"My sweet, crazy child, you said a thousand things to me yesterday that sleep and daylight have driven right out of your mind. Wait a minute, don't look at me too much with those adorable eyes, Claudine! Eyes I shall never forget—that were too kind to me. All last night and the rest of that other night, I've been fighting against a mad, ridiculous hope. I'd ceased to be aware that I was forty," he went on with an effort, "but I realised you would remember the fact, if not today or tomorrow, at any rate very soon. My darling with the too-loving eyes, my little curly shepherd," he said, even lower for there was a lump in his throat and his eyes were wet, "don't tempt me any more. I'm nothing but a poor dazzled man, utterly swept away by you. Defend yourself, Claudine! My God, it's monstrous; in other people's eyes, you might be my daughter!"

"But I am your daughter too!" (I held out my arms to him.) "Don't you *feel* that I'm your daughter? I was that from the very beginning—ever since those very first days—I've been your obedient, astonished child. And much, much more astonished a little later on to feel that so many things were coming to her all at once—a father, a friend, a master, a lover. Oh, don't say no, don't stop me, let me say a lover too! A lover—one can find that any day—but someone who's everything all the same time—someone, who, if he goes away, leaves you a widow and an orphan and utterly friendless—isn't that an incredible miracle? *You're* that miracle! I adore you!"

He lowered his eyes, but too late. A tear trickled down on to his moustache. Desperate, I flung my arms round his neck.

"Are you unhappy? Have I hurt you without meaning to?"

The great arms I was waiting for closed tight round me at last; the blue-black eyes told me what I wanted to know.

"Oh my girl, my girl beyond all hope! Don't give me time to be ashamed of what I'm doing! I'm keeping you, I can't do anything but keep you . . . your little body is the loveliest thing to me in the whole world. Shall I ever be completely old if I have you? My darling, my bird, if you only knew how possessive my love is, how boyishly jealous. And what an intolerable husband I shall be!"

A husband? Why, of course, he didn't know! I came to, tore myself away from my dear place, after one furtive kiss, and brusquely untwined my arms.

"No, not my husband."

He stared at me, his eyes intoxicated and tender, and kept his arms open.

"It's very serious. I ought to have told you at once. But . . . you upset all my resolutions when I saw you come in. And then I'd waited for you so long, I just couldn't say a word. Sit down there.

Don't hold my waist . . . nor my arm . . . nor my hand . . . please!
It would be almost better not to look at me, Renaud."

Seated in the little tub-chair, I put out my arms and thrust away
his eager hands with all the resolution I had left. He sat down, very,
very close, on the Breton chair.

"Marcel came here yesterday afternoon. Yes. He asked me to tell
him all about the night before last . . . as if it *could* be told, Renaud!
And he congratulated me on my artfulness! Apparently, you're still
quite rich, and, by becoming your wife, it's his fortune, Marcel's, I
should be pinching for my own advantage."

Renaud had leapt to his feet. His nostrils were quivering in the
most menacing way; I hastily ended my speech.

"So, I don't want to marry you . . ."

The shuddering sigh I heard urged me on to finish.

". . . but I *do* want to be your mistress."

"Oh! Claudine!

"What do you mean, Claudine?"

He considered me, with his arms dropped and his eyes full of such
admiration and such distress that I no longer knew what to think. I
had been expecting a triumph, a wild embrace, perhaps almost too
eager acquiescence.

"Don't you think it's a good idea? Do you imagine I'd ever let
people think that I don't love you better than anything in the world?
I've got money, too. I've got a hundred and fifty thousand francs.
There, what do you say to that? I don't need Marcel's money."

"Claudine!"

"I'd better own up to everything," I said, looking up to him
coaxingly. "I scratched him—Marcel, I mean. I . . . I tore off a little
bit of his cheek and I threw him out of the flat."

The remembrance made me stand up and begin to act the scene
for him and my amazon-like gestures forced him to smile under his
moustache. But what was he waiting for? Why didn't he accept my
offer at once? Hadn't he understood, then?"

"So . . . so you see," I said in a voice that was becoming rather
embarrassed, "I want to be your mistress. It won't be difficult, you
know how much freedom I'm allowed. Well, I give you all that
freedom, I'd like to give you my whole life. But you have to go away
on business quite a lot. When you're free, you can come here and I'll
come to your flat too—your famous flat! You won't think your

home's too much like an eighteenth-century engraving any more, will you? Not for a Claudine who completely belongs to you?"

My legs were shaking a little, so I sat down again. He sank down on his knees, with his face on a level with mine; he stopped me talking by laying his mouth on mine for barely a second, without any pressure. He drew it back, alas, at the moment when the kiss was beginning to make my head whirl. With his arms round me, he talked to me in a voice he could not quite control.

"Oh, Claudine! Little girl, who's got all her knowledge out of nasty books, is there anything in the world as pure as you are? No, my darling, my delight, I'm not going to let you get away with this lunatic generosity! If I take you, it's for good, for ever and ever. And, in front of everyone, in the ordinary, decent, conventional way, I shall marry you."

"No, you won't marry me!"

I needed courage, for, when he called me 'my darling', 'my delight', all my blood drained away and my bones turned soft.

"I'll be your mistress, or nothing."

"My wife, or nothing!"

Suddenly struck by the strangeness of this debate, I broke into a nervous laugh. As I was laughing, with my mouth open and my head thrown back, I saw him leaning over me, so tortured with desire that I trembled, then, bravely, I opened my arms, thinking he was accepting me.

But he shook his head and said, in a choked voice:

"No!"

What could I do? I clasped my hands; I implored; I offered him my mouth, my eyes half-closed. He repeated again, almost as if he were being strangled:

"No! My wife or nothing."

Slowly, I stood up, feeling utterly helpless and lost.

During those few seconds Renaud, as if suddenly inspired, had reached the drawing-room door. He already had his hand on the study-door when I guessed. The wretch! He was going to ask Papa for my hand!

Without daring to scream, I hung on to his arm, imploring him under my breath:

"Oh, if you love me, don't do it! Mercy, anything you like. Do you want Claudine this very minute? Don't ask Papa anything, wait a few days. Do think . . . it's revolting, this money business! Marcel's venomous. He'll tell everyone, he'll say I seduced you by force. I love you, I love you. . . ."

He took me in his arms, the coward, and kissed me slowly on my cheeks, on my eyes, on my hair, under the ear just where it makes you shudder. What could I do, in his arms?

And, noiselessly he opened the door, as he gave me one final kiss. I had only just time to break away quickly.

Papa, sitting cross-legged on the floor among his papers, his beard dishevelled and his nose pugnacious, glared at us ferociously. We had chosen a bad moment.

"What the devil are you doing, butting in here? Ah, it's you, my dear Sir, I'm delighted to see you!"

Renaud recovered a little of his self-possession and formality, though bereft of hat and gloves.

"The fact is, Sir, I should like to have a minute's serious conversation with you."

"Impossible," said Papa categorically. "Absolutely impossible before tomorrow. This," he explained, pointing to Monsieur Maria who was writing—writing too fast—"this is of the utmost urgency."

"But, Sir, what *I* want to say to you is of the utmost urgency."

"Say it straight out then."

"I want—I implore you, try not to think me too outrageously absurd—I want to marry Claudine."

"Is that business going to start again?" thundered Papa, who had leapt to his feet and looked really formidable. "God's thunder, ten thousand herds of sacred swine, all sons of bitches! But don't you realise this she-donkey doesn't want to get married? She'll tell you so herself, that she doesn't love you!"

Under the storm, Renaud regained all his swagger. He waited for the oaths to come to an end, then, looking down at me quizzically under his drooping lashes, he said:

"She doesn't love me? Claudine, do you dare to say you don't love me?"

Goodness me no, I didn't dare. And, with all my heart, I murmured:

"Yes, of course I love you."

Papa, dumbfounded, contemplated his daughter as if she were a slug that had fallen from Mars.

"Well, this is staggering? And you, do you love her?"

"Definitely," said Renaud, nodding his head.

"Extraordinary!" marvelled Papa, with sublime unconsciousness. "Oh, I'm perfectly willing! But personally, when it comes to marrying, she wouldn't be at all my type. I prefer women more . . ."

And his hands sketched the outline of the breasts of a nursing mother.

What could I say? I was beaten. Renaud had cheated. I whispered to him very softly, standing on tiptoe to reach his ear:

"You know, I don't want Marcel's money."

His face, young and radiant under his silver hair, he pulled me into the drawing-room, as he replied, lightly and spitefully:

"Pooh! He'll still have all his grandmother's to batten on!"

And the two of us went back to my room, his arms tight round me, carrying me off as if he were stealing me; both of us as ecstatic and silly as the lovers of romance.

Claudine Married

1

DEFINITELY, there is something wrong with our married life. Renaud knows nothing about it yet; how should he know?

We have been home for six weeks now. It is over, that lazy, feverish, vagabond life that lasted for fifteen months and in which our wanderings took us from the Rue de Bassano to Montigny, from Montigny to Bayreuth, from Bayreuth to a village in Baden that I thought at first, to Renaud's huge delight, was called "Forellen-Fischerei" because an enormous signboard above the river announces you can catch trout there and I don't know German.

Last winter, in a thoroughly hostile mood and clinging tight to Renaud's arm, I saw the Mediterranean. A cold wind was brushing it up the wrong way and it was lit by a thin, harsh sun. Too many parasols, too many hats and faces ruined this meretricious south of France for me. What ruined it most of all was the inevitable meeting with first one, then at least a dozen of Renaud's friends; with families whom he provided with complimentary tickets; with ladies at whose houses he dined: this appalling man makes himself agreeable to everyone and puts himself out most for the people he knows least. As he explains, with impudent charm, it is not worth while doing violence to one's nature to please one's real friends, since one's sure of them anyway. . . .

My puzzled simplicity has never been able to see the point of those winters on the Côte d'Azur where lace frocks shiver under sable stoles!

Moreover, the abuse I showered on Renaud and the abuse he showered on me overstrained my nerves and made me ill able to bear the petty irritations of everyday life. After being dragged from pillar to post in a half-painful, half-delicious state of physical intoxication and a kind of giddy daze, I ended up by demanding mercy and rest and a fixed abode. Well, here I am back at home! So what is it that I need? What is it I still feel lacking?

Let's try and put a little order into this hotch-potch of memories still so recent, yet already so remote.

What a fantastic comedy my wedding-day was! By the time that Thursday arrived, three weeks of being engaged to this Renaud whom I love to distraction, with his embarrassing eyes, his still more embarrassing (though restrained) gestures, and his lips, always in quest of a new place to kiss, had made my face as sharp as a she-cat's on heat. I could make no sense at all of his reserve and abstention during that time! I would have been entirely his, the moment he wanted it, and he was perfectly aware of this. And yet, with too epicurean a concern for his happiness—and for mine?—he kept us in a state of exhausting virtue. His uncontrolled Claudine often gave him angry glances after too brief a kiss, broken off before the proper time. "But, goodness, in a week's time or less—what difference does it make? You're exciting me for nothing, you're wearing me out with frustration. . . ." With no mercy for either of us, he left me, against my will, completely intact until after that slap-dash wedding.

Genuinely annoyed by the necessity of informing His Worship the Mayor and His Reverence the parish priest of my decision to live with Renaud, I refused to help Papa or anyone else in any way at all. Renaud dealt with the matter with expert patience; Papa with unwonted, furious, ostentatious zeal. Mélie alone, radiant at being present at the climax of a love-story, sang and day-dreamed at the window overlooking the gloomy little courtyard. Fanchette, followed by Limaçon, still unsteady on his legs and "fairer than a son of Phtah", sniffed at open cardboard boxes, new materials and long gloves that made her retch slightly and diligently kneaded my white tulle veil with her front paws.

This pear-shaped ruby that hangs round my neck on such a thin gold chain was given me by Renaud two days before our wedding. How well I remember his bringing it! Enchanted by its clear wine-colour, I held it up against the light, at eye-level, to admire it, with my other hand resting on Renaud's shoulder as he knelt in front of me.

"Claudine, you're squinting, like Fanchette when she's after a fly."

Without listening to him, I suddenly put the ruby in my mouth "because it ought to melt and taste like a raspberry fruit-drop"! Renaud, baffled by this new way of appreciating precious stones, brought me sweets the following day. Honestly, they gave me as much pleasure as the jewel.

On the great morning, I woke up irritable and surly. I raged against the Town Hall and the Church, the weight of my long-trained dress, the scalding chocolate, and Mélie, who had put on her purple cashmere at seven o'clock and kept gloating, "My precious, what a time you're going to have!" I raged against those people who were going to come: Maugis and Robert Parville, Renaud's witnesses, Aunt Coeur in Chantilly lace, Marcel, whose father had forgiven him—on purpose to annoy and make fun of him, I believe—and my own witnesses: a very eminent (and very dirty) malacologist whose name I have never discovered, and Monsieur Maria! Papa, serenely forgetful, saw nothing in the least odd in this remarkable devotion on the part of my martyred suitor.

And Claudine, ready long before the time, a little sallow in her white dress and precariously-balanced veil—this short hair can be a nuisance at times—sat beside the basket where Fanchette was having her stomach massaged by her striped Limaçon, thinking: "It revolts me, this wedding! The ideal thing would have been to have had it here, for the two of us to have dinner and then lock ourselves up in this little room where I've gone to sleep thinking of him, where I've thought of him and not been able to go to sleep, and . . . But my little four-poster bed would be too small. . . ."

Renaud's arrival, and his slightly flurried gestures, did nothing to drive away these preoccupations. Then, at the urgent request of Monsieur Maria who was going demented, we had to rout out Papa and hurry him up. My noble father, surpassing himself in a manner worthy of the rare occasion, had quite simply forgotten that I was getting married; we discovered him in a dressing-gown (at ten minutes to twelve!) calmly smoking his pipe. He greeted the unfortunate Maria with these memorable words:

"Come along in, Maria. You're devilish late today, just when we've got a very difficult chapter. What's the idea of turning up in dress clothes? You look like a waiter!"

"But, Monsieur . . . Monsieur . . . Mademoiselle Claudine's wedding . . . We're only waiting for you. . . ."

"Hell!" replied Papa, consulting his watch instead of the calendar. "Hell! Are you sure it's today? If you go on ahead, they can begin without me."

Robert Parville bewildered as a lost poodle because he was not trotting at the heels of his mistress; Maugis glazed with mock solemnity; Monsieur Maria pale as death; Aunt Cœur supercilious and Marcel stiffly formal—they hardly constituted a crowd, did they? To me, there seemed to be at least fifty of them in the poky flat! Isolated under my veil, I was acutely conscious of my failing, twittering nerves. . . .

What followed gave me the impression of one of those confused and muddled dreams in which you feel as if your feet were tied together. A pink and purple ray falling on my white gloves through the stained-glass windows; my nervous laugh in the sacristy when Papa insisted on signing his name twice on the same page, "because my first flourish isn't impressive enough". A stifling sensation of unreality; Renaud himself far away and insubstantial. . . .

When we returned home, Renaud, thoroughly anxious at the sight of my drawn, unhappy face, questioned me tenderly. I shook my head, saying, "I don't feel much more married than I did this morning. What about you?" His moustache quivered and, at that, I blushed and shrugged my shoulders.

I wanted to get out of that ridiculous dress and they left me to myself. My darling Fanchette found me easier to recognise in a pink linen blouse and a white serge skirt. "Fanchette, am I going to leave you? It's the first time ever. . . . I've got to. . . . I don't want to drag you about in railway trains, along with your precious child." A slight desire to cry, an indefinable uneasiness, a painful contraction of the ribs. "Oh, let my beloved friend take me quickly and deliver me from this idiotic apprehension which is neither fear nor modesty. How late night comes in July, how this white sun makes my temples throb!"

At nightfall, my husband—my husband!—took me away. The

noise of the rubber-tyred wheels did not stop me from hearing my heart-beats and I clenched my teeth so tight that his kiss did not unclench them.

In the Rue de Bassano, I hardly caught more than a glimpse of that flat "too like an eighteenth-century engraving" that he had hitherto refused to let me enter. The only light came from shaded writing-lamps placed on the tables. To intoxicate myself still more, I breathed in that smell of light tobacco and Russian leather that permeates Renaud's clothes and his long moustache.

I seem to be still there, I can see myself, I *am* there.

So, the moment had come? What should I do? For a split second, I thought of Luce. Without realising it, I removed my hat. I took my loved one's hand to reassure myself and I gazed at him. Carelessly, he threw off his hat and gloves and drew back a little, with a trembling sigh. I looked lovingly at his beautiful dark eyes and his arched nose and his faded gold hair that the wind had artfully ruffled. I went up close to him, but he retreated mischievously and contemplated me from a little distance, while all my splendid courage drained away. I clasped my hands.

"Oh! Please do be quick!"

Alas, I did not realise how funny that remark was.

He sat down.

"Come here, Claudine."

Sitting on his knees, he could hear that I was breathing too fast; his voice became tender.

"Are you my very own?"

"You know I am. I've been yours for so long."

"You're not frightened?"

"No; I'm not frightened. To begin with, I know everything!"

"What, everything?"

He slid me down, so that I lay on his knees, and bent over my mouth. I put up no defence and let his lips drink deep. I wanted to cry. At least, I felt as if I wanted to cry.

"You know everything, my darling little girl, and you're still not frightened?"

I almost shouted:

"No! . . ."

Yet, all the same, I was and I clung desperately round his neck.

With one hand, he was already trying to unhook my blouse. I sprang to my feet.

"No! All by myself!"

Why? I have no idea why. A last vestige of the impulsive Claudine? Completely naked, I would have gone straight to his arms, but I didn't want him to undress me.

With clumsy haste, I undid my clothes and scattered them everywhere, kicking my shoes in the air, picking up my petticoat between two of my toes, and flinging away my corsets, all without one glance at Renaud sitting there in front of me. I had nothing on now but my little chemise and I said: "There!" with bold defiance as, with my usual gesture, I rubbed the imprint the stays had left round my waist.

Renaud did not move. He merely thrust his head forward, gripped both arms of his chair and stared at me. The heroic Claudine, panic-stricken by that stare, fled in terror and flung herself on the bed—on the bed that was still fully made.

He came and lay on it with me. He held me close, so tense that I could almost hear his muscles quivering. Fully dressed, he embraced me and held me down on it—heavens, whatever was he waiting for to get undressed himself?—and his mouth and his hands forced me to stay there, without his body touching me, from my shuddering revolt to my wild consent, to the shameful moan of voluptuous pleasure I would have liked to hold back out of pride. Only after that did he fling off his clothes, as I had done mine, and laugh mercilessly to annoy an angry and humiliated Claudine. But he demanded nothing, only freedom to give me all the caresses I needed to send me to sleep, in the small hours, still lying on the fully-made bed.

I was grateful to him later on—very grateful indeed—for such active self-denial, for such stoical and frustrated patience. I made up to him for it, when, tamed and curious, I would avidly watch his eyes glaze as he tensely watched mine glaze too. Moreover, for a long time, I retained—and, to tell the truth, I still retain—a slight terror of . . . how can I put it? I think "marital duty" is the usual term. This potent Renaud made me think, by analogy, of that great gawk Anaïs, who had a mania for cramming her large hands into gloves too tight for them. Apart from that, everything is perfect; everything is even a little *too* perfect. It is pleasant to begin in complete ignorance and then to learn so many reasons for giving nervous laughs and nervous cries, for uttering little muffled moans, with your toes curled up with tension.

The only caress I have never been able to grant my husband, is to use the familiar *"tu"*. I always use the formal *"vous"*, on every possible occasion, even when I am imploring him, even when I am consenting, even when the exquisite torture of suspense forces me to speak in jerks, in a voice that is not my own. But isn't this calling him *"vous"* a special, unique caress from this Claudine who is rather uncivilised and apt to be lavish with *"tu"*?

He is handsome, I swear he is! His dark, smooth skin glides over mine. Where his great arms join his shoulders, there is a feminine, cushioned roundness where I lay my head, night and morning, for a long while.

And his hair, the colour of a grebe's plumage, his slender knees, his slow-breathing chest, marked with two dark brown specks, the whole of that tall body where I have made so many exciting discoveries! I often tell him, sincerely: "I do think you're marvellous to look at!" He holds me very tight and says: "Claudine, Claudine, I'm old!" And his eyes darken with such poignant regret that I stare at him, uncomprehending.

"Ah! Claudine, if I'd known you ten years ago!"

"You'd have known the inside of a law-court if you had! Besides, you were only a young man then, a horrid, filthy brute of a young man who made women cry, while I . . ."

"*You* wouldn't have known Luce."

"Do you imagine I regret her?"

"At this very moment, no . . . don't shut your eyes, I implore you, I forbid you to. . . . That look in them belongs to me . . ."

"So does my whole self!"

My whole self? No. That is the flaw.

I have evaded this certainty as long as I could. I hoped so ardently that Renaud's will would curb mine, that his tenacity would eventually overcome my fits of rebellion; in short, that his character would match the expression of his eyes, accustomed to command and to fascinate. Renaud's will, Renaud's tenacity! He is suppler than a flame, just as burning, just as flickering; he envelopes me without dominating me. Alas! Are you to remain your own mistress for ever, Claudine?

All the same, he knows how to subjugate my slim, golden body, this skin that clings to my muscles and refuses to obey the pressure of hands, this little girl's head with the hair cut like a little boy's. . . . Why do they have to lie, his dominating eyes, his stubborn nose and his attractive, clean-shaven chin that he displays as coquettishly as a woman?

I am gentle with him, and I make myself small; I bend my neck meekly under his kisses; I demand nothing and I avoid any kind of argument in the virtuous fear of seeing him give in to me at once and smiling a too-facile *yes* with his good-natured mouth. He has no. authority except when he is making love.

I realise that, at least, is something.

I told him about Luce, every single detail, almost in the hope of seeing him frown and get angry and ply me with furious questions. . . . Oh dear no, not at all! On the contrary, even. He plied me with questions, yes, but not furious ones. And I cut short my answers because my mind was harking back to his son, Marcel (it irritated me to remember how that boy too used to harass me with questions), but certainly not out of defiance. For, if I have not found my master, I have found my friend and ally.

All this hotch-potch of feelings would get short shrift from Papa. Contemptuous of the psychological mix-ups of a daughter who quibbled and dissected and pretended to be a complex person, his answer would be: "The bloody little fool's got a bee in her bonnet and nothing will stop it buzzing!"

My admirable father! Since my marriage, I haven't thought enough about him, or about Fanchette. But, for months, Renaud has loved me too much, taken me about too much, made me too drunk with landscapes, too dazed with movement and new skies and unknown towns. . . . Little knowing his Claudine, he has often smiled in amazement at seeing me more impressed by a landscape than by a picture, more excited by a tree than by a museum, or by a river than a jewel. He had a great deal to teach me and I have learnt a great deal.

Sexual pleasure appeared to me like some overwhelming, almost sombre marvel. When Renaud, seeing me suddenly still and serious, would question me anxiously, I turned red and answered, without looking at him: "I can't tell you. . . ." And I would be forced to explain myself without words to that redoubtable questioner who battens on looking at me, who watches every nuance of shame on my face and finds exquisite pleasure in heightening it.

It would seem that for him—and I feel this is what separates us—sexual pleasure is made up of desire, perversity, lively curiosity and deliberate licentiousness. To him pleasure is something gay and lenient and facile, whereas it shatters me and plunges me into a mysterious despair that I seek and also fear. When Renaud is already smiling as he lies panting beside me, no longer holding me in his arms, I am still hiding my terrified eyes and my ecstatic mouth in my hands, however much he tries to stop me. It is only a little while after that I go and huddle up against his reassuring shoulder and complain to my friend of the too-delicious pain my lover has caused me.

Sometimes, I try to persuade myself that perhaps love is still too new to me, whereas, for Renaud, it has lost its bitterness. I doubt if this is true. We shall never think the same about love, apart from the great affection that drew us together and still binds us.

In a restaurant, the other night, he smiled at a slim, dark woman who was dining alone and whose beautiful made-up eyes responded willingly.

"Do you know her?"

"Who? The lady? No, darling. But she's got a very pretty figure, don't you think?"

"Is that the only reason why you're looking at her?"

"Of course, my precious child. That doesn't shock you, I trust?"

"No, not a bit. Only . . . I don't like her smiling at you."

"Oh, Claudine!" he pleaded, putting his swarthy face close to me. "Do let me go on believing that people can still look at your old husband without repulsion; he so much needs to have a little self-confidence!" He added, tossing his fine, light hair, "The day when women stop looking at me at all, there'll be nothing for me but to . . ."

"But whatever does it matter about other women? Because *I* shall always love you."

"Hush, Claudine," he cut in deftly. "Heaven preserve me from seeing you become a unique monstrosity!"

There you are! Talking of me, he says *women*; do I say *men* when I'm thinking of him? Oh, I know the answer. The habit of living in the public eye and having constant illicit love-affairs affects a man, subjects him to humiliating worries unknown to little brides of nineteen.

I could not resist saying spitefully:

"No wonder Marcel's like a flirtatious girl who can't live without admiration. He's obviously inherited your temperament."

"Oh, Claudine! Don't you like my defects?" he asked a little sadly. "Certainly, I can't see where else he got them from. . . . At least, you must admit that I exploit my charms for less perverse reasons than he does!"

How quickly he switched back to light-hearted frivolity! I believe that, had he answered me sharply, knitting those beautiful eye-brows, like the velvet lining of a ripe chestnut-burr, "That's enough, Claudine. Marcel doesn't come into this," I should have begun to feel a great joy and a little of that timid respect that I want to feel for Renaud and cannot.

Rightly or wrongly, I need to respect, to be a little afraid of the man I love. I was a stranger to fear for as long as I was a stranger to love and I should have liked both to have come together.

My memories of the past fifteen months mill about in my head like specks of dust in a dark room barred by one shaft of sunshine. One after the other they pass into the beam, glitter there for a second while I smile or pout at them, then go back into the shadow.

When I returned to France, three months ago, I wanted to see Montigny again. But this deserves what Luce calls commencing at the beginning.

Eighteen months ago, Mélie hastened to announce loudly and triumphantly to Montigny that I was getting married "to ever such a fine man, a bit on the old side, but still good and lusty".

Papa despatched a few printed announcements at random, one of them to Darjeau the carpenter "because he made a devilish good job of the packing cases for my books". And I myself sent two, with the addresses inscribed in my best handwriting, to Mademoiselle Sergent and to her disgusting little Aimée. This earned me a somewhat unexpected letter.

"My dear child," wrote back Mademoiselle Sergent, "I am sincerely happy" (keep a straight face, Claudine!) "about this marriage of affection" (her language goes beyond the bounds of decency) "which will be a sure safeguard against a slightly dangerous independence. Do not forget that the School eagerly awaits a visit from you, should you return, as I hope, to see a part of the country that so many memories must have endeared to your heart."

This final irony was blunted by the universal kindliness I felt for everything and everyone just then. All that persisted in my mind was amused surprise and the desire to see Montigny again—oh, woods that had enchanted me!—with sadder, more sophisticated eyes.

And, as we were returning from Germany via Switzerland last September, I begged Renaud to agree to break our journey and spend twenty-four hours with me in the very heart of Fresnois, at Montigny's mediocre inn, Lange's in the Place de L'Horloge.

He consented at once, as he always consents.

To re-live those days, I have only to close my eyes for a minute.

In the slow train that pottered irresolutely through that green, undulating countryside, I thrilled at the well-known names of the deserted little stations. Good heavens! After Blégeau and Saint-Farcy, it would be Montigny and I should see the ruined tower. . . . I was so excited that my calves prickled with nerves: I stood up in the compartment, clutching the cloth arm-straps with both hands. Renaud, who was watching me, with his travelling-cap pulled down over his eyes, came and joined me at the window.

"Darling bird, are you fluttered at getting so near your old nest? . . . Claudine, do answer. . . . I'm jealous . . . I don't like seeing you so tensely silent except in my arms."

I reassured him with a smile, and once again I scanned the forest-fleeced back of the hills as they fled whirling past.

"Ah!"

With my outstretched finger, I pointed to the tower, its crumbling red-brown stone draped with ivy, and to the village that cascades below it and looks as if it were pouring out of it. The sight of it gave me such a fierce, sweet pain that I leant on Renaud's shoulder. . . .

Broken summit of the tower, mass of round-headed trees, how could I ever have left you? And must I feast my eyes on you only to go away and leave you again?

I threw my arms round my husband's neck; it was to him I must look now for my strength and my motive for living. It was for him to enchant me, to hold me fast; that was what I hoped, that was what I wanted.

The gate-keeper's little pink house at the level-crossing whisked by, then the goods station—I recognised the foreman!—and we jumped out on the platform. Renaud had already put the suitcase and my handbag into the one and only omnibus while I was still standing rooted to the spot, silently registering the humps and the holes and the landmarks of the beloved, shrunken horizon. There, right above us, was the Fredonnes wood that joins up with the Vallées one . . . that yellow, sandy serpent is the path to Vrimes, how narrow it was! And it would no longer take me over to see the girl who made her First Communion with me, my delicious Claire. Oh! They had cut down the Corbeaux wood without my permission! Now you could see its rough skin, all bare. . . . Joy, joy, to see Quail Mountain again, blue and misty: on sunny days it was clothed in a rainbow haze but you can see it close and clear when it's going to rain. It is full of fossil shells and purple thistles and harsh, sapless flowers and haunted by little butterflies with pearly blue wings, tortoiseshells speckled with orange half-moons like orchids, and heavy Camberwell beauties in dark, gilded velvet. . . .

"Claudine! Don't you think sooner or later, we'll have to face climbing into this bone-shaking contraption?" asked Renaud, who was laughing at my blissful stupor.

I got into the bus with him. Nothing had changed; old Racalin was drunk, as in the old days. Immutably drunk, he sent his creaking vehicle lurching from one ditch to another with authoritative self-assurance.

I scrutinised every hedge, every turning, ready to protest if they had touched *my* country. I said nothing, not another word, till we reached the first tumbledown cottages at the bottom of the steep slope, and then I exclaimed:

"But the cats won't be able to sleep in Bardin's hayloft any more. There's a new door!"

"'Pon my soul, you're right," agreed Renaud, impressed. "That brute of a Bardin's had a new door put in!"

My previous dumbness burst into a spate of gay, idiotic chatter.

"Renaud, Renaud, look quick, we're going to go right past the gate of the castle! It's deserted; we'll see the tower in a minute: Oh, there's old Madame Sainte-Albe on her doorstep! I'm sure she saw me; she'll go and tell the whole street . . . quick, quick turn round; there, those two tree-tops above old Madame Adolphe's roof, they're the big fir-trees in the garden, *my* fir-trees, my very own ones. . . .

They've haven't grown; that's good. . . . Who on earth's that girl I don't know?"

Apparently I asked this last in a tone of such comical asperity that Renaud roared with laughter and displayed all his white, square teeth. But there were snags ahead; we had got to spend the night under Lange's roof and my husband might well laugh less light-heartedly up there, in the gloomy inn. . . .

Mercifully, it was all right! He found the room tolerable, in spite of the tent-shaped bed-curtains, the minute wash-basin and the coarse sheets that were greyish, but, thank heaven, very clean.

Renaud, excited by the poverty of the setting, by all the childishness that Montigny brought out in Claudine, flung his arms round me from behind and tried to pull me on to the bed. But I wouldn't let him . . . the time would pass too quickly.

"Renaud, Renaud, dear, it's six o'clock. *Please* come over to the School and let's give Mademoiselle a surprise before dinner!"

"Alas!" he sighed, anything but resigned. "That's what comes of marrying a stuck-up little child of nature—she deceives you with a country town numbering 1,847 inhabitants!"

A dab of the brush on my short hair (the dry air made it light and fluffy), an uneasy glance in the mirror—had I aged in eighteen months?—and we were outside in the Place de L'Horloge. It is so steep that, on market days, any number of little stalls find it impossible to keep their balance, turn *oopsidaisy* and collapse with a tremendous clatter.

Thanks to my husband, thanks to my shorn locks (feeling a trifle jealous of myself, I thought of the long chestnut ringlets that used to dance well below my waist), nobody recognised me and I was able to take it all in at leisure.

"Oh, Renaud, just imagine, that woman with a baby in her arms, that's Célénie Nauphely!"

"The one who used to suck her sister's milk?"

"None other. Now she's the one who's being sucked. Lawks a mercy, did you ever! It's disgusting!"

"Why disgusting?"

"I don't know. Little Madame Chou has still got the same peppermints in her shop. Perhaps she doesn't sell any more now that Luce has gone . . ."

The main street—nearly ten feet wide—runs down so steeply that Renaud asked where they sold alpenstocks here. But Claudine danced on, her straw boater over one eye, dragging him along by his little finger. As the two strangers passed by, the doorways filled with familiar and rather malevolent faces; I could put a name to all of them, check up all their wrinkles and blemishes.

"I'm living in a drawing by Huard," declared Renaud.

An angrily exaggerated Huard, he might even have said. I had not remembered that the slope of the whole village was so abrupt and steep, or the streets so flinty, or old Sandré's hunting costume so aggressively warlike. . . . Had the aged Lourd really been as smiling and drooling in his dotage when I saw him last? At the corner of the Rue Bel-Air, I stopped and laughed out loud:

"Good Lord! Madame Armand is still wearing her curl-papers! She twists them up at night when she goes to bed, forgets to take them out in the morning and then it's too late, it's not worth the bother, so she keeps them in the following night. Next morning, the same thing happens and so it goes on. I've never seen her without them, writhing like worms on her greasy forehead! . . . For ten years, Renaud, just here, where these three streets meet, I used to admire a wonderful man called Hébert who was Mayor of Montigny, though he could hardly sign his name. He used to attend all the Council meetings, nodding his fine official head—he had a red face and almost white flaxen hair—and making speeches that have remained famous. For example: 'To make a gutter in the Rue des Fours-Baneaux? *Tattistykestion*, as the English say.' Between sessions he used to stand here at the crossroads, looking purple in winter and scarlet in summer, and observing—what? Nothing! It was his entire occupation. He died of it. . . ."

My husband's indulgent laugh was growing a trifle strained. Was he beginning to find me a bore? No; he was only feeling a jealous resentment at seeing me completely reabsorbed in the past.

And then, at the bottom of the hill, the street opened out into a roughly cobbled square. A stone's-throw away, behind iron-grey railings, loomed the huge square block of the slate-roofed School, its whiteness hardly soiled by three winters and four summers.

"Claudine, is that the barracks?"

"No, of course not! It's the School!"

"Poor kids . . ."

"Why 'poor kids'? I assure you we were anything but bored there."

"*You* weren't, you little she-devil. But the others! Are we going in? Is one allowed to visit the prisoners at any time?"

"Wherever were you brought up, Renaud? Don't you know that this is the holidays?"

"No! You mean to say you dragged me here just to see this empty gaol? Was that the exciting prospect all the throbbing and panting was about, you fussy little steam-engine?"

"You lumbering old push-cart!" I said triumphantly. A year of foreign travel has been enough to enrich my native vocabulary with "typically Parisian" insults.

"Suppose I deprived you of pudding?"

"Suppose I put you on a diet?"

Suddenly serious, I fell silent. As I put my hand on the latch of the heavy iron gate, I had felt it resist, just as in the old days. . . .

By the pump in the courtyard, the little rusty mug—the same one—hung from its chain. Two years ago, the walls had been all white and chalky; now they were scratched, shoulder-high, as if by the nails of restive prisoners. But the thin grass of the summer holidays was pushing up between the bricks of the gutter.

Not a soul in sight.

With Renaud following meekly behind me, I climbed the little flight of six steps, opened a glass-topped door, and walked along the paved, echoing corridor that runs from the playground to the three downstairs classrooms. That gust of fetid coolness—hasty sweeping, ink, chalk-dust, blackboards washed with dirty sponges—stifled me with a very strange feeling. Surely at any moment, the importunate, loving little ghost of Luce, in her black apron, would slip round the corner of the wall, swift and light on her rope-soled shoes, and bury her face in my skirts?

I gave a start and felt my cheeks quiver; swift and silent on rope-soled shoes, a little ghost in a black apron was pushing open the playground door. . . . But no, it was not Luce; a pretty little face that I had never seen before was staring at me with limpid eyes. Reassured, and feeling almost at home, I went forward:

"Mmmzelle anywhere about?"

"I don't know, Mada . . . Mademoiselle. Upstairs, I expect."

"Right, thanks. But . . . aren't you on holiday?"

"I'm one of the boarders spending the summer holidays in Montigny."

She was utterly charming, the boarder spending the summer holidays in Montigny! Her chestnut plait fell forward over her black apron as she drooped her head, hiding a fresh, sweet mouth and reddish-brown eyes that were lovely rather than lively—the eyes of a doe watching a motor-car go by.

A biting voice (Oh! how well I recognised it) interrupted us from the staircase:

"Pomme, whoever are you talking to?"

"Somebody, Mmmzelle!" cried the innocent little thing, running off up the stairs that led to the private rooms and the dormitory.

I turned round to give Renaud a laughing look. He was interested, his nose was twitching.

"Hear that, Claudine? Pomme! Someone'll eat her up, with a name like that. Lucky I'm only an old gentleman past the age! . . ."

"Shut up, schoolgirl's dream! Someone's coming."

A rapid whispering, a brisk step coming downstairs, and Mademoiselle Sergent appeared. Dressed in black, her red hair blazing in the setting sun, she was so like herself that I wanted to bite her and fling myself round her neck for the sake of all the Past she brought back to me in that direct, black gaze of hers.

She paused for a couple of seconds; that was enough, she had seen everything; seen that I was Claudine, that my hair was cut short, that my eyes were bigger and my face smaller, that Renaud was my husband and that he was still (I could read her thoughts!) a fine figure of a man.

"Claudine! Oh! you haven't changed a bit. . . . Whyever didn't you warn me you were coming? How d'you do, Monsieur? Fancy this child not telling me a word about your visit! Don't you think she deserves two hundred lines as a punishment? Is she still as much of a young terror as ever? Are you quite sure she was fit to get married?"

"No, Mademoiselle, not at all sure. Only I hadn't enough time ahead of me and I wanted to avoid being married on my death-bed."

Things were going well; they'd "clicked"; they'd get on with each other. Mademoiselle likes handsome males, even if she doesn't make much use of them. I left them to enjoy each other's company.

While they were chatting, I went off to ferret about in the Senior Classroom, hunting for my desk, the one Luce used to share with me. I ended by discovering under all the spilt ink, under the new and old scars, the remains of an inscription cut with a knife . . . *uce* et *Claudi* . . . 15th February 189 . . .

Did I put my lips to it? I will not admit it. . . . Looking at it so close to, my mouth must have brushed that scarred wood. But, if I wanted to be absolutely truthful, I should say, now that I realise it, that I was very harsh in my repudiation of poor Luce's slavish affection. And I should say that it took me two years, a husband and the return to that school to understand the true worth of her humility, her freshness, and her gentle, frankly-offered perversity.

The voice of Mademoiselle Sergent roughly banished my dream.

"Claudine! I presume you've taken leave of your senses? Your husband informs me that your suitcases are over at Lange's!"

"Well, where else should they be? I couldn't leave my nightdress in the station cloakroom!"

"That's simply absurd! I've heaps of empty beds upstairs, not to mention Mademoiselle Lanthenay's room. . . ."

"What! Isn't Mademoiselle Aimée here?" I exclaimed, sounding far too surprised.

"Now, now, where's your head?"

She came close to me and ran her hand over my hair with thinly-veiled irony.

"During the summer holidays, Madame Claudine, the assistant mistresses return to their own homes."

Bother! And I'd been counting on the spectacle of the Sergent-Lanthenay *ménage* to edify and delight Renaud! I had imagined that even the holidays could not separate this exceptionally united couple. Ah, well, that little bitch of an Aimée wouldn't trail around long with her family! I understood now why Mademoiselle had welcomed us with such surprising affability; it was because Renaud and I were not disturbing any intimate scene . . . what a pity!

"Thank you for your offer, Mmmzelle; I'd be delighted to recover a little of my lost youth by spending the night at school. Who on earth is the little green apple—I mean that child Pomme—we met just now?"

"A noodle who's failed her oral in the elementary exams, after having asked for an exemption. An absurd business. The little fool's fifteen! She's spending her holidays here as a punishment, but otherwise she doesn't seem in the least upset. I've got two others like her upstairs, two girls from Paris rusticating here till October. . . . You'll see them all later . . . but come along first and get settled in. . . ."

She slipped me a sidelong look and asked in her most natural voice:

"Would you like to sleep in Mademoiselle Aimée's room?"

"I should love to sleep in Mademoiselle Aimée's room!"

Renaud followed us, alert now and enjoying himself. The crude chalk and charcoal drawings fixed to the passage wall with drawing-pins made his nostrils quiver with amusement and his moustache twitch ironically.

The favourite's bedroom! . . . It had been embellished since my time. That white bed for one and a half people, those Liberty draperies at the window, those mantelpiece ornaments (ugh!) in copper and alabaster, the shining order everywhere and the faint perfume that hovered in the folds of the curtains absorbed me so much I could think of nothing else.

When the door had closed behind Mademoiselle, Renaud turned to me.

"Why, my darling child," he said, "these staff bedrooms are very pleasant indeed! They quite reconcile me to your secular school."

I burst out laughing.

"Oh, my goodness me! You don't really imagine this is the official furniture? Come on, use your memory! I've told you at great length about Aimée and the part that flaunting favourite plays here. The other assistant mistress has to put up with a three-foot iron bedstead, a deal table and a basin I couldn't drown one of Fanchette's kittens in."

"Oh! Then you actually mean it's here, in this very room that . . ."

"Yes, of *course* it's here in this very room that . . ."

"Claudine, you can't imagine what a sensational effect this has on me, all that it conjures up. . . ."

Oh yes I could; I could imagine it only too well. But I remained resolutely blind and deaf and I studied the scandalous bed with distaste. It might be wide enough for them but not for us. I was going to suffer. Renaud would be unbearably close. I should be hot and I shouldn't be able to spread my legs. And there was that worn hollow in the middle, ugh!

It took the open window and the beloved landscape it framed to restore my good temper. The woods; the narrow, poor-soiled fields, all stubble after the harvest; the Pottery glowing red in the dusk. . . .

"Oh, Renaud, look—see that tiled roof over there! They make little glazed brown pots there and two-handled pitchers with indecent little tubular navels. . . ."

"Sort of peasant-ware pisspots? I know. Rather charming."

"Ages ago, when I was quite a little girl, I used to go and see some of the potters and they'd give me little brown pots and cider-mugs. And they used to tell me proudly, waving their hands all covered with wet clay, like gloves: 'It's us as does all the pottery for the Adrets' Inn in Paris.'"

"Really, my little curly shepherd-boy? Being an old man, I remember the place. I've drunk once or twice from those cider-mugs without realising that your slim fingers might have brushed against them. I love you. . . ."

A tumult of fresh voices and small, trampling feet drove us apart. The steps in the passage slowed down outside the door; the voices lowered to whisperings; there came two timid knocks.

"Come in!"

Pomme appeared, flushed and overwhelmed with her own importance.

"It's us, with your bags. Old Racalin's just brought these over from Lange's."

Behind her was a cluster of black aprons; a red-haired child of about ten with a quaint, amusing little face, and a brunette of fourteen or fifteen with an ivory skin and black, luminous, liquid eyes. Frightened by my stare, she shrank aside, disclosing another brunette of the same age, with the same eyes and the same ivory skin. . . . How amusing! I caught hold of her sleeve:

"How many copies of this model are there?"

"Only two. She's my sister."

"I had a sort of vague suspicion she might be. . . . You don't come from these parts, I realise that."

"Oh no! . . . we live in Paris."

The tone, the little half-suppressed smile of disdainful superiority on the curved mouth—honestly, she was delicious enough to eat!

Pomme was dragging the heavy suitcase. Renaud relieved her of it with zealous eagerness.

"Pomme, how old are you?"

"Fifteen and two months, Monsieur."

"You're not married, Pomme?"

They all burst out laughing like clucking hens! Pomme split her sides artlessly; the dark-haired, white-skinned sisters managed their mirth more elegantly. And the little thing of ten, buried in her carroty hair, was definitely going to make herself ill with laughing. Splendid! Here was my school, just as I'd always known it!"

"Pomme," went on Renaud, without moving a muscle, "I'm sure you like sweets!"

Pomme gazed at him with her reddish-brown eyes as if she were yielding up her soul to him.

"Oh yes, Monsieur!"

"Good, I'll go and get some. Don't bother, darling. I'll find them perfectly well on my own."

I remained with the little girls, who scanned the passage nervously, terrified of getting caught in the lady's bedroom. I wanted them to feel relaxed and at home.

"What are your names, you little black-and-white ones?"

"Hélène Jousserand, Madame."

"Isabelle Jousserand, Madame."

"Don't call me Madame, silly infants. I'm Claudine. You don't know who Claudine is, do you?"

"Oh, yes we do!" cried Hélène (the younger and prettier). "Mademoiselle always tells us, when we've done something naughty. . . ."

Her sister nudged her; she stopped.

"Go on, go on. You intrigue me! Don't listen to your sister."

"All right, then; she says: 'My word, it's enough to make me wash my hands of the whole place! Anyone would think we were back in the days of Claudine!' Or else: '*That*, young ladies, is worthy of Claudine!'"

I broke into an exultant "goat-dance."

"What luck! *I'm* the scarecrow, *I'm* the monster, the legendary terror! . . . Am I as ugly as you expected me to be?"

"Oh no," said little Hélène, tenderly and shyly, quickly veiling her soft eyes behind a double fence of lashes.

The caressing spirit of Luce haunted this house. It was possible, too, there were other examples. . . . I'd make them talk, these two little girls. We must get the other one out of the way.

"I say, you, go and look outside in the passage and see if I'm there."

The red-head, devoured with curiosity, looked sullen and refused to budge.

"Nana, will you do as the lady tells you!" cried Hélène Jousserand, quite pink with fury. "Listen, old thing, if you stay in here, I'll tell Mademoiselle that you take letters from the girl who shares your desk over to the boys' playground. All for filthy bribes in the shape of chocolates!"

The little girl had already vanished. With my arms round the shoulders of the two sisters, I looked at them from close to. Hélène was the more charming, Isabelle the more serious; she had a barely visible down of moustache that would be troublesome later on.

"Hélène, Isabelle, is it a long time since Mademoiselle Aimée went away?"

"It's . . . twelve days," replied Hélène.

"Thirteen," corrected Isabelle.

"Tell me, just between us, does she still get on well, *very* well with Mademoiselle?"

Isabelle blushed, Hélène smiled.

"Right. I don't need to ask any more. That's how things were in my time; this . . . friendship . . . has lasted three years, my children!"

"Oh!" they exclaimed simultaneously.

"Exactly, it's about two years since I left the School, and I saw them together for a whole year . . . a year I'm not likely to forget . . . And, do tell me, is she still pretty, that loathsome little Lanthenay?"

"Yes," said Isabelle.

"Not as pretty as you," murmured Hélène, who was beginning to eat out of my hand.

By way of caress, I dug my nails into the nape of her neck, as I used to do to Luce. She did not blink. The atmosphere of this School where I could still assert my power intoxicated me.

Pomme, her arms dangling and her mouth half-open, listened affably, but without real interest. Her mind was elsewhere. Every other second, she leant forward to look through the window and see whether the sweets were coming.

I wanted to know more.

"Hélène, Isabelle, tell me a little of the School news. Who are the seniors in the First Division now?"

"There's . . . Liline, and Mathilde."

"*No!* Already? Yes, of course, it's two years . . . Is Liline still good-looking? I used to call her the Gioconda. Her green and grey eyes, that silent mouth with the tight corners . . ."

"Oh!" broke in Hélène, pouting her moist pink lips. "She's not as beautiful as all that—anyway, not this year."

"Don't you believe her," Isabelle-the-Downy snapped very quickly. "She's the best-looking of them all."

"Coo! Everyone knows why you say that *and* why Mademoiselle won't let you sit next to each other at the evening class any more, even though you're mugging up the same book!"

The elder one's lovely eyes filled with bright tears.

"Will you let your sister alone, you little pest! And you needn't put on that saintly air either! After all, this child's only imitating the example set by Mademoiselle and Aimée. . . ."

Inwardly, I was delirious with joy; things were going well, the School had made considerable progress! In my time, Luce was the only one who wrote me love-letters; Anaïs herself had got no further than boys. How charming they were, this new lot! If Doctor Dutertre still carried on his job as Regional Inspector, he had nothing to complain of.

Our group was worth looking at. A brunette to the right, a brunette to the left, Claudine's curly, excited head in the middle, and that fresh Pomme innocently contemplating us . . . bring on the old gentlemen! When I say "the old gentlemen" . . . I know some, who, though still young . . . It would not be long before Renaud returned.

"Pomme, do go and look out of the window and see if the gentleman with the sweets is coming! . . . Is her name really Pomme?" I asked my pretty Hélène, who was leaning trustfully against my shoulder.

"Yes; her name's Marie Pomme; she's always called 'Pomme'."

"Not exactly a brilliant genius, eh?"

"Goodness gracious, no! But she doesn't make a nuisance of herself and she agrees with everybody."

I went off into a daydream, and they stared at me. Like reassured little animals they investigated everything about me with curious eyes and light paws. "It curls naturally, doesn't it?" they asked, touching my short hair. Fingering my white buckskin belt, a hand's-breadth wide, with its dull gold buckle, a present—like everything I have—from Renaud, one cried: "There, you see! *You* insisted broad belts weren't being worn any more." They studied my stiffly starched butterfly collar, my pale blue linen blouse with its broad tucks. . . . Time was slipping by . . . I realised that I was leaving tomorrow; that all this was a brief dream; that I was jealous of a present that was already my past and wanted to leave a mark on it. I wanted to imprint a sweet and searing memory on something or on somebody. . . . I tightened my arm about Hélène's shoulder and whispered almost inaudibly:

"If I were your school friend, little Hélène, would you love me as much as your sister loves Liline?"

Her Spanish eyes, with their drooping corners, opened wide, as if almost frightened: then the thick lashes were lowered and I felt her shoulders stiffen.

"I don't know yet. . . ."

That was enough; *I* knew.

Pomme, over at the window, burst into shrieks of joy: "Bags and bags! He's got simply *sacks* of them!"

After this explosion, Renaud's entrance was greeted with a reverent silence. He had bought everything Montigny's modest sweet-shop could provide: from chocolate creams to striped bull's-eyes and English sweets whose smell reminds you of sour cider.

All the same, such a quantity of sweets! . . . I wanted some too! Renaud, who had stopped in the doorway, gazed at our group for a minute with a smile—a smile I had sometimes seen on his face before—and at last took pity on the palpitating Pomme.

"Pomme, which do you like best?"

"All of them!" cried Pomme, intoxicated.

"Oh!" the other two exclaimed indignantly. "How *can* you!"

"Pomme," went on Renaud, bubbling over with pleasure, "I'll give you this bag here, if you'll kiss me. . . . You don't mind, Claudine?"

"Heavens, *I* don't care!"

Pomme hesitated for three seconds, torn between her furious greed and regard for the proprieties. Her frank, red-brown gaze wandered beseechingly to her hostile schoolmates, to me, to heaven, to the bags Renaud was holding out to her at arm's length. . . . Then, with the slightly foolish grace of her whole small person, she flung her arms round Renaud's neck, received the bag and went off, scarlet, to open it in a corner. . . .

I meanwhile was pillaging a box of chocolates, helped silently, but swiftly, by the pair of sisters. Hélène's small hand went to and from the box to her mouth, sure and indefatigable. . . . Who would have thought that little mouth could take in so much!

A shrill bell interrupted us and broke off Renaud's contemplative trance. The little girls fled in terror, without saying "Thank you", without even glancing at us, like thieving cats. . . .

Dinner in the refectory amused Renaud prodigiously, but I was slightly bored by it. The uncertain hour, the purple twilight I could feel thickening and falling on the woods . . . I escaped, in spite of myself. . . . But my dear man was so happy! Ah, how craftily Mademoiselle had found the right way to rouse his curiosity! Sitting beside Renaud, in this white room, at the table covered with white oilcloth, opposite those pretty little girls, still in their black aprons, who were fiddling disgustedly with their boiled beef after their orgy of sweets, Mademoiselle talked about me. She talked about me, lowering her voice now and then, because of the pricked-up ears the two little Jousserands were straining in our direction. Wearily, I listened and smiled.

"She was a terrible tomboy, Monsieur, and, for a long time, I didn't know what to do with her. From fourteen to fifteen, she spent most of her time twenty feet above ground and her sole preoccupation appeared to be to display her legs right up to her eyes. I've sometimes seen her show the cruelty children show to grown-up people." (*That was a good one!* . . .) "She's remained just what she was, a delicious little girl. Although she didn't like me at all, I used to enjoy watching her move . . . such suppleness, such precision of movement. The staircase that leads to this room—I've never seen her come down it except astride the banisters. Monsieur, what an example to the others!"

The perfidiousness of that motherly tone ended up by amusing me and by kindling a well-known dark and dangerous light in Renaud's eyes. He looked at Pomme, but what he was seeing was Claudine, Claudine at fourteen and her legs displayed "up to the eyes" (up to the eyes, Mademoiselle! The tone of the establishment has risen considerably since I left it). He looked at Hélène and saw Claudine astride a banister rail, Claudine cheeky and defiant, blotched with purple ink-stains. It would be a warm night. And he burst into a nervous laugh when Mademoiselle turned away from him to exclaim: "Pomme, if you take salt with your fingers again, I shall make you copy out five pages of Blanchet!"

Little Hélène was very silent; she kept trying to catch my eye and avoiding it when she succeeded. Her sister Isabelle was decidedly less pretty; that shadow of a moustache, now that it was no longer silvered by daylight, made her look like a child that has not wiped its mouth properly.

"Mademoiselle," said Renaud, coming to with a start, "will you authorise a distribution of sweets tomorrow morning?"

The voracious little red-head, who had licked all the plates clean and eaten up all the crusts during dinner, let out a little yelp of greed. No! said the contemptuous eyes of the three big ones, who were already gorged with sticky filth.

"I authorise it," replied Mademoiselle. "They don't deserve anything; they're a lot of ticks. But the circumstances are so exceptional! Well, come along, aren't you going to say thank you, little sillies? Have you lost your tongues? . . . Off to bed with you now! It's nearly nine o'clock."

"Oh, Mmmzelle, may Renaud see the dormitory before the kids go to bed?"

"Kid yourself! Yes, he may," she conceded, rising from her chair. "And you, Miss Untidies, if I find one brush lying about!"

Grey-white, blue-white, yellow-white; the walls, the curtains, the narrow beds that looked like babies swaddled too tight. Renaud sniffed the peculiar smell in the air; the smell of healthy little girls and of sleep, the dry, peppery fragrance of marsh peppermint, a bunch of which hung from the ceiling; his subtle nose analysed, savoured and took it all in. Mademoiselle, from force of habit, thrust a redoubtable hand under the bolsters in search of booty to confiscate—a half-nibbled tablet of chocolate or an instalment of a forbidden book, serialised in ten-centime paper-backs.

"Did you ever sleep here?" Renaud asked me, very low, drumming his burning fingers on my shoulders.

Mademoiselle's sharp ear had caught the question and she forestalled my reply.

"Claudine? Never in her life! And I'm extremely glad she didn't. Whatever state should we have found the dormitory in next day—not to mention the boarders!"

"Not to mention the boarders"—she had actually said that! It was the giddy limit! My modesty was up in arms. I just could not tolerate these broad hints any longer. High time we got off to bed.

"Seen everything you want to see, Renaud?"

"Everything."

"Then let's go to bed."

There was much whispering as we turned to go. I could guess pretty well what the little brunettes were muttering: "I say, is she going to sleep with the gentleman in Mademoiselle Aimée's bed? . . . First time it's ever had even one man in it, Mademoiselle Aimée's bed!"

The sooner we got away, the better. I flashed a smile at little Hélène, who was plaiting her hair for the night, her chin on her shoulder. More than ever, I wanted to be gone.

The cramped, light bedroom, the lamp that gave out too much heat, the pure blue of the night through the window; a cat creeping like a little velvet ghost along the dangerous window-ledge.

The reviving ardour of my lord and master, who had been titillated all the evening by too-youthful Claudines, the nervous excitement that drew the corners of his mouth into a horizontal smile . . .

My own brief slumber, lying on my stomach with my hands clasped behind my back "like a bound captive", as Renaud says . . .

The dawn that drew me from bed to stand at the window in my nightdress, so as to see the mist sailing over the woods up by Moutiers, so as to hear the little anvil at Choucas from closer to. It rang that morning, as it had rung all those other mornings, a clear G sharp. . . .

Every detail of that night is still clear in my mind.

In the school, nothing was stirring yet; it was only six o'clock. But Renaud woke up because he could no longer feel me there in the bed; he listened to the blacksmith's silvery hammering and unconsciously whistled a motif from *Siegfried*. . . .

He is not ugly in the morning, and that after all is a great asset in a man. Invariably, he begins by combing his hair over to the left with his fingers, then he flings himself on the water-jug and drinks a huge glass of water. This is quite beyond me! How can anyone drink something cold first thing in the morning? And, since I don't like it, how can *he* possibly like it?

"Claudine, what time are we leaving?"

"I don't know. So soon?"

"So soon. You aren't truly mine in this place. You're unfaithful to me with all the sounds and the smells, all the old, remembered faces; there isn't a tree that doesn't possess you. . . ."

I laughed. But I did not make any reply, because I thought there was some truth in his accusation. And, besides, I no longer have my home here. . . .

"We'll leave at two."

Reassured, Renaud looked thoughtfully at the candies piled up on the table.

"Claudine, suppose we go and wake the little girls up with the sweets? What do you think?"

"Let's! Only, suppose Mademoiselle sees us . . ."

"Afraid she'll punish you with two hundred lines?"

"'Course not. . . . And, anyway, it'd be lots more fun if she caught us!"

"Oh, Claudine! How I love your schoolgirl soul! Come and let me bury my nose in you, dear little reopened exercise-book."

"Ouch! You're crumpling my covers, Renaud! . . . And Mademoiselle will be up, if we don't hurry . . ."

Laden with sweets, we walked silently along the passage, he in his blue pyjamas, I in my long, white billowing nightdress with my hair over my eyes. I listened outside the dormitory door before going in. . . . Not a sound. They were as silent as little corpses. I opened the door very softly. . . .

How *could* those wretched little girls sleep in broad daylight, with that sun blazing through the white curtains!

Promptly, I searched for Hélène's bed: her charming little face was buried in the pillow and all one could see was her black plait, like an uncoiled serpent. Next to her, her sister Isabelle lay flat on her back, her long lashes on her cheeks, wearing a virtuous, absorbed expression. Further on, the red-headed kid, sprawled like a dropped puppet, an arm here, an arm there, her mouth open and her red mop standing out like a halo, was snoring gently. . . . But Renaud was staring chiefly at Pomme, Pomme who had been too hot, and was curled up like a dog on the outside of her bed, muffled in her long-sleeved nightdress, her head level with her knees and her charming little round behind thrust out. . . . She had plaited her hair in a tight rope and plastered it smooth like a Chinese girl's; she had one pink cheek and one red one and her mouth and her fists were closed.

They were a charming sight, all of them! The standard of looks in the School had definitely gone up! In my time, the boarders would have inspired chastity even in that notorious "fumbler", Dutertre. . . .

Finding them as attractive as I did, and in another way, too, Renaud went up close to Pomme's bed—she was quite definitely his favourite—and dropped a large green pistachio fondant on her smooth cheek. The cheek quivered, the hands opened and the charming little muffled behind shifted.

"Good morning, Pomme."

The red-brown eyes opened roundly in startled welcome. Pomme sat up, still dazed. But her hand clapped down on the harsh green sweet. Pomme said "Oh!" swallowed it down like a cherry and exclaimed:

"Good morning, Monsieur."

At the sound of her clear voice and my laugh, the sheets on Hélène's bed rippled, the tail of the uncoiled serpent swished, and, darker than a blackcap, Hélène suddenly sat up. Sleep was difficult to shake off; she stared at us, trying to connect up today's thoughts with yesterday's; then her amber cheeks turned pink. Dishevelled and charming, she pushed back a big, obstinate lock that fell across her little nose. Then she had a good view of Pomme, sitting up, with her mouth full.

"Ah!" she squeaked in turn. "She'll go and eat the lot."

Her squeal, her outstretched arm, and her childish anguish enchanted me. I went and squatted cross-legged on the foot of her bed, which made her draw her feet up under her and blush still more.

Her sister yawned, mumbled and put up modest hands to where the ample nightdress had come a little unbuttoned. And the carrot-headed kid, Nana, moaned covetously at the far end of the room, twisting her arms with longing . . . for Pomme, conscientious and indefatigable, was eating more and still more sweets.

"Renaud, it's cruel! Pomme is a bundle of charms, I don't deny it, but do give Hélène and the others some sweets too!"

Solemnly, he nodded his head and moved away.

"Right! Now, listen to me, all of you! I'm not giving anybody one single more sweet" . . . (palpitating silence) . . . "unless she comes and gets it."

They looked at each other in consternation. But little Nana had already thrust her stocky little legs out of bed and was examining her feet to see if they were clean enough to be presentable. Swiftly, holding up her long nightdress so as not to stumble, she ran up to Renaud on her bare feet that went flic, flac on the wooden floor. With her tousled head, she looked like a child on a Christmas card. Then, catching tight hold of the full bag Renaud threw her, she went back to her bed like a contented dog.

Pomme could stand it no longer and sprang out of bed in turn. Heedless of a plump calf, gilded for a second by the sun, she ran to Renaud, who held the coveted fondants high above her head:

"Oh," she wept, too little to reach them. *"Please,* Monsieur!"

And then, since this had been successful last night, she flung her arms round Renaud's neck and kissed him. It was highly successful today as well. This game was beginning to irritate me. . . .

"Go on, Hélène," muttered Isabelle, furious.

"Go on yourself! You're the bigger. *And* the greedier too."

"That's not true?"

"Oh, it isn't true, isn't it? All right, then. I'm not going. Pomme will eat the lot. . . . I jolly well wish she'd be sick, just to teach her. . . ."

At the thought of Pomme eating the lot, Isabelle jumped to the floor while I held Hélène back by her slim ankle, through the sheet.

"Don't go, Hélène. *I'll* give you some."

Isabelle returned triumphant. But, as she was hurriedly climbing back into her bed, the shrill voice of Nana was heard yapping:

"Isabelle's got hair on her legs! Her legs are all over hair!"

"Indecent little beast!" cried the accused. By now she was huddled up under the sheets, leaving only her shining, angry eyes visible. She reviled and threatened Nana, then her voice turned hoarse and she collapsed on her bolster in tears.

"There, Renaud! Now look what you've done!"

He laughed so loud, the mischievous fiend, that he dropped the last paper-bag on the floor and it burst.

"I'll pick them up for you. What can I put them into?" I asked my little Hélène.

"I don't know. I haven't anything here—ah, I know, my basin, the third one on the wash-stand. . . ."

I put all those multicoloured horrors into the enamel basin and took it over to her.

"Renaud, do just look out into the passage. Didn't I hear footsteps?"

And I remained seated on my little Hélène's bed while she sucked and nibbled and glanced at me stealthily. While I smiled at her, she promptly blushed, then plucked up courage and smiled back. She had a moist, white smile that looked fresh and appetising.

"What are you laughing at, Hélène?"

"I'm looking at your nightdress. You look a bit like a boarder, only it's linen—no, batiste, isn't it?—and you can see through it."

"But I am a boarder! Don't you believe me?"

"No, of course not . . . but it's such a pity you aren't."

Things were going well. I moved closer.

"Do you like me?"

"Yes . . . awfully," she whispered. It sounded like a sigh.

"Will you kiss me?"

"No," she protested fiercely, in a very low, almost frightened voice.

I leant forward very close and said:

"No? I know those *noes* that mean *yes*. I've said them myself in the old days. . . ."

Her imploring eyes indicated the other girls. But I felt so mischievous and so curious! And I was just going to tease her again, at even closer quarters . . . when the door opened and Renaud entered, followed by Mademoiselle in a dressing-gown. Whatever am I saying? In a house-coat, with her hair already done to face the public gaze.

"Well, Madame Claudine, do you find the boarders tempting?"

"I must say there'd be some excuse for being tempted this year."

"Only *this* year? How marriage has altered my Claudine! . . . Come along, young ladies, do you know it's nearly eight o'clock? At a quarter to nine, I shall look under the beds, and, if I find the least thing, I shall make you sweep it up with your tongues!"

We left the dormitory with her.

"Mademoiselle, will you forgive us for this double invasion at this hour of the morning?"

Amiable and ambiguous, she answered in a low voice:

"Oh, well, in the holidays! And, as for your husband, I like to see it as a charming piece of indulgence, entirely paternal."

I shall not forgive her for that word.

I remember the walk before lunch, the pilgrimage I wanted to make to the threshold of "my" house of the old days which that hateful sojourn in Paris had made dearer to me than ever. I remember the clutch at my heart that kept me standing motionless before the double flight of steps with their blackened iron railings that led to the front door. I stared fixedly at the worn copper ring I used to tug at to peal the bell when I came home from School; I stared at it so hard that I could feel it in my hand. And, as Renaud was gazing at the window of my bedroom, I looked up at him with eyes misty with tears.

"Let's go away. I can't bear it. . . ."

Overcome by my misery, he led me away in silence, my arm clutched tight against his. In my mind, I turned the knob of the ground-floor window shutter with my finger—I could not stop myself . . . and it was over.

It was over, and now I regretted having wanted to come back to Montigny, impelled by regrets, love and pride. Yes, by pride as well. I had wanted to show off my husband. . . . Was he really a husband, this paternal lover, this sensual protector? . . . I had wanted to cock a snook at Mademoiselle and at her absent Aimée. . . . And then—*that* would teach me—look at me now, nothing but an anguished little girl, no longer sure where I really belonged, my heart prostrate between two homes!

Entirely due to me, lunch was a thoroughly uncomfortable meal. Mademoiselle could not make out why I looked so distressed (neither could I); the little girls, sickened with sugary stuff, could not eat. Renaud was the only one who laughed, as he teased Pomme with questions.

"Do you say yes to everything you're asked, Pomme?"

"Yes, Monsieur."

"Pomme, I certainly don't pity the lucky man who will seek your favours, you round, pink apple. I foresee the happiest possible future for you, a future made up of fair shares for all and no quarrelling."

Then he glanced at Mademoiselle in case she might be annoyed, but she shrugged her shoulders and said, in reply to his look:

"Oh, it doesn't matter what you say to her, she never understands."

"Perhaps a practical demonstration would help?"

"You wouldn't have time before your train. Pomme never grasps anything till it's been explained four times, at the very least."

I made a sign to stop the outrageous thing my wicked wretch of a husband was going to retort; my little Hélène, who was listening with all her ears, was already on the alert for it. ("My little Hélène" was the name I had privately given her from the first.)

Goodbye to all that! For, while I was strapping up the suitcase, there was a clatter in the courtyard, punctuated by old Racalin's oaths. Goodbye!

I had loved—and I still loved—those echoing white corridors, that barracks with the pink-brick corners; I had loved the aversion inspired in me by Mademoiselle; I had loved her little Aimée, and Luce, who had never known that I did.

I stopped for a moment on that landing, with my hand on the cool wall.

Renaud, down below, beneath my feet, was having a private conversation (yet another!) with Pomme.

"Goodbye, Pomme."

"Goodbye, Monsieur."

"Will you write to me, Pomme?"

"I don't know your name."

"The excuse won't hold water. I'm called 'Claudine's Husband.' At least, you'll be sorry to see me go?"

"Yes, Monsieur."

"Especially on account of the sweets?"

"Oh, yes, Monsieur!"

"Pomme, your shameless candour inspires me with enthusiasm. Kiss me!"

Behind me, something rustled very softly. . . . My little Hélène was there. I turned round; she stood there, pretty and silent, a study in black and white; I smiled at her. She wanted very much to say something to me. But I knew it was too difficult and she could only gaze at me with lovely black-and-white eyes. Then as, down below, Pomme clasped herself round Renaud's neck with placid docility, I put one arm round this silent little girl who smelt of cedar-wood pencils and sandalwood fans. It was on her resilient mouth that I said goodbye to my youthful past. . . .

To my youthful past? . . . Here, at least, I might as well not lie. . . . Hélène, trembling and already passionate as she ran to the window to watch me go, you will never know something that would surprise and hurt you: what I kissed on your clinging, inexpert mouth was only the ghost of Luce. . . .

Before talking to Renaud, in the train that carried us away, I gave one last look at the tower, hooded over by a woolly mass of thickening storm-clouds; I watched it till it vanished behind the round back of a hill. Then, relieved, as if I had said goodbye to someone, I returned to my dear, frivolous man, who so as not to break the habit, was saying admiring things and holding me close and . . . but I interrupted him.

"Tell me, Renaud, is it awfully nice, kissing that Pomme?"

I looked earnestly into his eyes, without being able to see into the blue-black depths of them; it was like looking into a bottomless lake.

"That Pomme? Darling, you wouldn't be doing me the great honour of being jealous? Nothing would give me more intense pleasure!"

"Oh, don't think it's an honour! Pomme isn't my idea of an honourable victory."

"My slenderest, loveliest of girls, if you'd said: 'Don't kiss Pomme!' it wouldn't even have been any merit for me to have kept off her!"

Yes. He would do whatever I wanted. But he had not given a straight answer to my question: "Is it awfully nice, kissing that Pomme?" He is adept at never giving himself away, at sliding out of things, at smothering me with evasive tenderness.

He loves me, there is no doubt whatever of that, more than anything in the world. Thank God, I love him—that is certain too. But how much more feminine he is than I am! How much simpler I feel I am, how much more ruthless . . . more sombre . . . more passionate.

I expressly avoid saying: more upright. I could have said it a year and some months ago. At that time, I would not have given in so quickly to temptation, up there on the dormitory landing. I would not have kissed that young mouth, cold and moist as a split fruit, under the pretence of saying goodbye to my schoolgirl past, to my black-overalled childhood self. I would only have kissed the desk over which Luce had bent her stubborn brow.

For a year and a half, I have been aware of the progress of the slow and pleasant corruption within myself that I owe to Renaud. When one looks at them through his eyes, big things grow small and all that is serious in life is reduced to triviality. On the other hand, futile trivialities, especially if they are harmful, assume an enormous importance. But how can I defend myself against the incurable and engaging frivolity that prevails over everything else in him and sweeps me along in his wake?

There is something worse: through Renaud I have discovered the secret of giving and receiving sensual delight, and the possession and use of it gives me the thrill of a child wielding a deadly weapon. He has revealed to me the sure and urgent power of my tall, lithe, muscular body—hard buttocks, scarcely any breasts, an even-textured skin as smooth as porcelain—of my Egyptian-tobacco eyes that have grown deeper and more restless, of a short, bushy mane the colour of ripening chestnuts. . . . All this new strength I exert, only half-consciously, on Renaud—just as, had I stayed two days more at the School, I should have exerted it on that charming Hélène.

Yes, yes, I admit it, but do not press me further. Otherwise I shall say that Renaud was responsible for me kissing my little Hélène on the lips.

3

"SMALL and silent Claudine, what are you thinking about?"

He asked me that, I remember, on the hotel terrace at Heidelberg, while my eyes were wandering from the ample curve of the Neckar to the sham ruins of the Schloss down below us.

Sitting on the ground, I raised my chin from the props of my two fists.

"I'm thinking of the garden."

"What garden?"

"Oh! 'What garden!' The garden at Montigny, of course!"

Renaud threw away his cigarette. He lives, like a god, in clouds of fragrant Egyptian tobacco smoke.

"Funny little girl. . . . With *that* landscape in front of you! Are you going to tell me it's more beautiful than this, the garden at Montigny?"

"Of course not. But it's mine."

That was just it! Over and over again we had discussed it, but neither could understand the other. Renaud would kiss me affectionately, a little contemptuously, and call me a lazy little stay-at-home and a gipsy who wouldn't leave her tent. I would laugh and retort that *his* home was in a suitcase. We were both right, but I blamed him because he did not think as I did.

He has travelled too much and I not enough. There is nothing nomadic about me, except my mind. I cheerfully follow Renaud in his wanderings because I adore him. But I like journeys that have an end. He is in love with travel for travel's sake; he gets up happily under a foreign sky, thinking that today he will be off somewhere else. He longs for the mountains of one nearby country, for the harsh wine of another, for the artificial charm of this dolled-up watering-place ablaze with flowers, for the solitude of that high-perched hamlet. And he goes off, with no regrets for the hamlet or the flowers or the potent wine.

I follow him. And I enjoy—yes, truly I enjoy them too—the friendly town, the sun behind the pine-trees, the echoing mountain air. But round my ankle I feel a thread whose other end is wound and knotted round the old walnut-tree in the garden at Montigny.

I don't think I am an unnatural daughter! And yet there is something I have to admit: I have missed Fanchette during our travels almost as much as Papa. The only time I really missed my noble father badly was in Germany, where those Wagnerian chromolithographs and picture-postcards reminded me of him. All the representations of Odin and Wotan, apart from the missing eye, resembled him. Like him, they were handsome, they brandished harmless thunderbolts and they displayed tempestuous beards and commanding gestures. And I could imagine that, like his, their vocabulary included all the coarse expressions of a mythical bygone age.

I wrote to him seldom and he rarely replied. His letters were affectionate and higgledy-piggledy, written in a juicily hybrid style, in which periods whose cadence would have delighted Châteaubriand (I am flattering Papa a little) harboured in their bosom—their august bosom—the most scarifying oaths. I learnt from these anything but commonplace letters that, apart from the silent, faithful Monsieur Maria, who was still the perfect secretary, nothing was going right. . . . "I don't know whether to blame your absence for it, little donkey", my dear father confided to me, "but I'm beginning to find Paris pestilential, especially since that specimen of the dregs of humanity by the name of X . . . has just published a treatise on *Universal Malacology* stupid enough to make even the squatting lions outside the Institute vomit. How can the Eternal Justice still pour forth the light of day on such filthy skunks?"

Mélie wrote to me also, well describing Fanchette's state of mind since my departure; how she had wailed in desolation for days and days. But Mélie's handwriting is so hieroglyphic that it is impossible to keep up a sustained correspondence with her.

Fanchette was mourning me! The thought of this haunted me wherever I went. All the time I was on my travels, I started at the sight of every lean tom-cat fleeing round the corner of a wall. Over and over again, to Renaud's surprise, I have let go his arm to run up to a she-cat, sitting sedately on a doorstep and say to her: "My Sweeeet!" Often the little animal would be shocked and tuck in her chin, with a dignified movement, against her ruffled shirt-front. But I would insist, adding a series of shrill onomatopoeic noises in a minor key until I saw the green eyes melt into gentleness and narrow in a smile. Then the flat, caressing head would rub hard against the door-post in polite greeting and the cat would turn round three times, which clearly meant: "I like you."

Never once did Renaud show any impatience during these bouts of cat-mania. But I suspect him of being more indulgent than understanding. He is quite capable, monster that he is, of never having stroked my Fanchette except out of diplomacy.

How willingly I look back over this recent past and dwell on it! But Renaud lives in the future. This paradoxical man who is devoured by the terror of growing old, who studies himself minutely in looking-glasses and desperately notes every tiny wrinkle in the network at the corner of his eyes, is uneasy in the present and feverishly hurries Today on Tomorrow. I myself linger in the past, even if that past be only Yesterday, and I look back almost always, with regret. It is as if marriage (be honest and say sex!) had developed certain modes of "feeling" in me that were older than myself. This amazes Renaud. But he loves me, and if, as my lover, he no longer understands me, I can still take refuge in the other Renaud, my dear, great fatherly friend! For him, I am a trusting daughter who leans on her self-chosen father and confides in him, almost without the lover's knowledge. Better still, if Renaud-the-lover tries to insinuate himself as a third between Papa-Renaud and Daughter-Claudine, the latter gives him a ruthless reception. She pushes him away like a cat who's jumped up on one's desk. So then the poor thing has to wait, impatient and disappointed, until the other Claudine returns, light-hearted and rested, to bring him her swiftly-overcome resistance, her silence and her fire.

Alas, all I have put down here, more or less at random, does not make me see where the rift between us lies. Nevertheless, how conscious, how terribly conscious of it I am!

Here we are, in our own place at last. All the tiring shopping expeditions of our return are over; Renaud's fevered anxiety that I should like my new home has calmed down.

He begged me to choose between two flats, both of which are his. (Two flats; that's none too many for one Renaud. . . .) "If you don't fancy them, darling child, we'll find another one that's prettier than these two." I resisted the desire to reply: "Show me the third one," and, overcome once more by my insurmountable horror of moving, I examined the two quite conscientiously; above all, I had a good sniff at them. And, finding the smell of this one more sympathetic to my hypersensitive nose, I chose it. It needed very little more in the way of furniture, but Renaud, scrupulous over details and much more feminine and house-proud than myself, used all his ingenuity ferreting round for objects to complete a flawless whole. Anxious to please me, anxious too not to include anything that might offend his over-critical eye, he consulted me twenty times over. My first answer was sincere: "It's all the same to me!" My second too. But on the subject of the bed, "that keystone of conjugal bliss", to use Papa's expression, I gave my opinion very definitely.

"I'd like my little four-poster with the chintz curtains."

At which, my poor Renaud flung up his arms in despair.

"Misery me! A four-poster bed in a Louis XV bedroom! Besides, my darling, monstrous little girl, do use your imagination! We should have to add an extension to lengthen it. . . . I mean, widen it. . . ."

Yes, I realised that only too well. But what could you expect? I couldn't feel much interest in furniture that I didn't know—not yet. The big low bed has become my friend, and so have the dressing-room and a few vast padded armchairs. But the rest continues to regard me, if I dare use the expression, with a mistrustful eye; the wardrobe with the long mirror squints at me when I pass, the drawing-room table with its curved legs tries to trip me up and I kick it back good and hard.

Two months, Lord, two months—isn't that long enough to break in a flat? And I stifle the voice of reason that growls: "In two months, you can tame plenty of pieces of furniture, but not one Claudine."

Would Fanchette consent to live here? I saw her again at Papa's flat in the Rue Jacob, my darling white beautiful. She had not been warned of my return and it made my heart heavy to see her prostrate with emotion at my feet, unable to utter a sound, while, with my hand on her warm pink stomach, I tried vainly to count the wild pulsations of her heart. I laid her on her side to comb her dulled coat; at that familiar gesture, she raised her head with a look full of so many things—reproach, unfailing love, torment accepted with joy. . . . Oh, little white animal, how close I feel to you because I understand you so well!

I have seen my noble father again, tall and broad with his tricoloured beard, brimming over with sonorous words and ineffective pugnacity. Without being consciously aware of it, we love each other and I understand all the genuine pleasure implied by his first words of welcome: "Would you deign to give me a kiss, you vile slut?" I think he has grown larger in the last two years. I'm not joking! And the proof is that he confessed to me that he felt cramped in the Rue Jacob. I admit that he did add afterwards: "You know, this last year or two, I've been picking up books, for nothing, in the sale-rooms. Nineteen hundred at least. . . . A thousand herds of sacred swine! I've been forced to stuff them away in the boxroom! It's so small, this pig-sty. . . . Whereas, in that room at the back at Montigny, I could . . ." He turned away his head and pulled his beard, but our eyes had had time to meet and exchange an odd look. He's b . . . well, I mean, he's *quite* capable of going back there just as he came here, for no reason at all. . . .

I am avoiding the thing that is painful to me to write. Perhaps it isn't in the least serious? If only it weren't in the least serious! Here it is:

Since yesterday, everything has been in place in Ren . . . in our flat. We shall see no more of the fussy niggling of the carpet-layer nor of the incurable absentmindedness of the curtain-hanger, who, every five minutes, kept mislaying his little brass gadgets for a quarter of an hour. Renaud feels at ease, and wanders about smiling approval at a clock that is right, bullying a picture that is not hanging straight. He tucked me under his arm to take me round on our proprietorial tour, then left me (no doubt to go off and do his work on the *Diplomatic Review*, to settle the fate of Europe with Jacobsen and treat Abdul Hamid as he deserved), alone in the drawing-room. He left me, after a satisfying kiss, saying: "My little despot, your kingdom is yours to rule."

Sitting there, with nothing to do, I drifted off into a long day-dream. Then an hour struck—I have no idea which—and brought me to my feet, quite unaware that I was living in the present. The next thing I knew, I was standing in front of the glass over the chimneypiece, hurriedly pinning on my hat . . . *to go home.*

That was all. But it was a shattering experience. It conveys nothing to *you*? You're lucky.

To go home! But where? Isn't this my own home, then? No, no, it isn't, and that's the whole source of my trouble. To go home? Where? Definitely not to the Rue Jacob, where Papa has piled up mountains of papers on my bed. Not to Montigny, because neither the beloved house . . . nor the School . . .

To go home! Have I no real dwelling then? No! I live here with a man, admittedly a man I love, but I am living with a man! Alas, Claudine, plant torn up from its soil, did your roots go as deep as all that? What will Renaud say? Nothing. He can do nothing.

Where would I find a burrow? Within myself. I must dig into my misery, into my irrational, indescribable misery, and curl myself up in that hole.

I sat down again and, with my hat still on my head and my hands clenched tight together, I burrowed.

My diary has no future. It is five months now since I abandoned it on an unhappy note, and I feel resentful towards it. In any case, I haven't time to keep it up-to-date. Renaud is taking me about and exhibiting me in the social world—almost every variety of it—far more than I like. But since he's proud of me, I can't hurt him by refusing to accompany him. . . .

His marriage—I hadn't realised this—has made a great stir among the variegated (I nearly wrote "motley") crowd of people he knows. No, he doesn't know them. He himself is tremendously well-known. But he's incapable of putting a name to half the individuals with whom he exchanges cordial handshakes and whom he introduces to me. Frittering himself away, incorrigibly frivolous, he is not seriously attached to anything—except to me. "Who's that man, Renaud?" "It's . . . Bother, I can't remember his name." Well! Apparently, his profession demands this sort of thing; apparently the fact of writing profound articles for serious diplomatic journals infallibly necessitates your shaking hands with a horde of affected people, including painted women (of the world and the half-world), clinging and pushing "actresses", painters and models. . . .

But Renaud puts so much husbandly and fatherly pride (the

ingenuous tenderness of it touches me, coming from this blasé Parisian) into those three words, "My wife, Claudine", that I draw in my claws and smooth out the angry creases between my eyebrows. And, besides, I have other compensations: a revengeful pleasure in answering, when Renaud vaguely points out to me a "Monsieur . . . Durande":

"You told me the day before yesterday that his name was Dupont!"

"Did I tell you that? Are you sure? I've mixed them both up with . . . well, the other one. That moron who calls me 'Old Boy' because we were in the Sixth together."

All the same, I find it hard to get used to such nebulous intimacies.

Here and there, in the lobbies of the Opéra-Comique, at Chevillard and Colonne concerts, at soirées, particularly at soirées—at the moment when the fear of music casts a gloom over faces—I have overheard remarks about myself that were not entirely benevolent. So people are gossipping about me? Ah! of course, here I am Renaud's wife, just as, in Montigny, he is Claudine's husband. These Parisians speak low, but people who come from Fresnois can hear the grass grow.

They say: "She's very young." They say: "Too dark . . . she looks bad-tempered. . . ." "What, too dark? She's got chestnut curls——" "That short hair, it's to attract attention! All the same, Renaud has taste." They say: "Where on earth does she come from? . . . She's from Montmartre. . . . It's Slavonic, that small chin and broad temples. She's straight out of one of Pierre Loüys' homosexual novels." . . . "Surely it's a bit early to have got to the stage of only liking little girls. How old *is* Renaud?"

Renaud, always Renaud. . . . Here is something characteristic: No one ever refers to him except by his first name.

4

YESTERDAY my husband asked me:

"Claudine, will you have an at-home day?"

"Heavens above, whatever for?"

"To gossip, to 'argle-bargle' as you say."

"With whom?"

"With women of the world."

"I don't much like women of the world."

"With men too."

"Don't tempt me! . . . No, I won't have an at-home day. Do you imagine I know how to be a society hostess?"

"*I* have one, you know!"

"You *do?* . . . All right, keep it: I'll come and visit you on your at-home day. Honestly, it's much less risky. Otherwise, after an hour I'm quite likely to say to your gorgeous lady friends: 'Get out. I'm fed up with you. You make me sick!'"

He did not insist (he never insists); he kissed me (he always kisses me) and went out of the room, laughing.

My stepson, Marcel, overwhelms me with polite contempt for this misanthropy and this frightened dislike of the "world" I am always proclaiming. That little boy, so completely unsusceptible to women, assiduously seeks their company; he gossips, fingers materials, pours out tea without staining delicate dresses and adores talking scandal. I am wrong in calling him "that little boy". At twenty, one is no longer a little boy and *he* will remain a little girl for a long time. On my return to Paris, I found him still charming, but all the same a little worm. He is excessively thin now, his eyes are bigger and have a wild, strained look and there are three premature fine wrinkles at the corner of the lids. . . . Is Charlie the only one responsible for them?

Renaud's anger against this two-faced little cheat did not last very long. "I can't forget that he's my child, Claudine. And perhaps, if I'd brought him up better . . ." I myself forgave Marcel out of indifference. (Indifference, pride, and an unadmitted—and rather low-down—interest in the aberrations of his love-life.) And I feel a keen pleasure that never loses its edge every time I look under the left eye of that boy who ought to have been a girl and see the white line left by my scratch!

But that Marcel amazes me! I had been expecting implacable resentment and open hostility. Not a trace of anything of the kind! Irony frequently, disdain too, curiosity—and that's all.

His one and only preoccupation is himself! He is constantly gazing into mirrors, putting his two forefingers on his eyebrows and pushing up the skin of his forehead as high as it will go. Surprised by this gesture, which is becoming a morbid habit, I asked him the meaning of it. "It's to rest the skin under the eyes," he replied with the utmost seriousness. He lengthens the curve of his eyelids with a blue pencil; he risks wearing over-ornamental turquoise cuff-links. Ugh! At forty, he will be sinister. . . .

In spite of what happened between us, he feels no embarrassment at making me partial confidences, either out of unconscious bravado or as a result of his increasing moral perversion. He was here yesterday, languishing the tired charm of his too-slender body and his brilliant, fevered eyes.

"You look utterly exhausted, Marcel!"

"I *am* utterly exhausted."

We always adopt an aggressive tone with each other. It's a kind of game and means very little.

"Charlie again?"

"Oh, for goodness' sake! . . . A young woman oughtn't to know about certain disorders of the mind. Or, if she does, she ought to have the decency to forget them. 'Disorders' *is* what you call them, isn't it?"

"'Disorders' is certainly what they're called. . . . But I would hardly say 'of the mind'."

"Thanks for the body. But, between you and me, my tiredness

has nothing whatever to do with Charlie, so he needn't flatter himself it has. Charlie! A waverer, neither one thing nor the other. . . ."

"I say, come now!"

"Believe me. I know him better than you do. . . ."

"So I should hope! Thanks for the compliment."

"Yes, at bottom he's a coward."

"When you really get to the bottom. . . ."

"It's ancient history, our friendship. I'm not repudiating it; I'm breaking it. And because of some not very savoury incidents. . . ."

"What, the beautiful Charlie? Has he been twisting you over money?"

"Worse than that. He accidentally left a wallet behind at my place—full of women's letters!"

With what hatred and disgust he spat out his accusation! I stared at him, profoundly thoughtful. He was a pervert, an unfortunate—almost irresponsible—child, but his fury was justified. One had only to put oneself in his place in imagination. Yes, I should have felt the same.

It is laid down that everything—joys, sorrows, trivial events—should come upon me suddenly. Not, goodness knows, that I go in for the extraordinary . . . apart from one exception—my marriage. But time goes by for me like the big hand of certain public clocks; it stays perfectly still where it is for fifty-nine seconds, then all at once, with no transition, it jumps to the next minute with a spasmodic jerk. The minutes grab it roughly as they do me. . . . I am not saying that is entirely and invariably unpleasant, but . . .

My last jump was this: I went to see Papa, Mélie, Fanchette and Limaçon. This last, striped and splendid, fornicates with his mother and takes us back to the worst days of the House of Atreus. The rest of the time, he prowls about the flat, arrogant, leonine and fierce. Not one of the virtues of his lovable white mother has been passed down to him.

Mélie rushed to meet me, holding the globe of her left breast in her hand, like Charlemagne holding the terrestrial orb.

"My darling, precious lamb . . . I was just going to drop you a line! If you knew the state we're in here. All upside-down, you'd think the end of the world was come. I say, aren't you fetching in that hat? . . ."

"Pipe down, pipe down! So the end of the world's come! Why? Has Limacon overturned his . . . spittoon?"

Wounded by my sarcasm, Mélie withdrew.

"You think I'm joking? All right, go and ask Monsieur—you'll see with your very own eyes.

Intrigued, I walked into Papa's study without knocking. He turned round when he heard me, unmasking an enormous packing case that he was filling with books. His handsome, hirsute face wore an entirely new expression; harmless rage, embarrassment, childish confusion.

"Is that you, little donkey?"

"It would seem so. What on earth are you doing, Papa?"

"I . . . I'm putting some papers in order."

"Funny kind of file you've got there! But—I know that packing-case. . . . That comes from Montigny, that does!"

Papa resigned himself to the inevitable. He buttoned up his tight-waisted frock-coat, sat down, taking his time about it, and crossed his arms over his beard.

"That comes from Montigny and that is going back there! Do I make myself clear?"

"No, not in the least."

He stared at me under his bushy, beetling eyebrows, lowered his voice and risked coming right out with it:

"I'm buggering off!"

I had understood perfectly well. I had felt that this irrational flight was coming. Why had he come? Why was he going away? Idle to ask. Papa is a force of Nature; he serves the obscure designs of Fate. Without knowing it, he came here in order that I might meet Renaud; he is going away, having fulfilled his mission of irresponsible father.

As I had made no answer, that terrible man recovered his self-confidence.

"You realise, I've had enough of it! I'm ruining my eyes in this pitch-dark hole. I'm surrounded by rogues and scoundrels and bunglers. I can't stir a finger without banging against the wall, the wings of my spirit are broken with beating against universal ignorance. A thousand herds of abysmal, mangy swine! I'm going back to my old hovel. Will you come and see me there with that highwayman you married?"

That Renaud! He has captivated even Papa, who rarely sees him, but never speaks of him except in a special tone of gruff affection.

"You bet I'll come."

"But . . . I've got all sorts of important things to say to you. What's to be done with the cat? She's used to me, that animal. . . ."

"The cat?"

The cat! It's true . . . he's very fond of her. Besides, Mélie would be there, and I feel apprehensive for Fanchette when I think of Renaud's manservant and Renaud's cook. . . . My darling, my sweet girl, nowadays I sleep beside a warm body that is not yours. . . . I made up my mind.

"Take her with you. Later on, I'll see; perhaps I'll have her back with me."

But what I was most conscious of was that, on the pretext of filial duty, I would be able to see the house of enchanted memories again, just as I had left it, revisit the dear and dubious School. . . . In my heart, I blessed my father's exodus.

"Take my bedroom with you too, Papa. I'll sleep in it when we come to see you."

With one gesture, the bulwark of Malacology crushed me to powder with his contempt.

"Ugh! You wouldn't blush to co-habit with your husband under my unpolluted roof, impure animals as all you females are! What does it mean to you, the regenerating power of chastity?"

How I love him when he's like that! I kissed him and went away, leaving him burying his treasures in the vast packing-case and gaily humming a folk-song he adores:

> There was a young maiden as I have heard tell,
> And the language of flowers she knew passing well;
> She would finger and fondle her sweet Shepherd's Purse:
> You can all take my meaning for better or worse.

A hymn, presumably, to regenerating Chastity!

"Definitely, darling, I'm going to start having my day again."

Renaud broke this grave news to me in our dressing-room where I was taking off my clothes. We had spent the evening at old Madame Barmann's and assisted, by way of a change, at a good old squabble between that fat female screech-owl and the noisy boor who shares her destiny. She said to him: "You're common!" He retorted: "You bore everyone to tears with your literary pretensions!" He bellowed; she screeched. The altercation continued. Running out of invectives, he flung down his napkin, left the table and stormed upstairs to his room. Everybody sighed and relaxed and we went on with our dinner in peace. When we reached the sweet course, our amiable hostess despatched her personal maid, Eugénie, to soothe the fat man down (by what mysterious process?) and he finally came downstairs again, calmed, but offering not the slightest apology. However, Gréveuille, the exquisite member of the Academy, who is terrified of rows, laid the blame on his venerable mistress, flattered the husband and helped himself to some more cheese.

My own personal contribution to this charming milieu consists of my curly head, my soft, suspicious eyes, the discrepancy between my full, firm neck and my thin shoulders revealed by my *décolletage,* and a mutism that embarrasses my neighbours at dinner.

The men do not make up to me. My recent marriage still keeps them at a distance and I am not the kind of female who tries to attract flirtatious admirers.

One Wednesday, at that old Barmann woman's, I was politely pursued by a young and attractive literary man. (Beautiful eyes, that boy, a faint touch of blepharitis, but no matter. . . .) He compared me—my short hair as usual!—to Myrtocleia, to a young Hermes, to an Eros by Prud'hon—he raked his memories of private art collections for me and cited so many hermaphroditic masterpieces that I began to think of Luce and Marcel and he nearly ruined a marvellous dish for me. It was a heavenly *cassoulet,* a speciality of the Barmann's cook, served in little silver-handled *cocottes.* "Such an advantage having one's own *cocotte,* isn't it, Cher Maître? One can be sure of getting enough to eat," whispered Maugis in Gréveuille's ear and the sixty-year-old sponger, who was the hostess's lover, agreed with a one-sided smile.

After dinner, the little flatterer, excited by his own evocations, would not leave me alone. Huddled up in a Louis XV armchair, I could hear him, though I was hardly listening, going on with his endless literary comparisons. He gazed at me with his caressing, long-lashed eyes, and murmured so that the others could not hear:

"Ah, your dreaming is the dreaming of the boy Narcissus, your soul, like his, is full of bitterness and sensuous delight."

"Monsieur," I told him firmly, "you are completely off the track. My soul is full of nothing but haricot beans and little strips of bacon."

Dumbfounded, he said no more.

Renaud scolded me a little and laughed a great deal.

"You're going to start having your day again, dear Renaud?"

He had ensconced his large body in a wicker armchair and I was undressing with my usual chaste unselfconsciousness. Chaste? Let us say, innocent of any ulterior motive.

"Yes. What do you intend to do, my darling child? You looked very pretty and very wan just now at the hook-nosed Barmann's."

"What do I intend to do when you start your day again? Why, I intend to go and see you."

"Is that all?" said his disappointed chin.

"Yes, that's all. It's *your* day, isn't it? How else do I come into it?"

"But, hang it all, Claudine, you're my wife!"

"And whose fault is that? If you'd listened to me, I'd be your mistress, tucked away all nice and quiet in a little hide-out somewhere, miles away from all your social world. Then your receptions could go on in their old normal way. I do wish you'd behave as if you were my lover. . . ."

Good heavens, he took me at my word! Because I had just picked up my mauve silk petticoat from the floor with an agile foot, my big husband advanced on me, excited by the double Claudine reflected in the glass.

"Get away from me, Renaud! That gentleman in evening dress, that little girl in her knickers, no, really! It's like a scene out of Marcel Prévost . . . when he's being licentious in a big way. . . ."

The truth is, Renaud likes tell-tale mirrors and their bright, lewd connivance, whereas I fly from them, disdaining their revelations, instinctively seeking darkness, silence and blind ecstasy. . . .

"Renaud, you wretch! We were talking about your day."

"To blazes with my day! I prefer your night!"

5

So Papa has gone away exactly as he came. I did not accompany him to the station, having little desire to witness his tempestuous departure. I did not need to be there to know what it would be like. Wrapped in a stormcloud, he would rage against the "filthy rabble" of railway employees, shower them contemptuously with sumptuous tips, and forget to pay for his ticket.

Mélie is sincerely sorry to leave me but "at moment", the permission to take Fanchette with her will be staunching all her regrets. Poor Mélie, her *lammy* remains incomprehensible to her! What, I've married the man of my choice; what, I sleep with him as much as I want to—and even more—I live in a pretty *höam*, I have a manservant, a carriage hired by the month—and I don't put on any more swank? Mélie thinks I ought to go about positively flaunting my good fortune.

I wonder . . . is there possibly a grain of truth in her criticism? In Renaud's presence I don't think of anything—except him. He is more engrossing than a petted woman. His intense vitality manifests itself in smiles, in words, in constant humming, in amorous demands; tenderly, he accuses me of not wooing him, of being able to read in his presence, of having my eyes too often fixed on some point in space. Out of his presence, I feel the embarrassment of an abnormal, illicit situation. Am I totally unsuited to the "estate of matrimony".

Yet I ought to be able to get used to it. After all, Renaud has only got what he deserves. All he had to do was not to marry me. . . .

Oyez! Oyez! My husband has resumed his at-home day.

Word has gone round.

What can Renaud have done in the sight of the Lord to deserve so many friends? The manservant Ernest has ushered at least forty people into the leather-upholstered study that smells pleasantly of Turkish tobacco and the long hall to which we banished all drawings and sketches, whoever the artist. The crowd included men, women and Marcel.

At the first ring of the bell, I leapt to my feet and ran and locked myself into the comforting dressing-room. It rang—it rang again. At every trill, the skin of my back stirred unpleasantly and I thought of Fanchette who, on rainy days, watches the big drops dripping from the broken gutter with the same nervous ripples running down her spine. . . . Alas, I was all too like Fanchette! For, in a few moments, Renaud was parleying with me through the locked door of my refuge.

"Claudine, little girl, this is becoming impossible. At first I said you hadn't come home yet, but, I assure you, the situation's getting critical: Maugis is insisting that I keep you in a cellar, God only knows where. . . ."

I listened to him, looking at myself in the glass and laughing in spite of myself.

"People are going to think that you're frightened. . . ."

The beast! He had said the one thing that would have any effect! I brushed my hair over my forehead and made sure my skirt was properly done up; then I opened the door.

"Can I appear in front of your friends like this?"

"Yes, of course. I adore you in black."

"Oh, you adore me in all colours!"

"Most of all in flesh-colour, it's true. . . . Come quick!"

People had already been smoking a lot in my husband's flat; the smell of tea hovered in the air along with that of ginger—and those strawberries, and those ham and *foie gras* and caviar sandwiches. How quickly a hot room begins to smell like a restaurant!

I sat down and I "paid a call". My husband offered me tea, as if I were simply the latest arrival, and it was the pretty Cypriot with the paradoxical name, Madame van Langendonck, who brought me cream. What luck!

Here, at . . . Renaud's, I could identify various figures I had vaguely met at theatres and concerts: critics, great and small, some with their wives, some with their mistresses. That was just as it should be. I had insisted that my husband should not do any purging—horrible word! the thing itself would have been just as ugly. And, as I have said, I was not the hostess.

Maugis, with a claret glass full of Kummel in his hand, was questioning, with marvellously simulated interest, the author of a feminist novel, who was explaining at length the theme of his next book. The novelist talked on, indefatigably: the other never stopped drinking. When he was sufficiently drunk, he finally asked in a thick voice:

"And . . . and the title of this powerful work?"

"It isn't decided yet. Not till I've polished off the book."

"I hope you'll polish yourself off first."

With which he moved quickly away.

Among the numerous foreigners, I picked out a Spanish sculptor with beautiful eyes, like a horse's, a clear-cut mouth, and an incomplete knowledge of our language. He was mainly interested in painting and I admitted, without embarrassment, that I hardly knew anything in the Louvre and felt no particular passion to enlighten my ignorance.

"You no know the Rubens'?"

"No."

"You have not the wish to see them?"

"No."

At this, he rose to his feet, "made a leg" with Andalusian grace, and, with a deep, respectful bow, announced crushingly:

"You are a swine, Madame."

A lovely lady who belongs to the Opéra (and to one of Renaud's men friends) gave a start and stared at us, hoping for a scene. But she wasn't going to get it. I had completely understood this Spanish aesthete, who had only one disparaging term at his disposal. He only knows the word "swine"; in France we have only one word for all the different varieties of "love", which is every bit as ridiculous.

Somebody had come in and Renaud exclaimed:

"I thought you were in London! So it's sold, then?"

"It's sold. We're living in Paris," said a tired voice with a faint, hardly perceptible English accent.

The man was tall and fair, and held himself very upright, carrying his small head, with its brick complexion and opaque blue eyes, very straight on his square shoulders. He was, as I say, square-shouldered and well-built, but he had the stiffness of a man who is thinking all the time about holding himself straight and appearing robust.

His wife . . . we were introduced to each other without my really listening, I was too busy looking at her. I noticed almost at once one of the most definite sources of her charm: all her movements, the turn of her hips, the arching of her neck, the quick raising of her arm to her hair, the sway of her seated body, all described curves so nearly circular that I could see the design of interlacing rings, like the perfect spirals of sea shells, that her gentle movements left traced on the air.

Her long-lashed eyes, of a changeable amber-shot grey, looked darker under the light gold wavy hair that had a greenish tinge in it. A black velvet dress, its too sumptuous material very plainly cut, clung to her round, mobile hips and her slim but not squeezed-in waist. A tiny diamond star, the head of a long pin, glittered among the drooping feathers of her hat.

She drew a swift, hot little hand out of her fox muff and put it in mine, while her eyes looked me up and down. I was almost sure she was going to speak with a foreign accent. I don't know why, but, in spite of the faultless dress, the absence of jewellery—she did not even wear a necklace—she struck me as a trifle flashy. Her eyes did not look like a Frenchwoman's. She spoke. . . . I pricked up my ears . . . and she spoke without the faintest trace of accent! How stupid one is to get preconceived ideas! Her fresh mouth, tight in repose, became flower-like and tempting when she opened it. She broke at once into complimentary remarks:

"I'm so delighted to meet you. I was sure your husband would unearth a little wife who would surprise and ravish us all!"

"Thank you on my husband's behalf! But now won't you pay me a compliment that doesn't flatter anyone but me?"

"You don't need one. Just resign yourself to looking unlike anyone else."

She hardly moved and made only restrained gestures, yet, merely in the act of sitting down beside me, she seemed to swirl round twice inside her dress.

Were we already mutually attracted or hostile? No, definitely attracted: in spite of her praise just now, I felt not the slightest desire to scratch her; she was charming. From closer range, I counted her spirals and her multiple curves; her supple hair swirled on her nape, her ear traced complex and delicate whorls, while her ray-like lashes and the quivering plumes swathed round her hat seemed to be whirling round, independent of her, in invisible gyrations.

I was tempted to ask her how many spinning dervishes she numbered among her ancestors? But I knew I mustn't; Renaud would scold me. And, anyway, why be in such a hurry to shock this endearing Madame Lambrook?

"Have you heard Renaud talk about us?" she enquired.

"Never. Do you know each other very well?"

"I should think we do! . . . We must have dined together at least half a dozen times. And I'm not counting big dinner parties."

Was she laughing at me? Was she sarcastic or silly? That was something I should find out later on. For the moment, I was enchanted by her slow speech, and her caressing voice that lingered now and then, cooingly, on a rebellious *rrr*.

I let her go on talking and, all the while, she gazed closely into my eyes with her short-sighted ones, coolly verifying their colour that matches my short hair.

And she told me about herself. In a quarter of an hour I knew that her husband was a retired British officer sapped and burnt-out by India, where he had left the last of his physical strength and his mental activity. He was nothing now but a handsome carcass—she made that very clear. I knew that she was rich, but "never anything like rich enough," she said passionately, that her Viennese mother had given her beautiful hair, a skin like a white convolvulus (I quote) and the name of Rézi.

"Rézi . . . it sounds like a delicious fruit. . . . What an unusual name!"

"In France, yes. But in Vienna I believe it's anything but unusual. Almost as common a diminutive as Nana or Titine here."

"I don't care. . . . Rézi. How charming it is, that name Rézi!"

"It's charming because you say it charmingly."

Her bare fingers stroked my bare nape, so swiftly that I started, more as a nervous reflex than in surprise. For I had been aware, for the past two minutes, of her darting eyes encircling my neck with a chain of glances.

"Rézi. . . ."

It was her husband this time, wanting to take her away. He had come to say goodbye to me and his opaque blue eyes embarrassed me. A handsome carcass! I thought it might still house a good deal of jealousy and tyranny, for, at his laconic summons, Rézi rose at once, making no demur. That man expresses himself in slow, spaced-out phrases (like an actor being prompted every three words, Maugis says). Obviously, he is careful about his diction so as to suppress all trace of English accent.

It was agreed that "we would see each other often" and that "Madame Claudine was a marvel". If I keep my promise, I shall go and see that blonde Rézi in her flat, only two steps away, in the Avenue Kléber.

Rézi. . . . Her whole person gives off a scent of fern and iris, a respectable artless, rustic smell that I find surprising and enchanting by contrast. For I can discover nothing artless or rustic in her, least of all anything respectable, she is far too pretty! She talked to me about her husband and her travels, but I know nothing about herself, except her charm. . . .

"Well, Claudine . . . ?"

My dear giant, worn out and happy, was contentedly surveying the drawing-room, empty at last. Dirty plates, little cakes nibbled at and left, dead cigarettes on the arms of chairs and the edges of tables (have they no shame, these beastly visitors?), glasses sticky with appalling mixtures of drinks. I had caught a classically hirsute poet from Provence busy combining orangeade, kummel, cognac, cherry brandy and Russian anisette! "A liquid *Jezebel*," little Madame de Lizery (Robert Parville's mistress) had exclaimed, and then told me that at Les Oiseaux, the girls, well up in *Athalie*, used to call all *"horribles mélanges"* Jezebels.

"Well, Claudine, aren't you going to say anything to me about my at-home day?"

"Your at-home day, my poor sweet! I think you're as much to be pitied as censured . . . and that we must open the windows. Several of these little walnut cream cakes left over look quite appetising. Are you sure nobody's 'wiped their feet on them', as my noble father would say?"

Renaud shook his head and pressed his temples. He could feel a migraine threatening.

"Your noble father always shows commendable prudence. Follow his example and don't touch those dubious cakes. I saw Suzanne de Lizery brush her hands over them, hands that had just been touching goodness knows what and had been 'in mourning' a good while, judging by their black-rimmed nails."

"Ugh! . . . Shut up or I shan't be able to eat my dinner. Let's go to the dressing-room."

My husband had received so many people that I felt abominably tired. But he—young Renaud with the silver hair—seemed more animated than ever. He wandered about, chattering and laughing, inhaled deep breaths of my person (which apparently drove away any hint of migraine) and kept circling round my chair.

"Why *do* you keep on gyrating like a buzzard?"

"A buzzard, eh? I've no idea what a buzzard is. Let me guess. . . . I imagine the buzzard as a little animal with a hooked nose. . . . Buzzard! A little chestnut beast that kicks with its hooves and has a horrid disposition. Right?"

This picture of a four-legged bird-of-prey threw me into a paroxysm of such youthful gaiety that my husband stopped and stood still in front of me, almost offended. But I only laughed louder than ever and his eyes changed and became excited.

"My little curly shepherd, is it as funny as all that? Laugh again, so that I can see right to the back of your mouth."

It was a warning! I was in danger of being made love to somewhat violently. . . .

"No, really . . . not before dinner."

"After?"

"I don't know."

"Very well, before *and* after. Don't you admire my genius for compromise?"

Feeble, cowardly Claudine! There are certain kisses that are "Sesames" . . . and after which I want to be conscious of nothing but darkness, nakedness, and the vain, silent struggle to hold myself back one minute, just one minute longer, on the edge of delight.

"Renaud, who *are* those people?"

Now that the light was out, I had sought my place in the bed, my place on his shoulder, where the rounded joint of the arm made me a soft, familiar bolster. Renaud stretched out his long legs and I cuddled my chilly feet against them; then he settled the back of his neck on the exact centre of the small pancake cushion, stuffed with horsehair, that serves him as a pillow. Invariable ritual preparations for the night, followed or preceded almost as regularly by other rites. . . .

"What people, my own child?"

"The Rézis . . . the Lambrooks, I mean. . . ."

"Ah! . . . I was sure you'd like the wife. . . ."

"Tell me quick, who are they?"

"Well, they're a couple . . . charming, but ill-assorted. What I appreciate in the wife is a bosom and shoulders with milky blue veins that she displays at dinner parties. No young creature anxious to give pleasure to others could display more of them. Also an insinuating coquetry—of gesture, rather than word—and something gipsyish about her . . . a taste for pulling up her stakes and moving on. In the husband, what interested me was that inner collapse, disguised by his square shoulders and rigidly correct deportment. Colonel Lambrook has remained behind in the Colonies; all that has come back is his physical wreck. He goes on living a mysterious unknown life out there; the moment you mention his beloved India he stops answering you and immures himself in haughty silence. What magnet keeps him eternally fixed out there? Suffering, beauty, cruelty? No one knows. And it's such a rare thing, little girl, a mind so firmly sealed that it can keep its secret."

Is it such a rare thing, dear Renaud?

"The first time I dined with them, a couple of years ago, in the fantastic bazaar that served them as a home at the time, they gave me an extremely attractive Burgundy. I asked whether I could get hold of some of it. 'Yes,' said Lambrook; 'it isn't dear.' He searched his memory for a moment, then raised his terra-cotta face and added: 'Twenty rupees, I think.' And he had been back in Europe ten years!"

I mused for a minute in silence, nestled against the warmth of my friend.

"Renaud, does he love his wife?"

"Maybe yes, maybe no. He treats her with a mixture of brutality and politeness that strikes me as sinister."

"Is she unfaithful to him?"

"My darling bird, how on earth should I know?"

"Why, she might have been your mistress."

The tone of conviction in which I said this convulsed Renaud with untimely mirth.

"Do keep still, or you'll have me on the floor. I've said nothing outrageous. There's nothing in the suggestion to shock either of you. Does she have women friends, do you know?"

"But this is an inquest . . . why, it's worse, it's a conquest! Claudine, I've never seen you so interested in a woman you've only met once."

"I admit it. Anyway, I'm getting myself into training. You accuse me of being unsociable, so I propose to make some acquaintances. And, as I've just met a pretty woman with an attractive voice and a hand that's pleasant to touch, I ask about her, I . . . ."

"Claudine," broke in Renaud, half teasing, half serious. "Doesn't Rézi remind you a little of Luce? A resemblance that's more than . . . skin deep?"

The hateful man! Why deflower everything with a word? I turned over in one bound like a fish, and went off to seek sleep in the chaste and chilly regions of the far side of the great bed.

A big gap in my diary. I have not put down a daily account of my impressions and I am sure I should get them wrong in a general summing-up. Life goes on. It is cold. Renaud bustles about, in the highest spirits. He rushes me round from one first night to another, loudly proclaiming that the theatre bores him to tears, that the compulsory coarseness of the average play revolts him. . . .

"Then why on earth do you go, Renaud?" asks the simple Claudine, genuinely puzzled.

"Simply . . . you'll despise me, my little judge . . . to see people. To see whether Annhine de Lys is still going with Miss Flossie; whether pretty Madame Mundoë's hat is a success, whether the strange, seductive Polaire with those eyes like an amorous gazelle's still holds the record in wasp-waists. To be there on the spot half an hour after midnight when Mendés is holding forth lyrically at a supper-table, *talking* his dazzling review. To blossom out myself in the presence of the grotesque old Barmann and her 'cameleer', as Maugis calls Gréveuille. To admire the Field-Marshal's plume surmounting the face of that ferret run to fat, Madame de Saint-Niketês."

No, I don't despise him for all that frivolity. And, besides, it wouldn't matter if I did, because I love him. I know that audiences at first nights never listen to the play. I do listen, I listen passionately . . . or else I say: "This revolts me." Renaud envies me such simple and emphatic convictions: "You're young, my little girl. . . ." Not as young as he is! He makes love to me, works, visits people, gossips, dines out, gives a party at home at four every Friday, and finds time to choose a sealskin jacket for me. From time to time, when we are by ourselves, he relaxes his charming, tired face, holds me close against him and sighs, with profound unhappiness: "Claudine, my darling child, how old I am! I can feel the minutes adding wrinkles one by one, and that hurts, that hurts so much!" If he only knew how I adored him like that, and how I hope that the years will calm his fever for showing-off! Only then, when he'll be willing to stop parading and throwing out his chest, shall we at last come together completely. Only then shall I stop panting with the effort to keep up with his forty-five-year-old's gallop.

6

ONE day, with an amused memory of the Andalusian sculptor and his "You are a swine, Madame!" I decided to discover the Louvre and to admire these new Rubens' without a guide. Wearing my sealskin bolero jacket and the matching toque that looks as if a little animal were curled up asleep on my head, I set off boldly on my own. Having not a scrap of sense of direction I kept getting lost at every turning of the gallery like a wedding-party in a Zola novel. For though, in a wood, I know by instinct where the east lies and what time it is, I go astray in a suite of rooms all on one floor.

I found the Rubens'. They disgusted me. Just that, they disgusted me! I tried loyally, for a good half-hour, to work myself up into a state of excitement about them, but no! That meat, all that meat; that heavy-jowled powdered Marie de' Medici with her sweating breasts, that plump warrior, her husband, being carried away by a victorious—and robust—Zephyr . . . no, no, *no*! I shall never understand. If Renaud and Renaud's female friends knew that! . . . Well, it can't he helped! If I'm pushed, I shall say what I think.

Depressed, I walked away, taking small steps to avoid the temptation of sliding on the polished parquet between the rows of masterpieces observing me.

Ah! here was something better, some Spanish and Italian fellows really worth looking at. All the same, it was cheek of them to put the label "St. John the Baptist" on that seductive painted face by Da Vinci, drooped forward and smiling like Mademoiselle Moreno.

Heavens, what a beautiful young man! I had discovered, quite by chance, the boy who could have made me commit sin. Lucky he was only on canvas! Who was he? "Portrait of a Sculptor", by Bronzino.

I wanted to touch that forehead, just where it swelled above the eyebrows under the thick black hair, and that ruthless, undulating lip; I wanted to kiss those eyes that looked like a cynical page's. Did that white, naked hand really model statuettes? I could well believe it. From the hue of the face, I imagined that the downless skin was of the kind that darkens to the colour of old ivory under the armpits and in the hollows behind the knees. . . . A skin that would be warm all over, even on the calves. . . . And the palms of the hands would be moist. . . .

Whatever was I doing? Blushing, and only half-awake, I looked about me. . . . What was I doing? I was being unfaithful to Renaud!

I shall have to tell Rézi about this aesthetic adultery. She will laugh, with that laugh that breaks out suddenly and dies away listlessly. For we are two good friends, Rézi and I. A fortnight has been enough to make us so; it is what Renaud would call "an agelong intimacy".

Two good friends, yes indeed. I am enchanted by her. She is fascinated by me. Nevertheless, we do not really confide in each other. No doubt, it is still a little too soon for that. Too soon for me, very definitely. Rézi does not deserve Claudine's inmost soul. I give her my physical presence, my short, curly hair that it amuses her to "do"—vain effort!—and my face that she seems to love without any hint of jealousy when she takes it between her two soft hands to "watch my eyes dance", as she says.

She treats me freely to her beauty and grace, with an insistent coquetry. For the past few days, I have been going to see her every morning at eleven.

The Lambrooks live in the Avenue Kléber, in one of those modern flats where so much space has been sacrificed to the concierge and the staircase, the front and back drawing-rooms—rather fine panelling, a good copy of Van Loo's portrait of Louis XV as a child—that the private rooms have to snatch air and daylight as best they can. Rézi sleeps in a long, dark bedroom and dresses in a gallery. But I like this inconvenient, perpetually overheated dressing-room. And Rézi dresses and undresses in it by a kind of magical process. Sitting very demurely in a low armchair, I watch her admiringly.

While still in her chemise, she does her hair. That marvellous hair, tinted pink by the blinding electric light, green by the low streak of blue daylight, shimmers when she tosses her head to shake

428 The Complete Claudine

it out. At all hours of the day, this false double light from the inadequate window and the over-bright bulbs illuminates Rézi with a theatrical glare.

She brushes her dancing cloud of hair. . . . A wave of her wand and, in a flash, thanks to a magic comb, all that gold is gathered up into a shining, twisted knot on the nape of her neck, with every ripple subdued. How on earth does it stay put? Wide-eyed, I am on the verge of imploring: "Do it again!" Rézi does not wait for my request. Another wave of the wand and the pretty woman in the chemise rises up, sheathed in a dark cloth dress and wearing a hat, ready to go out. The straitlaced corsets, the impertinent knickers, the soft and silent petticoat, have flung themselves on her like eager birds. Then Rézi gives me a triumphant look and laughs.

Her undressing is just as magical. The garments drop all at once, as if they were stuck together, and this charming creature retains nothing but her chemise . . . and her hat. How that hat irritates me and amazes me! She pins it on her head before she puts on her corsets, she leaves it on till she has taken off her stockings. She wears a hat in her bath, she tells me.

"But why this worship of headgear?"

"I don't know. Something to do with modesty, perhaps. If I had to escape in the middle of the night because the house was on fire, I wouldn't mind running out in the street completely naked, but not without a hat."

"Honestly? The firemen would have a treat!"

She is prettier and not so tall as my first impression suggested; small, but perfectly proportioned, with a white skin that rarely flushes to pink. Her short-sightedness, the changeable grey of her eyes and her fluttering eyelashes dissemble her thoughts. In fact, I do not know her at all, in spite of the spontaneous sudden way she came out at our fourth meeting, with this:

"I'm crazy about three things, Claudine: travelling, Paris . . . and you."

She was born in Paris and loves it like a foreigner; she has a passion for its cold, dubious smell, for the hour when the gaslight reddens the blue dusk, for its theatres and its streets.

"Nowhere else in the world, Claudine, are women as pretty as they are in Paris! (Let's leave Montigny out of it, darling. . . .)It's in Paris that you see the most fascinating faces whose beauty is waning—women of forty, frantically made-up and tight-laced, who have kept their delicate noses and eyes like a young girl's. Women who let themselves be stared at with a mixture of pleasure and bitterness."

A woman who thinks and talks like that is not a fool. That day, I seized hold of her pointed fingers that were drawing invisible spirals to illustrate what she was saying, as if to thank her for having charming thoughts. The next day she was in a flutter of ecstasy over Liberty's window display, a facile colour harmony of pink and saffron satins!

I regularly stay later than I mean to at the Avenue Kléber, and it is just on noon when I reluctantly decide to leave the low armchair and return home to my husband and my lunch. I am in no hurry to get back to Renaud's eager embraces and his appetite for red meat (for he doesn't live, as I do, on quails and bananas). Almost every day, just as I am about to go, the door of the dressing-room opens noiselessly and reveals the deceptively robust figure of Lambrook framed in the doorway. It happened again yesterday. . . .

"Wherever did you spring from?" exclaimed Rézi irritably.

"From the Avenue des Champs Élysées," replied that phlegmatic man. Then he hung about, kissing my hand, inspecting my unfastened jacket, staring at Rézi in her corsets and finally said to his wife:

"My dear, what a lot of time you waste dolling yourself up!"

Thinking of my friend's fantastic speed in dressing, I burst out laughing. Lambrook did not blink, but his terra-cotta skin faintly darkened. He asked how Renaud was, hoped we should both come and dine with him soon, and went away.

"Rézi, whatever's the matter with him?"

"Nothing. But don't laugh at him, Claudine, when he's talking to me; he thinks you're making fun of him."

"Really? I don't care if he does."

"But I do. It means I shall have a scene with him. . . . His jealousy gets me down."

"Jealous of *me*? On what grounds? Is the man out of his senses?"

"He doesn't like my having a woman friend. . . ."

Might he have his reasons, the husband?

Yet nothing in Rézi's behaviour leads me to think so. . . . Sometimes she looks at me for a long while without blinking her short-sighted eyes, whose eyelids are almost parallel—a detail that makes them seem longer—and her thin, tight-shut mouth half opens and becomes childish and tempting. A little shiver runs over her shoulders, she gives a nervous laugh and exclaims: "Someone's walking over my grave!" . . . and kisses me. That is all. It would show considerable vanity on my part if I imagined. . . .

I encourage nothing. I let the time slip by, I study every subtle shade and shimmer of this rainbow-like Rézi, and I wait for what will come. I wait, I wait . . . more out of laziness than virtue.

I saw Rézi this morning. That did not stop her from rushing round to me about five o'clock, all impatience. She sat down, just as Fanchette lies down, after turning right round twice. Her dark blue tailor-made gave her golden hair a reddish tinge; a complicated feather hat crowned her with embattled grey seagulls, so swirling with life that I should not have been greatly surprised to hear those entangled beaks twittering.

She installed herself, like someone taking refuge, and sighed.

"What's the matter, Rézi?"

"Nothing. I'm bored at home. The people who come to see me there bore me. One admirer, two admirers, three admirers today. . . . I've seen enough of them! The monotony of those men. I nearly hit the third one!"

"Why the third?"

"Because he told me, half an hour after the second—and in exactly the same terms, the tiresome creature—that he loved me! And the second had already been a repetition of the first. That trio will be seeing precious little of me in future. Oh Lord, all those men, all exactly alike!"

"Only take one of them; you'd get more variety."

"I'd get more exhausted too."

"But . . . your husband . . . doesn't he make a fuss?"

"He doesn't turn a hair. What makes you think he would?"

Honestly, did she take me for an utter fool? What about all those precautions the other morning, those warnings full of dark hints? Yet she was looking at me, with her clearest, most candid gaze, her eyes shot with gleams of moonstones and grey pearls.

"Now, come, Rézi! The day before yesterday, I mustn't even laugh at what he said. . . ."

"Ah!" (her hand twirled gracefully in the air, as if she were whipping up an invisible mayonnaise). "But, Claudine, that's not at all the same thing . . . these men who buzz round me . . . and you."

"I should hope not! And since your reasons for liking me can't be the same as theirs . . ."

She gave me a sudden, swift glance, then promptly looked away.

". . . you might at least tell me, Rézi, why you don't dislike seeing me."

Reassured, she put down her muff, so as to be freer to use her hands, her neck and her whole torso to emphasise what she wanted to tell me; she settled herself deeper in the big armchair and gave me an affectionate, mysterious smile.

"Why do I like you, Claudine? I could simply tell you: 'Because I think you're pretty,' and that would be enough for me, but it wouldn't be enough for your pride. . . . Why am I fond of you? Because your eyes and your hair are made of the same metal, and they're all that remain of a little light bronze statue; the rest has turned into flesh. Because your harsh gestures make a good accompaniment to your soft voice; because you tone down your fierceness for me; because, whenever one guesses one of your secret thoughts or you let one out, you blush as if someone had slipped a rude hand under your skirt. . . ."

I interrupted her with a gesture—yes, it was a harsh one. I was irritated and disturbed that so much of myself should show through without my knowledge. . . . Was I going to be angry? To leave her altogether? She forestalled any hostile resolve by kissing me impetuously, close to my ear. Drowned in fur, brushed by pointed wings, I hardly had time to be conscious of Rézi's own smell and the deceptive simplicity of her scent—when Renaud came in.

I leant back, embarrassed, in my chair. Embarrassed, not by Rézi's swift kiss, but by Renaud's keen look and the amused, almost encouraging indulgence I read in it. He kissed my friend's hand, saying:

"Please don't let me disturb anything."

"But you're not disturbing anything at all," she cried. "Anything or anyone! On the contrary, you can help me make Claudine stop frowning. She's angry because I've just paid her a very sincere compliment."

"Very sincere, I'm sure, but did you put enough conviction into your tone? My Claudine is a very serious and very passionate little girl, who's incapable of accepting . . ." (here, because he belonged to a generation that still read Musset, he hummed the accompaniment to the serenade from *Don Juan*) . . . "who's incapable of accepting certain words if they're underlined by certain smiles."

"Renaud, I implore you, no marital revelations!"

In spite of myself, I had raised my voice in exasperation, but Rézi turned her most disarming smile on me.

"Oh, *yes*, oh *yes*, Claudine! Do let him tell. I take a very real interest in them and it's an act of charity to let my ears have a little dissipation! They're getting to the point of forgetting what the word 'love' means."

Hmm! This excited eagerness of a sex-starved wife struck me as coming rather oddly after her recent assurance that she was sick and tired of men wanting to make love to her. However, Renaud knew nothing of that. Moved with generous compassion, he studied Rézi from her chignon to her ankles and it was impossible for me not to laugh when he exclaimed:

"Poor child! So young, and already deprived of what gives beauty and colour to life! Come to me. Consolation awaits you on the couch in my study. I am prepared to sacrifice myself—and it'll cost you less than going to a specialist."

"You're not a professional. Besides, either one's a man of honour or one isn't. . . ."

"And you aren't? Thanks, no!"

"You shall give me . . . whatever you like."

"Whatever I like?" She half-veiled her smoke-coloured eyes. "Well . . . perhaps you might amuse yourself with a little preliminary trifling."

"I should be only too delighted to trifle with you."

Enchanted at feeling a little outraged, Rézi arched her neck and tucked in her chin, exactly as Fanchette does when she finds an exceptionally large grasshopper or a stag-beetle in her path.

"No, I tell you, benefactor of humanity! In any case, I haven't got to that stage yet!"

"And what stage have you got to . . . already?"

"To compensations."

"Which particular ones? There are so many species—at least two."

She turned pink, overdid her short-sightedness, then, with a little twist, turned to me, imploring:

"Claudine, protect me!"

"I'll protect you all right . . . by forbidding you to let Renaud console you."

"Why, I believe you're really jealous! Are you?"

She sparkled with a malicious delight that immensely enhanced her beauty. Poised on the edge of her chair, with one leg outstretched and the other bent back and clearly outlined under her skirt, she leant towards me in a tense attitude, as if about to run. Her cheek, close to mine, was gilded with a down paler than her hair and her eyelashes fluttered incessantly, transparent as a wasp's gauzy wings. Overcome with so much beauty, it was with the utmost sincerity that I replied:

"Jealous? Oh, no, Rézi; you're far too pretty! I'd never forgive Renaud for being unfaithful to me with an ugly woman!"

Renaud caressed me with one of those intelligent looks that bring me back to him when my fierce unsociability or an unusual sharp attack of loneliness and abstraction have carried me rather far away. . . . I was grateful to him for saying so many loving things to me like that, in silence, over Rézi's head. . . .

However, Rézi-the-Golden (had she entirely understood me?) drew herself upright, gave a nervous stretch with her hands clasped inside her muff, made a face and said, with a little snort:

"Oh dear . . . your complicated psychology has made me feel quite faint, and I'm awfully hungry."

"Oh, my poor dear! And here have I been letting you starve!"

I leapt up and rushed to the bell.

A little while later, peace and friendly understanding exhaled from steaming cups and slices of toast slowly soaking up butter. But personally I despised those smart people's tea. With a basket in my lap, I was peeling withered apples and pricking and squeezing flabby medlars, winter fruits from home sent me by Mélie that smell of store-cupboards and over-ripeness.

And because a piece of burnt and blackened toast was making the room smell of creosote and fresh coal, off I went on the wings of imagination to Montigny, to the big open fireplace with the canopy over it. . . . I thought I could see Mélie throwing a damp faggot on it, and Fanchette sitting on the raised hearthstone, shift back a little, shocked by the boldness of the flames and the crackling of the green wood. . . .

"My own girl!"

I had been dreaming aloud. And, at the sight of Renaud's mirth and Rézi's stupefaction, I flushed and gave a shamefaced laugh.

7

THE mild winter drags on, warm and enervating. January is nearly over. The days go by, alternating between a feverish rush and incredible idleness. Theatres, dinners, matinées and concerts, up to one o'clock in the morning, often two! Renaud struts, throws out his chest, and I sag and wilt.

I wake up late, in a bed submerged under newspapers. Renaud divides his attention between "the attitude of England" and that of Claudine, lying on her stomach and lost in hostile dreams, trying to catch up on the indispensable sleep of which this artificial life deprives her. Luncheon is a brief affair of red meat for Renaud and various sugary horrors for myself. From two to five, the programme varies.

What does not vary is the five o'clock visit to Rézi or from Rézi; she is becoming more and more attached to me without trying to hide it. And I am becoming attached to her, God knows, but I conceal it. . . .

Almost every evening, at seven o'clock, coming away from a tea-shop or a bar where Rézi revives herself with a cocktail and I nibble potato chips with too much salt on them, I think with silent fury that I have got to go home and dress and that Renaud is already waiting for me, adjusting his pearl studs. Thanks to my convenient short hair, I have to admit—my modesty blushes!—that men and women find me equally disturbing.

Because of my shorn mane and my coldness towards them, men say to themselves: "She only goes in for women." For it is obvious to the meanest understanding that, if I don't like men, I *must* be pursuing women; such is the simplicity of the masculine mind!

Moreover, the women—on account of my shorn mane and my coldness' towards their husbands and lovers—seem inclined to think as they do. I have caught charming glances in my direction; curious, shamed, fugitive glances and even blushes if I let my eyes rest for a moment on the grace of a bare shoulder or a perfect neck. I have also sustained the shock of extremely explicit approaches; but these drawing-room professionals—the square lady of fifty or more; the thin, dark little girl with a flat behind; the monocled Jewess who plunges her sharp nose into *décolletages* as if she expected to find a lost ring in them—these temptresses found Claudine so lacking in response that they were obviously shocked. And that nearly ruined my promising reputation. To make up for it, the night before last, I saw one of my "women friends" (i.e. a young literary lady I had met five times) give such a malicious smile when she mentioned Rézi's name that I understood the implication only too well. And I thought that Rézi's husband might "cut up rough" the day rumours began to reach his brick-red ear.

A letter from Papa arrived for me, grandiloquent and heart-broken. In spite of the active bee that buzzes incessantly in his bonnet and keeps him happy, Papa is getting upset by my absence. In Paris, it didn't worry him in the least. But down there he has found the old house empty, empty of Claudine. No more silent little girl curled up, with a book on her knees, in the hollow of a big armchair bursting at the seams—or perched in the fork of the walnut-tree, shelling nuts with a noise like a squirrel—or stretched full length on the top of a wall with a predatory eye on the next-door neighbour's plums and old Madame Adolphe's dahlias. . . . Papa doesn't *say* all this; his dignity forbids it, as does the nobility of his style which does not condescend to such puerilities. But he thinks it. So do I.

Thoroughly upset, brimming over with memories and regrets, I rushed to Renaud to hide myself in the hollow of his shoulder and find oblivion there. My dear giant whom I was distracting (without his grumbling) from virtuous industry, does not always understand the causes of what he calls "my shipwrecks". But as usual, he sheltered me generously, without asking too many questions. In his warmth, the mirage of Fresnois melted into a mist and vanished. And when, swiftly excited by holding me close, he tightened his embrace and bent down his gold-streaked moustache that smelt of Egyptian tobacco, I was able to look up at him and laugh.

"You smell like a blonde who smokes!" I told him.

This time, he retorted, teasingly:

"And Rézi, what does she smell of?"

"Rézi?" . . . (I thought for a moment.) "She smells of untruthfulness."

"Untruthfulness! Are you trying to make out that she doesn't love you and is pretending to have a crush on you?"

"No, I'm not. I said more than I meant to. Rézi doesn't lie; she dissimulates. She shuts things away at the back of her mind. She isn't like the pretty Van Langendonck, who informs you, with a wealth of detail, 'I've just come from the Galeries Lafayette' at the beginning of a sentence and ends up: 'Five minutes ago I was at Saint-Pierre de Montrouge.' Rézi doesn't gush, and I'm thankful that she doesn't. But I *feel* that she hides things, that she decently buries any number of little horrors, pawing away as scrupulously as Fanchette in her tray. Commonplace little horrors, if you like, but symmetrically neat."

"What makes you so sure?"

"Nothing, of course, if you need proofs! I'm going by my instincts. There's another thing—her maid often has a way of coming in the morning, giving her a crumpled piece of paper and saying: 'Madame left this in yesterday's pocket. . . .' By chance, I happened one day to glance at the crushed-up contents of 'yesterday's pocket' and I can assure you that the envelope was still unopened. What do you think of that as a postal system? The suspicious Lambrook himself would think it was nothing but an old bit of paper."

"It's ingenious," mused Renaud aloud.

"So you realise, my dear giant, that this secretive Rézi who turns up here all white and gold, with eyes so clear you can see right to the bottom of them, who envelopes me with a pastoral scent of fern and iris . . ."

"Oho! Claudine!"

"Whatever's come over you?"

"Come over *me*, indeed? What about *you*? Am I dreaming? What, my remote, disdainful Claudine getting interested in someone, in

Rézi, to the point of studying her, to the point of thinking deeply about her and making deductions! Now then, Mademoiselle" (he was scolding me in jest, with his arms folded, like Papa). "Now then, isn't it a fact that we are in love?"

I drew sharply away from him and glared at him from under such frowning eyebrows that he was startled.

"What? Angry again? Really, you do take everything tragically!"

"And you don't take anything seriously!"

"Only one thing: you . . ."

He waited expectantly, but I did not budge.

"Come here, my little silly! Come here, then! What a lot of trouble I have with this child! Claudine," he asked (I was sitting on his knee again, silent and still a little tense), "tell me one thing."

"What?"

"Why, when it comes to admitting one of your secret thoughts, even to your old husband-papa, do you jib so fiercely? You couldn't show more outraged modesty if you were asked to display your behind at an imposing gathering of Paris celebrities. In fact, I believe you'd show less."

"Dear, simple man, that's because I *know* my behind, which is firm, pleasantly coloured and agreeable to touch. I am not so confident about my thoughts, about their clarity and the welcome they'll receive. . . . My modesty is very clear-sighted; its job is to hide anything in me that I'm afraid may be ugly and weak."

I surprised Renaud this morning in a fierce and gloomy rage. In silence I watched him throwing balls of screwed-up paper on the fire, then suddenly sweep a whole pile of pamphlets off his desk and toss the lot on the spluttering coke. A little ashtray, hurled with a deadly aim, buried itself in the waste-paper basket. Next it was the priestlike Ernest who came in for his wrath and, because he had not appeared the moment the bell rang, heard himself threatened with instant dismissal like a mere layman. Things were hotting up!

I sat down, with my hands folded, looking on and waiting. Renaud's eyes discovered me and softened:

"Why, you're back, my sweet. I didn't see you. Where have you been?"

"At Rézi's."

"I ought to have known that! . . . But forgive me for being absent-minded, darling. I'm annoyed."

"Lucky you hide it so well!"

"Don't laugh. . . . Come over here, close to me. Soothe me. I've had some infuriating, quite odious news about Marcel. . . ."

"Oh?"

I thought of my stepson's last visit. He really is going too far. An incredible desire to swagger drove him to tell me a hundred things I had not asked him, among others a fairly detailed account of an encounter in the Rue de la Pompe, at the time when the Lycée Janson releases a covey of boys in blue berets into the street. . . . That particular day, Marcel's Odyssey was interrupted by Rézi, who, for a good three-quarters of an hour, wasted all her wiles on him, vainly trying the whole armoury of her glances and a series of her most alluring swirls. Finding all her weapons blunt, she finally wearied of the fight and gave it up. She turned to me with a pretty gesture of discouragement and so plainly said: "Ouf! I've had enough!" that I began to laugh and Marcel (that pervert is far from being a fool) smiled with infinite disdain.

This disdain quickly changed to undisguised curiosity when he saw the eclectic Rézi bring all the same battery of allurements to bear on me. . . . At that, with an illtimed pretence of being tactful, he left.

What new prank had that boy been up to?

With my head resting on Renaud's knees, I waited to be enlightened.

"Always the same story, my poor darling. My charming son is bombarding some brat of good family with neo-Greek literature. . . . You don't say anything, my little girl? I ought to be used to it by now, alas! But these affairs make my gorge rise. I find them utterly revolting."

"Why?"

Renaud started at my quietly asked question.

"What do you mean? Why?"

"What I meant, my dear man, was why do you smile excitedly, almost approvingly, at the idea that Luce was too loving a friend to me? . . . And at the hope . . . I repeat the hope! . . . that Rézi might become a luckier Luce?"

How very odd my husband's face looked at that moment! Extreme surprise, a kind of shocked prudery, a shamefaced, ingratiating smile passed over it in waves like cloud-shadows running over a meadow. . . . Finally, he exclaimed triumphantly:

"That's not the same thing!"

"Thank heavens, no, not quite. . . ."

"No, it isn't at all the same thing! You women can do anything. It's charming and it's of no consequence whatever. . . ."

"No consequence? . . . I don't agree with you."

"I mean what I say and I'm right! Between you pretty little animals it's a . . . how can I put it? . . . a consolation for *us*, a restful change . . ."

"Oh?"

". . . or, at least a kind of compensation. It's the logical search for a more perfect partner, for a beauty more like your own, which reflects your own sensitiveness and your own weaknesses. . . . If I dared (but I shouldn't dare), I would say that certain women need women in order to preserve their taste for men."

Frankly, no, I did *not* understand! How singularly painful it is to love each other as much as we do and to feel so very differently! . . . I could only see what my husband had just said as a paradox that flattered and disguised the touch of the *voyeur* in his sexual make-up.

Rézi has turned herself into my shadow. She is there at all hours of the day, lassoing me with her harmonious gestures whose line prolongs itself into the void, throwing a spell over me with her words, her looks, her stormy thoughts that I expect to see bursting out in sparks from the tips of her tapering fingers. . . . I am getting uneasy, I am conscious of a will in her more consistent, more obstinate than my own which goes by leaps and bounds and then turns sluggish.

Sometimes, irritated and enervated by her soft persistence, by her beauty that she flourishes under my nose like a bouquet and adorns, barely veiled, before my eyes, I feel like asking her abruptly: "What are you driving at?" But I am frightened that she might tell me. And I prefer to keep a cowardly silence, so as to be able to stay with her with a clear conscience, for, during the last three months, she has become my cherished habit.

Indeed, apart from the insistence of her soft grey eyes and the

"Heavens! how I love you!" she often lets out as innocently and spontaneously as a little girl, there is nothing I need to be scared about.

In actual fact, what is it she loves in me? I am perfectly aware of the genuineness, if not of her affection, at least of her desire. And I am afraid, yes, afraid already—that this desire is the only thing that animates her.

Yesterday, blinded by a migraine and oppressed by the twilight, I let Rézi lay her hands over my eyes. With my lids closed, I could imagine the supple curve of her body leaning over me, slim in a clinging dress of a leaden grey that made one uncertain of the exact colour of her eyes.

A dangerous silence descended on us both. Nevertheless, she did not risk a gesture and she did not kiss me. After some minutes, she just said: "Oh my dear, my dear . . ." and fell silent again.

When the clock struck seven, I shook myself sharply and rushed to the switch to turn on the light. Rézi's smile, revealed pale and enchanting in the sudden glare, encountered my harshest, most forbidding face. Repressing a little sigh, she picked up her gloves with a supple movement, straightened her irremovable hat, murmured "Goodbye" and "Till tomorrow" into my neck, and I found myself alone in front of a mirror, listening to her light escaping footsteps.

Don't lie to yourself, Claudine! That meditation of yours, leaning on your elbows in front of that glass, with that air of suppressing a pang of remorse, was it anything else but the pleasure of verifying that your face was still intact—that face with the Havana-brown eyes, that face Rézi loves?

8

"My darling little girl, what are you thinking about?"

His darling little girl was squatting, tailor-fashion, on the big bed she had not yet quitted. . . . Enveloped in a vast pink nightdress, she was thoughtfully cutting the toe-nails of her right foot with a pretty little pair of ivory-handled clippers and not breathing a word.

"My darling little girl, what are you thinking about?"

I raised my head, adorned with snaky curls, and I stared at Renaud—who, already dressed, was knotting his tie—as if I had never set eyes on him before.

"Yes, what are you thinking about? Ever since we woke up, you haven't said a word to me. You let me prove my affection without even noticing it."

I raised a protesting hand.

"Obviously, I'm exaggerating. But you were decidedly absent-minded, Claudine. . . ."

"You amaze me!"

"Not as much as you amaze me! I'm used to your showing more consciousness during these diversions."

"They're not diversions."

"Call them nightmares, if you like, but my remark holds good. Where have you been wandering all the morning, my bird?"

"I'd like to go to the country," I said, upon reflection.

"Oh!" he exclaimed in consternation. "Claudine! Just look!"

He raised the curtain; a deluge was streaming down on the roofs and overflowing gutters.

"This morning dew whetted your appetite for it? Conjure up dirty water running all over the ground, the bottom of your skirt clinging to your ankles; think of cold drops dripping off the lobes of your ears. . . ."

"I am thinking of it. You've never understood the first thing about country rain, about *sabots* that go 'sluck' when they leave their wet imprints. Or about the rough hood with a bead of water stuck on the end of every woolly hair, the pointed hood that makes a little house for your face that you snuggle into and laugh. . . . Of course, the cold stings, but you warm your thighs with two pocketfuls of hot chestnuts and you wear thick, knitted gloves."

"Don't go on! My teeth are on edge at the thought of woollen gloves rasping against the ends of my fingernails! If you want to see your Montigny again, if you've really set your heart on it as much as all that, if it's a 'last wish'" . . . (he sighed) . . . "we'll go."

No, we won't go. Talking out loud, I had sincerely found myself thinking the words I was saying. But that morning, I was not tormented by regret for Fresnois; my silence was not due to homesickness. There was something else on my mind.

It was that . . . that hostilities had commenced and that, confronted with Rézi's amorous treachery, I found myself irresolute, without any plan of defence.

I had gone to see her at five o'clock, because, at the moment, half my life is spent in her company. And this enrages me and fascinates me and I can do nothing about it.

I found her all alone, roasting herself at a fire like the fires of hell. The glare from the hearth seemed to glow right through her, turning her tousled hair to a halo of pink flames, blurring the lines of her figure to a haze of coppery red and the crimson of molten metal. She smiled at me without getting up and held out her arms to me so lovingly that I took fright and only kissed her once.

"All alone, Rézi?"

"No. I was with you."

"With me . . . and who else?"

"With you . . . and me. I don't want anything more. But it isn't enough for you, I realise that."

"You're wrong, darling."

She shook her head with a swaying movement that rippled right down to her feet, tucked in under a low pouffe. And the gentle, dreamy face, where the bright flame carved two dimples of shadow at the corners of the mouth, looked long and searchingly into mine.

So, it had come to a head! And was that all I could find to say? Couldn't I, before letting her overwhelm me and permeate herself with me, have had it out with her, clearly and explicitly? Rézi was not a Luce whom you could beat, who would leave you in peace for twenty-four hours if you smacked her. It was my fault; it was all my fault. . . .

She gazed up at me sadly and thoughtfully and said, hardly above a whisper:

"Oh, Claudine, why are you so suspicious of me? When I sit too close to you, I always find a defensive leg, stiff as a chair-leg, thrust out under your skirt to stop me coming nearer. It's unkind of me, Claudine, to think you have to put up a physical defence! Have I ever let my mouth make one of these deliberate mistakes, pretending afterwards I was in such a hurry or it was so dark I couldn't be sure where your face was? You've treated me like a . . . a diseased person, like a . . . a professional, whose hands you keep watching, who makes you self-conscious about your every movement. . . ."

She stopped, and waited. I said nothing. She went on, with a more tender reproach:

"My dear, my dear. Is this really you, the intelligent, sensitive Claudine who's setting these conventional limits to love? They're so ridiculous!"

"Ridiculous?"

"Yes, there's no other word. You're my friend; you're only to kiss me here and here. You're my lover; you can kiss me wherever you like."

"Rézi . . ."

She checked my incipient gesture.

"Oh, don't be frightened! There's nothing of *that* sort between us. But I wish, dear, that you'd stop hurting me and setting your modesty up in arms against me, because I don't deserve it. Be fair to me," she implored (she had crept closer to me without my noticing it, with an invisible, snakelike slither). "What is it about my fondness for you that puts you on the defensive?"

"Your thoughts," I said in a low voice.

She was close to me, close enough for me to feel the warmth she had received from the fire radiating on my cheek.

"Then I ask your forgiveness," she whispered, "for an affection too strong for me to disguise. . . ."

She seemed docile, almost resigned. My breath, that I drew more slowly so that she should not guess I was in the least disturbed, brought me her smell of overheated silk and iris, a smell even sweeter because she had raised her arm to smooth the golden coil on her nape. . . . What could stop me from losing my head? . . . Pride restrained me from trumping up some obvious excuse to make a diversion. Rézi sighed and stretched her arms. . . . Her husband had just come in, in that silent, indiscreet way of his.

"What, no light yet, Rézi, my dear?" he said with apparent astonishment, after he had shaken hands.

"Oh, don't ring!" I begged, without waiting for Rézi to answer. "It's the time I love, the hour between the dog and the wolf, as we say in France."

"It strikes me as considerably nearer the wolf than the dog," that insupportable man replied very quietly.

Rézi, obstinately silent, followed him with a look of black hatred. He walked away with an even tread, entered the zone of shadow in the open doorway of the great drawing-room and continued his promenade. His measured step brought him back to us, right in front of the fire that lit up his hard face and opaque eyes from below. Having come within six inches of me, he made a military half-turn and walked away again.

I remained seated, not knowing what to do.

Rézi's eyes became diabolical; she calculated her spring. . . . Rearing up with a swift, silent movement, she pounced on me, mastering me with a fantastically soft mouth and an arm round my neck. Above my own, her wide-open eyes listened to the retreating footsteps and her free hand, held high, marked the rhythm of her husband's walk and of the quivering of her own lips that seemed to be counting my heart-beats: one, two, three, four, five. . . . Like a snapped link, the embrace broke off; Lambrook turned round; Rézi was once again sitting at my feet, apparently seeing pictures in the fire.

In my indignation, my surprise, my anxiety about the real risk she had just run I could not surpress a shuddering sigh and a cry of distress.

"You were saying, dear lady?"

"Why, dear sir, only that you must throw me out at once!

It's appallingly late. . . . Renaud must be looking for me at the Morgue!"

"I flatter myself that he would look for you here first."

I could have hit that man!

"Rézi . . . goodbye. . . ."

"See you tomorrow, darling?"

"Yes. Till then."

And that is why Claudine was so pensive this morning, as she cut the toenails of her right foot.

Cowardly Rézi! The expertness of her gesture; the abuse she made of my discretion, knowing she could rely on it; the unforgettable perfection of the perilous kiss, all that Yesterday plunged me into deep and heavy thoughts. And Renaud thought I was depressed. Doesn't he know then, will he never know, that in my eyes, desire, vivid and recent regret and sensual pleasure, are all invariably tinged with sombre hues?

Lying Rézi! Liar! Two minutes before the assault of her kiss, her humble, sincere voice had been reassuring me, telling me how hurt she was by my unjust suspicion. Liar!

In my innermost self, the suddenness of her trap pleaded in her favour. This Rézi, who had complained that I might at least have appreciated her restraint, had not been afraid to reverse her decision all at once, to risk my anger and the jealousy of that hollow Colossus.

Which does she love better, danger or me?

Me, perhaps? Once again, I saw that animal spring of the loins, that thirsty gesture that flung her on my mouth. . . . No, I would not go and see her today!

"Are you going out, Renaud? Will you take me with you?"

"With the greatest joy in the world, my charming child! Is Rézi engaged elsewhere, then?"

"Leave Rézi out of it. I want to go out with you."

"A quarrel, already?"

I answered only with a gesture of fending something off and sweeping it away. He did not insist.

Gracious as a loving woman, he hurried through his shopping in half an hour to rejoin me in the carriage—a hired coupé, a little shabby but well sprung—and drove me to Pépette's to drink tea and eat cheesecakes and lettuce and herring sandwiches. . . . We were sitting there all warm and cosy, saying silly things to each other like a badly-behaved young married couple . . . when my appetite and gaiety vanished simultaneously. Staring at a sandwich I had just bitten into, I had run up against a tiny, already distant memory.

One day, at Rézi's (it was barely two months ago) I had left a piece of toast, out of which I had bitten a half-moon shaped slice. . . . We were chatting and I did not notice Rézi's hand shyly and deftly steal that nibbled toast. . . . But, all at once, I saw her fiercely biting it and enlarging the crescent marked by my teeth, and she realised that I had seen her. She blushed, and tried to save the situation by saying: "Aren't I shockingly greedy!" That tiny incident, why did it rise up and trouble me at that moment? Suppose she were really unhappy because I hadn't come?

"Claudine! Hi, Claudine!"

"What?"

"But, my dear, this is a positive illness! There, there, my poor bird, the moment the fine weather comes, we'll go spanking off to Montigny, to your noble father, to Fanchette and Mélie! . . . I don't want to see you glooming like that, my precious child."

I smiled at dear Renaud in an ambiguous way that did not reassure him in the least, and we returned home on foot in weather muggy after rain and with the roads and pavements so greasy that horses and pedestrians staggered and slid with the same drunken unsteadiness.

At home, an express letter awaited me:

"Claudine, I implore you, forget, forget! Come back, so that I can explain, if such a thing needs to be explained. It was a game, a bit of teasing, a wild desire to fool that person who kept on walking about so close to us and whose steps on the carpet exasperated me. . . ."

What? Could I really believe my eyes? So, according to her, it was to fool "that person who kept on walking about?" But I was the stupid idiot who had been fooled! "A bit of teasing?" She would see if I could be teased in that sort of way with impunity!

My fury writhed inside me like a kitten sucking the teat; savage plans of revenge rushed through my mind. . . . I refused to admit how much disappointment and jealousy there was in my rage. . . . Renaud caught me unawares with the little blue letter open in my hands.

"Aha! She's given in? Splendid! Remember this, Claudine, it must always be the *other* who gives in!"

"You have such brilliant insight!"

My tone made him realise that I was in a stormy mood and he became anxious.

"Come now, what's happened? Anything you can tell me? I'm not asking for details."

"Nothing to tell! You're right off the track. We've had a quarrel and that's all there is to it."

"Would you like me to go round there and try to straighten things out?"

My poor, big man! His kindness and his unawareness relaxed me and I flung my arms round his neck with a laugh that had a touch of a sob in it.

"No, no. I'll go tomorrow. Calm yourself!"

"A bit of teasing!"

A remnant of common sense checked my hand as I was on the point of ringing Rézi's doorbell. But I know that common sense, because it is my own particular brand; it allows me, precisely one minute before fatal blunders, to enjoy the lucid pleasure of telling myself: "This *is* a fatal blunder." Forewarned, I hurry on serenely towards disaster, steadied, like a ship well down in the water, by a reassuring load of total responsibility.

"Is Madame at home?"

"Madame is not very well, but she will be delighted to see Madame."

Not very well? Hmmm! Not ill enough to stop me from saying what I intended to say! Anyway, all the better; it would make her feel worse. "A game!" A game two people could play. . . .

She was as white as her crêpe-de-chine dress, her eyes ringed with a mauve border that made them look blue. Slightly startled and moved, furthermore, by her grace and the look she gave me, I stood still:

"Rézi, are you really ill?"

"No; not now I see you."

I gave a rude shrug. Then I was utterly taken aback. For, seeing my sarcastic smile, she was suddenly beside herself with rage.

"You can laugh? Get out of here, if you want to laugh!"

Knocked off my high horse by this sudden violence, I tried to get back into the saddle:

"You surprise me, my dear. I thought you had such a sense of humour, with your taste for *games*, for rather elaborate *bits of teasing*."

"You did? You believed what I said? It isn't true. I lied when I wrote to you, out of pure cowardice, so as to see you again, because I can't do without you, but . . ."

Her eagerness melted into incipient tears.

". . . but it wasn't a joke, Claudine!"

She waited, fearfully, for what I would say and was frightened by my silence. She did not know that everything in me was fluttering in wild confusion, like a nest of agitated birds, and that I was flooded with joy. . . . Joy at being loved and hearing myself told so, a miser's joy at a treasure lost and recovered, victorious pride to feel I was something more than an exciting toy. It was the triumphant downfall of my feminine decency. I realised that. . . . But because she loved me, I could make her suffer still more.

"Dear Rézi . . ."

"Ah! Claudine! . . ."

She believed I was on the verge of yielding completely; she stood up, trembling all over, and held out her arms; her hair and her eyes glittered with the same pale fire. . . . Alas! how the sight of anything I love, my friend's beauty, the soft shade of the Fresnois forests, Renaud's desire, always arouses in me the same craving to possess and embrace! Have I really only one mode of feeling? . . .

"Dear Rézi . . . am I to suppose, from the state you're in, that is the first time anyone has resisted you? When I look at you, I can so well understand that you must always have found women only too delighted and willing . . ."

Her arms, raised imploringly above the white dress that wound tightly about her, its train vanishing into the shadow like a mermaid's tail, dropped again. With her hands hanging limp, I saw her almost instantaneously recover her wits and turn angry again. She said defiantly:

"The first time? Do you imagine that after eight years of living with that hollow brick, my husband, I haven't tried everything? That, to kindle any spark of love in me, I haven't searched for the sweetest, most beautiful thing in the world, a loving woman? Perhaps what you value more than anything else is the novelty, the clumsiness of a first . . . transgression. Oh, Claudine, there is something better, there is deliberately seeking and choosing. . . . I have chosen you," she ended in a hurt voice, "and you have only put up with me. . . ."

A last grain of prudence stopped me from going closer to her; also, from where I was, I could admire her to the full. She was using every weapon of her charm—her grace, her voice—in the service of her rejected passion. She had told me, truthfully: "You are not the first," because, in this case, truth struck home more shrewdly than a lie. Her frankness, I could swear, had been calculated, but she loved me!

I was dreaming of her, with her standing there before me, feasting my eyes on the sight of her. A movement of her neck conjured up the familiar Rézi, half-naked, at her dressing-table. . . . I gave a sudden shiver, it would be wise not to see her again like that. . . .

Irritated and exhausted by my silence, she strained her eyes into the shadow, trying to make out mine.

"Rézi . . ." (I spoke with a great effort) . . . "please . . . let us give ourselves a rest today from all this and just wait for tomorrow to come . . . tomorrow that straightens out so many tangles! It isn't that you've made me angry, Rézi. I'd have come yesterday, and I'd have laughed or I'd have scolded, if I weren't so fond of you. . . ."

With the alert movement of an animal on the watch, she thrust out her chin, faintly cleft with a vertical dimple.

". . . You must let me think, Rézi, without enveloping me so much, without casting such a net over me—a net of looks, gestures that come close without actually touching, persistent thoughts. . . . You must come and sit over here near me, put your head on my knees and not say anything or move. Because, if you move, I shall go away. . . ."

She sat down at my feet, laid her head on my lap with a sigh, and clasped her hands behind my waist. I could not stop my fingers from trembling as I ran them through her lovely hair, combing it into ringlets whose gleam was the only brightness left in the dark room. She did not stir. But her scent rose up from the nape of her neck, her burning cheeks warmed me and, against my knees, I could feel the shape of her breasts. . . . I was terrified lest she should move. For, had she seen my face and how profoundly disturbed I was . . .

But she did not move, and, this time, too, I was able to leave her without admitting my disturbance, so painfully like her own.

Out in the sharp, cold air, I calmed my jangled nerves as best I could. In situations of that kind, one's still undamaged "self-esteem" is definitely supposed to brace one up, isn't it? Well, all I can say personally is that I felt I had been rather a mug.

Today, I wager that the people who appear regularly on my husband's "day" must have said to themselves as they left the house, "Why, she's getting quite sociable, that little wife of Renaud's! She's becoming civilised!"

No, good people, I am not becoming civilised. I was sociable simply because I was in a daze. That woolly affability, those feverish hands that were a menace to teacups, were not for you! It was not you, old gentleman addicted to Greek literature and Russian vodka, whom I waited on with the zeal of a young Hebe! That unconscious smile with which I greeted your proposal to visit me in my own home (like the manicurist) to read Pierre Leroux to me, was not for you, novelist with socialist pretensions and a sharp eye to the main chance! Nor, Andalusian sculptor, was the earnest expression with which I followed your flood of Hispano-French invectives against contemporary art: my passionate attention was registering not only your aesthetic axioms ("All men of talent, he is dead seence two centuries"), but listening to Rézi's laugh—Rézi, in a close-fitting sheath of white cloth, the same dull, creamy white as her flowing crêpe-de-chine négligé. Andalusian sculptor, you must have renounced all hope of my aversion when I said: "I've seen the Rubenses."—"Ah! And what do you think?"—"They're tripe!" How feeble the word "swine" seemed to you and how you wished I'd fall dead at your feet!

Nevertheless, I am still alive, and I am living in the most revolting respectability. The violence of Rézi's attraction, the vanity of my resistance, the sense that I am behaving ridiculously, all urge me to get it over and done with; to intoxicate myself with her till I have exhausted her charm. But, to make a wretched pun, I rezist! And I despise myself for my own stubborn obstinacy.

Today again, she went off with the chattering throng of men who had been smoking and drinking and women who were a little tipsy from the extreme heat of the room, after the cold outside. She went off, kept well in sight by her husband, without my having told her: "I love you. . . . I'll see you tomorrow." Went proudly, the wretch, as if she were sure of me in spite of myself; sure of herself, menacing and passionate. . . .

When Renaud and I were left alone at last, we gazed at each other dejectedly, like weary victors on a battlefield. He yawned, opened a window, and leant his elbows on the sill. I went and stood beside him to drink in the cool misty air, the clean wind, damp from a shower. The feel of his great arm round me soon turned my thoughts from the path they were pursuing, now racing in a confused rush, now trailing along, broken, like shreds of clouds.

I wished that Renaud, who stands a head and shoulders higher than myself, were even taller still. I wanted to be the daughter, or the wife, of a giant Renaud so that I could nestle into the hollow of his elbow, inside the cavern of his sleeve. . . . Snug in the shelter of his ear, he would carry me away over endless plains, through enormous forests and, when the storm raged, his hair would moan in the wind like a pine-tree. . . .

But Renaud (the real one not the giant) made a movement and, at that, my fairy-tale took fright and vanished. . . .

"Claudine," he said in his full voice, velvety as his eyes. "I rather think you've made it up, you and Rézi. Am I right?"

"It depends on whether I'm willing to. . . . I'm letting her do all the pleading."

"No harm in that, Claudinette, no harm in that! And is she still crazy about you?"

"She is. But I'm still keeping her languishing after . . . after my forgiveness. 'The greater the labour.'"

"'The greater the prize,'" he chanted in an operatic baritone. "She looked very pretty today, your friend!"

"I've never seen her look anything but pretty."

"I believe you. Is the small of her back attractive?"

I was thoroughly startled.

"The small of her back? Why, I haven't the faintest idea! Do you imagine she receives me in her bath?"

"Why, yes. I did imagine so."

I shrugged my shoulders.

"It's unworthy of you, setting little traps like that! You might believe that I'm sufficiently honest and sufficiently fond of you . . . Renaud, to own up to you frankly, when the day comes: 'I've let Rézi go further than I meant to. . . .'"

The arm that encircled my shoulders turned me round to face the lighted room.

"Will you, Claudine?"

His face was bent down over mine; on it I could read curiosity and eagerness, but not a trace of anxiety.

"So in fact you can see it coming, the day when you'll have to own up?"

"That isn't what I've got to tell you tonight," I said, averting my eyes.

I was being evasive, because I felt more tremulously agitated than a little moth, one of those little reddish moths with phosphorescent eyes that flutter over asters and flowering laurels. When you hold one in your hand, you can feel its velvet body breathing and suffocating as you linger over its poignant warmth. . . .

Tonight, all my self-possession has gone. If my husband wants me—and he will—I shall be the Claudine who terrifies him and wildly excites him, the one who flings herself into love-making as if it were for the last time, and who clings, trembling, to Renaud's arm, with no resource against herself. . . .

"Renaud, do you think Rézi may be a vicious woman?"

It was nearly two in the morning. In the total darkness, I lay resting, huddled close against Renaud's side. He was still in a state of rapture, perfectly ready to plunge me back into the dizzy vortex from which I had just surfaced; I could hear his hurried, irregular heartbeats beneath my head. . . . Querulous and shattered, with my bones turned to water, I was enjoying the convalescence that follows moments of too fierce intensity . . . but, along with sanity, I had recovered the obsession that never leaves me, and, with it, the image of Rézi.

Whether I see her—a white figure with outstretched arms swathed in her long dress—lighting up the darkness where coloured specks dance before my exhausted eyes; whether she is sitting, absorbed, at her dressing-table, her arms raised and her face hidden, so that all I see is the nape whose amber melts into the pale gold of the hairline, it is Rézi, always Rézi. Now that she is no longer there, I am not sure that she loves me. My faith in her is limited to an exasperated desire for her presence.

"Renaud, do you think she may be vicious?"

"My sweet lunatic child, I've told you that, as far as I know, Madame Lambrook hasn't any lovers."

"That's not what I'm asking you. Having lovers doesn't mean that a person's vicious."

"No? Then what do you understand by vice? Homosexuality?"

"Yes and no. It depends how it's practised. But that still isn't vice."

"I'm longing to hear your definition! It must be something quite out of the ordinary."

"Then I'm afraid you're going to be disappointed. Because, after all, it's self-evident. I take a lover . . ."

"Do you, indeed?"

"It's a supposition."

"A supposition for which you'll get your bottom smacked if you don't look out!"

"I take a lover, without loving him, simply because I know it's wrong: *that's* vice. I take a lover . . ."

"That makes two."

". . . a lover whom I love or whom I simply desire—keep still, Renaud, will you?—that's just obeying the law of nature and I consider myself the most innocent of creatures. To sum up, vice is doing wrong without enjoying it. . . ."

"Let's talk about something else, shall we? All these lovers you've taken. . . . I need to purify you. . . ."

"All right, purify me, then."

All the same, if I had talked of taking "a girl-friend" instead of "a lover" he would have thought my little bit of reasoning eminently sound. For Renaud, adultery is a question of sex.

She makes me uneasy. In her artful gentleness, her shrewd avoidance of anything that might arouse my mistrust, I can no longer recognise the pale, passionate Rézi who beseeched me in a fever of tears. . . . But a glance, bright with mischief and loving defiance, has revealed the secret of all this discretion: she knows that I . . . love her—I wish there were a less crude word, a word that conveyed subtler shades of meaning. She has noticed my confusion at being left alone with her; when we exchange a brief kiss at meeting and parting (I daren't avoid kissing her altogether!), she must feel me tremble, as she does herself. She knows now, and she is waiting. Commonplace tactics, if you like. A lover's trap, as old as love itself, yet, forewarned as I am, I dread falling into it. Oh, calculating Rézi! I was able to resist your desire, but can I resist my own?

"Giving oneself up to the intoxication of cherishing and desiring, forgetting everything one has loved before, beginning to love all over again, being rejuvenated by the freshness of a new conquest—that's what makes life supremely worth living! . . ."

It was not Rézi who spoke thus. It was not myself. It was Marcel! His perversity has attained a certain grandeur, now that the excitement of a new passion is heightening his tired beauty and his flowery romanticism.

Sitting opposite me, slumped in a big armchair, he was talking like someone in delirium, his eyes lowered, his knees together. And all the time he kept making a compulsive, maniacal little gesture, stroking his eyebrows that were pencilled to lengthen their curve.

He certainly has no love for me, but I have never jeered at his peculiar affairs, and perhaps that is why he confides in me.

I listened to him seriously, and not unperturbed. "Giving oneself up to the intoxication of cherishing and desiring, forgetting everything that one loved . . ."

"Marcel, why must one forget?"

He raised his chin in token of ignorance.

"Why? I don't know. I forget, in spite of myself. Yesterday turns pale and misty behind today."

"Personally, I'd prefer to bury Yesterday and its withered flowers in the fragment casket of my memory."

Almost unconsciously, I was imitating his metaphorical redundancy.

"I can't argue about it," he said, dismissing it with a careless gesture. "Anyway, give me news of your Today and her rather sensual Viennese charm."

I frowned and lowered my head in a threatening way.

"Gossip busy already, Marcel?"

"No. Only intuition. After all, I've had so much practice! . . . Besides, you so *definitely* prefer blondes!"

"Why the plural?"

"Aha! Rézi's got you on a string now, but there was a time when you didn't find *me* unattractive!"

What cheek! His spoilt vanity is mistaken. Ten months ago, I would have slapped him; but at this moment I wonder whether I am any better than he. All the same! I stared at him from quite close to, fastening my eyes on his frail temples that would soon shrivel, on the tired crease that already marked his lower lid. And, having ruthlessly scrutinised him, I announced spitefully:

"Marcel, when you're thirty, you'll look like a little old woman."

So he had noticed it! So it was visible, then? I dared not reassure myself by admitting that Marcel had a special flair. The lazy and fatalistic passion that guided me whispered this advice: "Since people believe it is so, it might just as well be so!"

It was easy enough to say! If Rézi continues to woo me silently with her presence and her glances, at least she seems to have renounced any effective attack. She adorns her beauty in front of me like someone polishing a weapon, incenses me with her fragrance and mockingly flaunts all her perfections at me. She puts an audacious childish mischievousness into the game, but plays fair as regards her gestures so that I cannot complain.

"Claudine, look at my toe-nails! I've got a marvellous new nail-powder. My nails are little convex mirrors. . . ."

The slender foot kicked off the mule and rose up, brazen and naked, displaying the gleaming, deliciously artificial pink of the nails that tipped the pale toes . . . then at the very moment when I might have been about to seize it and kiss it, it vanished.

There is also the temptation of the hair; Rézi lazily entrusts me with the task of combing it. I acquit myself brilliantly, especially at the beginning. But prolonged contact with this golden stuff that I unravel and that is so electric that it clings to my dress and crackles under the tortoiseshell comb, like burning bracken, is too much for me. The magic of that intoxicating hair penetrates all through me and makes me torpid. . . . Weakly, I let fall the loosened sheaf and Rézi becomes impatient—or pretends to.

Yesterday night at dinner—a dinner for fifteen at the Lambrooks'—while everyone was busy coping with lobster *à l'Américaine,* she even dared to look me full in the face and make the adorable mime of a kiss—a silent, complete kiss, with her lips first pursed, then parted, and her sea-grey eyes open and imperious, then veiled.

I was terrified that someone might see her and even more shaken by seeing her myself.

Sometimes this nerve-racking game embarrasses Rézi herself. This happened this morning, in her flat.

Wearing a straw-coloured petticoat and corsets, she was twisting and undulating in front of the mirrors, trying to do the back-bends like a "Spanish" dancer in Montmartre and get the nape of her neck on a level with her hips.

"Claudine, can you do that?"

"Yes, and better than you can."

"I'm sure, dear. You're like a well-tempered foil, hard and supple. . . . Ah!"

"What's the matter?"

"Are there mosquitoes at this time of year? Quick, quick. Look at my precious skin I love so much . . . and I've got to wear a low neck tonight!"

She made an effort to see a bite (imaginary?) behind her bare shoulder. I bent forward.

"There, there, a little above the shoulder-blade, higher, yes, that's it . . . something stung me. . . . What can you see?"

I could see, close enough to touch, the perfectly curved shoulder, Rézi's anxious profile, and, lower down, two bared young breasts, round and far apart, like the ones gallants toy with in naughty eighteenth-century engravings. I saw all this, stupefied, and did not say a word. I was unaware, at first, of the intense gaze she had fixed on me. That gaze attracted mine at last, but I averted it to dwell on the peerless whiteness of that flawless, even-tinted skin where the breasts broke abruptly into pink at the tips, the same pink as her nail-varnish. . . .

Triumphant, Rézi followed my wandering eyes. But because they had become fixed and urgent, she weakened herself and her eyelashes fluttered like wasp-wings. . . . Her eyes turned bluer and rolled upwards and it was she who whispered, "No, no . . . *please* . . ." as palpably shaken as I was myself.

"*Please* . . ." That word, breathed on a sigh, with a mixture of sensuality and childishness, has done more to precipitate my defeat than the most searching caress.

9

"My darling child, whatever time's this you're coming in? When for once we're dining alone at home! . . . Come along, quick; you look perfectly all right as you are; don't rush off to your bedroom on the excuse of tidying up your curls—or we'll be here till midnight! Come along, sit down, sweet! I've ordered something special for you tonight—those revolting aubergines with parmesan that you adore."

"Yes. . . ."

I heard what he said without taking it in. Leaving Renaud holding my hat, I dug my fists into my hair and rubbed my overheated head, then collapsed on to the leather chair opposite my husband, under the kindly, shaded light.

"No soup?"

I wrinkled my nose in disgust.

"Tell me where you've come from, with that sleepwalking expression and those eyes burning holes in your face. From Rézi's, eh?"

"Yes. . . ."

"Claudine, my girl, you must admit I'm not a jealous husband!"

Not jealous enough, alas! That was what I ought to have answered, instead of merely being content to think it. But he thrust a swarthy face towards me, barred by a moustache lighter than the skin and softened by a feminine smile. He looked so radiant with amorous fatherliness that I did not dare.

To occupy my restless hands, I broke off some golden crumbs to convey them to my mouth, but my hand dropped again; the obstinate perfume that clung to it made me go suddenly pale.

"Are you ill, my little one?" Renaud asked anxiously, flinging away his table-napkin. . . .

"No, no! Tired, that's all. Please, I'm awfully thirsty. . . ."

He rang the bell and asked for the sparkling wine I like, the musty Asti I can never drink without a smile. . . . But this time, I was tipsy before I had drunk a drop.

All right, yes, I had come from Rézi's! I wanted to scream, to stretch my arms till the sinews cracked so as to melt the maddening stiffness in the nape of my neck.

I had gone to see her, as I do every day, about five o'clock. Without ever making an appointment, she always faithfully waits in for me then; without having made any promise, I faithfully arrive at that hour.

I go to her on foot, walking fast. I watch the days drawing out and the March showers washing the pavements; the daffodils from Nice, heaped on the little barrows, fill the rainy air with their precocious, intoxicating, vulgar spring.

It is on that short road that I study the march of the seasons now, I who used to watch as alertly as an animal for the first pointed leaf in the wood, the first wild anemone like a glimmer of mauve-streaked white flame, for the first willow catkins, whose little furry tails smell like honey. Wild creature of the forest, you are caged now and you do not want to escape.

Today, as always, Rézi was waiting for me in her green-and-white bedroom. The bed is painted dull white and the late Louis XV armchairs are upholstered in almond-green silk, scattered with little white bows and big white bunches of flowers. Against this tender green, her skin and her hair look dazzling.

But today . . .

"How dark it is in here, Rézi! And there's no light in the hall! Say something. I can't even see you."

Her voice answered me sulkily, coming from a deep armchair, one of those wicked chairs that are too wide for one person and a little too narrow for two. . . .

"Yes; gay, isn't it? Something's gone wrong with the electricity. Apparently they can't fix it till tomorrow morning. Naturally, we've got nothing here to use instead. The maid was actually talking of sticking candles in the bottles on my dressing-table! . . ."

"Well, wouldn't that look rather attractive?"

"Thanks! . . . You always side with evil Fate against me. . . . Candles! I'd feel I was lying on my bier! They're too funereal for words. Instead of coming and consoling me, you stand over there all by yourself, laughing. I can hear you laughing! Come and sit with me in the big armchair, Claudine darling. . . ."

I did not hesitate for a second. Huddled in the big chair, with my arms round her waist, I could feel her body warm and untrammelled under a loose dress, and her scent rose up in my nostrils.

"Rézi, you're like the white tobacco flower that waits for the dark to release all its scent. . . . Once evening comes, you can't smell anything else; it puts the roses to shame."

"Do I really wait for the dark before I give off any scent?"

She let her head fall on my shoulder. I held her close, feeling her living warmth throbbing under my hands, like a trapped partridge.

"Is your husband going to rise up out of the shadows again like an Anglo-Indian Satan?" I asked in a muffled voice.

"No," she sighed. "He's taking some compatriots round Paris."

"Indians?"

"Englishmen."

Neither she nor I were paying any attention to what we said. The darkness covered us. I did not dare loosen my arms and, besides, I did not want to.

"Claudine, I love you. . . ."

"Why say it?"

"Why not say it? For your sake, I've given up everything, even the flirtations that were the only thing that relieved my boredom. Can you ask me to be more restrained? Don't I torture myself because I'm afraid of making you angry?"

"Torture yourself? Oh, Rézi . . ."

"It's the only word. It *is* torture to love and desire unappeasably; you know it is."

Yes, I knew it. . . . How well I knew it. . . . What was I doing at that moment except delighting in that useless pain?

With an imperceptible movement, she had turned still more towards me, clinging close against me from shoulder to knee. I had hardly felt her move; she seemed to have swivelled round inside her dress.

"Rézi, don't talk to me any more. I'm in a trance of laziness and well-being. Don't force me to get up from here. . . . Imagine that it's night and we're travelling. . . . Imagine the wind in your hair . . . bend down, that low branch might wet your forehead! . . . Squeeze close against me—mind out, the water in the deep ruts is splashing up under the wheels. . . ."

All her supple body followed my game with a treacherous compliance. Her hair, tossed back from the head that lay on my shoulder, brushed against my face like the twigs I had invented to distract me from my inner turmoil.

"I'm travelling," she murmured.

"But shall we arrive?"

Her two hands nervously gripped my free one.

"Yes, Claudine. We shall arrive."

"Where?"

"Bend down, and I'll whisper it to you."

Credulously, I obeyed. And it was her mouth that I encountered. I listened for a long time to what her mouth told mine. . . . She had not lied: we were arriving. . . . My haste equalled her own, then surpassed and outstripped it. In a revelation of self-knowledge, I thrust away Rézi's caressing hands. She understood, trembled all over, struggled for a brief second, then lay back, her arms hanging limp.

The dull thud of a distant street-door brought me to my feet. Rézi's warm lips were pressed to my wrist; all I could make out was the pale blur of her seated figure. With one arm round her waist, I pulled her up and crushed her whole body against me, bending her back and kissing her at random on her eyes, on her dishevelled hair, on her moist nape. . . .

"Tomorrow!"

"Tomorrow. . . . I love you."

I ran down the street, with my head buzzing. My fingers still tingled from the slight scratchiness of lace, still seemed to be slithering on the satin of an untied ribbon, still felt the velvet of a peerless skin. And the evening air hurt me like a knife, tearing the veil of perfume she had woven all about me.

"Claudine, if even aubergines with parmesan leave you cold . . . I know where to look for the reason!"

I started at the sound of Renaud's voice; I had been a very long way away. It was true I was not eating. But I was so thirsty!

"Darling, isn't there something you want to tell me?"

This husband of mine is certainly not like other husbands! Vexed by his persistence, I implored him:

"Renaud, don't tease me. . . . I'm tired, I'm nervous, I'm embarrassed in front of you. . . . Let's get the night over, and for heaven's sake, don't imagine so many things!"

He said no more. But, after dinner, he kept watching the clock and, at half-past ten, insisted that he was shockingly sleepy, a thing that he never admits. And, once we were in our great bed, he lost not a moment before seeking in my hair, on my hands, on my mouth the truth I did not want to tell him!

"Tomorrow!" Rézi had implored. "Tomorrow!" I had consented. Alas! this Tomorrow did not come. I hurried round to her, sure of a longer, more perfectly savoured bliss now that there would be light again to show me this marvellous, vanquished Rézi. . . . But I had completely forgotten her husband! He disturbed us twice, the fiend; twice, by an abrupt entrance, he made our timid, hungry hands fly apart! We stared at each other, Rézi and I, she on the verge of tears, I in such a furious rage, that had there been a third intrusion, it would have been all I could do not to throw my glass of orangeade in the face of that stiff, suspicious, polite husband. . . . And that throbbing "Goodbye," those stolen kisses, those furtive pressures of our fingers are no longer enough to satisfy us now. . . .

What can we do?

I came home, alternately building up and sweeping away impossible plans. It was hopeless!

Today I went back to Rézi's flat to tell her of my utter helplessness, to see her, to breathe in her sweetness.

She rushed to meet me, as anxious as I was myself.

"Well, darling?"

"I haven't found any solution. Are you angry with me?"

Her eyes caressed the curve of my mouth as I spoke and her lips trembled and parted. . . . I caught the infection of her desire and my whole being was hungry for her. Was I going to seize her then and there in that smug drawing-room and kiss her to death?

She guessed what I was thinking and drew back a step. "No," she said in a low, hurried voice, pointing to the door.

"Then in my flat, Rézi?"

"In yours, if you like. . . ."

I smiled; then I shook my head.

"No! The bell keeps ringing all the time; Renaud is always in and out; the doors bang. . . . Oh, no!"

She wrung her white hands in a little gesture of despair.

"Then it's to be never again? Do you imagine I can live for a month on the memory of yesterday? It ought never to have happened," she ended, turning away her head. "If you can't quench my thirst for you every day . . ."

Tenderly sulky, she went over and collapsed in the big armchair, the same one. . . . And though today she was sheathed in a tight-fitting wool street-dress, honey-pale as her hair, I recognised only too well the curve of her half-reclining hips and the tapering line of her legs that were silvered with almost invisible velvet down.

"Oh, Rézi!"

"What?"

"The carriage?"

"The carriage? Jolts, starts, cricks in the neck . . . curious faces suddenly glued to the window, a horse falling, a zealous policeman opening the door, the driver discreetly tapping with the handle of his whip: 'Madame, the road's blocked. Should I turn back?' No, Claudine, definitely *not* the carriage!"

"Then, my dear, find somewhere possible for us yourself . . . up to now you've found nothing but objections!"

Swift as a snake when you touch it, she reared up her golden head and darted me looks full of tearful reproach.

"Is that all your love amounts to? You wouldn't dream of being offended if you loved me as much as I love you!"

I shrugged my shoulders.

"Then why keep putting up all these barriers? The carriage paralyses you, this drawing-room bristles with matrimonial traps . . . have we got to take in the Saturday *Journal* and look for a shelter you hire by the day?"

"I'd do that gladly," she sighed ingenuously, "but all those places are watched by the police so . . . so somebody told me."

"I don't care a fig about the police."

"*You* don't have to, thanks to the sort of husband you have, thanks to Renaud. . . ."

Her voice changed.

"Claudine," she said slowly and thoughtfully, "Renaud—Renaud's the only person who can . . ."

I stared at her, dumbfounded, without finding any reply. She was thinking very earnestly, sitting there, slim in her honey-coloured dress, her fist under her childish chin.

"Yes, Claudine, our peace of mind depends on him . . . and on you."

She held out her arms, and her impenetrable, tender face appealed to me.

"Our peace of mind, oh! my dear, our happiness, call it what you like. Only realise that I can't bear to wait, now that I have felt your strength, now that Rézi is yours, with all her passion and all her weakness!"

I slipped into her arms, and bent over her lips, prepared to resign myself to tight, hampering garments, prepared to ruin our delight by over-haste.

She wrenched herself out of my hands: "Sshh! I heard footsteps."

How terrified she was! Her whiteness had gone whiter still; she was listening, bending forward, her pupils dilated. . . . Oh, if only a chimney would fall and flatten out that accursed Lambrook and deliver us from him!

"Rézi, my golden, why do you think that Renaud . . . ?"

"Yes, Renaud! *He's* an intelligent husband and he adores you. You must tell him . . . well, almost everything. He's so fond of you and so clever, he must arrange a 'hide-out' for us."

"You aren't afraid of *my* husband being jealous?"

"No."

Curious, that little smile of hers! . . . A crazy confidence in her had been growing almost as fast as my desires, why did she have to check it by an ambiguous gesture, a sly inflexion of the mouth? But it was the merest shadow, and if I were to have no more of her than her sincere sensuality, the double softness of her skin and her voice, her glorious hair and her enthralling mouth . . . was not that more than enough? Whatever it cost me, I would ask help—not now, a little later, I wanted to go on searching on my own!—I would ask help from Renaud. For her sake, I would humble my fierce modesty and the loving pride I should have put into discovering a safe haven for our passion entirely on my own.

Enervating sulks, angry tears, tender reconciliations, electric hours when the mere contact of our hands maddened us . . . that is the summary of this last week. I haven't spoken to Renaud. It would cost me so much to do that! And Rézi is resentful because I haven't. I haven't even admitted to my dear giant that Rézi's feeling for me and mine for Rézi is becoming clearer than words can say. . . . But he knows almost everything, apart from details, and this certainly induces a strange fever in him. What fantastic, loving pandarism leads him to keep urging me to go and see Rézi, to make sure I look my best for her? At four o'clock, when I throw down the book with which I was cheating the time of waiting, Renaud gets up, if he is in the room, and becomes agitated: "You're going over there?—Yes?" He runs his deft fingers through my hair to fluff up my curls, bends his great moustache down close to me to re-knot my thick knitted silk tie and verify the spotlessness of my boyish collar. Standing behind me, he makes sure that my fur turban is firm and straight, then holds out the sleeves of my sable coat. . . . And, finally, it is he who slips into my dazed hands a bunch of dark red, almost black roses, my friend's favourite flower! I admit that I would never have thought of that!

And then comes a big, affectionate kiss.

"Run along, my little girl. Be very good. Be proud, not too humbly loving, make yourself desired. . . ."

"Make yourself desired. . . ." I am desired, alas! . . . but not as a result of my strategy.

10

WHEN it is Rézi who comes to see me, the strain on my nerves is even worse. There she is in my bedroom—which is simply *our* bedroom, Renaud's and mine—one turn of the key and we should be alone. . . . But I don't want to lock us in. Above all I hate the idea of my husband's maid (a taciturn girl with a silent tread who sews such slack stitches with her flabby hands) knocking and explaining in a hushed voice through the closed door: "It's Madame's blouse . . . I want it to repair the armholes." I dread the spying of Ernest, the manservant with a face like a bad priest's. Those servants of his don't belong to me; I employ them with caution and repugnance. To tell the whole truth, there is something I dread even more—Renaud's curiosity. . . .

And that is why all I let Rézi do in my bedroom is weave her most seductive spirals and put on every shade of reproachful expression.

"You haven't found anything for us, Claudine?"

"No."

"You haven't asked Renaud yet?"

"No."

"It's cruel. . . ."

At that word, sighed almost in a whisper, with her eyes suddenly lowered, I felt my will collapse. But Renaud came and knocked with little cautious taps and received a "Come in" ruder than a brick in his face, in reply.

I don't at all like the suppliant charm Rézi puts on with Renaud, nor that way he has of trying to find out what we are hiding from

him by sniffing at her hair and her dress as if to detect the fragrance
left by my kisses.

He did it again today, in front of me. . . . He kissed both her
hands when he came in, for the pleasure of saying:

"So you've taken to using Claudine's scent, that sweet, dusky
Chypre?"

"Why, no," she replied innocently.

"Funny, I thought you had."

Renaud switched his gaze on me with a knowing, flattering look.
My whole soul flared up with rage. I was so exasperated, I wondered
should I tug the ends of his big moustache with all my might till he
screamed, till he beat me? . . . No. I managed to contain myself; I
preserved the stiff, correct calm of a husband whose wife is being
kissed during some innocent party game. To make matters even
worse, he was about to make his exit with the insulting discretion of
a waiter serving a couple dining in a private room. I stopped him:

"Do stay, Renaud. . . ."

"Not on your life! Rézi would tear my eyes out."

"Why?"

"My little curly shepherd, I know only too well how precious a
tête-à-tête with you is."

An ugly fear poisoned me: suppose Rézi, with her fluctuating,
untruthful nature, took to preferring Renaud! He was particularly
handsome today, in a long jacket that suited him and drew attention
to his broad shoulders and small feet. . . . And there was that Rézi,
the source of all my trouble, furred in nutria the colour of rye and
wearing a prematurely summery hat of lilacs and green leaves. . . . I
was aware of an old feeling surging up in me again, the brutality that
had made me beat and scractch Luce. . . . How poignantly sweet
Rézi's tears would be to my torment!

She looked at me in silence, putting all her words into her
eyes. . . . I was going to yield. . . . I yielded.

"Renaud, dear, are you going out before dinner?"

"No, little girl, why?"

"I want to talk to you . . . to ask you to do something for me."

Rézi sprang up from her chair and settled her hat, all gaiety and
confusion . . . she had understood.

"I must fly. . . . Yes, literally, I can't stay another moment. . . .
But tomorrow I'll see you for a long time, Claudine. Ah! Renaud,

how one ought to envy you this child of yours!"

She disappeared with the rustling of her dress, leaving Renaud confounded.

"She's mad, I take it? Whatever's come over the two of you?"

Oh, heavens! Could I really say it? How hard it was! . . .

"Renaud . . . I . . . you . . ."

"What is it, little one? You've gone all pale!"

He drew me on to his knees. Perhaps it would be easier there. . . .

"The fact is . . . Rézi's husband's an awful nuisance."

"He certainly is . . . especially to her!"

"To me too."

"The devil he is! . . . You mean he's had the impertinence to try something on?"

"No. Don't move; keep me in your arms. Only this wretched Lambrook is always on our backs."

"Ah! I see."

Of course, I ought to know by now that Renaud is anything but a fool. He understands at the first hint.

"My dear little amorous pussy-cat! So you're being tormented, you and your Rézi? What's to be done about it. You're quite aware that your old husband loves you enough not to deprive you of a little pleasure. . . . She's charming, your fair-haired friend. She loves you so tremendously!"

"Does she? Do you really think so?"

"I'm certain of it! And your two beauties complement each other. Your amber can hold its own against her dazzling whiteness. . . ."

His arms had trembled. . . . I knew what he was imagining. Nevertheless I relaxed at the sound of his voice; overflowing with tenderness, genuine tenderness.

"What do you want me to do, my darling bird? Leave this flat empty the whole of the afternoon?"

"Oh! no. . . ."

I added, after an embarrassed silence:

". . . If we could . . . somewhere else. . . ."

"Somewhere else? Why, nothing easier!"

He rose to his feet with one bound, set me on the floor and walked up and down with long, very youthful strides. . . .

"Somewhere else . . . let's see . . . of course there's . . . No, not that—it's not good enough. . . . Ah! I've got the very thing for you!"

He came back to me, flung his arms round me and searched for my mouth. But, quite frigid with confusion and shyness, I turned slightly away. . . .

"My charming little girl, you shall have your Rézi. Rézi shall have her Claudine. Don't you worry about any thing any more . . . except having to be patient for one day . . . two days at the most. . . . That's not long, is it? Kiss your faithful giant who will be blind and deaf as he keeps guard over the threshold of your room and those soft whisperings inside. . . ."

The joy, the certainty of possessing Rézi in all the glory of her scented whiteness, the relief of having confessed the ugly secret, did not prevent me from feeling another kind of unhappiness. Oh, dear Renaud, how I would have loved you for a sharp, scolding refusal!

I had hoped that night of waiting would be happy, alternating between flutters of sweet apprehension and half-waking dreams through which Rézi drifted in a haze of golden light. . . . But the very fact that I was waiting conjured up another vigil in my little bedroom in the Rue Jacob. That had been a younger, more fierily impetuous Claudine. . . . Would Rézi find me beautiful enough? Ardent enough, oh yes, I was sure of that. . . . Weary of lying awake, I put out a slim cold foot to disturb Renaud's light sleep so that I could huddle my body, prickling all over with nerves, in the shelter of his arm. And there, at last, I dozed off.

Dreams succeeded each other and melted into each other in a tangled, confused blur, impossible to analyse: sometimes a young, supple figure would appear in the fog, then vanish, like the moon shining through clouds, then veiled again. . . . When I called "Rézi," she turned round, showing me the gentle, rounded forehead, the velvety eyelids and full, short lips of little black-and-white Hélène. What was she doing in my dreams, that schoolgirl, glimpsed for a moment and very nearly forgotten?

Renaud has wasted no time. He arrived home for dinner last night excited, boisterous and demonstrative.

"Tell Rézi to prepare!" he said as he kissed me. "Bid that young witch wash and anoint herself for tomorrow's Sabbath!"

"Tomorrow? Where?"

"You'll know in due course! Tell her to meet us here; I'll take you both with me. It's not good for you to be seen going in by yourselves. And besides, I'll see you comfortably settled in."

This arrangement chilled me a little: I would have liked the key, the address of the room, freedom. . . .

Rézi arrived before the appointed time, looking anxious. Making an attempt to laugh, I said to her:

"Will you come with me? Renaud has found us a . . . a 'bachelor-girls' flat'."

Her eyes danced and a golden glint came into them.

"Ah! . . . So he knows that I know that he . . ."

"Of course! How else would it have been possible? You yourself suggested . . . and I'm thankful now, that you were so persistent, Rézi . . . my asking Renaud's help. . . ."

"Yes, yes. I did. . . ."

Her sly, caressing grey eyes became anxious and sought mine; her hand went up to her hair and kept circling round and round as she tucked in stray gold wisps on her nape.

"I'm afraid you don't love me enough, today, not enough for . . . that, Claudine!"

Her mouth was too close as she said it; I could feel her breath and that was enough to make me clench my jaws and bring the blood to my ears. . . .

"I always love you enough . . . too much . . . madly, Rézi. . . . Yes, I would far rather that no one in the world had authorised us or forbidden us to have an afternoon alone together, safe behind a locked door. But if in that room, wherever it is, whoever found it, I can believe for one moment that you belong to me, that I am the only one . . . I shall regret nothing."

She listened to the sound of my voice as if in a day-dream; perhaps she did not even hear the words. When Renaud entered, we started simultaneously and, for a minute, Rézi lost a little of her self-assurance. He dissipated her embarrassment with a kindly, conspiratorial laugh, then, looking mysterious, produced a small key from his waistcoat pocket.

"Hist! To whom shall I entrust it?"

"To me," I said, holding out an imperious hand.

"To me!" Rézi implored coaxingly.

"*How happy could I be with either*," warbled Renaud, "*were t'other dear charmer away*."

At this Maugis-like joke, and the shrill laugh with which Rézi greeted it, I felt on the verge of a clumsy outburst of rage. Did Renaud divine this? He stood up:

"Come along, children. The carriage is down below."

Sitting opposite us on the penitential, pull-down seat, he could hardly disguise his excitement over this escapade. His nose whitened and his moustache quivered when his eyes wandered over Rézi. The latter tried, uncertainly, to make conversation, gave it up and looked enquiringly at me in my sad, haughty impatience. . . .

Yes, I was eaten up with impatience! Impatience to savour all that Rézi's urgency had promised me during this week of stress and strain; impatience above all to arrive, to end this shocking expedition as a threesome.

What? We were stopping in the Rue Goethe? So near home? It seemed to me that we had been driving for half an hour. . . . The staircase of number 59 wasn't bad. There were stables at the bottom of the courtyard. Two storeys. Renaud opened a noiseless door and, the moment one entered the hall, one was conscious of the thick, heavy air of rooms hung with material.

While I was examining the little drawing-room with a slightly hostile eye, Rézi ran to the window and, in a prudent (I don't want to write experienced) way, inspected the outside without raising the white net curtains. Presumably satisfied, she wandered, like myself, about the minute drawing-room, where an amateur of Louis XIII Spanish furniture had indulged his mania to the full. It was crammed with carved and gilded wood, heavy ornamental frames, crucifixes on moth-eaten velvet, hostile *prie-dieus* and an enormous sedan chair, ponderous and splendid, with a cornucopia of autumn fruits, apples, grapes and pears, carved in full relief on its sides. . . . This sacrilegious austerity pleased me and I relaxed my frown. A half-drawn curtain in the doorway revealed the corner of a light, English-style bedroom, the knob of a brass bedstead and a pleasant couch covered with flowered material. . . .

"I like the look of it. Definitely."

"Renaud, it's charming!" declared Rézi. "Whose place is this?"

"Yours, fair Bilitis! Here's the electric light switch. Here's some tea and some lemon, here are some black grapes, and lastly, here is my heart that throbs for both of you. . . ."

How utterly at ease he was and with what good grace he fulfilled his dubious rôle! I watched him bustling about, arranging the saucers with his deft, feminine hands, smiling with his blue-black eyes, holding out a bunch of grapes to Rézi that she nibbled coquettishly . . . Why was I astonished at his behaviour when he was not astonished at mine?

. . . I was holding her against my heart, against the whole length of my body. Her cool knees touched me, her little toe-nails scratched me deliciously. Her crumpled chemise was nothing but a rag of muslin. My bent arm supported the precious weight of her neck, her face was half-buried in the torrent of her hair. The day was ending, the shadow was dimming the bright leaves on the hangings whose unfamiliarity galled me. Rézi's mouth was very close to mine; from time to time a glint of light, like a sun-gleam on a river, shone on her teeth as she talked. She talked in a fever of gaiety, one bare arm raised and her forefinger drawing what she said. In the twilight, I followed that white and sinuous arm whose gestures made a rhythmic accompaniment to my languor and the adorable sadness that drugged me. . . .

I wanted her to be sad, as I was; I wanted her too to be quiet and fearful at the thought of the minutes flying past; I wanted her, at least, to leave me to brood on my memory. . . .

As if the first caress had wounded her, she had turned a marvellous, animal face towards me; eyebrows lowered, upper lip raised and snarling, an expression of frenzy and supplication. . . . Then everything melted into wild surrender, into murmuring, imperious demands, into a kind of amorous fury, followed by childish "Thank-yous" and great, satisfied sighs of "Ah!" like a little girl who had been dreadfully thirsty and drunk everything down at a gulp, leaving her out of breath. . . .

Now she was talking, and her voice, dear as it was, disturbed the precious hour. . . . She was, in fact, chattering her joy aloud, just like Renaud. . . . Couldn't they savour it in silence? There was I, sombre as that unfamiliar bedroom. . . . What a bad after-love-making companion I am!

I roused myself to life again by straining close the warm body that adapted itself to mine and flexed when I flexed; the beloved body, so fleshy in its tapering slimness that nowhere could I feel the resisting skeleton beneath. . . .

"Ah! Claudine, you crush me so tight in your arms! . . . Yes, I assure you that his frigidity, his outrageous jealousy justify everything."

She was talking of her husband? I was not listening. And what need had she of excuses? That word rang false here. With a kiss, I dammed the flow of her soft chatter . . . for a few seconds.

"Claudine, I swear no one's ever made me suffer the torture of waiting as *you* have. So many weeks wasted, my love! Think, it'll soon be spring and every day is bringing us nearer the summer holidays that will separate us . . ."

"I forbid you to go away!"

"Yes, do forbid me something!" she implored, invincibly tender, clinging close to me. "Scold me, don't leave me, I don't want to see anyone but you . . . and Renaud."

"Ah! So Renaud finds favour with you?"

"Yes, because he's kind, because he's got the soul of a woman, because he understands us and protects our privacy. . . . Claudine, I don't feel ashamed in front of Renaud. Isn't that odd?"

Odd indeed, and I envy Rézi. For *I* am ashamed. No, that's not quite the right word. . . . What I am rather is . . . a little . . . scandalised. That's it. My husband shocks me.

". . . And, in any case, darling," she wound up, raising herself on one elbow, "the three of us are involved in a little adventure that's far from commonplace!"

"Far from commonplace! A little adventure!" That babbler! If I kissed her mouth rather cruelly, didn't she guess why? I wanted to bite off her pointed tongue; I wanted to love the mute, docile Rézi, perfect in her silence, eloquent only in look and gesture.

I annihilated myself in my kiss, aware only of her quick, fluttering breath fanning my nostrils. . . . It had grown dark but I cupped Rézi's head in my two hands like a fruit, ruffling her hair that was so fine that I could have guessed its colour merely by the feel of it. . . .

"Claudine, I'm sure it's seven o'clock!"

She leapt out of bed, rushed over to the switch and flooded us with light.

Left solitary and chilly, I curled up in the warm place where she had lain to keep the heat of her body a little longer, to permeate myself with the smell of her blonde skin. *I* had plenty of time. *My* husband was not anxiously expecting me home . . . quite the reverse!

Dazed by the light, she spun round for a moment, unable to find her scattered underclothes. She bent down to pick up a stray tortoiseshell hairpin, stood up again and her chemise slid to the ground. Unembarrassed, she coiled up her hair again, with that swift, deft grace that amuses and charms me. . . . The frizz of gold in the hollow of the raised arms and at the base of the youthful stomach was so pale that, in the light, my Rézi seemed as naked as a statue. But what statue would dare display those full, resilient buttocks, so bold and assertive after the slimness of the torso?

Looking very serious, with her hair as irreproachably done as if she were going to a formal party, Rézi pinned her spring-like hat on her head and stood for a moment admiring herself in the glass, arrayed only in a toque of lilac-blossom. I laughed and thereby unfortunately spurred her to hurry. The next moment, the corset, the diaphanous knickers, the dawn-pink petticoat flung themselves on her, undoubtedly summoned by three magic words. Another minute, and the fashionable, sophisticated Rézi stood before me, furred in nutria, gloved in ivory suède, proud of her conjuror's dexterity.

"My blonde girl, it's dark now that all your white and gold doesn't shine brighter than the light. . . . Help me to get up. I'm too weak to battle with these sheets that hold me down. . . ."

On my feet, stretching up my damp hands to ease the stiff little ache between my shoulder-blades, I studied myself in the huge, well-placed mirror. I was proud of my muscular tallness, of my slender grace, more boyish and clear-cut than Rézi's. . . .

The nape of her neck slid caressingly under my raised arm and I turned away from the two figures, one dressed, one naked, that the mirror reflected back.

I hurried into my clothes, helped by Rézi. Close to me, she gave off a smell of love-warmed flesh and of fur. . . .

"Rézi dear, don't try to teach me your magical speed! Compared to your fairy hands, I shall always look like someone dressing themselves with their feet! What, aren't we going to have any tea?"

"We haven't time," demurred Rézi, smiling at me.

"Just some black grapes at least? I'm so thirsty. . . ."

"All right, some black grapes. . . . Come and take them."

I took them from between her lips, crushing out their juice in my parched mouth. . . . I was staggering with exhaustion and desire. She escaped from my arms.

The lights were switched off, the door stood ajar on the cold, bright, echoing staircase. Rézi, all warm and glowing, offered me her mouth, that tasted of black grapes, for the last time. . . . And suddenly I was in the street, being elbowed by passers-by, and because of that unnatural getting dressed again, feeling shivery and faintly sick, as if I had had to get up in the middle of the night.

"Darling child, come here and I'll make you laugh!"

It was Renaud who had come into the dressing-room and interrupted the prolonged morning curry-combing of my short hair. Wedged in the wicker armchair, he was already laughing himself.

"Listen! A devoted female who's willing to keep the Rue Goethe tidy for sixty centimes an hour returned an object (found in the storm-tossed sheets) to me this morning, neatly folded in a scrap of the *Petit Parisien*, with the sole comment: 'It's Monsieur's chin-strap.'"

"!!! . . ."

"There! You'll promptly get the most unseemly ideas into your head! Look!"

At the end of his fingers dangled a narrow rag of minutely-pleated linen, edged with Malines lace. . . . The shoulder-strap of Rézi's chemise! . . . I snatched it from him in mid-air. . . . I shan't give it back to him.

"What's more, I suspect that concierge of providing 'gags' for our most popular music-hall comedians. Yesterday, about six, I went round there—very discreet—and a trifle anxious about my darling, who was so long coming home—to ask for news of you. She replied, full of respectful censure, 'Those two ladies have been waiting nearly two whole hours for Monsieur.'"

"So then?"

"So then . . . I didn't come up, Claudine. Kiss me as a reward for that."

11

THIS will no longer really be Claudine's diary any more, because in it I can talk of nothing but Rézi. What has happened to the old, quick-witted Claudine? She is nothing but a fevered, unhappy creature drifting weakly in Rézi's wake. The days go past without incident, except for our meetings once or twice a week in the Rue Goethe. The rest of the time I follow Renaud as he performs his various duties: first nights, dinners, literary parties. I often take my mistress to the theatre, accompanied by Lambrook, just for the craven assurance that at least during those hours she cannot deceive me. I suffer from jealousy and yet . . . I do not love her.

No, I do not love her! But I cannot deprive myself of her, and in any case I do not try to. Away from her, I can imagine, without a tremor, her being knocked down by a motor car or killed in a railway accident. But I cannot, without my ears buzzing and my heart accelerating, say to myself: "At this very moment she is yielding her mouth to a lover, man or woman, with that hurried flutter of the lashes, that backward tilt of the head as if she were drinking, that I know so well."

What does it matter that I do not love her, I suffer as much as if I did!

I find it hard to endure Renaud's presence, his all-too-readiness to be involved as a third. He has refused to give me the key of the little flat, alleging, no doubt with good reason, that we must not be seen going into it alone together. And each time it means the same humiliating effort for me to say to him: "Renaud, tomorrow we're going *over there*. . . ."

He always consents eagerly; he is invariably charming—rejoicing, no doubt, like Rézi in the "far from commonplace" situation. . . . That need, common to both of them, to proclaim themselves vicious and ultra-modern, disconcerts me. Yet I do what Rézi does—and even more—and I do not feel I am vicious. . . .

Nowadays, Renaud lingers when he accompanies us *over there*. He pours out the tea, sits down, smokes a cigarette, chats, gets up to straighten a picture-frame or flick a moth off the velvet of a *prie-dieu* . . . he makes it obvious that he is at home. And when he finally makes up his mind to go, pretending to apologise for staying so long, it is Rézi who protests, "Oh, don't go yet . . . do stay another minute. . . ." But *I* say nothing.

Their conversation leaves me out of it: gossip, backbiting, jokes that quickly turn bawdy, thinly veiled allusions to what will happen when he has gone. . . . She laughs, she plays up to all this boring drivel, exerting the charm of her soft, myopic gaze, of those supple twists of her neck and waist. . . . I swear, yes, I swear I am so shocked by it all that I feel as embarrassed and outraged as a decent girl confronted with obscene pictures. . . . Sensual delight—my form of it—has nothing to do with cosy, giggling "fun and games".

In the bright bedroom, where Rézi's Iris and Claudine's harsh sweet Chypre mingle in the air, in the great bed that is fragrant with our two bodies, I avenge myself silently for many a hidden, bleeding wound. . . . Afterwards, curled up against me in an attitude blessedly familiar now, Rézi talks and questions me. She is irritated by the brevity and simplicity of my answers, avid to know more, incredulous when I assure her of my former virtue and the novelty of this madness of mine.

"But, after all, what about Luce?"

"Luce? All right, she loved me."

"And . . . nothing happened?"

"Nothing! Do you think I'm ridiculous?"

"Of course not, my Claudine."

With her cheek on my breast, she seemed to be listening to some inner voice of her own. Memories brought sparkles into her grey eyes. . . . If she spoke, I knew I should want to hit her, yet I longed for her to talk. . . .

"Rézi, you didn't wait till you were married?"

"Oh, yes I did!" she cried, sitting up, yielding to the impulse of telling me about herself. "The beginning couldn't have been more ridiculous, more utterly commonplace. . . . My singing-mistress, a peroxide blonde with bones like a horse. Because she had sea-green eyes, she affected arty clothes and a sphinx-like personality. An Anglo-Saxon sphinx! . . . With her, I didn't merely increase my vocal range. I learnt to use the whole gamut of perversity. . . . I was very young, newly-married, frightened and a little swept off my feet by her. . . . I stopped the lessons at the end of the month—yes, exactly a month—appallingly disillusioned because of a little scene I'd witnessed through a half-open door. The sphinx, swathed in Liberty scarves, was bitterly accusing her cook of having done her out of something less than eighty-five centimes. . . ."

Rézi had grown animated; she rocked to and fro, tossing her silky hair and laughing at her comical reminiscence. Sitting, doubled up, in the hollow of my thigh, with one foot in her hand and her chemise slipping off, she seemed to be enjoying herself enormously.

"And, after that, Rézi? Who came next?"

"After that . . . it was . . ."

She hesitated, gave me a swift glance, closed her mouth again, and then made up her mind.

"It was a young girl."

I could swear, from the way she looked, that she had omitted someone, man or woman.

"A young girl? Really? How interesting!"

I longed to bite her.

"Interesting, yes. . . . But I suffered. Oh, never again have I wanted to have anything to do with a young girl!"

Her mouth drooped; sitting there thoughtful and half-naked, she looked like an amorous child. How sharply I would imprint my teeth in two little red curves on that shoulder, pearly in the dimming daylight!

"You . . . loved her, that girl?"

"Yes, I loved her. But now I love no one but you, darling!"

Whether from true fondness or instinctive apprehension, she flung her flawless arms round me and drowned me in the loosened flood of her hair. But I wanted the end of the story. . . .

". . . And she—did she love you?"

"Oh! how can I tell? Claudine, my dearest dear, there's nothing to equal the cruelty, the cold, critical demandingness of young girls! I mean decent young girls; the others don't count. They lack all awareness of suffering, all sense of pity and fairness. . . . That one was more ruthless in search of pleasure, more avid than a last year's widow, yet she kept me in suspense for weeks. She'd only see me when her family were there, she would watch my unhappiness with that frank, pretty face and those hard eyes. . . . A fortnight later, I learnt the cause of my punishment . . . being five minutes late for a meeting, too lively a conversation with a man friend. . . . And the spiteful remarks, the bitter allusions made out loud in public, with the shrill, crude recklessness of girls who haven't yet been softened and scared by their first fall from virtue!"

My pinched and shrunken heart beat faster. I wanted to annihilate the woman who was talking. Nevertheless, I respected her more, carried away into making a truthful admission. I preferred her stormy eyes, darkened by her memory to the childish, provocative gaze she turns on Renaud—and on any man—and on any woman—even on the concierge. . . .

Heavens, how changed I am! Not fundamentally changed maybe—I hope not—but . . . disguised. Spring is here, the Paris spring, a little bronchitic, a little tainted, quickly tired, never mind, it *is* spring. And what do I know of it but Rézi's hats? Violets, lilacs and roses have blossomed in turn on her charming head as if the sunshine of her hair had brought them out. She has presided authoritatively over my sessions with dressmakers and milliners, annoyed to find that certain smart women's hats look so ridiculous on my short, curly hair. She forced me to go along with her to Gauthé's to have myself fitted with this corset-belt of overlapping ribbons, a supple girdle that gives with every movement of my hips. She has fussed busily among materials, picking out the blues that enhance the yellow of my eyes, the strong pinks against which my cheeks look so exotically amber. . . . I am dressed by her. I am inhabited by her. I find it hard to resist her. Before I reach her doorstep, I throw away the bunch of wild narcissus, bought from some man in the street. I love their over-rich, southern scent, but Rézi does not like it.

Oh, how far I am from being happy! And how can I relieve this anguish that oppresses me? Renaud, Rézi, they are both necessary to me, and there is no question of choosing between them. But how I wish that I could keep them separate, or, better still, that they had never met!

Have I found the remedy? At any rate, it's worth trying.

Marcel came to see me today. He found me in an odd mood, at once gloomy and aggressive. That is because, for the past week, I have been putting off a meeting, though Rézi keeps imploring me, Rézi looking deliciously fresh, excited and stimulated by spring. . . . But I can no longer endure Renaud's presence between us. How is it he doesn't see this? The last time we were at the Rue Goethe, my husband's fondly perverse, Peeping Tom mood came up against such savage rudeness that Rézi jumped up anxiously and made him some sign or other. . . . He departed at once. . . . This kind of understanding between them exasperated me still more, I turned obstinate and, for the first time, Rézi went away without removing the hat that she takes off after her chemise.

So Marcel teased me about my sour expression. He has long ago discovered the secret of my trouble and my joy; he guessed where the sore spot lay with a sureness that would have amazed me had I not known my stepson. Seeing me in a black mood today, he maliciously turned the knife in my little wound.

"Are you a jealous lover?"

"Are you?"

"Me? . . . Yes and no. Do you keep a sharp eye on *her*?"

"What's that got to do with you? Anyway, why *should* I keep an eye on her?"

He shook his delicate, made-up head and lengthily arranged his cravat, shot with changing, iridescent gleams in the hues of a scarab; then he shot me a sidelong glance:

"No reason at all. I hardly know her. It's just a superficial impression *she* gives me—that she's a woman who needs watching."

I smiled unkindly.

"Really? Your own experiences must make you quite an authority on women. . . ."

"Charming," he conceded, without losing his temper. "That was a nasty dig. As a matter of fact, you're perfectly right. I saw all three of you at the first night of the Vaudeville. Madame Lambrook looked quite delicious, I thought—maybe that hair-style was a *little* too severe. But what grace! And how obviously she adores you . . . you and my father!"

I controlled myself rigidly and gave no sign. Disappointed,

Marcel stood up, with a provocative sway of his hips . . . goodness knows for whose benefit!

"Goodbye. I must get back. You'd depress a writer of gay pornography if they weren't all so dreary already!"

"Who is it you're leaving me for?"

"Myself. I'm on honeymoon with my latest little find."

"You've got a new . . . ?"

"Home, dear, not homo. What, haven't you heard that I'm a free man again?"

"No. *They're* so discreet!"

"Who?"

"Your boy-friends."

"They have to be. Yes; I've got a little love-nest. But absolutely *minute*! You can just get two in with a tight squeeze."

"And they do squeeze tight?"

"You said it, not me. Won't you come and see it? By the way, I'd just as soon you didn't bring my dear father. Your girl-friend, if it would amuse her. . . . What about it?"

Suddenly, impelled by an idea, I grabbed hold of his wrist.

"You aren't ever out in the afternoon, are you?"

"The afternoon? Yes. . . . On Thursdays and Saturdays. But don't imagine," he added with a charming smile, like a modest girl's, "that I'm going to tell you where I go."

"I'm not interested. . . . Tell me, Marcel . . . it wouldn't be possible to see it while you were out . . . your little haven of rest?"

"Rest? Hardly that! Except *afterwards*, of course. . . ."

He looked at me with a vicious glint in his eyes—blue eyes, shot with sombre grey. He had understood.

"It might be managed, at a pinch. . . . Is she discreet, your pretty Madame Lambrook?"

"Oh, yes!"

"I'll give you the key. Don't break my little knick-knacks. I'm attached to them. The electric kettle, for the tea, is in a little green cupboard to the left as you go in. You can't possibly lose your way about; I've just got one room to work (!) in, another to talk in, and a bathroom. You'll find the biscuits, the Château-Yquem, the arrack and the ginger brandy in the same cupboard. Next Thursday?"

"Next Thursday. Thank you, Marcel."

He is a little blackguard, but at this moment I could positively hug him. When he had gone, a wild joy sent me pacing from one window to the other, with my hands behind my back and whistling my loudest.

He has *given* me the key!

The tiny key of a Fichet lock made a lump in my purse; I could feel it against my palm. I was taking Rézi there, in the crazy hope that we were hastening towards a "solution". To see her in secret, to keep my dear Renaud right out of this business which doesn't concern him. . . . I love him too much—oh, indeed I do—to be able to see him mixed up in these intrigues without feeling appallingly uncomfortable. . . .

Rézi accompanied me meekly, amused at the idea, happy that my severity had melted at last after a week of sulking.

It was warm. In the victoria, she opened the boyish jacket of her rough blue serge suit, and sighed, turning her head to get some air. Secretly, I studied the simple, fleeting line of her profile; the small girl's nose, the lashes shot through with light, the velvet of the ash-blonde eyebrows. . . . She held my hand, waiting patiently, and now and then leant forward a little to look at a flower-barrow that puffed its damp fragrance at us, a shop-window, or a well-dressed woman going past us. Heavens, how sweet she was! Wouldn't anyone say she loved me, that she wanted no one but me?

We arrived at the address in the Chaussée d'Antin. A big courtyard, then a little door, a minute, well-kept staircase and landings so small that you practically had to stand on one foot. Having climbed three flights without pausing, I stopped: the air already smelt of Marcel; sandalwood and new-mown hay, with the faintest whiff of ether. I opened the door.

"Wait, Rézi, we can only go through one at a time!"

Honestly, I wasn't exaggerating! This doll's flat amused me immensely at first sight. An embryonic hall led to a scrap of a study; only the bedroom-drawing-room attained normal proportions.

Like two cats in a strange house, we advanced step by step, stopping to examine every piece of furniture, every picture-frame. . . . Too many scents, too many scents. . . .

"Look, Claudine, there's an aquarium on the mantelpiece."

"See—fishes with three tails. . . ."

"Oh! There's one with fins that look exactly like flounces! What's this, an incense-burner?"

"No, an ink-pot, I imagine. . . . Or a coffee-cup . . . or something else."

"What marvellous old material, darling! It would make heavenly revers on the jacket of a suit. . . . Look at that charming little goddess with her arms crossed."

"It's a little god."

"No, Claudine, you're wrong!"

"One can't see properly; there's a drapery. Ow! Don't sit down where I did, Rézi—on the arms of this green English chair!"

"Goodness, you're right! What a fantastic notion, these sort of shiny wooden lance-heads! You could impale yourself on them! Oh, quick, do come and look, my little shepherd!"

I didn't like her calling me "my little shepherd"; it is one of my Renaud's special names for me. I felt offended with her, but even more with him.

"Look at what?"

"His portrait!"

I joined her in the drawing-room-bedroom. It was unmistakably a portrait of Marcel dresssed as a Byzantine lady. A rather curious pastel, boldly coloured, but feebly drawn. Red hair, coiled in plaits over his ears, the forehead loaded with jewels, she . . . he . . . oh, I give up! Marcel was holding one loose panel of the stiff, transparent dress away from him, with an affected gesture. The dress itself was of gauze, heavily embroidered with pearls, dripping down straight, like a curtain of rain. Between the folds you could see the pink of the tapering hips, the calf and the slender knee. With his face looking thinner, and his disdainful eyes bluer under the red hair, it was quite definitely Marcel.

Gazing at it dreamily, with Rézi leaning against my shoulder, another picture came back into my mind. I visualised again the dark, ambiguous youth of Bronzino's brilliant portrait in the Louvre who had so suddenly vanquished me. . . .

"What pretty arms that boy has!" sighed Rézi. "Pity he's got queer tastes. . . ."

"Pity for whom?" I asked, my suspicions promptly roused.

"For his family, of course!"

She laughed and put up her laughing mouth for a kiss. My mind switched to other things.

"Oh, yes. . . . What concerns me now is where does he sleep?"

"He doesn't lie down . . . he sits up. Going to bed is far too ordinary."

In spite of what she said, I had found a kind of narrow bed-recess behind a pink velvet curtain. In it was a divan draped in the same pink velvet, patterned with greyish-green plane leaves like the imprints of five fingers. I pressed an electric push-button and amused myself by flooding this altar with the light that poured down from an inverted crystal flower. . . . It *would* be an orchid!

Rézi pointed a slim forefinger at the cushions strewn on the divan:

"There's all you need to prove that no woman's ever laid her head here. . . ."

I laughed at her malicious perspicacity. The well-chosen cushions were all covered in rough brocade or embroidered with spangles or gold and silver thread. A woman's hair would have got pitifully tangled by them.

"All right, we'll remove them, Rézi."

"Let's remove them, Claudine. . . ."

Perhaps that afternoon will be our most charming memory. I was unrestrained, and less harsh. She displayed her usual ardour, her usual submission to being mastered, and the inverted flower shed its opalescent light over our brief repose. . . .

A little while afterwards, from down below, came the sound of a tinny, broken-down piano and an equally broken-down tenor combining to hammer out insistently:

Jadis—vivait—en Nor-mandie . . .

At first it was annoying to have such an acute sense of rhythm as I have. But I got used to it. I adapted myself to it. And then it wasn't annoying any more . . . on the contrary.

Jadis—vivait en Nor . . .

If anyone had ever foretold to me that, one day, a tune in six-eight time from *Robert Le Diable* would affect me to the point of bringing a lump into my throat . . . But it needed a very special concatenation of circumstances.

About six o'clock, when Rézi, appeased, was asleep with her arms round my neck, the doorbell rang so imperiously that it shattered our nerves. Terrified, she stifled a scream and dug all her nails into the back of my neck. Reared up on one elbow, I listened.

"Darling, don't be frightened. There's nothing to be afraid of.

Someone's made a mistake. . . . One of Marcel's friends—he can't have warned them all that he wouldn't be here."

Reassured, she uncovered her white face and lay back, in a disarray that could not have been more like a "gay" eighteenth-century print. But, once again, came that *trrr* . . .

She leapt up and began to get dressed. Terrified as she was, her conjuror's fingers did not falter. The ringing went on, insistent, persistent; it was intelligent and teasing, it played tunes on the bell. I clenched my teeth with nervous irritation.

My poor friend, pale, and already ready to leave, clasped her hands over her ears. The corners of her mouth quivered each time the ringing started up again. I took pity on her.

"Now, now, Rézi. It's obviously a friend of Marcel's."

"A friend of Marcel's! Goodness, can't you hear the malice, the purposefulness of those exasperating rings? . . . Nonsense. It's someone who knows we're here. If my husband . . ."

"Oh! You've no courage!"

"Thanks! It's easy to be brave with a husband like yours!"

I said no more. What was the good? I hooked up my corset-belt. As soon as I was dressed, I tiptoed to the door, silent as a cat, and strained my ears. I could hear nothing but that ringing, that infernal ringing!

At last, after a final, prolonged trill, a kind of exclamation mark, I heard light footsteps running away. . . .

"Rézi! He's gone!"

"At last! Don't let's leave at once; someone may be spying on us. . . . If you think I'll ever come back here! . . ."

What a sad ending to that meeting that was to have no sequel! My pretty coward was in such a hurry to leave me, to get right away from this building and this neighbourhood, that I dared not ask to go back with her. . . . She went downstairs ahead of me, while I stayed behind to switch off the inverted flower and pick up the spangled cushions. Marcel's portrait stared at me with its contemptuous chin and its painted, tight-shut lips.

Today I was confronted with the original of the compromising Byzantine pastel, now wearing a tight, very short black jacket. He was sizzling with curiosity, just as in the days when he was violently intrigued by Luce.

"Well, how about yesterday?"

"Really, I must thank you. What a delicious little temple you have there! It's worthy of you."

He bowed.

"Of you too."

"Too kind. I found your portrait particularly interesting. I'm delighted to know that your soul is a contemporary of Constantine's."

"It's the rage nowadays. . . . Tell me, are you neither of you greedy? Didn't even my Chateau-Yquem—it's a present from Grandmother—tempt you?"

"No. Curiosity muzzled all our other instincts."

"Oh! *curiosity*," he said sceptically, with the smile in his portrait. . . . "What good little housewives you are. . . . I found everything in perfect order. I hope, at least, you weren't disturbed?"

His flashing smile, that look so swiftly darted, then withdrawn. . . . Oh, the little beast, it was he who had rung—or got someone to ring. . . . I ought to have suspected that! But I wasn't going to let that wicked boy catch me out.

"No, not in the slightest. The calm of a well-ordered house. I believe someone did ring once . . . but, again, I couldn't be sure. At that moment I was completely absorbed in contemplating . . . your little androgynous goddess, the one with the folded arms. . . ."

That would teach him! And, as we are both good deceivers, he assumed the expression of a satisfied host.

12

A LETTER from Montigny that I was obliged to read aloud in order to understand it, the writing was so hieroglyphic.

"Aren't you going to come and see us, my little maidie? The big 'imp's thigh' rose-bush wants to flower; it's nearly out. And the little 'weepy ash' has grown a lot. Monsieur is as usual."

Monsieur was "as usual"—I didn't doubt that, Mélie! The weeping ash had grown, good. And the big "nymph's thigh" rose-bush was going to flower. It's so lovely, it covers an entire wall, it flowers hurriedly, abundantly, tirelessly, and exhausts itself towards the autumn, after constant re-flowerings and fresh bursts of fragrant life; it's like a thoroughbred horse that will work itself to death. . . . "The nymph's thigh rose tree wants to flower." At this news, I felt the fibre that binds me to Montigny revive, full of new sap. It wants to flower! . . . I thrilled with a little of the proud joy of a mother who has been told: "Your son is going to get all the prizes!"

All my vegetable family was calling me. My forebear, the old walnut-tree, was growing old waiting for me. Under the clematis, it would soon be raining stars. . . .

But I can't, I can't. What would Rézi do if I were away? I don't want to leave Renaud in her vicinity; my poor giant is such a lover of women and she is so . . . lovable!

Take Renaud with me? Rézi all alone, Rézi in the dry, scorching Paris of summertime, alone with her desires and her taste for intrigue. . . . She would deceive me.

Heavens! Is it true that four months have gone by in just drifting from hour to hour, alternating between kisses and sulks? I have done nothing during all this time, nothing at all but wait. When I leave her, I wait for the day when I will see her again; when I am with her, I wait for her pleasure, swift or slow in coming, to yield me a lovelier, sincerer Rézi. When Renaud is with us, I wait for him to go and I wait for Rézi's departure so that I may talk to my Renaud a little while, without jealousy or bitterness, because, since Rézi, he seems to love me more than ever.

This would go and happen! I have fallen ill, and now three whole weeks have been wasted. Influenza, a chill, overstrain—the doctor who is attending me can call it what he likes. I've had a very high temperature and a great deal of pain in my head. But, fundamentally, I'm robust.

Dear big Renaud, how much I appreciated your gentleness. Never have I known you take so much pains to talk in moderate, cadenced, rounded tone of voice. . . .

Rézi has looked after me too, in spite of the fear of appearing ugly to her that made me hide my burning face in my arms. Sometimes her way of looking at Renaud and her way of sitting on the edge of my bed "for his benefit", with one knee raised, as if she were gracefully riding side-saddle, in a chip hat and a *broderie anglaise* dress with a velvet belt, shocked me. Her whole way of going on was too affected and coquettish for someone visiting a sick friend. Thanks to my temperature I was able to scream "Go away!" to her and she really believed I was delirious. I also thought that, whenever she entered, I saw Renaud smile as if a puff of cool wind had blown in. . . .

I felt resentful of my friend's fresh beauty and her unshadowed, matt ivory cheeks. And though, when she left, she very gently laid long-stemmed, black-red roses on the couch where I was recovering my strength, the moment she had gone, I snatched up the hand-glass hidden under the cushions and stared for a long time at my bleached pallor, thinking of her with jealous rancour. . . .

"Renaud, is it true the trees on the boulevards are already turning rusty?"

"Yes, it's true, little girl. Would you like to come to Montigny? You'd see greener ones there."

"They're too green. . . . Renaud, I could go out today. I'm feeling so well. I ate all the lean part of a cutlet after my egg, I drank a glass of Asti and picked at some grapes. . . . Are you going out?"

Standing in front of the window of his "work sanctum", he looked at me undecidedly.

"I'd simply love to go out with a handsome husband like you. That grey suit is very becoming, that piqué waistcoat accentuates your distinguished Second Empire look I like so much. . . . Is it for me that you're so young today?"

He reddened a little under his dark skin and smoothed his long, silver moustache.

"You know quite well it hurts me when you talk about my age. . . ."

"Who's talking about your age? On the contrary, I'm seriously afraid that your youth is going to last as long as you do, like a disease you're born with. Take me out with you, Renaud! I feel strong enough to stagger the whole world!"

My grandiloquence did not make him decide in my favour.

"Certainly not, my Claudine. The doctor told you: 'Not before Sunday.' Today's Friday. Just another forty-eight hours' patience, my darling bird. Ah! Here comes a friend who'll know how to keep you at home. . . ."

He profited by Rézi's entrance to make a hasty exit. This was entirely unlike the Renaud I knew, who was so anxious to please me, however contrary to the dictates of prudence. . . . That doctor was a fool!

"Why are you making such a face, Claudine?"

She was so pretty that I relaxed my frown. Blue, blue, blue, in a blue at once misty and frothy as soapsuds.

"Rézi, the fairies have washed their linen in the water of your dress."

She smiled, sitting close against my hip. I was looking at her from below. A long dimple, like an exclamation mark, divided her obstinate chin. Her nostrils described the simple, classic curve I used to admire in Fanchette's little nose. I sighed.

"Oh dear, I wanted to go out, and that idiot of a doctor doesn't want me to. But, at least, *you'll* stay with me, won't you? Do! Give me your freshness, the breeze that ripples in your skirt, and flutters the wings of your leafy hat. Is it a hat? Is it a wreath? My dear, I've never seen you look so irresistibly Viennese; your hair is like foaming lager. . . . Do stay with me, tell me about the streets and the sun-baked trees . . . and about what little affection you have left for me since our separation."

But she refused to sit down, and, all the time she was talking to me, her eyes kept darting from one window to another, as if looking for a way of escape.

"Oh! I'm too miserable for words! My sweet, I'd have liked to spend the day with you, especially as you're all alone. . . . It's such a long time, Claudine darling, since your mouth was close to mine!"

She bent down caressingly, offering me her moist, shining teeth, but I turned away.

"No. I must smell of fever. Off you go and have your nice walk."

"Don't think I'm walking for pleasure, Claudine darling! It's a dreary duty expedition. Tomorrow's the anniversary of my engagement—there's nothing to laugh about!—and I'm in the habit of giving my husband a present that day."

"Well?"

"Well, this year I've gone and forgotten my duty as a grateful spouse. And I must rush off, so that Mr. Lambrook shall find something or other under his mitred table-napkin tonight—a cigar-case, some pearl studs, a case of dynamite—well, anyway, *something*! Otherwise it means three weeks of icy silence, oh, no reproaches— that would offend his dignity. . . . Lord!" she cried, raising her clenched fists. "And there's the Transvaal needing men! What the hell is he doing here?"

Her voluble, self-conscious bantering filled me with extreme mistrust.

"But, Rézi, why don't you entrust your purchase to the infallible taste of a manservant?"

"I did think of that. But all the domestics, except my 'Abigail', are under my husband's thumb."

Decidedly, she had set her heart on going out.

"Run along, virtuous spouse, go and celebrate the feast of Saint Lambrook."

She had already pulled down her white veil.

"If I'm back before six, could you put up with a little more of me?"

How pretty she was, bending forward like that! Her skirt, swirled tight round her by the swiftness of her movement, revealed all the lines of her body. . . . I was moved only to a Platonic admiration. Was my convalescence to blame? I no longer felt the old desire beating up on great, tempestuous wings. . . . And, besides, she had refused to sacrifice Saint Lambrook's Day for me!

"It all depends. Come up, anyway, and you'll be rewarded according to your merits. . . . *No*, I tell you, I smell of fever!"

So, there I was, all alone. I yawned, I read three pages, I walked about the room. I began a letter to Papa, then I became absorbed in assiduously polishing my nails. Seated at the dressing-table, I cast a glance every now and then at the mirror like someone watching the clock. I didn't look so awful, after all. . . . My curls were a little longer; that was not unattractive. That white collar, that little red muslin blouse with hundreds of fine white stripes, irresistibly suggested a walk in the street. . . . I read in the glass what my eyes had decided. It was soon done! A black-banded boater, a jacket over my arm so that Renaud couldn't scold me for taking risks and I was out of doors.

Heavens, how hot it was! It didn't surprise me that the nymph's-thigh rose-bush was flowering with zest. Filthy place, this Paris! I felt light; I had grown thinner. The fresh air was a little intoxicating, but I got used to it as I walked. I had no more thoughts in my head than a dog being taken out after being cooped up in a flat for a week of rainy days.

Without doing so on purpose, I mechanically took the route to the Rue Goethe. . . . I smiled when I arrived outside number 59 and I threw a friendly glance up at the white net curtains that veiled the windows of the second floor. . . .

Ah! the curtain had stirred! . . . That tiny movement riveted me to the pavement, stiff as a doll. Whoever was up in "our" flat? Maybe it was the wind blowing in from a window on the courtyard that had lifted that net. . . . But while my logical self was reasoning, the beast in me, bitten by a suspicion, then suddenly enraged, had guessed before it had understood.

I raced across the street; I climbed the two flights, as in a nightmare, treading on steps of cotton-wool that sank and rebounded under my feet. I was going to drag with all my might on the brass bell-pull, ring till I brought the house down. . . . No, *They* would not come!

I waited a minute, my hand on my heart. That wretched, banal gesture cruelly brought back a phrase of Claire's, the girl who made her First Communion with me: "Life's just like it is in books, isn't it?"

I pulled the brass handle timidly, starting at the unfamiliar sound of that bell that had never rung for us. . . . And for two long seconds, seized with a childish cowardice, I kept saying to myself: "Oh! If only they wouldn't open it!"

The approaching step brought all my courage back on a wave of anger. Renaud's voice enquired irritably:

"Who's there?"

I had no breath left. I leant against the sham marble wall that chilled my arm. And the sound of the door he had opened a little way made me want to die. . . .

. . . but not for long. I *had* to pull myself together! Hell, I was Claudine! I was Claudine! I flung off my fear like a coat. I said: "Open the door, Renaud, or I'll scream." I looked straight into the face of the man who opened it; he was completely dressed. He recoiled, in sheer astonishment. And he only let out one mild expletive, like a gambler annoyed by ill luck:

"The deuce!"

The impression of being the stronger stiffened my courage still more. I was Claudine! And I said:

"I saw someone at the window from down below. So I came up to say 'Hullo' to you."

"It was wicked of me to do it," he muttered.

He made no move to try and stop me, but stood back to let me pass, then followed me.

In a flash, I crossed the little drawing-room and raised the flowered curtain in the doorway . . . Ah! Just as I thought! Rézi was there, of course she was there—and putting on her clothes again. . . . In corset and knickers, her lace and linen petticoat over her arm, her hat on her head, just as for me. . . . I shall always see that fair-skinned face decomposing, looking as if it were dying under my gaze. I almost envied her for being so frightened. She stared at my hands and I saw her thin lips go white and dry. Without taking her eyes off me, she stretched out a groping arm towards her dress. I took one step forward. She nearly fell, and threw up her arms to protect her face. That gesture, which revealed her downy armpits whose warmth I so often inhaled, unleashed a hurricane in me. I would snatch up that water-jug and hurl it . . . or maybe that chair. The lines of the furniture quivered before my eyes like hot air over the fields. . . .

Renaud, who had followed me, lightly touched my shoulder. He was hesitant, a trifle pale, but, above all, worried. I asked him, speaking with difficulty:

"What are you . . . you two . . . doing here?"

He smiled nervously, in spite of himself.

"Why . . . we were waiting for you, as you see."

I was dreaming . . . or he had gone out of his mind. . . . I turned again towards the woman there. While my eyes were averted from her, she had put on the blue dress in which fairies had washed their linen. . . . *She* would not have dared to smile!

"Life's just like it is in books, isn't it?" No, sweet Claire. In books the woman who arrives on the scene fires two shots at least to avenge herself. Or else she goes off, slamming the door on the guilty couple after crushing them with one contemptuous remark. . . . But *I* could find no gesture; the truth was I had not the faintest idea what I ought to do. You don't learn the part of an outraged wife in five minutes, just like that.

I was still barring the door. I thought Rézi was going to faint. How odd that would be! *He*, at least, wasn't frightened. Like me, he was following, with more interest than emotion, the succeeding phases of terror on Rézi's face. He seemed finally to have grasped that this hour was not going to bring the three of us together. . . .

"Listen, Claudine. . . . I meant to tell you. . . ."

With a sweep of my arms, I cut short his sentence. In any case, he seemed none too anxious to continue it, and he shrugged his left shoulder with a rather fatalistic air of resignation.

It was Rézi who roused all my fury! I advanced on her slowly. I could see myself advancing on her. This double consciousness made me uncertain what I meant to do. Was I going to strike her, or only increase her shameful fear to swooning-point?

She drew back and moved round behind the little table on which the tea stood. She had reached the wall! She was going to escape me! Ah! I wasn't going to let her.

But already her hand was on the door-curtain, she was groping at it, walking backwards, keeping her eyes fixed on me. Involuntarily, I stooped down to pick up a stone. . . . There were no stones. . . . She had disappeared.

I let my arms drop; all my energy suddenly drained away.

There we were, the two of us, looking at each other. Renaud's face was—almost—his kind, everyday face. He looked troubled. His beautiful eyes were a little sad. Oh heavens, the next moment he was going to say: "Claudine," and if I voiced my anger, if I let the strength that still sustained me ebb away in reproaches and tears, I should leave the place on his arm, plaintive and forgiving. . . . I *wouldn't*! I was . . . I was Claudine, hang it! And besides, I should be too furious with him for having made me forgive him.

I had waited too long. He stepped forward, he said: "Claudine . . ."

I leapt back, and, instinctively, I started to flee, like Rézi. Only *I* was fleeing from myself.

I did well to make my escape. The street, the glance I threw up at the betraying curtain revived all my pride and resentment. Moreover, I knew now where I was going.

It took less than a quarter of an hour to rush home in a cab, grab my suitcase, and be downstairs again, having flung my key on the table. I had some money, not much, but enough.

"Gare de Lyon, driver."

Before getting into the train, I sent a telegram to Papa, then another to Renaud: "Send clothes and linen to Montigny for an indefinite stay."

13

THOSE cornflowers on the wall, faded from blue to grey, shadows of flowers on a paler paper. . . . That chintz curtain with the fantastic pattern—yes, there was the monstrous fruit, the apple with eyes in it. . . . Over and over again I had seen them in my dreams during my two years in Paris, but never so vividly. . . .

This time, from the depths of my transparent sleep, I actually heard the creak of the pump!

I sat up, with a start, in my little four-poster. The first smiling welcome of the bedroom of my childhood made me burst into floods of tears. Tears as bright as the sunbeam that danced in golden coins on the windowpanes, as soothing to my eyes as the flowers on the grey wallpaper. So it was really true that I was here, in this bedroom! There was no other thought in my head till I came to wipe my eyes with a little pink handkerchief that had no connection with Montigny. . . .

My unhappiness dried my tears. I had been hurt. A salutary hurt? I could almost believe it was, for, after all, I could not be thoroughly unhappy in Montigny, in this house. . . . Oh! there was my little ink-stained desk! It still contained all my school exercise-books: *Arithmetic . . . Dictation.* For in Mademoiselle's day, we no longer put *Sums* or *Spelling. Dictation, Arithmetic* sounded more distinguished, more "Secondary School . . .".

Hard nails scratched on the door and scrabbled at the keyhole. An anguished, imperious "Meow!" summoned me to open it . . . "O my darling girl, how beautiful you are! My ideas are in such a muddle that, for a moment, I'd forgotten you, Fanchette!"

I took her into my arms, into my bed and she thrust her wet nose and her cold teeth against my chin, so excited to see me again that she kneaded my bare arm with all her claws out. "How old are you now? Five, six? I can't remember. Your white fur looks so young. You'll die young . . . like Renaud. Oh dear, that memory's gone and spoilt everything for me. Stay under my cheek so that I can forget myself, listening to all your purring machinery vibrating at full blast. . . . Whatever must you have thought of me, arriving suddenly like that without any luggage? Even Papa smelt a rat!"

"Well? And where's the other animal? Your husband?" he had asked.

"He'll come as soon as he's less busy, Papa."

I was pale and absent-minded; I was still there in the Rue Goethe, between those two people who had hurt me. Though it was past ten o'clock, I refused to eat anything; all I craved for was a bed, a warm, solitary burrow where I could think and weep and hate. . . . But the darkness of my old bedroom sheltered so many kindly little ghosts that they lulled me into deep, dreamless sleep.

There was a slither of slipshod feet. Mélie entered without knocking. She had dropped back at once into all the old ways. In one hand she held the little tray that had lost most of its varnish—the very same one!—in the other, her left breast. She was faded and slatternly, with a touch of the procuress in her make-up, but the mere sight of her warmed my heart. What that ugly servant was bringing me in the steaming cup on the scabbed little tray was "the philtre that annihilates the years! . . ." It smelt of chocolate, that philtre. I was dying of hunger!

"Mélie!"

"What, my precious lammy?"

"Do you love me?"

She paused long enough to put down her tray before answering, with a shrug of her flabby shoulders:

"You bet I do."

It was true: I could feel it was true. She remained standing, watching me eat. Fanchette watched me too, sitting on my feet. Both of them admire me unreservedly. Nevertheless, Mélie shook her head and weighed her left breast with a disapproving expression on her face.

"Don't look any too hearty, you don't. What have *they* been doing to you?"

"I've had influenza. I wrote and told Papa that. By the way, where *is* Papa?"

"Messing about in his den, I'll be bound. Leastways, you'll see him soon enough. Be you wanting me to fetch you a porger? I'll go get un."

A "porger" in our parts is a big wooden basin.

"Get un for what?" I said, slipping back into the beloved dialect.

"Why, to wash Lord Behind and Lady Titty for sure!"

"Deedy, yes. A good big one too!"

In the doorway, she turned round and asked point-blank:

"When be *he* coming . . . Monsieur Renaud?"

"Be *I* like to know? He'll write and tell you. Now, trot along, do!"

While waiting for the porger, I leant out of the window. There was nothing to be seen in the street but a tumble of roofs. On account of the very steep slope, each house has its first floor on the level of the ground floor of the one above it. I was quite certain that the slope had grown steeper in my absence! I could see the corner of the Rue des Soeurs, which runs straight—I mean, crooked—to the School. . . . Should I go and see Mademoiselle? No; I wasn't looking pretty enough. . . . Besides, I might find little Hélène there—that future Rézi. . . . No, no, no more girls, no more women! . . . Spreading out my fingers, I shook my hand with slightly disgusted irritation, as if a long, smooth hair had got caught in my nails. . . .

I slipped, barefooted, into the drawing-room. . . . Those old armchairs, the very rents in them were like welcoming smiles! Here, everything was in its right place. Two penitential years in Paris had not eclipsed the gaiety of their round backs and their pretty Louis XVI feet, still whitened with a remnant of paint. . . . That Mélie, what a dolt she was! The blue vase that, for fifteen years, I had always seen on the left of the green vase, she had gone and put it on the right! Quickly, I restored everything to its proper place till I had completely recreated the setting in which I had lived nearly all my life. Nothing, in fact, was missing except my former gaiety, my cheerful solitude. . . .

On the other side of the shutters, closed against the sun, lay the garden. . . . No, garden, no, I would not go and look at you for another hour! The mere whisper of your foliage would move me too much, it was so long since I had eaten green leaves!

Papa probably thought I was asleep. Or else he had forgotten that I had arrived. No matter. In a little while, I would go into his lair and bring down a few maledictions on my head. Fanchette followed me step by step, terrified I might escape again. "My swee-ee-eet! Have no fear! I tell you, my telegram said: *clothes and linen . . . for indefinite stay. . . .*" Indefinite. What did that mean? I was no longer any too sure. But it certainly seemed to me that I was here for a long, long time. . . . Ah! how good it was to give one's misery a change of scene!

My brief morning drifted by in the enchanted garden. It had grown. The temporary tenant had touched nothing, not even the grass on the paths, I believe. . . .

The enormous walnut-tree bore thousands and thousands of full nuts. Just breathing in the strong, funereal smell of one of its crumpled leaves made me close my eyes. I leant against it, the protector of the garden, but its destroyer too, for the chill of its shade kills the roses. What does it matter? Nothing is lovelier than a tree—than that particular tree. At the far end, against old Madame Adolphe's wall, the twin fir-trees nodded an unsmiling greeting, stiff in their sombre raiment that serves for every season. . . .

The wistaria that climbs up to the roof had lost all its charming flowers. . . . So much the better! I found it hard to forgive wistaria blossom for having adorned Rézi's hair. . . .

Inert at the foot of the walnut-tree, I felt myself becoming a plant again. Over there, Quail Mountain looked blue and far away; it would be fine tomorrow, if Moustiers was not covered with cloud.

"My lammykin! Look—see, a letter!"

. . . A letter. . . . Already! How brief the respite had been! Couldn't he have left me a little time, a little more of sunshine and animal life? I felt very small and frightened, faced with the pain about to assault me. . . . Oh, to wipe out everything that had been, wipe it out and start again quite fresh! . . ."

"My darling child . . ."

He might just as well have stopped there. I knew everything he was going to say. Yes, I was his child! Why had he deceived me?

"My darling child, I cannot console myself for the pain I have caused you. You have done what you had every right to do and I am nothing but a wretched man who loves you and is desolate. You know, Claudine, you must surely know that nothing but imbecile curiosity impelled me to *that*, also that it isn't about *that* I feel guilty: I tell you this at the risk of making you feel even harsher towards me. But I have hurt you and I can't get a moment's peace. I'm sending you everything you asked for. I entrust you to the country you love. Remember that, in spite of everything, you are my one and only love, my one and only source of life. My 'youth' as you used to call it when you still used to look up into my eyes and laugh—that dismal youth of a man already old—has vanished at one stroke with you. . . ."

How it hurt, how it hurt! I sobbed, sitting there on the ground with my head against the rough flank of the walnut-tree. My own pain tormented me; so, alas, did his. . . . I had never before known what a "broken heart" was, and now I was enduring the anguish of two, and suffering even more for his than for mine. . . . Renaud, Renaud! . . .

Sitting there, I gradually became numb; my sorrow slowly congealed. My burning eyes followed the flight of a wasp, the "frrt" of a bird, the complicated journey of a ground-beetle. . . . How blue the blue of those aconites was! a fine full-bodied colour, strong and plebeian. . . . Where did that honeyed breath come from, smelling of attar of roses and spiced cake? . . . It was the great nymph's-thigh rose-bush wafting me its incense. . . . That bush brought me to my feet, that were swarming all over with ants, to go over and greet it.

So many roses, so many roses! I wanted to say to it: "Rest. You have flowered enough, worked enough, exhausted enough of your strength and your fragrance. . . ." It wouldn't have listened to me. It wanted to beat the rose record in number and in scent. It had stamina, it had speed, it gave everything it had. Its innumerable daughters were pretty little roses, like the ones on Holy Pictures, barely tinted at the edges of the petals, with little hearts of vivid carmine. Taken singly, they might seem slightly insipid, but who would dream of criticising the mantle, murmurous with bees, they had thrown over this wall?

"Swine of a donkey! Will someone flay the skin of that infamous beast vomited up by the jaws of hell? . . ."

No possible doubt that was Papa giving signs of life. Delighted at the thought of seeing him, of distracting myself with his extravagant absurdity, I ran. I saw him leaning out of a window on the first floor, the library one. His beard had whitened a little, but it still poured in a tricoloured flood over his vast chest. His nostrils snorted fire and his gesture struck consternation into the universe.

"What's the matter, Papa?"

"That filthy cat has walked all over my beautiful wash-drawing with her dirty paws, ruined it for ever! She bloody well deserves to be chucked out of the window!"

So he was perpetrating wash-drawings now? I trembled a little for my darling Fanchette.

"Oh, Papa, you haven't hurt her?"

"No, of course not! But I might have done and I ought to have done, d'you hear, you daughter of a wheezy horse?"

I breathed again. Seeing him so rarely now, I had forgotten how harmless his thunderbolts were.

"And you, my Dine, are you well?"

His infinitely tender voice, that pet name of my very earliest childhood, reopened fountains of youth in me; I listened to bright, fleeting memories plashing drop by drop. Thank goodness, he had started thundering again!

"Well, she-ass, I'm talking to you, I believe?"

"Yes, Papa dear, I'm well. Are you working?"

"It's insulting to me even to doubt it. Here, read this; it appeared last week; it produced an earthquake. All my oafs of colleagues pulled long faces. . . ."

He threw me down the number of *Reports* that included his precious contribution.

Malacology, malacology! To thy faithful devotees, thou dispensest happiness and oblivion of humanity and all its woes. . . . Flicking through the little magazine (its cover was a cheerful pink), I came across the authentic slug in this word that trailed its slimy length of fifty-four letters right across the page. *Tetramethylmonophenilsulfotripara-amidotriphenylmethane.* . . . Alas! I could hear Renaud's laugh at the discovery of such a gem.

"Would you let me keep this, Papa? Or is it your only copy?"

"No," he replied from his window, like Jupiter from Olympus. "I've ordered ten thousand private reprints of it from Gauthier-Villars."

"That was wise. What time do we have lunch?"

"Ask the domestic staff. I am nothing but a brain. I don't eat. I think!"

With a noise like thunder, he slammed his window shut and the sunlight glittered on the panes.

I knew him; this man who was nothing but a brain would shortly be "thinking" a large beef steak.

My entire day drifted by in searching step by step, crumb by crumb, for all the fragments of my childhood scattered in the corners of the old house; in staring, through the bars of the gate that the powerful wistaria had wrenched out of shape, at Quail Mountain changing and growing paler, then turning purple in the distance. The thick woods whose rich, dense green took on a blue tinge towards evening, those I would leave till tomorrow. I was not ready to love them yet. . . . Today, I dressed my wound, and nursed my hurt in a sheltered place. Too much light, too much clean wind and the green briars blossoming with wild roses might rip off the light cotton-wool of healing that swathed my sorrow.

In the reddening evening, I listened to the kindly garden settling down to sleep. Above my head, the black shape of a little bat zigzagged in silent flight. . . . A Saint-Jean pear-tree, lavish and hurried, dropped its round fruits one by one—those pears that are sleepy as soon as they are ripe and bring tenacious wasps down with them as they fall. . . . Five, six, ten wasps in the hole of one little pear. . . . They go on eating as they fall, merely beating the air with their light wings. . . . That was just how Rézi's golden lashes used to flutter under my lips.

This reminder of my treacherous mistress did not make me double up inwardly with the pain I dreaded. Ah, I had been right in my surmise that I had not loved *her*.

Whereas there was something else I could not conjure up without a torturing pang, without clasping my hands in anguish—Renaud's tall figure in the dimness of that flowered bedroom, watching my face for my decision, his sad eyes fearing the irrevocable. . . .

"My pettikins, a telegram for you!"

Honestly, it was too much! I turned round, menacing and furious, ready to tear the paper to shreds.

"It's reply paid."

I read: *Urgently request news of health.*

. . . He had not dared say any more. He had been conscious of Papa, or Mélie, of Mademoiselle Mathieu, the postmistress. *I* was conscious of them too, in my reply:

Comfortable journey. Father very well.

I cried in my sleep, but I cannot remember what I dreamt. Yet it was a dream from which I woke with a sense of oppression, heaving great trembling sighs. Day was just breaking; it was only three o'clock. The hens were still asleep, only the sparrows were twittering, making a noise like gravel being shifted. It was going to be fine; the dawn was blue. . . .

I wanted, as I used to do as a little girl, to get up before the sun and go to the wood of Fredonnes to catch the nocturnal taste of the cold spring and the last shreds of the night that retreats into the undergrowth before the first rays and buries itself there. . . .

I jumped out of bed. Fanchette, asleep and deprived of the hollow between my knees, coiled herself round like a snail without so much as opening an eye. She gave a little moan, then pressed her white paw more firmly over her closed eyes. She is not interested in dewy dawns. She only cares for clear, bright nights when, sitting upright and austere as an Egyptian cat-goddess, she stares interminably at the white moon moving across the sky.

My hasty dressing and that uncertain early half-light took me back to winter mornings when I used to get up shivering and set off to school, through the cold and the unswept snow. A skimpy little urchin, brave under my red hood, I would crack boiled chestnuts with my teeth as I slid along on my small pointed *sabots.*

I passed through the garden and climbed over the spikes of the gate. I wrote on the kitchen floor, with a piece of charcoal: "Claudine has gone out. She'll be back for lunch." Before climbing over the gate, with my skirt hitched up, I smiled at *my* house, for nothing is more my very own than that big granite dwelling with its peeling shutters open day and night over unsuspicious windows. The mauve slate of the roof was adorned with close-shaven little yellow lichens and, on the flag of the weathercock, two swallows were puffing out their white chests, offering them to be scratched by the first sharp ray of sunlight.

My unwonted appearance in the street disturbed dogs who were doing duty as scavengers, and grey cats fled silently, their backs arched. Safe on a window-sill, they gazed after me with yellow eyes. . . . In a minute or two, they would come down again, when the noise of my footsteps had decreased round the turning. . . .

These Paris boots were no good at all for Montigny. I would get some other, less elegant ones, with little nails in the soles. . . .

The exquisite cold of the blue dusk struck my skin, so long unused to it, and pinched my ears. But up there on the heights, lilac mists drifted like gauzy sails and the edges of the roofs had suddenly turned a violent orange-pink. . . . I almost ran towards the light till I reached the Saint-Jean gate, half-way up the hill, where a cheerful, tumble-down house, stuck there all by itself at the edge of the town, guards the entrance to the fields. There I stopped, heaving a great sigh. . . .

Had I reached the end of my troubles? Up here, would I feel the last impact of the cruel blow die away? In that valley, narrow as a cradle, I had laid all the dreams of sixteen years of solitary childhood. . . . I seemed to see them sleeping there still, veiled in a milky mist that rippled and flowed like a sea. . . .

The clatter of a shutter being thrown open chased me away from the heap of stones where I had been daydreaming in the wind that almost froze my lips. . . . It was not the people of Montigny I had come out to see. What I wanted was to descend the hill, go through that bed of mist, climb the sandy yellow path on the other side up to the woods whose crests were tipped with fiery rose. . . . Onwards!

I walked on and on, in anxious haste, keeping my eyes on the ground all along the hedgerows, as if I were searching for the herb that would heal me. . . .

I returned home half an hour after midday, more exhausted and dishevelled than if three poachers had set upon me in the woods. But while Mélie moaned and lamented, I stared at my reflection with a passive smile. My tired face was striped with a pink scratch near my lip, my hair was matted with burrs, my soaking skirt was embroidered with little, green hairy beads of wild millet. My blue linen shirt was split under the arms, and a warm, damp smell rose up in my nostrils, that smell that so madly excited Ren. . . . No, I never wanted to think of him again!

How beautiful the woods were! How soft the light! How cold the dew on the edges of the grassy ditches! I had been too late to find that charming population of small, frail flowers in the fields and copses, forget-me-not and bladder campion, daffodils and spring daisies; Solomon's seal and lily of the valley had long since shed their hanging bells. But at least I had been able to bathe my bare hands and trembling legs in thick, deep grass, sprawl my tired limbs on the dry velvet of moss and pineneedles, rest without a thought in my head, baked by the fierce, mounting sun. . . . I was penetrated with sunlight, rustling with breezes, echoing with crickets and birdsong, like a room open on a garden. . . .

"That's a nice sight, to be sure! A pretty dress like that!" scolded Mélie.

"Don't care. I've got other ones. Oh, Mélie, I don't think I'd have come home if I didn't need my lunch so! . . . But I'm simply dying of hunger."

"That's a good thing. The food's all cooked. . . . But I ask, where's your sense got to, doing such a thing? And Monsieur yelling after you everywhere and rolling his eyes like a stuck pig. You're just the same as ever. You little tramp, you!"

I had run about so much and looked at so much and loved so much that morning that I stayed in the garden all the afternoon. The kitchen garden, that I had not visited yet, presented me with warm apricots and peaches, which I ate afterwards, lying on my stomach under the big fir-trees with an old Balzac between my elbows.

How marvellously light-hearted I felt, how blissfully tired from physical exertion! Didn't that mean I was happy again, that I had forgotten everything and recovered my joyous solitude of the old days?

I might have deceived myself into believing it, but no, Mélie was wrong; I wasn't "the same as ever". As the day declined, the wound began to throb again, the uneasiness returned, the torturing uneasiness that forced me to keep moving, to keep changing from one room, one chair, one book to another as one tries to find a cool place in a fever-tossed bed. . . . I went into the kitchen and, after long hesitation—I was helping Mélie beat a mayonnaise that refused to thicken—I finally asked her, in a casual voice:

"There weren't any letters for me today, were there?"

"No, my lammy; nothing came but Monsieur's papers."

I went to sleep so tired that my ears buzzed and the exhausted muscles of my calves went on quivering automatically. But my slumber was not pleasant; it was shot through with confused dreams, dominated by a nerve-racking sensation of waiting for something. It was so strong that I lingered on in bed this morning, between Fanchette and my cooling chocolate.

Fanchette, convinced that I have come back solely for her sake, has enjoyed perfect bliss since my return. A little too perfect, perhaps. I don't torment her enough. She misses my constant teasing of the old days when I used to hold her upright on her hind-paws, or dangle her by her tail, or swing her to and fro, two paws gripped in either hand, crying: "Here's a fine white hare, weighing eight pounds!" Now I am always gentle. I caress her without pinching her or biting her ears. . . . Really, Fanchette, one can't have everything; look at me, for example. . . .

Who was that walking up the front doorsteps? The postman, surely. . . . As long as Renaud hadn't written to me!

Mélie would have brought me his letter by now. . . . She wasn't coming. . . . All the same, I listened with my ears and nostrils stretched to their utmost. . . . She wasn't coming. . . . He hadn't written. . . . So much the better! Let him forget and allow me to forget!

That sigh, what did it mean? It was a sigh of relief. What else *could* it be? But if Claudine was reassured, why was she trembling all over? . . . Why hadn't he written? Because I hadn't answered him. . . . Because he was frightened of making me even angrier. . . . Or else he had written, and torn up his letter. . . . He had missed the post. . . . He was ill!

With one bound, I was out of bed, pushing away the dishevelled cat, who blinked at this rude awakening. This movement restored me to consciousness; I felt thoroughly ashamed of myself. . . .

Mélie was such a dawdler. . . . She would have put the letter down on a corner of the kitchen table, beside the butter they bring wrapped in two beet leaves. . . . That butter would make a greasy mark on the letter. I pulled a cord that let loose a din like a convent bell.

"Is it for your hot water, my pet?"

"Yes, of course. . . . Oh, Mélie! Didn't the postman bring anything for me?"

"Nothing, my lamb."

Her faded blue eyes crinkled up with ribald affection.

"Aha! Hankering after your man? You blessed little newlywed, you! Fair itching for him."

She went off, chuckling very low. I turned my back to my looking-glass so as not to see the expression on my face.

Having finally recaptured my courage, I climbed up, preceded by Fanchette, to the attic where I had so often taken refuge when it rained for days on end. It is huge and dim; laundered sheets hang over the wooden rollers of the drier; a pile of half-gnawed-away books occupies an entire corner; an antique night-commode, with one foot missing, gapes open, awaiting a ghostly behind. A great wicker hamper conceals remnants of wallpapers that date back to the Restoration; plum-coloured stripes on a bilious yellow ground; imitation green trellises overgrown with strange vegetation among which fluttered improbable marrow-green birds. . . . All this jumbled pell-mell with the tattered remains of an old herbarium in which I used to admire the delicate skeletons of rare plants from goodness knows where before I destroyed them. . . . Some of them were still left, and I turned over the pages, inhaling the old dust with its sweetish, faintly chemist's shop smell, and the odour of mildewed paper, dead plants and lime blossoms gathered last week, spread out to dry on a sheet. . . . When I pushed up the skylight I saw the same old little landscape framed in its aperture when I raised my head; a distant, complete little landscape with a wood to the left, a sloping meadow and a red roof in the corner. . . . It was composed with care, naïve and charming.

From below came the sound of the door-bell. I listened to doors opening, indistinct voices, something like a heavy piece of furniture being dragged along. . . . Poor, unhappy Claudine, how the slightest thing upset you now! . . . I could not bear to stay up there any longer; I would rather go down to the kitchen.

"Wherever had you got to, my pet? I looked for you; then I

thought you'd gone off tramping again. . . . It's your trunk Monsieur Renaud's sent express. Racalin's took it up to your bedroom by the back stairs. . . ."

That big parchment trunk depressed and upset me as much as if it had been a piece of furniture from *over there*. . . . One of its sides still bore a large red label with white letters: HÔTEL DES BERGUES.

It dated from our honeymoon. . . . I had begged for that label to be left on because it enabled the trunk to be seen a long way away at stations. . . . At the Hôtel des Bergues . . . it had rained all the time, we had never gone out. . . .

I pushed up the lid violently, as if I wanted to throw off the searing, beloved memory that rose up before me, wearing the face of hope.

At first sight, I did not think the maid had forgotten anything to speak of. The maid. . . . I saw traces of other hands than hers here. . . . It was not she who had put in, under the summer blouses and the layers of fresh, fine underlinen threaded with new ribbons, the little green leather case. Inside it, the ruby Renaud had given me shone lucent, like transparent blood, like rich, mellow wine. . . . I hardly dared to touch it. No, no; let it go on sleeping in the little green case!

In the lower compartment lay my dresses, their bodices empty and their sleeves like deflated balloons; three simple dresses that I can keep here. But shall I also keep that enchanting little old silver box here, a present from him, like the ruby, like everything I possess? It had been filled with my favourite sweets, extra sugary fondants and chocolate creams. . . . Renaud, wicked Renaud, if only you knew how bitter sweets taste, wetted with hot tears! . . .

I hesitated now over lifting each layer, for the past clung to every fold and everything spoke of the tender, imploring solicitude of the man who had betrayed me. . . . Everything here was full of him; he had smoothed the folded underclothes with his own hands, he had tied the ribbons of those sachets they were packed in. . . .

Working slowly, my eyes misty with tears, I lingered long over the emptying of this reliquary. . . .

I would have liked to linger even longer! Right at the bottom, in one of my little morocco mules, a white letter was rolled up. I knew perfectly well that I should read it . . . but how cold that sealed paper felt! How unpleasantly it crackled under my trembling fingers! I had to read it, if only to silence that odious little noise. . . .

"My poor, adored child, I am sending you all that remains to me of you, everything that still kept your scent lingering here, a little of your presence. My darling, you who believe in the soul of things, I still hope that these will speak of me without anger to you. Will you forgive me, Claudine? I am mortally lonely. Give me back—not now, later on, when you feel you can—not my wife, but just the dear little daughter you have taken away. Because my heart is bursting with grief at the thought of your pale, intense little face smiling at your father while all that remains to *me* is the cruel face of Marcel. I implore you to remember, when you are less unhappy, that one line from you would be as dear and blessed to me as a promise. . . ."

"Wherever be you off to now? And lunch on the table, waiting for you!"

"It'll have to be disappointed. I'm not having any lunch. Tell Papa . . . oh, anything you like, that I'm going to walk as far as Quail Mountain. . . . I shan't be home till this evening."

As I spoke, I was feverishly stuffing things into a little basket, the crusty top of a cottage loaf, some windfall apples, a leg of chicken pinched from the dish ready for the table. . . . Definitely I was *not* lunching here! To see clear into my troubled mind, I needed the sun-striped shadow and the beauty of the woods as counsellor.

In spite of the harsh sun, I did not stop once as I followed the narrow path that leads to Les Vrimes, more of a ditch than a path, hollow and sandy like a river-bed. My footsteps sent *verdelles* scurrying away, those big, emerald-green lizards who are so timid that I have never managed to capture one. Clouds of common butterflies, beige and brown like labourers, rose in front of me. A Camberwell beauty zigzagged past, brushing the hedge as if it were an effort to raise its heavy brown velvet wings any higher. . . . At long intervals, a shallow, undulating furrow made a hollow imprint in the sand; a snake had passed there, slate-coloured and shining. Perhaps the green legs of a frog, still kicking, had protruded from its flat little tortoise-like mouth. . . .

Often I turned round, to watch the ivy-clad Saracen tower and the decrepit castle growing smaller. I wanted to go as far as the little gatekeeper's lodge that, maybe a hundred years ago, lost the floorboards of its single storey, its windows, its door and even its very name. . . . For here it is called "the-little-house-where-there-are-so-many-dirty-things-written-on-the-walls". That's the sort of place it is. And it really is a fact that it would be impossible to see more obscenities and naïve bits of gross scatology than are carved or scrawled in charcoal there. They cover the entire length and breadth of the walls so thickly that they intertwine and they are illustrated with sketches, done with chalk or a pen-knife. But I am not concerned with the little six-sided house to which rude boys and bands of sly girls make their pilgrimage on Sundays. . . . What I want is the wood it used to guard and that is never sullied by young Sunday pleasure-seekers because it is too dense, too silent and broken by damp gulleys brimming over with ferns. . . .

Ravenous, with all thought put to sleep, I ate like a woodcutter, my basket between my knees. The sheer delight of feeling a lively animal, conscious of nothing but the flavour of crisp, crunchy bread and juicy apple! The gentle landscape awakened a sensuality in me that was almost like the rapture of the hunger I was appeasing; those dark, close-knit woods smelt like the apple, this fresh bread was as gay as the pink-tiled roof that pierced them. . . .

Then, lying on my back, with my arms flung out sideways, I waited for blissful torpor.

No one in the fields. What would they be doing in them? Nothing was cultivated there. The grass grew, the dead wood fell, the game walked into the snare. Little girls on holiday from school led the sheep along the slopes and everything, at this hour, was taking a siesta, like myself. A flowering briar-bush exhaled its deceptive smell of strawberries. The low branches of a stunted oak sheltered me like the porch of a house.

While I was slithering a little way to change my bed of cool grass, a crackling of crumpled paper chased away approaching sleep. Renaud's letter palpitated inside my blouse, that imploring letter. . . .

"My poor adored child" . . . "the dear little daughter you have taken away" . . . "Your pale intense little face . . ."

He had written, perhaps for the first time in his life, without weighing the words he wrote, without any attempt at literary style—he who, normally, was as shocked to see a word repeated only two lines later as to find an inkstain on his finger.

I carried that letter as engaged girls do, next to my heart. That and the other one of the day before yesterday were the only two love-letters I had ever received. For, during our brief engagement, Renaud had been with me every day, and, ever since, gaily, meekly or indifferently I had always followed him wherever his roving, worldly temperament took him. . . .

What good had I done him or myself, in eighteen months? I had rejoiced in his love, been saddened by his frivolity, shocked by his ways of thinking and behaving—all this without saying a word and deliberately avoiding discussions. And more than once I had felt resentful towards Renaud for my own silence.

There had been egotism in my suffering without trying to find a remedy; there had been obstinate pride in my silent reproaches. Yet what was there he would not have done for me? I could have obtained everything from his passionate tenderness; he loved me enough to guide me—if I had guided him first. And what had I asked him for? A place for assignations!

We must begin all over again. Thank God, it was not too late to make a fresh start. "My dear giant," I would say to him, "I order you to dominate me! . . ." And I would say too . . . oh, so many other things. . . .

It was growing late. The sun was dipping, delicate butterflies were emerging from the woods with a hesitant, already nocturnal flight; a shy, sociable little owl appeared too early on the fringe of the wood, blinking its dazzled eyes; as the daylight faded, the undergrowth was coming alive with a thousand uneasy rustlings and little cries. But for all these things I had only inattentive ears and absently tender eyes. . . . Suddenly, I was on my feet, stretching my numbed arms and cramped calves; the next moment I was rushing away towards Montigny, spurred on by the time—the time of the post, of course! I wanted to write, to write to Renaud.

I had made my resolution. . . . Ah! how little it had cost me!

"Dear Renaud,—I find it difficult to write to you because this is the first time. And I feel I shall never be able to say all I want to say to you before the evening post goes.

"I've got to ask your forgiveness for having gone away and to thank you for having let me go. It has taken me four days, all alone in my home with my misery, to understand something you could have convinced me of in a few minutes. . . . All the same, I think these four days have not been wasted.

"You have written me all your loving tenderness, dear giant, without saying a word to me about Rézi, without telling me: 'You did with her just what I did, with so little difference. . . .' Yet that would have been very reasonable, almost flawless as a piece of logic. But you knew that *it was not the same thing* . . . and I'm grateful to you for not having said it.

"I don't want ever, ever again to make you unhappy, but you must help me over this, Renaud. Yes, I am your child . . . something more than your child, an over-petted daughter whom you ought sometimes to refuse what she asks for. I wanted Rézi and you gave her to me like a sweet. . . . You've got to teach me that some kinds of sweets are harmful and that, if one eats them all, one must be on the look-out for bad brands. . . . Don't, dear Renaud, be afraid of making your Claudine unhappy by scolding her. I like being dependent on you and being a little frightened of a friend I love so much.

"I want to tell you something else too; it's that I shan't come back to Paris. You have entrusted me to the country I love, so come and find me again here, keep me here, love me here. If you have to leave me sometimes, because you have to or because you want to, I will wait here faithfully and with no mistrust. There is enough beauty and sadness here in Fresnois for you to have no fear of boredom if I am with you all the time. For I am more beautiful here, more loving, more sincere.

"Whatever happens, come, because I can't go on any longer without you. I love you, I love you; it's the first time I've written it to you. Come! Remember that I have just been waiting four whole long days, my dear husband, for you not to be too young for me any more. . . ."

Claudine and Annie

H<small>E</small> has gone! He has gone! I keep saying those words to myself; now I am writing them down on paper to find out if they are true and if they are going to hurt me. As long as he was there, I did not feel as if he were going. He bustled about methodically. He kept giving precise orders and insisting: "Annie, be sure not to forget . . ." then breaking off to say: "Goodness, how miserable you look! Your distress distresses me more than the prospect of going away!" Did I really look so miserable? I was not suffering, because he was still there.

Hearing him pity me like that made me shiver inwardly. Shrunk into myself, I kept wondering fearfully: "Am I really going to be as unhappy as he says? This is terrible."

At the moment it is all too true. He has gone! I am afraid to move, to breathe, to live. A husband ought not to leave his wife—not when it is this particular husband and this particular wife.

Before I had turned thirteen, he was already the master of my life. Such a handsome master! A red-haired boy, with a skin whiter than an egg and blue eyes that dazzled me. When I lived with my grandmother Lajarrisse—she was all the family I had—I used to look forward and count the days to his summer holidays. At last the morning would arrive when she would come into my nunlike little grey and white bedroom (they whitewash the walls down there because of the fierce summer heat and they stay fresh and clean in the shadow of the shutters) and say, as she entered: "Alain's bedroom windows are open, cook saw them when she came back from town." She would announce this calmly without suspecting that those mere words made me curl up into a tight little ball under my sheets and draw my knees up to my chin . . .

Alain! At twelve years old I loved him, as I do now, with a confused, frightened love that had no trace of coquetry or guile in it. Every year we were inseparable companions for close on four months because he was being educated in Normandy at one of those schools modelled on English lines where the boys have long summer holidays. He would arrive all white and golden, with five or six freckles under his blue eyes, and push open the garden gate as if he were planting a flag on a conquered citadel. I used to wait for him in my little everyday frock . . . not daring to dress up for him in case he noticed it. He would take me off with him and we would read or play. He never asked for my opinion; he jeered at me a good deal; he issued decrees. "This is what we're going to do. You're to hold the foot of the ladder and stretch out your pinafore so that I can throw the apples into it." He would put his arm round my shoulders and look about him menacingly as if to say: "I dare anyone to take her from me!" He was sixteen and I was twelve.

Sometimes—I made that gesture again, humbly, only yesterday—I would lay my sunburnt hand on his white wrist and sigh: "How black I am!" He would give a proud smile that displayed his square teeth and reply: "Sed formosa, Annie dear."

I have a photograph here, taken in those days. I am dark and slight, as I am now, with a small head dragged back a little by the heavy black hair and a pouting mouth that seems to be pleading "I won't do it again." Under the very long lashes that grow in one dense, perfectly straight sweep, the eyes are of such a liquid blue that they embarrass me when I look at myself in the glass—they are so ridiculously light against a skin as dark as a little Kabyle girl's. However, since Alain found them attractive . . .

We grew up very virtuously, without any kissing or erotic behaviour. That was not due to me! I would have said "Yes" without even uttering a word. Sometimes, when I was with him towards evening, I found the scent of jasmine too oppressive and my throat felt so constricted I could hardly breathe . . . Since words failed me to tell Alain: "This jasmine, this twilight, this down on my own skin that caresses my lips when they brush it . . . they're all you . . ." I would press my lips together and lower my lashes over my too-light eyes in an attitude so habitual to me that he never once suspected anything . . . He is as upright and decent as he is handsome.

At twenty-four, he announced: "Now we're going to get married" just as eleven years earlier he would have announced: "Now we're going to play Indians."

He has always known so infallibly what I ought to do that without him I am lost. I am like a useless mechanical toy that has lost its key. How am I to know now what is right and what is wrong?

Poor weak, selfish little Annie! Thinking of him makes me feel sorry for myself. I implored him not to go away . . . I said very little because his affection, always reserved, dreads emotional outbursts. "Perhaps this legacy doesn't amount to much . . . We've got enough money as it is, and it's a long way to go on the off-chance of finding a fortune . . . Alain, suppose you commissioned someone else . . ." His astonished eyebrows cut me short in the middle of my tactless suggestion, but I plucked up courage again. "Well then, Alain, couldn't you take me with you?"

His pitying smile deprived me of all hope.

"Take you with me, my poor child? You . . . delicate as you are . . . and . . . I don't want to hurt your feelings . . . such a bad traveller? Can you see yourself enduring the voyage to Buenos Aires? Think of your health, think . . . and I know this is an argument that will convince you . . . of the trouble you might be to *me.*" I lowered my lids, which is my way of retiring into my shell, and silently cursed my Uncle Etchevarray, a hothead who disappeared fifteen years ago and of whom we had heard nothing till now. Tiresome idiot, why did he take it into his head to die rich in some unknown country and leave us . . . what? . . . Some *estancias* where they breed bulls, "bulls that sell at up to six thousand piastres, Annie." I can't even remember what that adds up to in francs.

The day of his departure is not over yet and here I am in my room, secretly writing in the beautiful notebook he gave me for the purpose of keeping my "Diary of his journey". I am also re-reading the list of duties he drew up for me with his usual solicitous firmness. It is headed *Timetable.*

June. Calls on Madame X . . . , Madame Z . . . , and Madame T . . . (important).

Only one call on Renaud and Claudine. Too fantastically unconventional a couple for a young woman to frequent while her husband is away on a long journey.

Pay the upholsterer's bill for the big armchairs in the drawing-room and the cane bedstead. Don't haggle because the upholsterer works for our friends the G.s. People might gossip.

Order Annie's summer clothes. Not too many 'tailored' things; light, simple dresses. Will my dear Annie not obstinately persist in believing that red and bright orange make her complexion look lighter?

Check the servants' account books every Saturday morning. See that Jules does not forget to take down the tapestry in my smoking-room and that he rolls it up sprinkled with pepper and tobacco. He's not a bad fellow but slack and he'll do his jobs carelessly if Annie doesn't keep a sharp eye on him.

Annie will take a daily walk in the Avenues and will not read too much nonsense. Not too many 'realistic' novels or any other kind.

Warn the 'Urbaine' that we are giving notice on July 1st. Hire the Victoria by the day during the five days before you go off to Arriège.

My dear Annie will give me much pleasure if she frequently consults my sister Marthe and goes out with her. Marthe has a great deal of good sense and even common-sense under her rather unconventional exterior.

He has thought of everything! Don't I have, even for one minute, any shame about my . . . my incompetence? Inertia would be a better word perhaps . . . or passivity. Alain's active vigilance overlooks nothing and spares me from the slightest practical worry. By nature I am as indolent as a little Negress but, in the first year of our marriage, I did attempt to shake myself out of my silent languor. Alain made short work of destroying my noble zeal. "Leave it alone, Annie, the thing's done. I've seen to it myself." "No, no, Annie, you don't know, you haven't the remotest idea . . .!"

I don't know anything . . . except how to obey. He has taught me that and I achieve obedience as the sole task of my existence . . . assiduously . . . joyfully. My supple neck, my dangling arms, my too-slender, flexible shape . . . everything about me, from my eyelids that droop easily and say "yes" to my little slave-girl's complexion, predestined me to obey. Alain often calls me that, "little slave-girl". Of course he says it without malice, with only a faint contempt for my dark-skinned race. He is so white!

Yes, dear "timetable", that will continue to guide me in his absence and until his first letter arrives, yes, I will give notice to the "Urbaine", I will keep an eye on Jules, I will check the servants' account-books, I will pay my calls and I will see Marthe frequently.

Marthe is my sister-in-law, Alain's sister. Although he disapproves of her having married a novelist, albeit a well-known one, my husband is aware of her lively, scatter-brained intelligence and her intermittent clear-sightedness. He readily admits: "She's clever." I am not quite sure how to assess the value of that compliment.

In any case, she knows infallibly how to handle her brother and I am sure Alain has not the least suspicion how she plays up to him. How artfully she glosses over the risky word she has allowed to slip out, how deftly she glances off from a dangerous topic of conversation! When I have annoyed my lord and master, I just remain completely miserable, without even pleading to be forgiven. Marthe just laughs in his face, or tactfully admires some remark he has just made or is amusingly scathing about some particularly odious bore—and Alain's scowling eyebrows relax.

Clever, certainly, at using her wits and her hands. I watch her in amazement when, all the time she is chattering, her fingers are busy creating an adorable hat or a lace jabot with the professional skill of a 'first hand' in a good fashion-house. All the same, there is nothing of the 'little milliner' about Marthe. She is dimpled and rather short, with a tight-laced, very slim waist, and a shapely, provocative behind. She carries her head of flaming red-gold hair (Alain's hair) very high and she has glittering, ruthless grey eyes. Her face is the face of a young incendiary—a fierce little female 'comrade'—and she composes it into a charming pastiche of an eighteenth century court lady. She uses powder and lipstick and wears rustling silk dresses patterned with garlands of flowers, pointed bodices and very high heels. Claudine (the amusing Claudine whom one mustn't see too much of) calls her "The Marquise of the Barricades".

This revolutionary Ninon de Lenclos has completely subjugated the husband she conquered after a brief struggle—there again I recognise her kinship with Alain: Léon is rather like Marthe's Annie. When I think of him, I mentally call him "poor old Léon". Nevertheless, he does not look unhappy. He is dark, good-looking, with regular features, a pointed beard, almond-shaped eyes and soft hair plastered close to his skull. A typical Frenchman of the mild, unassertive kind. He would be more impressive if his profile were a little more forceful, his chin squarer and his brows more emphatically drawn, also if his brown eyes were not so eagerly anxious to please. He is a trifle—it's malicious of me to write it—a trifle "head salesman in the silk department" as that wicked Claudine suggested when she nicknamed him one day: "And-what-next-Madam?" The label has stuck to poor old Léon whom Marthe treats merely as a productive piece of property.

She shuts him up regularly for three or four hours a day, with the result that he furnishes, she told me confidentially, a good average yield of one and two-thirds novels per year—"enough for our bare necessities," she added.

It is beyond me that there should be women with enough initiative and enough constant, persevering will—enough cruelty too—to build up an income large enough to sustain an extravagant way of life on the bent back of a man who is forced to write and write till he nearly kills himself. Sometimes I condemn Marthe; at others, she inspires me with admiration, tinged with fear.

Thinking of her masculine authority that exploited Léon's meekness, I said to her one day, when I was feeling extraordinarily bold:

"Marthe, you and your husband are an unnatural couple."

She stared at me in stupefaction, then she laughed till she nearly made herself ill.

"No, really . . . the things our little Annie says! You ought never to go out without a dictionary. An unnatural couple! Luckily, there's no one to hear you but me, considering what those words imply nowadays . . ."

The fact remains that Alain has gone! I can't forget him for long while I run on like this, talking to myself on paper. What am I to do? This burden of living alone overwhelms me . . . Suppose I go off to the country—to Casamène—to the house my grandmother Lajarrisse left us, so as to see no one, no one at all till he comes back?

Marthe came in at that point, sweeping away all my splendid, ridiculous plans with her stiff skirts and her rustling sleeves. Hurriedly, I hid my notebook.

"All by yourself? Are you coming to the tailor's? All alone in this dreary room? The inconsolable widow, in fact!"

Her ill-timed jest . . . and also her likeness to her brother in spite of the powder, the Marie-Antoinette shepherdess hat and the tall parasol . . . made me start crying again.

"There, now I've done it! Annie, you are the most abject of . . . wives. He'll come back, I tell you! In my simple-minded, unworthy way, I imagined his absence . . . anyway for the first few weeks . . . would give you a holiday feeling—that it would actually be rather a lark . . ."

"A lark? Oh! Marthe . . ."

"Why, 'Oh! Marthe'? . . . I admit it feels empty here," she said, wandering round the room, *my* room, where nothing, in fact, has changed.

I dried my eyes, which always takes a little time because I have such thick lashes. Marthe says, with a laugh, that I have "hair on my eyelids".

She turned her back to me and leant with both elbows on the mantelpiece. She was wearing—a little early for the time of year, I thought—a high-waisted beige voile dress sprinkled with little old-fashioned roses with a gathered skirt and a cross-over fichu in the style of Madame Vigée-Lebrun. Her red hair, swept up from the nape, was typical of a very different painter—Helleu. The two styles clashed a little, but not crudely. But I shall keep these remarks to myself. After all, what remarks do I *not* keep to myself?

"What are you studying for such a long time, Marthe?"

"I'm contemplating the portrait of his lordship, my brother."

"Alain?"

"Right first time."

"What do you find so striking about him?"

She did not answer at once. Then she burst out laughing and said, turning round:

"It's extraordinary how like a cock he is!"

"A cock?"

"Yes, a cock. Just look."

Horrified to hear such a blasphemy, I mechanically picked up the portrait, a photograph printed in reddish sepia. It's one I'm very fond of. My husband is standing, bare-headed, in a summer garden, with his red hair bristling, his eyes glaring haughtily and his calves braced taut. That is his habitual stance. He looks like a robust, handsome young man with a fiery disposition and an alert eye; he also looks like a cock. Marthe was right. Yes a red, shiny-plumaged, crested and spurred cock . . . As miserable as if he had just gone away all over again, I relapsed once more into tears. My sister-in-law threw up her arms in consternation.

"No, really, if one can't even mention him! You're a case, my dear. It's going to be a gay expedition to the tailor's with your eyes in that state! Have I hurt your feelings?"

"No, no, it's just *me* . . . Take no notice, I'll be all right in a minute."

The fact is that I couldn't admit to her that I was appalled that Alain should look like a cock and even more appalled that I should have realised it . . . A cock! Why did she have to make me notice that?

2

"Madame didn't sleep well?"

"No, Léonie."

"Madame has black rings round her eyes . . . Madame should take a glass of brandy."

Léonie knows only one remedy for all ills—a glass of brandy. I imagine she tests its good effects daily. She intimidates me a little because she is tall, and very decisive in her movements. She has an authoritative way of shutting doors and when she is sewing in the linen-room she whistles military bugle-calls, like a coachman who has just returned from his regiment. Nevertheless she is capable of devotion and she has worked for me, ever since my marriage four years ago, with affectionate contempt.

That solitary awakening! There I was, all alone, telling myself that a day and a night had gone by since Alain left, summoning up all my courage to order meals, telephone to the "Urbaine", go through the account books! . . . A schoolboy who had not done his holiday task could not have woken up more depressed on the first morning of term . . .

Yesterday, I did not accompany my sister-in-law to her fitting. I felt angry with her about that business of the cock. I pleaded tiredness and the redness of my eyelids.

Today I want to shake myself out of my nervous depression and—since Alain has ordered me to—go to Marthe's at-home day, though crossing that immense drawing-room, full of the babel of women's voices, alone and unsupported has always been a torture to me. Suppose, as Claudine says, I "reported sick"? Oh, no, I can't disobey my husband.

"Which dress does Madame want?"

Yes, which dress? Alain would not have hesitated for a moment. With one glance, he would have considered the state of the weather and of my complexion, then the names on Marthe's visiting-list and his impeccable choice would have satisfied every contingency . . .

"My grey crêpe dress, Léonie and the hat with the butterflies."

They amuse me, those grey butterflies with their soft feather wings speckled with pink and orange crescents. At least I must admit that my great sorrow hasn't had too disastrous an effect on my looks. With the butterfly hat set very straight on my smooth, thick hair, parted on the right and knotted in a low chignon and my pale, disturbing blue eyes, more liquid than ever from recent tears, I could count on infuriating Valentine Chessenet. She is one of my sister-in-law's most faithful 'regulars' and she loathes me because (I can sense this) she finds my husband very much to her taste. That creature looks as if she had been dipped in a bleaching bath. Her hair, her skin, her eyelashes are all of the same uniform pinkish fairness. She makes her face up pink and plasters her lashes with mascara (Marthe told me this herself) without managing to liven up her insipid, anaemic colouring.

She would already have taken up her post at Marthe's, with her back to the light to hide the bags under her eyes, as far away as possible from the lovely, stupid Cabbage-Rose whose healthy radiance she dreads. She would screech nasty things at me over the heads of the other women and I should be incapable of making any retort; my intimidated silence would make the other parakeets laugh and call me "the little black goose" again. Alain, it is only for you that I am off to expose myself to all those painful pin-pricks.

The moment I reached the hall, my hands went cold at the sound of that hen-house cackle, punctuated by the clatter of little spoons like the sound of pecking beaks.

Of course that Chessenet woman was there! They were all there and all chattering away, except Candeur, the child-poetess, whose silent soul only blossoms in beautiful verses. *She* kept quiet, slowly rolling her mottled eyes and biting her lower lip with a voluptuous, guilty air, as if it were someone else's.

There was Miss Flossie who, when she refuses a cup of tea, utters such a prolonged, guttural "No" that she seems to be offering her whole self in that throaty purr. Alain (why?) does not want me to know her, that American woman, supple as a piece of silk, with her sparkling face glittering with tiny gold hairs, her sea-blue eyes and her ruthless teeth. She smiled at me without a trace of embarrassment, her eyes riveted on mine, till a curious quiver of her left eyebrow, as disturbing as an appeal, made me look away . . . At that, Miss Flossie gave me a more nervous smile while a slim, red-haired young girl huddled in her shadow glared at me with inexplicable hatred in her deep eyes.

Maugis—a fat music critic—his protruding eyes flashing for a second, stared straight at the two Americans so insolently that he deserved to be hit and mumbled almost inaudibly as he filled a claret-glass with whisky:

"Some Sappho . . . if that sort of thing amuses you!"

I didn't understand. I hardly dared look at all those faces suddenly fixed in a malicious rigidity because I was wearing a pretty frock. How I longed to escape! I took refuge by Marthe who revived me with her firm little hand and her audacious eyes, courageous as herself. How I envy her for being so brave. She has a sharp, impatient tongue, and she is very extravagant; she could easily be a target for unkind gossip. She is well aware of it and has a method of forestalling any spiteful innuendo: she gets her teeth into any treacherous female friend and shakes her with the tenacity of a good ratting terrier.

Today, I could have hugged her for her retort to Madame Chessenet who shrieked as I entered the room:

"Ah! Here comes the Hindu widow!"

"Don't tease her too much," Marthe flashed. "After all, when a husband goes off, it leaves a void."

A penetrating voice behind me, a voice that rolled its *r*'s, acquiesced:

"Cerrtainly . . . a verry considerrable and painful void!"

And all those women burst out laughing. I turned round in confusion and was more confused than ever when I saw that it was Renaud's wife, Claudine. "Only one call on Renaud and Claudine, too fantastically unconventional a couple . . ." Alain treats them so distantly that I feel stupid and almost guilty in their presence. Nevertheless, I find them charming and to be envied, that husband and wife who never leave each other and are as united as lovers.

One day, when I was admitting to Alain that I didn't blame Claudine and Renaud in the least for posing as married lovers, he asked me rather sharply:

"My dear, where did you get the notion that lovers see each other and enjoy each other's company more than married people?"

I replied sincerely:

"I've no idea . . ."

Ever since then, we have only exchanged occasional formal visits with this "fantastic" couple.

This doesn't embarrass Claudine in the slightest, for nothing embarrasses her. Renaud doesn't mind either, for the only thing in the world he minds about is his wife. Yet Alain has a perfect horror of breaking with people unnecessarily.

Claudine seemed perfectly unaware that she had raised a laugh. She lowered her eyes and went on eating a lobster sandwich, announcing calmly when she had finished it: "That's the sixth."

"Yes," said Marthe gaily, "you're an expensive acquaintance. The soul of Madame Beulé has passed into you."

"Only her stomach, the one thing she had worth taking," Claudine corrected her.

"Take care, dear," insinuated Madame Chessenet. "You'll get fat on that diet. It struck me the other night that your arms were filling out into a charming, but dangerous roundness."

"Pooh!" retorted Claudine, with her mouth full. "I only wish you had thighs as round as my arms. So many people would be pleased if you had."

Madame Chessenet, who is skinny and bitterly laments it, swallowed this rebuff with difficulty. Her neck was so tense that I feared there was going to be a little scene. However she merely glared in mute fury at the insolent young woman with the short hair and rose to her feet. I was on the point of getting up to go myself, but I sat down again so as not to have to leave the room with that bleached viper.

Claudine valiantly attacked the plate of little cream cakes topped with praline and offered me one (if Alain had seen us! . . .). I accepted, and whispered to her:

"That Chessenet woman's going to invent most appalling scandals about you!"

"I defy her to. She's already brought out everything she's capable of imagining. There's nothing she hasn't attributed to me except infanticide and I wouldn't even be too sure of that."

"She doesn't like you?" I asked her shyly.

"Oh yes, she does. But she conceals the fact."

"Don't you mind?"

"Of course I do."

"Why?"

Claudine's beautiful tobacco-brown eyes stared at me.

"Why? *I* don't know. Because . . ."

Her husband's approach broke off her reply. Smiling, he unobtrusively pointed towards the door. She rose from her chair, supple and silent as a cat. I had no idea why.

All the same, it seemed to me that the all-embracing look she gave him was definitely an answer.

I wanted to leave too. Standing in the middle of that circle of men and women, I felt ready to faint with embarrassment. Claudine noticed my misery and came back to my side; her sinewy hand gripped hold of mine and held it tight while my sister-in-law started asking me questions.

"Any news of Alain yet?"

"No, not yet. Perhaps I'll find a telegram when I get home."

"Well, good luck, and my blessing. Goodbye, Annie."

"Where are you spending your holidays?" Claudine asked me very gently.

"At Arriège, with Marthe and Léon."

"As long as it's with Marthe! . . . Alain can sail the seas without a qualm."

"You don't imagine, that, even without Marthe . . ."

I realised I was blushing. Claudine shrugged her shoulders and replied, as she joined her husband who was waiting for her by the door with no sign of impatience:

"Good Lord, no! He's trained you too well!"

3

THAT telephone message of Marthe's embarrassed me considerably: "Impossible to come and pick you up at home to go for a fitting at Taylor's. Come and fetch me at four o'clock at Claudine's."

An indecent picture could not have upset me more than that piece of blue paper. At Claudine's! Marthe suggests it quite casually; the Timetable says . . . What does it *not* say?

This appointment arranged by Marthe . . . ought I to consider it as an official call on Renaud and Claudine? No . . . Yes, of course . . . I got in a state, and wondered whether to shuffle out of it, torn between the fear of offending my sister-in-law and the dread of Alain and my own conscience. However, my enfeebled conscience was too unsure of the right course to follow not to yield to the more immediate influence of Marthe. It yielded most of all to the delightful prospect of seeing this Claudine who is forbidden me like an outspoken, over-truthful book.

"Rue de Bassano, Charles."

I had put on a dark, unassuming dress and I wore a plain net veil and neutral-tinted suède gloves, with the sole idea of removing any trace of "official character" from my "deportment". I know how to use those words, for Alain's social experience has made me acutely conscious that, according to the occasion, one's "deportment" should or should not assume an official character. When I mentally pronounce those words, they accompany a quaint, childish, puzzle-picture in the form of a caption . . . Deportment, a little person with threadlike limbs, stretches out his arms towards the proffered sleeves of an Academician's uniform, round whose collar 'officialcharacterofficialcharact . . .' is embroidered in a delicate garland . . . How silly I am to write all this down! It's only a little bit of maundering. I shall never put down my other maunderings; if I were to read them through again, this notebook would drop from my hands . . .

On Claudine's landing, I glanced at my watch: ten past four. Marthe would be sure to have arrived and would be sitting nibbling sweets in that extraordinary drawing-room that I had hardly taken in on my earlier visits—I had been too suffocated by shyness.

"Is Madame Léon Payet here yet?"

A hostile old female servant gave me an absentminded stare; she was far more interested in preventing a big brindled cat from escaping.

"Limaçon, just you wait . . . I'll scorch your backside for you, so I will . . . Madame Léon . . . what's her name? Floor below, very like."

"No, I meant to say . . . Is Madame Claudine at home?"

"So now it's Madame Claudine? You don't seem to know your own mind. Claudine, she lives here all right. But she's gone out."

"Oh, you monstrous liar!" shouted a gay, tomboyish voice. "I'm here and I'm at home. In one of your nasty moods, eh, Mélie?"

"No such thing," retorted Mélie, unperturbed. "But another time, you can open the door yourself. That'll larn you."

And she retreated with much dignity, the tabby cat at her heels. I was left standing in the hall, waiting for some being to emerge from the shadows and be good enough to show me in . . . Was this the witch's home? "Sugar-house, sweet, pretty sugar-house . . ." as Hansel and Gretel sang outside the alluring castle . . .

"Come in! I'm in the drawing-room but I can't budge," cried the same voice.

A tall shadow rose up and blotted out the window; it was Renaud coming to meet me.

"Come in, dear lady. The child's so desperately busy that she can't say how d'you do to you for a minute."

The child? Ah, there she was, almost squatting on the hearth where a wood fire was blazing in spite of the season. I went forward, intrigued: she was holding out some mysterious object to the flames. More than ever, she made me think of the witch in the stories that frightened me and enraptured me in my credulous childhood. I half-feared, half-hoped to see strange creatures writhing in the flames that gilded Claudine's curly head—salamanders and tortured animals whose blood mingled with wine makes the victim languish to death . . .

She rose to her feet, perfectly calm.

"How d'you do, Annie."

"How d'you do, Mad . . . Claudine."

It was a slight effort for me to address her by name. But it was impossible to say "Madame" to this childlike young woman whom everyone called Claudine.

"It was just on the point of being done to a turn, so you see I couldn't possibly leave it."

She was holding a little square grille made of silver wire on which a tablet of chocolate was blackening and swelling up. Toasted chocolate?

"You know, this utensil isn't perfect, even now, Renaud! They've made the handle too short and I've got a blister on my hand . . ."

"Show me quick."

Her tall husband bent down, and tenderly kissed the slender, scorched hand, caressing it with his lips and fingers, like a lover . . . They were no longer paying the slightest attention to me. I wondered whether I ought to go. This spectacle made me feel anything but inclined to laugh.

"All better!" cried Claudine, clapping her hands. "We're going to eat our toasted chocolate now, Annie. Just the two of us. My great big beautiful man, I'm going to entertain a visitor in my drawing-room. Go into your study and see if I'm there."

"Am I in the way, then?" that white-haired husband of hers whose eyes are those of a young man asked, still bending over her.

His wife stood on tiptoe, raised the ends of Renaud's long moustache with both hands and gave him a fierce, straining kiss. I was the one in the way. I got up to make my escape.

"Hi, Annie! Where are *you* rushing off to?"

A despotic hand grabbed hold of my arm and Claudine's ambiguous face with its mocking mouth and melancholy eyelids searched mine severely.

I blushed as if I felt guilty at having seen that kiss . . .

"I thought . . . I mean, since Marthe hasn't turned up . . ."

"Marthe? Is she supposed to be coming?"

"But of course! It was she who told me to come and meet her here . . . Otherwise . . ."

"What d'you mean—'otherwise'—you rude little thing? Renaud,

did *you* know Marthe was supposed to be coming?"

"I did, darling."

"You never mentioned it to *me*."

"Sorry, little one. I read you all your letters in bed, as usual. But you were playing with Fanchette."

"That's a barefaced lie. Why don't you admit *you* were tickling me all down my ribs with your nails? Sit *down*, Annie! Goodbye, you great bear . . ."

Renaud softly shut the door behind him.

I seated myself a little stiffly, right on the edge of the sofa. Claudine settled herself on it, tailor-fashion, with her legs drawn up and crossed under her orange cloth skirt. A supple white satin blouse, its whiteness emphasised by Japanese embroidery, of the same colour as her skirt, gave a subtle glow to her matt complexion. What was she thinking of, all of a sudden so serious, sitting there pensively and looking like a little Bosphorus boatman with her embroidered skirt and her short hair?

"Beautiful, isn't he?"

I find her laconic utterances and her quick movements, as sudden and unexpected as her immobility, as shattering as blows.

"Who?"

"Renaud, of course. It's quite possible he did read me Marthe's letter . . . I couldn't have been paying attention."

"He reads your letters?"

She gave a preoccupied nod; the tablet of toasted chocolate had stuck to the little silver grille and was threatening to crumble . . . Emboldened by her absentmindedness, I asked:

"He reads them . . . before you do?"

The mischievous eyes looked up at me.

"Yes, Lovely-Eyes. (You don't mind my calling you 'Lovely-Eyes'?) What's it got to do with you?"

"Nothing, of course. But I shouldn't like it myself."

"On account of your beaux?"

"I don't have beaux, Claudine!"

It burst from my lips with so much fervour, so much shocked sincerity that Claudine doubled herself up with delight.

"She's risen! She's risen! Oh, the simple soul! Well, Annie, I *have* had beaux . . . and Renaud used to read me their letters."

"And . . . what did he say?"

"Oh . . . nothing. Not much, anyway. Occasionally he'd sigh:

'Odd, Claudine, the number of people one meets who are convinced that they *aren't like everyone else*—and of the need to put it in writing.' So that's that."

"That's that . . ."

In spite of myself, I repeated the words in the same tone as hers.

"So it means nothing at all to you?"

"What? . . . Oh, all that . . . yes. In fact nothing means any-thing to me but one single human being . . ." She corrected herself . . . "No, that's not true. I'm not indifferent to the sky being warm and clear. Or to cushions being deep enough to sink into and pamper my laziness or to the year being rich in sweet apricots and floury chestnuts. I care passionately that the roof of my house in Montigny should be solid enough not to scatter its lichened tiles on a stormy day . . ." Her voice which had trailed away to a sing-song hastily recovered its firmness and went on ironically: "As you see, Annie, I'm interested, like you and everyone else, in the external world. And, to speak as simply as your sophisticated novelist of a brother-in-law, 'in what devouring time bears away on its changing, restless tides'."

I shook my head, not quite sure that I believed her. Then, to please Claudine, I accepted scraps of grilled chocolate that tasted a little of smoke and very much of burnt sugar.

"Divine, isn't it? You know it was I who invented the chocolate grille, this nice little gadget that they've made, in spite of all my careful directions, with too short a handle. I also invented the flea-comb for Fanchette, the stove without holes for roasting winter chestnuts, pineapples in absinthe and spinach tart . . . Mélie says *she* did but it isn't true. I also invented my drawing-room-kitchen which you see here."

Claudine's humour made me alternate between laughter and uneasiness. At one moment she troubled me; the next I admired her. Her long tobacco-brown eyes that ran right up to her temples had the same fervour, the same candid, direct look in them when she was proclaiming her inventor's rights in the chocolate grille as when she was proclaiming her passion for Renaud.

Her drawing-room kitchen added still further to this disquieting impression. I wanted desperately to know whether this woman I was talking to was an out-and-out lunatic or an expert hoaxer.

It was like a kitchen or the public room of an inn, one of those gloomy, smoky inns you find in Holland. But where, on the wall of an inn, even a Dutch one, would you find that exquisite, smiling fifteenth century Virgin, so enchanting in her pink tunic and blue mantle—a frail, childish Madonna, on her knees yet seeming half-frightened to pray?

"It's beautiful, isn't it?" said Claudine. "But what I like most about it is the vicious—yes, vicious is the only word—contrast between that dress, all tender rosy pinks and that appalling, desolate landscape in the background. As desolate as you were, Annie, the day your lord and master Alain set sail. Don't you think about that voyager any more now?"

"Whatever do you mean . . . not think about him any more?"

"Well, anyway, you don't think about him so much. Oh, you needn't blush about it . . . It's perfectly natural when you've got an impeccable husband like yours . . . Just look at that Virgin's charmingly contrite expression; she seems to be looking down at her baby Jesus and saying, 'Honestly, it's the very first time such a thing's happened to me!' Renaud thinks it's a Masolino. But the great Panjandrums of the art world attribute it to Filippo Lippi."

"What do *you* think?"

"Me? I don't care a fig who painted it."

I did not press the point. This very individual art critic rather disconcerted me.

In one corner, a Claudine in marble smiled under lowered eylids like a St. Sebastian who was revelling in his torments. A huge divan, covered with a dark bearskin that caressed my ungloved hand, retired into the shelter of a kind of alcove. But all the rest of the furniture astonished me; five or six public-house tables of shining dark oak and as many heavy, clumsy benches; an ancient rustic clock that did not go, some stone jugs and a cavernous, canopied fireplace guarded by tall copper fire-dogs. Added to all this, the room was in a state of temporary disorder; books were strewn everywhere and gutted Reviews littered the dull rose carpet. Intrigued, I studied everything closely. It gave me a kind of melancholy . . . the peculiar melancholy I associate with long voyages. I felt as if I had been staring for a long time through those small greenish panes, behind which the light was fading, at a grey ocean, flecked with a little foam, under a transparent veil of rain falling as lightly as fine ashes . . .

Claudine had followed my thoughts and when I was back with her again we looked at each other with the same expression in our eyes.

"Do you like it here, Claudine?"

"Yes. I loathe bright, cheerful rooms. Here, I can travel. Look, those green walls are the glaucous colour of daylight seen through a wine-bottle. And those oak benches must have been polished by the depressed behinds of generations of poor wretches who only got drunk to drown their sorrows . . . I say, Annie, it looks as if Marthe isn't going to turn up. Typical of your precious sister-in-law, eh!"

How abruptly, almost brutally, she had snapped off the thread of her sad little reverie! I had been following it so willingly, forgetting, just for this one hour, my anxiety about that husband of mine at sea . . . Besides, Claudine's changeableness was beginning to weary me with its mixture of childishness and savagery. I could not keep pace with the mind of this young barbarian that leapt in a flash from greed to shameless passion, from a despairing drunkard to that bustling, aggressive Marthe.

"Marthe . . . oh yes . . . She's very late."

"I'll say she is! No doubt Maugis has found some weighty reasons for keeping her."

"Maugis? Was she supposed to be seeing him today?"

Claudine wrinkled up her nose, tilted her head sideways like an inquisitive bird, and stared deep into my eyes. Then she leapt to her feet and burst out laughing.

"I know nothing, I've seen nothing, I've heard nothing," she cried like a voluble schoolgirl, jumping up and down. "I'm only terrified of boring you. You've seen the chocolate-grille, the drawing-room-kitchen, Renaud, the marble statue of me, the lot . . . Still I can call in Fanchette, can't I?"

One never has time to answer Colette. She opened a door, bent forward and chirruped mysterious summonses.

"My lovely, my precious, my snow-white . . . pussalina pussi-love, mrrroo, mrrraow . . ."

The animal appeared, like a somnambulist, like a little wild beast under a spell. It was a very beautiful white she-cat who looked up at Claudine with green, obedient eyes.

"My little coalheaver, my little slut, you've gone and done pipi again on one of Renaud's patent-leather boots. Never mind, he won't know. I'll tell him it's poor-quality leather. And he'll pretend to believe it. Come along and I'll read you some lovely things Lucie Delarue-Mardrus has written about cats."

Claudine grabbed the cat by the scruff of its neck, lifted it high above her head and cried:

"Look, lady, the drowned cat hanging up on a hook!" She opened her fist and Fanchette fell from the height, landing expertly on her soft paws. Not in the least perturbed, she remained where she was on the carpet. "You know, Annie, now that my girl lives in Paris, I read poetry to her. She knows everything Baudelaire has written about cats by heart. Now I'm teaching her all Lucie Delarue-Mardrus's cat poems."

I smiled, amused at this inconsequent childishness.

"Do you think she understands?"

Claudine crushed me with a long, withering look over her shoulder.

"What an idiot you are, Annie! Sorry, I only meant to say: 'Of course she does!' Sit Fanchette! Now just you watch and listen, you little sceptic. This one's unpublished . . . It's marvellous . . .

FOR A CAT

Majestic cat, mysterious and wise,
Through whose black velvet mask gleam jewelled eyes,
Do my ring-laden fingers not presume too much,
When they caress you, monarch in disguise?

Lithe, furry serpent, coiled up in repose,
Warmer than living feathers to my touch
Save for the coolness where your small bare nose
Buds through the black and white, a glistening rose.

Jungle-fierce still for all your ribbon bows
And feigned docility. Let some hapless toy
Catch your disdainful eye, at once peremptory paws
Pounce on the prey with grappling-irons of claws.

Tonight, here in the dusk, no wile of mine
Can lure your still remoteness, make you
                    glance from where
You sit, a Buddha-cat of stone, gold eyes astare:
You are remembering you were once divine."

The cat was half-asleep, vibrating with a faint, muffled purr that made a muted accompaniment to Claudine's peculiar voice, now grave and full of harshly rolled *r*'s, now so soft and low that it sent a shiver down my spine . . . When the voice ceased, Fanchette opened her slanting eyes. The two gazed at each other for a moment with the same grave intentness . . . Then raising her forefinger and touching her nose, Claudine turned to me and sighed:

" 'Peremptory . . .' It took some finding, that word! They're good, aren't they, those verses of Fervid's. Just to have hit on 'peremptory', *I'd* gladly give ten years . . . of the Chessenet's life!"

That name seemed as shockingly inappropriate here as a piece of gimcrack in a flawless collection.

"You don't like Ch . . . Madame Chessenet, Claudine?"

Claudine, now semi-recumbent, stared at the ceiling and put up a lazy hand.

"She means nothing to me . . . A carved yellow beetroot . . . Means no more to me than the Cabbage-Rose."

"Ah, the Cabbage-Rose . . ."

"Rose or cabbage? That buxom girl with cheeks like the buttocks of little Cupids."

"Oh!"

"Why that shocked 'Oh!'? Buttocks isn't a dirty word. Anyway the Cabbage-Rose bores me too . . ." She yawned.

"And . . . Marthe?"

I was animated by an indiscreet curiosity, as if, by questioning Claudine, I was about to discover the secret, the 'recipe' of her lucky disposition that detached her from everything, and made her indifferent to gossip, petty quarrels, even to the conventions. But I was not adroit enough and Claudine made fun of me. With a carp-like leap, she turned over on her stomach and said mockingly, with her nose in her cat's silvery fur:

"Marthe? I think she's missed her appointment . . . I mean the one she made with us. But . . . is this an interrogation, Annie?"

I was shamed. I leant towards her and said, in a sudden burst of frankness:

"Forgive me, Claudine. The fact is I was beating about the bush . . . I couldn't bring myself to ask you . . . what you think of Alain . . . Ever since he went away, I just haven't known how to go on living and nobody talks to me about him, at least not in the way I want them to talk . . . Is it usual in Paris to forget people so quickly when they've gone away?"

I had come straight out with what was in my mind, and I was surprised at my own vehemence. Claudine's triangular face, propped up on two small fists, its smooth, rather sallow skin lightened by pearly reflections from the white satin blouse, took on a wary expression.

"Is it usual to forget? . . . I don't really know. I suppose it depends on the person who goes away. As a husband, Monsieur Samzun—'Alain' as you call him—impresses me as . . . impeccable. As a man? He aims at being distinguished, but all he manages to be is correct. He's always talking in aphorisms . . . no man ever had such a store of them. And his whole manner, all his typical gestures are highly . . ."

" 'Peremptory'," I said with a timid smile.

"Yes, but *he* hasn't any right to be 'peremptory' because he isn't a cat. No, he most certainly isn't a cat! He's got snobbery in his heart and a ramrod in his arse . . . Heavens, what an idiot I am! For goodness' sake, don't start crying as if I'd hit you, my poor child! As if it mattered what *I* say! You know perfectly well that Claudine's got a hole in her head . . . Oh, very well then, she wants to go! Kiss me first to show me there's no ill-feeling. Do you know what she looks like with her great knot of hair and her straight little frock and those dewdrops on the end of her lashes? A little girl who's been married against her will!"

I smiled to please her, to thank her too for giving me a glimpse of her honest, rebellious mind instead of the conventional lies I was used to.

"Goodbye, Claudine . . . I'm not angry with you."

"I should hope not. Will you give me a kiss?"

"Oh yes!"

Her tall flexible body bent over me; she laid both hands on my shoulders.

"Put up your mouth! Goodness, what am I saying . . .? Force of habit . . . Put up your cheek. There! See you soon, in Arriège? This is the way out. Remember me to that trollop of a Marthe. No, your eyes aren't red. Goodbye, goodbye . . . chrysalis!"

I went down the stairs slowly, pausing on every step, irresolute and disturbed. She had said: "A ramrod in his . . ." Honestly, I believe it was the metaphor, the picture of that ramrod that had shocked me, not Claudine's opinion in itself. She had blasphemed and, abashed for a moment in the presence of this uninhibited child, I had let her blaspheme.

"My dear Alain,

I promised you to show I could be brave. So I'll only show you my brave side . . . forgive me for hiding all the other. You can guess it only too well.

I've done everything I possibly can to see that our home that you like to be tidy and properly kept up isn't suffering too much from your absence. I go through the servants' books on the appointed day and Léonie is being very kind to me . . . that is to say, I am sure her intentions are good, anyway.

Your sister is charming, as usual. Seeing her as much as I do, I wish I could acquire a little of her courage and her never-failing will-power. However, I won't pretend that this isn't a very lofty ambition. Anyway, you don't really want me to be like that and you are so intelligent and strong-minded yourself that it's more than enough for the two of us.

I don't know where this letter will reach you and this feeling of uncertainty makes me all the more nervous and awkward when I write to you. A correspondence between us is something so new to me now; I've got so much out of the habit of it. I wish I need never have to get into the habit again. Yet I realise that, in my weak moments, it will be my one great stay and comfort. I can only say in a few words, putting it badly, I am sure, and saying much less than I think, that my heart follows you wherever you go with all my devoted love, and that I remain

Your little slave,
Annie."

I wrote this letter with extreme constraint, without ever letting my love and grief burst out spontaneously to him. Was it lack of confidence in myself, as usual, or, for the first time, in *him*?

Which Annie would he prefer? The Annie, softer and more silent than a feather; the one he knew, the one he had accustomed to be mute, to veil her thoughts under her words as she veiled her eyes under lashes or the lost, troubled Annie, defenceless against her crazy imagination, whom he has left behind here—the Annie he does not know?

Whom he does not know . . .

Letting my thoughts run on like this, I feel guilty. Hiding something is almost like lying. I have no right to hide two Annies in myself. Suppose the second were only half of the other? How exhausting this all is!

As for Alain, you know the whole of him when you've known him an hour. His mind is as regular as his face. He detests the illogical and dreads the unconventional. Would he have married me, if one evening long ago when we were engaged I had flung my arms round his neck and said: "Alain, I can't endure another minute unless you make love to me . . ."?

The mere fact of his being away is upsetting my reason. Already there are so many tormenting thoughts that I must not admit to him when he returns. This is not going to be anything like the "Diary of his journey" I was expected to keep: it will be the diary of a wretched, distraught creature . . .

"Madame, a telegram!"

That brusque military manner of Léonie's frightened me. My fingers are still trembling with apprehension.

> "Excellent journey. Sailing today. Letter follows.
> Affectionate remembrances.
>
> > > Samzun"

Was that all? A telegram is not a letter and this one should have reassured me on every vital point. But it arrived at a moment when I was completely demoralised. Somehow, I would have liked something very different. Besides, I don't like his signing himself "Samzun". Do I sign myself "Lajarrisse"? My poor Annie, what hornet has stung you today? And what madness to go and compare yourself to a man . . . to a man like Alain!

I shall go and see Marthe to escape from myself.

When I arrived, it was Léon I found at home. As every day, at this time, he was busy in his study which Marthe calls "the torture-chamber". Bookcases with gilded lattice-work, a beautiful Louis XVI table on which this model writer never lets a drop of ink spill, for he writes carefully, with a blotter under his hand . . . altogether a very commodious prison.

As I entered, he rose and dabbed his temples.

"This heat, Annie! I can't produce anything the least good in it. Besides, somehow, it's a languid, depressing day in spite of the sunshine. A bad, immoral day."

"It is, isn't it?" I broke in eagerly, almost gratefully. He stared at me with his beautiful spaniel-like eyes, without the faintest idea what I meant . . .

"Yes. I'm going to find it hard to grind out my sixty lines today."

"You'll be scolded, Léon."

He languidly shrugged his shoulders, as if inured to it.

"How's your novel going? Well?"

Pulling his pointed beard, he answered with a vanity as discreet as his modest talent:

"Not too badly . . . much as the others."

"Tell me how it's going to end."

Léon appreciates me as a willing, easily-interested, audience. I have at least managed to acquire a taste, however mild, for his tales of adulteresses in high society and noble suicides and princely bankrupts . . .

"The end's giving me a good deal of trouble," sighed my unhappy brother-in-law. "The husband has taken his wife back, but she's tasted freedom and found it intoxicating. It would be better, from the literary point of view, if she stayed with him. But, as Marthe points out, it would sell better if she went off again and hopped into bed with someone else."

Léon has retained some expressions from his journalist days that I find quite revolting.

I said: "The point is, does she want to go off?"

"Of course she does!"

"Well, then, she must."

"Why?"

"Because she's 'tasted freedom'."

Léon sniggered as he continued to count his pages.

"That sounds funny . . . coming from you, of all people! . . . Marthe's waiting for you at the Fritz," he went on, picking up his pen again. "Forgive me for hustling you off, Annie dear, won't you? I've got to deliver this thing in October, so . . ."

He indicated the still meagre pile of manuscript.

"Yes, of course . . . Get on with your work, poor old Léon."

"Place Vendôme, Charles!"

Marthe has become passionately addicted to these five o'clock teas at the Fritz. I infinitely prefer my little "Afternoon Tea" in the Rue d'Indy with its low-ceilinged room that smells of cake and ginger

and its mixed clientèle of elderly English ladies in sham pearl
necklaces and demi-mondaines who use it for discreet assignations.

Marthe, however, loves that long white gallery at the Fritz. She
walks through it, peering about as if she were short-sighted and were
searching for someone when, all the time, from the moment she
entered, her menacing grey eyes have been taking in every detail.
She has been counting the people there and summing them up;
noting familiar faces and scanning them sharply; noting, most of all,
the hats she will copy with that infallible hand when she gets home.

What a horrible nature I have! Here I am, thinking almost
spitefully of my sister-in-law whose company has cheered me up
and distracted me ever since Alain went away . . . The fact is, I
tremble every time I have to walk by myself down that redoubtable
gallery at the Fritz, under the eyes of those people devouring little
cakes and even more eagerly devouring their neighbours.

Once again, I launched myself into that rectangular hall with the
foolhardiness of the very shy and traversed it with long strides,
thinking with terror: "I'm going to catch my foot in my dress and
twist my ankle . . . perhaps my placket-hole is gaping, I'm sure my
hair is coming down at the back . . ." I was so preoccupied that I
walked right past Marthe without seeing her.

She caught me by the crook of her parasol and laughed so
uproariously that I thought I would die of shame.

"Who are you running after, Annie? You look like a woman
hurrying guiltily to her first assignation. There, there, sit down, give
me your parasol, take off your gloves . . . Ouf! Saved once
again in the nick of time! I must say that little face could be a lot
worse, even if you *are* in torture. It suits you to look scared to death.
Who were you running away from?"

"Everybody."

She contemplated me with pitying disdain and sighed:

"I've almost given up hope of ever making anything of you. Do
you like my hat?"

"Yes."

I said it with genuine conviction.

Till then, I had been too busy pulling myself together to look at
Marthe. I suppose you could, by stretching a point, call it a hat, that
muslin mob-cap, falling in pleats round the face? Hat or not, it
"came off". The linen dress, the inevitable fichu that revealed the
milky neck, completed a charming fancy-dress of the French

Revolution period. She was still Marie-Antoinette, but already in the Temple prison. Never would I have dared to go out arrayed like that!

Radiating with self-confidence, she flashed her formidable eyes all about her; there were not many men who could sustain those glances. As she crunched her toast with relish, she stared at people, chattered and simultaneously reassured me and dazed me.

"Did you look in at our place?"

"Yes . . ."

"Did you see Léon?"

"Yes."

"Was he working?"

"Yes."

"He mustn't let up, the thing's simply got to be in in October. I've got some heavy bills . . . Any news of Alain?"

"A telegram . . . he says there's a letter coming."

"You know we're leaving in five days' time?"

"Whenever you like, Marthe."

"'Whenever you like!' Honestly, you wear me out, my good girl! Look, quick, there's the Cabbage-Rose. Her hat's a disaster!"

Hats play a considerable part in my sister-in-law's life. Moreover, it was undeniable that the hat the Cabbage-Rose (a lovely, fresh, slightly overblown creature) was wearing *was* an utter failure.

Marthe wriggled with delight.

"And she wants us to believe that she ruins herself buying her hats at Reboux! The Chessenet, who's her best friend, told me the Cabbage-Rose cuts all the labels out of her mother-in-law's smart hats and sews them inside her own."

"Do you believe that?"

"One should always believe the worst first go, there's always time to find out the facts later . . . What luck! Here come the Renaud-Claudines . . . we'll call them over to our table. Maugis is with them."

"But, Marthe . . ."

"But what?"

"Alain doesn't like us to see too much of the Renaud-Claudines."

"I'm quite aware of that."

"So I oughtn't to . . ."

"Since your husband isn't here, stop worrying . . . I'm the one who invited you, so you're relieved of all responsibility . . ."

After all, since Marthe *was* my hostess . . . my Timetable might forgive me!

Claudine had seen us. From a yard away, she greeted Marthe with a resounding: "All hail, Goldilocks!" that made heads turn in our direction.

Renaud followed her, indulgent as usual to all her crazy ways and Maugis brought up the rear. I don't much like that Maugis, but I put up with his cheerful drunken effrontery and now and then find it amusing. I shan't say a word to Alain about this meeting; being so sober and correct himself, he positively abhors this great fat untidy Bohemian who always wears a stove-pipe top-hat.

Marthe fluttered like a white hen.

"Claudine, will you have tea?"

"Ugh, not tea! It turns my stomach."

"Chocolate?"

"No. I'd like some cheap wine. The twelve sous a litre kind."

"Some *what*?" I asked, staggered.

"Ssh, Claudine!" Renaud gently remonstrated, smiling under his whitening moustache. "You'll scandalise Madame Samzun."

"Why?" exclaimed Claudine. "What's wrong with wine at twelve sous a . . ."

"Not here, my pet. You and I will go off and have some on our own. We'll drink it, with our elbows propped on the zinc counter of that little pub in the Avenue Trudaine—the one with the shady but extremely affable proprietor. Would you like that—" (he dropped his voice) "—my darling bird?"

"Oh yes, yes! Oh, I'd adore it!" cried the incorrigible Claudine.

She gazed at her husband with so much childish enthusiasm and loving admiration that I was suddenly choked with an overwhelming desire to cry. If I had asked Alain for wine that cost twelve sous a litre he would have given me . . . permission to go to bed and take some bromide!

Maugis drooped his moustache towards me, a moustache bleached by a cosmopolitan taste in liquor.

"Madame, you appear to be suffering certain pangs of remorse occasioned by this tepid tea and these vomitively chocolatious éclairs . . . You most certainly will not be able to imbibe the necessary cordial here at the Fritz. The liquid refreshments they serve here would wreck the livers of hardened drinkers in the lowest type of military canteen . . . I cannot say the sixty-centime claret recommended by Madame Claudine excites me either, except to cynical merriment . . . What *you* need is a nice green."

"A nice what?"

"Call it a blue, if that appeals to you more. A Pernod for babies. I am the president of a Feminist Society: 'The Right to Absinthe'. I can tell you the members don't half put it away."

"I've never drunk absinthe in my life," I said with some disgust.

"Oh!" exclaimed Claudine, "there are so many things you've never tasted, good little Annie!"

She put so much meaning into the words that she made me feel foolish and embarrassed. With a laugh, she gave a mocking glance at Marthe who replied:

"She needs educating. We're counting a lot on 'the easy relaxed life of fashionable watering-places', as someone puts it in Léon's latest novel."

"In '*The Tragic Hearts*'?" exclaimed Maugis effusively. "A powerful work, Madame, and one that will live. The torments of an ill-starred but aristocratic love affair are depicted in letters of fire by a pen dipped in gall!"

To my amazement, Marthe burst out laughing. There they were, all four of them, making fun of that poor, wretched man back at home, grinding out his daily sixty lines. I was embarrassed and shocked, yet forced to seem amused in self-defence. I studied the bottom of my cup, then I furtively glanced up at Claudine who happened to be looking at me and who murmured very low to her husband, as if she were talking to herself:

"What marvellous eyes Annie's got, hasn't she, Renaud dear? Wild chicory flowers, growing out of brown sand . . ."

"Yes," agreed Renaud, and added: "When she raises her eyelids it's as if she were taking off her clothes."

All four stared at me with a far-away expression. I suffered agonies of shame, coupled with agonies of appalling pleasure, as if my dress had suddenly dropped off.

Marthe was the first to pull herself together and change the conversation.

"When will you two be coming down there?" she asked Renaud and Claudine.

"Down where, my dear Marthe?"

"To Arriège, naturally. It's a sad fact, but nowadays all good Parisians harbour a sleeping arthritic under their skin."

"Mine suffers from insomnia," said Maugis pompously. "I douse it with whisky. But you and your cures, that's all a lot of chichi, lady Marthe. You just want to be in the fashion."

"Not at all, you insolent man! I take Arriège very seriously. Those four weeks of treatment set me up for the winter so that I can eat truffles, drink Burgundy and go to bed at three in the morning . . . Talking of that, it is next Tuesday, isn't it, that we all make our pilgrimage to the shrine of the Lalcade? It should be a good party, much gayer than Arriège."

"Oh, certainly," replied Claudine. "It'll be crammed with Dukes, with some princes thrown in for good measure. You'd go if you had to stand on your head, wouldn't you, Marthe?"

"I could stand on my head here and now," said Marthe rather superciliously. "My underclothes are nice enough to survive it . . ."

"And besides," Maugis grumbled into his moustache, "she wears closed knickers."

I had heard. We had all heard!

There was a brief, chilly silence.

"What about you, pensive one?" Claudine was asking. "Are you Arrièging?"

The "pensive one" was myself . . . I started . . . I was already far away.

"Me? Oh, I shall follow Marthe and Léon."

"And *I* shall follow Renaud to see he doesn't follow other petticoats (I'm only joking, dearest!). What luck! We'll meet again down there. I shall watch you all drinking water that tastes of rotten eggs and be able to compare your respective grimaces and now which of you has the most stoical soul. *Your* face should be a study taking the waters, Maugis, you bloated old wine-skin."

They laughed, but I had an anguished vision of how Alain's face would look if he suddenly came in and saw me in such improper company. For after all, Marthe's presence doesn't justify everything and one really can't be on intimate terms with that crazy Claudine who calls people "bloated old wine-skins".

"Alain, I shan't go to Madame Lalcade's."

"You must go, Annie."

"But I shall be so lonely, so sad with you not there."

"So sad . . . my modesty prefers not to discuss that. But not lonely. Marthe and Léon will escort you."

"I'll go if you want me to."

"Do try and develop a little social sense, dear child, and not regard every function I consider it expedient for you to attend as some kind of dreary duty. This party of Madame Lalcade's will be reckoned as a . . . a manifesto of art and your absence will delight certain ill-natured people . . . Don't neglect this very agreeable house, perhaps the only one whe people in society can safely rub elbows with any number of interesting artists . . . If you knew how to put yourself forward a little more, you might get yourself introduced to the Comtesse Greffulhe . . ."

"Ah?"

"But I haven't much hope, that, especially without me, you'll be able to do yourself justice . . . Ah well!"

"What ought I to wear?"

"Your white dress with the shirring at the waist seems to me to be indicated. Great simplicity, that night, Annie. You'll see a slight excess of Gismonda coiffures and Laparcerie dresses at Madame Lalcade's . . . There must be absolutely nothing about your appearance to warrant your feeling embarrassed . . . Be just as you are now, simple, reserved, unaffected; don't add anything, don't change anything. Isn't that a handsome compliment I'm paying you?"

A very handsome one, certainly, and I fully appreciated its worth.

That conversation took place a fortnight ago and I can still hear every word Alain said in that firm, unhesitating voice of his.

Tonight I shall put on my white dress and I shall go to Madame Lalcade's party and listen to Fauré's sad and frivolous music which is to be mimed by people in fancy-dress . . . I am thinking of Marthe's delight. She is replacing, almost at the last moment, a pretty Marquise who has a cold. In forty-eight hours, my sister-in-law has confected something out of shimmering silks, tried on a whalebone bodice, consulted engravings and hairdressers and rehearsed a rigadoon.

"What a crowd of people, Léon!"

"Yes. I recognised the Voronsoffs' carriage and the Gourkaus' and the . . . Be so kind as to button my glove, Annie . . ."

"Your gloves are terribly tight!"

"Not tight, Annie, only new. The woman at the glove-shop always says to me 'Monsieur's hands seem to get smaller and smaller' . . ."

I did not even smile at his childishness. Vain of his hands and feet, my poor brother-in-law endures a thousand small tortures but will not concede even a quarter of a size to his mangled fingers.

Such a flood of light wraps overflowed through the door of the conservatory being used as a cloakroom and right out into the garden, that, for a minute, I was agitated by the fear and the hope that I would not be able to get into it . . . Léon forced a slow passage for me through the crowd with an insinuating elbow. Obviously I should get in but my dress would be ruined . . . I looked frantically for a corner of a looking-glass, quite convinced that my heavy knot of hair was coming undone . . . Between two sumptuous dowdies, I caught a glimpse of a fragment of myself. Yes, that was Annie, slim and brown as a coloured girl . . . those were her blue eyes, blue as the turned-down gas-flame, so meekly submissive they seemed to be treacherous.

"All's well, all's well. Very much in form, tonight, the whipped child!"

Now the mirror reflected, quite close to mine, Claudine's vigorous profile and the sharp-pointed décolletage of her yellow dress that rippled like a flame . . .

I turned round to ask her, idiotically enough:

"I've lost Léon . . . You haven't seen him?"

The yellow female fiend burst out laughing.

"Truth and honour, I haven't got him on me! Are you really in such a desperate state?"

"About what?"

"About mislaying your brother-in-law."

"It's just . . . You see, Marthe's playing in this mime and I haven't anyone but him."

"Perhaps he's dead," said Claudine with macabre solemnity. "It's of no importance. I'll chaperone you just as well. We'll sit down, we'll look at the greasy shoulders of old ladies, we'll hit them over the head if they talk during the music, and I shall eat all the strawberries on the buffet!"

This alluring programme (or was it Claudine's irresistible authority?) decided me. With my head bent low, I made my first step into the studio where Madame Lalcade paints and gives parties. It was filled to overflowing with massed flowers and human beings.

"She's invited all her models," whispered my companion.

It was glittering with women, so closely packed that, at each sensational new arrival, only their heads turned and nodded like a field of heavy poppies in the wind.

"Claudine, we'll never be able to sit down in there . . ."

"Oh yes we shall. Just you wait!"

Claudine's smiling unceremoniousness admitted no rebuff. She conquered half a chair, agitated her hips till she had invaded the whole of it and installed me, heaven knows how, beside her.

"There! Look-see the pretty stage-curtain with the garlands. Oh, how I love everything you can't see behind! Look-see also Valentine Chessenet in red with her rabbit's eyes also in red . . . Honestly, has Marthe got a part? Look-see again, Annie, there's Madame Lalcade saying how d'you do to us over fifty-three ladies. How d'you do, Madame? How d'you do, Madame! Yes, yes, we're very well, thank you. Three quarters of our behinds have somewhere to lay their head."

"People will hear you, Claudine!"

"Let them hear me!" retorted the redoubtable creature. "I'm not saying anything dirty. My heart is pure and I wash every day. So there! How d'you do, Maugis, you great tun-belly! He's come to see Marthe décolletée to her very soul and possibly for the music as well . . . Oh, how lovely the Cabbage-Rose is tonight! I defy you, Annie, to distinguish from a yard away where her skin ends and her pink dress begins. And what healthy, abundant meat. At four sous a pound there must be a hundred thousand francs' worth! No, don't try and work out how many kilos that makes . . . Look, there's Renaud over there in that doorway."

Without her realising it, her voice had all at once softened.

"I can't see anything."

"Neither can I, except the tip of a moustache, but I know it's his."

Yes, she knew it was he. Passionate, instinctive animal that she is, she could pick up his scent, through all those other warm effluences, all those perfumes, all those breaths . . . Why is it that every time I am forcibly reminded of their love, I feel unbearably sad?

The electric lights suddenly went out. There was that *Ah*! of vulgar surprise that bursts from the crowd when the first firework goes off on the fourteenth of July, followed by enraged chattering. Then that too was abruptly quenched . . . On the still invisible

stage harps were already pattering like raindrops; plucked mando-
lines were softly twanging an invocation: "Come, all you fair
ladies . . ." Then, slowly, the curtain rose.

"Oh, this is bliss," Claudine whispered, enraptured. Against a
grey-tinted backcloth of a formal park, Aminte, Tircis and Clitan-
dre, the Abbé, the Ingénue and the Roué lay about in languorous
attitudes as if just returned from Cythera. The swing hardly swayed
under the light weight of a panniered shepherdess at whom a
shepherd in reddish-purple gazed up adoringly. An exquisite creature turned over the pages of a music-book, bent forward so low that
her charms were exposed as she followed the song her lover's languid
fingers were tracing . . . Far too soon, all this enchantment—the
disillusioned dreamers, the sweetly ironical music—was dispersed
by the lively chords that announced the Rigadoon.

"What a pity!" sighed Claudine.

Grave couples in shimmering costumes paraded, pirouetted,
curtsied and bowed. The last Marquise, all in frosty silver on the
arm of a sky-blue Marquis, was Marthe, so dazzling that a
murmur greeted her appearance and I could hardly believe it was
she.

The will to be beautiful had transfigured her. Here and there the
fire of her hair glinted through the ash of powder that could not
extinguish it. With her eyes burning paler against her make-up, her
firm round breasts disclosed almost beyond the limits of decency,
her face serious and concentrated, she pivoted on perilous pointed
heels, plunged into curtsies, raised her little painted hand and, at
each pirouette, darted her most terrible Ninon-turned-anarchist
glance at the audience . . . With no real beauty and no more than
superficial grace, Marthe eclipsed all the pretty women who danced
alongside her.

She *willed* to be the most beautiful . . . Such a thing would be
impossible to a poor creature like me. The sad, pompous music
mocked me, melted me, moved me to the point of tears. But my
self-consciousness would not let me indulge my feelings. Everything
was ruined for me by the effort to stop myself crying, by the thought
of the cruel lights that would go on in a moment and of Claudine's
too-penetrating gaze.

My very dear Annie,
    Your letter arrived just before I sailed so if this one is brief, you

must blame it entirely on the hurry of departure. I am delighted to know you are showing yourself to be so courageous and so attached to everything that makes up the life of a simple woman in good society: your husband, your family, your charming well-kept and well-ordered home.

For it seems to me that, being away from you, I may, perhaps even should, pay you the compliments I refrain from paying you when I am with you. Do not thank me for it, Annie, for, to some extent, it is my own work I am admiring; a lovable child, fashioned little by little and without great difficulty into an irreproachable young woman and an accomplished housewife.

The weather is superb; we can count on a perfect crossing. So you can hope that everything will proceed normally till I reach Buenos Aires. You know that my health is excellent and that the sun has no terrors for me. Therefore you must not fret if the posts are rare and irregular. I shall contain myself and not await your letters too impatiently, though they will nevertheless be precious when they arrive.

I embrace you, my very dear Annie, with all my unshakeable affection. I know you will not smile at my rather solemn form of expression; the feeling that attaches me to you has nothing frivolous about it.

Your
Alain Samzun.

With my forefinger pressed to one throbbing temple, it was a labour to read his letter. For once again I was in the grip of that prostrating migraine that recurs at almost regular intervals to make life a misery. With my jaws clenched and my left eye closed, I listened to an incessant hammer in my wretched brain. Daylight hurts me: darkness stifles me.

In the old days, at my grandmother's, I used to inhale ether till I almost lost consciousness. But, during the first months of our marriage, Alain found me one day, half-swooning on my bed, with a bottle clutched in my hand and he forbade me ever to use it again. He spoke to me very seriously and lucidly about the dangers of ether, about his horror of these "hysterics' remedies", about the harmlessness, in short, of migraines: "All women have them!" Ever since, I have endured the pain with as much patience as I could muster, limiting myself quite unsuccessfully to hot compresses and general hydrotherapy.

But today I was suffering so much that I wanted to cry. The sight of certain white objects, a piece of paper, an enamelled table, the sheets of the bed on which I was lying produced that contraction of the throat and that nervous nausea I know and dread only too well. Alain's letter . . . so longed for, none the less! . . . seemed to me cold and colourless. I realised this must be a really vicious attack . . . I would re-read the letter later.

Léonie came in. She took great care not to make a noise: she opened the door very softly, but banged it loudly behind her. At least her intentions were good.

"Is Madame's head still bad?"

"Yes, Léonie . . ."

"Why doesn't Madame take . . .?"

"A glass of brandy? No, thank you."

"No, Madame, a little ether."

"Monsieur doesn't like me to drug myself, Léonie. Ether won't help me."

"It's Monsieur who makes Madame believe that. Monsieur is a nice man in every way and he imagines it might do Madame harm, but, when it comes to knowing anything about women's troubles, don't you talk to me of men. *I* always take ether when I get my neuralgia."

"Ah! You . . . you've actually got some here?"

"A brand-new bottle. I'll go and fetch it for Madame."

The divine, powerful odour relaxed my nerves. I lay back full-length on my bed, the bottle under my nostrils, weeping tears of weakness and pleasure. The cruel blacksmith retreated, there was only a discreet, padded finger tapping my temple now. I breathed in so hard that there was a sweet taste in my throat . . . my wrists turned heavy.

There followed vague, fleeting dreams, all barred by a line of light—the one that filtered through my half-closed eyelids. I saw Alain in a tennis shirt he wore one summer eight years ago, a white cellular one that his flesh tinted pink . . . I myself was the very young Annie of those days, with my heavy plait that ended in a soft ringlet . . . I touched the supple flesh of the pink shirt and it excited me like living skin, warm as my own, and I told myself confusedly that Alain was a little boy and it didn't matter, didn't matter, didn't matter . . . He was passive and vibrant; over his burning cheeks he drooped long black lashes that were Annie's eyelashes . . . How velvety that skin felt to the touch! Didn't matter . . . didn't matter . . .

But a tennis-ball suddenly hit me hard on the temple and I caught it in flight. It was warm and white . . . a nasal voice, quite close to me, announced: "It's a cock's egg." I was not in the least surprised, since Alain was now a cock, a red cock on the bottom of a plate. He scratched the china with an arrogant claw till it squeaked maddeningly and crowed "*I* always . . ." What was he saying? I couldn't hear. The bar of greyish-blue light cut him in half like the President of the Republic's sash. Then came blackness, blackness, a delicious death, a slow falling sustained by wings . . .

A wicked act, a wicked act, yes Annie, there is no other word for it! A piece of deliberate, complete disobedience to Alain's will. He was right to forbid me this ether that makes me quite irresponsible . . . Thus I accused myself in all humility two hours later, alone with my own reflection in the glass, sitting at my dressing-table where I was brushing and redoing my dishevelled hair. My head was free, clear and empty. Only the dark circles under my eyes, my pale lips, and my lack of appetite, though I had been fasting all day, gave evidence of my debauch with the beloved poison. Ugh! The stale, cold fumes of ether clung to the curtains. I must have air, I must forget—if I could . . .

My window, on the second floor, has a dismal outlook. I opened it and gazed at the narrow courtyard where Alain's horse was being rubbed down by a stout groom in a check shirt. At the sound of my window being opened, a black bull terrier sitting on the cobbles raised his square muzzle . . . It was my poor Toby, my banished, disgraced Toby! The next second, he was on his feet, a small, dark figure, waving the remnant of his cropped tail at me.

"Toby! Toby!"

He jumped up and down, making wheezy little grunts like moans. I leant out.

"Charles, send Toby up to me by the back stairs, please."

Toby had understood before the man and bounded forward. Another minute and the poor black French bulldog was at my feet, in a delirious convulsion of humility and love, his eyes and his tongue nearly bursting out of his head.

I had bought him last year from one of Jacques Delavalise's

stablemen, because he was really a beautiful little eight-month old bull-pup with an uncropped tail, no nose, limpid slits of eyes and ears like trumpets. And I had brought him home, feeling rather proud but slightly apprehensive. Alain examined him with an expert but not unfriendly eye.

"A hundred francs, you say? That's not dear. The coachman will be pleased, the rats are destroying everything in the stable."

"In the stable! But that's not what I bought him for. He's pretty. I wanted to keep him for myself, Alain."

"For yourself? A stable bulldog in a Louis XV drawing-room? Or on the lace covers of your bed? If you really want a dog, my dear child, I'll find you a little floss-silk Havanese for the drawing-room, or perhaps a big Saluki . . . Salukis go with all styles."

He rang the bell and, when Jules appeared, he indicated my poor black Toby who was innocently chewing the knob of a chair.

"Take this dog to Charles, say he's to buy him a collar, keep him clean and tell me if he's a good ratter. The dog is called Toby."

Since then I have never seen Toby, except through the window. I had watched him suffering and thinking of me, for we had loved each other at sight.

One day, I kept back some little pigeon bones and carried them out to him in the yard, taking care no one saw him. I came back indoors with a heavy heart and with an uneasy feeling I thought I could dissipate by confessing my weakness to Alain. He hardly scolded me at all.

"What a child you are, Annie! If you like, I'll tell Charles he can take the bull-terrier with him under the seat sometimes when you go out in the carriage. But don't let me ever find Toby in the flat, will you? Never, is that understood? You'll oblige me greatly by remembering this."

Today, admitting to Alain that I had let Toby into my bedroom would not be enough to relieve me of all anxiety—I may as well be frank—of all remorse. This crime which, last week, would have made me tremble, is a trifle compared to my guilty, delicious ether-intoxication.

Go on sleeping on the carpet patterned with grey roses, black Toby; go on sleeping with the great sighs of an animal worn out by emotion: you are not going back to the stable.

4

ARRIÈGE.

A smell of orange-blossom and sulphur baths comes up through my open window. "The local smell," the hotel porter who brought up our luggage obligingly explained to me. Marthe assures me one gets used to it in a couple of days. To the scent of the flowering oranges planted in a hedge in front of the hotel, granted. But the other, that sulphurous smell that clings to one's very skin, it's revolting!

I leant on the sill, already discouraged, while Léonie whose felt travelling hat made her look like a policeman in mufti unpacked my great wicker trunk and disposed the silver trinkets from my dressing-case like soldiers on parade.

What on earth was I doing here? I felt less alone in Paris, in my yellow bedroom with Alain's portrait for company, than between these four walls distempered in pink with an undertone of grey. A brass bed whose weary mattress and bedclothes I have inspected suspiciously. A dressing-table that is too small, a writing-desk I shall use to do my hair at, a folding-table I shall use to write on, some commonplace upholstered chairs and some white-painted wooden ones. How many days had I got to live in this room? Marthe had said: "That all depends."

From the other side of the flagged corridor, I heard her piercing voice. Léon's muffled replies, which I could not catch, made a blank between her remarks. I sank into a torpor, isolated from everything, from the place I was in, from Marthe, from Alain, from the disturbing future, from all sense of passing time . . .

"Shall we go down, Annie?"

"Oh, Marthe! You gave me a fright! But I'm not ready!"

"Good heavens, whatever do you imagine you're doing? Not even got washed or done your hair? For mercy's sake, don't start being a dead weight the moment you get here."

My sister-in-law was arrayed as if for the Fritz, fresh, made-up and rosy. Eleven hours of railway journey had dealt kindly with her. She declared she wanted to go and listen to the music in the park.

"I'll hurry up. What about Léon?"

"He's washing his godlike body. Come on, Annie, get on with it! What's stopping you?"

I hesitated, standing there in my corsets and petticoat, to undress completely in front of Marthe . . . She stared at me as if at some rare animal.

"O Annie, saintly Annie, are there two mugs in the world like you? I'll turn my back, then you can scrub your fair body in peace."

She went over to the window. But the room itself embarrassed me and I could see myself in the glass, long and brown like a date . . . Suddenly, Marthe shamelessly turned round. I shrieked, I plastered my arms against my dripping thighs, I contorted myself, I implored her . . . Appearing not to hear me, she put up her lorgnette and stared at me curiously.

"Funny creature! It's obvious you're not from these parts. You look like one of those females in an Egyptian mosaic . . . or a serpent standing on its tail or a slender brownstone jar . . . Staggering! Annie, you'll never convince me your mother didn't have an affair with a donkey-boy in the shade of the Pyramids."

"Marthe, *please*! You know perfectly well how that kind of joke shocks me . . ."

"I'm quite aware of it. Here, catch your chemise, you great silly! At your age, behaving like a prudish schoolgirl! . . . *I'd* go stark naked in front of three thousand people, if it was the fashion. To think one always hides one's best features!"

"Does one? Madame Chessenet certainly wouldn't agree with you."

"What perspicacity! (You don't like her, do you? That amuses me.) She must have breasts she could wear as the very last word in fashion, as a flat stole with the end coming down to her knees."

Her chattering presence acted as a tonic on my laziness and ended by overcoming my childish prudery. Moreover, Marthe has the gift of making one forgive her almost anything.

While I was arranging my white tulle jabot in front of the glass, Marthe leant out of the window and described what was going on under her eyes.

"I can see, oh! I can see some wonderful sights . . . I can see Léon searching for us, looking exactly like a lost poodle . . . He thinks we've gone to listen to the music. Good riddance!"

"Why?"

"For fear he should bore me, of course! I can see a staggering lady, dressed from head to foot in real Valenciennes, but with a mug as wrinkled as a withered greengage . . . I can see the idiotic backs of men in dented panamas that look like squashed meringues . . . I can see . . . Aha!"

"What is it?"

"Hi! Hi! All right, nothing to be alarmed about! Yes, yes, it's us, come up!"

"You're crazy, Marthe! Everyone's staring at you. Who are you talking to?"

"The little Van Langendonck."

"Calliope?"

"None other!"

"Is she here?"

"Presumably, since I'm calling out to her."

I frowned involuntarily; still another connection Alain would like to break off and which he keeps as distant as possible. Not that this little Cypriot, the widow of a Walloon, gets herself talked about as much as Chessenet but my husband objects to her flamboyant, languorous beauty which offends his sense of good taste. I had not realised that there was a code of strict conventions for beauty, but Alain assures me there is.

Calliope Van Langendonck, known as "the violet-eyed Goddess", announced her arrival by an elegant rustle of silks, made an effective theatrical entrance, overwhelmed Marthe with kisses, exclamations, trailing laces and lapis-lazuli glances veiled by eyelids armed with lashes that glittered like lances, then flung herself on me. I was ashamed of feeling so stiff and unresponsive, so I offered her a chair. Marthe was already bombarding her with questions:

"Calliope, which is the lucky vessel you've got in tow here this year?"

"Qu'est-ce, vessel? . . . Oh, yes . . . No vessel, I am by mine own self."

She frequently repeats what one has just said with a charming, puzzled air of listening to herself and mentally translating. Is it coquetry or a ruse to give herself time to choose her reply?

I remember, last winter, she was mixing up Greek, Italian, English and French with an ingenuousness too overdone to be sincere. Her "babelism", as Claudine, who finds her wildly amusing, calls it, and her carefully cultivated gibberish, attract attention like an additional charm.

"Alone? Tell that to the marines."

"But it is true. One must take care, two months each anno, to keep looks."

"It's worked very well up to now, hasn't it, Annie?"

"Oh, yes. You've never looked prettier, Calliope. The Arriège waters obviously do you good."

"The waters? I take jamais . . . never . . ."

"Then, why . . .?"

"Because the altitude's excellent here and I meet people I know and I can dress economically."

"Admirable woman! All the same, sulphur's good for the skin, isn't it?"

"No, it's kakon . . . bad for skin. I take care skin with a special recipe—Turkish."

"Tell us quick. I'm panting with excitement and I'm sure Annie hasn't a dry stitch on her."

Calliope who has left practically all her definite and indefinite articles behind in the isle of Cyprus, spread out her glittering hands magisterially.

"You take . . . old glove buttons, mother-of-pearl, you put in avothiki . . . egg-cup . . . and you squeeze lemon quite whole over . . . The next day, she's paste . . ."

"Who's *she*?"

"The buttons and the lemon. And you spread on face and you are whiter than, whiter than . . ."

"Don't bother to find the word. Thanks immensely, Calliope."

"I can ancora give recipe for removing spots woollens . . ."

"No, that's enough, good Lord! Not all the same day! How long have you been in Arriège?"

"One, due, trois . . . seven days . . . I'm so happy to see you! I want not to leave you again. When you suddenly called from the fen . . . window, I had spavento and I dropped my sunshade!"

I was disarmed. Alain himself could not have kept a straight face under this flood of crazy polyglottism. If this frivolous creature can make the long hours of my "season" seem shorter, I'll see her as much as she likes, in Arriège.

What need had Marthe to drag me round that bandstand? I came back with a splitting migraine and feeling as if my skin bore the almost physical imprint of all those stares directed at us. Those people, the bathers and water-drinkers of Arriège, stripped us and devoured us with their cannibal eyes. I feel sick with apprehension at the thought of all the tittle-tattle and spying and scandalmongering going on among these people with nothing to do and riddled with boredom. Luckily, very few faces I knew except the little Van Langendonck. Renaud and Claudine arrive in three days' time; they've booked their suite.

What a dreary bedroom this is! The harsh electric light glares down from the ceiling on my dead, empty bed . . . I feel lonely, lonely to the point of weeping, so lonely that I made Léonie stay and take down my hair so as to have a familiar presence with me as long as possible . . . Come, my black Toby—warm, silent little dog who adores my very shadow—come and lie at my feet. Your sleep is feverish after the long journey, agitated by simple straightforward nightmares . . . Perhaps you're dreaming that we're being separated again?

Don't be frightened, Toby. At this moment, the severe master is asleep on the colourless ocean, for his bed-time is as carefully regulated as all the rest of his life . . . He has wound up his watch, he has laid his tall white body, cold from the icy tub, between the sheets. Is he dreaming of Annie? Will he sigh in the night, will he wake up in the blackness, the deep blackness that his dilated pupils will pattern with gold half-moons and processions of roses? Suppose, at that very minute, he were calling his docile Annie, searching for her smell of roses and white carnations with the tortured smile of an Alain I have only seen and possesed in dreams?

No. I would have felt it through the air, over all those miles of distance . . .

Let's go to bed, my little black dog. Marthe is playing baccarat.

"My dear Alain,

I am getting used to this hotel life. It's an effort I hope you'll put down to my credit, just as I give you credit for every victory gained over my apathy.

All the same, the days are longer for me than for the people who are taking the cure. Marthe, valiant as usual, is submitting herself to a very severe régime of douches and massage. Léon only drinks the waters; I just look on.

We've met Madame Van Langendonck who is here on her own. Believe me, dear Alain, I did not in any way seek this meeting. Marthe is only being affable to her and says that watering-place friendships are the easiest things in the world to break off in Paris. So I hope you are reassured that our relations are purely superficial. Besides, she is staying at the Casino and we are at the Grand-Hotel.

I also believe the Renaud-Claudine couple will be arriving in a few days. It will be almost impossible for us to avoid seeing them; in any case I get the impression that you consider the husband acceptable socially because he knows everyone. As to his wife, we shall deal with the situation as best we can. For that I rely on Marthe, who has acquired from you some of your unerring sense of the right thing to do on any occasion.

I am writing only about Marthe and myself, dear Alain. You have forbidden me to pester you with my solicitude, useless but so well-intentioned! So now you shall also be told that we get up at quarter-to-seven, and that on the stroke of seven we are sitting at little tables in the dairy. A glass of warm, frothy milk is put in front of us and we drink it slowly, watching the sun suck up the morning mist.

We have to breakfast as early as seven because the medicinal baths are at ten. People arrive in dressing-gowns without even taking time to make the most cursory toilet. This early rising is not becoming to all the women and I admire Marthe for surviving the ordeal so well. She appears swathed in linens and muslins, wearing snowy frilled caps in which she looks charming.

Your Annie does not deploy so much art. She turns up in a tailored shirt and a soft silk blouse, and the absence of corsets makes not the slightest difference to my waistline. My night plait is tied up in a "door-knocker" with a white ribbon and I wear a cloche hat of woven straw. Not an outfit to cause a sensation!

After two cups of milk and as many little *croissants*, a walk in the park, then back to the hotel to see if there are any letters and to get properly dressed. At ten o'clock, Marthe disappears to her douche and I am left alone till mid-day. I stroll, I read, I write to you. I try to imagine your life, your cabin, the smell of the sea, the throbbing of the screw . . .

Goodbye, dear Alain, take good care of yourself and of your affection for

Annie"

That was all I could find to write to him. I broke off a dozen times, some clumsiness on the verge of dropping from my pen. What evil spirit inhabits me, so that I am already writing "clumsiness" where the word ought to be "frankness"?

But could I write everything? I dread my husband's anger, even at a distance, if I had told him that I live in the constant company of Calliope, and of Maugis who arrived three days ago and never leaves us . . . The ten-five train tomorrow brings Claudine and her husband . . . Like a coward, I tell myself that a complete confession when Alain returns will earn me no more than a serious sermon. He won't have seen Calliope in the dairy in the morning in "wanton disarray"—so disarrayed and so wanton that I turn my eyes away when I talk to her. Clouds of tulle that keep slipping down, flounced negligés yawning wide open over the golden skin and extraordinary lace mantillas to veil her dishevelled hair. Yesterday morning, however, she turned up in a vast dust-coat of silvery glacé silk, so hermetic and so decent that I was amazed. All round us, the panamas and the check caps were regretfully searching for glimpses of amber skin.

I complimented her on her correct attire. She burst into her ear-splitting laugh and shrieked: "Oh this thing! I had to wear it! I haven't a stitch on underneath!"

I didn't know where to look. All the caps and panamas had bent towards her, with an automatic jerk, like puppets bowing . . .

Luckily, Calliope is alone. Alone? Hmm! Sometimes, when we are walking together, we run into extremely presentable gentlemen who swerve aside with rather too much affected discretion, rather too much sublime indifference. She sweeps past them, her small figure stiffly upright, with a fan-like flutter of her eyelids which she has tried unsuccessfully to teach me.

The hour of the sulphur bath draws us together by creating a desert all round us. Léon, extremely depressed these days, often comes and sits at our table and risks startling ties and vivid waistcoats that suit his ivory complexion. He goes off every quarter of an hour to drink one of the four glasses of the water. He is trying hard to make an impression on Calliope and keeps paying her literary compliments.

To my great astonishment she receives his advances with barely-concealed disdain and a cold, lofty blue stare which implies: "What does this slave want?"

There is also . . . Marthe. Yes, Marthe. I hesitate even to write it . . . That Maugis dogs her heels far too closely and she endures his presence as if she were unaware of it. I cannot believe it. Marthe's glittering grey eyes see everything, hear everything, pounce on the thought behind the eyes they look into. How is it she doesn't tear that delicate, dimpled little hand of hers away from the lips of that creature that say a prolonged good-morning and good-night to it twice a day? Maugis reeks of alcohol. He is intelligent, yes, and extremely well-informed under all his half-drivelling banter; Alain tells me he is a redoubtable swordsman and that absinthe has not yet made his wrist tremble. But . . . ugh!

She's just amusing herself—that's what I'd like to hope. She's flirting for the pleasure of seeing her adorer's globulous eyes become bloodshot and yearning when they look at her. She's just amusing herself . . .

I've just come back from accompanying Marthe to her douche. I am still shaken by the experience.

In a hideous rough pine cabin, dripping on every wall and impregnated with sulphur and steam, I assisted, behind a wooden screen, at the nameless torture this douche-massage is. In a flash, Marthe was naked. I blinked at so much shamelessness and so much whiteness. Marthe is white, like Alain, with more pink underneath. Without a flicker of embarrassment she turned a pair of impudent, deeply-dimpled buttocks towards me while she strapped a rubber cap round her temples, a revolting head-dress that made her look like a fishwife.

Then she swung round . . . and I was struck dumb by the character this pretty woman's face assumed, deprived of its wavy hair: eyes so piercing they looked almost maniacal, a short, solid jaw, a coarsely-modelled ruthless brow. I searched in vain for the Marthe I knew in this one who frightened me. This disturbing face was laughing above a plump, dainty, almost too feminine body, all exaggerated taperings and exaggerated curves . . .

"Hi, Annie, are you falling asleep on your feet?"

"No. But I've had quite enough already. This cabin, that rubber cap . . ."

"I say, Catherine, shall we see if she's a brave girl, this little sister-in-law of mine? What about the two of us giving her a good douche, with the full jet on?"

I looked apprehensively at the sexless creature in an oilcloth apron, perched on a pair of wooden clogs. She laughed, displaying red gums.

"If Madame will kindly lie down . . . we've lost quite a bit of your fifteen minutes . . ."

"I'm coming, I'm coming."

With a bound, Marthe cleared the edge of a kind of sloping open coffin I had not noticed before and lay down, her hands over breasts to protect them from too rude a shock. The daylight from above lit up the veins in her skin, sculptured the fine creases, harshly illuminated all the red gold fuzz with which her body was fleeced. I blushed in the shadow. I could never have believed Marthe was so hairy . . . I blushed even more at the thought that Alain's body was covered with the same reddish-gold fuzz, like fine copper wire. Marthe waited with her eyes closed and her elbows trembling, then the sexless creature aimed two great rubber hoses that hung from the ceiling at her.

There was an outburst of piercing shrieks and imploring supplications. Under the cold jet, thicker than my wrist, Marthe twisted herself like a severed caterpillar, sobbed, ground her teeth and swore. When the hot jet succeeded the cold one, she sighed, appeased and comforted.

The creature douched with one hand and with the other great solid hand kept remorselessly slapping the delicate body that was now marbled with fiery red.

After five minutes of this appalling torture, a big warmed towel-robe, a dry friction and Marthe, delivered of the revolting rubber cap, was looking at me, still breathless and panting, with big tears in the corner of her eyes.

In a choked voice, I asked her if it was like that every morning.

"Every single one, my child. As Claudine remarked last year: 'Apart from an earthquake, they haven't found a more effective method of stimulating the circulation'."

"Oh, Marthe, it's atrocious! That jet's more brutal than any bludgeon . . . it made you cry and sob . . . The whole thing's too horrible!"

Already half-dressed, she gave me a curious, one-sided smile; her nostrils were still quivering.

"I don't find it so," she said.

Meals here are a torture to me. We have a choice between two restaurants, both of which are attached to the Casino, for the hotels serve no meals and Arriège is a town only in name, since it consists entirely of the Casino, the thermal establishment and four big hotels. These refectories, where we present ourselves like boarding-school pupils or prisoners, where at mid-day one is roasted by the harsh mountain sun, are enough to destroy my appetite entirely. I thought of having meals sent up to my room but all they would bring me would be warmed-up left-overs, and besides, it would be unkind to Marthe for whom meals are a pretext for tattling and poking one's nose into other people's affairs . . . I'm beginning to talk like Marthe myself!

Calliope always sits at our table and so does Maugis to whom I find it hard to be civil. Marthe devotes her attention to him, appears to be interested in his critical articles and tries to coax, or rather bully, him into doing one on "*The Tragic Hearts*", my brother-in-law's latest novel, to whip up the sales and to publicise water-places . . .

Léon devours the tough meat with an anaemic man's appetite and goes on paying assiduous court to Calliope who persists in sending him back to his sixty lines with the contempt of a royal princess for a paid scribe. Funny little woman! I have to admit it is I who seek her out now. She talks about herself with embarrassed volubility, fishing in some foreign language for the word she lacks in ours, and I listen to the jerky narrative of her life as if it were a fairy story.

I forget myself in listening to her—most of all while Marthe is having her douche, at the hour when the place is deserted. I sit opposite her in a big wicker armchair, behind the dairy, and, while she talks, I admire her adorned and disarrayed beauty.

"When I was little," Calliope said one morning, "I was very beautiful."

"Why, 'I *was*'?"

"Parceque I am less. The old woman who did our washing always used to spit in my face."

"The disgusting creature! Didn't your parents sack her?"

Calliope's lovely blue eyes enveloped me in disdain.

"Sack her? In my country, old women must spit on pretty little girls, saying 'Phtu! Phtu!'. It's to keep beautiful and guard against evil eye. I was kept kallista too on account my mother, the day I baptised, had meal put on table at night."

"Oh?"

"Yes. You put many things to eat on table and you go to bed. Then the mires come."

"Who?"

"The mires. You don't see them but they come to eat. And you put each chaise, chiesa, how you say? chair, right against wall because if one of the mires bumped her elbow passing to s'asseoir at table, she would give . . . bad spell on little child."

"How charming these old customs are! The mires, as you call them, are they fairies?"

"Fairies? I not know. They're mires . . . Oh dear, I've got a headache."

"Would you like some aspirin? I've got some in my room."

Calliope ran a hand with rose-tinted nails over her smooth forehead.

"No, thank you. It's my own fault. I not made the crosses."

"What crosses?"

"Like this, on the pillow."

With the flat of her hand, she traced a series of hurried little crosses on her knee.

"You make the little crosses and quick, quick you lay your head on the place and the bad visitors doesn't come in sleep nor mal-de-tête nor anything."

"You're sure?"

Calliope shrugged her shoulders and stood up.

"Of course I'm sure. But you . . . you is a people without religion."

"Where are you running off to, Calliope?"

"It's devtera . . . Monday. I must do my nails. Here's something again you not know! Do the nails Monday: health. Do the nails Tuesday, wealth."

"And you prefer health to wealth? How I agree with you!"

She was already walking away but she turned round, clutching armfuls of her dishevelled laces.

"I not prefer . . . Monday I do one hand, and Tuesday the other."

Between noon and five o'clock an inhuman heat prostrates all the bathers. The majority shut themselves up in the huge vestibule of the Casino which looks like a waiting-room in some modern station. Lying back in rocking-chairs, they flirt—poor wretches!—they suck iced coffee and doze to the sound of an orchestra as drowsy as themselves. I often absent myself from these predictable pleasures, embarrassed by people's stares, by Maugis' ill manners, by the noise of some thirty children and their already affected unselfconsciousness.

For I have seen little girls of thirteen there, already developing a woman's calves and hips, shamelessly exploiting the so-called privileges of childhood. Straddled over the leg of a grown-up male cousin or perched on a bar-stool with her knees up to her chin, one adorable little blonde with knowing eyes shows all she can of herself and studies the shamefaced excitement of the men with an icy, catlike gaze. Her mother, a fat, blotchy-faced cook, says ecstatically: "What a baby she is for her age!" I cannot run into this impudent brat without feeling uncomfortable. She has invented a game of blowing soap-bubbles and chasing them with a woollen racquet. Now males of all ages blow into clay pipes and run after soap-bubbles so as to brush against the little girl, steal her pipe and snatch her away with one arm when she leans out of the bay window. Oh, what a vile beast must lie dormant in certain men!

Thank heaven, there still remain some real babies, little boys with bare cigar-brown calves and the clumsy charm of bear-cubs; little girls growing too fast, all angles and long thin feet; tiny tots with arms like pink sausages, dented with soft creases as if they had been tied up with string—like that fat little cherub of four, who had had an accident in his first knickerbockers, and who whispered, very red in the face, to his severe and disgusted English governess: "Does ev'yone know I've been in my trousers?"

Today, I slipped away after lunch and went back to the hotel. I crossed the dangerous tract of sunlight that separates it from the Casino. For twenty-five seconds I savoured the scorching pleasure of feeling as if I were being swept off my feet by the blast of heat; my back sizzled and my ears buzzed. On the verge of falling, I took refuge in the cool darkness of the lobby where a smell of old casks came up through an open door leading down to the cellars, a smell of red wine turning to vinegar. Then I was back in my silent room that already smells of my scent, back on the less hostile bed where I flung myself in my chemise to lie there half-undressed and daydream till five o'clock.

Toby lightly licked my bare feet with a hot, red tongue, then fell prone on the carpet. But this caress not only gave me gooseflesh; it left me shuddering as if I had been outraged and switched my thoughts on to a dangerous path . . . My semi-nakedness reminded me of Marthe's douche, of what she was seeking in those jets that buffeted her, of the whiteness of my husband's—my dream-husband's—body . . . To free myself from the obsession—was it really to free myself? . . . I jumped out of bed and ran to look for Alain's latest photograph that I had hidden between two sachets.

Whatever had happened? . . . Was I actually dreaming? I could not recognize that handsome young man there . . . Those harsh eyebrows, that arrogant stance like a cock! No, surely I was mistaken . . . or perhaps the photographer had absurdly overdone the re-touching?

But no, that man there was my husband who is far away at sea. I trembled before his picture as I tremble before himself. A slavish creature, unconscious of its chains—that is what he has made of me . . . Shattered, I searched obstinately for one memory in our past as a young married couple that could delude me again, that could give me back the husband I *believed* I had. Nothing, I could find nothing—only my whipped child's submissiveness, only his cold condescending smile.

I wish I knew I were delirious, or dreaming. Ah! the cruel, cruel man! When did he hurt me most deeply . . . when he left me and sailed away—or the very first time he spoke to me?

5

WE were waiting, behind closed shutters, in Marthe's bedroom which is bigger than mine for Claudine and Calliope who were coming to tea. Claudine had arrived last night with her husband and was making an exception and coming alone as Marthe was excluding men today "to give herself a rest". By way of resting, she was pacing round the room; even when she stopped for a moment, she did not stand still but shifted impatiently from one foot to another like a soldier marking time. She was wearing a green muslin dress—a harsh, impossible green that exaggerated the whiteness of her skin and kindled her tempestuous hair to a blaze. Into its low neckline, she had tucked a great pink richly-scented common rose. Marthe has an infallible eye for violent, yet successful colour contrasts in the things she wears.

She was obviously extremely agitated: her eyes were menacing and her mouth unsmiling. Finally she sat down, did some rapid scribbling on a sheet of paper and muttered some figures.

"It's two louis a day here . . . fifteen hundred francs due to Hunt when we get back . . . and that fool who wants us to take in Bayreuth on the way . . . Life's somewhat complicated!"

"Are you talking to me, Marthe?"

"I'm talking to you and not talking to you. I'm saying that life is complicated."

"Complicated . . . very, in some ways."

"Exactly. 'Very, in some ways.' Suppose you had to find five hundred louis?"

"Five hundred louis?"

"Don't wear yourself out making calculations . . . it comes to ten thousand francs. If you'd got to produce them out of a hat in three weeks from now, what would you do?"

"I . . . I should write to the bank manager . . . and to Alain."

"How simple!"

She sounded so acid that I was afraid I had offended her.

"Why did you say it so bitterly, Marthe? . . . Is it . . . is it because you need money?"

Her hard grey eyes softened:

"My poor innocent child, you distress me. Of course I need money . . . All the time, all the time!"

"But, Marthe, I thought you and Léon were well-off. His novels sell, and there's your dowry . . ."

"Yes, yes. But one's got to eat. Porterhouse steak costs the earth this year. All in all, we've only thirty thousand francs a year—to cover everything. Do you imagine a woman can live decently on that unless she's a dim little moth?"

I looked thoughtful for a moment to give the impression of making calculations.

"Well . . . perhaps it is rather a tight squeeze. But, Marthe, why on earth didn't you . . .?"

"Didn't I what?"

"Come to me. *I've* got some money and I'd be only too pleased . . ."

She kissed me—a kiss that sounded like a slap—and pulled my ear.

"You're sweet. I'm not saying no. But not now. Leave it for the moment, I've still got one or two strings to pull that haven't been overworked. I'll keep you as the last resort. Besides it amuses me, fighting against money—waking up and finding a bill that's come in for the tenth time with 'urgent' on it and staring at my empty hands and telling myself: 'Tonight, there have got to be twenty-five louis in that little fist'."

I stared flabbergasted at her—at this diminutive Bellona in a grasshopper-green dress. "Fight . . . struggle . . ." the alarming words conjured up images of murderous gestures, tensed muscles, blood-stained victories . . . I sat there as if paralysed, my hands inert, gazing at her and thinking of my recent tears over Alain's photograph, of my crushed, ineffective life . . . Then a thought suddenly disturbed my inertia.

"Marthe . . . how do you manage?"

"What d'you mean?"

"How do you manage, when you need money so badly?"

She smiled, averted her head, then looked at me again with a sweet, far-away expression.

"All right, I'll tell you . . . I touch Léon's publisher . . . I get round the tailor, or else I terrorise him . . . And besides, now and then, I get unexpected repayments . . ."

"You mean money you were owed . . . that you'd lent to people?"

"Something of the kind . . . I can hear Claudine. Who's she talking to?" She opened the door and leant out into the corridor. I followed her with my eyes, painfully aware of having dissembled. For the first time, I had just feigned ignorance and pretended to be as idiotically naïve as the Cabbage-Rose. "Unexpected repayments! . . ." Marthe troubles me.

Claudine was certainly talking in the corridor. I could hear her saying gutturally, "My girrrl . . ." What girl? And why such a tender voice?

She appeared, holding her Fanchette on a lead. The cat minced in with a calm, undulating gait but its green eyes blackened at the sight of us. Marthe, in raptures, clapped her hands as if she were at the theatre.

"What a marvellous idea, Claudine! Where did you get that delicious animal? At Barnum's?"

"Certainly not. At home. In Montigny. Sit, Fanchette."

Claudine removed her boy's hat and shook out her curls. I find that ivory skin and that fierce, yet sweet expression of hers extraordinarily attractive. Her cat sat down primly with her tail wrapped round her front paws. It was a good thing I had sent Toby out for a walk with Léonie; she would have scratched him.

"Hullo, you, princess in the tower."

"Hullo, Claudine. Did you have a good journey?"

"Very good. Renaud charming. He flirted with me all the time, so ardently that I didn't feel for one minute as if we were married . . . Would you believe it . . . a man wanted to buy Fanchette from me? I gave him a look as if he'd raped my mother . . . It's hot in here. Are there a lot of ladies coming?"

"No, no, only Calliope Van Langendonck."

Claudine nimbly swung her foot over a chair—a very high chair.

"What luck! I adore Calliope. Trireme ahoy! She'll keep us in fits. Besides which, she's pretty and she's the last reincarnation of the 'soul of antiquity'."

"What nonsense!" exclaimed Marthe. "Why she's as cosmopolitan as a croupier in a casino!"

"That's what I meant. In my over-simple imagination she's the living embodiment of all those people down below us."

"The moles?" I chaffed her, shyly.

"No, you sly little bitch. Down below . . . on the map. Here she is! Appear, Calliope, Hebe, Aphrodite, Mnasidika . . . I'm trotting out all my Greek for you!"

Calliope gave the impression of being naked in a too-sumptuous dress of black Chantilly lace over flesh-coloured crêpe-de-Chine. She almost collapsed on the threshold.

"I'm dead . . . three flights . . ."

"Is bad for skin," Claudine finished for her.

"But is good for pregnant woman. It makes child drop."

MARTHE (*horrified*) Are you pregnant, Calliope?

CALLIOPE (*serene*) No . . . *jamais*, never.

MARTHE (*bitter*) You're lucky. Neither am I, as it happens. But what a ghastly bore it is, having to take all these precautions. How do *you* prevent it?

CALLIOPE (*modest*) I am widow.

CLAUDINE Obviously, that's one method. But not inevitably sufficient in itself. What did you do when you weren't a widow?

CALLIOPE I made crosses on, before. And I cough, after.

MARTHE (*bursting with laughter*) Crosses! . . . On which of you? You or your partner?

CALLIOPE On both, *cherie*.

CLAUDINE Ah! Ah! And you coughed afterwards? Is that the Greek rite?

CALLIOPE No. You cough like this (*coughing*) and it's gone.

MARTHE (*dubious*) It gets in quicker than it gets out . . . Claudine, just pass me the peach salad . . .

CLAUDINE (*absorbed*) No one could call me curious, but I would like to have seen his face . . .

CALLIOPE Whose face?

CLAUDINE The face of the late Van Langendonck when you were 'making crosses over'.

CALLIOPE (*candid*) But I didn't make them on face!

CLAUDINE (*unable to control herself*) Oh, this is bliss! (*suffocating with laughter*) Calliope . . . you incredible woman . . . you'll make me choke to death in a moment . . .

She shrieked and doubled herself up with delight; Marthe too was convulsed with laughter. In spite of being shocked and disgusted by them, I could not help smiling in the dimness that protected me. But it did not protect me enough; Claudine had noticed the silent amusement for which I rebuked myself sternly.

"Aha! Saint Annie, I saw you! Run away and play in the park at once or else don't look as if you understood. No, on second thoughts, smile again!" (Her harsh voice had suddenly become gentle and sing-song.) "When the corners of your mouth go up, your eyelids come down. Your smile is far more ambiguous than Calliope's stories, little Annie . . ."

Marthe thrust the screen of an open fan between Claudine and myself.

"If you go on like this, you'll be calling my sister-in-law 'Rézi' in a minute! Thanks, I don't want that sort of thing going on in my respectable bedroom!"

Rézi? Whatever did that mean? I plucked up my courage.

"You said . . . Rézi? Is that a word in a foreign language?"

"You couldn't have put it better!" retorted Claudine, while Marthe and Calliope exchanged knowing smiles. Then, all at once, her gaiety vanished. She stopped sucking her iced coffee through a straw, and fell into a momentary day-dream. Her darkened eyes looked exactly like the eyes of her white cat who was staring pensively into space, as if at some invisible menace . . .

What else did they say? I can't remember much . . . I withdrew further and further into the shadow of the shutters. I daren't write down the scraps I do remember. All sorts of horrors! Calliope retailed them quite naturally, with an exotic shamelessness; Marthe, crudely and bluntly; Claudine with a kind of languid ferocity I found less revolting.

Finally they began to question me, with much laughter about

gestures and positions, about things I daren't name even to myself. I didn't understand everything, I stammered and pulled my hands away; in the end they let me alone, though Claudine murmured, looking deep into my pale eyes that are too receptive to other people's will: "This Annie of ours—she's as engaging as a young girl." She was the first to leave, leading her white cat with its green collar and yawning in our faces: "It's too long since I've seen my great man; time's beginning to pall on me!"

Maugis "sticks" closer and closer. He incenses Marthe with his homage which rises up in fumes of whisky. These meetings at the five-o'clock concerts put me out of all patience. Calliope is invariably there, surrounded by men staring at her like a pack of hounds and the Renaud-Claudine couple, amorous and irritating. Yes, irritating! The way they smile into each other's eyes and sit knee to knee, as if they'd only been married a fortnight! Besides, *I* have seen people married a fortnight who didn't behave in a way that attracted attention.

I remember a very recently-married couple dining at a small table in a restaurant; he red-haired, she exaggeratedly dark, whose faces never betrayed desire, whose hands never touched, whose feet never met under the tent of the tablecloth . . . Often she would droop her eyelids over her transparent eyes "the colour of wild chicory flowers", she would pick up her fork and put it down again, cool her hand against the beaded side of the water-jug like a fever-patient grown used to her fever. *He* ate with an appetite as healthy as his teeth and spoke in an authoritative voice: "Annie, you're wrong; this meat isn't underdone. It's exactly the right degree of rareness . . ." So blind, so indifferent, he was unaware of that sweet fever, he did not even see those too-heavy lashes veiling the blue eyes. He never guessed my anguish nor how I was longing for, yet dreading, the moment that had not yet come when my pleasure would respond to his . . . How painful it is even to write this . . . It was always the same . . . I yielded myself, frightened and obedient, to his simple, robust caress which broke off too soon, at the instant when rigid and choking back tears, I thought I must be on the brink of death itself, when my whole being was crying out for and expecting . . . I did not know what.

I know now. Boredom, loneliness, an afternoon of atrocious

migraine and ether have turned me into a sinner full of remorse. A sin which is always threatening me and against which I struggle desperately . . . Ever since I took to writing this diary, I can see myself emerging a little more clearly every day, like a blackened portrait being cleaned by an expert hand. How did Alain, who was so little concerned about my moral miseries, guess what had happened between me and . . . Annie? I have no idea. Perhaps the jealousy of a betrayed animal illuminated him that day . . .

What is it that has suddenly made me see clearly? His absence? Have a few hundred miles of land and water worked this miracle? Or have I perhaps drunk the philtre that restored Siegfried's memory to him? But the philtre also restored his love, and, in my case, alas! . . . What have I to cling to now? All the people about me are speeding and striving towards the goal of their life . . . Marthe and Léon are toiling with all their might, he for big editions, she for luxury. Claudine loves and Calliope permits herself to be loved . . . Maugis intoxicates himself—Alain fills his life with a thousand exacting vanities: respectability, cutting a brilliant, but eminently correct figure in society, the necessity of living in a well-ordered house, of weeding out his address-book as one weeds out servants' references, of training his wife whom he rides on too short a rein like his half-bred English horse . . . They go about, they do things, and *I* stay here, listless and empty-handed . . .

Marthe burst in in the middle of this fit of black depression. She herself seemed less cheerful than usual, or else less valiant, and her red mobile mouth drooped at the corners, even when she laughed. But perhaps it was I who was seeing everything warped?

She sat down without looking at me, arranged the folds of a lace skirt that she wore under a little eighteenth-century jacket of stiff Chinese silk. White plumes quivered in her white hat. I don't much care for that costume—it's too elaborate, too suggestive of a society wedding. Secretly I prefer my own ivory voile dress with fine tucking everywhere, on the yoke, above the flounce of the skirt, at the top of the sleeves that flare out below it in wings . . .

"Are you coming?" demanded Marthe brusquely.

"Coming where?"

"Oh, why must you always look as if you'd just dropped from the moon? To the music . . . it's five o'clock."

"The fact is I . . ."

Her gesture cut me short.

"No, spare me that! You've said it already. Get your hat on and let's be off."

Normally I would have obeyed, half-unconsciously. But today had been a troubled day and it had changed me.

"No, Marthe, I assure you, I *have* got a headache."

She wriggled her shoulders impatiently.

"Yes, I know. The air will do you good. Come along."

Gently, I continued to say no. She bit her lips and her red, brown-pencilled eyebrows drew together in a frown.

"Look here, Annie. The fact is I need you—there!"

"Need me?"

"Yes, need you. I don't want to be alone . . . with Maugis."

"Alone with Maugis? You must be joking. There'll be Claudine and Renaud and Calliope."

Marthe fidgeted and turned a little pale; her hands were trembling.

"I implore you, Annie—don't make me lose my temper."

Taken aback, but defiant, I remained seated. She did not look at me but spoke, with her eyes staring at the window.

"I . . . I *particularly* need you to come because . . . because Léon is jealous."

She was lying. I could feel she was lying. She guessed it and, at last, turned her blazing eyes on me.

"Yes, all right, it's a fib. I want to talk to Maugis without anyone seeing us. I need you to make the others believe you're accompanying him and me a little way up the path . . . thirty paces behind like an English governess. You can take a book or a piece of needlework or anything you fancy. There! Got it? What's your answer? Will you do me this small favour?"

I blushed for her. With Maugis! And she had counted on me . . . for . . . oh, no!

As I shook my head, she gave me a furious stamp.

"Idiot! Do you imagine I'm going to sleep with him in a ditch in the park? Get it into your head that everything's gone wrong, that I can't lay hands on a penny, that I've got to get, not just one article on Léon's novel that's coming out in October but two articles . . . *three* articles . . . in the foreign reviews that'll get it sold in London and Vienna! That soak is as tricky as a monkey and we've been pitting our wits against each other for a month, but he'll come across with those articles or I'll . . . I'll . . ."

She was spluttering with fury, her fist clenched and her face savage. She looked like a stocking-knitter at the foot of the guillotine disguised as an aristocrat. Then, with a magnificent effort, she calmed herself and said coldly,

"That's the situation. Are you coming to the music now? In Paris, I shouldn't be reduced to asking you this. In Paris, a woman with her wits about her can manage these things on her own! But here, in this place where we all live in each other's pockets, where your next-door-neighbour in the hotel counts your dirty nightdresses and the jugs of hot water the maid brings up in the morning . . ."

"Just tell me one thing, Marthe . . . is it out of love for Léon?"

"Out of love that I'm . . . what?"

"Doing all this . . . Sacrificing yourself, being friendly with this horrible man . . . it's for your husband's glory, isn't it?"

She gave a harsh laugh as she powdered her flaming cheeks.

"All right, if you like, for his glory . . . If he's to wear laurels on his brow, he may have to wear something else. You needn't look wildly round for your hat. It's on the bed."

How much further are these women going to lead me astray? There is not one of them I wish to resemble! Marthe, who sticks at nothing; Calliope who is as cynical as a harem woman; Claudine who is as unashamed as an animal of all her instincts, even her good ones. Since I can judge them so clearly, heaven preserve me from becoming like any of them!

Yes, I accompanied Marthe to the band-stand, then into the park, with Maugis walking between us. In a deserted path, Marthe said to me casually: "Annie, your shoelace is coming undone." Meekly I pretended to re-tie the silk lace, though the knot was perfectly secure, and made no attempt to catch up with them. I walked at some distance behind, my eyes on the ground, not daring to look at their backs and not hearing what they were saying, only a rapid murmur of voices.

When Marthe, excited and triumphant, came to relieve me of my shameful sentry-duty, I heaved a great sigh of relief. She took my arm in a friendly way.

"It's done. Thank you, pet. You've helped me arrange things satisfactorily. But imagine the difficulty! If I'd asked Maugis to meet me alone in the park or the dairy or at one of those little tables where they serve iced coffee, some busybody, male or, worse still, female would have crashed in on us before we'd been there five minutes. My little game would have been ruined. And seeing him in my room would have been far too risky . . ."

"So you're going to get them, Marthe?"

"Get what?"

"The articles in the foreign Reviews."

"Ah . . . yes . . . Yes, I'm going to get them and everything else I wanted."

She was silent for a moment, fluttering her wide sleeves to cool herself. Then she muttered, as if to herself:

"He's rich, the swine."

I stared at her in amazement.

"Rich? Why should that bother you, Marthe?"

"What I meant by that," she explained very fast "is that I envy him for being able to write for his own pleasure instead of slaving away like poor old Léon over there. There he is, as usual, laying siege to Calliope without the faintest success. That Cypriot town has no ramparts but it's amazing how it defends itself!"

"Besides, perhaps the assailant isn't very heavily armed," I risked shyly.

"Mercy, what next! Annie coming out with improper remarks! I didn't know you were *quite* so well informed about Léon, dear!"

All animation, she rejoined the group of friends we had left. However, I pleaded my migraine again as an excuse to get away and here I am back in my bedroom, with my black Toby at my feet, troubled about myself, dissatisfied with everything, humiliated by the menial service I have just rendered my sister-in-law.

All the things Alain does not suspect! It makes me smile maliciously to think how little he knows about me, even about his favourite sister. I am beginning to hate this Arriège, where my life has been revealed to me with such depressing clarity, where you cannot get away from this restricted little crowd of people who, when you see them so close, seem to be distorted into caricatures of human beings . . . I've exhausted any amusement I had in watching these creatures' antics. In the daily procession to the dairy, I see too much plastered-over ugliness in the women's faces, and, in the men's, bestial desires or else utter fatigue. For among them are the sinister faces of the baccarat fiends—drawn and green, with blood-shot eyes. Those faces belong to the numbed bodies of men who have been sitting all night on a chair. As Marthe says, it is not only arthritis that ossifies so many joints here.

I've no longer the least desire to go to the pump-room or to assist at Marthe's douche or to gossip in the hall of the casino or to giggle at *Jeannette's Wedding* with Claudine. That perverse creature, who is mad about Debussy, has taken a sadistic fancy to going to the most hackneyed old musical comedies and applauding them frantically. Day after day, at the same hours, the same amusements, the same dressing-up, the same collection of faces . . . I simply cannot stand it any longer. Through the window, my eyes keep straying to the open breach at the western end of the valley—a break in the dark chain that hems us in, a rift of light in which distant mountains, powdered with mother-of-pearl, sparkle against a sky whose pure faint blue is the exact blue of my eyes . . . It is through there now that I can fancy I am escaping . . . Through there I can divine (or only imagine, alas!) another life that will be *my* life, not that of the broken mechanical doll they call Annie.

My poor black Toby, what am I going to do with you? Now we are going off to Bayreuth! Marthe has decided this with an emphatic authority that spares me any need to argue. All right, Toby, I'll take you with me—it's much the simplest, most honourable thing to do. I promised you I'd keep you and I need your mute, familiar presence, your short square shadow beside my long one. You love me enough to respect my sleep, my sadness, my silence and I love you like a little guardian monster. I feel young and gay again when I watch you gravely escorting me with your jaw distended by a big green apple that you'll carry about for a whole day, like a precious treasure, or obstinately scratching a pattern on the carpet to try and make it come off. For you live in a state of ingenuous surprise, surrounded by mysteries. The mystery of the coloured flowers on the upholstery of the armchairs; the deceitfulness of the mirrors out of which a phantom bull-terrier glares at you, a black bull-terrier who resembles you like a twin brother; the trap of the rocking-chair that tilts away under your paws . . . *You* don't obstinately try to penetrate the unknown. You sigh or you growl or else you smile rather sheepishly, and you resume your chewed green apple.

Only two months ago, I too would have said: "I give up. My

master knows how to deal with it." Now I torment myself and I flee from myself. I flee from myself. Understand what I mean by that please, little dog, full of a faith I have lost. It is better, a hundred times better for me to drivel in this diary and to listen to Claudine and Calliope than to linger dangerously alone with myself . . .

Nowadays, we talk to nothing but our going away. Calliope keeps dinning into my ears how heart-broken she is over our departure, larding her laments with constant ejaculations of "Dio almighty!" and "poulaki mou!"

Claudine observes all this agitation with kindly indifference. Renaud is with her, what does all the rest matter? Léon, embittered by his failure with Calliope (he cannot forgive her) talks far too much about his novel and about the Bayreuth he means to describe in it—"a Bayreuth perceived from a particular angle."

"It's a new subject," Maugis gravely declared today—Maugis who for ten years has been Bayreuth correspondent to three daily papers.

"It's a new subject when you know how to rejuvenate it," Léon affirmed pompously. "Bayreuth seen through the eyes of a woman in love with all her sensual perceptions intensely sharpened by gratified—and illicit!—passion . . . All right, laugh . . . it could make a very good subject and run into twenty editions!"

"At least," muttered Maugis through a cloud of smoke. "Anyway, I always agree with the husband of a pretty woman."

The pretty woman was half-asleep, recumbent in a rocking chair. Marthe never takes more than a cat-nap.

We were grilling in the park; it was two o'clock, the longest, most stifling hour of the day. The iced coffee was melting in our glasses. I rejoiced in the torrid sun, lying back in a wicker armchair and I did not even flutter my eyelids—at school they used to call me the lizard . . . Léon kept glancing at his watch, careful not to overstep the time-limit of his recreation. The carcass of Toby, which appeared to be uninhabited, lay prone on the fine sand.

"Are you taking that dog with you?" Marthe sighed faintly.

"Certainly, he's such a well-behaved boy!"

"I don't much care for well-behaved boys, even on railway journeys."

"Then you can get into another compartment."

Having made this reply, I silently marvelled at myself. Last month I should have answered: "Then I'll get into another compartment."

Marthe made no comment and appeared to be asleep. After a moment, she opened her vigilant eyes wide.

"I say, you two, don't you think Annie's changed?"

"Hmm . . ." Maugis mumbled, very vaguely.

"Do you think so?" asked Calliope, in a conciliating voice.

"I'm delighted to observe you all agree with me," mocked my sister-in-law. "So I shan't surprise you by saying that Annie walks faster, stoops her shoulders less, doesn't keep her eyes always fixed on the ground and talks almost like a normal human being. Alain's the one who's going to get a surprise!"

Embarrassed, I got up to go.

"It's your activity that galvanises me, Marthe. Alain won't be so surprised as you think. He always prophesied that you'd have an excellent influence on me. Excuse me, but I'm going indoors to write letters . . ."

"I'll come with you," said Calliope.

She did indeed come with me, without any encouragement on my part. She slipped her dimpled arm under my thin one.

"Annie, I've got a very great favour to ask you."

Her face was infinitely seductive. Between the sharp-pointed lashes, the lapis-lazuli eyes glittered at me in a suppliant stare, the Cupid's bow mouth was half-open as if on the verge of pouring out the most intimate confidences . . . One has to be prepared for anything with Calliope.

"Tell me, dear . . . you know if it's anything in my power . . ."

When we reached my bedroom, she took my hands with an overdone imitation of an Italian actress.

"Oh, you will, won't you? You're such a pure! That's what decided me. Je suis . . . lost if you refuse me! But you'll be kind for me . . . no?"

She rolled a little lace handkerchief into a ball and dabbed her eyelashes with it. They were dry. I felt extremely uneasy.

Then she stood very still, fumbling the dozens of curious charms that jingled on her chain (Claudine says Calliope sounds like a little dog when she walks) and staring at the carpet. She seemed to be muttering something to herself.

"It's a prayer to the Moon," she explained. "Annie, come to my aid. I need a letter."

"A letter?"

"Yes. A letter . . . *epigraphion*. A good letter, that you'll dictate."

"But to whom?"

"To . . . to . . . a very dear friend. A man."

"Oh!"

Calliope flung up a tragic arm.

"I swear, on oath, on head of my dead parents that he is only Platonic friend!"

I did not answer at once. I wanted to know more.

"But, my dear, why do you need *me* for that?"

She wrung her hands but her face was extremely calm.

"Understand! A very dear friend I love . . . Yes, I love him, I swear, Annie! But . . . but I not know him too well."

"Yet you love him!"

"Yes. He wants to marry me. He writes passionate letter and I *réponds* . . . answer very little . . . because I not know very well how to write."

"I never heard such nonsense!"

"The truth . . . on oath! I speak . . . two, *tree*, four, *cinq*, languages, enough to travel with. But I can't write. Especially French . . . so complicated if . . . if I not find the word . . . My friend thinks me . . . educated woman, unique, walking encyclopedia . . . and I'd so like to appear as he thinks! Otherwise . . . as you say in France, don't you? . . . the affair's in a cart."

She looked piteous, she blushed, she twisted her little handkerchief, she turned on all her charm. I asked reflectively, in a very chilly voice:

"Tell me, Calliope, whom did you count on before me? After all, I'm presumably not the first . . ."

She shrugged her shoulders tempestuously.

"A little boy of my country, who wrote well. He was . . . in love with me. And I copied his letters . . . but in the other gender of course."

This calm villainess, instead of arousing my indignation reduced me to helpless laughter. I can't help it, I can't take Calliope seriously, even as a wicked woman. She had completely disarmed me. I opened my blotter.

"Sit down there, Calliope, and we'll try. Although you'll never know how strange it is to me to be writing a love-letter . . . Come on. What am I to say?"

"Everything!" she cried with passionate gratitude. "That I love him! . . . That he's far from me! . . . that my life has no savour

. . . that I am fading away . . . In fact, all the things one usually says."

That I love him . . . that he is far from me . . . I had already treated that theme, but with so little success! Sitting beside Calliope, with my elbows on the table and my eyes on the hand that glittered with rings, I dictated as if in a dream . . .

"My beloved friend . . ."

"Too cold," interrupted Calliope. "I shall write 'My soul on the sea!' "

"Just as you like . . . 'My soul on the sea . . .' I can't do it this way, Calliope. Give me the pen . . . you can copy it out and alter it afterwards."

And I wrote feverishly:

"My soul on the sea, you have left me like a house without a master where a forgotten candle still burns. The candle will burn down to the end and passers-by will think the house is inhabited but the flame will burn low in an hour and die out . . . unless another hand restores it to glowing life . . ."

"Not that, no!" Calliope intervened, leaning over my shoulder. "Not good, 'another hand!' Write 'the same hand'."

But I was no longer writing anything. With my head on the table, buried in the crook of my elbow, I was suddenly weeping, furious with myself for being unable to hide my tears . . . The game had ended disastrously. Kind little Calliope understood . . . not quite correctly . . . and overwhelmed me with hugs, with her scent, with condolences and cries of despairing self-reproach:

"Darling! *Psychi mou*! How bad I am! I not think you were all alone! Give me, is finished. I not want more. And, besides, it's enough! The begin, good if I change little. I shall put *palazzo* instead of house and I shall search in French novels for the rest . . ."

"Forgive me, Calliope dear. This thundery weather has put my nerves in a wretched state."

"Nerves! Ah! if we women only had nerves!" said Calliope sententiously, rolling her eyes up to the ceiling. "But . . ."

The simple cynical gesture she made completed her sentence so oddly that, in spite of myself, I smiled. She laughed.

"That's so, eh? Addio, *mille remerciements*, and forgive me. I take away beginning of letter. Be with your courage."

Already outside in the corridor, she reopened the door and thrust her face round it, the face of a mischievous goddess:

"And I'll even copy it twice. Because I have another friend."

"'Being of a saline and sulphurous nature, the waters of Arriège are indicated in the case of chronic affections of the skin . . .'"

Claudine was reading aloud the little panegyric, bound in an attractive cover, that the thermal establishment provided for the benefit of people taking the cure. We were listening for the last time to the dismal orchestra that always played *fortissimo*, with a rigid strictness of rhythm and not the slightest variation of tone. Between a *Selection from the Dragoons of Villars* and a *March* by Armande de Polignac, Claudine was initiating us, against our will and not without acid comments, into the virtues of the sulphurous spring. Her diction was impeccable, her tone magisterial, her calm imperturbable.

Her white cat, on a lead, was asleep in a wicker chair. "A chair that costs two sous, like a lady's," Claudine had insisted. "Not an iron one because Fanchette feels the cold in her behind!"

"I'm going to play a game!" she cried, suddenly inspired.

"You make me slightly apprehensive," said her husband, with his usual loving glance.

He was smoking fragrant Egyptian cigarettes and sat, for the most part, silent and detached as if he had transferred all his life to the woman he called his "darling child".

"A nice party game! I'm going to guess from your faces what diseases you've come here to cure, and, when I make a mistake, I'll pay a forfeit."

"Pay me one straight away," cried Marthe. "I'm as fit as a fiddle."

"Me too," growled Maugis, whose face was purple under the panama pulled down as far as his moustache.

"Me too," said Renaud quietly.

"So am I!" sighed Léon, pale and exhausted.

Claudine, enchantingly pretty in a white straw bonnet, tied under the chin with white tulle strings, menaced us with a pointed finger.

"Attention, all! You're going to see that every one of you has come here for pleasure . . . just like me!"

She picked up her little book again and distributed her diagnoses like so many bouquets.

"Marthe, for you 'acne and eczema'! For you, Renaud . . . let's see . . . ah! 'furunculosis'. Pretty, isn't it? It sounds like the name of a flower. In Annie, I divine 'intermittent erysipelas' and in Léon 'scrofulous anaemia' . . ."

"He won't thank you much for that," broke in Renaud who saw a sickly smile on my brother-in-law's face . . .

"And in Maugis . . . Maugis . . . oh, bother, I can't find anything else . . . Ah! I've got it! In Maugis, I diagnose . . . 'recurrent pruritus of the genital parts'."

There was an explosion of laughter! Marthe showed all her teeth and impudently directed her laugh straight at the furious Maugis who lifted his panama to pour out a stream of invectives against the brazen hussy. Renaud tried half-heartedly to impose silence, for a respectable group behind us had just taken flight with much scandalised clatter of overturned chairs.

"Pay no attention," cried Claudine. "Those people who've gone are just plain jealous," (she picked up her book again) "they've only got miserable little dieases not worth having . . . they're just . . . 'chronic metritises', petty 'aural catarrhs' or miserable two-penny-halfpenny 'leucorrheas'!"

"What about you yourself, you poisonous little thing?" burst out Maugis. "What the hell have you come here for, besides making yourself a thorough pest and disturbing everyone's peace?"

"Hush!" She leant forward, with an impressive, mysterious air. "Don't tell anyone. I've come here for the sake of Fanchette, who suffers from the same complaint as you."

6

B AYREUTH.

Rain. Rain . . . The sky melts into rain, and the sky here is coal-dust. If I lean on the window-sill, my hands and elbows are smeared with black. The same impalpable black powder snows down invisibly on my white serge dress, and if I absentmindedly stroke my cheek with the palm of my hand I crush a gritty sticky smut into long black streaks. Drops of rain have dried on the flounce of my skirt in little grey spots. Léonie is eternally brushing my clothes and Martne's. As she does so, she wears a blissful expression that makes her look like a sentimental policeman. It reminds her of her native Saint-Etienne, she declares.

In the west, the sky is turning yellow. Perhaps the rain is going to stop and I shall see Bayreuth otherwise than through this fine, open veil, otherwise too than through the distorting prism of my tears.

For, the moment I arrived, I dissolved into water like the clouds. I feel a little ashamed to write down the puerile reason for such a crisis of misery, but I will.

At Schnabelweide, where we changed from the Nürnberg-Carlsbad line, the train rushed on in a heedless hurry most untypical of German trains, carrying my trunk and my dressing-case off on their way to Austria. As a result I found myself—after fifteen hours of travelling and sticky all over with this German coal-dust that smells of sulphur and iodoform—without a sponge, without a clean handkerchief, without a comb, in fact without everything absolutely essential. This blow demoralised me, and while Léon and Maugis tore off to the Information Bureau, I began to cry. I just stood there on the platform, shedding great tears that made little pellets in the dust.

"This Annie of ours was obviously born under Aquarius," murmured Claudine philosophically.

As a result, my arrival in the "Holy City" was pitiable and absurd. I was not amused by Marthe's snobbish ecstasies over the postcards, the red glass Grails, the carvings, the plates and the beer-jugs, all stamped with the image of the god Wagner. Even Claudine, unkempt, with her boater over one ear, hardly raised a smile from me when she brandished a smoking sausage she was clutching triumphantly, right under my nose.

"Look what I've bought!" she cried. "It's a sort of postman who sells them. Yes, Renaud, a postman! He's got hot sausages in his leather satchel and he fishes them out with a fork, like snakes. You needn't make a face, Marthe, it's delicious! I shall send one to Mélie—I shall tell her it's called a Wagnerwurst . . ."

She went off, dancing, dragging her gentle husband towards a lilac-painted *konditorei* to eat whipped cream with her sausage . . .

I recovered my luggage, thanks to the zeal of Léon, egged on by Marthe, and the polyglottism of Maugis. The latter speaks as many German dialects as there are tribes in Israel and, with one sentence I found totally intelligible, he galvanised the smiling, apathetic officials into action. I got my own things back at the very moment when Claudine, moved by my plight had just sent me one of her linen chemises . . . so brief, it made me blush . . . and a little pair of Japanese silk knickers patterned with yellow moons. With them was this note: "Take them, anyway, Annie, if only to dry your tears, and remember I'm a St. Martin type. Query: would St. Martin have given away his trousers?"

I am waiting, without impatience, for lunchtime, and for the rain to stop. Now and then a rift of blue shows through two heavy sailing clouds, then vanishes. My window looks out on the Opernstrasse, over a boarded footpath that conceals the stagnant water below. The staircase smells of cabbage. My curious coffin-like bed is boxed in during the day under a lid covered with sprigged material. The top sheet buttons on to the eiderdown and my mattress is composed of three pieces, like a Louis XIV chaise longue . . . Do I feel the faintest touch of the sacred fever? No, most decidedly no. I envy

Marthe who, the moment we arrived at the station, began to sparkle with conventional enthusiasm, already breathing what her husband pompously calls "the fervour of all the nations who have come to worship the man who was greater than man . . ." On the other side of the wall, I can hear that neophyte furiously banging about among her trunks, and emptying the tiny jugs of hot water with a single splash. Léon's voice reaches me only as an inarticulate buzz. Marthe's total silence seems to me ominous. I was not altogether surprised just now when I heard her exclaim in a loud, shrill voice, anything but suggestive of Marie-Antoinette:

"Hell! What a filthy hole!"

Only one pleasurable sensation makes me almost content to sit perfectly still in front of this window, at this rickety little mahogany table: the feeling of being very far away, beyond anyone's reach . . . How long is it since Alain went away? A month, a year? I have lost all count of time. I shut my eyes and try to conjure up his fading image; sometimes I strain my ears, as if I thought I heard his footsteps . . . Am I awaiting his return or am I dreading it? Often, I turn round sharply with the vivid impression that he is there, that he is going to lay his heavy hand on my shoulder, and my shoulder automatically droops to receive it . . . It is over in a second, but it is like the flash of a danger signal. I know all too well, that if he returned, he would once again be my master. Once again, my neck would bow meekly to the yoke that it has hardly had time to miss. After all, it is as used to wearing it as my hand is to the ring Alain put on it the day we were married, the ring that is a little too tight and has worn a permanent groove in my finger.

For people on a pleasure-trip, how gloomy the three of us were, in that *Restauration* this evening! Certainly the novelty of the place, the feeble, hissing gas-light, the cold wind blowing through the gaps of the tent did not excite me personally to gaiety but I was surprised that Marthe and her husband looked equally lost and constrained. Marthe stared at the chicken and stewed pears on her plate. Léon made notes in a little pocket-book. On what? The place seemed in no way remarkable. This restaurant, the Baierlein, whose vogue is due to its serving meals on a terrace under a striped tent, seemed to me, apart from the stewed pears, much like the one at Arriège. More English women dining there perhaps, and little brown jugs of *Seltz-wasser* on the tables. What a lot of English women! Whoever told me they were stiff and reserved? Léon informed me they had come straight from *Parsifal*. Flushed, their hats askew, their admirable hair clumsily twisted up anyhow, they shrieked, wept over their memories of the opera, waved their arms and never, for a moment, stopped eating. I stared at them—I who was not hungry, who was not weeping, I who was keeping my chilly hands sedately folded inside my wide sleeves—as if they were drunk, wondering half-enviously, half-disgustedly: "Shall I be like that on Sunday?" To tell the truth, I hope I shall.

Marthe uttered not a word as she studied the diners with her insolent eyes. She must have found their hats unworthy of interest. My brother-in-law went on taking notes. So many notes! People were staring at him. I stared at him too. How extraordinarily French he looked!

In spite of an English tailor, a Swedish bootmaker and an American hatter, this effeminately handsome man is a supreme example of the French type in all its colourless correctness. I began to wonder what betrayed him at once as a typical average Frenchman, with no great qualities and no great defects. Was it no more than the suavity of his over-frequent gestures and the total lack of character in his regular, well-proportioned features?

Marthe brusquely interrupted my ethnological speculations.

"Please don't all talk at once. Honestly, this place bores me to tears. Isn't there somewhere even *more* giddily exciting?"

"Certainly," said Léon, consulting his Baedeker. "The Berlin restaurant. It's smarter, more French, but it has less local colour."

"I don't care a fig about local colour . . . I've come here for Wagner, not for Bayreuth. All right, let's go to the Berlin tomorrow . . ."

"We shall have to pay ten marks for a *truite au bleu* . . ."

"Why worry? Maugis is good for . . . for standing us a meal . . . maybe a couple . . ."

I decided to intervene.

"But Marthe, *I* feel embarrassed letting Maugis pay for me . . ."

"All right, my dear girl, you can go off by yourself and eat in some cheap little restaurant."

Léon irritably put down his gold pencil.

"Really, Marthe, you needn't be so cutting! In the first place there aren't any cheap little restaurants . . ."

Marthe's nerves were thoroughly on edge. She gave a sarcastic laugh.

"No one like Léon for summing up a situation in a few well-chosen words! . . . Now, now, Annie, stop looking like a martyr . . . It's this chicken with pears that's driven me frantic . . . Are you two coming? I'm fed up, I'm going home."

With a peevish gesture, she gathered up her fleecy, trailing skirt and, sweeping the terrace with a contemptuous gaze, observed:

"Never mind, one day we'll have a little Bayreuth in Paris. And that, my children, would be far more chic . . . and far more sought after!"

This first night has been so appalling, it would be better not even to mention it. Wedged in the middle of the hard mattress, scratched by the coarse cotton sheets, I cautiously breathed in the—imaginary . . .? smell of cabbage that filtered through the windows, under the doors, through the walls. In the end I sprayed an entire bottle of White Carnation over my bed and fell into a sleep filled with absurd voluptuous dreams. It was like looking at slightly caricatured illustrations in a dirty book . . . a debauch in Louis-Philippe costume. Alain, in nankeen, and more enterprising than he had ever been; myself in organdie, more revolted than I had ever dreamed . . . But, in any case, those voluminous trousers rendered any consent impossible.

7

OWING to our having booked our seats almost at the last moment, I could not sit with Marthe and Léon. Secretly I was glad to be on my own, away from them. Standing up, in the dim light of the round lamps that encircled the auditorium like a broken necklace, I cautiously analysed the odour of burnt rubber and mildewed cellars. I was not shocked by the grey ugliness of the sacred fane. Everything, including the low stage and the black gulf out of which the music would rise, had been so over-described to me, that it hardly came as anything new. I waited. Outside, the second fanfare sounded (I think it was Donner's call). Some foreign women removed their hatpins with a bored, accustomed gesture. I did the same. Like them, I stared vaguely at the *Fürstenloge*, where I could see black shadows moving about and large bare foreheads tilted forward . . . There was no interest to be found there. I had to wait a little longer, for the last padded door to be opened for the last time, showing a patch of blue sky in the aperture, for the last old lady to have finished coughing once and for all, before finally the E flat rose from the abyss and growled like a hidden beast.

"Obviously, it's very fine," decreed Marthe. "But it doesn't have any intervals."

I was still throbbing, but I concealed my emotion like a sensual desire. I merely replied that it had not seemed long to me. But my sister-in-law who was wasting a new orange dress, the same shade as her hair, thought poorly of this "fairy-prologue".

"My dear, the intervals here are part of the performance. They're something one simply must see . . . ask any of the regular habitués. You eat during them, you meet your friends, you exchange impressions at length . . . The spectacle's almost unique. Isn't it, Maugis?"

The great boor imperceptibly raised his shoulders.

" 'Unique', that was the word I was looking for. Nevertheless, in here, at least they don't have the cheek to serve that f . . . filthy dish-water tasting of furniture-polish instead of decent beer. To come to Bayreuth to drink that muck makes one wonder how people can be such fatheads!"

He looked as slovenly and dissipated as ever: I searched in vain for some trace of fanatical enthusiasm that might have rehabilitated him in my eyes. For Maugis is one of those who "discovered" Wagner in France. He has stubbornly imposed him on the French year after year in articles which are an extraordinary mixture of bald scepticism and drunkenly lyrical fervour. I know that Léon despises his flatulent, slangy style and that Maugis calls Léon "a society scribbler" . . . In every other respect, they get on marvellously . . . especially these last two months.

I felt so lost in the theatre's huge restaurant, so far away . . . no, more than that, so *cut off* from everything. I was still inhabited by the demon of the music, the lament of the Rhine maidens was still wailing in my head and conflicting with the deafening clatter of crockery and knives and forks. Frenzied waiters, their black dinner-jackets positively stiff with grease, dashed about, their hands loaded, and the pinkish froth of the beer spilled over into the gravy . . .

"As if we hadn't enough of their beastly 'gemischtescompote'," grumbled Marthe with extreme resentment. "That Logi was particularly poor, wasn't he, Maugis?"

"Oh no, not particularly," he retorted, with an expression of mock indulgence. "I heard him seventeen years ago in the same part and I thought him undeniably better today."

Marthe was not listening. She had turned, first her eyes, then her lorgnette, towards the far end of the room.

"But it is . . . it really is her."

"Is who?"

"Why, the Chessenet! With people I don't know. There, right at the end, at the table against the wall."

Feeling horribly shaken, as if I had suddenly been dragged back to my old life, I nervously explored the vast chessboard of tables. Yes, that pinkish-flaxen chignon was undoubtedly Valentine Chessenet's.

"Lord, what a bore!" I sighed dejectedly.

Marthe lowered her lorgnette to scrutinise my face.

"Why should it worry you? You can hardly be afraid—here—of her nabbing your Alain again!"

I gave a slight start.

"Again? I wasn't aware . . ."

Maugis, obviously meaning well, broke in with an idiotic, irrelevant remark that silenced Marthe. She tightened her lips, but she watched me out of the corner of her eye. My fork was trembling a little in my hand. Léon gnawed his gold pencil and looked about him with a reporter's eye. Quite suddenly I had a violent desire to take that mollusc by the scruff of his neck and bang his pretty, lifeless face against the table . . . Then my rush of hot blood subsided and I was left amazed at my absurd burst of feeling . . . I think music must have a bad effect on me. The sight of that Chessenet woman had brought Alain back to me and, for one brief instantaneous flash, I saw him lying asleep, unconscious and white as a corpse.

My husband's mistress! Suppose she had been my husband's mistress! . . . For two hours, I have been saying this over and over to myself without its conveying any clear picture . . . I cannot evoke any image of Madame Chessenet except in full evening dress or in an elegant afternoon outfit, wearing one of those absurdly small hats with which she tries to create a style peculiarly her own . . . the Chessenet style! Yet if she had been his mistress, she must have taken off that tight dress, delicately removed that absurd little hat . . . But my weary head cannot imagine further than that . . . Besides, neither can I see Alain ardently wooing a woman. He never wooed me. He was never imploring, pressing, anxious, jealous . . . All he ever gave me was . . . a cage. I was contented with that for so long . . .

His mistress! Why doesn't that idea make me feel more heartbroken resentment against my husband? Don't I love him at all any more?

I can't think any longer, I'm exhausted. Let's put it all aside. Think, instead, Annie that now you're alone and free . . . that you've still many more weeks of freedom . . . Free! it's a strange word . . . There are birds who think they are free because they are hopping about outside their cage. Only—their wings are clipped.

"Good gracious, aren't you even up yet?"

This morning, all ready dressed to go out, I went into Marthe's room to ask her to come and explore Bayreuth a little with me. I found her still in bed, her red hair loose and dishevelled about her dimpled white shoulders. As I entered, she gave a leap like a carp and turned her plump behind over under the sheets. She yawned and stretched—she goes to bed with her rings on—then she threw me a rapid grey glance from under frowning eyebrows:

"You've already got your outdoor things on! Where are you off to?"

"Nowhere special. I'm just going for a walk. Are you feeling ill?"

"Bad night, headache, feeling lazy . . ."

"What a pity! Now I'll have to go all alone."

I went out, after shaking hands with poor old Léon who did not get up from his mahogany table—every bit as ugly as mine—where he was despatching his sixty lines before luncheon.

I felt diffident, all alone in the street. I would not have the courage to buy anything—I spoke German too badly—I would simply look round. The next minute I was gazing into a "modern-style" shop that was a world in itself—a Wagnerian world. There was a photograph of the Rhine Maidens with their arms twined round each other's shoulders; three hideous stout women, one of whom squinted, wearing flowered headdresses like the one my Luxemburger cook wears on her day out . . . Round the poker-work frame writhed seaweed—or earthworms. Price complete with frame? Ten marks. I paid it.

Why so many portraits of Siegfried Wagner? And why only of him? Yet other children of "Cosima's late" as Maugis calls him are certainly no uglier than this young man with a caricature of a nose. The fact that Siegfried conducts the orchestra—and incidentally conducts it rather badly—hardly seems a sufficient excuse . . . Everywhere, there was that persistent smell of cabbage . . . None of these streets had any character, and, at the end of the Opernstrasse, I hesitated whether to turn right or left.

"The poor lost child, abandoned by its mother,
Ever finds refuge in the holy place,"

said a cheeky, birdlike voice behind me.

"Claudine! . . . Yes, I don't know which way to go. I'm so unused to going out by myself."

"Unlike me. At twelve, I used to scamper about like a little rabbit . . . incidentally *I* had a white behind too."

The . . . posterior . . . really occupies an excessive place in Claudine's conversation. Nevertheless, I find her entirely delightful.

I reflected, as I walked beside this free creature, that it was odd Alain should have allowed me to visit women of dubious—not even dubious!—reputation like that Chessenet female and the Cabbage-Rose, who makes sure beforehand that her lovers are expert, and yet forbidden me to see Claudine, who is charming and who makes no secret of the fact that she adores her husband. Weren't those other women far more dangerous for me to frequent than this one?

"I must say, Claudine, I'm surprised to meet you without either Renaud or Fanchette."

"Fanchette's asleep and, anyway, the coal-dust dirties her paws. My Renaud's working at his *Diplomatic Review* in which he's abusing Delcassé as a stinker. So I've come out so as not to disturb him. And moreover, I've got maggots in my brain this morning."

"You've got . . .?"

"Yes, maggots. But what about you, Annie? What does this mean, you independent little thing, running about alone in a foreign city, without your governess! And where's your leather satchel? And your drawing-book?"

She stood there teasing me, a quaint figure in her abbreviated skirt, her coarse straw boater tilted over her nose, her curly short hair and her triangular face quite brown above the white silk blouse. Her beautiful almost yellow eyes seemed to light up her whole person, like fires blazing in an open field.

"Marthe's resting," I replied at last. "She's tired."

"Tired of what? Of being fumbled by Maugis? Oh! Whatever have I said?" she corrected herself, hypocritically putting her hand over her mouth as if to crush back the impudent words . . .

"You think? . . . You think she does . . . that he does what you just said?"

I could not keep the tremor out of my voice. Fool that I was! I knew Claudine would tell me nothing now. She shrugged her shoulders and spun round on one foot.

"Oh, if you listen to everything *I* say! . . . Marthe is like heaps of women I know . . . it amuses her to be raped a little in front of everybody. Alone with a man, it's a different story, somehow, it doesn't make them any less respectable." I walked pensively beside Claudine. We met Englishwomen—still more of them!—and Americans in silk and lace at ten o'clock in the morning. My companion received a great many glances. She became conscious of this and returned stare for stare with cool self-possession. Only once did she turn round excitedly and pull me by the sleeve.

"What a pretty woman! Did you see her? That blonde with eyes like black coffee?"

"No, I didn't notice."

"Little fathead! Where are we going?"

"I wasn't going anywhere. I wanted to see a little of the town."

"The town? Not worth the trouble. It's nothing but postcards and all the rest is hotels. Come along, I know a pretty garden; we can sit down on the grass."

I had no strength to resist her turbulent will: I adapted my steps to her long, quick stride. We walked down an ugly street, and then, some way beyond the Schwarzes Ross, we found ourselves in a great empty square, one of those pleasant, melancholy squares, full of lime-trees and statues, so typical of provincial towns.

"What is this square, Claudine?"

"This? I've no idea. Margravine's Square. When in doubt here, I christen everything Margravine's. Come along, Annie, we're nearly there."

A little gate in the corner of the big square led us into a trim flower-garden that soon expanded into a park, a slightly neglected park that might have belonged to some cool, sleepy château in provincial France.

"This park is . . . what?"

"The Margravine's Park!" asserted Claudine confidently. "And here we have one of the Margravine's benches, one of the Margravine's soldiers, one of the Margravine's Nannies . . . Green, isn't it? It's restful. You could almost imagine you were in Montigny . . . except it's not nearly, nearly so good."

We sat down side by side on the soft, crumbling stone of an old bench.

"You love your Montigny, don't you? Is it beautiful country?"

"Beautiful country? I'm as happy there as a plant in a hedge, as a lizard on its wall, as . . . *I* don't know. There are days when I don't come home from morning to night—when *we* don't come home," she corrected herself. "I've taught Renaud to realise how beautiful that country is. When I go there now, he comes too."

Once again, her intense love for her husband brought on that depression that almost makes me want to cry.

"He follows you everywhere . . . in everything . . . wherever you go, whatever you do."

"But I follow him too," said Claudine, surprised. "That's how we go on . . . We follow each other . . . without being like each other."

I bent my head and scratched the sand with the tip of my umbrella.

"How you love each other!"

"Yes," she answered simply, "It's like a disease." She stared into space for a moment, then turned her eyes back to me.

"And you?" she asked abruptly.

I started.

"Me? . . . What about me?"

"You don't love your husband?"

"Alain? Why yes, naturally . . ."

I drew back, uneasy. Claudine moved closer and burst out impetuously:

"Ah! 'Naturally'. Right, if you love him naturally, I know what that means. What's more . . ."

I wanted to stop her, but it would have been easier to stop a run-away pony!

"What's more, I've often seen you together. He looks like a stick and you look like a wet handkerchief. He's a clumsy idiot, a booby, a brute . . ."

I flinched at her gesture as if she had raised her fist at me . . .

"Yes, a brute! That carrot-headed fool has been given a wife, but not the faintest glimmering of how to treat her . . . Why, it would be glaringly obvious to a seven-months-old baby! 'Annie, you can't do this . . . Annie, you can't do that . . . it simply isn't *done!*' The third time he said that to *me*, I should have answered: 'And suppose I make you a cuckold . . . would that be considered correct?'"

She brought it out with such comical fury that I burst into simultaneous laughter and tears. The extraordinary creature! She was so heated that she had actually pulled off her hat and was tossing her short hair as if to cool herself.

I did not know how to control myself. I still wanted to cry but most of all I wanted to laugh. Claudine turned to me with a severe face that made her look like her cat.

"There's nothing to laugh about! Nothing to cry about either! You're a softy, a pretty little scrap of chiffon, a crumpled bit of silk and you've no excuse because you don't love your husband."

"I don't love my . . ."

"No, you don't love anyone!"

Her expression changed. She became more serious:

"For you haven't got a lover. Love . . . even a forbidden love . . . would have made you blossom, you supple, barren branch . . . Your husband! Why, if you'd loved him in the real sense of the word, loved as I love!" she said, clasping her delicate hands over her breast in a strangely proud, firm gesture, "you'd have followed him over land and sea, whether he kissed you or beat you, you'd have followed him like his shadow and like his soul! . . . When one loves in a certain way," she went on in a lower voice, "even betrayals become unimportant . . ."

I listened, straining towards her, straining to catch what she was uttering like a prophetess revealing strange truths. I listened with a passionate sense of desolation, never taking my eyes off hers that were staring into the distance. Then she calmed herself and smiled at me as if she had only just noticed my presence.

"Annie, in our fields at home, there's a fragile grass that looks like you . . . a grass with a slender stalk and a heavy head of seed-pods that weighs it down. It has a pretty name that I give you whenever I think of you—'Drooping Melic'. It shivers in the wind, as if it were frightened . . . and it only stands up straight when all its seed-pods are empty . . ."

She threw an affectionate arm round my neck.

"Drooping Melic, how charming you are, more's the pity! I haven't seen a woman since . . . for a long time . . . who was so appealing. Look at me, chicory-flowers, eyes fringed like a pool among black rushes, Annie who smells like a rose . . ."

Utterly broken with misery, utterly melted with tenderness, I laid my head on her shoulder and raised my still-wet lashes towards her. She bent down her face and dazzled me with her eyes, bright as a wild animal's and suddenly so dominating that I closed my own, overwhelmed . . .

But the affectionate arm was suddenly withdrawn, leaving me tottering . . . Claudine had leapt to her feet. She had stretched herself taut as a bow and was harshly rubbing her temples.

"Too bad!" she muttered. "Another minute and . . . After I'd absolutely promised Renaud . . ."

"Promised what?" I asked, still all at sea.

Claudine laughed in my face, with an odd expression, displaying her short teeth.

"To . . . to . . . be back at eleven, my child. I've cut it a bit too fine . . . Buck up, we might just make it if we hurry . . ."

8

THE first act of *Parsifal* had just finished and sent us out into the disenchantment of broad daylight. During the three days that followed *Rheingold*, these long intervals which were Marthe's and Léon's delight, have always interrupted my illusion or my intoxication in the most inopportune way. To have to leave Brünnhilde, abandoned and menacing, to return to my beflounced sister-in-law, to Léon's finical niggling, to Maugis' inextinguishable thirst, to Valentine Chessenet's washed-out fairness was intolerable. Not to mention the "Achs" and the "Kolossals" and the "Sublimes" and the whole stream of polyglot exclamations poured out by these undiscriminating fanatics! No, no, *no*!

"I'd like to have a theatre entirely to myself," I declared to Maugis.

"In which you resemble Ludwig of Bavaria," he replied, taking his lips for a moment from the straw of his hot grog. "Look where *his* morbid fancy led him. He died after building residences in a style which is only esteemed by the most provincial of pastry-cooks. Meditate on the sad result of solitary self-indulgence."

I started violently. Leaving that drunkard sitting there and refusing the enormous glass of lemonade Claudine was holding out to me, I went and stood with my back against a pillar, facing the declining sun. Swift clouds were hurrying towards the east and their shadow was all at once chill. Over Bayreuth, the black smoke from the factory chimneys swayed over heavily till a stronger wind swallowed it up in one breath.

A group of Frenchwomen, in straight corsets that flattened their hips and exaggeratedly long skirts that fitted closely in front and swept out in folds behind them, were talking in high, shrill voices. Their conversation was extremely uninhibited and had nothing to do with the magnificent music. They were talking with that cold animation that is attractive for a minute but becomes exasperating after a quarter-of-an-hour. They were pretty creatures and, even without hearing what they were saying, one could have guessed they belonged to a frail, nervous race, contemptuous and lacking will-power—a race very different, for example, from that calm, red-haired Englishwoman whom they were taking to pieces from top to toe. The latter completely ignored them from where she sat on one of the steps of the porch, displaying her large, ill-shod feet with chaste tranquillity . . . Then it was my turn to be stared at and whispered about.

The one who seemed to know everything declared: "I think she's a young widow who comes every year to the festival on account of one of the tenors . . ." I smiled at this ingenious calumny and moved away towards Marthe. Marthe was in her element. Wearing white and mauve and leaning on a tall parasol, she was parading about in her most gracious Marie-Antoinette manner, acknowledging friends from Paris, distributing greetings, making inventories of hats . . . But there was that odious Maugis, brushing her skirts as usual! I preferred to retrace my steps and go back to Claudine.

But Claudine was deep in conversation—clasping a huge cream-stuffed cake in her ungloved hand—with a most strange little creature . . . That brown Egyptian face, in which the mouth and eyes seemed to be drawn with two parallel strokes of the brush, framed in dancing ringlets like those of a little girl of 1828 . . . could it belong to anyone but Mademoiselle Polaire? All the same, Polaire in Bayreuth seemed so wildly improbable that I could hardly believe my eyes!

Both were supple and slender, both intensely lively, each wore a little bow on her forehead at the edge of her parting—Polaire's white, Claudine's black. The people who were avidly staring at them declared they looked like twins. I did not agree. Claudine's hair was more boyish and rebellious and her eyes did not evoke the east as Polaire's did. Those admirable Egyptian eyes of Polaire's have more gloom, more defiance—and more subservience—in their expression. All the same, there was a resemblance. Passing behind them, Renaud gave their two short manes a quick, affectionate tweak; then, laughing at my stupefied face, he said:

"Yes, Annie, it positively is Polaire, our little lily."

"Their Tiger-Lily," added Maugis, who was mimicking a cake-walk with extravagant nigger-minstrel's hip wrigglings. I was ashamed to find myself laughing at his contortions as he sang with a nasal twang:

> *"She draws niggers like a crowd of flies*
> *She is my sweetest one, my baby Tiger-Lily!"*

So now I had all the information I needed!

Insensibly, I had drawn closer to the two friends in my curiosity . . . Claudine caught sight of me and beckoned me with an imperious gesture. Feeling very self-conscious, I found myself confronting this little actress who barely glanced at me, being far too busy standing on one foot, tossing back her dark hair that had tawny glints in it, and feverishly explaining something or other in a throaty, twanging voice.

"You see, Claudine, if I mean to do serious drama, I've got to know all the serious drama before my time. So I've come to Bayroot to get educated."

"It was your duty," said Claudine with grave approval—though her tobacco-brown eyes were dancing with jubilant mischief.

"They've put me up right at the other end of the town, at the back of beyond—over there, at the Bamboo Cabin . . ."

Claudine saw my astonishment at the peculiar name of the hotel and informed me, with angelic kindness:

"It's the Margravine's bamboo."

"It doesn't matter," went on Polaire. "I don't regret coming all this way, although! . . . You know, at Madame Marchand's, they produced it quite differently from here, and besides, their Wagner isn't anything to make you fall flat on your fanny! . . . As to his music, why it's just like a band! Makes me want to salute and slap my right thigh."

"Just the way Annie expresses it," slipped in Claudine, with a glance at me.

"Ah, Madame says that too? Pleased to meet you . . . What was I saying? Oh, yes . . . This makes it twice I've been to *Parsifal* to make sure wherever you go, you find lousy people. You saw

Kundry, that bandeau she had round her forehead, and then those flowers, and that veil hanging down? Well, that's exactly the head-dress Landorff designed for me for the Wintergarten in Berlin, that year I bored myself stiff singing '*Little Cohn*'!"

Polaire exulted for a moment, then paused for breath, oscillating on her high heels and wriggling her abnormally small waist which she could have belted with a man's collar.

"You ought to sue," Claudine advised fervently.

Polaire started like a fawn and launched forth again:

"Never, it's beneath me . . ." (her beautiful eyes darkened). "*I'm* not like other women. Anyway, what's the good? Sue these Boches? Oh, bother . . . where's my nail buffer got to? . . . Besides there'd be no end to it . . . Actually again in their *Parsifal* . . . just listen . . . in act three when the fat man's dipping in the water and that hairy bloke's sprinkling him, well that chap's attitude, with his hands folded flat and his body turned at that three-quarter angle is *absolutely* my gesture in *Berber Song*, that he's pinched from me. Just imagine my agony! And all my side, Claudine, the right of my corsets, all the bones are broken!"

I studied her fascinating face, so mobile that it was like watching a cinema film as it swiftly registered in turn excitement, rebellion, a negro ferocity, an enigmatic melancholy whose shadow was dispersed by an abrupt, jerky laugh as Polaire flung up her pointed chin like a dog baying the moon. Then all at once, she simply left us standing, with a grave childish goodbye, like a well brought-up little girl's.

For a moment, I followed her with my eyes, watching her swift walk, the deft way she threaded her way through the groups, with a quick swing of her hips and broken gestures that reminded one of her broken syntax, her whole body leaning slightly forward, like a clever animal walking on its hind legs.

"A sixteen-inch waist!" said Claudine reflectively.

"It's a size in shoes, not in belts."

"Annie? . . . Annie, I'm talking to you!"

"Yes, yes, I'm listening!" I said, coming to with a start.

"What have I just been talking about?"

Under my sister-in-law's inquisitorial eye, I became confused and averted my head.

"I don't know, Marthe."

She shrugged her shoulders which one could almost see showing pink under a white lace bodice with deep-cut armholes. A wildly indecent bodice . . . but since it is high-necked, Marthe displays herself like that in the street and remains perfectly cool and collected under the gaze of the men. I am the one who is embarrassed.

Armed with a spray, she was over-lavishly scenting her pinkish-red hair—her beautiful hair that is as vital and rebellious as she is.

"That's enough, Marthe, that's enough, you smell too good as it is."

"Never too good. For one thing, I'm always afraid of people saying I smell like a red-head! Now that you've come down from your cloud, I'll start all over again. We're dining tonight at the Berlin . . . Maugis is standing treats."

"Again!"

The word had slipped out in spite of me and Marthe spiked it in mid-air with a glance as sharp as a dagger.

"What d'you mean—'again'? Anyone would think we were sponging on Maugis. It's his turn, we invited him the day before yesterday."

"And last night?"

"Last night? That was entirely different—he wanted to show us that Sammet place—it's supposed to be a historic eating house. Anyway, the food was revolting in that hole—tough meat and flabby fish. He definitely owes us a decent meal to make up for it."

"Owes you and Léon, maybe, but not me."

"It shows his good manners, always including you too."

"Good manners . . . how much I wish that just for tonight he'd revert to his normal ones!"

Marthe combed her back hair with savage little tugs.

"Charming! Quite a neat sarcasm! You're definitely coming on. Is it seeing so much of Claudine?"

She put so much acidity into the question that I shivered as if she had scratched me with the tip of her nails.

"I've less to lose by seeing so much of Claudine than you have by seeing so much of Maugis."

She turned on me; her piled up hair was like a helmet of writhing flames.

"Advice? You've got a ruddy cheek! Yes, a ruddy cheek to meddle in my affairs and take it on yourself to tell me how to behave. I've got a husband to do that, you know! And I'm amazed you *dare* to find anything improper in something Léon accepts as perfectly all right!"

"*Please*, Marthe . . ."

"Had enough, eh? Well, mind you don't let it happen again! Monsieur Maugis is simply a very devoted friend."

"Marthe, I implore you not to go on. Insult me as much as you like but don't try and set up 'Monsieur Maugis' as a perfectly blameless, devoted friend and Léon as a despotic husband . . . You can't think me quite such a fool!"

She had not expected this. She held her breath, with an effort, for she was panting with fury. She struggled hard with herself for a long minute, and finally mastered herself with a power that proved to me how frequent these rages were.

"Now, now Annie . . . don't take advantage of me. You know how easily I flare up. I believe you're teasing me on purpose . . ."

She smiled, the corners of her mouth still quivering.

"You're coming to dinner with us, aren't you?"

I still hesitated. She put her arm round my waist, clever and coaxing as when she wanted to smooth down Alain.

"You owe that to my reputation! Just think if people see all four of us together, they may think it's you that Maugis is running after!"

We were good friends again, but I could feel our friendship cracking like a white frost in the sun. I was very tired. Ever since yesterday a migraine had been dully threatening me; this little scene had brought it on in full force. Nevertheless, I felt it was almost worth it. Only a month ago, I would not have had the courage to tell Marthe even half what I was thinking . . .

As we drove to the *Flying Dutchman*, I sat perfectly mute in the carriage, with my finger pressed to my temple, too stupefied to utter a word. Léon asked compassionately:

"Migraine, Annie?"

"Yes, unfortunately."

He nodded his head and gazed at me sympathetically with his gentle, spaniel-like eyes. For some time, I too have felt extremely sorry for him. If Marthe wears the trousers, *he* may well be wearing . . . Claudine would have brought out the word without the slightest hesitation. My sister-in-law, sitting tranquilly beside me was flouring her cheeks in an effort to overcome the heat.

"We shan't see Maugis up there," observed my brother-in-law, "he's keeping to his room."

"Ah!" ejaculated Marthe indifferently.

Her lips had tightened as if to suppress a smile.

"Is he ill?" I asked. "Perhaps slightly too many grogs last night?"

"No. But he says the *Flying Dutchman* is a piece of sentimental filth, the dregs of Italian-German opera and all the performers lousy. I assure you, Annie, those were his exact words. He also added that the mere thought of Daland the fisherman, Senta's father, gives him a violent pain in his guts."

"It's a somewhat personal type of criticism," I said ungraciously.

Marthe looked away and did not seem anxious to pursue the conversation. On our left, the empty carriages were returning at a fast trot, raising clouds of dust, whereas we were climbing the hill almost at a walk, jammed in the file of traffic . . . I have only seen it four times, that brick theatre (Claudine is perfectly right, it *does* look like a gasometer) the brightly-dressed crowd surrounding it, the row of local inhabitants stupidly sneering at the visitors, yet every time I look at that scene again, I feel the same almost physical impatience that used to come over me sometimes in Paris when I stared at the restricted, intolerably well-known view from my bedroom window. But in those days I had less sensitive nerves and a master who made it his business to keep me dull-witted. I was almost afraid to think and to look about me.

I would not admit to anyone but myself and to these useless pages of my diary, how disillusioned I am with Bayreuth. There is nothing much to choose between an interval during *Parsifal* and a Paris tea-party—a "five o'clock" at my sister-in-law Marthe's or at that loathsome Valentine Chessenet's. The same ill-natured tittle-tattle; the same passion for gossip and scandal, even for out-and-out slander; the same trivial small talk in which the latest fashions, the latest composers, greed and indecency are all equally entertaining topics.

Once again, I longed to get away. At Arriège, I used to gaze at the rift of light between two mountain peaks: here my eyes follow the trails of smoke as they stream away to the east . . . Where could I escape from monotonous sameness, from the all too well-known, from mediocrity and malice? Perhaps I ought to have done what Claudine said . . . accompanied Alain in spite of himself? No, for with Alain—and in him—I should only have found once again the very things I want to escape from . . . Migraine, alas, is a depressing and realistic adviser and I listened to it more attentively than I did to the *Flying Dutchman* . . . Ether, oblivion, cool unconsciousness . . . those were the only things that attracted me . . . A mark in the hand of the old man who showed us into our seats bought me my liberty and authorised my silent escape . . . "This lady is ill . . ."

I ran, I jumped into a carriage, and soon I was in my room where Toby, who was sleeping sentimentally on my slippers, barked affectionately to see me back so soon. *He* loves me! And someone else loves me—*I* do! I take more pleasure in looking at myself nowadays. Away from that white man whose gleaming skin made me seem so black, I find myself prettier and exactly, as Marthe said, like a slender fine brownstone jar, with two wild chicory flowers in it. Claudine talked as if she were thinking aloud: "Blue flowers, look at me—eyes fringed like a pool among black rushes . . ." But her friendly arm had withdrawn . . .

At last, at last, I was lying half-undressed face down on the bed with the heavenly bottle under my nostrils. Suddenly, I could feel myself flying; I could feel the cool sting of imaginary drops of water all over my body; the cruel blacksmith's arm grew slacker and slacker . . . But I was still awake under my semi-drunken stupor; I did not want that heavy sleep, that swoon from which one emerges nauseated. All I wanted from the little Genie of ether, that crafty comforter with the sweet, ambiguous smile was the fanning of wings and the gentle rocking that turned my bed into a swing . . .

The brief, furious barking of the little dog awakened me. Frozen with terror, I groped for my watch. Nonsense, they wouldn't search for me up there, by the "gasometer" . . . They were far too concerned with their own affairs to be concerned about me . . . All told, my escape and my brief drunken stupor had taken up only an hour. I thought it had been far longer. "Oh, be quiet," I implored Toby, "for goodness' sake be quiet . . . my ears cannot bear noise just now . . ."

He obeyed regretfully, laid his square nose on his paws and blew out his long dewlaps, still barking internally. My good little watch-dog, my little black friend, I shall take you wherever I go . . . He listened and I listened too: a door shut in the room next to mine—Marthe's room. No doubt it was the ever-obliging Madame Meider who had gone in to "tidy things"—to open the little silver boxes and straighten out the illustrated Paris papers scrunched up into balls in the waste-paper basket.

Yesterday, as I passed through the hall, I caught the four little Meider girls in pinafores, carefully smoothing out a crumpled number of *La Vie en Rose* with their grubby hands. The four little Meider girls will learn French from it—and something else into the bargain.

No, it was not Madame Meider. They were speaking French . . . Why, it was Marthe! Marthe who had come to enquire after me: I had not expected such devoted solicitude! Marthe's voice and a man's. Léon? No.

Half-undressed, sitting on my bed with my legs dangling over the edge, I strained my ears to hear but I could not manage to. The ether was still buzzing, faintly, in my ears . . .

My chignon was coming down. A tortoise-shell hairpin slid down the nape of my neck, soft and cold as a little snake. Whatever must I have looked like, with my bodice undone and my skirt pulled up showing my dusky skin and my shoes still on my feet! The greenish mirror reflected my ravaged face—pallid lips; glazed eyes, puckered at the outer corners, with purple shadows under them like bruises . . . But whoever was that talking in Marthe's bedroom?

There was an incessant murmur of voices, punctuated now and then by a loud laugh or by an ejaculation from my sister-in-law . . . Definitely, a very peculiar kind of conversation . . .

Suddenly there was a shriek! A man's voice let out an oath, then Marthe's voice exclaimed irritably: "Keep your foot still, can't you?"

Shocked to the core, for Marthe had used the familiar "*tu*" which she never used to her husband, I did up my blouse with trembling hands and pulled down my skirt as if someone had suddenly come into the room. My clumsy fingers kept ineffectively sticking the same pin into my hair a dozen times without making it stay up . . . Whoever could it be behind that wall, alone with Marthe?

There was complete silence now. What ought I to do? Suppose the *man* had hurt Marthe? Ah, how I wished he *had* only done her some physical injury, that he had been a thief, a prowler armed with a knife, for now I was imagining all sorts of things more revolting than any crime going on behind that door. I wanted to see, I wanted to know . . .

I grabbed the handle and pushed the door open with all my might, one hand put up to shield my face as if I were afraid someone was going to hit me . . .

What I saw, without fully taking it in at first, was Marthe's milky-white back and her plump shoulders naked above her pulled-down chemise. Then I realised, to my horror, she was sitting on Maugis's knees. Maugis, scarlet in the face, was slumped in an armchair . . . apparently fully dressed. Marthe screamed then leapt to her feet revealing the disarray of that loathsome man with her.

Planted there squarely in front of me, in a pair of long linen drawers with voluminous, frilly legs, with her white face and her wobbling red chignon, she irresistibly suggested a female clown at a carnival. But what a tragic clown, paler than the traditional flour could make her, her eyes dilated and deadly! I stood there, unable to speak.

Maugis found his tongue first. He said in a caddishly flippant way:

"Come on, Marthe, now the kid's caught us out, we might as well finish our little orgy . . . What's the risk?"

With a curt nod, she showed him the door. Then she bore down on me and pushed me into my room so roughly that I staggered and nearly fell.

"What are you doing here? Did you follow us?"

"Good heavens, no!"

"You're lying!"

I straightened myself up and dared to look her in the face.

"No, I'm not lying. I had a migraine and I came home. I gave something to the man at the door so that he'd let me through. I . . ."

Marthe laughed, without opening her mouth, as if she had hiccups.

"Ah, so you know that dodge too . . . the mark to the man at the door? You're ripe for the big stuff now, Alain had better watch out . . . I admit your migraine, but why the hell did you come bursting into my bedroom?"

How bold a woman can be! This one was back in her element, she was once again the indomitable little flame-thrower on the barricade.

With her hands on her hips, she would have braved an army, with the same white face, the same hard, unflinching eyes . . .

"Are you going to talk? What do you expect to get for running off to Léon to tell him he's a cuckold?"

I blushed, both at the word and at the suspicion.

"I shan't do that, Marthe. You know that quite well."

She stared at me for a moment, her eyebrows raised.

"Nobility of soul? No. I can't swallow that. More likely a trick, to keep a hold on me for the rest of my life. You can get rid of that notion. I'd rather go and tell that other imbecile myself."

I made a gesture of weary impatience.

"You don't understand me. It isn't only the . . . the thing itself that shocks me . . . it's your choosing that cad . . . Oh, Marthe, *that* man of all men . . ."

That wounded her, and she bit her lip. Then she shrugged her shoulders, with a gesture at once sad and cynical.

"Yes, yes. You're another of those simpletons for whom adultery . . . a conventional word you like, eh? . . . ought to be hidden in bowers of flowers, and to be ennobled by passion, by the beauty of the lovers, by their oblivion of the world . . . There, there my poor girl, keep your illusions! Personally I'll keep my own particular worries and my own particular tastes . . . That cad as you call him, possesses among other qualities an open purse, a kind of lewd wit I rather enjoy, and the tact to ignore jealousy. He smells of the bar? Maybe he does. Even so, I much prefer that smell to Léon's—who smells of cold veal."

As if suddenly exhausted, she collapsed on a chair.

"Everyone hasn't the luck to sleep with Alain, my dear. In fact it's a privilege reserved to a small number of females . . . whom I don't envy all that much."

What was she going to say next? She flashed me a malicious smile before adding:

"Anyway, without wishing to be unjust to him, that delicious brother of mine must be a rotten lover. 'Toc, toc, that's that. See you again soon, dear lady.' Eh?"

I turned away my head; there were tears in my eyes. Marthe swiftly hooked up her dress, pinned on her hat and went on talking in a dry, feverish voice:

". . . So I can't understand why Valentine Chessenet was crazy about him for so long . . . considering she's an expert in men . . ."

It was indeed the name I was dreading. But I too was brave in my own way; I waited for what was to come without flinching.

My sister-in-law put on her gloves, grabbed her parasol and opened the door.

"Eighteen months, my dear, eighteen months of letter-writing and regular meetings. Twice a week . . . as regularly as a piano lesson."

I stroked the little bull-terrier with a hand that had gone quite cold. Marthe lowered the veil of a hat entirely covered with roses, licked the superfluous rouge off her lips and studied me covertly in the glass. But I made sure she saw nothing.

"Was it a long time ago, Marthe? I certainly heard plenty of rumours but nothing very precise."

"A long time ago? Yes, quite a long time. It's been over since last Christmas . . . so I'm told. Nearly eight months—it's ancient history . . . Farewell, noble soul!"

She slammed the door. She was undoubtedly telling herself: "I've hit back. A good, telling blow! Let Annie talk now if she likes! I've had my revenge in advance."

She did not know that what she thought was a mortal blow had been dealt not at a person but only at his empty garment.

When she had gone, I felt utterly exhausted, physically and mentally. Every muscle in my body was stiff and aching; my mind was a whirling fog in which depression, the shame and shock of what I had seen, the inability to decide what I ought to do all mingled together in wearying confusion. At last I was clearly conscious of one thing—the impossibility of seeing Marthe every day, every hour without seeing the odious face of that gross, almost fully-clothed man beside her insolent grace . . . Was that adultery and could one believe that what they were doing bore any resemblance to love? Alain's brief, monotonous love-making did not soil me as much as that, and, thank God, if I had to choose . . . But I did not want to choose.

Neither did I want to stay on here, even though I would not hear *Tristan*, and not see Claudine again . . . Goodbye, elusive Claudine! For, ever since that troubled hour when she guessed so much of my misery, when I felt so close to loving her, Claudine has avoided any occasion of seeing me alone and smiles at me from a distance as if at some place she were sorry to leave.

No, I must look for some other way out! The summer was nearly over. For the first time, I realised that Alain would soon be embarking on his return voyage and I childishly pictured him loaded with great sacks of gold, red gold like his hair . . .

A paragraph from his last letter came back to my mind: "I have noticed, my dear Annie, that certain of the women in this country resemble you in type. The most pleasing of them have, like you, long, heavy black hair, beautiful thick eyelashes, smooth brown skins and the same taste for idleness and day-dreaming. But the climate here explains and excuses these tendencies of theirs. Perhaps living here might have altered many things between us . . ."

What! Could that clear-cut, positive mind become hazy too? Was he confusedly thinking of revising and modifying our . . . our "time-table"? Mercy, how many more changes, surprises, disillusions! I was weary at the prospect of having to begin my life all over again. Some clean, quiet corner; new faces which conveyed nothing to me of what was going on behind them . . . that was all, absolutely all, I wanted!

With a great effort, I got up and went off to look for my maid . . . I found her in the kitchen, surrounded by the four ecstatic little Meiders to whom she was singing in a robust baritone voice:

> *"I lov-er yew with love so trew*
> *Night and day, I dream of yew . . ."*

"Léonie, I want you to pack my things. I'm leaving at once."

She followed me, too dumbfounded to answer. The four little Meiders would never know the end of that waltz . . .

Cantankerously, she dived into my trunk.

"Am I to pack Madame Léon's trunk too?"

"No, no, I'm leaving alone, with you and Toby." I added nervously: "I've received a telegram."

Léonie's back expressed complete disbelief.

"You'll take a cab to the station with the luggage as soon as you're ready. I'll meet you there with the dog."

I was so terrified they would return! I kept glancing every minute at my watch. For once I blessed those interminable performances. At least they would cover my escape.

I paid my bill without looking at it and left an enormous tip that made the four little girls in pinafores jump for joy. The Franconians have no false pride!

At last, there I was alone with Toby, wearing his leather and badger-hair travelling collar. His little black face followed my every movement; he understood and sat patiently waiting, his metal lead trailing on the carpet. I had still a quarter-of-an-hour to spare. I wrote a hurried note to Marthe and sealed it in an envelope. "I'm leaving for Paris. Make whatever explanation you like to Léon."

My heart was heavy at the thought of how alone I was in the world. I would like to have left a more affectionate farewell message to someone . . . but to whom? Suddenly, I thought I knew.

"My dear Claudine,

Something unexpected forces me to leave immediately. It's a very upsetting, very hurried departure. But don't go and suppose some accident has happened to Alain or Marthe—or to me. I am leaving because everything here oppresses me. Bayreuth is not far enough from Arriège, nor Arriège far enough from Paris, to which I am returning.

You have made me see only too clearly that where there is no great love, there is only mediocrity or misery. I do not yet know what remedy I shall find: I am going away to make a change, and to wait.

Perhaps you could have kept me here, you who radiate faith and tenderness. But, ever since the Margravine's garden, you no longer seem to want to. No doubt you are justified. It is right that you should keep that flame that you warmed me with for a moment whole and intact for Renaud.

At least write me a letter—just one letter. Comfort me and tell me, even if you have to lie, that my misery is not beyond all alleviation. For the thought of Alain's return fills me with such troubled apprehension that even hope seems dim and unreal to me.

Goodbye . . . give me some advice. Let me lay my head, in spirit, on your shoulder as I did in the Margravine's garden.

Annie"

9

Iᴛ was eleven in the morning when I arrived in Paris. It looked arid and dejected as Paris always does at the end of summer. I felt empty and sick: I seemed to have come back from the other end of the world with only one desire, to lie down on the spot and go to sleep. Leaving Léonie to struggle with the Customs, I fled straight home in a cab . . .

When it stopped outside the house, the concierge, out of uniform and in his shirtsleeves, came out on the doorstep with his wife, my cook. Her mottled cheeks turned streaky white and red at the sight of me . . . Absent-mindedly, I read on their dull faces surprise, embarrassment and the offended dignity of correct servants confronted with someone who has behaved incorrectly . . .

"It's Madame! . . . But we never received Madame's telegram!"

"That's because I didn't send one."

"Ah, that's what I said too . . . Monsieur is not with Madame?"

"Obviously not. Get me some lunch as soon as possible . . . Anything will do . . . some eggs, a cutlet . . . Léonie's following on with the luggage."

I walked slowly up the stairs, followed by the concierge who hastily put on a green livery coat with tarnished buttons. I stared, feeling like a stranger, at this little house Alain had insisted on buying . . . Personally, I had not wanted it in the least. But my opinion had not been asked . . . Nevertheless, I think that, below a certain price, a small town house is more commonplace and more uncomfortable than a flat . . .

What did all that matter now? I felt as indifferent as if I were a traveller arriving at a hotel. There were dirty finger-marks on the white door of my bedroom . . . the electric light bulb in the passage had gone . . . From force of habit I opened my mouth to order the paint to be washed, and the bulb renewed . . . Then I changed my mind and turned away.

When I opened the door of my yellow and white bedroom, I softened a trifle and lost some of my courage. On that little lacquered desk, where not much dust was visible, I had written the first lines of my notebook . . . In that great flat bed where my light weight barely makes a hollow, I had experienced, as if in a dream, migraine, fear, resignation, the fleeting shadow of love, unsatisfied desire. What should I dream about in it now, deprived of my fear, my resignation, of even the shadow of love? It was extraordinary that a creature as weak as myself, so dependent on physical and moral support, should somehow find herself alone and not perish at once like a convolvulus whose tendrils have been torn away from what they clung to? Perhaps one did wither away like that—so quickly . . . Mechanically, I went over and looked at myself in the glass over the chimney-piece.

I would not have been astonished to see a wasted, diminished Annie appear in the glass, an Annie with even narrower shoulders and an even more drooping body than before the summer began . . . My reflection surprised me and I leant on my elbows to study it at closer range.

The dark hair, matted by a night in the train made a harsh frame to the still slender oval of a brown face. But that pucker of weariness at the corners of the lips was not the only thing that altered the line of the mouth, a mouth firmer and less beseeching than formerly . . . As to the eyes, their gaze was more direct; the eyelids kept steady instead of constantly fluttering and drooping under the weight of the silky lashes. I would never be able to look at you again, "wild chicory-flowers", my amazingly clear eyes, my one real beauty, without thinking of Claudine bending down over them and saying teasingly: "Annie, they're so clear, you can see right through to the other side." Alas, it was true. Clear as an empty bottle. Moved by that memory, vaguely intoxicated by the novelty of my reflected image, I bent my head and touched my ungloved hand with my lips . . .

"Am I to unpack Madame's trunk?"

Léonie had come in, out of breath, and was running a hostile eye over the room which would have to be given "a thorough good do".

"I don't know, Léonie . . . I'm waiting for a letter . . . Only take out the silk dresses and petticoats—the rest can wait . . ."

"Very good, Madame. Actually I've got a letter for you here from Monsieur that the porter was going to send on to Germany."

I snatched the unexpected letter from her. So as to read it by myself, I went off into Alain's study where I pushed back the shutters myself.

"My dear Annie,

It is a very tired husband who is writing to you. Don't be alarmed; I said 'tired', not 'ill'. I have had a hard struggle. I have already told you of the difficulties of converting bulls into ready money and I will tell you again in more detail when I see you. I am delighted to have emerged from them honourably and to be bringing back a handsome sum. You should be grateful to me, Annie, for undertaking this journey which enables me to increase the amenities of our home and to offer you a sable stole as handsome as the one belonging to Madame . . . you know whom I mean? . . . my sister disrespectfully calls her: 'the Chessenet'.

The sun is oppressive at this hour so I am profiting by it to catch up with my correspondence. Out in the courtyard a girl is sitting sewing, or pretending to sew. There is really a quite singular resemblance, which I have remarked many times, between her bent, motionless profile, with the chignon on the nape of the neck, and yours, Annie. The red flower is an addition, of course, so is the little yellow shawl. All the same, it amuses me to watch her and makes my thoughts stray towards you and towards my return which is now only a matter of days . . ."

Of days! It was true, he had been gone a long time . . . But days! . . . I had begun to believe he would never return. And now he was going to come back, he was going to leave that distant land, that dark girl who looked like me and whom perhaps, on stormy nights, he called Annie . . . He was going to come back and I had not yet decided my fate and plucked up courage against myself and against him!

Without picking up the letter I had dropped on the carpet, I gazed about me reflectively. This study, which serves as a smoking-room had not kept any imprint of its master. There was nothing lying about in it and nothing in it to charm. The tapestry that had been taken down for the summer left a great panel of white, unpapered wall. I felt thoroughly miserable here; I would not stay on in Paris.

"Léonie!"

The good policeman came running, a skirt dangling from each of her forefingers.

"Léonie, I want to leave tomorrow for Casamène."

"For Casamène. Oh, goodness me, no!"

"What do you mean, no?"

"Madame hasn't written to the gardener's wife, the house is shut up and hasn't been cleaned, there won't be any food got in. And besides I need a good two days for the things that needs doing here—there's Madame's everyday skirts that's got their lining torn, there's the white linen dress what we couldn't find a cleaner for in Germany and the petticoat what goes with it as needs new lace putting on, and then there's . . ."

I put both hands over my ears—Léonie's grammar showed she was seriously upset.

"That'll do, that'll do! You shall have two days for all that. Only write yourself to the gardener's wife and tell her . . ." (I hesitated for a moment) ". . . tell her I'm only bringing you. She's to do the cooking."

"Very good, Madame."

Léonie made a dignified exit. Once again, I had offended her. One has to be so careful with one's subordinates! All the servants who have passed through this house have been hypersensitives, illtempered ones too, who fiercely resented other people's changes of mood and let it appear on their faces—when Alain was absent.

I am leaving tomorrow. It is high time, my patience is worn out. All this setting of my married life has become intolerable to me, even the Louis XV drawing-room where on Fridays I used to wait, meek and terrified, for the ring that announced the first caller. I exaggerate: in those days which seem strangely far away I was more meek than terrified and almost happy in a timid, colourless way. Is my lot any better today, wandering hither and thither, demoralised yet more self-willed? It's a very arduous problem for such a tired brain.

I am leaving nothing of myself behind in this little house, tall and narrow as a tower. Alain did not want Grandmother Lajarrisse's furniture; it has remained at Casamène. Some books, two or three photographs of Annie—the rest belongs to my husband.

Three years ago I gave him a little English desk which he has graciously kept ever since in his study. Today I indiscreetly pulled the brass handle of the drawer, which resisted. A methodical man locks his drawers when he goes off on a long journey. Looking at it closer, I discovered it was sealed with a little, almost invisible strip of gummed paper . . . Obviously my husband did not completely trust his domestic staff. But had he only been thinking of his man-servant when he devised such a carefully concealed precaution? . . . Suddenly, I had a vision of Marthe's venomous face: "Eighteen months, my dear, eighteen months of continuous correspondence and regular meetings . . ."

I felt I would rather like to know what Valentine Chessenet's style was like. I can swear that it was not a sudden access of physical jealousy or some feverish compulsion that made me want to open that drawer . . . It was simply that I reached a stage where scruples seemed an absurd luxury . . .

One after another, all the keys on my little bunch proved useless for the English lock. I disliked the idea of asking anyone's assistance. I looked round and saw a flat metal ruler lying on the writing-table . . . Yes, it would do to make a lever under the drawer. What hard work it was! The exertion made me hot and I broke my thumb-nail, such a well-manicured little pink nail on my brown hand. There was an appallingly loud crack . . . suppose the servants came in, thinking there had been an accident? I listened for a moment, terrified. Thieves must often die of heart-failure!

The light ash-wood had split. A little more work and the whole front of the pretty desk was smashed and ripped off. It fell to the ground, followed by an avalanche of papers.

I felt as abashed as a little girl who has upset a box of chocolates. Where should I begin? It would not take long; each little bundle, methodically secured by a rubber band, bore a label.

Here were *Receipted Bills*, here were *Title Deeds*, here were *Papers concerning lawsuit over building-plots* (what building-plots?), then came *Receipts from Marthe* (ah?), *Letters from Annie* (three in all), *Letters from*

Andrée (but which Andrée?), letters . . . letters . . . letters . . . ah, at last! *Letters from Valent*:

I went over to the door and quietly locked it. Then, sitting on the floor, I spread the quite thick bundle out on my lap.

"My beloved Carrots . . ." "My little white man." (She too!) "Dear Friend." "Monsieur." "Naughty boy." "Fickle brute." "My copper coffee-pot . . ." The appellations certainly varied considerably more than the theme of the letters. Nevertheless, it had been a complete idyll. One could follow it chronologically from the first little note: "I made a fatal error by giving myself so quickly . . ." up to "There is nothing I shall not do to get you back. I shall even seek you out at home with your little black goose . . ."

In the margin on the back of these letters, Alain had noted in his stiff writing: "Received the . . ." "Answered the . . . by telegram." I would have recognised him just by that trait. Ah! *She* could call him beloved Carrots, white pussy-cat, tea-pot, coffee-pot, whatever she fancied . . . he would still be the same man!

What should I do with all this stuff? Send the packet of letters to Alain's address, in a sealed envelope addressed in my writing? That was what people did in novels. But he would think I still loved him and was jealous. No . . . I left all the papers on the floor at the foot of the ravaged desk, along with the flat ruler and my bunch of little keys. The only thing I took away was *Letters from Annie.* My pillaging had made glorious havoc of that tidy soulless room . . . I would give a good deal to see Alain's face when he returns!

A blue envelope lay beside my cup on the breakfast tray. I guessed more by the fat round handwriting than by the Bavarian stamp that it was Claudine's reply. She had taken pity on me and answered quickly . . . Her handwriting was like her; sensual, lively and upright. The loops were short and graceful; the crosses of the T's exaggerated and masterful.

"My sweet Annie,

So it will be a long time before I see them again, those unique eyes that you hide so often behind your lashes, like a garden behind a grille, for I imagine you have gone off on a long journey . . . And whatever gave you the idea of asking me for an itinerary? I am neither Cook's nor Paul Bourget. Anyway, we'll see about that in a moment. First I must tell you the most urgent thing, which is as banal as a sensational news item.

On the day after your departure, I did not see the Léon ménage at *Tristan*. Your brother-in-law's absence was nothing—but Marthe missing the intervals of *Tristan*, the most sensational ones after *Parsifal*! We returned from the theatre on foot as usual, me hanging on the arm of my dear great man, and we thought we'd both go a little out of our way to enquire after Marthe. Horrors! The respectable Meider home was open to all comers and four little girls in pink pinafores were scurrying about like rats. Finally, I caught sight of Marthe with her red mane standing on end, who slammed the door in our face to prevent us from entering . . . Renaud parleyed with a maid, listened to what she was moaning in Bavarian punctuated by cries of *Yo!* and led me away, so astonished that he almost looked stupid . . . I exaggerate.

Do you know what, Annie? Léon had just poisoned himself like a shop girl whose young man has chucked her! He had drunk laudanum and so enthusiastically that he had given himself appalling indigestion! You'll immediately think that Liane's suicide must have haunted that eminently Parisian brain. Not at all. In the course of a lively scene, Marthe, in a very irritable mood—history does not record why—had called her spouse 'cuckold' so frequently and with so much conviction that the wretched man no longer doubted what is called in journalese 'the extent of his misfortune'.

The next day I went out to reconnoitre on my own. Marthe received me like a model wife, told me about the 'fatal mistake' and got up a dozen times to rush to the invalid's bedside . . . Maugis was not there because an urgent telegram had summoned him to Béziers the night before. It's curious, all the same, Annie, how many urgent departures one sees among the French colony at Bayreuth!

Don't be alarmed, nervous child; the suicide is going on well. Marthe nurses him like a horse who's due to run in the Grand-Prix. In a few days he'll be fit enough to get back to his work at the rate of eighty lines a day instead of sixty to make up for lost time. Your sister-in-law is an intelligent woman who understands to perfection that the situation of a married woman is far superior to that of a divorced one, or to certain widowhoods, even of a lucrative kind.

Now you are up to date with the news. Let us talk about you.

About you, you embarrassing little creature, so slow at getting to know herself; so swift, when the appointed day came, to fly away, silent and black-capped, like a migrating swallow.

You are going away, and your flight and your letter are like a reproach to me. How much I regret you, Annie, who smells like a rose! You mustn't be angry with me for that. I am only a poor brute who loves beauty and weakness and trust and when a little spirit like yours leans on mine, when a mouth yearns, like yours, towards mine, I find it very hard to understand why I must not embellish both the one and the other with a kiss. I tell you I still don't properly understand the reason, although it has been explained to me.

People must have spoken to you, Annie, about me and a woman friend whom I loved too simply, too completely. She was a vicious, fascinating seducer, that Rézi; she tried to put her naked blonde loveliness between me and Renaud to give herself the literary pleasure of betraying us both . . . Because of her, I have promised Renaud—and Claudine too—to forget there may be weak, tempting, pretty creatures whom a gesture of mine might charm and enslave . . .

You are going away and I can guess that you are all confused in your mind. I hope, for your sake and his, that your husband will not be coming back at once. You are neither sufficiently clear-sighted nor sufficiently resigned. The fact that you do not love him is an unhappiness, a calm grey unhappiness—yes, Annie, an ordinary unhappiness. But think that you might have loved without return, or loved and been deceived . . . That is the only great unhappiness, the unhappiness for which one kills, burns, annihilates . . . Forgive me, Annie, I was on the point of forgetting that, here, we are only concerned with you . . . A woman in love finds it very hard to conceal her egoism.

'Advise me . . .' you implore. How easy that is! I feel you are ready for all sorts of silly acts—which you will perform quietly, with a gentle obstinacy, with that young girl's grace that gives such hesitance and charm to your gestures, soft, supple Annie.

All the same, I can't very well say to you straight 'One can't live with a man one doesn't love, it's filthy indecency,' though that opinion does not differ appreciably from what I really think. But I can at least tell you what *I* did.

Loaded with a great weight of misery and very little luggage, I went back to my native earth. To die there? To recover there? When I went, I had no idea. The heavenly solitude, the pacifying trees, the blue night that was a good counsellor, the peace of wild animals—those were the things that prevented me from doing something irreparable and gently brought me back to that other land I thought I had lost forever—happiness.

My dear Annie, you can always try.

Goodbye. Don't write to me—except to say that the treatment is working. For I shall be too regretful at being unable to suggest another.

I kiss, from the eyelashes to the chin, your whole face that has the tapering shape and almost the exact colour of a ripe filbert. From so far away, kisses lose their poison and, for a minute, I can pursue our dream in the Margravine's garden—without remorse.

Claudine."

10

CLAUDINE has deceived me. No, that is unjust. Claudine has deceived herself. The "country cure" is not a panacea. Besides, it is difficult to cure a sick person unless he has faith.

In the first pages of this diary . . . (I had to break off here to scold Toby who, with his ears pricked and his eyes starting out of his head, had once again dragged it away by one corner like the corpse of an enemy.) In the first pages of this diary which has no end and no beginning, which is depraved and diffident, vacillating and rebellious just like myself, I read these words: "the burden of living alone". Ignorant Annie! What does *that* burden weigh, compared with the chain I have worn, without respite, for four years and which I must assume again for life? But I do not want to resume it. It is not liberty in itself that I crave for—I need no further proof of that than my feverish need to keep changing my surroundings and the bitter awareness of my own solitude that makes me see it reflected in this lonely landscape of sky and fields and harsh, grey, red-gashed rocks . . . Yet to be able to choose one's own misery . . . there are certain people for whom that represents their ideal of happiness . . .

Alas! I am one of them. I have hardly arrived and already I want to leave. Even though Casamene belongs to me, it is too much associated with my whole life with Alain. There is not a corner of this old-fashioned estate where I could not easily identify traces left by our childhood games; in the romantic shrubbery, under the trees of the "little forest"—a modest copse which I called by this grandiose name—in the dark gloomy shed where the rusted tools suggest some medieval torture-chamber. Near the ravine, a chestnut-tree still bears the cruel scars of a wire Alain fastened tight round its trunk, maybe twelve years ago; the bark has broken out in a blistered swelling. That was where my stern companion was Snake's-Eye, chief of a tribe of Redskins, and I was his domesticated little squaw who tended the fire of pine-cones. It was one of his favourite games and part of it involved his being extremely severe with me and constantly scolding me.

He has never liked Casamène. My impractical dreamer of a grandfather laid out these few acres in an exaggeratedly picturesque style: a ravine, *wild*, of course; two mounts; a dell; a grotto; a belvedere; a great avenue to give a long vista; exotic shrubs; a paved carriage-drive sufficiently winding to give the impression of traversing miles on his property . . . Everything about the place, Alain used to say, was utterly ridiculous. Very likely it is. At this moment all I see in it is the poignant sadness of an abandoned garden. Under this white sun, already as pallid as in October, it has the mournful luxuriance of a cemetery.

"The pacifying trees! . . ." Ah, Claudine, I could sob if I were not so scared, so petrified by loneliness. The unhappy trees here know no peace themselves and can give none to others. Beautiful, twisted oak with the fettered feet, how many years have you stretched your trembling branches up to the sky, like trembling hands? What straining effort towards freedom bent you under the wind, then forced you upright again so that your limbs are all tortured angles? All round you, your stunted, deformed, earth-bound children are already stretching up beseeching arms.

Other captive creatures, like that silver birch-tree, resign themselves to their fate. So does that delicate larch, but it weeps and shivers under its torrent of silky hair and I can hear its shrill lament from my window as the gusty wind buffets it . . . Oh, the sadness of all these tormented trees, tethered fast by their roots! How could any pliant, uncertain spirit ever have looked to them for peace and oblivion? It was not in trees, Claudine, or in frisking animals, it was only in yourself there lay strength and vitality and joy at once dazzling and blinding.

It is raining, which makes everything worse. I have lit the lamp early and shut myself up in my room. I am in a state of acute nervous tension; even the heavy closed shutters and the sound of Léonie having a loud conversation with the gardener's little girl do little to reassure me. The fire crackles—we need fires already—so does the woodwork. When the flame is quiet, the buzzing silence fills my ears. The clawed feet of a rat are distinctly audible running overhead, above the joists of the ceiling and Toby, my little black guardian, looks up ferociously in the direction of this inaccessible enemy. For heaven's sake, Toby, don't bark! If you bark, the shattered silence will fall in fragments on my head, like the plaster of an old—too old—house . . .

It is late, but I dare not go to bed yet. I shall sit up by the dying fire, till the wick of the lamp burns low. I listen to muffled rustlings, to the breath of the wind blowing the leaves along the gravel, to all the footsteps of small, unknown animals. Just now, to give myself courage, I touched the broad blade of a hunting-knife. But the chill feel of the metal, instead of reassuring me only frightened me more.

What idiotic panic! Don't these friendly pieces of furniture know me any more? Yes, but they know I am going to leave them and they will not shelter me. Old piano with the fluted carving, I wearied you with my scales. "More energy, my little Annie, more energy!" Even then! This portrait of a wasp-waisted student, copied from a daguerreotype, is my grandfather. He dug wells on the tops of mountains, started an enterprise for cultivating truffles, tried to illuminate the bottom of the sea "by means of whale-oil burning in transparent vessels, hermetically sealed"(!); in short he light-heartedly ruined his wife and daughter, showed not the slightest remorse and was adored by both of them. What an elegant waist he had, if the likeness is a true one! A modern woman might envy it. A beautiful, dreamy forehead, the inquisitive eyes of a child, small white-gloved hands—that is all that I know of him.

Above the piano, on the wall, is a bad photograph of my father; I only knew him as old and blind. A distinguished-looking man with white whiskers—how do I come to be the daughter of anyone so . . . ordinary?

Of my mother, nothing. Not a single picture, not a single letter. Grandmother Lajarrisse refused even to talk of her to me; all she ever said was: "Pray for her, my child. Ask God to have mercy on all those who have disappeared, on all exiles, on all the dead . . ." Really, it is rather late in the day to begin worrying about my mother! Let her remain for me what I always imagined her: a pretty, unhappy creature who ran away or who killed herself. I feel sorry for her but not really concerned.

Two letters arrived for me this morning—enough to make me doubly uneasy. The huge one, thank heaven, was from Claudine; the other from Alain. I woke up feeling stronger and more alert, soothed by the freshness of the early hour—the cuckoo-clock in the kitchen had just croaked its two notes eight times—by the fragrant tea steaming in my blue cup, by Toby's delirious jumping up and down and whining as he waited hungrily for me to finish my breakfast and give him his. I could breathe a new lightness and excitement in the air, a holiday atmosphere of going away. That is *my* way of enjoying the peace of the country, Claudine— daydreaming to the jingle of harness-bells on the road . . . I imagined myself as a young woman of the 1830's. A Creole maybe? They were in fashion then. An unhappy marriage—an elopement—my flimsy, inappropriate clothes, my ribboned sandals scuffed by the pebbles on the drive—the heavy chaise—the steaming post-horses—what else? The broken spring, the surprises on the road, the providential encounter . . . All the charming, absurd, sentimental romancing of our grandmothers!

In the envelope with the French stamp, there were only a few lines from Claudine.

"My dear little Annie, I do not know where to find you. I only hope this reaches you to tell you that Marthe, who is back in Paris, explains your flight in a few brief words: 'My sister-in-law is having a difficult pregnancy and has gone to the country to rest.' That was the respite I wished for you! Perhaps everything will seem simpler as a result? This is also to tell you that Léon and his wife appear to be in perfect health—and in perfect harmony.

Goodbye, I just wanted to reassure you—and to warn you. Only that . . . and to have some news of you for I can't be satisfied with Marthe's explanation. I envisaged you menaced by every kind of danger—barring myself. I said: 'Don't write to me if the remedy fails.' But that only applies to the remedy! I want to know everything about *you* . . . about you whom I have so virtuously renounced. A note, a picture-postcard, a telegram, *some* sign . . . Make that my reward, Annie. Cured, or ill, or 'lost' as they say, or even—what Marthe says . . . Ugh! no, not that! Remain the slim fragile amphora that two clasped arms can encircle so easily.

Your

Claudine."

That was all! Yes, that was all. Even Claudine's tender anxiety did not satisfy me. When, like me, one has nothing in oneself one hopes for everything from another . . .

A weary lassitude had clouded that bright hour. Why did I have to be reminded of those other people and those other days? I re-read Claudine's letter and its tiresome solicitude revived dim, almost effaced pictures in my mind. Through a haze of them I stared at the square envelope addressed in Alain's stiff writing without really seeing it . . . Dakar, Dakar . . . where had I seen that name inscribed in black in a little circle? Why Dakar? The last time, it was Buenos Aires . . .

With a cry, I emerged from my daze. Dakar! Why, he was coming back, he was on the way, he was getting nearer, he would be here tomorrow, any moment now! So that was what the treacherous calm of this morning had in store, was it? In opening it, my clumsy fingers tore the letter as well as the envelope, the incredibly neat handwriting danced before my eyes . . . I read at random:

"My dear Annie . . . at last . . . return journey . . . met our friends X . . . travelling for pleasure . . . insist on my staying with them . . . matter of ten days . . . find house ready, Annie happy . . ."

Ten days, ten days! Fate had granted me no longer than that to make up my mind. It was not much. But it would be enough.

"Léonie!"

"Madame?"

She was holding three new-born kittens in her apron and explained, laughingly, to excuse herself:

"I was just a-going to drown 'em."

"Then hurry up and do it. The trunks, the dressing-case—the whole lot strapped up and ready to catch the five o'clock express. We're going back to Paris."

"What, again!"

"Does that annoy you? I should hate to force you to remain a minute longer in service with someone who goes against your wishes."

"I didn't say that, Madame . . ."

"Hurry up. Monsieur tells me he will soon be arriving home."

She went upstairs and I heard her taking her revenge by violently pulling open drawers and slamming the doors of cupboards.

11

A<small>LL</small> these parcels, all these cardboard boxes! The room is permeated with a composite smell of new leather, black tarred paper, and rough, unworn wool, to which the big waterproof cape contributes a quota of bitumen. I have spent my time to some purpose since my hurried return. I have been incessantly at the bootmaker's, the tailor's, the hatter's . . . That sounds like a man talking, not a woman, but fashion is more to blame for that than I am.

In five days I have ordered so many, many things and had them delivered! I have climbed so many stairs, instructed so many obsequious tradesmen, taken off my blouse and skirt so many times and felt my bare arms shiver under the cold fingers of "head fitters" that my head is whirling. Never mind, it's worth it. I am slipping my collar.

At the moment, I am sitting here, slightly dazed, admiring my treasures. Those beautiful big lace-up shoes, flat and tapered as skiffs on their low English heels! One ought to be able to tramp steadily for miles on those little yellow boats. At least, I presume so! My husband preferred me to wear Louis XV heels—more "feminine" . . . Because he preferred them, I don't want any! Neither would he approve in the least of this rust-coloured coat and skirt, the colour of red squirrel's fur, whose trim skirt flares out so simply and neatly. Personally, I love it. Its sober, tailored line makes me look slimmer than ever and its tawny colour emphasises the blue of my eyes—exaggerates it so that it positively makes one's mouth water . . . And those masculine stitched gloves, that severe felt hat trimmed with an eagle's feather! So many novelties, so many gestures of defiance, go to my head as does the unexpected charm of this hotel bedroom. An eminently respectable hotel . . . two steps from our house—no one would ever guess I was in hiding.

Without bothering about probability, I told Léonie: "The house needs urgent repairs. Monsieur will join me at the Impérial-Voyage." Ever since, the poor thing has come round every morning to take orders and to complain.

"Madame, would you believe it? The builder still hasn't come to do those repairs what Madame wrote to him about."

"It's not possible, Léonie! The only thing is . . . perhaps Monsieur has sent him special instructions?"

And I dismiss her with a smile so benevolent that it intimidates her.

I am feeling tired. While I am waiting for tea-time, I am caressing the finest of my new toys with my eyes—but only with my eyes because I am frightened to touch it. My very latest toy; I only bought it a few minutes ago. It is a dainty, dainty little black revolver that looks like Toby. (Toby, *don't* lick that shiny cardboard, you'll give yourself stomach-ache!) It has two safety-catches, six chambers, a cleaning-rod, all sorts of things. I bought it from Alain's gunsmith. The man who sold it to me carefully explained the mechanism, all the while glancing at me furtively with a fatalistic expression as if he were thinking: "Another of them! What a tragedy! So young! Still, after all, I've got to sell my knick-knacks . . ."

I feel remarkably well. I am enjoying the kind of rest I have not known for a long time. Someone with quite good taste must have furnished this little yellow drawing-room and the Louis XVI bedroom that opens out of it. Here, my irritable, fastidious instinct does not suspect dirty carpets or dubious corners in the upholstery. The light falls softly on smooth, polished furniture and matt woodwork painted a restful greyish white. When I go out, an old gentleman in a morning-coat, enthroned behind the desk, smiles at me as if I were his daughter . . . At night I sleep for hours, on a good plump firm mattress.

I had gone off into a momentary daydream that I was a tranquil, middle-aged, dried-up English spinster and that I was staying as a paying guest with a delightful French family when suddenly there was a knock at the door.

"Come in!"

The knock was repeated.

"I said, 'Come in' . . ."

The quaint little chambermaid who looks like a mouse put her head round the door.

"Is it my tea, Marie?"

"Yes, Madame, and a visitor for Madame."

"A visitor!"

I leapt to my feet, still holding my yellow shoes by their laces. The mouse's face looked scared.

"Why yes, Madame! It's a lady."

I trembled all over; there was a buzzing in my ears.

"You're sure it's . . . it's a lady?"

Marie burst out laughing like a stage maid in a comedy: I could hardly blame her.

"Did you say I was in? . . . Tell her to come up."

I leant against the table for support, and waited. A hundred idiotic notions flashed through my mind . . . This lady was Marthe and Alain was with her . . . They were going to take me back . . . I stared insanely at the black toy . . .

A footstep brushed the carpet . . . Good heavens, it was Claudine! How pleased, oh how pleased I was to see her!

I threw myself on her neck with such an "Ah!" of relief that she drew back a little in surprise.

"Annie . . . who were you expecting?"

I pressed her hands, I slipped my arm under hers and pulled her towards the gilded cane sofa with nervous, urgent gestures that she gently repulsed, as if she were uneasy . . .

"Who was I expecting? No one, no one! Oh, I'm so glad it's you!"

Suddenly a suspicion clouded my joy.

"Claudine . . . you haven't been sent? You haven't come on behalf of . . ."

She raised her mobile eyebrows, then frowned impatiently.

"Look here, Annie, we're behaving as if we were acting a scene in a drawing-room comedy . . . you in particular . . . What's happened? And what are you frightened of?"

"Don't be angry, Claudine. It's all so complicated!"

"Do you think so? It's nearly always so simple!"

Meekly, I did not contradict her. She looked pretty, as always, in her own way; her face mysteriously shadowed by a black hat wreathed with blue and white thistles under which I could only make out her eyes, her curly hair and her ironical, pointed chin . . .

"I'd like to tell you everything, Claudine . . . But, first of all, how did you know I was here?"

She raised her forefinger.

"Shh! . . . Once again you must thank Chance—Chance with a capital C, Annie—which is my servant when it isn't my master . . . It led me to the Louvre—the shop not the gallery—which is one of its temples, then under the arcade of the Théâtre-Français, not far from a famous gunsmith's where a slim little creature with burning blue eyes was buying . . ."

"Ah! So that was why . . ."

So she had been frightened too . . . She had supposed . . . It was kind but a little naïve. I smiled surreptitiously.

"What, you mean you thought . . . No, no Claudine, don't be alarmed! People don't do it just like that, for no definite reason . . ."

"Blow their brains out? . . . I fear your argument doesn't convince me. On the contrary, nine times out of ten, it *is* for no definite reason . . ."

She was making fun of me, but all my heart was swelling with gratitude to her. Not for her slightly melodramatic apprehensions just now but because in her, and only in her, I had met with pity, loyalty, affection that had blazed for a moment into passion . . . everything life had denied me.

Her speech was harsh, but her eyes were tender. There was anxiety behind the raillery. She was not quite sure what she ought to prescribe for me. She was an ignorant, intelligent, superstitious little doctor, an osteopath with a touch of divination but lacking in experience . . . I could sense all this but took care not to tell her so. It was too late to change my habits.

"This place might be a lot worse," observed Claudine, looking about her. "This little drawing-room is rather charming."

"Yes, isn't it? And the bedroom—look . . . You wouldn't think you were in a hotel."

"You most certainly wouldn't. It's much more like a delicious little flat people hire for assignations."

"Is it? I don't know anything about those."

"Neither do I, Annie," she laughed. "But I've had them described to me."

This revelation left me brooding. "A flat people hired for assignations . . ." It was an ironical suggestion to make to a woman who was expecting no one!

"Have some tea, Claudine."

"Ugh! How strong it is! Lots of sugar, for goodness' sake. Ah, here's Toby! Come here, Toby, you charming black angel, you square frog, you noble-browed thinker, you sausage on four paws! What an extraordinary mug you've got—like a sentimental murderer—my darling, my precious! . . .

All at once, she had become completely Claudine again. Her hat had fallen off and she was on all fours on the carpet, hugging the little dog with all her might. Toby, who bares his strong, uneven teeth menacingly at everyone, was completely bewitched and let her roll him about like a ball . . .

"Is Fanchette well?"

"Very well thank you. Believe it or not, she's had another three children. That makes nine this year. I shall write to a birth-control specialist. Most shaming children, moreover—greyish, badly marked . . . their father must have been the coal-man or the laundryman . . . But who cares? it does her good."

She drank her cup of tea with both hands, like a little girl. That was how she had held my head tilted back for a minute, for just one minute, in the Margravine's garden . . .

"Claudine . . ."

"What?"

"Nothing . . ."

"Nothing what, Annie?"

"Nothing . . . new. It's for you to question me."

Her eyes changed back from those of a mischievous schoolgirl into a woman's eyes, sombre and penetrating.

"May I? With no subject barred? . . . Good! Has your husband come back?"

Sitting beside her, I lowered my eyes on my folded hands as if I were in the confessional.

"No."

"Is he coming back soon?"

"In four days' time."

"What have you decided?"

I admitted, under my breath:

"Nothing! Nothing!"

"Then what's all this equipment?"

With her chin, she indicated the trunk, the clothes, the cardboard boxes strewn everywhere . . .

"Just some odds and ends for the autumn season."

"Hmm. I see."

She scrutinised my face suspiciously . . . I could not stand it any longer. Let her blame me, if she liked, but I could not bear her to imagine some sordid escapade, some kind of ridiculous elopement. Hurriedly, with the words tumbling over each other, I brought out a wildly disjointed story.

"Listen . . . Marthe told me that Alain . . . with Valentine Chessenet . . ."

"Oh! the bitch!"

"So I came back to Paris . . . I . . . I nearly demolished Alain's desk . . . I found the letters."

"Excellent!"

Claudine's eyes were sparkling and she was twisting a handkerchief. Encouraged, I became feverishly worked up.

". . . And then I left everything on the floor, letters, papers—everything . . . he'll find them, he'll know it was me . . . Only I can't stand any more, I can't stand any more, do you realise? I don't love him enough to stay with him. I want to get away, get away, get away . . ."

Choking with tears and my spate of words, I raised my head to get a gulp of breath. Claudine delicately stroked both my hands and asked very gently:

"So . . . you want to get a divorce?"

I stared at her, dumbfounded.

"A divorce . . . whatever for?"

"Really! You are the most extraordinary girl! Why, because you don't want to live with him any more!"

"I most certainly don't. But is it necessary to have a divorce?"

"Well, it's still the surest, if not the shortest method. What a babe-in-arms you are!"

I had not the heart to laugh. I was beginning to panic.

"But do realise I don't want to see him again! I'm frightened!"

"Bravely said. Frightened of what?"

"Of him . . . that he'll make me go back . . . that he'll talk me round . . . I'm frightened of seeing him . . . Perhaps he'll be very nasty . . ."

I shuddered.

"You poor little thing!" Claudine murmured very low, without looking at me.

She seemed to be thinking very hard.

"What do you advise me to do, Claudine?"

"It's difficult. I'm not at all sure, myself. We must ask Renaud."

Terrified, I cried:

"No! Nobody . . . nobody!"

"You're very unreasonable, child. Wait a minute . . . Did you take the lady's letters?" she asked me suddenly.

"No," I admitted, slightly taken aback. "What for? They don't belong to me!"

"Of all the reasons!" exclaimed Claudine very contemptuously, with a shrug. "Hell . . . I can't think of anything. Have you any money?"

"Yes . . . Very nearly eight thousand francs. Alain left me a lot when he went away."

"I'm not asking about that . . . Money of your own—any private means?"

"Wait . . . there's the three hundred thousand francs of my dowry . . . And then there's the fifty thousand francs in cash Grandmother Lajarrisse left me three years ago."

"That's fine, you won't die of starvation. Looking ahead, would it worry you if *he* divorced you?"

I replied with a haughty gesture.

"Nor me either," said Claudine quaintly. "Well then, my dear child . . . go."

I did not stir: I did not say a word.

"My opinion and my prescription don't produce loud cries of enthusiasm, Annie? I can understand that. But I've come to the end of my tether and my genius."

I raised my eyes and looked at her through a mist of fresh tears.

Without speaking, I indicated the trunk, the tough clothes, the long shoes, the waterproof cape . . . all that puerile globe-trotter's gear I had bought in these last few days. She smiled and her piercing gaze softened.

"Yes, I see, I see. I saw at once. Where are you going, my Annie, whom I'm going to lose?"

"I don't know."

"Is that true?"

"I swear it."

"Goodbye, Annie."

"Goodbye . . . Claudine."

I implored her, huddled close against her:

"Tell me again . . ."

"What, darling?"

"That Alain can't hurt me if he catches me up?"

"He won't catch you up. At least, not at once. Before you see him, you'll see various unpleasant people who'll fiddle about with papers, then will come the divorce, the blame laid on Annie—and freedom."

"Freedom." (I spoke almost in a whisper, as she had.) "Is it a very heavy burden, Claudine? Is it very difficult to manage? Or will it be a great joy—the cage open—all the world before me?"

She answered, very low, shaking her curly head:

"No, Annie, not all at once . . . Perhaps never . . . You'll carry the marks of the chain for a long time. Perhaps, too, there are people who are born submissive? . . . But there's something worse than that . . . I'm afraid for you . . ."

"Whatever of?"

She looked me in the face. I saw Claudine's eyes and Claudine's tears shining in all their beauty—small tears that did not fall, golden eyes that had refused me their light . . .

"I'm afraid of the Meeting. You will meet him, the man who has not yet crossed your path. Yes, yes," she insisted as I made a gesture of violent dissent, "that man is waiting for you somewhere. It's right, it's inevitable. Only Annie, my dear Annie, do you know how to recognise him, don't be deceived, because there are doubles, there are any number of shadows who simulate him, there are caricatures of him. Between you and him there are all the ones you have to step over or push aside . . ."

"Claudine—suppose I got old before I met him?"

"She raised her graceful arm in a gesture that transcended herself:

"Still keep going on! He is waiting for you on the other side of life."

I was silent out of respect for this faith in love. I was a little proud, too, of being the only person . . . or almost the only one . . . to know the true Claudine, exalted and fierce as a young druidess.

Just as in Bayreuth, I was ready to do her will, good or evil. She gazed at me with those eyes in which I wanted to see the light that had dazzled me in the Margravine's garden . . .

"Yes, Annie, wait. Perhaps there isn't a man who deserves . . . all this."

Her hand lightly brushed and caressed my shoulders. I leant towards her and she saw in my face my offering of my whole self, my utter abandonment, the very words I was going to say . . . Quickly she put her warm hand over my mouth, then raised it to her lips and kissed it.

"Goodbye, Annie."

"Claudine . . . one second . . . only one second! I want . . . I want you to love me from a distance—you who could have loved me—you who are staying here."

"I'm not staying, Annie. I've already gone. Can't you feel that? I've left everything . . . except Renaud . . . for Renaud. Friends are traitors, books are deceivers. Paris will see no more of Claudine. She will grow old among her relatives the trees, with her lover and friend. He will grow old more quickly than I shall, but solitude can work miracles. Perhaps I can give a little of my own life to prolong his."

She had opened the door, and I was going to lose my only friend . . . What gesture, what word would retain her? Ought I not to have . . . ? But already the white door had hidden her dark slenderness and I could hear the light rustle of footsteps, that had announced her arrival, dying away . . . Claudine had gone!

I have just read Alain's telegram. In thirty-six hours he will be here, and I . . . Tonight I am catching the Paris-Carlsbad express on which we travelled only last month to Bayreuth. From there, I do not know yet. Alain does not speak German—that puts another little obstacle between us.

Since the day before yesterday, I have done so much thinking that my head is exhausted. My maid is going to be as astonished as my husband. I am only taking my two little black friends, Toby the dog and Toby the revolver . . . I shall be a very well-protected woman, shall I not? I am going away resolutely, not hiding my tracks, but not marking them with little pebbles either . . . This escape of mine is not a crazy flight on the spur of the moment. For four months I have been slowly gnawing away at my rope till it has finally frayed and parted. All that was needed was simply that the gaoler should carelessly leave the prisoner unguarded. Once his back was turned, she became aware both of the horror of the prison and of light shining through the chinks of the door.

Before me lies the troubled future. Let me know nothing of tomorrow, let no presentiment warn me of what is in store— Claudine has told me too much already! I want to hope and to fear that there are countries where everything is new, unknown cities whose only lure is their name, skies under which an alien soul replaces your own . . . Somewhere in the whole wide world, shall I not find the nearest thing to paradise for a little creature like me?

Standing in front of the glass, dressed all in tawny frieze, I have just said goodbye to the Annie who once lived here. Goodbye, Annie! Feeble and vacillating as you are, I love you. Alas, I have no one but you to love.

I am resigned to whatever may come. Just for a passing moment, I can foresee with sad clairvoyance what this new life of mine will be like. I shall be the woman travelling alone who intrigues a hotel dining-room for a week, with whom schoolboys on holiday and arthritics in spas suddenly fall violently in love . . . I shall be the solitary diner, whose pallor provides scandal with an excuse for inventing all kinds of drama . . . the lady in black, or the lady in blue, whose melancholy reserve frustrates and repulses the compatriot she meets on her travels . . . Also the one whom a man remorselessly pursues because she is pretty and a stranger, or because of the big, lustrous pearls he has noticed on her fingers . . . The one who is murdered one night in a hotel bedroom and whose body is found outraged and bleeding . . .

No, Claudine, I do not shudder. All that is life, time flowing on, the hoped-for miracle that may lie round the next bend of the road. It is because of my faith in that miracle that I am escaping.